BOOK ONE

ARBAT SQUARE

By

John S. Halbert

"Arbat Square," by John S. Halbert. ISBN 978-1-62137-332-2 (Softcover)

Library of Congress Control Number: 2013912428

Published 2013 by Virtualbookworm.com Publishing Inc., P.O. Box 9949, College Station, TX 77842, US. ©2013, John S. Halbert. All rights reserved. No part of this publication may be reproduced, stored in a retrieval system, or transmitted in any form or by any means, electronic, mechanical, recording or otherwise, without the prior written permission of John S. Halbert.

Manufactured in the United States of America.

To Cate

PROLOGUE

A NEW NIGERIA

Lagos, Nigeria; Tuesday, August 9, 2011:

Stooping out through the little airliner's curved open door, at the top of the steps Kip Leeds gripped the tubular handrail and started down. With his first breath, the West African air was just as he remembered it from that first time—steamy and salt-laced from the nearby equatorial Atlantic. Still stiff after the droning flight from Frankfurt, the American swayed down the spindly steps of the diminutive *'Gulfstream'* jetliner onto the shimmering, sun-baked concrete apron and gazed about. Before him, on the face of the monstrous, multi-storied concrete-and-glass main terminal, a big lighted sign proclaimed the place to be the *'MURTALA MOHAMMED AIRPORT LAGOS'*. Below it was a newer-looking billboard: "Welcome to Lagos," it declared. Kip gave an involuntary shudder. If the signs were telling the truth, things had changed greatly since his first trip to Nigeria, when he had felt anything *but* welcome—or safe. Had it really been nearly two decades since he came to Lagos that time with the fifty-thousand dollars strapped underneath his clothes to meet with all those men who had turned out to be criminals?

A trim-looking black man in casual slacks and a pullover shirt was stepping across the way toward him, his hand extended. "Leeds!" The man gave a grin, his perfect white teeth contrasting with his very dark, shiny face.

"Colonel Ajiboy!" Kip grabbed the man's hand. The African pulled the American to him in a hug. "It is good to see you, again . . . it has been a long time, my friend!" He looked the pale-skinned newcomer over and grinned again. The Nigerian motioned his guest toward a side door of the terminal. "By the way, I am now *'Major General Solomon Ajiboy—retired'*." The

i

slender, fit-looking older man pulled on a door handle. "When the political situation got better, I gave it all up to be with my grandchildren." Inside, the cool air was in sharp contrast to what Kip remembered about the gigantic structure on his first visit to the cavernous place, with its humid atmosphere that time and the stomach-turning smells inside the vast building. Ajiboy glanced at his visitor. "You are going to see many changes in Nigeria since you were here, before."

As they stepped along the concourse, he gestured at a mahogany door, beside which was a sign that read, "Chapel". "That was once the terrible 'Interrogation Room', where that Ukrainian *'General Retchko's'* 'murder-squad' beat people to death." Just then, the door opened and an African couple in flowery native dress and ribboned headpieces came out, followed by a smiling black man in clerical garb, a Crucifix in his hand. The woman was fingering a rosary. Ajiboy nodded at the two. A happy look crossed his face. "I say, Nigeria is much better, now."

'I'm looking forward to getting around . . . I've heard many good things, lately."

"You will be here for some time?"

"I've planned a couple of days, here. Then, I'm returning to Frankfurt. My wife and our teenaged son are visiting her relatives, there. Then, we're traveling to Moscow, to a wedding."

"You are going to Moscow to a wedding?"

"You remember that Russian soldier, *'Terenty Suslov'?* The fellow about my age who came here that time with the others to blow up the refinery down at Tanuta City?"

"Yes, a diplomat-military officer. *'Russian Special Forces',* he was."

"His daughter is getting married to a young American whose mother is an old friend of mine in Texas. Her husband was an agent of the American 'Investigation Bureau' and now works with us. We all became friends after what happened that time in Madrid—at *'Plaza Mayor'.*"

Ajiboy led the way into a suite. "This is the 'Security Office'."

Kip looked around; the place was palatial; elegant, even. He took the plush leather seat the African offered him.

"Tea?"

"Sure."

Ajiboy nodded at a soldier who came back with a pot of water and a pair of teacups.

As the fellow poured the men cupfuls, Kip went on. "When Suslov came here with the others and destroyed that refinery, it was the end of the 'Cartel'."

Ajiboy shrugged. "But their former clients still cause much trouble for the world." The Nigerian narrowed his eyes. "Suslov was with the Americans and that older Russian—what was his name?"

"Golubko—*'General Rodion Golubko'* He was a colonel, then . . . he's now retired from the Russian military and is working with us. I'll see him in Moscow at the wedding." Kip produced a wry grin. "It was pretty amazing, actually, how it all worked out."

A big smile creased Ajiboy's face. I know your people were behind the overthrow of the old dictator here in Nigeria—". The African gave a smirk. *"They say he died 'naturally', but we know better, do we not?"* He looked thoughtful. "Give Golubko my regards. That Russian was a good soldier—a fine man." Ajiboy looked at Kip. "So tell me . . . what have *you* been doing these many days?"

"When I got all that money, I invested a lot of it in the private crime-fighting operation out of Zurich . . . as an investment, it's worked out very well for me." The American stirred his cup. "Since I got out of the oil trading business, I've worked with the Swiss Inspector, *'Tarliani'*, along with *'Livshits'*, the Russian . . . and *'Watering',* in Washington." The American went on, "Even though all of us came from different parts of the world with different politics, working together, we've captured or killed some important 'terrorists' and criminals." He paused. "Except for the *'September-Eleventh'* attacks, of course—*that* was our big failure." Kip stirred the tea slowly, thoughtfully, then downed the cup's contents all at once. "That big terrorist—*'Agent U',* they called him—he was the mastermind of much trouble we went through for a long time."

"Thank God he is dead, now."

"We believe it was the Israelis who killed him. But Retchko is still up there, somewhere."

"Ah, yes . . . the old Soviet general—we've come to know *plenty* about *him.*"

"Retchko controlled the old crime "Cartel" from the *'Tanuta Refinery'.* He was—and is—an evil man."

Through the glass door Kip saw well-dressed people going about in the corridor.

Ajiboy smiled. "We've made a lot of progress, here in Nigeria" He reached for his hat. "I will show you around the airport . . . then we will go downtown. I believe you will find the changes—since you were here last—to be interesting . . . for one thing, they say Lagos will be the biggest city in the world, in a few years." The retired, civilian-dressed general motioned to a soldier in fatigues, who came to respectful attention. "Corporal, bring around the staff car . . . we are leaving, now."

* * *

Dusk, the Next Day, Wednesday, August 10, 2011:

"You say it will be an all-night flight to Frankfurt?" General Ajiboy squinted into the penetrating orange glare of the setting sun. Out on the apron the fuel truck was pulling away from the little airliner. As the two pilots came out of the briefing room and stepped across the concrete in the direction of the corporate jet, Ajiboy looked the aircraft over with obvious admiration. "It is your organization's airplane?"

Kip Leeds nodded. "We use it to fly our people to assignments around the world . . . they carry weapons and other gear with them." He gave a shrug. "We couldn't do that on a regular airliner, of course—not with the security issues after 'Nine-Eleven'." He watched as the pilots took their places in the cockpit. In a minute he would have to get aboard.

A wistful look came over the African's creased face. "Well, Mister Leeds, this has been a pleasant time for me . . . seeing you again, like this. It was certainly better than that first time we met in *'Busa's'* living room!"

Who could forget that scene! You were pretty intimidating."

"I had to be—I was responsible for the safety of all that money. You certainly put it to good use, didn't you!"

"Next to marrying my wife, it was my best investment!"

The cockpit window slid open. "We must leave, now, sir---"

"See you next time!" Kip said, shaking the Nigerian's hand.

Inside the cabin, he took a left-side seat, buckled the belt, and looked out. Solomon Ajiboy was giving a final wave. As the jet nosed toward the taxiway and the African was lost from view, an unexpected pensive feeling came over Kip.

For this short, pleasant trip had been a closure, of sorts, to that intense, anxiety-ridden first journey he had made to Nigeria, now almost two decades past. It was hard to believe it had been that long ago.

* * *

A few minutes later, when the trim little airliner lifted from the runway and set a northerly course toward Europe, Kip stared down at the nondescript grassy landscape, waving in the slanted rays of the sun, now low on the horizon. As darkness settled over West Africa, the American's thoughts drifted back to that time when he first came to Nigeria with the fifty-thousand dollars strapped beneath his clothes and those desperate moments when he was not sure if he would ever again see his homeland.

~~~

PART ONE

THE AMERICANS

-1-

The upfront screen map and the countdown clock in the Airbus cabin showed they were getting close to Lagos. Kip Leeds looked out the window and saw that night had fallen over West Africa. Squirming about, he could feel the new hundred-dollar bills in the money harness—beneath his clothes, he was surrounded by money. Every time he moved, there came the confining sensation of the fifty-thousand dollars strapped to his body—nervous sweating had molded the new bills into what amounted to a form-fitting second-skin. He felt in his pocket for the jagged-edged "identification" they had told him to paste onto an index card. It was still there.

Just then, the sound of the engines dropped, and he could feel the airliner starting to descend.

"Here we go," he said to himself, as the cabin lights came full-up and the flight attendants started bustling about. He gave an involuntary shudder—the old nerves were back and there were worrisome questions yet unanswered. Who will be meeting me? Where will we be going? Why did the Nigerians want him to come to Lagos in the first place? Couldn't they have done the transaction by *wire*, as he did with oil deals? The Africans had insisted everything was on the level. But what if the Customs officers discovered all this money? He had heard some bad stories about such things. More nerves.

For the hundredth time, he re-played in his mind how all this had come about. It had started with the fax from a "Masobe Busa", in Lagos, Nigeria, claiming he and some "Associates" had twenty-million dollars to transfer out of the country, and they needed someone to help them. For that, the men would pay a six-million-dollar commission.

At first, Kip and Brad Holdon, his partner at *'H & L Petroleum Marketing'*, had thought it was a put-on. Hadn't everyone heard about the infamous "Nigerian Scams"? To play

3

along, they had faxed the fellow back, but after some more letters, including a convincing-looking one from a "Doctor Krasheev" of the *'Nation Bank of Nigeria'*, whom Kip had learned was real; another from a lawyer named "Adwadube", and some impassioned telephone calls from Busa, himself, he and Brad had decided he would go to Lagos to see what the deal—to be called an "Oil-Buy" as a cover—was all about. He was supposed to take fifty-thousand dollars in cash with him to set up a bank account there, which had struck Brad and him as unusual, but worth a try, they had reasoned. At the very least, Kip figured he would have an interesting story to tell the folks when he got back home. Maybe he would even have six-million dollars.

But other concerns kept nagging at him. Before he had left for the airport, Ned Ferry, an older friend of his who owned a detective agency, had sat him down and advised him sternly about this trip. "Kip, when you're in Nigeria, you must remember that you're strictly on your own," he had said, "the embassy there won't be able to help you . . . and for God's sake, don't let anybody know you have all that money on you—over there, they'd kill you in a second for it . . . and that goes double for the military and the Nigerian Customs officers. They like to do-away with Americans carrying money, I'm told."

"Yes, sir, I'll do that, sir," he had blanched, startled by the crusty man's intense words.

"There's something else to keep in mind," Ned Ferry had gone on, ". . . *everybody and anybody* can be your friend or your enemy—you might not know who is which—watch out for the double-cross." The detective had leaned forward, his voice in an earnest whisper. "People will try to shake you down for money at every turn . . . I'd advise you to have a few hundred dollars in your pocket for payoffs. Remember that you're going to a part of the world that's very different to what you're used to. They say the airport at Lagos is the most dangerous one in the world—be very careful."

As Kip had stood up to leave, the private investigator had added, "Call us when you get there, so we'll know you arrived all right." He would try to remember to do that.

The aircraft banked and below were the myriad lights of a huge city. With juddering thumps, the big airplane returned to earth. Kip gazed out the window at what looked like any other nighttime runway he had ever seen—he guessed he had expected to see flaming torches from the African jungle, or something.

In a few minutes, the airliner pulled up to an enormous, but dimly-lighted, multi-story building and the engines whined to a stop.

He had arrived in Lagos.

Kip pulled his bag from the overhead bin and joined the jostling passengers exiting the airliner down a set of wheeled steps. Inside the Lagos terminal, the scene he came upon was about like any other airport he had ever seen, except that this crowd was made up almost entirely of Africans in native dress.

Then, it hit him—the soggy, sponge-like humidity and the smells—of sweat and strange fragrances. A squad of soldiers in full battle gear with rifles on their shoulders goose-stepped past; their jarring jackboots whamming down in thunderous cadence.

Up ahead were tables with uniformed officers standing behind them. With a chill of alarm he realized they were directing him toward the Customs inspectors! *Were the Nigerians about to find the fifty-thousand dollars strapped underneath his clothes?*

At that moment, a very dark, fierce-looking man in khaki pants and a white, open-collar shirt stepped in front of him, blocking his way. "Kip Leeds?" the man intoned in a heavy, accented voice, his piercing black eyes boring straight into Kip's.

With a start, the American realized he must be his airport contact! Kip nodded, swallowing.

"Identification?"

With nervous fingers Kip pulled out the pasted-on card Masobe Busa had faxed him.

The muscular African thrust a card he was holding at the one in Kip's hand. The serrated edges were a perfect match. "Follow me!" he ordered.

Kip's heart was pounding as the man led him around a corner of the shadowy concourse to a bench. "Put two-hundred dollars in your passport and sit right there," he said. "I will be back to get you in a few minutes."

The man took his precious passport with the money inside it and headed back in the direction from which they had just come.

Kip sat down on the bench and looked around at his dingy surroundings. No one else was nearby, a fact he was not sure was to his benefit or not. The odor of humid sweat hung in the air. On the paint-peeled wall right across from where he sat hung a huge *'Pepsi'* poster. From a loudspeaker came a continuous jabber of announcements in accented English—was *'English'* the language of Nigeria? Kip had more or less assumed that everyone would be speaking in some sort of native tongue.

While he was pondering this, the man in the khaki pants and the white shirt came back. To Kip's relief, he was holding the passport. The American stuffed it into his back pocket. "Come with me!" the African motioned, "everything is arranged!"

Kip grabbed his bag and followed him past the immigration area, through the vast main terminal, to the outside. At once, they were surrounded by gawking, chattering beggars and others not so impoverished-looking. "Give this woman twenty dollars!" the man said, pointing to a wizened crone, "she is with us!" Kip pulled out a twenty and handed it to her. The doddering old female snatched it and stepped back, cackling and grinning. She had no teeth.

The man glared at the rest of the bunch, who shrank back into the shadows.

The two went down a long, curving, grass-lined sidewalk to the street. Under a street lamp at the curb, Kip turned about and stared at the huge terminal building, with its big lighted sign on the front: *'MURTALA MOHAMMED AIRPORT LAGOS'*. He could see that others were being shaken-down for money just as the old woman had done to him. It looked like an extortion racket was in full swing back there.

A half-dozen youngsters, including a one-legged boy hobbling on a tree-limb crutch, came up with their hands outstretched. The man swore at them; they turned and fled.

There was a scruff of tires and a blue, older-model, four-door Toyota swept up to the curb. "Get in!" the man said, opening a rear door, "these men will take you to the hotel."

Kip tossed his gear onto the floorboard and ducked into the right-rear seat. The car pulled away into the traffic. By the flickering light of other cars' headlamps and intermittent street lights, he could see that two men were in the front seats. Both stared straight ahead.

They had gone about a block when a police officer in a "Colonial-style" uniform stepped off the curb. *WHAM!* His hand slammed onto the car's hood like a thunderclap! The driver jammed on the brakes and gaped at the scowling lawman, who was pointing at *Kip*. "I want to see *that* backseat passenger, outside!" He repeated the demands. "*You!* Get out of that car! That is an order!" Kip's eyes were wide—should the officer find all that money on him, the American knew he might have but moments to live.

The officer pulled out a billy-club and lunged at the door. Just as his fingers gripped the handle, the driver floorboarded the gas pedal and the Toyota shot forward! The policeman spun around and fell, yelling, to the pavement! Kip looked back, aghast, and saw the officer reach for his gun. The driver jerked the car around a corner, out of the policeman's line of fire, and they sped off into the night!

"Oh! Oh!" Kip gasped, as the sedan careened down a shadowy back street at the outskirts of the airport.

The African male in the front passenger's seat spoke. "We will be all right—this happens all the time." They were the first words either of the two men had said. "Mister Busa is waiting for you at the hotel," the fellow went on in a heavy accent, "everything is arranged."

Kip remembered the white-shirt-khaki-pants man at the airport had also said, "everything is arranged." *Everything, what?* he wondered. And what had the front-seat man meant by, "this happens all the time"?

While he was still thinking about this, they came to a ramp and the driver whipped the Toyota up onto a divided highway.

As they raced along, Kip looked closely at the two men. In the flickering lights of the road, he could tell that the driver appeared to be the younger of the two—probably in his late-twenties; the other man was stocky and middle-aged. Both had very dark complexions. Neither had much to say, but he got the impression they were following someone else's orders.

After they had been on the freeway-like thoroughfare for about ten minutes, the driver twisted the wheel and they bounded down an exit ramp onto a rutted service road, where the sedan presently drove up in front of a brightly-lighted, modern-looking six-story building. According to the marquee the establishment was the *"Roomland Hotel"*.

The front-seat passenger yanked open the rear door while the driver hopped from the other side.

Kip tugged his luggage bag from the floorboard and got out.

"Come!" the stocky one said, "the man is waiting for us." Kip guessed he meant Busa.

The African motioned toward the other end of the lobby. "We will take the stairs. "

The three strode through the paneled space in the direction of a staircase off to one side of the registration counter. "You are already registered," the man said. As they started up, Kip spotted a uniformed officer seated before a bank television monitors— evidently the "security center". On the sixth floor, at the very end of the hallway, they stopped. The heavyset man knocked on a door in what sounded to Kip like a code. A second or two later, the knock was repeated from the inside, then the door cracked open and a shiny African face peered out.

"Okay!" the Nigerian said. The door swung aside. The three stepped into a room where they were greeted by a clean-cut, twenty-something fellow who bowed to the first man. "This is Ivan," the older man said, "he will be your bodyguard while you are here."

As they shook hands, Kip wondered what the leader had meant by "bodyguard". Ivan gestured toward a varnished wooden *armoire* in the corner. Evidently, the luggage bag was to go in it.

After he had hung it up, the four stood around, as if no one quite knew what to say or do next. The older man broke the silence. "Mister Busa will be here in a few minutes." Kip noticed Ivan and the young driver visibly tense; the two kept glancing at the entrance. "Take seats," the man motioned

They were hardly settled on the sofas when loud knocks sounded in the same cadence as when they had arrived. Ivan made for the door, where he rapped back the sequence.

An overlarge, very dark-skinned man dressed in a ballooning, flower-print, African-style outfit bustled into the room and headed straight toward the American, his hand outstretched. "Kip Leeds?"

When Kip answered, the man, beaming with a tooth-enhanced smile, grabbed him in a smothering hug. "Masobe Busa! Glad you could finally be here with us—you have the fifty thousand dollars with you?"

Kip nodded.

"Good!" Busa gestured for him to sit down. "Give it to me and we will go in the morning to the 'Imperial Industrial Bank' to deposit it!"

Kip sat on the sofa and began to unwrap the cash that was strapped on him.

Busa counted it out. "It is all here!" he grinned, stuffing the bills into a pocket.

The other two men, who had stood almost attention for several minutes, looked at Busa, who gave a quick motion of his head toward the door. Without a word, they left the room.

"Be ready at ten-o'clock," Busa said to Kip, "we will pick you up and go to the bank."

The American nodded. He knew these men literally had his life in their hands.

The heavy man glanced at Ivan. "Ten o'clock!" he repeated, stepping into the corridor. The door swung shut with some automatic-sounding "clicks" that Kip heard. *A special door?*

With Busa gone, the two looked at each other. "I guess you're my 'bodyguard'," Kip said. The Nigerian nodded. The American got the impression the young African would rather be somewhere else. Kip went to the front window and cracked the curtain. Down below, Busa and the two other men were getting into the blue Toyota.

Kip yawned. "I missed a whole night's sleep on the plane." He pulled out some shorts and a T-shirt from the bag.

Ivan took off his shoes. "Mister Busa wants me to sleep fully-clothed," he said.

The youth dragged over a chair and propped it under the doorknob. Kip watched him, frowning. "Why are you doing that?"

"Security . . . Mister Busa's orders—" He hung a ribbon with a bell on it over the doorknob. "This will wake us if somebody tries to break into the room."

Kip was glad the bodyguard was going to all this trouble on his behalf—but why did these people think he needed all this "protection"?

"Don't worry," Ivan said, as he turned out the light over his bed, "all this is just a 'precaution'."

Kip switched off the wall lamp over his pillow and lay back in the shadowy gloom. Why *are* these men so concerned with security? Was there something he didn't know—something he s*hould* know for his own sake? What would the morrow bring? *Could he trust these strangers with his life*? For now, these questions had no hard answers.

But right now, he was too keyed-up to sleep. Thoughts of some friends he had left back in Texas started moving across his mind. How long would it before he would again see them?

Ned Ferry's daughter, Sloane, had driven him to the airport. Kip had known the young woman since about the time her mother had died when she was twelve; almost a dozen years ago. During her teenage years he had suspected from time-to-time that the girl had had a crush on him that she had kept to herself. Now twenty-three and a newly-minted college graduate, Sloane was the single mother of a little boy by a French exchange student named "Dominique" she had met at the university, who had died a hero while rescuing some friends in a fraternity house fire. Now, she was Ned Ferry's partner in the detective agency.

Kip remembered her long, silky-black hair streaming back in the wind as the convertible had raced along the freeway with the top down on the drive to the airport. If she had been trying to get his attention with the short sundress outfit and strappy sandals she was wearing, she had definitely succeeded, he thought. Perhaps she had worn them on purpose to show herself off to him. His free-wheeling business partner, un-attached Brad Holdon, had once told him that women were cleverly conniving about such things. Men basically mis-understood women, he claimed, and most of the time never suspected what they were up to. Weddings, he had insisted, were something of, by, and for the *females.* Men would be perfectly happy just to wrap things up with a simple little ceremony—then bring on the honeymoon and the glorious bliss. Kip wondered if bachelor Brad was right.

For a fleeting second as they had ridden along, he had speculated what it would be like to be married to Sloane; then had pushed aside the thought as he always had—he was too old for her and she was too young for him—and that was that. Besides, how could he ever follow in the footsteps of her heroic, now-dead, former boyfriend?

Kip recalled an extremely attractive young widow he had known a few years earlier, whose husband, an Air Force pilot, had stayed at the controls of a burning bomber while everyone else bailed out. But before he could escape, the airplane had exploded, killing him. Kip remembered how every time he went to her house, the guy's medals and pictures were all over the place; she never stopped going on about how great he was. When he finally understood he could never compete with the ghost of a dead "All-American" hero, he had broken off the relationship.

On the other hand, the only mementos Sloane had of "Dominique", the father of her child, "Nicky", were an enlarged framed picture of him from the school's yearbook, plus some snapshots of their short relationship. Those few pictures were the sole connection the little boy would ever have to his father except for his name: "Nicky's" actual name was "Dominique."

When they had pulled up in front of the International Terminal at the *'DFW Airport'*, Sloane had gripped the steering wheel and looked at him. "Oh, Kip, take care of yourself."

"I told your dad I'll call him as soon as I arrive in Nigeria."

The scene was still vivid in his mind how she had stared at him for a long moment, then gunned the engine and sped off, leaving him standing at the curb holding his luggage. As he turned and trudged past the automatic glass doors into the cavernous terminal building, where a roaring racket of echoing announcements and people's voices awaited him, he had realized how much he would miss her on this trip.

Kip squirmed on the hotel bed, his thoughts going on. For now, there was *another* female to think about, as well. At the Frankfurt airport, while he had sat in the waiting area for the flight to Lagos, a very pretty young blonde woman had appeared at the check-in counter. After a few minutes, she came back to the gate area and stood off by herself, waiting. Kip was intrigued. What was this stylish-looking girl doing on the flight to *Nigeria?* he wondered. "Woman of Mystery," he thought to himself.

Later, when the inflight movie had finished and the lights came back up, Kip was startled to see her sitting in the seat to his left! "Mind if I sit here and smoke?" Kip had recognized a German accent. After lighting a cigarette, she turned to him with a smile. "What is your business in Nigeria?"

Her question caught him off guard. "I—I'm going to Lagos to look for some—'antique cars'," was the only thing he could think of to say. He didn't want to tell her the whole story.

"'Antique cars'?" The girl's eyebrows went up. *"In Lagos?"* She blew a long puff of smoke, brushed back her short platinum hair and looked straight into his eyes. "What *kind* of antique cars?" He could tell she didn't believe him.

Just then, an older woman had appeared at the front of the aisle and motioned for her to come forward. "I will return," the blonde said, stubbing out her cigarette, "I want to hear more about those old cars in Lagos."

He had stared at her well-proportioned backside as she strode up the aisle into the next cabin. "Who *is* this beautiful girl? he had asked himself. Maybe she's a spy! Perhaps Busa or someone else planted her on the plane to keep tabs on him—why else would she sit down next to *him*? But it could be she was just trying to be friendly. She was a "Woman of Mystery," all right.

He remembered how he would have to have a convincing story ready for her when she returned. It had already begun to look as if there was a lot more to this journey to Africa than he had ever imagined there would be. He needed some time to think.

In a little while, when the blonde came back down the aisle and dropped into the seat next to him, to his surprise, she was wearing a flight attendant's outfit. "We have to be dressed in our uniforms when we land in Lagos—it is a Nigerian rule." That explained what she was doing on this trip: she would be part of the crew on the return flight to Frankfurt. The girl lit another cigarette and looked Kip over with the most deep-blue eyes he had ever seen. "Tell me more about these 'antique cars' in Lagos."

This time, he was ready with a concocted story. "Back in 'World War Two' . . ." he had started, "there was a shipload of cars headed for South Africa that was diverted to Lagos when there was a warning about an enemy submarine—"

Kip stopped. He'd forgotten she was German—yesterday's "enemy".

"Amazing." The girl had looked at him with raised eyebrows, shaking her head slowly, "I have never heard about any of this," she went on in her Teutonic accent, "and I have been to Lagos many times." She didn't seem to be buying the story. "I would be really surprised if there were old cars hidden down there . . . Lagos is not like that. It is too dangerous for that sort of thing."

His face flushed, he had tried to grope for words. "It was a big secret for a long time after the war and so I decided to go there and try to find the cars. I understand they're stored somewhere in the Lagos area."

"Whatever you say . . ." She sounded skeptical.

To try to keep the conversation going, he had changed the subject. "What part of Germany are you from?"

The girl blew one last exhalation and squashed her cigarette in the seat arm's ash tray. "Hamburg."

He had told her he was an oil trader and would do some petroleum business in Nigeria, along with looking for the antique vehicles. When he had said that, the girl had seemed to relax.

"I have to go back up to the crew area," she said at length, " . . . 'been nice talking to you." With a smile, she had given his forearm a quick squeeze, then slipped out of her seat and swayed up the aisle. As before, he couldn't help but notice her stunning figure.

Kip tossed on the mattress some more, thinking about her firm touch on his arm and her plush shape; his blood pressure rising. He could not forget how she had looked back at him, and with a wave the blonde "Woman of Mystery" had stepped beyond the curtain into the next compartment.

It was then he had discovered the card she had dropped into his lap. *"Nixie Garten"* it stated, and gave a Frankfurt address and a telephone number. Printed at the bottom was: *Linguist— German, English, Spanish, French, Italian, Portuguese, Arabic, Russian.* It looked as if she could carry on a conversation just about anywhere. Just in case, from now on, he would keep her card in his wallet. As he lay there, he found himself hoping he would somehow, somewhere, someday again see her.

After a while, fatigue overcame him and he fell asleep in a strange bed; in a strange room; in a strange hotel; in a strange city; in a strange country; on a strange continent; where he would never have expected himself to be.

-3-

"Well, it is about time you woke up . . ." came an accented voice from nearby. Kip's eyes flew open; he bolted upright in an unfamiliar bed. Where was he? He looked about the room—then it all came back: he was in a hotel in Lagos, Nigeria; the dark-skinned young fellow was his "bodyguard", Ivan. Sunshine filtered through the window curtains and there was a vague sound of voices coming from somewhere outside the building.

"Better get moving," Ivan said, looking at Kip in the dresser mirror as he buttoned his shirt, "Mister Busa will be here in a little while and he will expect you to be ready."

As Kip drew his portable electric shaver across his face, he casually looked out the window at some sort of bazaar going on down below. The American watched, fascinated, as a scrawny little girl about ten years old walked along with what looked like a table-sized salad bar balanced on the top of her head. Men and women alike were carrying enormous packages and even big boxes, luggage, and briefcases on their heads, leaving their hands free. Kip wondered how they did it. He remembered how his grade-school teachers used to make him walk around with a book on his head to develop his posture. These people must have perfect posture.

Just then, there came the now-familiar knock on the door. Busa, wearing a three-piece suit, hustled into the room, grinning. "We are supposed to be at the bank at noon," the heavyset man said, "so let us be going."

Outside, the young driver was standing beside the same blue Toyota of the night before. Kip dropped into the right-rear seat; Busa eased his bulk into the other side. The car's springs groaned with his extra weight.

With a clash of gears, the vehicle pulled away down the bumpy service road. As they passed the bazaar next to the hotel he had looked down upon a little while before, Kip glanced out and did a double-take—hanging by their tails from a wooden "A-frame" crossbar were about a dozen huge dead rats! Other food items Kip couldn't identify were on a table underneath the hideous creatures. It looked as if the lunch stand was doing a good business.

While he was still thinking about this, the Toyota nosed up onto the highway and headed toward the center of Lagos city. The driver said it would be about a thirty-kilometer ride to the bank and would take two hours. Kip wondered why such a short trip—about the same distance as between Dallas and Fort Worth—would take so long.

It was becoming a hot, sticky day; the humid, salt-laden sea breeze coming off the nearby equatorial Atlantic already felt like a steam bath—the car was not air-conditioned. Busa pulled out a handkerchief and wiped his shiny forehead.

As they rode along, Kip observed caravans of troop-laden military vehicles going in all directions. Ahead was a line of heavy traffic. At a stop, an open Army truck pulled up beside them. Two-dozen uniformed soldiers were sitting in back, armed with automatic weapons. As if on command, they all turned and stared down at Kip in the Toyota. For a *very* long minute they held him fixed in their gaze; there came the unmistakable sound of rifles cocking. Kip swallowed, remembering that Nigeria was a military dictatorship. Trying to look calm, he looked straight ahead, as if to ignore them. When the traffic began moving again and the truck roared off, he was shaking and his business suit was damp with nervous sweat. Busa took it all in with aplomb, as if armed soldiers inspected his car every day.

After a few kilometers, the pace picked up again and the Toyota began to make better time. The car went by a gigantic stucco building surrounded by a milling crowd of Africans; most were wearing the flowery outfits. But Kip saw hardly any women in the throng. A faded sign painted on the building proclaimed it was a "Tabernacle".

Before long, they came to a lengthy bridge that carried them over the broad mouth of a river and a wide bay that fronted on the Atlantic. Kilometer-after-kilometer the Toyota thumped along on the bumpy concrete viaduct. Out on the shimmering water, scantily-clad men on dozens of big fishing sailboats hauled in their catches. About the time Kip was deciding it was the most drawn-out span he had ever been on, the driver glanced back at him. "This is the longest bridge in Africa," he said.

After some time, they drove back onto land, past a sign that read, *'Ikoye Lagos'*. Gazing about, Kip's first impression was that they had arrived in a war zone. Everywhere he looked, the abandoned shells of burned and blasted buildings stared back— the hulks of wasted twenty and thirty-story concrete structures stood vacant, their window openings gaping like empty eyesockets, even from the upper floors. Some of the gaps were patched-over with blotchy plywood; smoke stains enveloped many of the buildings, a number of which seemed to have been completely gutted; others had holes in them, as if they had been targeted by artillery fire. Abandoned and wrecked cars and trucks blocked many of the side streets. All around, paper and cardboard debris littered alleyways, lifting and swirling in the breeze. Everywhere was a rankling odor like old urine and burned rubber.

They turned off the highway onto a surface road into an immediate traffic jam. As far as Kip could see, up ahead, smoke-belching vehicles sat bumper-to bumper. He turned away from the window—the blaring of car horns was practically earsplitting. The American noticed that almost all the other vehicles in the line were taxis; some driverless. Had their owners either run out of gas or had given up and taken to the sidewalks, leaving their stalled vehicles in the street? All about them, men leaned out of their car windows, yelling and gesturing at each other—Kip could feel the tension in the sultry air.

"What's this all about?"

"People lined-up for 'petrol'," the driver said, drumming his fingers on the wheel, "there is a shortage in Nigeria."

" *'Petrol'*? You mean a *'gasoline shortage'*?" The American couldn't believe there was a lack of fuel in this oil-rich country— Nigeria was one of the biggest crude-oil exporters in the world. From his experience buying and selling oil futures, he knew that companies all over bought immense quantities of Nigerian crude;

to him, it was incomprehensible that there could be gasoline lines in Lagos.

"This is why it is taking us two hours to get to the bank," Busa wheezed, "everybody is coming here . . . this is one of the few petrol stations in Lagos that is still open."

"But why is there a shortage? Shouldn't there be plenty of gasoline here in Nigeria?"

The fat man blinked. "'Corruption' . . . it is all corruption."

As they sat in the stalled traffic, waves of heat from the pavement began to bake the men inside the un-air-conditioned Toyota. By now, Busa was on his second or third handkerchief. Kip took out his, as well. The unfortunate driver had no handkerchief and looked to be thoroughly sweat-soaked.

Kip leaned toward the window, trying to catch a breath of fresh air. Looking about, he noticed clusters of boys and girls wearing student-type uniforms walking along on the sidewalks, carrying schoolbooks. They all seemed to be headed toward a big building with a sign out front that said, "Christian Academy". A jitney bus full of young people pulled up alongside them; block letters on its side advertised the school. Kip found it hard to believe that a church school would be located in such an unsavory-looking neighborhood.

Minute-by-minute, meter-by-meter, they crept along in the withering heat. Finally, the Toyota passed the fuel yard, reeking of spilled oil, where the scene was akin to a riot. Swearing, shouting men challenged each other around the petrol pumps, some with their fists. Whatever the reason for the shortage, Kip decided, the result was obviously a high degree of civil unrest. The white American's blond looks drew threatening gestures from some of the agitated native drivers. He hoped the Toyota's tank had plenty of gas in it.

A couple of blocks farther on, they turned in at a dignified-looking, cream-colored stucco building. As they pulled up, Kip read the inscriptions, *Imperial Industrial Bank"*, on a pair of brass plaques flanking the mahogany front doors.

While the driver parked the car, Kip and Busa went inside to an air-conditioned waiting room.

But when the two sat down, Kip was jarred by an outsized oil painting hanging over the front door of Nigeria's military dictator in his bemedaled uniform, his grim face staring down at the room. Kip had seen the man's picture on posters everywhere since he had arrived in Lagos; evidently, "The Leader" wanted to remind everyone of his all-powerful presence—and what better place could there be for that, than a *bank?*

Two well-dressed Africans—a muscular, very dark-skinned man and a young woman of lighter complexion—quite attractive, as Kip observed—came in, took seats across from them and began speaking loudly, *almost as if they wanted to be overheard,* Kip thought. As they talked, it struck the American that their speech sounded stilted—like they had rehearsed what they were saying.

"You are here to see 'Doctor Nomoah'?" Kip turned about and saw a female employee at a glass door, clipboard in hand, motioning for Busa and him to follow her.

The young woman led the two through a bright open room, past a dozen or so workers sitting at computer screens and clacking office machines, back to a paneled office. A fussy-looking little baldheaded man in a brown three-piece suit sat in an enveloping maroon-leather chair at an oversized mahogany desk; the overhead lights caught his shiny pate. A picture window behind him gave a view of palatial formal gardens; a smell of incense suffused their surroundings. To Kip, it looked as if the bank was doing well.

"'I. M. Nomoah'," The Nigerian said with a half-smile, extending his hand, "what can we do for you, today?" Kip grinned to himself; it was a line any banker on earth would have used.

But then the American was sure he saw Busa narrow his eyes at the man, along with a barely-perceptible nod, *as if confirming something.*

Nomoah squared his shoulders and spoke again, this time in a more direct manner. "I understand you want to make a deposit."

Kip wondered how much he already knew about all this.

Busa pulled the big roll of money from his pocket. "This gentleman—" he nodded toward Kip— "wants to deposit a balance to lift a quantity of 'crude oil'."

Nomoah put his elbows on the arms of his chair and touched his fingertips together in an altogether typical banker's pose.

Busa spoke. "Ah, 'Chief'—"

Kip thought he saw a look of alarm on the banker's face; his eyes widened. Nomoah leaned far back in his chair and tapped his fingertips together, frowning. The slight Nigerian began swinging his foot back and forth. Busa seemed flustered—he took out a handkerchief and wiped his forehead.

The overweight man swallowed and went on. "This gentleman's 'chief' interest is 'oil', I should say . . . this is an unusual arrangement, as the 'crude' will require 'special handling'."

Kip knew the "oil" was actually the twenty-million dollars; all this was just a formality. But it was almost as if Busa moment ago had said something *wrong,* he thought.

The fat fellow's bulging eyes cast back and forth between Nomoah and Kip. "This man's firm in the 'States is going to lift a quantity of *'oil'.*"

"And you want our bank to act as fiscal agent?"

"Exactly."

"All right." Nomoah reached into a desk drawer and pulled out a pad of forms, wrote something on it and pushed it across the desk. "Sign here."

Kip read the pre-printed page that was an agreement to set up an account at the bank. Everything looked to be in order as far as he could tell, so he scratched his name on the line. Busa handed the money over to the banker.

Nomoah counted the bills. "Fifty-thousand dollars—" He wrote out a receipt and handed it to Busa.

"I'll make a copy of this, and give you the original," Busa told Kip. He stuffed it into a coat pocket.

The banker stood up and everyone shook hands all around. As they were leaving, Kip thought he saw the two Nigerians squint into each others' eyes for a long second.

". . . and I hope your transaction goes well—" the banker was saying.

Kip and Busa walked back through the outer office, past the clattering machines and blinking computer screens, to the outside. The dozing, sweat-soaked driver jerked to attention and hastily opened the back doors of the Toyota for them.

In a few minutes, they were back on the highway. They had just made it across the long bridge when a sudden on-and-off thunderstorm came up. Traffic slowed to a crawl as they crept along in yet another traffic jam. After a while, they passed the reason for the slow-up: a big semi-tractor had dropped head-first into a deep, water-filled sink-hole in the pavement and was pointed straight-down. Its driver stood in the roadway, wringing his hands while other vehicles slowly moved past.

As the Toyota splashed by people milling around in the middle of the broad highway, Kip noticed a husky-looking, very dark-skinned African in a business-suit standing on the pavement. With a start, the American saw that the man was staring back at him! Something about the fellow struck Kip as familiar, but try as he might, he could not place him.

They were just getting back up to speed when the sedan's engine began backfiring. Other vehicles began to pass them by as the car slowed to a crawl, while the driver frantically tried to coax the sputtering engine back to life. Kip gaped at the jiggling dials and blinking lights on the dashboard in consternation—the last thing he wanted right now was a breakdown in the middle of a Nigerian highway. Busa drew out his handkerchief and started wiping his forehead.

The car had just about coasted to a complete stop when the engine caught hold once more. "Bad petrol," the driver muttered.

Kip shook his head. How could there be poor-quality gasoline in a country literally awash with the world's highest-grade petroleum reserves?

In a little while, they again arrived at the "Roomland Hotel". Ivan ordered a room-service lunch for the two of them, the first real meal Kip had had since arriving in Lagos. As he didn't want to drink the local water, Ivan had the kitchen send up a case of bottled water. What they got was called 'Kada', with the name of a Nigerian town on it. The label looked interesting, so Kip peeled it off the bottle and stuck it in an outside pocket of his luggage bag as a souvenir.

Kip remembered he was supposed to call Ned Ferry back in the 'States, but when he lifted the receiver, all he got was silence—the phone was dead.

About that time, another thunderstorm came up and gave their part of Lagos a loud soaking. While the storm raged, the lights blinked and went out. Ivan was nonplussed. "Happens every day . . . there is an electricity shortage in Nigeria."

Kip rolled his eyes. First, not enough gasoline; now, no telephone, no electricity—Nigeria was beginning to look like a country of woeful shortages.

After a while, the lights blinked a couple of times, then came back on with an odd, dim hue. "This is a 'brownout'," Ivan said, "when they give us half our electricity." On the wall, the air conditioner moaned in protest. Just as Kip was wondering how long this "brownout" would last, the lights came back full-up. He checked the telephone. It was still silent.

All at once, there came the coded knock on the door! Kip and Ivan looked at each other, then the bodyguard jumped up to return the knock.

When he opened the door, Busa shuffled into the room, all out of breath. "Get ready, at once!" he gasped, "we are going to the 'Nation Bank' to see 'Doctor Krasheev'!"

In short order, they were in the Toyota, once more headed toward downtown. This time, the traffic was sparse, and the little car buzzed along at a fast clip. The middle-aged man who had brought Kip to the hotel the night before was with them.

A half-hour later, they came off the long bridge and drove past the "Ikoye Lagos" sign onto a littered secondary road. As they made their way down the narrow byway, skirting disabled vehicles that blocked the right-of-way here and there, Kip calculated that they were nearing the center of the city. At one point, as they passed an intersection, down a side street he caught a glimpse of the same traffic jam they had been in that morning.

Right after they passed a street sign announcing they were at *"Dinubu Square"*, the driver pulled onto a vacant lot. "Wait here," the stocky man said, "I will go and see if 'Krasheev' is ready for us."

He got out of the car and hustled off toward a big stone-faced building a block away. The remaining three settled back in their seats. The orange, late-afternoon sun beat down on the Toyota; Busa's handkerchief was hard at work. Fifteen, thirty, forty-five minutes went by, while they baked in the damp, late-afternoon heat, their clothes becoming more soggy with sweat by the minute. After a while, the searing equatorial sun moved behind a couple of buildings down the street; here and there, street lights came on. As they sat there in the stifling Toyota, early evening came to Lagos.

The door handle rattled, startling them. Outside in the half-light, the stout man's face was staring back at him through the glass. The American cranked down the window.

"Come! Doctor Krasheev is ready to see us!"

Kip, Busa, and the stocky man made their way down to the building on the next block. The multi-storied, stone-front structure had the solid, permanent look that Kip took to be from the days when Nigeria was part of the British Empire. Beside the lighted entrance, a polished brass plaque with a crown insignia on it announced the place to be the *"Nation Bank of Nigeria"*.

The three went up some broad stone steps, through a set of tall bronze doors into a musty, marble-floored lobby. The lights were off and the only illumination to speak of came from some outside street lamps that shone fitfully through narrow leaded windows, giving the place a shadowy, murky cast. A cat-sized gray rat scooted across the floor and scuttled down a ventilator shaft. Kip shuddered.

The man motioned for the others to follow him toward a wide marble staircase. As they came to the landing, Kip spotted a soldier in an Army uniform on each side standing attention, an automatic weapon at his side. Glancing around the cavernous room, Kip made out other rigid military men, all looking like ghosts in indistinct uniforms, standing in vague, unlighted spots. Then he remembered this was one of the main banks of the whole country. He hoped the guards were customer-friendly.

The trio trooped upstairs and made a turn to the left that took them down a long, darkened hallway where the only light came from flat rays that beamed out from under several closed doors. At the far end of the corridor, a yellowish glow came from inside a room where the door was open.

The stocky man motioned Kip and the other Nigerian into a well-furnished office to find an angular, middle-aged individual in a dark-gray, pin-striped suit sitting behind a mahogany desk. A nameplate in front of the African identified him as *"N. B. Krasheev, (Dr.) Director, Intercontinental Remittance Office"*.

So this is "Krasheev", Kip thought.

Another well-dressed man stood nearby. "Take seats," he said, and everyone settled into chairs. "This is Doctor Krasheev," the man went on, as the bank official extended his hand and shook the American's. But the banker was not smiling, and Kip saw that everyone else in the room had a serious expression on his face. It looked like this was going to be a solemn meeting.

While other introductions were going on, Kip looked around. The office was in what the American thought would probably be called "British Colonial" style; university degrees and other certificates hung on the wall behind the man's desk. A fixture that gave off only dim, half-hearted light was centered in an overhead tropical electric fan whose blades whirled the moisture-laden air so lazily that Kip wondered why they had even bothered to turn it on.

Glancing out the open window, he observed a three-story brick building across the street with rows of old-fashioned, push-out window-lights all up and down its block-long length.

" . . . and this gentleman here, will be signing for the funds regarding the 'oil' from the 'Tanuta Refinery'—" A rasping voice brought his reverie to an end.

Kip looked back into the room to see the stocky man pointing in his direction; everyone was staring at him, evidently waiting for him to speak.

"Y-yes," Kip stammered, as he tried to mentally shift gears and bring himself back into the conversation.

Krasheev leaned back in his chair and regarded Kip with expressionless eyes. "You are aware, I assume, that when you take possession of the 'oil' . . . the 'funds', actually—"

Kip nodded.

" . . . that the money has been considerably altered."

Altered? This was something new.

"It had been blackened when the authorities seized it at the airport."

Kip gaped at the man, uncomprehending.

"The bills will have to be restored chemically before they can be deposited in a bank. You must do that after we turn it all over to you."

"But why—how?" What had started out as a straightforward deal had now taken a whole new turn. "How do I do this?"

Krasheev looked impatient. "We will go into that, later. Right now, the main thing is to sign the funds into your possession." He nodded at his assistant, who produced a sheaf of papers. "These are the official transfer documents that will formally turn over the money to you . . . after that, we will deliver it to your designated location." He signed the page, then pushed it across the desk to Kip.

The Texan gaped at it, wide-eyed—the document, scripted in a classical font, was the most elaborate piece of paper he had ever seen—the heading, alone, could have been in twenty-four-carat gold, for all he knew. Blinking, Kip read the agreement that would transfer the twenty-million dollars of U.S. currency from the "Nation Bank of Nigeria" into his custody *in its current form.* Kip deducted that the money would have to be cleaned up before he could transfer it overseas.

Krasheev glanced around at the others, then bored his eyes at Kip. "We can arrange for the chemical cleaning of the bills after they are in your custody."

With nothing else to influence him, Kip scratched his signature onto the document. In short order, he read and signed the rest of the papers, all of which related to the funds transfer.

When he was finished, Krasheev passed the papers to his assistant, who handed one piece to Busa, then stuffed the rest of the pages into a briefcase.

Busa mouthed to Kip that he would give him a copy of the document.

Kip had no idea what to do with twenty-million dollars in discolored cash. "Where will I take the money?"

Busa spoke up. "Bring it to my house." Everyone turned to look at him. "We can clean the money in my garage. It will be safe, there."

Krasheev looked at Kip. "Is that all right with you?"

"I guess so."

"Fine. Then we will bring it tomorrow afternoon to Busa's place. We will show you how to chemically-clean the money so it can be deposited in the bank."

Kip gazed out the window trying to take it all in; everything was happening so fast. The lights were now on in the building across the street and throbbing machinery sounds came from inside it.

Krasheev saw him staring out his office window. "That is the 'National Government Defense Plant'." He leaned back and tapped his fingertips together. "That is where military uniforms come from. They also make shoes and underwear in there—" The American saw that the banker, for the first time, was making a half-way attempt to smile.

Then Krasheev extended his hand across the desk and shook Kip's.

The group filed out of the stuffy office, leaving the "Director of Intercontinental Remittance" sitting stiffly in his seat.

Passing through the lobby, they again made their way past the immobile guards, who looked as if they had not moved a molecule since the first time. Outside, the men stepped around a grimacing beggar lying on a threadbare blanket, to the curb, where Kip grasped the door handle of the awaiting blue Toyota.

In a few minutes, they were back on the highway, headed once more toward the city's outskirts.

A short distance beyond the long bridge, the driver suddenly slammed on his brakes! The car skidded and slewed from side-to-side, then came to a slithering stop in the midst of some people.

"Idiots!" the young fellow behind the wheel swore. In the car's headlights Kip saw a couple of men dashing across the highway in front of them, then several more loping past them into the darkness as other vehicles were loudly hitting their brakes behind them.

Kip stared in amazement as the driver threaded the sedan among clusters of gesturing, grinning individuals. "Why are they on the highway?"

"They think they can get away with it," the driver said, as more men materialized in the headlights. The young fellow winced, as yet another fellow dashed in front of the vehicle. "There are no rules, here."

Then Kip realized that some of the other cars didn't have their headlights on, or were only using parking lights.

". . . and these cars without headlights," the driver went on, as if reading Kip's mind, "they think they are so cool, or something." To the American, it was incredible that people were running about in the middle of the highway in front of vehicles that were speeding along with their headlights turned off.

A little farther on, they passed the big wrecked truck, still face-down in the watery sinkhole. They certainly do things differently in Nigeria, Kip concluded.

At length, they arrived back at the hotel. Busa walked with him upstairs to the room. "Tomorrow will be a big day," he wheezed," they will bring the cash to my house in the afternoon."

Then, the African turned and left.

Kip wondered what twenty-million dollars looked like.

-4-

At exactly three o'clock the next afternoon came the now-familiar knock. After returning the sequence, Ivan opened the door. Busa, who looked to be in a hurry, hustled in, almost bowling-over the younger Nigerian. "They are bringing the 'box' to my place in an hour!" the fat man puffed from the exertion of the stairs, "let us get going!"

Scant moments later they were at the front of the hotel, where the young driver was standing beside a shiny new Jaguar four-door sedan. The portly African eased his bulk into a rear seat. Kip took the other back seat. Busa's stocky associate from the night before was again with them.

After driving only about a kilometer on the highway in the direction of downtown, the car dropped off onto the service road and made a sharp right turn into a residential neighborhood. For some minutes, the expensive vehicle swerved and jostled down a rutted, muddy road. Kip looked about, frowning. Where were they going?

The driver navigated the car over a foot-deep trench onto a brick driveway. The American saw they were in a manicured, fenced compound; an iron gate was closing behind them. The Jaguar pulled up in front of a mansion-sized, two-story stucco, duplex-type house.

"Wait here!" Busa said. He got out and went into the elegant-looking place.

In a minute the man came back out and motioned for them. They trooped into a large open living area decorated in African artifacts; one whole plate glass wall looked out onto a lush, tropical garden. At the far end of the room was a black-mahogany dining set. What sounded to Kip like soft native music came from a stereo console at the other end of the space.

Busa clapped his hands twice. Right away, a stooped, bald-headed, very dark African man loped into the room and bowed at him. "Bring drinks to these men!"

The fellow put the palms of his hands together and bowed twice, then disappeared in a hurry out of the room. Seeing Kip's interest, Busa came over to him. "That is 'Mickey'," he said, "he came to me years ago."

Kip got the idea there was more to the story, but Busa moved off before he could ask any questions.

A couple of minutes later, "Mickey" came back through the doorway carrying a large silver tray. On it was a bottle of "Johnnie Walker Black Label", along with some glasses and a bucket of ice. The Nigerian motioned to the credenza where the fellow had placed the tray. "Have a drink!" Everyone helped themselves to the libations.

Glass in hand, Kip walked around the room, looking at the decorations. He wondered about a carved wooden crucifix hanging on the wall next to a plaque commending Busa for some achievement or other. The full name on the trophy, "Saleem Masobe Busa", to the American, looked decidedly un-church-like. "What is your religion?"

"Catholic," came the man's reply. For the time being, Kip decided to take his word for it, although he had some reservations as to whether the man was actually a Roman Catholic.

Just then, there came a loud sound from outside. A siren! As everyone made for the door, a throaty rumble became a ground-shaking roar of big diesel engines.

Out front, they were confronted by an intimidating procession of troop-laden military vehicles and police cars with flashing lights that had pulled up in front of Busa's house. A pair of military helicopters pounded overhead. The tall iron gate was again open.

A serious-looking Army officer in combat gear dismounted from a smoke-belching armored personnel carrier and came toward them with a searching face. "Busa? Busa, here?"

The fat man stepped forward. An animated conversation broke out between the two. Then Busa looked around and gestured for Kip to come over. Gulping, the blond Texan stepped across the front yard and came up to them.

"This is 'Colonel Ajiboy'," Busa told Kip.

The Army man looked the American up and down. "Identification?" Kip pulled out his Texas driver's license. The officer snatched the card and scrutinized it, glancing back and forth from the photo I.D. to him several times. He shoved the piece back at Kip, then turned toward the leading personnel carrier and shouted an order in a language Kip didn't understand.

At once, troops began quick-timing toward what seemed to be pre-planned positions around the property and snapped to attention, their weapons at the ready. It looked to Kip as if they had performed the maneuver many times. The commander of the detachment looked in turn at every one of the men in their positions, nodding in approval to each soldier

The Army leader told the civilians to go into the house. His voice had the ring of authority.

Inside, Busa's living room was a scene of furious activity as men shoved furniture back against the walls, creating a big open area in the middle. The overweight African clapped his hands twice, summoning Mickey. When the little servant appeared, Busa impatiently motioned for him to clear the drinks from the room.

Just then, the ramrod-straight military officer and another man in a dark suit strode through the front doorway. "Bring an iron and an ironing board in here!" the second man voiced at Mickey as the servant was stepping toward the kitchen with the Johnnie Walker paraphernalia. The harassed fellow was so startled at the man's strident command that he nearly dropped the tray. Kip wondered what was so important about a clothes-iron and an ironing board at a time like this.

There was a loud commotion at the front door. Through the entrance burst a half-dozen soldiers, their weapons at the ready. As Kip gaped, the troops formed two parallel lines into the living room facing each other. Through the open front door, the American could see more Army men out in the front yard. *What's going on?* he wondered. Then, four men in police uniforms clumped through the door bearing a meter-square, varnished, wooden platform with horizontal poles protruding from each corner. On the flat surface was a cube-shaped, gray-steel object about three-feet square that looked like a safe. Four of the soldiers detached themselves from the others at the doorway and stepped alongside the four at the corner poles, who shuffled into the middle of the open space and set down the object. The Army officer called out an order that brought all the troops in the room to guard position, their weapons cocked. Kip could hear someone shouting orders outside. Just then, a quartet of civilians in dark business suits appeared and made their way to the head of the gathering. The first civilian, who had entered with the Army officer and seemed to be the most important of the dark-suited delegation, nodded at the military man who then took one step backward and came to attention.

"I am 'Doctor Mobustu', of the 'Nation Bank of Nigeria'," the suited man addressed the gathering, "and we are here to demonstrate the method for chemically-removing the black alteration to the currency."

The African paused for what Kip thought was dramatic effect.

Out of the corner of his eye, Kip saw Mickey trot out of the kitchen with an ironing board that he set up at one end of the open room, then he returned a moment later with a clothes iron. Kip's attention again focused on what was going on. The man calling himself "Doctor Mobustu"—that to the American sounded like he was pronouncing as *"Mob-used-to"*—had motioned for one of the other well-dressed civilians to come forward and he was again speaking.

". . . of the Technical Division of the Nation Bank, and his associates, who will perform the demonstration—" The important-looking banker swept his hand at the other men.

Kip noticed Mickey's hunched frame ease into the crowded, sweltering room, where he hung back, watching. Off to the side stood Busa, his handkerchief working back and forth on his shiny forehead.

The Texan looked around, not quite believing what was happening—there was an air of unreality about all this, and an indefinable undercurrent of danger. The soldiers continued to stand in position, their eyes hardly blinking. He knew that his fate was entirely in the hands of all these strangers.

One of the suited men held an elongated wooden box, about a foot long, that he placed on the tea-table. Then, he knelt and inserted a key into a lock on the strongbox. There was a metallic "click", and the man stood up. The head of the bank detail motioned to another man, who squatted down and keyed open a second lock.

Mobustu knelt and, closing his eyes, appeared to meditate for a moment. Then he raised the heavy lid. Inside, on a top tray, was a blue plastic pouch about the size of a cigarette pack. He set aside the packet, then reached into his own coat pocket and pulled out another small bag, gray in color, that he placed next to the first. After stopping to wipe his forehead with a handkerchief, he lifted the tray up and out of the box. Curious, Kip leaned over and saw that the strongbox was packed with several dozen brick-sized objects, each covered by tissue paper.

The bank man went over for a low conversation with Busa, who clapped his hands twice.

"Bring a big pitcher of water and three trays!" he ordered Mickey.

The servant vanished into the kitchen, returning in a minute with a clear beaker of water along with some metal baking pans. Mobustu pointed at the tea table and Mickey placed the four items next to the pouches.

Then the little helper slunk back to his former place by the wall.

The bank official pointed to another civilian, who stepped forward and with a flourish poured the water from the beaker into a flat tray. The man picked up the blue pouch and emptied its contents—a grainy powder—into the tray. He took a shiny metal spoon-like object from the wooden box and stirred the contents with an air of formality. The concoction made an audible "sizzling" sound; a puffy little cloud of vapor lifted from the surface of the tray and drifted away with an acrid metallic odor that joined the sweat and body odors accumulating in the room that was feeling more closed-in by the minute. The assistant then poured the remaining water into the other trays. He un-wrapped the gray packet and dropped a powdery substance into the second tray. As he stirred the mixture with another spoon, it gave off a snapping, popping sound.

The bank man turned around and motioned his hand for Kip to come to the table. With all eyes in the room on him, the blond American made his way to where the man pointed, in front of the strongbox.

"Reach down in there and pull out one of the wrapped pieces!" he ordered in a thick brogue. "Pull it out at random! Do not select one!"

Taking a deep breath, Kip reached down into the tightly-packed safe and pulled one of the "bricks" from the tightly-packed stacks.

"Un-wrap it!"

With shaking fingers, Kip pulled the creased tissue-paper-like sheet from around the contents. What remained was a stiff rectangular block of compressed sheets of paper.

"Take one!"

Kip tugged on the packed papers, then pulled a piece from somewhere around the middle of the stack. He thought its texture seemed to have a vaguely familiar feel to it.

The bank officer nodded to one of the Nigerians who had helped open the strongbox. That man, who was now wearing rubber gloves, took the paper from Kip and immersed it into the first tray. Another African, who was holding a stopwatch, waited a short interval, then nodded. The first civilian pulled the paper from the solution.

Kip's jaw dropped—what had been a featureless black piece of paper moments ago, was now *a perfect-looking, United States one-hundred-dollar bill!*

In turn, the banker dropped it into the second and third trays. After the last tray, he carried it to another suited man at the ironing board, who ironed the bill on both sides, then handed it to the stupefied American.

Kip gaped, incredulous, at the chemically-cleaned money. "Is it real?"

Mobustu looked offended. "They are *ALL* real!" Get another one!"

Kip reached into the strongbox again and pulled out a second "brick"; in another minute, there were *two* authentic bills on the tea-table. They repeated the process until ten one-hundred-dollar U.S. currency notes were laid-out side-by-side.

Then Mobustu nodded at the two other men assisting him. They re-wrapped the blackened currency, then wedged the bundles back into the strongbox. Both men in turn re-locked the box.

The overheated room became very quiet.

"Order Arms!" Everyone jumped at the military commander's sudden shout. The soldiers un-cocked their weapons with loud *CLICKS!* and lowered them in jerky motions to their sides. "Left Face!" the officer in sunglasses called out. "Forward—march!"

Holding their weapons by the muzzles and stamping the marble floor, the troops tramped out of the house. Kip could hear more shouted orders outside, then the clatter of diesel engines starting. As everyone inside stood sweating, they heard, one-after-the-other, the trucks roar off.

The bank man turned to Kip. "This ends the demonstration! You will now be responsible for cleaning the bills for deposit into your bank!" The *entourage* headed for the exit. In another minute came the sounds of their vehicles driving away. Dust swirled in through the open front door.

Once again, silence took over the room.

A man in the rear was the first to say something. "I wish to speak privately with the American—"

With that, Busa, Mickey, and the others passed out through the kitchen doors.

The speaker was a man whom Kip had not noticed before. "Come over to the long table."

They sat down facing each other across the mahogany table-top. Kip had no idea what he wanted. A glass-faced clock on the wall struck the half-hour. The man interlaced his fingers; the diamond inset of an impressive-looking ring on the African's little finger caught the overhead light.

"Let me come to the point—I am 'Mike Adwadube' . . . and I am an attorney representing Mister Busa, *'General Retchko'* . . .

and the others involved in the 'transaction'." Kip remembered that this same "Adwadube" guy had sent a fax to his and Brad's office when all this business was just starting. The American looked at the fellow's face and felt a chill—the lawyer's eyes were cold, unfeeling-like; almost diabolical-looking. Right away, Kip sensed there was something unsavory about him.

Adwadube narrowed his mucosed eyes. "As you were told . . . the money must be cleaned-up before you can take it to the bank. It will cost money to do this."

"Money?" Kip felt the hair on the back of his neck begin to prickle. "How much money?"

Adwadube folded his hands together on the tabletop and stared straight at the lean Texan for long seconds. Kip blanched at the stare of the man's bleary, lifeless-looking eyes. The lawyer spoke slowly, deliberately. "'*One-million, six-hundred-seventy-five-thousand dollars'* . . . and we will need it right away to start processing the money."

"What! One-mil—what for? Why so much money?"

"The chemicals are expensive . . . and we must get started right now."

"I don't have that kind of money!" The idea was so preposterous he couldn't believe it.

"Have your associates in America send it."

"My 'associates' don't have that kind of money, either!"

A cloud came over the man's face. "Really, now—" His voice was chiding. "With this much at stake for you, surely you can make the arrangements."

Kip thought fast. "How about *this* arrangement . . . what if we could use the money already cleaned to buy a small amount of the chemicals to fix a few thousand dollars of the bills, then use *that* money to buy more chemicals! After a while, we would have *all* the money fixed-up and ready to deposit—"

The very-dark-skinned African shook his head. "Not acceptable! We must do all the bills at once!"

Kip knew that cleaning all the cash at one time was out of the question. If the fellow wouldn't budge from his demands, there was nothing else he could do. Right now, it looked as if he had no other choice but to try to get back to Texas and somehow work out things. "I'll tell you what . . . let me make a telephone call to my 'associates' in America—"

The lawyer shook his head; his filmy eyes unblinking. "The telephones are not functioning, now."

Kip suddenly realized that *wherever he went, the telephones did not work!* The whole time he had been in Nigeria, he had been cut-off from the outside world. *Now* he understood: Someone was purposely preventing him from contacting his home base! Kip thought about his one-way, one-time-only airline ticket in his luggage back in the hotel room with a reservation for the evening flight to Amsterdam. If he missed that plane, tonight, he would be stuck here in Lagos with no way to get out and unable to tell anyone on the outside world what was happening to him! Kip now knew he was in grave danger. He must get out of Nigeria at once.

" . . . with your plans—" the man was saying. Although Kip had not paid attention to all that Adwadube had just said, there was no question about what he had *meant.*

"I'll have to return to the 'States to get the money . . . I will leave, tonight."

The man nodded. "You can leave the box here with Busa. Go back to your headquarters to get the necessary funds and return."

Kip looked around. "By the way, where *is* Busa?" It seemed as if only he and the lawyer were now in the house.

"He has gone, and will meet you later." Adwadube glanced toward the front door. "The car is waiting for you, outside."

Kip was ready to get going. When he stood up, the African came around with his hand extended and was actually trying to smile. The American was having a hard time understanding some of these people. Knowing he might need Adwadube's good graces later, Kip shook the fellow's hand.

As he passed the tea-table on his way out, Kip looked down at the ten one-hundred-dollar bills still arrayed on the tabletop. Since technically, the money was his, and as the other man had gone ahead of him, he scooped up a fistful of the bills and stuffed them into his pocket.

At the front door, Kip turned about and took one last look at the room. The strongbox was still sitting in the middle of the floor.

Outside, the young driver was waiting in the Jaguar. In a minute, they had lurched across the ditch and were headed back toward the hotel.

As they rode along at what seemed to Kip to be a maddingly slow pace, he worried about his airline ticket—it would be a simple matter for Ivan or another of the men to take it, in which case he would be stranded in Lagos.

When they turned into the passenger drop-off at the "Roomland Hotel", Kip told the driver to wait on him; he would be checking-out right away and would need a ride to the airport.

The first thing he did when he returned to the room was to see about the ticket—thank God, it was still there! Breathing a sigh of relief, Kip shoved it into a rear pocket next to his passport. Next, he lifted the telephone receiver and heard nothing. Of course. It was then he realized Ivan was gone. Maybe it was just as well—he wanted to get away with a minimum of distractions. In haste he threw his things into the carry-on bag and with one last look-around at the room, closed the door and dragged his luggage, bumping, down the stairs.

At the front desk, he paid the room bill with two of the restored hundred-dollar bills. The clerk accepted the currency without question, a fact Kip noted with satisfaction; it looked as if the money was spendable. As he had snatched-up four of the bills back at Busa's tea-table, he now had two of the cleaned notes remaining.

Kip tossed the luggage bag onto the back floorboard of the sedan and dropped into the rear seat. "To the airport!" he told the driver. In short order, the Jaguar was racing up the highway.

As they rode along in the early-evening twilight, the Texan was torn by conflicting thoughts. Even though he could almost palpably feel the danger around him and wanted to get out of Lagos right away—there was still some unfinished business. In particular, Busa still had the bank receipt for the fifty-thousand dollars and the papers he had signed in Krasheev's office.

He leaned forward and tapped the driver's shoulder. "Where's Busa?"

" . . . the departure gate—" came the cryptic answer.

Presently, the lights of the hulking terminal of the "Murtala Mohammed Airport Lagos" came into sight. The Jaguar swept up the curving driveway to the airline building and slithered to a stop.

Kip grabbed his luggage and hopped out, mumbling something he hoped the young driver would regard as a satisfactory farewell.

No sooner had Kip stepped through the front doors into the terminal than he was surrounded by a gaggle of gesturing, jabbering people.

"I can carry your luggage!"

"Let me carry your ticket . . . your passport!"

Kip brushed them all off—in particular the last one. He shuddered at the thought of handing over anything of value to these people.

As the American trudged along, he observed that the airline ticket counters, all with familiar company names, were manned by uniformed soldier-types with pistols at their sides. "Where are the regular airline people?" he wondered, half-aloud.

Although the terminal was enormous, not many lights were on; the whole place had a dim, shadowy cast. All across the people-packed expanse, Africans, mostly in native attire, jostled along, many of them balancing bags and packages on their heads, shouting to each other in incomprehensible languages. Since there was no air conditioning in the terminal, to the heat and humidity were added the odors of sweat, strange incense, and some other smells he tried to ignore, but couldn't. By the time Kip had lugged his luggage all the way to the far end of the ticket terminal, he was adding his own sweat to the place.

"Your ticket?" An African female in a military uniform frowned at Kip through a smudgy glass window with iron security bars. The impression he had had when he first came into the terminal that the airline counters were run by soldiers was true: the grim-looking woman in the enclosure with the familiar airline logo sign behind her was wearing a holstered pistol. Kip handed his ticket to her, hoping she would not seize it, as he had been told happened sometimes at this airport. The woman turned the ticket folder inside-and-out while he stood there, sweating from the heat and anxiety. "Any electronic devices?" She motioned at a sign:

POSSESSION OF ELECTRONIC DEVICES OR APPLIANCES ILLEGAL. SEIZURE OF ITEMS AND ARREST FOR ILLEGAL POSSESSION

Kip's eyes went wide. *The battery-operated shaver!* He swallowed. "Does it mean *all* appliances?" He was sure everyone around could hear his pulses pounding.

The woman soldier glared at him. "If we find anything electric or electronic in your luggage we will seize it and you will be arrested!"

Kip knew if they were to look in his travel bag and find the little electric razor, it would be the end. He thought he was going to faint.

The female looked around for an inspector, but the only such person in sight was on the floor nearby, rifling through another man's things. A squad of male soldiers stood close-by the quaking other passenger, their sub-machine guns at the ready. For what seemed to Kip to be a *very* long minute, the woman waved at the official. The guard paid no attention to her.

She shrugged, stamped his folder, then stuck a boarding pass inside it. When he turned to leave, she held up her hand. "You must go to the 'Departure Tax' window." The military woman pointed at a booth located across the vast expanse of the terminal lobby.

Kip dragged the big bag over to the second window, which, like the ticket booth, had bars around it and what he took to be bulletproof glass in front. He reached into his pocket and pulled out one of the restored hundred-dollar notes and slid it under the thick pane.

The armed woman looked at it for a second, then shoved it back at him, shaking her head. "This is not a good bill!" she said through the glass, "I cannot take it!" She pointed at a sign behind her:

DEPARTURE TAX $35
U.S. FUNDS ONLY—
NO BILLS ACCEPTED
DATED PRIOR TO 1986

Kip stared at the message board in consternation; he had only *one* remaining hundred-dollar bill in his pocket! If it was dated *before* 1986, he was a goner. Because he had not been able to communicate with the outside world since he had been in Nigeria, no one back home knew where he was, or was doing, and would not be able help him in any way if the bill in his pocket was too old. *Whether he lived to board the plane or perhaps died tonight could very well depend on the date on the hundred-dollar bill in his pocket!*

Kip's heart was racing as he slipped the last hundred-dollar bill to the woman. She glanced at it, then looked up at him. "Give me your ticket!"

Just then, he heard the shuffling sound of jackboots close by. Turning about, he was horrified to see two soldiers with drawn pistols edging in his direction.

"Your ticket!"

With his heart in his throat, Kip pushed the packet underneath the inch-thick glass.

The Army woman stamped something on the ticket, inserted some American dollars into the folder and slid it back to him. With a shake of her head and a backhand motion, the woman waved away the soldiers. The disappointed-looking men re-holstered their semi-automatics and moved off.

Shaking from the close-call, Kip headed down the concourse, dragging the unwieldy luggage bag. He had gone only a few steps when another circle of people crowded about, trying to offer "services" for which he had absolutely no need. This time he shook them off by ducking through a gate, where a detail of armed guards stopped them.

* * *

A powerfully-built, very dark-skinned African followed closely behind Kip through the gate.

* * *

42

The departure lounge on the second level looked pretty much like what the American had seen at other airports, but there the comparison ended. Right away, it became obvious that the Lagos airport was indeed a military operation—up here at the gates, Army people were very much in charge. On the boarding pass was a statement that the airport was run by something called the "Nigerian Airplane Operating Company", that Kip guessed was a quasi-government outfit and as much confirmed his earlier suspicion that the airlines' presence were in name only. From all around the terminal, posters of Nigeria's malign-looking military dictator stared at him; up and down the concourse, goose-stepping troops, rifles on their shoulders, their combat boots slamming down with every jarring step, forced people aside. Kip had long since decided this airport was the most tension-filled place he had ever seen; an impression made even more pronounced by the fact that only half of the overhead lights were on, creating dim, uneven shadows all around.

Kip wandered across to a picture window and watched the *'DC-10'* he would soon board out on the concrete apron being loaded in preparation for its departure. Beyond the other side of the concourse, grounds-crewmen were also readying a brilliantly-lit *'Boeing 747'*. According to a placard by the gate, it would depart on its overnight journey to London at about the same time his DC-10 flight left for Amsterdam.

A squealing little blonde girl, chased by her mother who kept calling out to her in an English accent, was running up and down the way, oblivious to the dangers all around her. At one point, the moppet threaded herself between the goose-steps of a squad of soldiers as they tramped by, shoulder-to-shoulder. Everyone gasped—but, miraculously, she was not struck by the phalanx of kicking jackboots.

Kip was torn by the realization that there was still some unfinished business. His chief concern: where was Busa? The man was supposed be at the departure gate, but, so far, the obese Nigerian was nowhere to be seen. As he still had the bank receipt and the document from Krasheev, it was vital that the African bring them before he boarded the aircraft. On the other hand, since Kip wanted to get out of Nigeria as soon as possible, he was resolved to be one of the first passengers to board the airplane—Busa or no Busa. According to the information poster by the gate, the airliner would start loading passengers at nine-forty-five, with the departure set for ten-thirty.

As the clock crept toward boarding time, the realization finally sank-in to the American that Busa was not coming.

"Have your boarding passes ready!" came a loud voice. Kip looked around and saw a woman in military fatigues, with the now-standard semi-automatic at her side, standing at the gate, beckoning. There was a general shuffle as a line began to form. Kip dragged the big bag as close to the front of the procession as he could manage.

In the line, he reached into his ticket pack for the boarding pass. *It was not there!* Gulping, he frantically fished around in every pocket and in the folds and flaps of the luggage. It was gone! Casting about in desperation, he spotted a familiar-looking card lying on the linoleum toward the end of the line between some passengers' shoes. The boarding pass! It must have fallen out of the folder as he stood up to get in line! As he bolted back toward where it was, a soldier also noticed it and bent over to pick it up. With a lunge, Kip snatched the card just ahead of the man's groping fingertips!

While the female soldier ticket collector stood with her hand outstretched, Kip hesitated and took another look-around for the absent Busa. "Keep moving!" the armed agent snapped. With one last despairing glance backward, he handed her the pass. She tore off half of it and passed him through the gate to the plane.

* * *

A few steps behind Kip, the dark-skinned man pushed into the airliner, never taking his eyes off the American.

* * *

Kip's window-seat was on the right side in the very last row of the DC-10. While the airliner loaded, he watched the passengers as they came into the rear-most cabin. A thirty-something executive-looking chap speaking in a brisk British accent stuffed his briefcase into the overhead and sat down in the seat just ahead of him next to a younger-looking, very attractive Oriental girl. As Kip stared, astonished, right away the two lifted the seat-arm between them and began passionately making-out! This could be an interesting flight, Kip thought.

A sandy-haired fellow in his forties dropped into the aisle seat next to Kip. He said he worked with an oil company in Nigeria and was on his way to Memphis,Tennessee. Kip told him he was involved in oil marketing, which gave them something to talk about. The man said he had traveled from southeastern Nigeria on a domestic flight that had had some mechanical problems and was worried about safety and maintenance with the local airlines. He predicted there would soon be a spate of crashes. Kip and the oil worker swapped business cards.

The two watched as a turbaned, bearded, olive-skinned man in a white flowing robe appeared at the head of the nearest aisle, followed by more men in cloth headpieces and robes; all stepped in stately fashion down both aisles. They were followed by about three-dozen jiggling, giggling, long-legged young African women dressed in very short, clingy, low-cut, toga-like outfits. Every one of the girls was literally dripping in jewelry, bangles and beads. When they had occupied a substantial portion of the seats in the center section, there was a bustle of activity as an older, dignified-looking man with a crown on his head and holding a golden scepter in his bejeweled hands shuffled into the cabin, tended by several fawning men, also in robes and turbans. A thin man who was sitting at the front of the cabin next to the aisle, glanced up, then shot out of his seat and started bowing and genuflecting, reverently kissing and caressing the old man's hands, his rings and the scepter, all the while moaning something indistinguishable. Watching this, it seemed to Kip as if the man with the crown was some sort of "holy man" of extreme importance. He suspected that the girls constituted his harem. As the entourage and the mysterious man took their seats, a pronounced aroma of perfume began to waft about the cabin.

About that time, a disturbance broke out in the aisle a few rows in front of Kip. He looked up to see two armed soldiers pulling a passenger from his seat! Two other troopers stood in the aisle; their rifles aimed at the man. Over his American-accented protests, they handcuffed him, pushed him up the aisle with thumping noises and out the plane's front door.

Just then, another squad of troopers came tramping down the aisle. They stopped two rows in front of Kip and jerked another man—another American—out of his seat, and roughly shoved him up the aisle in a repeat of what had just happened.

"I've never seen anything like this!" the man next to Kip said, frowning, looking nervous, "it's like they're going after us Americans!"

He had hardly uttered those words when *a third* squad of about a half-dozen soldiers in all came down both aisles and yanked two more Americans from their seats and prodded them at gunpoint off the airplane!

Kip's acquaintance looked at him with concern in his eyes. *Were they going to be next?* The man slumped down in his seat as far as he could, motioning for Kip to do the same; both pretended to be reading a magazine held up in front of his face. After a minute, Kip peeped up and was shocked to see that soldiers at the front of both aisles were still scanning the passengers! *For more Americans?* He ducked down behind the periodical again, below the level of the top of the seat in front of him and once more feigned reading. His seatmate was doing the same.

Then there came a thumping of boots that seemed to be receding. A minute went by, then came sounds like the main cabin door up front being closed and latched. Kip lowered the magazine and stole a glance up the aisle. The armed men were not in sight.

All at once, the airplane gave a lurch and began moving backward! Was the ordeal of the soldiers over? As the massive aircraft rolled in reverse away from the terminal, from the relieved looks on the passengers' faces, everyone in the cabin had the same thought: "Let's get out of this country, *fast!*"

Then came the welcome whine of the engines starting. The three jets came up to idle speed and ran for about a half-minute, then shut down! Silence came over the cabin—the mystified passengers looked around at each other, frowning.

A flashing light outside the window caught Kip's attention—a vehicle with blinking blue-and-red lights was racing across the tarmac toward them. An appalling thought came to him: The soldiers are coming back! As he stared wide-eyed out the window, the streaking machine disappeared around to the left-side of the plane, out of his line of sight, where its flashing lights reflected on the cabin window frames. But they didn't seem to be moving, which brought on a whole new set of concerns. For some long minutes, everyone sat there, waiting and wondering in the overheating cabin. Kip could feel his clothes becoming soggy from sweat.

A crackling metallic voice burst from a loudspeaker overhead. "Ladies and gentlemen, this is the captain speaking . . . we apologize for the delay, but the ground crew wanted to inspect a cargo door. Everything is all right, so we will re-start the engines and be on our way in a few moments. Thank you for your patience."

There was a collective sigh of relief as once more the sound of the engines building up came from the outside. After a minute, they were back up to speed, and with a muffled roar the heavy, wide-bodied DC-10 made a waddling turn to the left. As the aircraft straightened and lumbered out the taxiway, through the window Kip saw the lights of the ladder-truck that had been the cause of so much anxiety receding into the distance.

Minutes later, there came the deep rumble of the three monstrous jet engines at full power as the huge aircraft began its take-off roll. As the lights of Lagos's airport flashed by, Kip was overwhelmed by a sense of relief to be finally getting out of this godforsaken country where he had endured so many nerve-wracking moments. It seemed incredible that everything that had happened in Lagos had taken place in only about forty-eight hours.

Then came the momentary downward dip of the rear of the plane where they were situated, followed at once by the welcome sight of the runway lights dropping away and the thumping sounds of the landing gear coming up.

As the airliner banked and started its climb toward cruising altitude, and as the glow of the city began to fade below and behind it, Kip bade good riddance to Lagos and its dreadful airport. Ahead was an overnight journey over the Sahara and the Mediterranean to Amsterdam that would take about seven hours.

While the airplane flew on, he leaned back in his seat and mentally replayed and analyzed the events in Lagos. The leading question was: What had happened to Busa? Without the receipt for the bank deposit, he was in an awkward position with Brad, and since a sizable portion of the fifty-thousand dollars had come from him, his partner was sure to have some pointed questions to ask. Same thing with the Krasheev document, which was Kip's proof that he had received the twenty-million dollars into his control. But Busa's mysterious failure to show up at the airport cast the man in a dubious light. His explanation would have to be a really good one.

And the twenty-million dollars was another big question. The elaborate production for his benefit in Busa's living room— whether it had been on the level or not—had been, as he saw it, a performance worthy of an award. Had it been for real? Kip preferred to think that it was. The fact that he had cast his hand into the strongbox at random ten straight times and had come up with a perfect hundred-dollar bill each and every time had to weigh heavily in favor of the money being authentic. And he had successfully passed them at the hotel and particularly at the airport, where two of the bills had undergone the utmost scrutiny by the female tax collector. By way of comparison, he figured the odds that one could hit the very biggest jackpot at Monte Carlo ten times in a row would be so unlikely as to be impossible, or else the high-stakes deck was completely stacked in his favor— and the stakes in Busa's living room had been stacked twenty-million dollars high.

The flight attendant came by with a glass of wine, and as the mellow glow of the *'Cabernet'* loosened his thoughts, he went on reflecting about all that had happened in Lagos. He had to marvel at all his narrow escapes back there: avoiding the immigration authorities; the policeman at the airport bent on his arrest; the Army truck on the highway with the trigger-happy soldiers;

48

getting in-and-out of the "Nation Bank" building with guards all around; the incredible scene at Busa's house; the events at the airport as he was leaving, including the lost boarding pass, capped by the bullying soldiers hauling the Americans off the airliner. Kip shuddered to think what would have happened to him if the last hundred-dollar bill had been the wrong date—he would surely not be on this airplane, and perhaps not even alive, by now. The same could be said for the electric shaver episode—had the inspector not been busy going through someone else's luggage, he would likely now be in custody and maybe dead. All the events at the "Murtala Mohammed Airport Lagos" had added-up to the closest-call of his life.

Then he remembered one more thing: the ground-crew had re-inspected the DC-10's cargo door. Kip recalled some news stories from the past about how some other DC-10's cargo doors had come off in midair, causing terrible crashes with hundreds of fatalities. In that regard, he was glad they had double-checked the plane's hatches, even though the truck and the flashing lights had caused so much worry to him and the other passengers.

Kip kept watching the video screen for the moment they would be out of Nigerian airspace, which took place about an hour after they had taken off. Then—and only then—did he feel they had escaped for certain the clutches of Nigeria's police and military. Up to then, he would not have put it past them to somehow have forced the plane back to Lagos for more soldier stuff.

Now that they were flying on the safe side of Nigeria—that to Kip, meant *outside* the country—and the Lagos episodes were behind him, he could again breathe freely. A movie came on the screen.

Kip still had not noticed the muscular, very dark-skinned Nigerian sitting on the far side of the cabin who was observing his every move.

After the film, the cabin lights dimmed even more and many of the passengers settled back to rest. Kip was too keyed-up to sleep, so he watched the entertainment on the airplane's big TV screen. Pretty soon, he discovered that the best "entertainment" was taking place in the seats right in front of him. As soon as the lights were turned down, the British guy and the Oriental girl had drawn a blanket unto themselves and snuggled down in the seat. Kip didn't pay any attention to them until a while later when he was startled to observe a bare feminine foot and a sleek calf straighten above the seat-back. As the "harem" girls giggled and the oil man next to Kip stared transfixed, the foot planted itself squarely on the window glass, squirmed about, then disappeared back beneath the undulating cover. As Kip saw it, the handsome Britisher and the beautiful Oriental girl were definitely doing their part to further international relations.

As the flight droned on, practically every passenger eventually dozed off. Up front, on what looked like a temporary throne, the man with the scepter was slumped over in snoring slumber; his jeweled crown had slid down onto his forehead. The fellow's male attendants were sprawled across nearby seats, likewise insensible. Kip stayed awake.

Hour-after-hour, the big airliner made its nighttime way northward over the featureless desert and the dark Mediterranean to a pre-dawn landfall over the south coast of France. From watching the map on the screen, Kip knew they were nearing Europe, and—right on time—Nice passed underneath, strung out like a shimmering necklace against the faint silver surf of the southern shoreline. Kip remembered that Sloane's late French-student boyfriend, the father of her little boy, Nicky, had been from somewhere around Nice.

Then the black landmass of France took over with its little light beads of towns here and there.

Not long after the DC-10 had left the Mediterranean behind, and as the forehead of the sun was poking up over the horizon off to the right side of the northbound airplane, Kip felt a prod on his shoulder. "Breakfast is served," came an attendant's voice.

The Important Man up front was now awake; his crown back in place on top of his head. Around him, anxious-looking manservants were trying to curry favor with his every move. As Kip watched, the old guy scowled and shook his head almost every time one of his lieutenants put a dish of food in front of him, whereupon the plate would be whipped away as soon as the fellow showed his displeasure.

Then came the familiar drop in the sound of the engines, as the airplane began its descent toward its Dutch destination.

A half hour later, the end of the Amsterdam runway shot by underneath the wings and with a couple of thumps, they were back in Europe—back in civilization, as Kip saw it.

While he waited in the surging Customs line, the very-dark-skinned African shuffled up close behind him. The man momentarily brushed up against the American. Kip turned about and saw for the first time the purposeful-looking individual who was looking him over, frowning.

-6-

6:30 AM; Friday, September 11, 1992:

"Paging arriving Lagos passenger Kip Leeds! Paging arriving Lagos passenger Kip Leeds!" As Kip trudged out of the Customs area into the main pavilion of Amsterdam's *'Schiphol Airport'*, he was startled to hear loudspeakers calling out his name. "Go to a white courtesy telephone for a message!" a woman's Dutch-accented voice echoed throughout the huge hall. Kip pushed his way past a crowd of people to a nearby wall-mounted white telephone. The operator told him he had a message from his office and to return the call at once

At a telephone kiosk he pulled out the restored bill that had failed the "date-test" back at the Lagos airport. They accepted it here without question—thank God, Kip breathed; at least in Amsterdam the once-black currency was spendable.

He bought a long-distance telephone card, then dragged the luggage bag to a nearby booth. "Is anything wrong?" he wondered, as he dialed Brad's number.

His business partner's distant voice came on the line. "Kip! Is it you?" Brad sounded agitated, impatient. "What's going on? We haven't heard from you since you left!"

Kip told him that he was okay and would be leaving Amsterdam in a little while.

"But what about the money? This guy Busa called a little while ago and said he has the twenty-million at his house! What's the deal?"

Not wanting to divulge too much over the telephone, Kip told his associate he would bring him up-to-date on everything when he returned to West Dallas later in the day.

Brad reminded him it was just past midnight in Texas—Kip had forgotten about the six-hour time difference; in Amsterdam, the morning sun was already climbing into the sky.

Kip hauled the heavy travel bag down a concourse to the gate at the far end of the corridor and got his boarding pass at the check-in counter. Continuing what by now had become something of a tradition for this trip, his seat assignment was a right-hand window seat on the very back row of a *'Boeing 747'*.

As he was turning away, a man's heavy voice came from the other end of the airline counter. "... I must be on this flight—!"

Kip looked over and saw the same dark-skinned man who had earlier bumped into him in the Customs line. The belligerent-acting individual was glaring at the young female ticket agent. "I insist you put me on this airplane!" He was pointing at the monitor screen behind the counter. "Do not argue with me! You *have* an available seat—*I found that out*—so I must have a ticket for this flight!" He reached inside his coat pocket. Kip's eyes went wide—for a split-second he thought the dark man was going for a weapon. The fellow withdrew his billfold. "Give me a ticket!"

The fresh-faced airline employee key-punched a ticket and a boarding pass. "Any checked luggage?"

The African, breathing hard, held up a leather travel bag. "Carry-on".

Boarding pass in his hand, the muscular man, huffing, dropped into a departure lounge seat and surveyed the big waiting room. Nostrils flaring, the fellow scanned the gathering until he spotted Kip standing off to the side. From across the way, the stranger began staring at the American. Out of the corner of his eye, Kip observed the man's piercing, beady eyes focused laser-like onto him. "Why does that guy keep looking at me?" Kip muttered under his breath. He was uneasy. *Could the mysterious African be a "hit-man" sent by the Nigerians to tail him?*

Inside the 747, Kip found his seat on the right side in the very back row of the fourth and rear-most main-deck cabin. He stashed his luggage bag behind the last row of seats across the aisle. Looking about at the sprawling rows that reminded him of a theater, he figured the seat-jammed space held close to a hundred people. It was amazing, he thought, that something this big could actually fly.

He was hardly settled when the fierce-looking African came down the opposite aisle. The man paused and cast about the cabin. Kip considered ducking down, like he had done when they were dragging the Americans off the plane back in Lagos, but decided instead to visually confront him. When the man located him, Kip held his eyes fixed on the fellow's squinting stare that lasted a long second. Then the stranger made what looked to be a showy diversion of stuffing his sport coat into the overhead bin. With another glance back at Kip, he sat down in an aisle seat on the other side of the cabin.

Before long, there came the engines at full power and the gigantic Boeing lifted from the runway.

As they flew along, he caught the dark-skinned African glancing at him repeatedly. Once, when he turned about to look at Kip, the Texan again boldly returned his gaze, and the man quickly averted his eyes. And there was something familiar about him. Kip racked his brain, trying to remember if he had seen him before; and, if so—where? Had he been in the gathering of men in Busa's living room? No, he didn't think he was there. Someone at the hotel, or maybe at the airport? Nothing came to mind. How about one of the men at the bank?

The bank! Now he remembered! Kip sucked-in his breath and goose-bumps came over him. Of course! *He was the man with the young light-skinned African woman in the waiting area of the 'Imperial Industrial Bank' when he and Busa were waiting to see Dr. Nomoah—the fellow who kept looking at him and talking loudly.* Then he remembered something else: the same man had been standing in the roadway by the wrecked truck, staring at Kip as he rode by! But what was he doing on this airplane? And if the man was trailing him—why?

After a while, to get away from the man's repeated glances in his direction, Kip wandered back to an open space and stood looking out a little window in the rear emergency door. Far below was an Arctic-like scene totally different from the equatorial tropics where he had been only a few hours earlier. As far as he could see, dazzling white icebergs floated on the gray water of the North Atlantic. According to the map on the screen, they were just south of Greenland. He stood there for some time, watching what looked like a winter wonderland glide by underneath them.

"Could you please take your seat?" came a woman's voice behind him. "Lunch is served." As on the other international flights, the food was excellent and the European wine flowed freely.

The liquid refreshment took off some of the edge of having to put up with the aggravating dark-skinned man. Kip decided not to let the guy rattle him—he would somehow deal with him when they landed.

As he thought about all that had happened in Nigeria, he began to suspect that there had been a lot more going on behind his back than he had realized at the time. Once more, he mentally re-played the events in Lagos, this time with the idea that anything that had happened and anyone he had seen, however insignificant-appearing at the time, could be important. Kip started with the dark fellow at the "Imperial Industrial Bank", whom he had hardly noticed at the time and who now sat across the airliner cabin from him. Did he have a part in Busa's money business? He thought back to when the man and the attractive young woman had come in and began speaking loudly while he and Busa sat there. Were they all in cahoots? *Had they been speaking to Busa in a code?*

Busa. Sometimes he had been very convincing; at other times, his behavior was hard to figure. The man, from what Kip had discerned, had seen to it that he remained safe in a decidedly unsafe environment. But then the Nigerian had disappeared from his own home while he and the lawyer Adwadube had talked. And his failure to show up at the airport with the documents, in addition to possibly having some serious other implications, was going to cause him problems with Brad. Kip also wondered about the quick way Busa had volunteered to have the currency brought to his house. Now, he had it in his possession! Perhaps Busa was under the control of someone higher-up! If so—who?

Kip squirmed in his seat, thinking. Had he been an unwitting pawn on some shadowy person's big, invisible chessboard? Kip had heard rumors that the Nigerian military dictator might soon be overthrown. Was the money somehow connected to that?

The money. The key to everything was the twenty million dollars. Kip thought about how he had gone all the way to Lagos to risk his life for the mysterious strongbox of black currency, and while there, had encountered the most inexplicable people he had ever met. With a sinking feeling he suspected he would probably have to deal with them again in the future.

A new angle occurred to him: Could there be *others* on this flight with whom he had crossed paths? Kip tried to connect each African passenger in the cabin with people he had seen while he was in Nigeria—but situated as he was in the rear corner of the airplane, he couldn't see everyone.

Pretending to stretch his legs, he strolled up through the third and second cabins, that were as spacious as the rearmost one, and just as filled with people. Since his access to First Class was barred, he turned across to the left walkway and made his way back to the rear compartment. He had to concede that if there were others on this flight who were involved with the black money, including anyone he could not see in First Class, he would have to find out who they were after they landed. As Kip took his seat once more, out of the corner of his eye he saw the aggravating dark-skinned stranger scrutinizing him. He ignored the man.

Sometime later, Kip glanced out the window and did a double-take—they were over land! The map that came on the screen about that time showed they were entering Canadian airspace over eastern Newfoundland. *North America!* After all that had happened, it almost seemed like home. He watched a featureless, desert-like landscape slide by below that reminded him of the isolated settlements in the middle of the Sahara he had seen the night before and thousands of miles back.

After more time, the captain came on the loudspeaker and announced they were in United States airspace. There was scattered applause; Kip breathed a sigh of relief at being back in home-territory. But as he stared out the window, he was weighed-down by the realization that in a few hours he would have to face his business partner without either the money, the receipt for the bank deposit—or even a convincing explanation who Busa and the others actually were.

He got up and stood by the emergency door once more. As he watched the United States scroll by below, Kip tried to draw some conclusions about the trip to Nigeria. He had never before gone overseas; now, he was returning from what was probably one of the most dangerous places on earth—where mural-sized images of the local dictator stared down from the sides of bomb-blasted buildings and armed soldiers goose-stepped up and down airport concourses; where grim military people thrust the boarding pass at you. In the 'States and in Western Europe, airline people smiled a lot and wore colorful uniforms instead of military fatigues and pistols—civilization, they called it.

He stepped around to his luggage bag behind the seat and pulled out an English-language newspaper he had bought in Amsterdam. Buried in one of the middle pages was a story about an outbreak of cholera in a particular northern Nigerian town. Tens of thousands of people there were sick, the report stated, and many had even died. The epidemic was believed to be tied to the water supply. As Kip read on, the name of the town in the news story sounded familiar—where before had he heard it? On a hunch, he went to his fold-over bag. Digging around in an outside pocket, he retrieved the "Kada" label he had peeled off the water bottle in the hotel room back in Lagos. *The bottled water was from the same town of the cholera epidemic!* The label stated the water was "produced from deep wells." Kip hoped the wells were *very* deep.

An hour later, Kip heard and felt the familiar drop in the sound of the turbines as the 747 began its long descent to the DFW Airport. After a while came the whine of the landing gear and then the tires brushed the concrete.

The journey was over. It seemed impossible that only four days earlier, he had started out expecting an uncomplicated business deal and a return home in triumph. In far-away Nigeria, he had come into a huge sum of as-yet unspendable money that was now in his name but still controlled by men who were most likely dangerous. Kip knew he would probably have to encounter those people again. His stomach tightened.

He tugged his travel bag from behind the nearby seat and joined the crowd leaving the plane. After passing through Customs, he headed toward the main terminal. A little farther on, a sign next to an elevator caught his eye:

NOTICE TO TRAVELERS:

THE UNITED STATES DEPARTMENT OF STATE HAS DETERMINED THAT THE AIRPORTS AT PORT-AU-PRINCE, HAITI AND LAGOS, NIGERIA ARE UNSAFE TO TRAVELERS.

Kip stared at the placard. So the Lagos airport was officially dangerous! He could believe it.

Just then, out of a restroom off to one side stepped the dark-skinned man! When Kip realized the African hadn't seen him, he scooted over and fell-in with a mass of people who were marching toward the baggage claim area. Out of the corner of his eye Kip saw the fellow searching about, and for an uncomfortable moment thought the man had spotted him as they surged by—at one point they were only a dozen feet apart—but he apparently didn't see Kip on the opposite side of the coursing parade.

When the people turned at a bend, Kip ducked into a crowded Texas-themed lounge, slid onto a stool at the far end of the bar and swung the luggage bag down at his feet. Seated next to him was a ruddy, overweight individual chugging down an outsized mug of beer.

Kip situated himself where the guy's beefy bulk partially shielded him from the entrance. After a quick look-around to make sure his pursuer was nowhere in sight, he took a deep breath and ordered a bourbon and water.

Just as the bartender was setting the glistening glass in front of him, Kip happened to glance up at the big wood-framed mirror behind the bar. His eyes went wide with alarm. In the mirror's reflection, the dark-skinned man was walking into the room! Without looking left or right, with purposeful steps the powerful-looking Nigerian was striding straight toward him.

The African was about midway across the room when a half-dozen well-dressed men around a center table stood up, blocking his way. One of the executive-types extended his hand to another. "It was good to see you!"

The scowling pursuer found himself momentarily entangled in their handshake. Kip scurried toward the kitchen door, a few feet away.

"What're *you* doing in here?"

Kip whirled around to confront a busboy who was gaping at him. The fugitive put his finger to his lips in a *"Shhh"* motion. "My brother is out there and he's not supposed to know I'm in town! It's a surprise family reunion!"

The youth winked. "Oh . . . you want to hide from them until—the party?"

Kip nodded, peering out the small, square window of the door, as if looking for someone.

The dark-skinned man was fingering his name tag on the luggage, frowning. Kip overheard the fellow speaking to the bartender, pointing at Kip's bag. "Did you see where this man went?"

"The blond guy at the end of the counter?"

"Yeah . . . where did he go?"

"Did you try the men's room?" The dark man hurtled off toward a door marked, "Restrooms".

Kip dashed back out, snatched up the bag and frantically pushed his way out of the bustling bar. He knew the man would be returning in a few seconds. He looked up and down the concourse. Not far away, was a down-escalator beneath a sign directing arriving passengers: "To Baggage Claim".

Kip raced over and jumped aboard. Taking two steps at a time, he bumped and elbowed his way past the others on the moving staircase, seething in impatience as it scrolled down toward the lower level at a maddeningly slow pace. At the bottom, across the open baggage claim area, a sign over a door pointed the way to "Ground Transportation". Puffing, Kip dragged the canvas bag out to the curb, where a cab was about to take on a passenger.

Kip nudged aside a little old lady with bluish hair whose bony fingers gripped a folded umbrella. "Excuse me, ma'am, but I'm late to a funeral!"

The surprised driver's eyes darted back-and-forth from the elderly woman to the puffing newcomer, who yanked open the rear door.

"To the downtown . . . *'Harland Plaza Hotel'* and hurry!" was the first thing that came to Kip's mind as he launched his luggage bag onto the rear seat and dived after it. He had to get out of the airport at once.

They pulled away, leaving the blue-haired woman standing at the curb, fuming. As the taxi turned into heavy traffic, Kip looked back and saw the dark-skinned man run out of the terminal, looking to and fro. Then the fellow elbowed aside the same old woman whom Kip had disposed and jumped into another taxi, pointing in Kip's direction. The old lady whacked her umbrella on the cab as it pulled away. Kip ducked down. "I hope the guy didn't see me!"

As they crept along in the molasses-like traffic, the driver looked into the rear-view mirror at Kip. "A funeral, you say? Who's funeral is it?"

"A 'friend's'". *Maybe my own funeral, if I don't lose this guy.*

As they drove slowly past the huge bulk of the terminal, a shuddery feeling came over Kip. The last time he had ridden from an airport was in that blue Toyota back at Lagos's creepy "Murtala Mohammed Airport Lagos"—and almost into the clutches of that native cop with the billy club. But Nigeria now seemed a long way off. As the taxi threaded through the jammed lanes, Kip reflected about the differences between civilization and the so-called *"Third World"*. In Lagos there had been a constant undercurrent of danger—Ivan's chair under the doorknob; the bell hung on the door; the billy-club policeman; the secret knocks; soldiers everywhere. Dangerous people had probably been around him at every turn. But then, if Busa and the others had seen him as their legal ticket to get the money out of Nigeria, they would likely have wanted to keep him safe and alive while he was there. Even Adwadube, the obnoxious lawyer, had been straightforward about what he had wanted. Next time— if there *was* a next time—he was going to be better prepared to deal with them.

The lugging cab finally broke into the clear and the driver speeded up. Kip kept looking back, but didn't see any taxis that might be tailing them. Maybe they had given the guy the slip.

Thirty minutes later, the cab pulled up in front of the Harland Plaza Hotel. He had decided to lay low for a day or so while he figured out a few things. At the front desk, Kip registered for an upper-floor room.

On the third ring, Brad Holdon answered the telephone. "I'm at the 'Harland Plaza'," Kip said into the mouthpiece, "meet me in the lounge . . . let's talk."

He was just starting on his second bourbon and water when there was a tap on his shoulder. His business partner eased into the seat across the table from him. "Okay, what happened?"

Kip flagged down a waiter and ordered Brad a bourbon, using change from the restored black bills. Over the next couple of hours and several more drinks, he told Brad about everything, from the first take-off to losing the mysterious man at the airport.

Brad's eyes were wide. "Who was he?"

Kip shrugged. "No idea . . . but he sure seemed to know who *I* was."

"You think the money was real?

"I'd bet my life on it—in fact, I *did* bet my life on it!"

"How can you be so sure?"

"Because I pulled the bills out of the box at random. Nobody could have rigged it to come out like it did, unless it was the real deal."

"Maybe—but we still owe the bank fifty grand for the deposit at that Nigerian Bank."

"They'll get it," Kip said. He hoped he was right.

Sloane says that next time you leave the country, she wants to go with you!"

After everything that had happened, Kip was anxious to again see her.

* * *

As Brad and Kip headed toward the door, they didn't pay any attention to a very dark, gnome-like, bald-headed older man who was sitting with his back to them in the next high-backed booth, fingering the stub of a First-Class airline ticket he had used from-Amsterdam-to-Dallas that day. Using a special amplifier in his ear, the hunched-over fellow had heard every word of their conversation.

* * *

9:16 AM; Saturday, September 12, 1992:

While Kip was taking a long, luxurious shower, the first since Africa, the hotel room's telephone started ringing. On and on it rang. Finally he couldn't take it any longer and stopped. Dripping, Kip splashed out to the phone by the bed. "Hello?"

"Kip? Is it you?' A familiar feminine voice sounded in the receiver. "I heard you were back from your trip! Daddy says somebody is following you!"

"Sloane! Why do you think I'm here at this hotel instead of at home? I'm on the run, kid."

There was a gasp at the other end of the line. "You mean somebody's *really* trying to get you? Oh, Kip! I guess that's why daddy wants me to bring you over here to our place to stay for a while."

"Your place?" The thought of staying in the same house with Sloane, even if for short time, sounded intriguing. Once again, he realized how much he had missed her. "Meet me at the back of the hotel near the service entrance in an hour."

Fifty minutes later, Kip left the key-card on the dresser and turned to open the door. As he did so, his eyes fell on a piece of paper that someone had slipped under the sill. On it was a handwritten printed message:

YOU ARE IN DANGER.
SERIOUS BUSINESS.
A FRIEND-

Kip jerked open the door and looked up and down the hallway. A couple of doors down, a maid was pushing a cleaning cart. "Did you see someone at this door, just now?" With a shrug, she shook her head. Not much English, he guessed.

A hotel guest stepped out of the next room. As the man was pulling his door shut, Kip called over to him with the same question.

"Ah, yes . . . you must mean the fellow who was at your door a few minutes ago," came the surprising answer.

"What did he look like?" Kip hoped for a clue.

"Well, a black fellow—a very black fellow, as I remember—stopped at your door and slid a piece of paper underneath it. I figured he was leaving you an invitation, or a message, or something."

"Anything else?"

He was bald-headed . . . sort of thin and underweight looking—kind of stooped over a little, I guess. You think he might have been a friend of yours?"

Kip smiled to cover his unease. "I guess I just missed him . . . well, thanks a lot."

Even though he was trying to appear casual, Kip was concerned—the description of the mysterious visitor didn't fit the African who had been following him. Now there was something else to worry about.

As he turned to leave, the man in the hallway called back to him. "Funny . . . even though he stood there for a half-minute or so, he never knocked on the door—I just remembered that. Well, if I see the guy again, I'll tell him you asked about him."

Kip was thinking about all this as he rode the elevator down to the lobby. "Where's the service entrance?" he asked the concierge. The woman pointed at an exit; in a few moments he was stepping up to a loading dock at the rear of the big building.

He had just gotten there when a convertible driven by a long-haired brunette slithered to a stop. The young woman flipped her sunglasses over her forehead and smiled at him. "Going my way, Buster?"

"Sloane! Are you a sight for sore eyes!"

She hopped from the car and grabbed him around his neck. He dropped the green luggage bag and hugged her.

"Oh, Kip, I was so worried about you! You didn't call us, and I didn't know where you were, or what you were doing, or *anything!*" She sniffed. "Brad said he had talked to you last night, but he didn't say much, except that you were back in town at this hotel!"

Kip slung his carry-all into the car's trunk. "I'll tell you all about it over some food. Let's find a restaurant—I'm about starved."

Sloane swung her car around and drove out into the flow of traffic.

* * *

A green sedan parked along a side street beyond the hotel's rear entrance pulled out behind them, then dropped back a few car lengths to allow a couple of other vehicles to move between it and Sloane's car. The husky, dark-skinned man at the wheel focused his eyes on the convertible up ahead.

* * *

Kip pointed. "There's a 'Denny's'." The car pulled into the diner's parking lot.

* * *

A block behind them, the green sedan drove up to a pump at a convenience store. As he fueled the car, the driver watched as the couple walked into the restaurant. After topping the tank, he drove around to a side street, where he parked a block back from the intersection. The dark man settled back to watch Sloane's car. "This could take a while," he said to himself, lighting a cigarette.

* * *

The man sat upright in his seat and squashed his smoke—the couple were coming out of Denny's. He could hear them faintly laughing. He observed the two get into the convertible, then the car backed out of its parking place. The dark man started his engine and eased the green sedan into the traffic. The leading car turned onto the roadway, and continued in the same direction it had been going.

Up ahead, the man saw the convertible just make it through a traffic signal before the light turned red. Cursing at the delay, he drew his car up behind a line of waiting vehicles. By the time the light changed back to green, the convertible was several blocks in front of him. He swung the sedan into the left lane and zoomed past several slow-moving cars and began to overhaul his quarry.

* * *

On the expressway. Sloane gave the convertible more speed.

"How's little Nicky?" Kip asked, over the wind noise.

She glanced at her passenger and smiled. "Sassy, as always."

* * *

The dark man whipped the green sedan off the freeway. Whoever that girl was, she was driving so fast he could hardly keep up with her. Spotting the convertible at a traffic light up ahead, he slowed down until the light turned green, then went faster to match her speed.

* * *

Sloane slowed the car and took the next exit. In a couple of minutes, they pulled up in a parking space at the Ferry Detective Agency.

"Kip, my boy!" Ned Ferry pumped the younger man's hand. "Come on in and tell us all about the trip . . . Brad says you have quite a story to tell."

* * *

The man drove another couple of blocks, then made a return loop. He turned down a side street, drove a half-block, did a U-turn and pulled up to the curb in a wooded residential area. The African turned off the ignition. He drew out a pair of binoculars and a legal pad.

The man squinted. A red Porsche was pulling into the driveway. A thirty-something-looking male got out and went into the house. The dark foreigner picked up the spyglasses and squinted at the rear of the coupé. He wrote down the car's license number.

* * *

Brad Holdon strode into Ned Ferry's office and greeted the group. He dropped a sheet of paper onto the detective's desk. "This fax came in just a little while ago."

SIR, AM MAKING ARRANGEMENTS TO MOVE THE BLACK CURRENCY TO EUROPE. LESS EXPENSIVE TO PROCESS THERE. WILL ADVISE YOU AS TO LOCATION AND WHEN SUBJECT BILLS WILL ARRIVE IN EUROPE.
—MASOBE BUSA---

Kip looked at the others. "There's not much we can do until they take the money to wherever they're going with it in 'Europe', as Busa puts it."

Brad was dubious. *"If* they go to Europe—"

Sloane glanced at Kip and spoke up. "Since Kip's going to be staying here a for a while, let me help him get settled-in."

"Tell you what," Brad put in. "I'll go over to his house and make sure everything's okay."

"That's a good idea." Kip made a list of things to bring from his place.

* * *

There was sudden movement across the way—the guy who had gone inside a half-hour ago was now leaving. The Nigerian debated whether to stay put or to follow him. He decided to see where he was going, now that he knew the current whereabouts of the others.

The red Porsche came down the driveway and stopped, facing him. For a split-second, the foreigner thought the fellow had spotted him even though they were a block apart.

But the American turned right and raced off, snicking through the gears.

The green sedan pulled up to the intersection. To the left, a couple of blocks away, the other car was threading its way through the lanes of traffic. The man swung the wheel, mashed down the accelerator; his car shot ahead.

After about a kilometer, as the African measured it, the other car made a right turn. Just as the Nigerianr passed through the intersection, for a fleeting moment he saw down the side street the sloping rear of the sports car turning into a wooded driveway. The green car went several blocks past where the Porsche had gone in, then made the same turnaround as before and parked a block down a side street under a shade tree.

The foreigner took his binoculars and the legal pad and walked across the street to a spot behind Kip's house. He edged into the woods and pushed through the underbrush up to where the back of the bungalow was in sight. The outline of the Porsche was visible through some leafy branches. Trying to be as quiet as possible, he stepped around the backsides of the house, taking notes of door and window openings. Satisfied that he had all the information he needed, the man retraced his way back through the foilage to the sidewalk in the middle of the block.

He got into the car and drove back in the direction of the Ferry office. As he passed by the house, he saw that the trunk lid of one of the cars—the convertible's—was open. The African slowed down just in time to catch a fleeting glance of a blond-haired man pulling a green canvas luggage bag from the compartment. The baggage was just like the one he had seen in the bar at the airport with "Kip Leeds's" name on it. What a stroke of luck! Now that he knew for sure the location of the American he had followed on the airplane, the rest of the job would be easy.

Having scouted the layout of the two houses, the Nigerian checked into a freeway motel.

In his room, he placed a telephone call to the "Chief".
"Hello? 'Ezego' here—yes, I have new information . . ." He gave his current address and telephone number then told the person on the other end of the line all that had happened since he had departed from Lagos. Then came an interval when other person was talking.

"Yes, I will do that . . . I will find that out when I get inside."

There was a pause, then the man's eyebrows went up." 'Retchko' and 'Betty Nkrume' are in West Dallas, you say? And tomorrow you will also be here?"

* * *

"Looks like you're stuck with me for a while!" Kip grinned at Sloane, as the throaty sound of Brad's Porsche faded away. "Your dad wants me to lie low until he finds out more about the guy who was on the plane. Brad's going to my house right now to get some files and papers."

You think that awful man who followed you is part of the black money crowd?"

"I wouldn't be surprised if he was connected with Busa or somebody else, all right."

Ned Ferry gestured at the door. "Sloane, take Kip upstairs and show him the guest room."

The girl opened the door of a room at the end of the upper hallway. "Well, this is it—" She motioned into a generic bedroom. ". . . your home for the next few days—enjoy!" She came about and their eyes met for a long second. Then Sloane turned and went downstairs, leaving Kip standing alone.

It was then he remembered his luggage was still in the trunk of her convertible. He dashed outside and opened the lid with the key Sloane had given him. In a jiffy he hauled out the fold-over bag from the rear compartment and double-timed back up the steps. He couldn't imagine that anyone would have seen him in those few seconds he had been outside.

* * *

9:17 AM; Sunday, September 13, 1992:

Sloane knocked on the door of the guest room. "Brad wants to talk to you on the telephone!" she called through the door.

Kip finished buttoning his shirt and picked up the receiver.

"I left a notebook at your house, yesterday," Brad said, "and I need you to go by and get it." He described the book. "It has important information, so I don't want anything to happen to it."

Kip remembered he was supposed to have a breakfast meeting with Ned Ferry. "I'll ask Sloane to go over there and pick it up."

* * *

Sloane Ferry drove her convertible into Kip's driveway. She unlocked the front door with the key he had given her and stepped inside. According to what he had told her, the notebook should be on the kitchen table.

But when she got to the kitchen, the young detective saw that the book was not on the table after all; it must be somewhere else.

As she passed through the doorway back into the living room, she heard a scraping behind her. Alarmed, the girl turned toward the sound, just as a muscular arm swung around her neck from behind and a heavy hand grabbed her mouth!

Before Sloane could react, she felt a smashing blow on the back of her head—then everything went black!

69

-8-

The ringing desk telephone interrupted Ned Ferry's breakfast conversation with Kip. Brad's voice crackled on the line. "I need to speak to Sloane . . . she has a notebook that I need."

"Sloane's not here."

"Not there?" Brad's voice sounded surprised. "She hasn't returned from Kip's house?"

The investigator peered at Kip over his reading glasses. "Did Sloane go to your house?"

"Yes, about an hour ago—she should have been back by now."

"Okay," Ned told Brad, "I'll call over there and tell her to hurry back." He tapped the cradle of the telephone and punched Kip's number. After a few seconds, the investigator frowned, then hung up the receiver. "That's strange—I got a recording that your telephone's out of order."

"Out of order?" Kip came out of his chair. "Something's wrong—the phone should be working!"

He scuttled down the steps to the driveway with Ned Ferry puffing along behind him. Even as the stout detective climbed into the front passenger seat of the big, brand-new Hummer, Kip was popping the gears into reverse. "I hope nothing's happened to her!" The younger man clenched his teeth as the massive vehicle with the big tires whirred out of the driveway onto the thoroughfare.

As they raced along toward his house, Kip blamed himself for asking Sloane to go over there in the first place. He knew he would never forgive himself if she had met with foul play. A few minutes later, when he swung the machine into his driveway, he saw her convertible parked next to his house. The front door of the bungalow was open. With his heart in his throat, he dashed inside. "Sloane!" Are you here?"

Nothing but silence came back to him. "Sloane! Where are you?"

He ran into the kitchen. She was gone! Then he gasped—the breakfast table and a couple of chairs were knocked-over, cabinet drawers were pulled open; other kitchen items were strewn about on the floor—the telephone, its wires dangling from the wall, was lying askew on the floor. All were obvious signs of a forced entry and an altercation. An object next to the back door caught his eye. *Sloane's handbag!*

Ned Ferry pointed. "Look!" On the floor next to the back door was a girl's sandal. "That's Sloane's shoe!" For the first time they noticed the back door was open. "Come on!" The older man shoved aside the screen door. "Let's look outside!"

At the bottom of the steps the detective's trained eyes made out a crushed line in the grass that led off behind the small house. He frowned at the furrows. "Somebody dragged her into the woods." They followed the tracks. "Here's Sloane's other shoe! Oh, God, something happened to her, all right . . ."

The two men pushed into the heavy growth, where a trail of disturbed leaves and the outlines in the soft earth of the soles of a man's shoes revealed that two people had recently passed through.

The men crashed through the underbrush, following the trail in the foliage.

Just before they reached the sidewalk, near the far edge of the thicket, Ned Ferry noticed that the markings in the soft ground became two pairs of footsteps, one of the large-size shoes and the other seemed to be bare footprints. At the sidewalk, they made out faint grass stains that led to the curb.

Kip knelt down. "There was a car parked here . . ." He pointed at the tracks of four tires that were outlined in some shallow mud next to a storm drain. The marks led out into the traffic lanes, where they were obliterated by the vehicles that had come along afterward.

The detective rubbed his chin. "We can make impressions of these tracks . . . I'll get the evidence kit from the office."

In a few minutes he was back on the scene with the plaster; before long, they had impressions of the tire tracks.

A gray-haired lady walking a dog came toward them. Ned Ferry held up his hand. "Did you see a man and a young woman here, a short while ago?"

"Oh, you must mean that nice man who was helping that poor, sick girl."

Kip and the detective glanced at each other. "What did they look like?"

"Well, I saw this man helping a girl get into a car."

"You say she was sick?"

"Um . . . he was holding on to her; she was wobbling, like she wasn't feeling well, or something."

"Do you remember how the girl *looked?*"

"Oh, she had long, dark hair—beautiful hair. My niece has hair just like—"

". . . what did the *man* look like?"

"A big guy; very dark-skinned; I remember that."

"What about the car?"

"It was green—that's about all I know. Is something wrong?"

"You've been very helpful, ma'am."

Back inside the Hummer, Kip was frowning. "Maybe I'm wrong—but that description sounds an awfully lot like the guy who was following me on the plane! But how did he find this place? And what would he want with Sloane?"

"We have to find her," Ned Ferry said.

* * *

Consciousness skidded back into Sloane's brain. Her head pounded from a terrific headache. Then it started to come back: She had been at Kip's house looking for a book—a notebook. She shook her head, trying to clear out the cobwebs. God, what a headache!

She opened her eyes and gasped: A muscular-looking, scowling, very-dark-skinned man was glowering into her face!

"Who—who are you?" Her voice sounded foggy, spongy; faraway. She tried to move, but her arms and legs were immobile. Then her eyes went wide in horror: she was sitting in a chair with her hands tied behind her and her ankles bound to the chair's legs! Sloane looked around. It looked as if she was in a hotel or motel room.

SLAP! The man backhanded her across her mouth. Her head jerked back and tears came to her eyes. There was a taste of blood in her mouth.

"All right, start talking!" The man had a thick, accented voice that she guessed was that of a native African. "What is the light-haired guy going to do with the money?"

"I—don't know what you're talking about. I don't know anything about any—"

The man slapped her again. Sloane's head spun to the side; pain shot through her face. "You do not understand; you either tell me what he's doing with the money, or you're dead!"

"Look, I—we . . . don't have any money. I don't know what you're talking about."

A look of rage came on the man's face. He grabbed her neck and began to squeeze. Sloane's eyes bulged—she couldn't breathe!

Just as she was about to pass out, the man released her. Gasping, she realized she would have to play along if she was ever going to get out of this. "Okay, okay," she swallowed, "I'll tell you all I know, but please untie my hands . . . they're hurting."

The man shook his head. "Start talking!"

"All I know is that he went somewhere."

"Where did he go?"

"I don't know exactly where he went."

"You lie!"

She winced as the man hauled back his hand to strike her again.

Just then, there came a knock at the door! The man's open palm froze in midair; a look of surprise came to his face.

He opened the door. Sloane's eyes were wide; her heart was racing as a stocky, hairless, middle-aged, pale-skinned white man and a younger woman with a cream-colored complexion stepped through the doorway. Behind them came a small, dark, bald-headed man in a brown three-piece suit.

73

The pallid, pudgy newcomer focused his blue eyes on Sloane, tied-up in the chair. "Who is *this?*" The young detective recognized an eastern-European brogue.

"The bitch showed up while I was looking for the stuff—I had to bring her."

"Did you get information?"

The assailant's eyes darted from the white man to the smaller black individual. "Yes, sir, *'General Retchko'* . . . *'Chief'*—I have a notebook with me, right now."

The hairless white man glared at the trussed-up girl then scowled at the black fellow. "Get rid of her!"

Sloane gave a pleading look at the light-skinned female who was frowning. The big black man pulled back the curtain and looked outside. "Good. It is almost dark."

Sloane's eyes went wide as he advanced toward her, rubbing his hands together.

* * *

"Here's a swatch of fibers." Ned Ferry dropped the tiny clump into a small evidence pouch with tweezers. "The guy must have snagged his coat or pants on a branch as he came through here."

Kip was exasperated. "We've gone over this area twice, now, and *this* is all we could find?"

"We'd better bring the police and the Federals into it." The detective had found something he had not mentioned to Kip that led him to believe this was not just an ordinary kidnapping. He fingered in his pocket the Nigerian-issued airline card he had picked up from the floor in Kip's kitchen. There was handwriting on the back of it in a language he did not recognize.

* * *

Daily Crier, Monday, September 14, 1992

POLICE SEARCH FOR MISSING DETECTIVE

(West Dallas)—Local and Federal officers are seeking

a missing female detective who police fear was the victim of foul play.

Sloane Marie Ferry, 23, an employee of the Ferry Detective Agency in West Dallas, failed to return to her office after an assignment Sunday morning.

James R. Randolph, of the local Federal Investigation Office, said a woman matching her description was seen getting into a dark-green Nissan on Fountain Grove Boulevard Sunday morning around eleven o'clock. One eyewitness said the driver was a well-built, very-dark-skinned man who was wearing a gray sport coat and dark trousers.

The missing young woman was described as having a slender build, long black hair; five-feet, six-inches in height and weighing about 115 pounds. She was last seen wearing an orange sundress.

* * *

9:22 P.M., Monday, September 14, 1992:

Mrs. Jackson came into Ned Ferry's study with a worried look on her face. "I don't know how I'm going to put off Nicky any longer . . . he's asking for his mother."

The detective sighed. "Tell him she's gone to visit some friends, and she'll be back, soon."

"But he knows something's not right."

"Keep him as busy as you can, while we try to find her."

As soon as she had left the room, he lifted the receiver and called the "Federal Investigation Agency" office on James Randolph's private number. "Jim . . . Ferry, here—anything new?"

"We have a license plate number on the green Nissan—it was a rental from *'DFW Airport'*. It had been rented to a Nigerian named 'Michael Mello'. There are some reasons to believe that is not his real name . . . he was listed on the passenger manifest of a flight that's already left the country." There was a pause, then the agent went on, "Mister Ferry, our people are going all-out on this . . . the TV and the papers are leaning on the story . . . we have out an *'All-Points-Bulletin'* with a picture and description of the 'subject '. . . I mean—your daughter."

"Okay, thanks." The detective hung up the phone and put his face in his hands. If it turned out that something had happened to Sloane he didn't believe he could go on any longer. Waves of remembrance rolled over him as he thought about the years of bringing her up alone after what had happened to his wife— Sloane's mother.

* * *

As a captain in the *'American Division'*, he and some of the other junior officers in his unit had gone to Australia on a "Rest and Recreation" furlough from the Vietnam War. Though most of the married ones had gone to Hawaii to meet their families there, he and some of the other young single officers went down to Brisbane, on the southeastern Australian coast—the word had gotten back from those who had already been there that the local beer flowed freely and the nearby beaches swarmed with good-looking, friendly females who liked American men.

He hadn't had to wait long. The first day after they had arrived at the "Gold Coast", as he learned they called it, and was stretched out on a beach towel soaking up some rays with the other guys, he had heard girlish voices nearby. "Look—there are some of them over there," came a tittering Australian accent.

Ned opened his eyes and, raising up onto his elbows, saw a half-dozen young women in about the tiniest bikinis he had ever seen, setting-up a volleyball net close by.

"You blokes care to join us?" came the same rollicking voice.

The young lieutenant focused on the source of the sing-song Aussie brogue—a tanned, leggy girl with swishy, dark-brown hair who was motioning at them. "We need some more people to

76

play volleyball with us!" Then she was striding with long barefoot steps across the sand toward the young men, followed by the others who were equally good-looking. The Americans scrambled to their feet. "Well, mates . . . how about it? Are you with us or must we look elsewhere for companionship?"

"Yes—yes, of course!" Ned was gaping at the girl, who was looking him up and down at the same time. The other fellows, from the expressions on their faces, could hardly believe their good fortune. "We'd be happy to play with you—I mean, to *play* you—isn't that right, guys?" The others nodded, grinning.

The tanned, toned Australian twirled the volleyball in her hands. "'Browning's' the name—'Browning O'Bryant'—what's yours?"

"Ned Ferry . . . Lieutenant, United States Army." He shook her hand, noting her long, slender fingers. She kept eying him as the others introduced themselves. "We're here on 'Rest and Recreation' from Vietnam."

"And just what brings you here to the 'Gold Coast'? I thought you 'Yanks' always went to Hawaii, or someplace like that."

"Brisbane sounded interesting, and I heard that the natives—"

The girl's eyes went wide. Ned flushed scarlet, grasping for words. "That is . . . we wanted to see your culture and scenery."

Browning rolled her eyes at the other Australians. "Well, 'natives' . . . I guess we must show these 'Yanks' some of our 'native culture and scenery'—as this bloody bloke puts it." Without any warning, she shoved the ball at Ned Ferry's stomach. He doubled over, grimacing and gasping for air. "Let's start with some volleyball—girls against boys!"

Right away, the Army fellows discovered that these lithe young women were far better net players than they were; after an hour, the boys had lost every single match.

"What's the matter, mates—volleyball a bit too much for you?" an auburn-haired girl jeered, after their latest lopsided triumph against the winded Americans.

"Let's go find some place to cool off!" one of the fellows called, "I'm getting a sunburn."

"I say, " a freckle-faced redheaded girl shook her head, ". . . and I used to believe you Americans were the toughest fellows in the world!"

Ned pointed up the road at a modern building facing the oceanfront a few blocks distant. "That's the hotel where we're staying. There's a pub in the lobby."

"We'll take our car and meet you there in a few minutes." Browning pulled on a terrycloth beach robe and stepped into a pair of flip-flops; the other young women were doing the same. The Americans took down the net and bundled the girls into their tiny Australian sedan, then headed along the seashore toward the inn.

A few minutes later, as the soldiers trudged into the lobby, Ned heard a female voice. "Over here!" The girls had pulled together two tables and were motioning at them. The perspiring Americans dropped into chairs; Ned found a seat next to Browning. The lithe, slender girl had dropped her flip-flops to the floor; her feet were propped on the front edge of the chair, her fingers laced around her pulled-up knees. She tossed her long brown hair over her shoulders, leaned back, and flexed her tanned toes.

We've ordered a pitcher of ale," she announced, as the other boys scraped their chairs to the table.

Ned wanted to get a conversation started. "'O'Bryant'— sounds Irish, or Scotch, to me."

"My great-great-grandfather went down from Belfast to London . . . somehow, he got into some sort of' problem'—so they threw him in jail." Ned's eyes were wide as she went on, "they put him on a ship to Australia, which in those days was a penal colony. When he got to Sydney, he got pardoned, and met a girl who had come from England 'to help populate the country,' as they put it, then they got married." Browning grinned. "I'm a distant result of that!"

* * *

Ned Ferry leaned back in his executive's chair, thinking; remembering. He would never forget those days and nights in Brisbane with Browning. They had been together every evening after she had gotten off work from her job as a typist, until his unit had returned to Saigon and on to the war. After he had gone back to that hellish, confused conflict, they had written countless letters to each other. When his Vietnam tour was finished and he was back in the 'States, he had proposed to her by long-distance telephone, and she had accepted. Early the next year, after he left the Army, he and Margaret Browning O'Bryant were married in the Anglican Cathedral in Brisbane.

After a snorkling *'Great Barrier Reef'* honeymoon they had made the long haul across the Pacific to West Dallas, where he began his career with the police department.

The two had been married three years when Sloane, named after her Australian grandmother, was born. The doctors had said her arrival was something of a miracle, as Browning had endured two earlier miscarriages.

* * *

Ned Ferry's eyes were still closed as he bathed his mind with the precious memories of his wife and daughter. As she grew up, Sloane had been a thoughtful child who was very selective of her friends. It was was remarkable, he thought, how well his gawky little girl had turned-out: by the time she was in high school, she had grown into an arresting-looking teenager with intelligence to match; extraordinary, considering what had happened to her mother during that time.

It was at Sloane's eleventh birthday party—a garden party— that a guest had noticed a bleeding mole on Browning's upper shoulder. At the dermatologist's came the stunning diagnosis: *'Melanoma'*, the rapidly-growing and deadly skin cancer. The Gold Coast sun had been the culprit.

Tears welled in Ned Ferry's eyes when he recalled how in only a few months, his beautiful Browning was gone.

Now, he was fearful he would never again see his daughter.

* * *

In the upstairs bedroom, Kip Leeds tossed and turned; his mind in a turmoil of worry over what might have happened to Sloane.

She would have been about thirteen and he was just out of college when he first saw her as a budding teenager whose mother had recently died. Sometimes, he had suspected Sloane had a crush on him, but he had always dismissed the idea.

Down through the years, he had put up with her foibles with indulgent humor. He remembered a dance recital one time, where she had turned the other direction from everyone else on the stage, bringing laughter from the audience and tears from her eyes he had had to console. Then there were the tennis matches with him, where she had had a hard time finding the base-line. But how could he have ever turned her down, and besides, in her own way she had always been good company.

Sloane had gone off to the university—then came the fraternity fire and the heroics of the young Frenchman, Dominique, who had lost his life rescuing the others. He never knew she was pregnant with his child. It had not been easy for Kip to connect the skinny little kid of the past with motherhood, but somehow she had seen it through. He remembered that Sloane had even had an emergency appendix operation halfway through the pregnancy. Recently, she had completed her university degree and become a licensed investigator, working with her father.

Once more he thought about her as his possible wife, but, as always, pushed the subject out of his mind, since, of course, he was sure she would not want anything to do with him in that way. He was, after all, nine years older than she; a huge age difference in the minds of young women, he figured. But the possibility that something terrible had happened to her was hitting him hard. Lovers they weren't—very special friends, yes—and he was missing her very much.

* * *

4:52 AM; Wednesday, September 16, 1992:

Tommy Perkis down-shifted the Kenworth up to the Laredo U.S. Border Patrol Station. Setting the brakes, he leaned against the steering wheel and ran his weary fingers through thinning, sandy-hued hair—since leaving West Dallas, it had been an all-night run; he had stopped only once, in Waco, for a snack and a fuel-up. As soon as he was across the border in Nuevo Laredo, he would take a long shower and get some sleep. Already, he could almost feel the water running over him. It had been really tough to make up the time he had lost back in the West Dallas yard when part of the load had not been ready on time. He had had to cool his heels for an hour until a "special shipment" had arrived for his truck. The "waybill" stated it was a crate of "dyed broadcloth" for delivery at the Nuevo Laredo terminal across the border.

The Customs inspector was motioning up to him. "Open the cargo doors, please."

Groaning, Perkis swung down and walked stiffly with the officer to the rear; it had been almost five hours since he had last stood on his feet.

The levered lock-handles clacked open. The inspector, whose name tag said, "Guzman", shined his flashlight into the trailer's cavernous, dark interior. "Lights?"

Perkis went back up to the cab and flipped a switch. A row of weak overhead lamps in the trailer came on. Piled high in a long row were wrapped pallets loaded with parts bearing destination stickers for an automobile assembly plant in Sonora, Mexico. Officer Guzman climbed up into the trailer and checked-off the pallets against the waybills.

Stapled to the back sheet was the supplementary "dyed broadcloth" bill. The inspector shined his flashlight around the shadowy interior. "Where's this shipment?"

Just then, a bumping sound came from the very rear of the van. Guzman turned to Perkis. "What's that?"

There it was, again—a thump.

The officer's flashlight flickered about, then stopped on an elongated wooden box about the size and shape of a casket. A sticker on its side read, "Dyed Broadcloth". The officer flipped the waybill to the hand-written description that seemed to match the box. It was addressed to the Nuevo Laredo terminal's dock. There, someone would pick it up.

Perkis squinted at the crate. "I guess this was the shipment I had to wait two hours for," he told the officer, "it's the first time I've actually seen it."

At that moment, something like a moan came from inside the box. For the first time, Guzman noticed rows of quarter-inch-wide holes that had been freshly drilled along the top and sides of the box.

"I want to see the contents of this crate." The officer motioned. "Get a crowbar."

With an uneasy feeling, the driver double-timed up front to the tractor and pulled open the toolbox. He grabbed a crowbar, then ran back to the rear of the trailer.

Perkis jammed the lever underneath a corner of the lid that came up with a loud squawk. It's not a very secure container, the driver thought, as only a half-dozen rusty nails held down the top. Guzman and the driver lifted aside the lid.

"Oh, my God!"

Guzman jumped down from the van and dashed toward the guardhouse. In moments, he was on the police radio. "Send 'E-M-S' to the Laredo Border Inspection Station! Emergency!" Get an ambulance to the guardhouse on the double!"

The officer stared at a faxed sheet of paper that was on the counter. "By God, it's her!"

With the paper in his hand, Guzman flung open the door and ran back to the trailer.

-9-

"What!" Ned Ferry sat upright. "'Laredo', you say?"

The voice on the other end went on for a few more seconds.

"We'll be there as fast as we can!"

Ned Ferry huffed down the hallway and rapped on the guest-room door. "Kip! Kip! They've found Sloane!"

The younger man, blinking, cracked open the door. "Where? How is she?"

She's at a hospital in Laredo!" The detective bustled back to his bedroom, flinging off his nightshirt. "Come on, let's get to the airport—fast!"

* * *

The doctor on duty in the Laredo hospital's emergency center had looked up at the clock on the wall: "5:22", the hands had pointed—in less than two hours he would be out of here. Then on to breakfast and some sleep.

A buzzer sounded and the red light began flashing over the big automatic swinging doors at the ambulance entrance.

"Emergency Room! *Code Blue! Stat! Stat!*" A strident voice burst from the loudspeaker and there went his plans for an easy end to the shift: "Stat" meant something extremely serious. He ran toward the rear doors and out onto the dock; his long, white smock coat swinging to and fro with each step. By the time he got there, others of the team were dashing up as well. Across the parking lot the flashing lights of an ambulance raced closer; its siren shrieking.

The blinking vehicle screeched to a stop and the driver leaped out. Snatching open the rear door, he bounded inside, where, in the brilliantly-lighted space, two other attendants were ministering to a patient. In a half-minute, the three medics were shoving the gurney through the big doors.

"What's the deal?"

"Female . . . heatstroke . . . dehydration . . . looks like she was assaulted."

A nurse was motioning. "To 'Room Six'!"

"Room Six" was the nearby space for patients who needed attention at once.

The doctor looked down at the pale, dark-haired female patient, whose condition he adjudged to be critical, and was at once struck by how attractive she was. He issued rapid orders: get her hooked-up to the monitors; do a blood work-up. He took the write-up from the driver. "What happened?"

"We think she's the girl recently in the news . . . the detective missing in Dallas. They found her nailed inside a wooden box in a cargo trailer—like a prisoner, or something—I'd never seen anything like it." The man shook his head. "She'd been inside it for days, maybe."

"Unbelievable." The doctor listened through his stethoscope "Heartbeat's not strong, but at least it's steady." He felt her forearm. "Skin's dry . . . dehydrated. Get a *'chilled I-V'* started."

"Blood pressure ninety over fifty," a nurse said.

"Temperature one-hundred-two-point-two."

"She's probably been overheated for no telling how long." The doctor had seen these types from people getting lost in the nearby desert—brain damage was a possibility in these cases. He turned to the nurse. "Get a 'brain-wave monitor'." The doctor looked again the patient and shook his head. "Who the hell locked her up like *that?"*

A nurse lifted her limp hand held it. "It's all right, honey . . . you're going to be just fine." It was important, the woman knew, to try to bolster their spirits, even if they weren't fully conscious. She had seen it make the difference between a patient's overcoming a trauma or dying from it.

"Get her into a gown," the doctor ordered, "and save her clothes for the police." He stepped outside the cubicle for a cup of coffee while the female nurses stripped the girl and put her into a hospital gown.

Minutes later, he re-entered the room. "Scratches on the neck and torso." A nurse marked his observations on a chart. Then he frowned. "I hate to say this, but we may need a rape kit."

* * *

84

The rented Learjet left the ground and made a sharp, nose-high turn over the end of the Love Field runway, then began its climb-out on a south-southwesterly heading. As the aircraft pulled for altitude, Ned Ferry and Kip Leeds, each lost in his own thoughts, stared at the jammed *'Metroplex'* traffic crawling along down below in the orange-hued, early-morning sunlight. The pilot had said it would take about an hour-and-a-half to get to Laredo.

"What did Randolph say?" Kip asked, over the roaring of the engines.

"She's in a hospital in Laredo. They found her in a semi-truck."

"In a *truck?* How? Why?"

"He didn't know."

* * *

Eighty-five minutes later, the aircraft's twin engines shut down in front of a general aviation hangar at the "Laredo International Airport".

As the two ran toward the building in the baking bordertown sunshine, a man in a sport coat with the badge of a police lieutenant in the palm of his hand stepped up to them. "Ferry?"

The detective nodded.

"Follow me," the man said, motioning toward a chain-link gate that led to the parking lot.

A minute later, they were in a police cruiser, speeding through the main gate onto a thoroughfare. The officer glanced back at them as he threaded the car between lanes of traffic "It'll take us about ten minutes to get to the hospital,"

The squad car slithered to a stop at the emergency entrance. At the nurse's station an older-looking lady in a striped seersucker coat picked up the telephone. "They're here . . . yes, the girl who was brought in. Her—"

" . . . her father".

". . . a friend."

A spare-looking man in a blue jumpsuit and a white smock-coat stepped toward them, fingering a stethoscope hung around his neck "I'm Doctor Sollis." He shook the newcomers' hands. "Could you come this way, please?"

"When can I see my daughter?"

"She's still in the emergency room; we're trying to stabilize her." The doctor told them how Sloane had been found. "I'll be honest with you . . . right now, it's touch-and-go—" The doctor looked uncomfortable. "Why don't you go to the waiting room and get a cup of coffee? We'll call you as soon as we can."

The detective was pale; there was a dry, bitter taste in Kip's mouth—"coffee" didn't sound very inviting, right now. The two men dropped into seats in an alcove off the emergency admitting office.

There was a commotion, and a gurney burst through some double-doors nearby, tugged along by an EMS crew. Bright-red flecks of blood streaked its sheets. The wheeled cot disappeared down a corridor into an examining room. A medical person ran past. "Hit-and-run," he gasped to someone else. Emergency people must have nerves of steel, Kip thought.

The doctor came back. "Come with me," he motioned.

"How is she?" Ned Ferry asked.

"You can see her for a few minutes." The two men followed him down a hallway into a small, over-bright room. Several 'I-V' poles stood around a narrow hospital bed. Under a white sheet lay a pale, motionless, dark-haired young woman.

Ned Ferry groaned. "Oh! it's her—" The man dropped down and caressed his daughter's face and hair. He reached for her hand, swathed in bandages over needles stuck into veins.

Kip blanched—it was hard to believe that the wan figure lying there hooked up to all those monitors and tubes was the same girl he had known all these years. The thought that she might be really hurt made his knees feel weak. He reached down and found her other hand. Kip stared in dismay at the dark-blue veins standing out in her translucent skin: her fingernails had a bluish tinge. A growing anger at whoever did this to her welled-up inside him.

"She's very weak," the doctor put in," but her vital signs are more stable, now. We're giving her fluids . . . she was overheated and dehydrated."

A nurse came into the room holding a clipboard. "Here's the lab report."

The doctor flipped through the pages for a minute while the two men gaped at him. He motioned toward the door. "Come with me . . . I want to talk to you some more about this."

In a nearby tiny, windowless office, the doctor motioned at two chairs as he took his own seat behind a small institutional desk. Framed hospital accreditation and public service certificates hung on the wall above the doctor's head. The two visitors settled into tubular leatherette chairs.

Ned Ferry spoke first. "Doctor . . . what has happened to my daughter?"

"They found her in the nick of time. A little longer in that crate—after the sun came up—and she would have been dead." He looked from one man to the other. "From the nature of bruises and other marks on her body, we know she was beaten, but I don't think she was sexually assaulted."

Kip stared at the doctor, trying to make sense of what the man was saying.

"We thought at first she had been raped, but there wasn't enough evidence to prove it . . . what we *do* know, is that she's been severely traumatized." He leafed through the report. "Her blood shows a high level of a sedative usually found in sleeping medicine."

"Sleeping medicine?"

"She was drugged."

"Is she going to be all right?"

Sollis took a deep breath. "She's not out of the woods—yet." The physician interlaced his fingers on the desktop. "With things like this, sometimes there are problems that go on, afterward."

"What kind of problems?"

"Heart rhythms, for one. Her whole system is out of balance from the heat overload she went through, and from the drug." The doctor saw that these two men were used to getting straight answers. "Her brain function could be affected, depending on how long she was overheated in that crate."

Kip was appalled that Sloane could have permanent injuries. Waves of remorse rolled over him—he had sent her to his house in the first place and there she had been waylaid.

The doctor was speaking. "We're hopeful that she'll come out of this coma, soon; then we can evaluate how much she's been affected."

"When will she wake up?"

"Perhaps in a few hours . . . after her liver and her kidneys have cleared out more of the drug. She'll do better as her temperature comes down." He looked at Ned Ferry, then at Kip. "I know it's tough, but if I were you, I'd go get some breakfast; nothing's going to change anytime soon. Meanwhile, we're watching her closely."

"I want to see my daughter again."

"All right." The doctor stood up and led the men back down the hallway.

The nurses stood back as Ned Ferry leaned over the inert girl and looked into her face with anguished expression. "Sloane, sweetheart . . . can you hear me?"

The girl stirred, but only the whirring, clicking sounds of the monitors came in reply.

A nurse tapped the clipboard she was holding. "She's still pretty much out of it."

"I guess you're right." He looked at Kip. "Let's go get something to eat."

The nurse forced a smile as the men passed through the doorway on their way out. "We'll page you if anything changes."

When the two went into the cafeteria, Kip's eye caught someone motioning at them from a table across the room. "Look, there's the police lieutenant who brought us from the airport." Kip returned the greeting. "It looks like he wants to talk with us."

The man was coming toward them with a police radio in his hand. "How's your daughter?"

Ned Ferry brought the officer up-to-date on Sloane's condition.

A few minutes later, the detective and Kip slid into seats across from the policeman with their breakfast trays. "I appreciate that you brought us here from the airport," the investigator said.

The officer shrugged. "Only doing what any officer would do under the circumstances . . . every department in the country had been notified of her disappearance—in fact, 'Guzman', the Customs Inspector who found her, recognized her from her picture."

"We owe this 'Officer Guzman' a vote of thanks."

"Then, you'll have the chance to do it in person; he's coming here as soon as his shift is over. Everybody's kind of gotten caught up in this—" The man stopped and dug a paper out of a pocket. "I almost forgot . . . you have a message from a guy named 'Randolph'. He wants you to call him. Says he has some new information for you."

Ned Ferry pulled his cell phone from his coat pocket. "Breakfast can wait."

The detective scrolled down a list on the miniature screen to Randolph's number. "Randolph . . . Ferry here." His face was impassive for a few seconds, then he cocked his head, frowning. "Is that so?" Another pause, then, "At the *'shipping yard'*, you say?"

The detective's eyebrows went up as he took in whatever the agent was telling him. "That's really something! Any report on where they went?"

He listened for more seconds, then told Randolph he had tire impressions of the suspect's vehicle at his office and to call Brad Holdon and arrange to get them. "Keep me posted."

He pocketed the receiver. The others were staring at him.

"Randolph says there were *three* men and a *woman* in the car when it returned to the airport rental place—a white, baldheaded fellow, and a tough-looking black man who seemed to match the description of the guy who followed you on the plane"—he nodded at Kip—"and a third man, a small, dark fellow, also bald." He glanced at Kip, whose eyebrows were up. "The woman was light-skinned and looked younger than the men. All four were on the flight to Frankfurt last night."

Kip groaned. "Looks like they gave us the slip."

"'*INTERNOL*' is working on it over there—but there's more. They're holding two warehouse-men from the dock in West Dallas where the crate was loaded onto the truck . . . Randolph thinks they arranged for it to look like it was a regular shipment."

Kip narrowed his eyes. "How is this guy Randolph so sure they were the ones who did it?"

"His agents found an electric drill in the garage of one of the warehousemen with a bit attached to it that matched the size of the holes drilled in the box, along with sawdust that was the same type of wood used in the crate."

"How did they know it was the same wood, so quickly?"

"They had the lab in Laredo do a spectro-analysis of samples and sent the results by satellite link to Dallas. Everything matched."

"What about the truck driver?"

"It looks like he was just a pawn. He was pretty upset, actually."

Just then, a uniformed officer stopped at their table. "Ferry?"

The detective nodded.

"They said you were here in the cafeteria . . . I'm 'Inspector Guzman', of the Border Patrol.

"Guzman!" Ned Ferry grabbed the man's hand and shook it. He introduced the others at the table. "Have breakfast with us!"

In a few minutes, the officer returned with a tray. "I'm glad to have had something to do with finding your daughter . . . it was a miracle."

He told how he and the driver had discovered Sloane inside the wooden crate in the back of the truck. "We're sure the driver didn't have anything to do with it. He was really shook up about it." Guzman gave a perplexed look "*Why* would anybody do such a thing to her?"

"She had been working on a case . . . maybe somebody wanted to get her out of the way."

When the men returned to the Emergency Room nurse's station, the woman behind the counter told them that Sloane had just been transferred to the Intensive Care Unit.

On the second floor, the head "ICU" nurse pointed at a hallway. "Ferry? She's in 'Room Number Two' . . ."

As they made their way down the corridor, a buzzer went off and a light began flashing over a door a few rooms before them. A woman's strident voice came out of an overhead loudspeaker. *"Code Blue! Room Two!"*

Nurses burst from several nearby doorways and ran down the hallway. Sollis, the doctor they had talked with earlier, dashed from the direction of the nurse's station and bounded into "Room Two".

Ned Ferry and Kip gasped; their eyes wide. *"Room Two" was Sloane's room!*

There was furious activity in the cubicle. As the two men watched, stunned, the doctor held what looked like a short paddle in each hand, connected to a wire. A nurse squeezed something from a tube onto both of them and he rubbed together the two paddles.

"Clear!" There was a loud *SNAP!* and the mattress jerked up and down. The doctor pulled back the paddles and looked at a monitor for a few seconds, frowning.

Then he called out again. "Clear!" Once more there came a slamming noise with the bed bouncing.

Sollis stared at the screen for several seconds, then handed the paddles to a nurse. "That was close!" He reached for the clipboard. "Do a blood electrolytes work-up and get Doctor Morin from Cardiology up here . . . I want to talk to him about this patient."

Just then, Kip heard a groan next to him. He whirled around just as Ned Ferry slumped senseless to the floor!

Inside the room, a nurse heard the sound and turned about. "Doctor! Out in the hallway!"

The physician hurried out and knelt down. Pulling a miniature flashlight from a coat pocket, he shined a tiny beam into each of Ned Ferry's eyes, then flipped it back into his pocket with a practiced air. "He just fainted . . . I guess all this has been a bit too much for him." He looked up at the nurse. "Smelling salts!"

After the doctor held a vial under the older man's nose for a few seconds, the detective began to revive. He hauled himself up and managed a wan smile. "I'm a fine one . . . going down like *that.*"

Sollis turned to the two Laredo officers. "Could you stay out here while I have a talk with these other two gentlemen?" He motioned Ned Ferry and Kip into a small anteroom.

"What's going on?" the detective asked, still pale from the fainting spell.

"I guess I can be honest with you . . . this patient has a very serious imbalance of what we call 'electrolytes.'" The doctor looked into the others' faces in turn. "Sometimes with heat stroke patients, it can cause sudden cardiac arrest. That's what happened, in there, just now."

"You mean she could *die* from these . . . electro—"

"'Electrolytes'. Yes, electrolyte imbalance *is* serious, since it relates to cardiac function. We hope that as she stabilizes, the danger should diminish. We are giving her potassium in the I-V."

The two officers re-joined them as they stepped into the room. Almost lost under the sheet lay the unconscious young woman whose long, dark hair draped across the pillow, framing her face. Tiny, clear-plastic oxygen tubes disappeared up into her nostrils.

"Sloane—?" Kip spoke into her ear, "it's Kip . . ."

The girl moaned and shuffled her feet under the sheet. But she did not awaken.

Kip thanked the police officers for all they had done, and promised to stay in touch with them. He stepped back into the cubicle and dropped into a chair. Ned Ferry had taken his coat off and was settled-down for the duration.

Kip glanced over at the girl and did a double-take. Did he just see Sloane's eyes blink two or three times? "Sloane?"

To his astonishment, the girl moved her head in his direction and looked at him."Kip?" She coughed twice.

Ned Ferry jumped to his feet, an incredulous look on his face. "Sloane!"

"Daddy . . . ?" Her thin voice trailed off. She looked around and saw him standing next to the bed. "What happened?"

"Just rest, honey. You had a little—.'accident'—but you're going to be fine. You're in a hospital in Laredo."

"*Laredo?* Why am I in—" She looked around, her eyes wide. "Where's Nicky?"

"Nicky's with the babysitter."

A shadow came into the room. Three well-dressed, crew-cut men stood in the doorway with small notebooks in their hands. At first Kip thought they were newspaper reporters, until they flashed what looked like police badges.

"Ferry?" one of the blond, gray-eyed men asked. The detective nodded.

"We are—going to ask the girl—some questions." The man was speaking in a measured voice. "We want to be—alone with the girl. All of you—must go away at—once."

Kip broke in, frowning. "But the patient's not ready to talk, right now." To him, there was something peculiar about these men.

Sloane, more fully awake now, was casting back and forth between the newcomers and her father. "Daddy, what are they talking about?"

Ned Ferry motioned toward the doorway and ushered two of the men out of earshot of the room. He did not notice that the third man had held back and was still standing just outside the door. The individual reached into an inside pocket of his sport coat.

Down the way, the detective frowned at the two men. "You must understand that she's been under a lot of physical and emotional stress."

"The 'Investigation' wants to—find out about her as soon as—possible."

"Who sent you here?"

"We are here to—find out about the girl they say was—found."

"Just a moment." Ned Ferry turned and walked down toward the ICU nurse's station. He pulled his cellular telephone from a case on his belt and scrolled down to Randolph's private number. "Randolph? Ferry, here." There was a pause, then, "Yes, she's awake . . . she's going to be all right, thank God." Another interval, and, "Three men who say they're investigators are here right now and want to see Sloane—alone."

The agent on the other end of the line said something, then Ned Ferry came back with, "No, I didn't get a close look at their 'I-D's'. Just a glance."

Then the older man looked surprised. "What!"

He looked up and down the corridor. "They're gone!"

-10-

Kip edged past the police guards into Sloane's room. She was propped up in the bed. He looked down at the empty dishes on the tray-table and nodded in exaggerated approval.

"So, my favorite 'left-hander' is finally eating, again!"

A wellspring of tears came to her eyes. "Oh, Kip—those awful men . . ." She reached for a tissue, then gave a start. "Where are my things?" Her eyes wide, Sloane cast about the room in a panic. "My dress! My under—"

"Leave it to a woman to worry about clothes at a time like this!"

"My handbag! Where's my purse? It has all my stuff in it."

"Your purse is fine; we found it back at my house." Sloane looked relieved. "But your *clothes* are 'evidence,' so they took away what you were wearing when you came here—*everything*."

"Oh, no! That was my favorite sundress!" She stared down in dismay at the crinkled, flowery hospital gown. "I can't go out of here like *this!*"

Kip smirked. "Tell you what . . . I'll go shopping for you."

"No!" She caught herself. "You don't know anything about—" The girl's eyes were wide.

Kip laughed. "Either I get you something to wear, or your 'disappearance' won't be the only thing the newspapers'll be writing about!"

The girl scrunched her nose at him. "Kip, I hate you!" Then she let out a sigh. "All right, I'll make a list—but don't you look at anything while you're buying it!"

* * *

A half-hour later, Kip stepped out of a taxicab in front of a shopping mall. Inside, he looked up and down the broad concourse and spotted a familiar-looking department store at the far end.

Even though Sloane sometimes drove him to distraction, he admired her good looks. And she was right about one thing: as a typical male he didn't know much about women's clothes—but he knew what he *liked*, so he would make this little shopping trip a creative exercise to decorate her *his way*. This could get interesting, he thought.

At a cosmetics counter just inside the store, a matronly middle-aged saleswoman caught his searching look. "May I help you?"

"Ah, yes . . . I'm here to buy some women's underwear."

The employee raised her eyebrows. *"Okay—"* She rolled her eyes toward the other side of the store, pointing. "Over there . . ."

He sauntered past displays of handbags and rows of women's blouses to what was obviously the lingerie section.

A teenaged salesgirl saw him coming. "Looking for someone?"

"Actually, I'm here to buy some women's underwear."

The young woman's eyebrows arched upward; her hand went to cover her mouth. "Oh, well, you certainly came to the right place," she blinked, with a discreet cough, "what kind of underwear would you like?"

"Something lacy, or with strings. I'm sort of new at this."

"We try to be helpful . . . what size do you want?" Kip did not notice she was trying hard to keep a straight face.

He pulled out Sloane's list and handed it to her. "I'm buying these for a friend. She's a girl."

Oh—this is a gift!" The salesgirl looked relieved. "I'll show you what's popular, right now." She led him to a display of thongs. "Your friend would probably go for some of these."

Kip's eyes got big. "Yes, I would . . . I mean—*she* would." He scanned the packages. All had provocative pictures on them. "They sure look tiny."

"It's because they *are* tiny; that's the whole idea."

Kip could feel his blood pressure rising; *'Sensory Overload'* was overtaking him. He lifted two packages of string underwear and a couple of lacy thongs from the rack and handed them to her. "I'll take these."

The girl looked at Sloane's list. "Bras are this way." She led him to a display of all kinds and shapes of brassieres.

Kip shook his head. "I'll let you be the judge."

The clerk grinned and lifted some of the cupped, sheer undergarments from the rack. Based on some color advertisements and pictures above the display, when fitted, Kip decided, they wouldn't leave much to anyone's imagination. "All the girls are wearing these," she said.

Kip thought "wearing" was not the right word—he had seen more cotton in the top of an aspirin bottle. But with nothing else to influence him, he shrugged, and the girl carried the lacy things to the counter. He hoped no one at the credit card company would notice he had bought women's underwear.

The next stop was the shoe department. Since he was doing the buying, he would get Sloane some shoes that would flatter her feet. That, of course, would automatically eliminate the chunky, squared-off, combat-boot-like clunkers that he saw young women wearing nowadays. Didn't they realize how un-lady-like those "clod-hoppers" looked? Somewhere he had heard the phrase, "women are slaves to fashion," and most of the shoes he saw on display confirmed it. Some people somewhere were getting rich foisting off these ugly things onto females, he decided. Kip was starting to believe *he* was a better judge of what looked good on women than the women themselves. In short order, he picked out a pair of flats and some strappy sandals in the size Sloane had written down.

In the summer clothes section, he told a young salesgirl he was buying a replacement wardrobe for a friend in the hospital. "I'll take whatever that girl's wearing," he said, pointing to a full-size display picture of a model. He knew Sloane would look great in it, and she deserved it, after all she had been through.

The last thing she had written on her list was a "make-up kit," so he went back across the store to the cosmetics counter. The same lady he had talked with earlier watched him coming toward her. "Oh, yes . . . I remember you—did you find your 'ladies' underwear'?"

97

"It's for a friend who lost all her things in a . . . *'burglary'*,"
he thought fast, "do you sell anything like—" he scanned down
Sloane's list, ". . . a 'make-up' kit?"

"Right this way." She motioned Kip around the glass counter
to a display of shiny, feminine-looking oval metal objects.
According to a printed advertisement above the little brass boxes,
they were called, "compacts". The woman pulled out one and set
it atop the counter. "This is probably what you're looking for."

Kip picked it up and turned it over, frowning. "Do women
really *use* these things?"

"Yes, and she'll need these too." The saleswoman opened a
slightly larger box that contained a little atomizer, tiny bottles of
liquids, something that resembled a miniature artist's palate;
other things that made no sense to him—for all he knew, it could
have been a surgical kit. Kip threw up his hands in bewilderment.
"All right . . . I'll take *all* of these!" No wonder it took women so
long to get dressed, he thought.

Even though female clothes and cosmetics were baffling to
him, Kip was actually having a good time of it, and was also
feeling rather pleased with himself, as he had been in the store
less than hour and was already finished. There were the standing
jokes among his male friends that women took all day to buy
even the most ordinary things. Guys of all ages considered it an
undisputed truth that girls and women went to the mall for the
emotional experience of just *being there*—not necessarily to buy
anything in particular, but rather to fill great chunks of time. This
usually meant hours of aimless poking around doing what they
called "shopping". And heaven help a fellow of any age she
dragged along with her; his day soon evaporated into thin air. It
had even happened to him, once or twice.

Kip and his buddies, on the other hand, considered
themselves much more sensible about such matters and always
went to a store *to buy something specific*, whether it be clothes or
merchandise. When they found it—which usually didn't take
very long—they paid for it and took it home. Kip laughed to
himself at the very idea that men could do better than women
when it came to buying things—even women's things.

* * *

Nuevo Laredo, 9:06 PM, Wednesday, September 16, 1992:

In the pale moonlight the two blond, husky, crew-cut men crawled up to the fence. One of them tapped the bottom strands with a palm-sized voltage detector: the webbed-screen wires were not electrified. He shook his head, and motioned toward the mesh barrier. The other man pulled out a set of hydraulic wire cutters, put the snips to the chain-link fence and in a few seconds there was a man-sized opening at the bottom of it.

The two men crawled through the gap and slithered across the brown, scrubby sagegrass up to the side of the helicopter company's lighted hangar office. From inside came the twang of a radio playing Mexican music. Both men synchronized their stop-watches, then the second man loped around to the rear door. He cocked his nine-millimeter pistol and waited; his eyes fixed on the luminous dial of his time-piece.

The other man hunched down and tiptoed underneath a lighted window around to the front door and held up. When their stop-watches showed that exactly sixty-seconds had elapsed, both men kicked open the doors, their silencer-equipped, nine-millimeter *'Barrettas'* whooshing.

Bright-red froth sprayed the walls behind them as the three paramedics flailed, staggering, backwards across desks and chairs. The assailants stared hard at the sprawled bodies for a second to make sure they were wasted, then the two commandos dashed into the hangar where the helicopter was parked underneath bright overhead lights. The first man motioned to the other, who tugged open the side door of the aircraft. The two pulled off their field packs; one contained a disassembled grenade launcher and rocket-propelled grenade rounds, directional mines and shaped-charge plastic explosives; the other held two *'AK-74'* assault rifles, re-load magazines, a burst-transmitter radio capable of communicating up to one-thousand kilometers; an electronic homing-device, and a laser gun. A

99

canvas satchel held the electronic module that would make the helicopter invisible and soundless.

The second man opened the heavy-cloth bag and withdrew a high-impact plastic object about the size and shape of a large pizza, then scooted underneath the aircraft. On the bottom of the fuselage, he pressed the plastic unit to the airframe, then struck it four times with the heel of his hand, activating the adhesive that held it to the helicopter's airframe. Then he pulled an insulated, small-diameter wire from the circular object and pulled it up one side of the fuselage. When he released it, the strand remained attached to the body of the aircraft. The man pulled more wires up the other side of the helicopter and along the bottom to the front and the rear. Both men pulled down yellow goggles over their eyes.

In a hurry the two heaved the other devices and the assault rifles into the back of the helicopter. Both men then shoved the aircraft outside onto the tarmac in front of the hangar.

The first man climbed into the right-front seat; the other individual locked the big right-rear side door in the open position, then strapped himself into the jumpseat. The man in the pilot's position pulled his safety belts snugly across his lap and shoulders since the aircraft would soon be put through violent maneuvers.

The three-bladed overhead rotor and the rear stabilizer fan began to turn; slowly at first; after about two minutes the noiseless blades were rotating at full speed. The pilot eased the rotor-pitch lever to takeoff position, and the soundless, invisible helicopter with no radar reflection lifted off, kicking out a ghostly cloud of swirling dust. The machine swung about, then in absolute silence flew northward toward the Rio Grande and the International Border.

* * *

Kip stepped into Sloane's "ICU" room and stopped short. The bed was empty. Looking-up-and-down the corridor, he spotted a nurse. "Where's this patient?"

The woman flipped through a sheaf of papers on a clipboard. "She's been moved downstairs to 'Room One-Two-Two'."

He took the elevator to the main floor and turned toward the end of the building.

As he was passing by the doors leading to the emergency center, a sudden thunderous explosion shook the building! Kip stopped as the lights blinked and came back on, followed by a chorus of screams and shouts from outside!

WHOOM! Another blast, more powerful than the first, rocked the hospital! The lights snapped off, plunging the whole place into darkness. At once, emergency lights took their place, their fitful beams casting shadowy illumination up and down the corridors. Immediately, the howl of alarm horns filled the air.

Kip pushed through the swinging doors to the emergency section and stood transfixed as a shouting crowd of people stormed toward him from the direction of the rear entrance.

A nurse screamed. "Someone's shooting at us!"

"Somebody's blowing up the building!" a doctor yelled.

Shards of metal and glass exploded from the rear doors and zinged across the admitting area.

A nurse fell screaming—a scarlet stain spread across the back of her blue hospital jumpsuit. A male orderly lunged out and pulled her back from the line of fire.

Two more big explosions shook the hospital—the hammering seemed to be concentrated against the backside of the second floor—the rear wing was taking a terrible beating.

Then the noises stopped. *Was the assault over?*

Grasping the department store shopping bags with Sloane's new things inside them, Kip turned and ran up the hallway. Shouts came from the Emergency Room behind him.

At the far end of the corridor, someone shined a flashlight at his face. "Oh, it's you!" came a voice.

One of the officers who had been guarding Sloane's room in the ICU recognized Kip. He pointed his flash toward a nearby alcove. "She's over there!"

Kip stepped inside to where Sloane was lying. In the dim light he could see she was crying; tears rolled down the girl's face. Her father brushed her cheek. "It's okay . . ." he was saying.

Kip touched her cheek, dampening his fingers with her tears. "I have your clothes."

She took his hand in hers and put it to her cheek. He felt her hand shaking.

The shriek of sirens came from outside; fire engines were arriving.

A doctor bustled into the room. "Is this patient named 'Ferry'?" Everyone nodded; there was a relieved look on his face. "Stay with these people," he told the nurse and the two security officers, "I'll be back." The doctor scurried away toward the bedlam of the Emergency Room.

In a few minutes, he returned and handed a tiny pill cup to the nurse. "This will calm her."

Kip motioned for Ned Ferry to step outside with him. "I'm going to find out what happened," he told the detective.

In the shadowy emergency center, where some low-level lights were now on, a security guard shined a flashlight at Kip, then waved him through. "We're evacuating this part of the building!" he said above the cries of confusion all around, "one of the upstairs rooms was shot-up by rockets and machine-gun fire!"

Kip made his way toward the blasted rear entrance, skirting chunks of broken glass and masonry; past disorderly heaps of unrecognizable rubble; around dark pools of blood here and there, and through the automatic doors that hung askew in their bullet-riddled frames; all their glass panes shot out.

Outside, shouting voices of lawmen and the impatient bullhorn-amplified commands of a fire chief competed with the roaring of emergency vehicles whose pulsating blue-red lights outlined the macabre scene with their strobe-like flashes. The pounding of rotors overhead caught Kip's attention; looking up, he spotted two stationary helicopters hanging above the treetops, their searching spotlight beams swinging back and forth.

Kip ducked under a line of yellow "Crime Scene" tape that stretched across the tops of orange traffic cones and stumbled around to the rear wing of the hospital. There, generator-powered arc lights cast bluish beams onto the darkened side of the building. In the gloomy half-light, he could make out streaks of smoke stains running up the side of the sagging facade; pieces of brick and mortar, along with a twisted window frame, lay in a jumbled heap on the ground. Kip stared aghast at the jagged hole on the second floor where the double windows had once been. On impulse, he counted the windows—Sloane's room had been the fifth from the end. Then he gasped, his eyes wide. *The center of the gutted, smoking ruin was the same Intensive Care room where Sloane had been!*

Stunned, Kip picked his way back through the wreckage to the first floor area where the girl had been moved. He pulled aside the detective and the two guards and told them what he had seen.

Ned Ferry clenched his teeth. "Those three men who came to Sloane's room this afternoon had something to do with this. I'm sure of it!"

"But, *why?*" Kip voiced aloud the question that was on all their minds.

Ned Ferry's cellular telephone sounded. "Yes, we're all right . . ." His eyes went wide. "*Sloane*, you say?" The detective sounded incredulous. "From *'Mexico'?*"

Another pause, then, "Yes, she's under guard, right now."

He pocketed the handset. "I was right—Randolph says the attack was probably meant for Sloane!"

The younger man's jaw dropped as Ned Ferry went on. "Someone hijacked a helicopter from an emergency medical hangar in Nuevo Laredo, across the border, tonight. They found three men there gunned-down—all dead."

The man wiped his forehead with his handkerchief. "Thank goodness we'd already moved Sloane out of that room."

"But why would those men target Sloane?"

"She knows something—and somebody's afraid she'll talk."

"Who—what could that be?"

Before the girl's father could reply, his cellular telephone again went off. "Yes?" Someone spoke to him for a full minute without stopping. "All, right, we'll do that," the detective said. "Randolph, again—he says they want to get Sloane out of this place right away—to another hospital. They're sending a special detail to pick her up."

At that moment, the main lights came back on.

The ambulance drove up outside the wreckage of the Emergency Center into a scene of shrieking confusion. Gesturing police officers shouted directions and orders to crowds of curious people who were gathered in the shadowy darkness up and the down the side streets, trying to catch a glimpse of what was happening at the targeted hospital. Every few moments another ambulance arrived or drove off, its siren screaming. The odor of burned wood and the clutching smell of explosive permeated the air around the backside of the stricken hospital.

A sweating policeman motioned at a spot for the driver to park the flashing emergency vehicle. While two other smock-coated men pulled a gurney from the ambulance, the driver ducked beneath the sagging, shored-up frames of the rear emergency doors and made his way to the admitting station.

There, frantic shouting and hurried bustling had taken over. Paramedic crews were arriving by the minute to pick up patients for transport to other hospitals; others tugged gurneys bearing waxen-faced elderly patients hooked to I-V lines and breathing machines toward ambulances waiting outside.

At the scarred emergency counter the man looked around at the carnage with a critical eye, then shoved a sheaf of papers across the counter.

A harassed-looking woman looked up. "You're here to pick up this patient for transport?"

The powerfully-built, crew-cut man nodded.

The woman initialed and stamped the documents in a hurry, as yet another paramedic crew was coming through the doorway in their direction. "Room one-twenty-two . . . down that way."

The man motioned to the others, who then pulled the gurney through the receiving area, around the corner and headed up the corridor.

Kip looked up to see a husky man in a paramedic uniform standing in the doorway of the hospital room, shuffling a packet of papers in his hands. "Ferry?"

Sloane's father nodded. "We are to take the patient to—another location."

The two other men in emergency-vehicle attire wheeled a chrome gurney up next to Sloane's hospital bed. The girl was sleeping; the sedative had done its job.

The man motioned toward the door. "You must leave the—room."

Ned Ferry, Kip, the two nurses and the security guards stepped out into the corridor while the three men lifted the insensible patient onto the narrow transporter. After strapping down Sloane, they tugged the wheeled cot out into the hallway.

The first paramedic's eyes surveyed the others for a long moment that Kip thought was almost like he was committing their faces to memory.

Kip pointed at the girl's belongings. "What about these?"

The man grunted and moved on.

Kip and one of the nurses snatched up the shopping bags and the bundles of her things and hurried out to catch up with the others.

The hallway procession made its way to the wrecked emergency center. At the desk a doctor came up with a bulky manila folder. "Are you men transporting a patient named 'Ferry?'"

The ambulance driver nodded.

Her chart—" The physician handed the package to the uniformed man. "Give it to the receiving center at the other hospital."

At the ambulance, the three men folded the legs of the gurney and shoved it into the boxy interior. The driver motioned to a seat along one side. "Get in," he said to Ned Ferry and Kip.

But when the first security guard started to get in, the man held up his hand, frowning. "They 'only' will be in the—ride . . . to the place—"

Before anyone could react, the driver and one of the other men swung shut the rear doors. Two of the paramedics climbed through a side entrance and took their places on a bench seat.

Engine roaring, the ambulance lurched by a motioning police officer, past television news trucks and emergency vehicles, and with a heavy tramp on the accelerator pedal, the machine broke out onto the main road.

The nurse looked up at the three uniformed paramedics who were standing with a sheet-covered gurney in front of the admittance desk. "May I help you?" she said, her voice raised above the sounds of the evacuation that was still in full swing.

"We're here to transport a patient named 'Sloane M. Ferry' to the other hospital," one of the men said, tapping a metal clipboard.

The woman frowned. "She's already been taken there."

"But that's impossible!" The man glanced at the others, who had surprised looks on their faces. "There's only one emergency medical crew that's supposed to pick up that patient, and this is it!"

* * *

As the ambulance sped down the divided highway, after a few minutes, Kip began to wonder where they were going—he had forgotten to ask.

"To which hospital are you taking us?" The paramedic next to him nodded and said nothing. Kip looked hard at the other ambulance man, who stared ahead with no expression. Kip felt a prickling sensation starting on the back of his neck; there was something unnatural about these men—they should have answered his questions at once. Kip glanced at Ned Ferry, who caught his eye and frowned. He, too, had noticed the mens' strange demeanor.

The crew-cut individual sitting at the front of the bench extended his fingers unnoticed into a sleeve pocket and moved a tiny lever on a flat metal canister. Just then, Kip was sure he saw the paramedic wink gravely at the other man, who momentarily narrowed his eyes in return. All at once, both men pulled out respirator masks and slapped them onto their faces!

Before Kip could react, the man at front held out his arm and sprayed a stinging mist from the sleeve pocket into the faces of Ned Ferry and Kip! Both men gasped, rolled their eyes, and slumped over, unconscious!

The front man pulled up his other sleeve, revealing a stop-watch. He pushed a button and stared at the dial for a few seconds; then back at the uncomprehending men slouched against each other. Then he rapped three times on the glass to the driver's compartment. The leader behind the wheel nodded and gave the ambulance more speed, at the same time flipping off the flashing lights. The emergency vehicle now appeared to be just an ordinary, off-duty ambulance going down the road.

A few minutes later, as the glowing lights of the International Bridge loomed up ahead, he turned back on the flashing emergency lights.

The driver stopped in line behind two eighteen-wheelers with Mexican license plates. All they had to do now was to get across the bridge and several problems would be solved. In Mexico, the girl whom "General Retchko" had said was dangerous to them would be disposed of once and for all. She would have been dead already, back in West Dallas like "Ezego" had wanted, except that "Betty Nkrume", the cream-colored girlfriend of the general, had been too squeamish to watch it being done. Over the border, these three Americans, unconscious in the ambulance, would be bayoneted and dumped in the desert.

A Border Patrol officer came back to the ambulance and motioned for the driver to roll down the window. "What is your destination?"

The eyes of the man behind the wheel bulged. "To the—hospital . . .we have to transport—this person from the burning—hospital."

The officer motioned toward the rear of the ambulance. "Please open the rear doors."

The driver, frowning, stepped outside and pulled the handle. The doors swung aside. Inside, a long-haired brunette female patient lay unconscious on a gurney; two paramedics were sitting alongside the patient, staring straight ahead. Two other men—one middle-aged, the other a good deal younger—sat on the opposite bench, stock-still; upright. The policeman took in the scene for a long second, then nodded at the driver, who closed the doors.

The border patrolman turned and walked back toward the guardhouse. The driver climbed back into the ambulance.

The gate arms lifted and the two trucks in front of the ambulance rumbled toward the International Bridge in the direction of the Mexico side of the Rio Grande.

An inspector waved the ambulance forward. "Please step out of the vehicle," the officer told the driver.

"We have a sick—patient . . . must get to—hospital."

"I understand that. Come with me, please."

Reddening, the driver dropped from the ambulance cab. "What is—delay?"

"Open the doors, again, please."

The driver had no such intention. He lifted his sleeve and a second later the officer slumped to the ground!

The paramedic jumped back behind the wheel, put the vehicle in gear and floorboarded the accelerator pedal. With a loud *CRACK!* the ambulance knocked aside the gate's wooden cross-arms and churned toward the bridge!

A volley of gunshots rang out as bullets tore into the ambulance's tires. The vehicle lurched, bounded over the curb, skidded across a sidewalk and slammed into the right-side bridge abutment a few meters short of the International Boundary. The hood flew up; steam erupted from the smashed radiator. Three men jumped out, and with Border Patrol bullets tearing after them, zig-zagged towards the middle of the bridge. In another second, they were across the border inside Mexico.

"Hold your fire!" The "paramedics" had made good their escape.

One of the officers pulled open the rear door. Inside, both male passengers were undoing straps that had held them upright. The female patient on the gurney was still unconscious.

"Sloane!" Ned Ferry spoke to her. The young detective moaned and stirred, but still slept.

The Border Patrolman frowned."Are you all right?"

"Y—yes . . . I guess so—" The younger man was rubbing his arms. "What happened?"

"We had a shoot-out!" When Ned Ferry and Kip dropped out of the vehicle, the officer told them what had taken place. Both men stared in amazement at the sight of the wrecked ambulance.

An officer stepped from the guardhouse. "Another ambulance—a *real* one—is on its way to take the patient to the second hospital!"

Just then, the officer who had been gassed by the bogus "paramedic" came up, rubbing his head. He told the others what had happened in the vehicle waiting line.

"So you knew they were the wrong paramedic crew?"

"When I looked inside, the two guys in the uniforms were staring ahead like statues. But what *really* tipped me off was that you two men—he nodded at Ned Ferry and Kip—were *strapped* to the wall, sitting up! I could tell you were unconscious, but the other guys must have wanted it to look like you were just sitting there. Everything inside that ambulance looked wrong, but I didn't want to arouse their suspicion, so I acted casual and came back to the guardhouse and told the others what I had seen. We were ready for them!"

Another officer spoke up. "We had our guns drawn when that guy drove the ambulance up to the guard gate, but I have to admit we weren't expecting anything like *this!*"

The men walked around the ambulance and stared in amazement at its smashed-in front end and at the ribbons of rubber; all that remained of the shot-out tires.

* * *

7:12 AM; Thursday September 17, 1992:

Kip yawned and stretched—his back was aching from the knobby waiting room sofa upon which he had spent the fretful, mostly-sleepless night. After the ambulance had finally taken Sloane to the new hospital, he and Ned Ferry had had to stay at the Border Patrol station for another hour, answering questions. By the time some officers had taken them to the hospital in a police cruiser, the girl was settled into a room, still sleeping.

In a restroom, Kip splashed water into his face, then shuffled down to Sloane's room—was he ever stiff and tired! Two sheriff's deputies stood guard outside the door. "Things have been quiet," one of them said, "other officers are posted at each hospital entrance." Through the doorway, Kip could see the girl's father sprawled across a stuffed chair.

When he stepped into the small space, the detective gave a start, then stretched. "Randolph called a little while ago. He's on his way to take over the investigation—he says this could be much bigger than they had at first thought."

A nurse edged into the room and handed Ned Ferry a national newspaper. He unfolded it and his eyes went wide. "Look at this!" He pointed at the front-page headlines:

-ATTACK ON TEXAS HOSPITAL

-EXPLOSIONS IN LAREDO EMERGENCY CENTER

-HOSPITAL ICU ATTACKED

-ORIGIN OF ASSAILANTS UNKNOWN

-INVESTIGATION KEYS ON POSSIBLE AERIAL ASSAULT

-SHADES OF PANCHO VILLA?

-1916 BORDER INCURSION RECALLED

Sloane moaned and moved underneath the sheets. "What's—?" she mumbled, blinking.

Kip spun around. "Well . . . look who's awake!"

He glanced up at the television set on the wall; the morning newscast was just coming on. Kip reached for the remote control and turned up the volume. "Let's watch the news."

". . . military implications of last night's commando-like raid on a South Texas hospital." The dark-haired newscaster turned to a screen behind him, where a middle-aged man in a gray suit stared rigidly into the camera. "We now go to Austin, Texas, where our military consultant, 'retired Army Colonel Morris Tredd', is with us."

The thin-lipped man nodded.

"Colonel Tredd, tell us what you know about the apparent attack on the hospital at Laredo, Texas that took place last night."

"Well, you do say 'apparent', because we don't know exactly yet how it happened . . . all we know for sure is that a series of explosions took place at the hospital."

"Then, it could have been something like, say, 'natural gas'?"

"Oh, no . . . they found spent rounds—automatic-weapons bullets and rocket-propelled grenade fragments—in the rubble." The man cleared his throat and went on in a gravelly voice. "My sources tell me that they were of recent Russian origin."

"*Russian* weapons fired on a Texas hospital?"

"I can say that there are some parallels here to the attack at Los Alamos last winter. If you recall, there was a commando raid on the 'National Laboratory', there, and a dozen or so U.S. Marines were killed in a particularly brutal fashion The same type rounds were found, there. The Pentagon won't say so, but my sources tell me they think that Russian Special Forces—known in military circles as the *'Spetsnaz'*—penetrated our most secure research laboratory. I would not be surprised if this was the same type operation."

"Are you saying that *Russian commandos* may have attacked a hospital in Laredo, Texas?"

"I'm told there are elements of 'Spetsnaz' operating across the border from *Laredo*—*that* much, I can say. But why they would go after a hospital, I *couldn't* say, unless they were trying to kill someone specific for some reason. It's interesting that only a relatively small section of the hospital was attacked."

"Could an aircraft have attacked it?"

"There is no evidence that an aircraft was involved."

The announcer came back on the screen. "Thank you, retired colonel Morris Tredd . . . and we'll be checking back with you, later."

The man in the gray suit was still nodding when the screen dissolved to a news logo.

Kip hit the "off" remote button and the television went blank.

Sloane turned to the men, her eyes wide. "*That* happened to my room?"

He handed her a tissue. "Don't worry . . . they've posted police officers all around the hospital."

Kip glanced at Ned Ferry; both were thinking the same thing—that there was nothing on the news about Sloane's abduction by the fake "paramedics" and the shootout at the International Bridge. He guessed the news agencies had missed the story—for the time-being, at least. In the meantime, since Sloane had slept through it, for now, they would not tell her about it.

The detective turned to Kip. "The Federals are coming to take over the investigation. Randolph will be here from Dallas in a couple of hours."

Sloane wiped her eyes. "Who's 'Randolph'?"

"The Government's 'Agent-in-Charge.'"

-11-

Federal Building, Dallas, Texas, 6:56 AM; Thursday, September 17, 1992:

James Richard Randolph hung up the telephone and leaned back in his office chair, thinking. If this "Sloane Ferry" individual had somehow become entangled in the case with which he was working, it could be the break he had been awaiting. Ned Ferry's description of the fake "paramedics" dovetailed with the profile the *"Agency"* had developed about the Russian paramilitaries whom they believed were operating out of Nuevo Laredo. The female's abduction and rescue from the cargo truck, along with the shootouts at the hospital and at the border bridge, plus other information he had, was, to him, convincing evidence that the suspects down there were involved in a far-flung subversive enterprise—an international crime cartel—that was supplying terrorist groups and their supporting governments with weapons, training, and expertise to develop and transport nuclear, chemical and biological weapons for use against Western interests. The *"International Criminal Control Organization"*, known as "INTERNOL", had learned the group was operating under an ironic code name: *"The Organization"*.

Although *INTERNOL* was sure the criminals' source of financing was in West Africa—most likely, in Nigeria—how the funds found their way into the hands of the militants was still a mystery, since, so far, every operative who had gone into Nigeria on the case had subsequently disappeared. The setup was always the same: a white American or European, operating under the cover of being an oil buyer, made contacts, sent out scanty, tantalizing information—then was never again heard from. What was most baffling about the disappearances was that investigators had almost always been able to trace the missing men to the "Murtala Mohammed International Airport" at Lagos, Nigeria—and no further. Something deadly was going on at that airport.

113

It was common knowledge in law-enforcement circles that Nigeria was the most dishonest country on the planet; long saturated with corruption that started at the top of the government and permeated down through all levels of society. *INTERNOL* had known for years that a large segment of the population lived off extortion, money laundering, kidnapping and murder.

Recent evidence suggested that international terrorists with Nigerian connections, trained by Russian paramilitaries, were infiltrating the United States across the Rio Grande; most likely at Laredo, Texas. According to recent situation reports, the crime cartel was using Laredo—and possibly, El Paso—as the gateways through which top-secret hardware and software, stolen from U.S. research laboratories, were passing across the border into Mexico, and on to terrorist organizations overseas. An example of this had been the event last winter at Los Alamos, New Mexico, where a leading researcher, now believed to have been a foreign agent, had disappeared with top-secret materials at the same time a detachment of nearby U.S. Marines had all been brutally murdered in a manner consistent with methods used by Russian Special Forces.

There was considerable new evidence that this same renegade organization was bringing nuclear materials, perhaps even atomic weapons, *into* the United States and was pre-positioning the deadly devices for possible future use against American cities—a horrifying prospect.

The "Agency" had recently learned that a small group of former *'Spetsnaz G-R-U'* troops, who were no longer with the Russian Special Forces and were now operating independently, had recently set up an operation in Nuevo Laredo, directly across the river from Laredo. The Mexican Government—which had a reputation for corruption sometimes only slightly less sordid than Nigeria's—seemed to be looking the other way.

American authorities believed they now faced a dangerous force of merciless Russian-trained terrorists—highly-proficient in infiltration, disruption, and assassination—who had taken a deadly aim at the United States's southern border.

From CIA briefings, Randolph knew that "Spetsnaz G-R-U", usually shortened to just "Spetsnaz", had had its origins under

Stalin during World War II and had grown from a ragtag guerilla band to a crack paramilitary organization under the Soviet—now Russian—General Staff. Spetsnaz had always been respected—feared, even—in the West for being audacious, efficient and ruthless in its methods. After the fall of Communism, the standard of recruiting and training had remained very high, and the "Troops," as they called themselves, were always ready for operations anywhere in the world. Once, after seizing an airfield in Bosnia, Spetsnaz troops had gotten into a vicious shooting battle against some U.S. forces that nearly set off "World War Three".

Randolph knew that Spetsnaz's confident, aggesssive soldiers had a régimen that they believed was superior to comparable American forces—the *'Green Berets'; 'Navy Seals';* the *'Delta Force'* and *'Marine Recon'*. Spetsnaz recruited members not only for their rugged physiques, but also for their political reliability; a matter of great importance in the Soviet and Russian schemes of things. Since they would be called upon to perform assassinations and reconnaissance deep inside other countries, the "Troops" were sworn to secrecy for life. It was a firing-squad offense for former members to divulge anything about Spetsnaz as long as they lived, which, to Randolph, made it even more remarkable that there was now a break-away group of such men, funded by the international terrorist cartel—the so-called "Organization"—operating out of Nuevo Laredo.

Randolph knew that since the real Spetsnaz looked upon them as traitors, they were now as much on the run from the Russians themselves as from *INTERNOL* and other law-enforcement agencies.

Although Jim Randolph had been with the Agency for fifteen years, the last two had been the worst of his life. He had come a long way since that day as a graduating senior at Penn when he had stopped at the "Agency's" recruiting table. Back then, most Ivy Leaguers he knew panned and ridiculed the military and anything else not related to social issues. The only reason he had talked with the recruiters in the first place was on a dare from some pacifist friends; the whole thing was supposed to have been a joke they would laugh about later at the fraternity house swilling bottles of beer: "Jim Randolph talked to the 'Agency', ha-ha!" But the "joke" had been on him; the government agents had offered him a well-paying job with a secure future that took advantage of his accounting background—he had been surprised to discover that all agents were accountants. During the detailed training he had learned about investigative procedures and such un-pacifist pursuits as self-defense and how to operate many types of weapons. After that, he had settled into a career of mostly gathering evidence against white-collar criminals.

It was while he was assigned to the Miami office he had met Sabina Torres, a Spanish-language television news reporter. Randolph would never forget that day. She had interviewed him—in Spanish, since he spoke the language—about Cuban boat refugees. When he had taken a hard-line stance against accepting any more such people into Florida, right there in front of the television cameras the "*Señorita* Torres" had delivered to him a lesson about fiery Latina temper. Recorders rolling, she had bristled that years before, her parents had fled Cuba's Communist régime and had spent many days drifting in a boat, nearly dying of thirst and sunstroke, before they had stumbled ashore in the Florida Keys and asked for political asylum. Furthermore, she had told him, when she had been born a few days later, the first child of boat people, her baby picture had even appeared on the front page of the Miami newspaper.

Taken by the girl's energy and stylish good looks, he had summoned the nerve to ask her out.

They were married a year later in the Catholic Church in Miami's "Little Havana" before hundreds of their friends and co-workers. The Director even came down from Washington.

Nine months later, Trini was born—his timing had drawn knowing winks from colleagues. They had named him after Sabina's uncle, *'Trini Torres'* who was still in Havana.

Then the Agency had transferred him to the Dallas office, and James Richard Randolph, at age thirty-four, became the youngest "Agent-in-Charge" in a major city in the country.

Then came that terrible day that began with a telephone call while he was in an early-morning staff meeting. A police officer he knew was on the line. "There's been an accident . . . they're transporting them to 'Parkland Hospital'—you'd better get over there, right away."

He would never forget how when he dashed into the Emergency Center and identified himself, a doctor had ushered him into small office and closed the door. There, he had learned the awful news.

She was driving to an aerobics class when another vehicle had broadsided her car. Witnesses said the other car—that turned out to be stolen—had shot through a red light straight into the driver's door of her BMW. Sabina had died instantly of blunt force trauma. Little Trini, even though he had been strapped into his child's seat, was dead on arrival—his neck had snapped with the side impact.

The other driver—who, according to the investigation, was an illegal just arrived from south of the border—had jumped out and run away. In a few hours, he was in Mexico, where U.S. authorities couldn't touch him.

In the two years since, Randolph had thrown himself into his work, trying to overcome what had happened. Fortunately for him, his superiors had indulged the young widower while he tried to work past his lost wife and son. In a way, this terrorism case that was taking up all his thoughts and energies these days was therapeutic; for the first time in a long time, his creative juices were again flowing. What he needed right now was a big case to kick-start his career, and the terrorists—as bad as they were— were giving him the opportunity.

* * *

Kip stood in the doorway of the hospital room, shaking his head in male amusement. "Is Sloane *still* in the bathroom? I was gone for an hour to have breakfast, and she hasn't come out!"

Ned Ferry gave a laugh. "She's in there trying on the new clothes and stuff. I think she's ready to get out of this place."

"Ferry—?" A male voice came from behind Kip. "Is this the 'Sloane M. Ferry' room?"

Kip turned about to face a man with sandy-colored hair, wearing a blue blazer and tan slacks, who looked to be in his late-'thirties. "And you are—?"

". . . Jim Randolph, 'Agent-in-Charge' of the Dallas office." The newcomer pulled a wallet from his inside coat pocket. "My badge."

Ned Ferry offered his Investigator's badge; Kip and the man shook hands. Two other crisply-dressed men stood nearby, both holding up their own badge identifications.

"We'll be moving this subject to a safer location as soon as she is recovered enough to do so." He looked around the room. "Where is she?"

Kip smirked. "She's putting on her face. She heard you were coming and wanted to—oh, here she is, now!"

The bathroom door had opened and Randolph forgot it was impolite to stare. A willowy young woman with long, shiny, black hair, wearing a short orange sundress, was stepping toward him.

"Sloane, this is 'Jim—Jim Randolph' . . . the Federal investigator who's taking over your case."

Randolph, gaping at the girl, whom he saw was beautiful, shook her extended hand. "Just call me 'Jim' " he said, swallowing.

She smiled at the newcomer. "Sloane Ferry."

"We'll move you to another location for the interrogations as soon as you're well enough."

"Well, I'm ready to get out of here right now!"

Randolph motioned to another agent. "Check with her doctors, and if they give us the 'okay', make the arrangements for the hospital to release her."

The man turned and left.

The remaining agent pulled out a device like a cellular telephone and began speaking into it. He flipped it closed and dropped it back into his coat pocket. "The plane will be ready for us as soon as you're released and we get to the airport."

Sloane was frowning. "The plane? What is all this?"

Randolph glanced at Kip and the girl's father. "You didn't tell her?"

The two men shook their heads. The girl's eyes darted back and forth among the men. He told Sloane about how she had been abducted by the fake "paramedics" and the shootout at the International Bridge; all of which she had slept through.

When he had finished the story, the girl's eyes were glistening. "But . . . *why?*"

Randolph closed the door and lowered his voice. "We believe those individuals who shot up the hospital and tried to kidnap you are part of a much bigger operation that's involved in smuggling weapons of mass destruction to terrorists and the money to finance it!"

Kip spoke up. "How come they are so interested in *Sloane?*"

"Somehow, she must have found out something they don't want her to tell us."

Sloane's eyes went wide. "They'—'who'? Tell—'what'?"

Just then, a nurse with a clipboard in her hand pushed open the door, sparing Randolph from having to offer any more details. "I'm told this patient is to be discharged."

At the front entrance, a few minutes later, they climbed into a white van, and with an escort of un-marked police vehicles, the procession pulled away.

As they rode along in the van, Kip had some questions. "Where are we going?"

"To a location outside of Santa Fe, New Mexico—it's in the mountains and very secure. We'll fly to Los Alamos, first, and transfer to vehicles. We might be there for a while."

"I want to see my son," Sloane said.

Randolph turned about and looked at her. "You have a son?"

It's a long story."

"If Miss Ferry—it's *'Miss Ferry',* isn't it?"

"Yes—I'm . . . not married."

Randolph turned to his assistant. "If 'Miss' Ferry would like, let's bring her son to her."

Sloane gasped, then tears came to her eyes. "That would be wonderful."

"Yes, ma'am."

"Just call me 'Sloane.'"

"Remember, it's 'Jim'—'Jim Randolph'."

Kip spoke up. "Have you found out anything about those men who attacked us?"

"We found the remains of a radio device with Russian writing on it in the wreckage of the Intensive Care room where you were." The agent glanced around at the others, who had surprised looks on their faces. "It appears that the three men who came to the room before the attack—pretending to be agents— left a homing device above the door . . . it acted as a beacon for the rockets they later fired at the room."

"By God, then my suspicions were correct!" Ned Ferry spluttered.

The three vehicles drove through the airport gates and pulled up in front of a hangar where a white *'Gulfstream'* jet airliner was parked on the tarmac. Kip read the letters, *'UNITED STATES OF AMERICA'*, painted in blue above the row of windows; on the fuselage next to the open front door was the *'Great Seal of The United States'*. A half-dozen U.S. Marines stood guard around the airplane.

As they piled out of the van, Randolph motioned toward the steps of the aircraft. "Everyone get aboard, quickly! There's no time to waste!"

In a half-minute, all had clambered up the aluminum steps, that began retracting into the bottom of the small airliner even as the twin jet engines were starting.

Five minutes later, the wheels lifted from the runway and the aircraft set a course toward the northwest.

Randolph turned about to Sloane. "We believe you were being followed by foreign agents! Now, we are going to a secret location to de-brief you . . . later, you can go home. We'll set up a guard for you."

* * *

Their departure from the hospital had been watched by an interested observer. When the group had hustled through the front lobby, a muscular, crew-cut young man had peered over his newspaper at them. As they drove down the curved driveway to the street, he pulled from his sport-coat pocket a palm-sized electronic instrument. With the punch of a single button, the device sent a coded burst-signal to a receiver across the border, a few miles to the south.

* * *

At an apartment in Nuevo Laredo, a buzzer went off and a red light flashed on a receiver. A Russian disguised as a Mexican looked around at the two other former "Spetsnaz" men who were lounging about, watching a *'fútbol'* game on television."They have left the hospital," he said, speaking in Russian.

One of the men fingered a Soviet-made *'Kalashnikov AK-74'* automatic weapon he was wiping-down with a cloth. "Very clever that we are using the American spy satellite without them knowing about it!"

There was laughter as the first Russian, calling himself *'Guido Lopez'* went on, *"The radio implant in the girl will now tell us exactly where they are going! We will follow them!"*

~~~~

PART TWO

THE RUSSIANS

-12-

Moscow, One Year Earlier, 2:55 PM; Monday, August 12, 1991:

Terenty Suslov swung from the screeching tram down to the curbside corner where the Selection Committee's instructions had told him to get off—but where was the "Academy"?

Looking up *'Soyuz Novaya Zemlya Prospekt'*, all he saw in that direction was a big stone-and-brick building behind an iron fence, topped with onion-shaped spires. Squinting, he read an inscription on a cornerstone that stated it was the *'Ol'ya Sovremniyy Monastery'*. Down the other way, on the opposite side of the street, above a hulking building, a red flag fluttering on a pole bore the yellow Hammer and Sickle of the Soviet Union.

Just then, a long, black *'ZIL'* limousine drew up in front of the structure. At once, the driver got out and tugged open the rear door. A bemedaled, uniformed man, obviously an important military officer, alighted from the vehicle. A pair of sentries flanking the entryway saluted smartly as the straight-shouldered man mounted the stone steps and strode through the opening dark-wood double-doors. To Terenty, it was an impressive sight. He broke into a run and, side-stepping a couple of cars passing along the street, reached the other side. At the entrance, a bronze plaque announced the big place to be the *'Tenetsk Military Academy'*.

Captain Suslov returned the salute of the guards as he walked past them into the building. At a desk just inside the foyer, an Infantry Major looked him up and down. "Your orders, captain?" The young Army officer reached into an inside pocket of his tunic and withdrew a sheaf of papers. The other man leafed through the pages, then handed them back with a motion. "Last door on the right."

Terenty made his way down a marble corridor and stopped at the entrance to an auditorium. Inside the white, high-ceilinged, gilt-trimmed room, about two hundred uniformed men sat in rows of theater-like seats. In a lighted alcove above and behind the raised stage was a larger-than-life-size bust of Lenin, his chin thrust out in an aggressive pose. A pair of glittering crystal chandeliers hung overhead; alabaster light sconces were arrayed around the walls. A quick look-around told him that, except for one or two lieutenant colonels, most of the other men were about his age: in their mid-to-late 'twenties; captains and majors in the Ground Forces and the Air Forces. Other officers represented the troops of National Air Defense; some even bore the insignia of the Strategic Rocket Forces, the most prestigious branch of the Soviet military. A few wore white Navy summer uniforms.

Just as Suslov dropped into an aisle seat near the back of the room, the low rumble of conversation abruptly stopped. He looked up to see that an older officer was stepping to the podium. Everyone stood; the man nodded at them and they again took their seats. "*Comrade* officers, I am Colonel General Antonin Krolov, the Commandant, and I welcome you to the 'Tenetsk Military Academy'." He gazed around at the men, who sat as still as statues, then gave a slight nod toward his left. A jowly, gray-haired man, his uniform hanging heavy with ribbons and medals, stepped onstage. The assembled multitude at once came again to their feet. "Comrade officers, I present to you . . . 'Hero of the Soviet Union' . . . 'the Minister of Defense' . . . 'Marshal of the Soviet Union'—Dmitri Yazov!"

Terenty recognized him as the man who had arrived in the limousine. The decorated officer stepped to the podium, looked around the room for several long seconds, then nodded. As one, the men sat down. "Comrade officers, you have been selected to attend here because your superiors are confident you have potential for advanced leadership in the armed forces." Terenty stared at the man who was entrusted with the entire defense of the country as the Marshal went on in a typically-stilted Russian manner of speaking. "The *'Motherland'* is constantly threatened by dark forces," the officer went on, "we must be ever prepared for all eventualities—you are here for advanced instruction to lead our mighty military forces." The room was silent as the

Soviet Union's top military officer's eyes swept around the room. "I wish you all success, here."

The Commandant again took the podium. "I have some further comments," he said to the gathered officers. "This is a three-year course . . . those who successfully complete it will be advanced one rank. Here we stress Marxist military theory and history of the Revolution. I am sure you will use this opportunity well."

A major general came to the podium. "I release you now to the barracks until tomorrow morning!"

As he headed toward the rear doors, Terenty noticed that most of the others had determined expressions on their faces—these men looked to be very professional. In the corridor, a line was forming. At a desk, the same major who had examined his papers when he had first arrived looked up at him. "Your name?"

"Suslov—Captain Terenty Suslov."

The frowning officer flipped through a list of names in front of him. "Yes . . . here are your credentials and your posting to quarters, and the schedules you are to follow." He handed a packet to Terenty. "The dormitory is in the next building."

When he got there, another major took his papers and scanned over them. "Ah, 'Spetsnaz'." The man took several pre-printed pages from the stack that he loudly rubber-stamped, then handed the remainder back to Terenty. "Your billet is on the third floor."

At the third level the young Captain Suslov found his lodgings. Opening the door, he was surprised to find a uniformed, close-cropped, blond-haired young man about his own age who sprang to his feet and offered his hand. "I have just myself arrived from the meeting," the other smiled, "we will be sharing these quarters."

Terenty put out his hand shook the officer's. "Terenty is my given name—Terenty 'Nicholovich' Suslov," he told the stranger.

"'Lychin'," the other officer said, "Gennady 'Illyich' Lychin—Infantry—what is your specialty?"

"Electronic Counter-measures. I am here for Special Forces training."

"Spetsnaz?"

"Of course."

Lychin's eyebrows raised. "I have *also* been selected for Spetsnaz. It looks as if the powers above think that Infantry, Electronics and Special Forces all go together!"

Terenty already liked the fellow's easy manner."Since you are Infantry . . . you can supply the muscles—we will *both* be the brains!"

The new roommate laughed. "But you are bigger than I am—*you* be the muscles!"

Terenty looked around. On the floor by a made-up bunk was a familiar-looking leather bag. "I see my things made it here, all right."

"Yes, your kit was here when I arrived this morning."

Terenty flipped through the schedule sheets. "I see we have the rest of the day off . . . where do we go for something to eat?"

"There is a kiosk down the street. I am hungry, also."

In a few minutes, the two Army officers were standing at a sidewalk food court on the next block from the Academy. The attendant wrapped two "blintzes" in waxed paper and handed both over the counter. On the way to a table, Gennady stopped to put coins into a drink machine. "I learned to like this drink when I was stationed at Sochi, on the Black Sea."

Terenty recognized his companion's foaming refreshment, as the two settled into seats at a weathered sidewalk table. "'*Kvas*', I see you have."

Gennady took a long swallow of the mildly-alcoholic liquid of fermented bread, then held the glass aloft with a satisfied air. "Next to Vodka, I would say 'kvas' is the 'national drink'."

Terenty got one and sat back down. The two officers dug into their rolled cheese pancakes with sour cream.

As they ate, a gray-bearded priest in a black robe and sandals stepped into the tiny garden of the nearby monastery. Gennady narrowed his eyes and watched as the older man picked a bunch of flowers and carried the bundle back into the stone structure. "I am glad I am not burdened by any religion . . . those people are not in the real world." He turned back to Terenty. "Tell me . . . are you a *'Party'* member?"

"Yes—" Terenty wanted to change the subject. "You were posted on the Black Sea?"

"Sochi was pleasant—very pleasant, indeed—lots of pretty girls at the beaches." A pained expression crossed his face. "But then we were called away to *'Chechnya'* on a mission to protect State property from counter-Revolutionary hoodlums. Those bloody, murdering bastards were killing our soldiers!" Terenty stared at his companion as Gennady went on, "We had to become ruthless, just to survive!" He stopped talking as a man and a woman passed by on the sidewalk. "Terrible things happened in that godforsaken place—things I cannot talk about."

The conversation stopped again while a tram squealed past.

"How did you come to Moscow?"

Gennady upended his glass and drained the few remaining drops of kvas. "I will start at the beginning. I was the son of workers."

"You seem to have done well."

I came from the city of *'Ul'yanovsk'*—does that city sound familiar?"

Terenty thought he recognized the name, but could not place it.

"It is the very town where Lenin was born! My 'patronymic' name is 'Illyich'—Gennady Illyich Lychin. My father was named after his great-uncle 'Vladimir Ilyich Ul'yanov,' which was Lenin's actual name!"

Terenty's eyes were wide. "You are related to *Lenin?*"

"Yes, but being related to the founder of the Soviet State has not meant any advantages for me. I have had to do everything for myself."

A grin flickered across Terenty's face. "Then, *I* must tell *you* something. *My* 'patronymic' name is 'Nicholovich'—as in 'Nicholas Romanov'—*the last Czar who your relative Lenin overthrew in the October Revolution!"*

Gennady looked stunned. "Oh, my God . . . that is—if I *believed* in God!" .

Terenty pushed back his chair. "This calls for more drinks!"

In a minute he returned with a bottle of Vodka in one hand a couple of small glasses in the other. "This will lubricate our senses!" He tugged the top from the bottle and poured the clear liquid into the glasses. "I believe we will be glad that we do not have any further business at the Academy, today!" He hoisted his glass. "To Lenin—your relative!"

"To the Revolution!"

What about Nicholas, the Czar—*my* relative?"

He was a reactionary." Gennady forced a smile. "Nothing personal, of course."

"Of course."

Gennady upended his glass. "As I was saying, I came from Ul'ynovsk, on the *'Mother Volga'*. I was an only child; my father worked in a truck factory; my mother worked in the childrens' nursery at the same factory. When I was ten years old, I joined the *'Pioneers'*."

Terenty nodded. "I know all about the Pioneers."

Gennady went on. "In the 'Pioneers', I had my first military training. I decided from that time that I wanted to have a military career."

"When I was very young, I also knew that *I* wanted to be an officer."

"At age sixteen, I joined the *'Komosomol'*," the 'Young Communist League'—" Gennady stopped.talking and looked at his companion, "I guess you did the same thing?"

Terenty nodded.

"One day about the time I was to graduate from secondary school, the local 'Political Officer' called me into his office. I thought I had done something wrong, but he shook my hand and invited me to apply to 'Officer Commissioning School'. . . he said my test marks and field leadership ratings had been noticed favorably by the 'Selection Committee' as having 'Party potential'."

"You joined the Party?"

"I had a provisional membership when I went off to the school in Kazan for two years. When I graduated, I became a Communist Party member."

"Where did you go from there?"

"I was posted to a little town on the 'Tobol River' called 'Kanzy-Mansiysk'—it was about as bad in real life as it sounded—the whole place was caked in mud!"

"Why were you there?"

"There was an enriched-uranium processing plant outside of town . . . very secret—we guarded it." Gennady rolled his eyes. "But that place had the ugliest women I ever saw. That was the hardest part—we drank a lot of Vodka!"

"How did you finally get out of there?"

"Another summons from the Political Officer." Gennady poured himself another drink, then went on. "The Comrade Officer told me I was appointed to the *'Ground Forces Academy'*. It was a two-year course. I came out a Captain of Infantry. After that, I was very fortunate—I was posted to the 'War Games Directorate' at the Ministry of Defense."

"Impressive."

"I participated in War Plans with 'Warsaw Treaty' commanders. It was a privilege to work under Kulikov."

"Kulikov! You were with *him?* "

"'Marshal of the Soviet Union Viktor Kulikov' was very tough, but fair." Gennady held up his glass and looked.at it. "I have strong respect for him. He is a man and a leader."

"How did you get appointed to the 'Tenetsk Academy'?"

"I was posted to Sochi, as adjutant of the garrison there. As I said, it was very pleasant duty, but it did not last long. The Chechnya uprising took our unit over to Grozny a few months later." Gennady stopped, as if in thought, then went on. "One day, our squad was driving down a street in a personnel carrier, when a rocket hit us. Only myself and the driver, who were up front, were still alive. But then the rebels—there were six of them—made a big mistake. When they came out of hiding, I guess they thought we were all dead. When one of them reached for my *'Kalashnikov'*, I shot him before he could react. My driver took out three of them before he was killed. I got the rest of them."

"I have heard of such things." Terenty poured another round of drinks."Go on."

"A few days later, my commanding officer called me to his quarters and told me I was being posted to 'Special Tactics.' He said I was suited for 'unconventional warfare.' When my orders came through, they were for the 'Tenetsk Military Academy'. Now, I am here."

Terenty rolled his glass in his hands. "Being a distant relative to the Czar did not do me any more good than being Lenin's nephew had helped you." He shrugged. "My advantage—if you want to call it that—was the fact that my father was related to 'Mikhail Suslov' . . . "

Gennady's eyes went wide. "Suslov! The 'theoretician' of the Communist Party? You are related to *him?*"

"But I still had to pass all the tests."

"Then, how *did* you get here—to 'Tenetsk'?"

"I was born in Leningrad', but my father came originally from a village called *'Shakhovskoye'*, over near the Urals."

Gennady looked startled. "There was a place by that name just a few kilometers from where I was born"—his eyes got big—"*it was the same town where Mikhail Suslov came from!*"

It was Terenty's turn to be surprised. "Something is going on, here—could there be a *reason* the Selection Committee brought us here and assigned us to the same quarters?"

"How well did you know Mikhail Suslov when he was still alive?"

"I was told he came to our flat only once, when I was very young. I knew he was an important man, but it was much later that I learned just *how* important he *really* was."

"He was on the *'Politburo'*."

"My uncle was a shrewd politician. I read that he was close to Stalin—you had to be *very* clever to survive in those days!" Terenty stopped and refilled the Vodka glasses. "Much later, he organized the coup that threw out Khrushchev for Leonid Brezhnev. From then, until he died, he was in charge of Party ideology."

Gennady nodded. "Mikhail Suslov was an important man."

"He found the right people and brought them to Moscow— that was how Gorbachev came here; my great-uncle brought him to the 'Central Committee' from down South. Later, of course,

Gorbachev became the General Secretary of the Communist Party of the Soviet Union." Terenty leaned forward. "But I am concerned about Gorbachev, right now," he said in a hoarse whisper.

"You are concerned? How?"

"There is tension in the air—you can feel it. The Party newspapers are critical of him in a way not possible before. Gorbachev has many enemies, right now."

"Are not Yeltsin and Gorbachev capable of keeping order?"

"Remember when Gorbachev threw Yeltsin off the Politburo? Those two have not gotten along, since then. Could they work together now in a crisis? I wonder."

As he spoke, Gennady's eyes were focused on something behind the other officer. Terenty noticed his wandering gaze and turned about to see what had caught his attention. A slender, auburn-haired young woman in a print dress, carrying a shopping bag and holding the hand of a little blonde girl, was coming up the sidewalk in their direction. As she passed by, Terenty caught her discreet nod and the suggestion of a smile.

Terenty's eyes were wide in admiration. "How pretty she is! Look at those legs and her figure. She has no wedding ring." He was still watching her. "I say, comrade, she is beautiful."

The young mother and the child made a turn past the jutting corner of a building.

Terenty slumped down in his seat and pushed his uniform hat to a precarious perch on the back of his head. "Perhaps her husband was killed in Afghanistan . . . there are a lot of those girls around these days, unfortunately." He stared at the monastery across the way. "And there will be many more pretty young widows if the rebellion in Chechnya goes on much longer." He shook his head. "I am afraid there will be no end to it. I worry they will bring the violence to Moscow."

"I would hope not! Those people are vicious murderers." Gennady downed his Vodka in one swallow. "You were telling me how you came here to the Tenetsk Academy—"

"My father was a diplomat with the Foreign Ministry. When I was young, I lived in France, in Spain and in the United States. We were in each country for three years. Last year, my father decided he had had enough intrigues, so he took his pension and now lives in Moscow."

"'Intrigues', you say?"

"Most of what went on at the embassies happened without my knowledge. But I *did* see and overhear some things that sounded interesting, even though I did not always understand what they meant."

Gennady gave Terenty a raised-eyebrow look. "Is there anything you can talk about?"

"I remember one day when I was about twelve or thirteen years old, my father took me with him to his office at the Embassy in Madrid. While I was there, we went by a room that was full of electronics. A man saw me staring at the equipment inside and closed the door in my face. It was then I realized that all kinds of things were probably going on in that building besides the parties my parents went to all the time. I guess my interest in electronic surveillance and countermeasures started from that moment—I wanted to be a part of that. Of course, I had no way of knowing that I would someday have that very type of career."

"How were you selected?"

"After we returned to Moscow from Washington, I had my *own* meeting with the 'Party-man'. He told me I had been selected for advanced entry into the Komosomol, due to my overseas experience. There, I got my first military training, along with the 'Pioneers'. We had tactical games with live ammunition, and we had to wear gas masks. It was very hard, as we also had to keep up our classroom grades. I am sure all of that is familiar to you."

Gennady nodded.

"But being the son of a diplomat did have its advantages. One day I mentioned to the Political Officer that I was interested in communications and electronic countermeasures and told him what had happened that time in Madrid. Not long after that, he summoned me to his office. He said that the Selection Committee had passed favorably on me; that after I graduated from the secondary school I would be entering the *'Higher Military Engineering School for Communications'*. I was there for three years. When I graduated, I was a Lieutenant in the Army, with an Electrical Engineering degree specializing in Military Electronic Intelligence. I also was certified as a Linguist in Romance Languages. At that time, I joined the Party."

"Then what did you do?"

"I was posted at the Madrid Embassy."

"Was that not the same place where you—"

". . . saw that room full of electronics!" Terenty laughed. "Everything had come full-circle from the time that door slammed in my face. Now, *I* was the man at the same door!"

"What did you do, there?"

"Things I cannot talk about much, but it was interesting. Let me just say that our NATO signal intercept specialists stayed very busy!"

"How were the women?"

"I used to go down to the *'Plaza Mayor'*, which was a big— really big—enclosed square in the center of the city that was hundreds of years old." A reminiscing look came onto Terenty. "At the outdoor cafes, and in the stores and shops in the area there were always plenty of girls from all over Europe . . . nice-looking and friendly. They also did not ask a lot of questions. Madrid was a good posting, all right."

"And what was *I* doing, at the same time?" Gennady threw in, "I will tell you—I was down by the mud of the Tobol River guarding artillery shells, looking at the world's *ugliest* women!"

Just then, the street lights came on up and down the way. Startled, Terenty looked at his watch. "I had not noticed that the evening is here."

"You must finish your story," Gennady said.

"I was in Madrid for two years, then the Selection Committee assigned me to another engineering academy. It was exciting to work and study in the very laboratories that were involved in the latest electronic warfare. We trained with captured Western equipment, then designed electronics to counter-act them. We were even able to duplicate NATO equipment we never actually saw, but knew all about through broken codes and cyphers. We read many of their messages, that way. It was much an electronic counterspy operation as a school.

The *K-G-B's* design bureau worked with us to devise programs and hardware to disrupt NATO communications—we even had an operation to jam American surveillance and communications satellites. Do you remember a few years ago when the American television programs went off the air for a whole day because all their relay satellites stopped working at the same time?"

"Ah, that was a great controversy—you were involved in it?"

"As I said, it was an interesting course of study . . . I was almst sorry it ended."

"Almost?"

"I graduated with an 'Engineering Degree First Class' and a rank of 'Captain' in the Army. The *'Council of Ministers'* gave our Bureau a commendation for what we accomplished. It was a great advantage to me when I went to my next postings at the *'Plesetsk' and 'Baikonur Cosmodromes'* as Electronics Security Officer."

"Baikonur! The cosmonauts blast-off from there to go into orbit."

Terenty looked around; no one was nearby to overhear them. "There were many security issues at the space centers. At the Plesetsk launch center one time we found that a module on one of our big intercontinental ballistic rockets breached security. Again, we worked with the K-G-B to solve that one. At Baikonur, there was a time when we had several rocket failures. We found a computer that was affected by sunspots. Several times, we had to devise countermeasures to defeat American attempts to penetrate our secret launches. Our group developed a reputation for doing such things."

"How long did you work with those things—those rockets?"

"The assignment was for two years, although my tour of duty at the space centers was actually a little shorter than that—I got another summons from our 'friends', the 'Selection Committee'."

"Where did you go, this time?"

"It happened like this: One day, I was called-in to the Security Office, where two men I had never seen before said they wanted to have a 'serious talk' with me. They said they were from the *'G-R-U'*, the Soviet General Staff's Intelligence Directorate. The men said they had some questions to ask: 'Was I a member of the Communist Party of the Soviet Union? Did I have any reservations about Marxism-Leninism? Did I have any Jewish blood as far back as the fourth generation? Were any of my relatives prisoners of war under German forces during the *'Great Patriotic War'?* Was there any compromising material in the files of any of my relatives?' I was concerned, but the Political Officer was casual, which reassured me. I later found out they already knew the answers—they were just double-checking on me. A few days later, I received my orders from the Selection Committee to report to Moscow—to the 'Tenetsk Military Academy' for training in Special Forces Administration under the Spetsnaz Bureau. Now, I am here."

Terenty poured the last of the Vodka into the two little tumblers. The two young officers clicked their glasses. "To success! To Moscow women!"

* * *

7:00 AM, Tuesday, August 13, 1991:

"Attention, comrade officers—students!" The major general who had addressed the men the previous afternoon stood at the podium and spoke. "I have some important announcements!" The uniformed man shuffled some papers and looked about at the assembly. "These officers are to go to the adjutant for special instructions."

He started reading names. After a minute, Terenty and Gennady were startled to hear, "Captain Gennady Lychin"—"Captain Terenty Suslov" ... "

The two looked at each other in surprise. They arose and made their way to the rear, where they joined others whose names had also been called. The adjutant motioned for the men to follow him to an anteroom. "Wait here, until you hear your name."

When the officer was gone, one of the nervous young men spoke. "Have we failed the course before it has even started?"

Soon the door opened and the adjutant called a name. After several minutes, the two came out and made their way down to

137

another room. As they passed by, Terenty thought he detected a pleased expression the young officer's face. As the others were called in turn, he and Gennady fidgeted. Finally, only the two of them were left in the waiting room.

At length, the major called both their names and motioned them through the door. The two presently found themselves inside a large, high-ceilinged office decorated in much the same fashion as the auditorium. At the far end of the room, behind an enormous polished mahogany desk, stood the school's Commandant. The two saluted the decorated officer, who returned their salutes and extended his hand to the young officers.

"You are Captains Suslov and Lychin, are you not?" he boomed in the same authoritative voice from the day before.

"Yes, comrade general."

"Excellent. I am Colonel General Krolov and I have been expecting you."

Terenty and Gennady glanced at each other as the school's Commandant motioned for them to be seated. The man folded his hands together on his desk. "I am sure you are wondering why you have been selected in this manner." As they nodded, he went on. "First of all, you have been carefully investigated for what I am about to say to you—" The older man squinted at both of them. "There exists an *'Academy'* that is keen to have you as students. You would find the work there very interesting, and conditions much different from what you have ever experienced."

Terenty and Gennady gave a quick look at each other with raised eyebrows.

"If you complete the course of study, your future success is assured."

Gennady spread his hands apart in a quizzical gesture. "Comrade general, may I ask a question?"

The senior officer nodded.

"Why were we brought in here together? You spoke to all the others separately."

"I am glad you asked that question, and it proves a point," the general said, "I do not know if you realize it, but you two young men have family and career backgrounds that—although they are quite different—for our purposes, complement each other."

"We have talked about that, sir,"

"It was no accident that we assigned you to the same room in the dormitory . . . we want you two officers to become well acquainted."

They glanced at each other; they had discussed that very point the day before.

"Your individual specialties are vital to the defense of the nation and you will be put together in future operations." Terenty started to speak, then held back. The general went on. "As I said, the course is interesting and different—but it will be intensive . . . and will involve extreme secrecy and, at times, great danger. If you decide to accept, the rewards can be substantial. If you decline, it will not be held against you."

The two young men looked at each other again, then spoke. "We accept, sir!"

The powerful man leaned forward; the shiny medals on his chest reflected the overhead lights. "Based on what we know about you already, I was sure you would say that." He gave a satisfied nod, then motioned to the major at the rear of the room, who had been standing by. "My adjutant will take you to another room for further processing and instructions." Colonel General Krolov returned their salutes and shook their hands. "I wish you great success," he said.

"Come with me," the major told them. Terenty and Gennady followed the man to the same doorway through which they had seen the others pass.

"Suslov? Lychin?" A bushy-browed officer sitting at a desk spoke their names. When Terenty and Gennady nodded, the man, who bore a major's insignia, pointed at a nearby table. "Answer the written questions and return them to me."

The two sat down to a stack of printed questionnaires about their family backgrounds, plus a section about general psychology. As he made his way through the pages, Terenty deduced from the questions that they already knew a lot about him. Gennady, at one point, glanced across the table with an expression that told his friend he had decided the same thing.

An hour later, they handed the questionnaires back to the major at the desk, who then motioned toward some chairs. "Be seated . . . the colonel will be with you in a few minutes."

The telephone on the Major's desk rang. After a short conversation, the man replaced the receiver in its cradle and looked across the room in their direction. "Come with me—"

The two captains were ushered into another office. A fit-looking colonel wearing thick eyeglasses returned the younger mens' salutes, then motioned for them to be seated. "I am 'Colonel Rodion Golubko'—you are Captains 'Suslov' and 'Lychin', are you not?"

"Yes, sir."

The colonel's spectacled eyes swept from one to the other of the two men sitting across from his desk. "You will be at the *'Soviet Military Intelligence Academy'* . . . it is the school every officer of every branch of the military forces seeks to attend."

"Yes, sir." Terenty felt a certain tension. Gennady was staring at the man.

"I will tell you that the régimen is very strict." The man's gray eyes—that looked larger than actual size from the eyeglasses he wore—-kept moving from one of the two young men to the other. "Not only is the course intense, the *existence* of this school is absolutely secret. Should you ever make any reference of any kind to anyone outside the walls of the Academy, the retribution will be swift and total."

Terenty and Gennady glanced at each other.

"The sentence for spreading any secrets about this Academy is ten years in prison, up to the *'ultimate sentence'.*" The man bore his eyes into the pair sitting before him. "We trust you will have professional success, but should you make a mistake here, you may be deprived of overseas work; you may be sent back to the Army—or you may be shot. You must understand and obey these rules completely—do I make myself clear?"

"Yes, sir." Terenty swallowed and stole a quick look at his fellow officer. *Had they made the right decision?* A purple vein stood out on the colonel's flushed temple; Terenty thought the man looked like Yuri Andropov, the tough former KGB head who had recently been the nation's leader.

Rodion Golubko surveyed the two young officers across from him, who were sitting very still. Then he leaned forward, crossed his arms on his desk and seemed to loosen a little. "The work you will do here will be very interesting," he said with the barest outline of a smile. "The benefits for successful graduates are privilege, overseas assignments, superior housing, and educational advantages for your children, should you decide to have any. We do know that at this time you have neither wives nor offspring."

To Terenty, the man's last statement confirmed that they already knew much about them.

The colonel was still speaking. "One more thing: we will dispense with the regular military hierarchy. You will dress as civilians."

Gennady looked surprised. "Civilians? Colonel, sir, why is that?"

"The school is a secret, so they do not want anyone else to know what they do there."

He tapped his fingertips together. "Civilian dress fits this requirement, perfectly." Colonel Golubko frowned. "There are other measures we take to insure that the secrets of the school are preserved, *as you will soon discover.*"

Terenty stared at a portrait of Lenin hanging on the wall behind the officer's desk as he tried to absorb all that the man was telling them.

". . . the agreements you will now sign," he was saying, bringing Terenty's attention back to the conversation, "the provisions will control your lives."

The colonel pushed a button the desk. At once, the major appeared at the door. "Bring the 'Agreement Memoranda'."

In a minute the assistant returned with two manila envelopes that he handed to the colonel. "These documents," the officer said, as he pulled sheafs of papers from both of the binders, "are the agreements that you will sign in order to enroll at the school. Read these carefully, as they contain strict protocols."

As Terenty and Gennady lifted the pages and began to read, Colonel Golubko leaned back in his chair and lit a cigar.

While the two young men read along, it became clear to them that by signing the papers, they would forever be under the control of the country's military; the pages outlined rules and regulations of the Soviet General Staff concerning military secrets. By signing the documents, the applicant agreed to never divulge in any manner whatsoever the existence of the school or its curriculum or purposes *for as long as the applicant should live.* Penalties for violating the edict would include a minimum of ten years in prison at hard labor, up to and including death by firing squad. Furthermore, the two men read, *the provisions would be enforceable anywhere in the world; now and at any time in the future.*

Terenty took a deep breath, then scratched his signature onto the document; his fellow officer did the same. The young men, now bound for life to the Soviet military, handed the papers across the desk to Colonel Rodion Golubko.

The officer scanned the signatures, then extended his hand to both of the two young men. "I welcome you to the 'G-R-U'!" His fleshy lips parted in a slight smile. "You will begin your duties at once." He pressed the button on the desk. When the major came to the doorway, he nodded at the two officers across from him. "These officers are now part of the 'G-R-U'."

Terenty and Gennady stood and saluted the colonel, who returned their salutes, then they followed the adjutant to a nearby room, where the other junior officers were sitting in stuffed chairs. "Your new quarters are prepared," the major said, "return to your rooms and bring your kits back here . . . I will expect you in fifteen minutes."

A quarter-hour later the young men, six in all, were once more standing in the room holding their valises. The major led them to the rear of the building where a pair of four-door sedans awaited them. Terenty observed that the cars, a blue *'Moskvitch'* and a gray *'Zhiguli'*, had very dark tinted glass; even on the windshields. The two automobiles, driven by men in civilian clothes who were wearing eyeglasses with unusual-looking yellow lenses, turned onto the main road. One of the cars drove off in one direction; the other went the opposite way. Even though Terenty said nothing, he was curious as to why the vehicles had parted. For security reasons?

For some time, the Moskvitch navigated around the streets of Moscow; several times making abrupt turns.

The sedan presently nosed into a driveway and pulled up in front of a pair of tall metal gates. A black-painted, wrought-iron, latticework fence extended in both directions. Behind it were thick woods. The major pushed a button on the car's dashboard. The barrier gate started to open.

As the heavy-looking roadblock swung aside and the automobile moved through the opening up a tree-shaded driveway, Terenty was struck by the symbolism: What *other* doors were opening for them?

After the vehicle had gone about fifty meters, it emerged from the leafy tunnel and approached a big building.

-13-

The Moskvitch pulled up onto a circular driveway and stopped in front of the three-story, yellow-stucco structure, trimmed in white, topped by a green-tiled roof. A middle-aged man in casual clothes stepped from the curb and walked briskly toward them. "We have been expecting you—" he said in a guttural voice, "the other vehicle has already arrived."

The driver drove around to the rear of the building to a parking space next to another automobile.

As soon as he got out, Terenty recognized the other sedan as the gray "Zhiguli" that had left the 'Tenetsk Academy' at the same time as they had. While they stood around, he observed that there was no identification on either the main structure or on any of the outbuildings that were set back in the woods some distance away. "We took a roundabout way to get here to throw-off any possible pursuers," the major said, confirming what Terenty had already suspected. The man motioned for the others to follow him toward a nearby rear entrance.

One of the young men spoke up. "What about our gear?"

"Everything is arranged," the officer said, as the group tramped into a foyer. There, they came across the four who had ridden in the other car, along with another man in civilian clothes Terenty took to be with the Academy. The major led the officers into a well-appointed dining-room. "We shall eat, now," he told the men as they filed into the paneled space.

While the officers took seats at tables covered with white, starched tablecloths embellished with bouquets of flowers, heavy silverware; candelabra and crystal goblets, waiters in formal attire appeared with bottled mineral water and appetizers. Looking around, Terenty could hardly believe that the place was connected to the Soviet military. Colonel Golubko had been absolutely right about one thing: being part of the "G-R-U" meant privileges far beyond what he could expect in the regular Army.

After the meal, the major took the men to a clothing-issue room, where they selected a wardrobe of civilian attire. "Until you graduate, you will have no need for military dress," the officer told them. "At that time, you will receive new uniforms for your higher rank."

One of the officers looked puzzled. "Major—why is all this necessary?"

"It is part of the secrecy of the Academy."

As soon as the men had changed into new street clothes, the officer led the group, each carrying a valise of their new outfits, down a paved pathway to an outbuilding that had no identification on it. These are the barracks," he said, answering the question that was on everyone's mind.

The man then read aloud their room assignments from a clipboard. As before, Terenty and Gennady would share the same room.

When they opened the door to their new quarters, they found that their kits had arrived ahead of them. Looking about, Terenty found a printed paper on the writing desk. "We will have an assembly in one hour," he read aloud from the page, which also had directions to the meeting place.

Gennady shook his head. "It feels strange to be wearing civilian things. I have worn only military uniforms for a long time."

"We may as well get used to it. They say we will be here for at least a year."

Now looking the part of regular Russian males, the two went back outside. A couple of others in their new group came up, and after introductions, the foursome headed out. As the young men paced about the tree-shaded grounds, they observed that the Academy took up an area about a quarter-kilometer square and was entirely enclosed by the high iron fence they had seen from the road, which in turn was backed by thick woods all around that blocked the view of the enclave from the outside.

The dozen or so yellow-stucco outbuildings, white-trimmed in the Russian style, included well-kept structures that seemed to be laboratories and lecture halls. Everywhere the men went, they observed cultivated flower gardens in the open spaces and formal-style shrubs and hedges skirting around all the buildings. This place must be very important, everyone agreed, to warrant all the physical effort that was obviously being expended on it.

One of the men pointed at what appeared to be a guardhouse set back into trees at the edge of an open area "Why is it *there?*" he wondered aloud, There was no entrance or exit in sight.

Terenty looked at his watch."It is time for the meeting," he told the others. The four young officers turned toward the main building, where the instructions had said the conference would take place.

As they stepped along, other men, also dressed in civilian outfits, began to emerge from barracks; all headed in the direction of the assembly hall.

As they came closer to the central building, to Terenty, its three-story facade reminded him of a school or a church—perhaps a former monastery that had been cleared of its religious underpinnings—then, "Sovietized."

At the front entrance, the four were directed to an auditorium where dozens of men were already filing into rows of red-velvet-covered seats. Since all were dressed as civilians, Terenty saw there was no way to tell the military ranks of the individual men—just as Colonel Golubko had said it would be.

That fact was reinforced a moment later when a man dressed in civilian attire stepped onstage. "Attention! I bring you the 'Commandant'... 'Colonel General Igor Kamblats'!"

The gathered officers rose to their feet as a middle-aged, barrel-chested man in plain clothes approached the podium. After placing his notes on the stand, he looked out at the men, who numbered about a hundred. "Comrade officers!" he said in a loud voice as the men sat back down, "I welcome you to the 'Soviet Military Intelligence Academy'. The purpose of this school is to train selected individuals for specific missions involving 'State Security'. He squinted his eyes around the room and went on. "Even though all of you have come from different military experiences—your paths have now led you to this place at this time for reasons very important to the 'Motherland'."

Terenty glanced about; his eye caught one of the men who had walked with him earlier. Without a doubt, new people and experiences would now become the focus of his life through this school. What lies ahead? he wondered.

"You will be divided into small groups according to your training régimens," General Kamblats was saying. The officer looked across the room at the new students. "Your assignments will be posted on the bulletin board at 'oh-seven-hundred' tomorrow morning." He nodded and took up his notes. "I wish you all success in your courses of study." The men stood as he left the stage, then took their seats again as a heavyset, civilian-dressed man approached the podium.

"Listen to me for important instructions!" said the dark-haired, middle-aged individual, in a bleating voice, "I am 'Major General Semen Putridchenko' . . . I am 'Chief of the Security Department' of the Academy."

The man paused a moment, as if waiting for everyone to absorb that information.

"There are specific rules you must follow that we will soon give in detail to you—for now, let me say this: you will be held to the highest standards of security . . . you signed an agreement that you will follow without fail. Should you violate the provisions—you are aware of the consequences."

As Terenty listened to the general, something about the man at the podium he could not define put the young officer on guard. Semen Putridchenko would not be a pleasant adversary, he decided.

General Putridchenko was going on. "You are not to say or do anything outside the walls of this institution that would divulge in any manner the existence of this school." Another pause, then, "Certain and powerful measures have been established to enforce this, as I shall now show you.'"

The lights went out as a screen lowered to the stage and a map of the campus came on. He flashed an arrow at various places while he named-off the individual features of the place; Terenty recognized some of them from the short walking tour he and the three others had taken earlier. A picture of a guardhouse—the same one that they had observed during their campus stroll—came on the screen. "This is a very special location, as I shall now describe," the general was saying, "the entrance gates that you came through, originally, are for one purpose only: *to enter the grounds of the Academy the first time.* You are forbidden to go near that entrance again unless instructed to do so." He paused as another slide came up. "This is the arrangement you shall use from now on."

Terenty was perplexed; the picture that filled the screen was of a red-brick building that looked like a factory. Squinting, he made out the words of a sign on the side of the building:

VULKON METALLURGICAL SCHOOL No. 6

"This is the entrance and the exit from the Academy, as it looks from the street. You will use it when you leave the grounds . . . you will identify yourself to the sentry using a special identification we will give you." Another picture came up. "From the outside it looks as if it is a regular school with 'metal shops' However, it is only a cover—the men in the place are part of the Academy. It is all for appearances. *No one must ever know the true nature of your activities."*

A picture of a man's wrist came on the screen. "This is the main security feature," General Putridchenko went on, as the next shot showed a close-up of the same wrist. "Look closely, comrades. and you will see a bump on the inside of this wrist—a chip will be implanted in your left wrist that will forever identify you as a member of the 'G-R-U'. The chip has a battery that is re-charged by the electrolytes of your blood and it will last you the rest of your lives."

There was a pronounced squirming in the seats.

The general's protruding eyes swept across the big room. "Each of you will have the implant procedure today. The recovery is minimal."

The man pointed again at the screen. "As you pass the guardhouse, hold your wrist out as the man in the picture is doing." The slide showed a man extending his left wrist toward a microphone-like device on a boom sticking out of the side of the guardhouse. "The instrument will automatically scan you and record the information. You will then go down a walkway that is covered with trees, into the rear of the next building . . . from there, you will pass on out the door as if you were a student leaving the 'Metallurgical School'."

The next picture flashed onto the screen. "The scanner records your return as you see demonstrated. Should anyone enter the compound without proper clearance, the intruder will immediately be shot dead—no questions asked." The general glared at the men for a second as if they were an enemy. "We have had to do that only once since I have been 'Chief of Security'. *But we would not hesitate to do it again.*"

Terenty felt cold sweat breaking out.

"Of course, you are free to leave the G-R-U at any time—but let me remind you that you signed an oath." A quick, unemotional grin flashed across his mouth, revealing nicotine-stained teeth. "But, really, comrades, you will find the life in the 'G-R-U' to be far better than it could ever be on the 'outside'."

General Putridchenko lifted his notes from the podium and shuffled offstage.

In his place came another plain-clothes individual whom Terenty recognized as the man who had eaten with them in the dining-room earlier. "Comrades! You will now go to the rear wing of the buildng, where they will do the procedure! We will again assemble in this room at 'oh-nine-hundred hours' tomorrow."

The men filed out of the hall. Outside, newly-placed signs guided the men down a corridor to a brightly-lit room where about a dozen tables were situated. On the wall behind each table was a short alphabetical list of names. Terenty stepped up to the table with his name over it, behind which sat a dour-looking man in a white smock with a stethoscope around his neck. Terenty stated his name.

"Your left wrist—" the florid-faced man, evidently a doctor, said. Turning the young officer's hand palm-side up, he took a hypodermic and injected a fluid into Terenty's forearm; at once, his hand wrist became numb. The doctor made a small incision, then, using tweezers, lifted a flat, object the size of a small coin from a labeled box and slid it underneath his skin.

* * *

8:50 AM, Wednesday, August 14, 1991:

Terenty elbowed into the jostling crowd of men gathered around the list that had just been posted on the bulletin board. Gennady came up behind him. "In what section are we?"

Terenty ran his finger down a list. "'*Special Forces Intelligence*'," he read aloud.

The two went into the assembly hall and settled into the red velvet, theater-type seats.

General Putridchenko was at the podium. "Comrades! We shall now get to business."

Terenty noticed for the first time the general's graying mustache. Again, the young captain had an uneasy impression about the senior officer he could not define.

". . . some information about the electronic chip that now is in your forearm—" the stocky, dark-haired man was saying. "It contains personal information about you, in addition to the identification function as we showed you, yesterday. The chip, as I mentioned, draws upon the natural electricity in your body to keep its energy cell charged. It will have its electrical function for the rest of your lives." The man looked around at his impassive audience. "It could be said that not only are you a part of the G-R-U—the G-R-U is now a part of you!"

Terenty glanced at Gennady, who was frowning.

The general was going on. "Twenty minutes after the chip was set into place under your skin, it imprinted the iron hemoglobin in your bone marrow, in your blood, in your liver, and in your spleen with the coded information contained on the chip. *Your body is now programmed!* We are now able to track your position by surveillance satellite, using the electro-magnetic properties that your bodies now have!"

There was a gasp across the room; some of the men looked around at each other with stunned looks on their faces.

"Comrades, this will be of great benefit to you. Should we ever need to recover you from a hostile location, for example— we could find your exact position within a few meters on earth and conduct a rescue . . . *undetected by the reactionary forces!*"

There was a shuffle of the men in their seats.

"We will accomplish this by utilizing a completely new technology we have developed . . . some of you will be testing it against actual adversary forces as part of your training!" With a smirk, the general turned and stepped from the stage.

Another plain-clothes man stepped to the podium and started speaking in a ranting voice. "Comrades, 'Minister of Defense' Yazov was scheduled to speak to you, but he has been called away to a very important meeting. However, we are much honored to have with us—the Military Advisor to the President . . . Marshal of the Soviet Union . . . 'Sergei Akhromeyev'!"

The assembled men stood as a slightly-built, spare-faced man in his full-dress unform approached the podium. Rows of medals flowed down a sash on the left side of his tunic; other decorations festooned the other side. He gave a nod; the men dropped back into their seats.

"Comrades, I come today to welcome you to this school—a revered institution in the Soviet Military." He paused for a moment, then went on."This academy exists to train men such as yourselves in the most secret and important elements of our struggle against Imperialism—'Counterforce Intelligence Operations'—under the command of the 'Soviet General Staff'."

As Marshal Akhromeyev spoke, Terenty decided there was something perhaps extraordinary about him; the man had none of the bombast of many of the upper-level officers. Terenty knew that he had been to America and had developed a professional relationship with the Chairman of the United States's *Joint Chiefs of Staff*. Terenty remembered that Akhromeyev had visited the "Pentagon"; had participated in Tank maneuvers in Texas, and had even addressed their Congress!

". . . full backing and support of the G-R-U, as you move forward in your training," the Marshal was saying.

Terenty re-focused his attention on the man's face that reminded him in a vague sort of way to a sad-looking old dog who was still trying to please his master after years of neglect.

Akhromeyev finished his talk. As the important "Marshal of the Soviet Union" walked from the stage, the men once again stood attention.

Back to the podium came General Putridchenko, who cast his baleful stare around the room.

"We will now take a break and return at eleven-hundred hours . . . we will have more information and assignments for you at that time."

Outside, Terenty, Gennady and several other young officers gathered to discuss the latest developments. "It is a bit frightening to have a computer chip in my body like this," one said.

It is already done," another put in. "Besides, we shall never eat this kind of food anywhere else in the military!"

A red-headed young man who had said his name was "Blagron", looked about, then spoke in a low voice. "I am not sure about this 'General Putridchenko', though."

"Something about him makes me nervous," another gave out in a hoarse whisper.

"I noticed it, too," someone else said. The others nodded.

Another spoke up. "I was impressed by Marshal Akhromeyev. According to what I have read about him, he has served the country long and well. He seemed very sincere."

"Terenty nodded. "But I thought he looked sad, or something. Perhaps he is tired. With all the concerns he now has, the Marshal's duties must be difficult."

"The Americans did well in the recent *'Gulf War'*. There have been rumors that our leaders are very concerned about that."

"There are the negative political developments in the 'Warsaw Treaty' states."

"'Special Forces Intelligence' will do important work in the future," Gennady said. "I am very excited to have the opportunity to be a part of—"

At that moment, the meeting hall doors swung open. At the entrance a man handed each officer a pair of yellow-lensed eyeglasses. When they took their seats, they saw that the curtains were pulled back; an electronic equipment rack with rows of blinking lights on it stood at one side of the platform; several tripod floodlights faced an open area in the center of the stage; a garage-type door at the rear was open to the outside.

General Putridchenko, fingering a pair of yellow eyeglasses, came back to the podium, which was now offset to one side. A technician stepped to the console.

"Your attention to the stage, please!"

The indicator lights started flashing; the technician moved a lever. Then followed an interval of about fifteen seconds while the General stood staring at the open area at center-stage.

"Put on your eyeglasses!"

An automobile, with a driver sitting at the steering wheel, was parked on the stage!

Loud gasps burst out.

The general turned to the men with a smirk. "This is a real car . . . this man drove it onto the stage through the open door a few seconds ago." As Terenty stared at the sedan, he recognized it as the blue Moskvitch in which he had ridden from the Tenetsk Academy to this place.

Even as everyone blinked at the incredible sight, General Putridchenko again spoke. "Take off your glasses!"

The car with the man inside it disappeared.

"Now, put back on the yellow eyeglasses!" When Terenty again looked at the stage, he was astounded to once more see the Moskvitch. The driver inside was grinning.

The man at the wheel stepped from the car. "Now, take off your eyeglasses!"

When Terenty lifted the frames, the car was once more invisible, but the driver was standing by himself at the edge of the stage. The General nodded, and the man, who was also wearing the saffron lenses, took one some steps forward with his hand outstretched. At once, he again vanished.

Now, back on with your glasses!"

With the yellow lenses in place, they could see the man again sitting behind the sedan's steering wheel. As the audience watched transfixed, the driver started the engine and turned the car out through the big opening, With a moaning clatter, the overhead door lowered into the closed position.

"Comrades!" General Putridchenko shouted, "this is the technology we will employ against the Imperialists!" A sneer came onto his face. "As soon as this technology is perfected, we will apply it on our intercontinental ballistic rockets and to their warheads to make them absolutely undetectable!" The general was almost giddy as he spoke. "All the efforts of the enemy to protect their threatening rockets in underground silos have now been wasted!"

While the man went on about how the new development would soon tilt the balance of power in favor of the Soviet Union, Terenty's mind was racing. How would his specialty in "Electronic Countermeasures", coupled with the "Special Forces" training he now faced, fit into this scheme of things? The demonstration he had just seen represented perhaps the greatest single military advance in history—bigger than atomic weapons, even—because, now, the country could face any adversary with confidence. What enemy could stand up to an opponent that had weapons against which they could not possibly defend? The Americans' vaunted, so-called *'Strategic Defense Initiative'* would now be worthless! Terenty was a military man, not a politician, but he understood that the new technology would have staggering diplomatic as well as military implications.

" . . . our great intercontinental ballistic rockets—standing-guard over the Motherland—have done their duty," the general was saying, "blocking the Imperialists while we developed this new means to protect our people." The man looked about. "The Academy will train you to carry out missions to preserve and protect these strategic advantages."

Another man whom Terenty had not seen before stepped to the podium. "Comrades! I will now assign you to training groups. Go to the corridor when your name is called." As the man began reciting names from a list, officers stood and left the auditorium one-by-one.

In a few minutes, Terenty and Gennady joined six other young men in the corridor around a major holding a clipboard. After taking a head-count, the officer motioned for the others to follow him.

Outside, he led them down a walkway to one of the outbuildings they had earlier observed. In a classroom, a gray-haired man in civilian clothes sat in a swivel chair at the instructor's desk at the front, facing away from them. A pungent cloud of cigar smoke hung over his head.

"Take your seats," the man spoke in a rasping voice, still facing the blackboard. When the young officers were all seated, the man swung around.

"Colonel Golubko!"

"Now, comrades, you did not think you would be rid of me *that* easily, did you?" The man gave a flickering grin. "We shall be working together for the next year!"

Rodion Golubko drew on his Cuban cigar and vented a roiling smoke cloud across the room. "You must understand that I personally selected young men because I have confidence in you," he said, with a trace of a smirk."I expect that you will not disappoint me."

Gennady glanced around at the others. "Comrade colonel, we have a lot of questions—"

With a little nod, the colonel's eyes narrowed as if in approval "That is why I am confident all of you will someday be successful G-R-U leaders. You are curious; you are intelligent, and you are politically loyal Soviet soldiers—these qualities will be very important in your future missions; that much I can tell you."

"Why did you select *us?*"

"Your profiles and your backgrounds qualify you for these assignments. Your future tasks will be intense and, at times— dangerous."

Terenty felt a nervous stab. *Where was all this leading?*

The older man glanced at his wristwatch."Let us now go to the Dining Hall."

* * *

2:05 PM, Wednesday, August 14, 1991:

Colonel Golubko reached above the blackboard and pulled down a roller-chart; on it were diagrams with color-coded illustrations. "This is how the new technology works," he said, raising a pointer. "Everything in the radiant energy spectrum such as light and heat—along with audio waves that our ears detect as sound, *can be neutralized."*

Terenty leaned forward with a surge of excitement about where this seemed to be going.

"If we reverse the light waves, they become invisible. In addition, the object now has no radar signature, since its identifying return pulse is cancelled. At the same time, if you take a sound wave and lay an exact reverse wave pattern on it at the same intensity—to our ears, the sound becomes silent . . . all you need is some means to instantly match all these wave patterns and reverse them, and an object is undetectible. Our Soviet 'academicians' are now able to do these things!"

One of the young men raised his hand."Colonel, what about the yellow eyeglasses?"

"The special lenses restore the properties of the light back into its original form so that we can see things as before. In a regular environment, they can also serve to brighten the visual senses. You probably noticed that the driver in the tinted-window car the other day was wearing the yellow eyeglasses—that was so he could see through the darkened windows normally."

"If an object is invisible—does it still exist?"

"It is still there—you can touch and feel it—but there is still an important limitation to the system at this time: total invisibility is only achieved by using very large-sized laboratory equipment." The colonel popped the pointer in the palm of his hand. "Our people are having a difficult time getting the hardware to a size small enough for field operations. Much of the technology is only available now in the 'West'. . . our scientists do have a working system that neutralizes sound, but so far have only been able to produce a portable light-wave device that takes out all the *colors* of an object. This still leaves it as a black shape—sufficient for nighttime operations, but it will have to be perfected for full-time use. We are working to obtain this capability by infiltrating American laboratories."

Terenty squirmed in his seat; *now* he understood how his "Electronic Counter-Intelligence" skills would be joined with the Academy's "Special Forces" training!

"This school is operated by the G-R-U, the Intelligence Directorate of the Soviet General Staff . . . you will train with the Spetsnaz, which will lead to your qualifying as Special Forces officers. As I said before, you men were selected for the Academy because your individual backgrounds match specific needs of the State. You will train as a unit . . . when the time comes for field exercises, you will remain together in both simulated and actual missions." The officer surveyed his new students.

"I cannot tell you details, but *the training will involve infiltrating the United States—*"

"Colonel, you mean we will train *inside* the United States?" Gennady voiced everyone's question.

"Ever since 'The Great Patriotic War', Soviet Special Forces have conducted exercises in that country without their knowing it!"

"Have *you* ever operated in the United States?"

"I can tell you that you will learn, as I did, to speak English without an accent . . ."

* * *

Gennady flipped his overnight pass through his fingers. "I am ready to get away from this place for a while!" He squinted at the list of rules.posted on the inside of their dormitory door. "We can stay out until seven o'clock tomorrow morning."

Terenty stuffed a coin clip into his pants pocket. "We can put the raise in salary we now receive into our social life."

Gennady snorted. *"Social life?* We will have no 'social life' for the next two years—Colonel Golubko will see to that."

As they stepped up the guardhouse, others were holding out their wrists to the detector, then were walking into the foilage tunnel that led to the outside.

"Let us see if this computer chip really works!" When Terenty lifted his wrist at the microphone-like sensing device, a lighted signal on a pole next to the opening flashed from an upraised palm of a hand to a walking figure, then repeated as Gennady did the same.

In minute, they were standing beside the "Vulkon Metallurgical School No. 6" sign; before them was a busy street. The two had to admit that the ruse looked perfect; from the outside no one would ever suspect that anything other than some sort of school was situated at the edge of the fenced woods.

Terenty squinted at a street sign down at the next corner. "We are in the northwest part of Moscow in the *'Tverskaya*

District'." When they reached the corner, the sign indicated the cross-street was the "Soyuz Novaya Zemlya Prospekt".

Gennady frowned. "This is the same street on which is the Tenetsk Military Academy!"

Some distance down the sidewalk was the entrance gate the blue Moskvitch sedan had used the first time they came to the Academy—the place of entry they were now forbidden to approach.

The two decided it would better to go in the opposite direction from the volatile iron entryway, so they crossed the street and made their way up Soyuz Novaya Zemlya Prospekt. Farther on, they came to another intersection. While they waited for a tram to pass, Terenty glanced at a stone building across the way—and did a double-take. "Is that not the *monastery* we saw the other day when we were eating at the kiosk?" Sure enough, even though they were looking at it from a different angle, its flower garden, the onion-shaped spires on top and the iron fence around it were unmistakable.

Gennady's eyes got wide as a realization struck him: "That means the Acad—" He caught himself—*that is . . . it is next to the Tenetsk Military Academy!"*

It occurred to Terenty that this was no time to be seen lurking near the secret schools. "Let us go in another direction," he suggested; Gennady nodded in agreement. The two young officers, looking the part of everyday civilians in casual clothes, turned and went up a tree-lined street that led them into a neighborhood of apartment blocks and small shops.

They had gone only a short distance when Gennady spotted a kiosk ahead of them on the next block. "We can eat there!" A few minutes later, the pair were standing at a sidewalk counter, ordering blintzes and a pitcher of kvas.

The young men spread out their food on a table underneath a hemlock's verdant canopy. For a while, the two ate in silence, watching pedestrians pass by.

"I wish things here in Moscow were like they were in Spain," Terenty stated at length with a fervor that caught Gennady by surprise. His eyes had been following a striking brunette in blue jeans and halter top as she strolled by arm-in-arm with a scruffy-looking boy. The girl's male companion caught Terenty's gaze and gave him a sour look. Terenty ignored the fellow. He re-filled both glasses; it was a warm evening and the kvas was going fast. "*'Plaza Mayor'* down in Madrid was a gold mine of girls."

Gennady swallowed a mouthful of his cheese roll. "They say the *'Arbat'* here in Moscow is popular, I have heard that even the 'Kremlin' is supposed to be a good place to meet women. I believe lots of—"

There was a loud ripping sound of paper tearing, followed by clattering thumps on the sidewalk not far from where they were sitting. "Oh, oh!" a female voice cried out.

The two young men turned in the direction of the noises and saw a little girl running toward the curb, chasing something that was rolling toward the street. Behind her, a female pressed her hands to her face. "Stop!" she screamed. "Do not go into the street!" The object, that Terenty now saw was a tin can, hopped off the curb and rolled out into the thoroughfare, still pursued by the child.

But the youngster did not notice that a tram was bearing down on her! With a shout, Terenty leaped from his seat and sprinted off the curb. Just as the little one reached down for the can, he snatched her up and away from the tracks. The rumbling streetcar, its wheels shrieking, crushed the tin flat as it whooshed over where they had been only a fraction of a second earlier!

As Terenty carried the frightened, crying child back to the sidewalk, an hysterical young woman ran up to them and knelt down. "Oh, my baby!" she held the little girl. "Are you all right?" When she looked up at Terenty in gratitude, he gasped—the youthful mother was the same auburn-haired beauty he and Gennady had seen a few days earlier! The blonde child who had been holding hands with her mother as they walked by the other kiosk was the same one he had just pulled from the tracks!

Gennady trotted up. "I saw what happened . . . you saved that little girl's life!"

Tears welled up in the young mother's eyes. "How can I ever thank you?"

"I—I only did what anyone would have done." Terenty swallowed, flustered by the wondrous creature who was looking at him with a rapturous expression her face. By now, the child had calmed down.

The girl stood and brushed back her reddish-brown hair. "I must be going. My parents are expecting me." The young woman wiped her eyes with the back of her hand. But when she turned about, she encountered the split-open grocery sack; tins and shredded brown paper were scattered across the cobblestones. "Oh, no! The bag is ruined! What will I do?"

Terenty spoke up in a hurry. "Allow us, Miss—"

". . . 'Tamara Kuznetsova'—this is my daughter, 'Larisa'." She batted her still-moist eyes and answered the question that was on his mind. "My daughter and I live with my parents."

"I am 'Terenty Suslov', and he is 'Gennady Lychin'. We are—ah, 'students'."

Her eyebrows went up. "Oh! I remember you from the other day! You were wearing—"

"Let us help you carry these things to your home!" Terenty glanced at Gennady, whose eyes were wide. She was saying too much! Terenty hurried over to the nearby table and came back with the empty bag. "We can put your groceries in here."

"Our apartment is over there," the girl pointed, "I would like for you to meet my parents."

Gennady gave his friend a wry grin as Terenty dropped the last item into the sack and grasped the lumpy bag.

A sudden breeze sprang up; it appeared that rain was not far distant.

Tamara Kuznetsova took little Larisa's hand, and after waiting for a tram to pass by, the four dashed across the thoroughfare toward a block-long row of six-story apartments.

As they hurried along, Terenty could hardly believe that only a few minutes ago he was complaining about his social life—and now, he was invited to the home of one of the most beautiful young women he had ever seen! And she was single, just as he had suspected the first time!

"We live on the fourth-level," Tamara puffed, as they trudged up the staircase at the end of the building. At a door near the landing, she turned a key in a lock. We have returned!" she called out as they shuffled into a small living room. Terenty glanced around at the plain apartment furnished with two venerable stuffed sofas and a chair; family pictures hung on the papered wall; lace curtains covered the windows. A middle-aged woman with graying hair stepped through an archway, followed by a thin, older man wearing suspenders.

"Mother . . . father . . . these are people I just met," the girl said.

Terenty and Gennady introduced themselves.

Tamara touched Terenty's shoulder. "He saved Larisa's life!" The young mother told how Terenty had pulled her daughter from in front of the speeding streetcar.

The older woman wiped her eyes; Tamara's father embraced him. "How can we ever repay you?" The man planted a wet kiss on both his cheeks.

Before Terenty could say anything, a brilliant flash of light burst through the window, followed by a crash of thunder. "I believe we will have a storm," the father said, over another peal that rattled the window panes.

The girl's mother patted Terenty's arm. "You must stay with us while we wait for the storm to pass. Let me prepare something for you to eat."

"Thank you very much, but we have already eaten."

The woman smiled. "Then we shall have refreshments!" She turned toward the kitchen.

More lightning bolts rent the outside; the thunder was so heavy that Terenty felt pressure on his chest. The little girl grabbed her mother's dress as the lights flickered and came back on; raindrops spattered on the outside of the window, then became a downpour. The older man glanced at the window. "This is going to be a big storm."

Terenty gave a wry shrug."I guess it is well that we are here and not trying to get back to the—school." Gennady shot him a hard look; he would have to measure his words with care.

The father eyed the young men. "You are students?"

"We go to the metallurgical school nearby," Terenty said. "We are learning to weld metals."

162

Tamara looked at the two, frowning. "Where are your uniforms? You had military—"

"Ah, we are in the—'*Reserves*'." Gennady cleared his throat, catching Terenty's eye. "That day we had just come from a—'Reserve' meeting."

The young woman seemed to be thinking this over. "Oh!" she said.

Tamara and her mother left the room. The older man motioned for the others to take a seat.

The little girl climbed up onto the sofa beside Terenty and looked into his eyes. "Are you my mommy's friend?" She stuck her thumb into her mouth.

"Yes . . . I am your mommy's—'friend'." The child wriggled in delight. Across the room, Gennady was having a hard time keeping a straight face.

Just then, the grandmother came back carrying a tray with a teapot and several little porcelain cups on it. Tamara was right behind her with another tray. "Croissants . . ." The girl set it onto a small table.

Terenty's eyes went wide as she bent over; for an instant a lamp behind her caught the outline of her figure underneath her loose dress, highlighting her long, reddish-brown hair that flowed down her face.

When Tamara sat down next to Terenty, the cushion shifted on the crowded settee; he could feel the subtle pressure and the warmth of her form against himself.

The little girl looked up at Terenty, then at her mother. "The 'mister man' is your friend . . ."

"Oh—?" Tamara glanced at Terenty, then back at her daughter, ". . . and how do you know that?"

The child blinked her eyes and squirmed some more on the seat. "He told me."

"That is very nice, honey." Tamara stole another look at Terenty.

With a grin, he spread his hands and shrugged. "She asked me and I told her the truth!"

How things could change in a half-hour!

A dazzling flash and a *BOOM!* rattled the walls over the sound of the downpour. Beady objects clattered against the window. *Hail!* In a second, the deluge was joined by a furious fusillade of rattling hailstones that slammed, banged and bounced against the building. *POP!* A glass pane cracked; the frozen projectiles seemed about to break through to the inside.

Then, there was only the rain, that began to slacken, then trailed off.

A loud knock at the front door gave everyone a start. "Fire!" a male voice shouted from the hallway. Tamara's father yanked open the door and was met by a cloud of gray smoke that rolled into the room. "Everyone get out of the building!" a frightened-looking youth cried. Down the corridor, someone else was beating on doors, shouting the same warning. All at once, the lights blinked and went out.

Tamara gasped and reached for the little girl, who was whimpering. Terenty felt for Tamara's hand; the older woman held onto Gennady's elbow. "Follow me down the stairs!" the father called out as everyone stumbled for the exit. In the darkness someone knocked over the refreshment tray, sending croissants scattering across the rug.

By now, the stairs were jammed with shouting, anxious tenants trying to escape the building. With Tamara's father leading the way, the group groped in single file down the darkened staircase, step-by-step, toward the main entrance. Their progress was made easier by occasional residual lightning that flickered through the window above each stairwell landing. When they reached bottom and ran outside, the storm had subsided to a light drizzle.

Someone gave a shout and pointed. An orange glow pulsated against the misty sky atop the other end of the block-long row of apartments.

"That is Galina's flat! Tamara put her hands to her face. "It is on fire! Come—we must see about this!" The older woman grabbed the child as Tamara began running down the street.

"Galina—is—my—cousin," the girl gasped, as Terenty and Gennady followed her splashing steps. Just as they reached the corner, a pair of fire engines swept up and a squad of firemen began dragging heavy canvas hoses toward the open passageway. Looking up, Terenty saw flames curling along the roofline at the very end of the block-long building; dark-gray smoke boiled from a blown-out side window on the top floor. Just then, the streetlights blinked and came back on.

"Galina! Galina!" Tamara called out, searching for a face in the murky shadows. "Galina!"

"Move back!" a fire captain shouted at the residents and other bystanders milling around.

Just then, a short-haired brunette rushed up and flung her arms around Tamara's neck, gasping. "Oh, Tamara . . . it was awful!"

Tamara patted the slender girl's shaking back. "Are you all right?"

The newcomer nodded, wiping her eyes with her hand.

Tamara caught sight of Terenty and Gennady, standing nearby with their hands in their pockets, gazing up at the building. "Over here!" she called. The two threaded their way over and around turgid hoses that snaked across the pavement, to where the young women stood. "These are men I just met," Tamara told the new girl, "and, *this* fellow"—she tugged Terenty's sleeve—"saved Larisa's life, just now." His name is 'Terenty'—Terenty'. . . ?"

As Tamara floundered for his last name, he came to her rescue. "'Suslov'—and this is my good friend, 'Gennady Lychin'. We are—'students'." Terenty felt a pang of guilt for having to mislead these people—then he remembered General Putridchenko's grim face. The deception would have to go on.

The girl extended a slim hand. "I am 'Galina Gavrona'." Terenty observed that she and Gennady held their gaze at each other some extra moments before letting their hands drop.

"Galina is a primary-school teacher," Tamara put in.

The young people looked up at the building, its facade glistening wet in the glare of the streetlights from the rain and water from the hoses. The fire is about out," Gennady said.

A man with a red armband came around. "Lightning started the fire," he told Galina, as the other residents gathered around, listening.

Galina shuddered. "There was a terrible noise and part of the ceiling in my kitchen fell. I smelled smoke and saw fire in there. I started screaming. I guess I was making a lot of noise, myself!" She gave a rueful grin "I ran outside—a neighbor rang the fire alarm." The girl patted her clothes. "It was raining . . . I am very wet."

Tamara spoke up. "Come up to my place and I will find something for you to wear."

The man with the armband came back. "The police will stay here, so your apartment will be safe." He motioned toward Galina's blackened flat on the top floor. "We will move you to another location in the morning when we start repairs."

Just then, the lights in the building came back on, although Galina's place remained dark. "You may return to your homes!" the official announced to the other tenants. He turned to Galina. "You have a place to stay?" The girl nodded.

The little group made their way back to the other end of the apartment row, where Larisa was asleep in her grandmother's arms.

"Let me take the little girl," Terenty offered. As the woman gingerly transferred the slumbering child to Terenty, Galina gave her cousin a knowing look.

With the child in his arms and oblivious to silent signals passing back and forth between the two young women, Terenty trekked with the others back up the four levels to the end apartment at the head of the stairs.

When they stepped inside the living room, Gennady turned to Galina. "Is there anything *I* can do?"

More significant glances passed between the young women as Terenty handed the little one back to Tamara. When the mother carried the sleeping child through the archway toward the rear of the flat, Galina went along.

Tamara's mother smiled at Terenty and Gennady." You boys have been most helpful . . . you *must* stay overnight with us." She motioned toward seats. "Please sit down." She pointed at her husband, then at the floor. "Vasily . . . pick up those croissants!"

"Of course, Vera." Without another word, the man got down on his hands and knees and began scooping the crusty bits and pieces from the carpet.

In the kitchen, the woman smiled to herself. *These young men have potential—real potential—she must not let them get away before the "glue" had time to set. An overnight stay could be most beneficial.* But why was she so curt with her husband, these days? Vasily was a good man; it was no fault of his he could not work regularly, anymore. It was just that the accident at the factory had put heavy burdens on her. Even though the Housing Board had sympathized and reduced the rent to as low as the law allowed, they were still barely making it. Her school principal job seemed secure, but for how long, no one could be sure; the news was so disturbing, these days.

Everyone she knew hoped Yeltsin could sort out the government mess before the whole country fell apart. The worst name these days was "Gorbachev". His ideas were taking the country nowhere. How ironic that he was more highly regarded in the West than here in the Soviet Union.

There had been Tamara's short marriage to that scum of a boy and the divorce. Everyone had warned her not to get involved with that hooligan, but she would not listen. So typical of youth and inexperience. The only worthwhile result of that disaster had been the baby. And lately, the awful boy had been pestering Tamara, trying to get her to go back with him, but she kept turning him away—she did not trust his motives. The girl was having a hard enough time these days trying to balance the part-time clerk's job with the child, Larisa; Tamara tired easily and had no social life. Those two young men in the living room right now represented the first time either she or her cousin had done anything "outside" to speak of in a long time. And both girls had had it so hard. Galina, bless her heart, had been only a few days away from being married to that nice boy last year when the taxi he was riding in collided with that big Army truck. No wonder the girl resented the military and its profane, uncouth men. Tamara said those two boys out there were going to some sort of "metal school". They were so polite and courteous. So different from military men.

167

* * *

"You say he saved Larisa's *life?*" Standing in front of a full-length mirror, Galina held up a short dress; then a long dress.

"She ran in front of a tram; he pulled her back just in time."

"Oh—a 'hero' type!"

"He seems to like Larisa. How about that other fellow . . . 'Gennady' his name was?"

"Nice eyes, good build—but he looks like an Army man, to me."

"I forgot to tell you; I saw both of them the other day in military uniforms."

"What! You know what I think about the military after what happened to Sergei."

"They said they had been to some sort of 'Reserve' meeting."

"You think they are actually military?"

"It does not matter to me—he likes my daughter and that is good. They both seem very nice."

"What if he really *is* connected with the Army, or something like that?"

"You cannot carry a grudge, Galina. Sergei was a good person—but you must move on; you must try again."

"It is just so—*different*—so strange talking like this to someone besides Sergei." She swapped the dresses back and forth in front of herself. "Which one of these looks best?"

"The short one . . . it shows off your figure!"

The muffled sounds of girlish conspiratorial laughter came through the closed door.

* * *

"You say you are in the 'Reserves?'" Vasily Kuznetsov looked at the two young men who sat on the sofa.

Gennady cleared his throat. "We go to meetings once a week . . . we do marching drills, we study history and tactics—that sort of thing."

"I see. You do not belong to the 'active' military, then?"

"No, we do not belong to the *'active'* military." *Technically, true—the 'Academy' is a specialized school; the 'G-R-U' is primarily an Intelligence organization that is not directly connected with the regular military. Justification. Justification. Keeping the secret of the Academy was going to be far more difficult than he had ever imagined.* A bitter taste was forming in his mouth.

The girl's father was looking hard at them. "You sit and walk like military men . . . and you are telling me you are *not* in the Army?"

The accusing face of Semen Putridchenko flashed before Terenty's eyes; he had absolutely no desire to ever be on the wrong side of the "Chief of Security's" firing-squad. There was only one way to answer the man's question. "No, sir, we are not in the active Army." *The truth—for now—but almost stretching it out of shape.*

"What are those bandages on your wrists?"

"Inoculations'." *God, the man was persistent!* Terenty felt unclean; he never thought he would ever have to carry the deception about the Academy into the living room of decent people like this. He stole a quick glance at Gennady; by his expression he knew his friend was having the same uncomfortable thoughts.

The father arose and stepped into the kitchen.

The sound of a door closing, then quick footsteps, came from the archway. Tamara twirled into the living room, followed by Galina.

The young men glanced—and did double-takes. The young women had changed into party outfits; Tamara's short, black dress revealed tight expanses of skin; Galina's short, satiny blue dress clung against her slender figure. Both wore strappy spike heels. The twosome swung around. "How do you like these?"

Terenty laughed; Gennady's eyes were wide. "Did you practice that maneuver, back there?"

Galina clasped her hands and dropped down next to Gennady on the sofa. Her cousin made tiny motions for her to get closer to him. Galina turned to Gennady, who had put his arm across the back of the sofa. "It was fortunate you and your friend came when you did."

All at once, Gennady felt awkward; compared to the soggy, disheveled shift she was wearing when they had first met at the apartment fire, the tight-fitting dress the short-haired brunette now had on made her look very different. "I am happy to be here—"

Tamara sat down next to Terenty on the other sofa. The girl dropped off her shoes and tucked her feet underneath herself. She leaned toward him; their shoulders touching. Rubbing his forearm with her fingertips, she looked into his face; her hazel eyes sparkling in the lamplight. "I want to thank you again for saving Larisa from the streetcar."

Terenty was about to say something when Mrs. Kuznetsova swept into the room holding a tray. "More croissants!"

"I will bring the drinks!" As Tamara scooted off the sofa and headed barefoot for the kitchen, Terenty was taken by her alluring, fluid stride; he thought she moved like a ballet dancer. An idea came to him: maybe he could take her to the *'Bolshoi'*, sometime.

Smiling, the woman passed around the crusty rolls. Just then, Tamara, followed by her father, returned with a brass teapot of hot water that she set on the table; her mother brought a tray of cups. To Terenty, it seemed that the older woman was exerting a lot of energy on his and Gennady's behalf.

Mrs. Kuznetsova motioned to her husband. "I believe we shall retire, now." The man arose and followed his wife through the archway. From somewhere in the rear of the apartment, came the sound of a door closing.

At the same time all four of the young people took a bite of croissant and a swallow of tea. "All together, now," Gennady said, with a laugh. There was a silence. He looked at Tamara. "Did your mother make these rolls?" The girl nodded, and there was another pause while everyone took a bite.

Gennady turned to Galina with a question he knew he must ask: "Have you a boyfriend?"

The girl stole a glance at Tamara, who was stifling a gasp; her eyes wide. "No . . . no, I do not," she said, looking down at her hands.

"Did I say something wrong?"

Galina took a deep breath. "My fiancé was killed in a car accident last year—we were about to be married." Gennady gaped at her. "Sergei was killed when an Army truck ran into his taxi."

"An *Army* truck, you say?"

"The truck drove straight into the taxi he was in . . . the military people did not even say they were sorry!" Galina wiped her eyes with her hands. "I hate the military, and everything and everyone connected with it!"

Gennady gave a sharp glance at Terenty, who was staring back at him. "I am sure the truck did not deliberately run into the taxicab."

"Yes, it did!" I do not know why, but I am sure it rammed his car on purpose . . . I just know it."

Tamara spoke up." Another croissant?"

"I will have one." Terenty picked up a pastry, took a bite, then turned to Tamara. "Your little girl is quite lively!"

"Larisa was the only worthwhile result of the marriage with that brute."

"He was *that* bad?"

"I know, now, that I was too young to get married, but I was stubborn and went ahead, anyway. I guess I thought I was in love, or something."

She seemed ready to talk and Terenty was curious, so he pressed on. "How long were you married? Why did you get divorced?"

"It lasted about a year; we divorced a year-and-a-half ago." The young mother paused, looking down. "The 'official' reason was 'physical cruelty'. He used to beat me—at night."

Terenty was dumbstruck; he could not imagine how anyone could deliberately hurt her.

Tamara turned the conversation in a different direction. "You are students, you say?"

The two young men glanced across at each other; the specter of Semen Putridchenko was once more in the room. Their stories would have to be vague but convincing.

Terenty spoke first. He told the girls about the years he had lived abroad with his diplomat parents in France, in Spain, and in the United States; how he later became an Army officer.

Galina was frowning. "But I thought you said you were *not* military men." Her voice became brittle. "I do not like the military."

"We are not *now* military men—we are 'students— so, we are all right!"

"*Students*? You went from being Army officers to a *'metal school'?*" Galina sounded skepical.

"Metal work is better than most jobs, and we will have the opportunity to *'travel'*, since we will be working with—'exotic' metals—in different places."

"You were in *America*?" Tamara and Galina seemed impressed. "Tell us about that."

Terenty went on, glad the conversation had moved away from the school. "Tall buildings; friendly people; good water. Terrible bread, though—ugh! Those Americans have to eat white, mushy stuff they call 'bread' that is nothing like our good Russian bread."

"Does everyone there have a car? I heard that all Americans have cars."

"The Americans do have a lot of cars, all right."

Galina, her elbows on her knees, chin cupped in her hands, turned her face to Gennady. "Now, tell us about *you*."

"I did not have the exciting life abroad as Terenty did, but I was with the 'Warsaw Treaty Forces' and in Chechnya."

Galina was startled. "Chechnya! Is it as bad there as we are being told?"

"Worse." I am concerned that the uprising will spread to Russia."

"Oh, that would be terrible," Tamara spoke up, "can the government do something?"

"It is a political as well as military matter." He wanted to get off the subject, but Galina did it for him.

"You are in the reserves?"

Gennady glanced at Terenty, who was gravely shaking his head. He told them about part-time "Reserve" meetings. He knew he was deceiving these trusting young women, but it was either tell them a "sanitized" story or perhaps be in danger of facing a firing squad.

"Then you will not be fighting anymore?"

"Not unless we are called up in an emergency, or our training calls for it." *The truth, as their training would include overseas operations, but not necessarily as regular Army officers.*

Terenty wanted to wrap up the topic. "I guess that is about all there is to say about us."

Tamara opened a varnished cabinet door. "Would you like music? We have waltz records. My father likes waltzes."

"A waltz would be fine," Terenty said; the others nodded.

Tamara put on a dance piece and reached for his hand. "Dance with me . . . I want to dance."

"I have not danced in a long time," he said, as they swung into the three-step movement. At once, the two bumped into the edge of the sofa. "We will have to take smaller steps," he grinned. When he pulled her close, to his delight, the beautiful barefoot dancer did not resist.

Gennady reached for Galina. The girl arose from her seat, and the two stepped into the beat of the music. When Gennady put his arm around her waist, he found that Galina followed his lead even though it had been a long time since he had danced like this.

Galina's foot bumped his shoe, dislodging her party shoe. She kicked them aside. "Take off *your* shoes, too," she grinned, "I do not want you stepping on my feet!"

Gennady, in his socks, held her even closer. As they danced, he looked about the room, trying to divert his attention from the stimulating female in his arms. In the lamplight, he saw his friend and the other girl gazing into each others' eyes as they swung to the waltz melody.

There was a sudden loud noise. Someone was rapping on the door! The dancing stopped; there came another loud beating at the entrance. Frowning, Tamara turned off the record player.

When the girl pulled open the door, a tousle-haired young man glared back at her. Tamara gasped. *"Pavel—!"*

The visitor noticed the others in the living room who were gaping at him. "Who are these people?" he rasped, in a harsh, unpleasant voice.

"These are my friends. But I want you to leave, this minute!"

"Why are they here?"

"Please go—now!"

"Pavel" grabbed her arm and pulled her out into the hallway, then kicked the door shut. Those inside heard an argument breaking out.

Terenty whipped the door back open and eased Tamara aside. The intruder clenched his fist and started toward her. Just as his hand touched the girl's shoulder the incognito Army captain grabbed Pavel's arm from behind and spun him to the floor, face-down.

You heard the *'madame'!* She wants you to leave!" Terenty hissed. "I am telling you to go away and stay away—understand?" He hauled the fellow to his feet.

Gennady stepped into the corridor. "Turn around, comrade, and start walking down the stairs," he put in through clenched teeth, "do not stop until you are far, far away." Pavel looked the two husky males up and down, turned on his heel and made for the staircase landing.

Down the hall, a scarfed older woman, who had been listening, in a hurry closed her door.

Tamara dropped onto the sofa, put her hands to her face and burst into tears. "He will not go away . . ." Her voice sounded despairing.

Galina sat beside her cousin and rubbed the girl's heaving shoulders. "That bastard . . . he does this to her all the time . . . he will not leave her alone—"

Terenty took the other seat on the sofa. "I am sure that hooligan will not bother you, again." She put her arms around his neck; Terenty could feel her warm tears. In that moment, an overwhelming feeling of tenderness toward her came over him.

Gennady put a slow waltz on the record player, turned the lamp down low and touched Galina's shoulder. "Let us dance," he whispered to her. She arose and drew herself into his arms.

Tamara and Terenty joined the other two on the tiny dance floor. "Hold me," she said to him, "hold me tight."

In the little living room, the two young couples, who did even not know each other until a short while before, swayed the night away to the slow strains of romantic waltzes.

When the music ended, the foursome returned to the sofas. Tamara pushed back her auburn hair from her face. "What an evening . . . you 'students;' 'Larisa and the tram'; 'the fire' . . . 'Pavel'—"

Terenty stroked her shoulder. "Do not worry about Pavel; I am sure he will leave you alone from now on."

"How can you say that?" Her voice was tiny.

"Such men are cowards, and since he knows that you have friends who will stand up for you, I believe he will leave you alone."

Tamara hugged his neck. "Thank you for saying that," she whispered, "I hope it is true." She stifled a yawn and looked up at Terenty, embarrassed. "I am very tired, all of a sudden."

"We must be back at the 'Acad'—back at the *'metallurgical school'* by seven o'clock." Terenty glanced at Gennady, whose eyes were wide.

"Do you want to sleep in my room?" Tamara asked. Seeing Terenty's upraised eyebrows, she put in, reddening, "That is . . . *Galina and I* can sleep here on the floor."

"Nonsense! All we need are blankets."

In a few minutes Tamara and her cousin came back with armloads of quilts and sheets. "I hope this will be all right," she said, dropping the bedclothes onto the oaken floor. Terenty pushed aside the tea table, then the four got down on their hands and knees and arranged the improvised beds.

Tamara handed Terenty an alarm clock. "This will get you going on time in the morning." With a grin, she motioned at the archway. "The bathroom is through there at the end of the hall."

* * *

175

Tamara closed the door to her room and turned to her cousin. "Well, what do you think?"

"They seem to be all right—they certainly took care of Pavel, did they not?"

"I do not know what would have happened, if they had not been here—or if Terenty had not saved Larisa from the tracks."

"Do you think they like us?"

"I would say so."

"He was very nice. I want to see him, again."

"And all of this because my grocery bag broke!"

"Can you *believe* this night?"

* * *

"Can you *believe* this night?" Gennady was speaking in in a low voice. The two young men were on their bedrolls in the darkness, whispering.

"Tamara is very pretty, is she not?"

"Yes, and I would like to know Galina better . . ."

* * *

Brrrriinng! The alarm clock jolted Terenty awake. It took him a moment to get his bearings; then he remembered last evening: Tamara and her cousin; the little girl with the tram; the fire; the dancing; the gross boy they had dispatched down the stairs.

"Good morning," came a female voice. Tamara stepped into the room and knelt down.

He grinned up at her. In the early morning's half-light that filtered through the window, he could make out the rounded outlines of her shoulders through her long, white nightshirt that draped onto her knees.

Tamara ran her fingertip from Terenty's forehead down to the end of his nose, then to his chin. "I had a wonderful time, last night—even if Pavel tried to ruin it."

"I am sure he will not bother you anymore." He reached up and was about to draw her down to him when his eye caught the clock on the floor next to him. "Ah, we must leave, now." He pulled himself to a sitting position. On the next bedroll, Gennady squirmed to his nudge. "Time to wake up!"

Just then, Galina padded into the living room. "Is it already time for you two to get up?"

"Unfortunately," Gennady croaked; stretching. He looked up at Galina and saw her slender form, backlit by the lamp that was shining behind her.

Terenty glanced at his friend. "We must go back at once to the—'school'."

Gennady put his arm around Galina's shoulder. "We must leave, now; our . . . ah . . . *passes* expire in a few minutes."

"The 'Rent Committee' is moving me to another apartment, today."

"We can come by this evening and help you—if we can get 'passes' from the 'school—'."

"Speaking of 'school,' we must be going at once!" Terenty pointed at the alarm clock; there were very few minutes left before their curfew was up.

The two made for the door and dashed down the steps, watched by the young women until they were out of sight.

Galina winked at her cousin. "I believe they had a good time,"

From far up the block, came the faint sounds of exultant whoops.

"We must hurry!" Terenty puffed, as the two rounded a corner.

In a few minutes, the "Vulkon Metallurgical School No. 6" came into sight; they trotted up the steps, loped down the leafy tunnel and turned the inside of their wrists to the detector on its pylon.

They had beaten the deadline by four minutes.

"That was *some* night, was it not?" Terenty laughed, as he pulled on a fresh outfit. "Would you have ever thought we would meet a couple of women like those two when we started out, yesterday? And to think—Tamara and her little girl were the same people we had seen that day walking up the sidewalk at the kiosk!"

"Galina is a very . . . ah . . . *interesting* girl. I can hardly wait to—"

"*CRACK!" A rifle shot!*

The two young men looked at each other in surprise. From the corridor came shouts and heavy footsteps. They bolted for the door and joined a cluster of students running toward the guardhouse at the edge of the woods, where some sort of disturbance had broken out.

As they came up to a circle of men standing around the tunnel opening that led to the outside, they saw a prone figure on the ground. Blood was spreading from underneath a young man's still form. sprawled face-down across the walkway. "He tried to get in without identification," someone said.

A paramilitary soldier holding a rifle stood off by the door of the guardhouse.

The two officers elbowed their way up through the gathering for a closer look."Look!" Terenty gasped, pointing at a dead youth lying on the sidewalk. "It is—it is—*Pavel!*"

-15-

Moscow, 7:14 AM, Thursday, August 15, 1991:

Major General Semen Putridchenko stood with two of his staff officers, conferring. As the scowling "Chief of Security" walked around, looking at the body; other men measured the death scene with tape, marking off the outline of the corpse in chalk; a photographer clicked his shutter from every angle; another official was speaking to the guard with the gun. The pool of blood underneath the body had already begun to coagulate around the edges.

Terenty and Gennady edged closer as they tried to overhear what the general and the others were saying, but they were only able to pick up confusing snatches of dialogue:

" ... Body—"

" ... 'Taxi—"

" ... Truck—"

A security officer came up and ordered the bystanders to clear out. "You have work to do!"

With one last look at the unfortunate Pavel lying dead on the ground, Terenty and Gennady headed back across the way toward the dormitory.

Gennady groaned as he closed the door to their room. "What if they find out we knew Pavel?" The two had no doubt that the troublesome fellow had followed them, and that General Pudridchenko had been true to his word that any intruder without the wrist-chip would be shot. What would happen if "Security" connected them with Tamara's former husband?

There was a loud knock on the door! Terenty opened it to one of the security guards he had seen a few minutes earlier.

"General Putridchenko wants to see you in his office, at once!" The man motioned to them. "Come with me!"

The two apprehensive young officers followed the man across the compound to a door at the rear of the main building. Next to a brass plaque with the hammer and sickle of the Soviet Union was a sign:

DIRECTOR OF SECURITY

In moments, they were in an office facing the general, who stood behind a massive mahogany desk, smoking a pipe. A heavy, masculine scent of tanned leather and tobacco smoke permeated the place.

The two saluted the dark-haired, mustached officer, who glared at them through thick reading glasses that exaggerated the size of his eyes—for a split-second, Terenty thought the man's face resembled a vicious insect. A corrugated frown etched the general's forehead as he looked them up and down. He returned a perfunctory salute. "Suslov? Lychin?"

"Yes, Comrade general."

"We found *your* names on *this* piece of paper in a pocket of the man we just shot!" The general slapped a handwritten white square onto his desk. You know the rules about divulging anything about the Academy—how do you explain this?"

"*I—I* do not know, sir," Gennady stammered, swallowing. He thought he would faint.

Terenty saw no alternative than to level with the general about the previous night. While the older man puffed on his pipe, the younger officer told how he and Gennady had met the two cousins; about the fire; how the former husband of one of them had created a scene. "But I do not know how he knew our names."

Gennady spoke up. "Comrade general, when we introduced ourselves to one of the girls— the one whose apartment burned— perhaps he overheard us talking. It was dark and there were a lot of people about . . . he could have been nearby without us knowing it." He spread his hands with a shrug. "Maybe he wrote our names down on the piece of paper you found."

"Did you mention anything about the Academy, at any time?"

"No, Comrade general; we were very particular about that . . . in fact, it was very difficult to always say the right words. We told everyone we were students at the 'metallurgical school'."

Terenty broke in. "Comrade general—if he had our names, it would be logical that he hung around nearby all night, and followed us here."

"You two must realize that things like this can adversely affect your careers."

"We understand, sir."

"You are dismissed—one condition: that I never again see you two in here."

They saluted the officer, who returned their salutes, turned on their heels, and left. As they made their way across the campus to the classroom building, the general's ranting voice still rang in Terenty's ears. His back tingled as if any second a heavy hand would grab him from behind for more questioning. The last thing they had wanted was to run afoul of Semen Putridchenko— but within three days it had happened. He knew that, from then on, no matter how correct their behavior should be, "Security" had them singled-out for special attention.

The two slid into seats at the rear of the classroom. Rodion Golubko stopped in mid-sentence as the others gave them chiding looks. "You know that prompt classroom attendance is mandatory!" the colonel glared; the stringy blue vein on his temple bulged. "Start taking notes!"

A little later, a messenger delivered an envelope to the classroom. Colonel Golubko glanced at the missive, then went on with the lesson. When the class broke at noon, the officer called out Terenty's and Gennady's names. "I want you two in my office, right now!"

Minutes later they were seated across from his desk. "You wanted to see us, sir?"

"I have a report from General Putridchenko that says you knew the man 'Security' shot this morning . . . is that correct?"

Terenty swallowed. "Yes, Comrade Colonel. That is, we—" '

The older man looked first at one, then the other of the two young officers in front of him. "You better tell me what is going on."

Terenty then repeated what he had told General Putridchenko. Gennady added his opinion that Pavel had overheard their introductions to the girls and had followed them

back to the Academy. "General Putridchenko seemed to believe that was what happened . . ."

The man glanced at the message from the Chief of Security. "Things like this"—he flipped the edge of the paper across the ends of his fingers—"can have a negative effect on your careers." Terenty looked down at the floor. The older officer frowned at the two. "Let me remind you that *I personally selected you for this program*—" The man's eyes bulged. "You must understand that you are here because you are among the brightest young officers in the Soviet military. But women have ruined many a promising man's career."

"Yes, comrade colonel."

"That is all I have to say, and I hope it is now ended." The colonel pushed himself back. "Let us go now to the dining hall and then get back to work."

* * *

1:40 PM, Thursday, August 15, 1991:

When they returned to the classroom, an athletic-looking, crew-cut man the young officers had never seen before stood by the window, smoking a cigarette. As the students took their seats, the man stubbed out his smoke and stepped to the lectern.

"I am 'Lieutenant Colonel Andrian Yelesiyev' of the G-R-U," he announced in a piercing voice much too loud for the size of the room, "and I will introduce you to the 'Spetsnaz' . . ."

There was a shuffling of shoes, almost as if the man had called for it.

"'Spetsnaz' stands for *'Spetsialnoe Naznachenie'*, and is under the direct command of the Soviet General Staff's Main Intelligence Directorate—better known as the 'G-R-U.'"

The lieutenant colonel arranged some papers on the podium. "Now some words about the history of the Spetsnaz. During the *'Great Patriotic War'* that the 'West' calls *'World War Two'*, there was a need for infiltration forces to combat the German invaders, so Comrade Stalin set up the Spetsnaz as a paramilitary force to operate behind enemy lines . . . eventually, there were

sixty-thousand such irregulars. Ask the Germans how successful they were."

The lieutenant colonel waited for the young men to absorb the implications of what he had just said.

The officer went on. "The purpose of the Spetsnaz is to carry out 'Special Reconnaissance'. You will learn how to subvert the military, political, and economic structure of an enemy by infiltration. As the course progresses, you will have the opportunity to *carry out covert operations inside the United States, where we have a special training facility that the Americans do not know exists!"*

There was a stirring of the men in their seats; several, including Terenty and Gennady, had grins on their faces.

"Let me tell you one thing: The very word, 'Spetsnaz' strikes fear at every Western soldier. When you are fully trained, you will have no equal in the world for fighting ability as our primary mission is to open the way for a Soviet occupation of Western Europe, should we be ordered to do so."

The men stirred. "Let me say something about the selection process. You are politically reliable, intelligent, and physically fit. You have signed the loyalty oath that binds you to the G-R-U for life—with the death penalty waiting for you if you reveal *anything.* to the outside."

The lieutenant colonel looked around at the faces staring at him.

"The training is extremely harsh—unless you are physically fit to the very highest level, you may not even survive!"

There was a collective deep breath in the room.

"You will train in hand-to-hand, close-in combat; techniques of infiltration; demolition; sabotage; reconnaissance . . . assassination and kidnapping—including silent-killing tactics. You will also learn sniping . . . chemical and biological warfare; all kinds of weapons—including foreign weapons—survival behind enemy lines; communications . . . parachuting . . . even how to steal, drive and operate the enemy's vehicles . . . you will learn how to operate up to one-thousand kilometers behind enemy lines without support."

He looked around at the roomful of young men, who were listening with attention. "As part of your training to operate in the United States, you will learn the English language to where you can speak it without an accent. This training course will lead to your being certified as 'Special Forces Leaders'." The man gave a smirk. "I can say that *two Cuban women have passed the course.*"

The speaker nodded at Rodion Golubko. "This is the colonel's third training unit; he has already trained men in the United States and on other overseas missions . . . you are privileged to have such an experienced and capable leader."

The instructor started passing out some books. "These are your 'training manuals'. They are not to be taken from the grounds of the Academy—in fact, you will *not* be able to remove them, as they have codes imbedded in the paper that will activate the sensors at the gate."

Terenty thought about Pavel and the shooting at the guardhouse. Tamara's former husband was now dead because he had triggered those same sensing devices.

". . . begins next week," Lieutenant Colonel Yelesiyev was saying, bringing Terenty's attention back to the man at the front of the room. "The Spetsnaz training center is at a location in the Moscow area. At the beginning, you will be taken there by automobile each Monday and returned here Saturday evenings. Later, you will go on extended field training in the Far North and in the Urals."

In his seat, Gennady thought about Galina; he would miss her very much when they would be away on those long training trips. Ever since they had left the apartment early that morning, images and sensations of the girl had flitted in and out of his mind—how she had felt in his arms; her warm breath on his neck as they held each other while they danced; the contours of her trim figure underneath the satin dress; the clinging cotton nightshirt. When he had arrived in Moscow, he had expected to find plenty of available and willing young women who would help him make up for the time he had lost at those dreary outposts—but a slender, dark-haired schoolteacher had stepped into his life and changed those plans. Something poignant and

sentimental about her kept tugging at him. Was it her shyness that she alternated with a subtle hint of seduction? Perhaps. But was he also trying to take advantage of her misfortunate apartment fire? As a military man, why did he not feel guilty that the *military* had caused the death of her fiancé? Was it because he was glad she no longer *had* a fiancé? In truth, they hardly knew each other. Maybe they could get together tonight at the new flat to which she was moving because of the fire. He very much wanted to see her, again, but did she feel the same about him? Would she remember him when he left for long-term training? How would he ever explain to her why a *metallurgical school* would even have "long-term-training"? The young officer let out a long, slow breath.

At the front of the room, Lieutenant Colonel Yelesiyev was finishing his monologue. "I will see you next week at the Spetsnaz training center."

Colonel Golubko stepped up. "This will conclude our classroom session for today. Next week, we will have an overview on 'Marxist theory' as applied to Special Forces."

Terenty rolled his eyes; he had already heard those droning lectures any number of times; "Marxism" was his least favorite subject.

The colonel went on. "We will issue the next passes for Saturday night."

Saturday night? Terenty groaned; that meant he would be unable to see or even talk to Tamara, until then! He glanced at Gennady: his friend's face was frozen in dismay.

"Tomorrow, you will be evaluated." He looked around the room at the men. "I suggest you rest well, tonight—it will be an exhausting day."

Without another word, he strode up the aisle, past the men and out the door.

One of the young men spoke up as they shuffled out into the afternoon sunshine. "What did he mean by 'evaluated'?"

Standing off by themselves, Terenty and Gennady had another concern. "What will the girls think if we do not see or talk to them until *Saturday* night?" Gennady shook his head as the two turned toward the dining hall.

"Straight, or on the rocks?" Semen Putridchenko popped open a Vodka bottle and turned to Rodion Golubko, who was settling into a chair in the general's quarters.

"Straight."

The general poured two glasses of spirits and drained his at once. "How is your new class?"

"A good group . . . perhaps the best, yet."

"You told me they will concentrate on 'Electronic Intelligence'."

"That is why we selected these candidates—for their infantry *and* electronic backgrounds—the Intelligence Directorate is telling us to prepare these men for a deep-penetration infiltration into the United States . . . they will need both special combat skills and electronic knowledge. We will train them to use both."

What is the régimen?"

"We have an agent at the *'Los Alamos Laboratory'* in America who is gathering hard Intelligence about the 'silent-invisible' technology. He believes he will have the material ready some months from now." He took a long swallow. "The men we are now training will be assigned to retrieve the agent and the information. We will accelerate the special training of these men for that task."

"What about those two whose names turned up in the pockets of the intruder we shot?"

"I believe they got caught up in a love-triangle and the boy followed them."

"We checked him out; his name was *'Pavel Drubkin'*. Until recently he worked at the *'ZIL'* automobile factory . . . no prior record."

"You disposed of him in the usual manner?"

"Just as with the other one last year."

"You certainly put a scare into those two boys."

"Makes them strong!" A twisted grin flickered across the general's pockmarked face. "I believe we will *need* strong men in high places, before long."

"Why do you say that?"

"My sources tell me something is about to happen—but I am not sure what it could be."

The colonel refilled both Vodka glasses. "Political . . . military?"

"Could be *both*—I have learned that General Lebed's *'Tula'* troops are just outside of Moscow. It is common knowledge that Alexander Lebed has political ambitions . . . I also know that mechanized units are assembling nearby; the *'Tank Brigade'* is on the move." Semen Putridchenko upraised one eyebrow. "Is it not interesting that all this happens just as Gorbachev is in the Crimea?"

"Are you suggesting a *'coup'*?"

"I am not suggesting *anything*—but I do find it extraordinary that Marshal Yazov cancelled his talk to our group yesterday to attend an—'important meeting'—as he put it."

"Perhaps the 'Minister of Defense' was too busy for us."

"Busy? Hah! The Academy is practically at the top of the list of priorities. No, something is going on—you will see." He drained his Vodka glass. "We will *all* see."

* * *

7:20 PM, Thursday, August 15, 1991:

"What time do you think they will be here?" Tamara glanced at Galina, as she set the table with her mother's best place-settings and silverware.

The girl's dark-haired cousin looked at the kitchen clock. "Any time, now, I would expect."

"You are sure they are coming?"

"Gennady told me they would be here tonight." Galina fingered the material of her shift. "I hope he likes this dress—I bought it last year for the wedding—before Sergei was killed."

* * *

Gennady paced the dormitory room, pounding his fist into the palm of his hand. "I told Galina we would be there, tonight. And now—*this!*"

"I hope they have not done something special for us—like a big dinner or something!" Terenty wrung his hands. "If they have, they will be disappointed."

"What can we tell them when we finally get out of this place? Remember: it will be Saturday before we have overnight passes."

"Ahh—!" Terenty slumped into a chair. "This 'Academy' is becoming very complicated."

"And we will have to keep doing this for the rest of our lives!"

* * *

Tamara looked at the clock on the kitchen wall; then at the muffins; at the two-liter bottle of kvas; at the silverware; at her mother's finest table settings—all arranged on the white linen tablecloth that she had hand-washed and ironed earlier that day. The clock's accusing hands were pointed at "9:27", as if mocking the young women's efforts.

Tamara went to the corner window and looked down onto the street. It had been raining, again; the pavement glistened in the fitful glare of the streetlights. She stood there for some minutes, hoping she would sight the pair hurrying down the walkway. But all she saw were a couple of other people with umbrellas trudging along the sidewalk.

Tamara felt as if heavy hands were squeezing her head and pushing down on her shoulders as she slumped into a chair. She blinked at her cousin. "I guess they could not be here, tonight."

Galina fought back her own tears as she stuffed a dish of food into the refrigerator.

"Let us not forget that we know very little about them—their 'student' story does sound strange, if you ask me."

"But Terenty did save Larisa's life . . . that must mean *something*."

"I just wanted to see Gennady, again."

188

The little girl came into the room and crawled up onto Tamara's lap. "Is the 'mister man'—your friend—coming to see us, yet?" The child batted her eyes at her mother's distressed face.

Tamara gave a despairing shake of her head. "No, he is not. I will change you out of that nice dress into pajamas, now."

* * *

8:05 AM, Friday, August 16, 1991:

"Follow the directions on the front page of the packet, comrades." Colonel Golubko passed out the big envelopes to the students. "You will have all the morning to complete these questions."

Terenty pulled a bundle of printed papers from its brown cover. The first sheet was a printed list of directions for taking what looked to be a psychological-profile test. He glanced around the room and caught the eye of several of the others, a couple of whom nodded, grinning, back at him. This could be interesting, he thought.

By the second page, he realized that this examination had a lot in common with the one of a few days earlier, except it was much more detailed. Terenty figured that no matter how disjointed the questions looked to him, they would probably make sense to someone who was used to looking inside other peoples' minds. What would the person who graded his test think of him? He chuckled to himself and turned to the next page.

Three-and-a-half-hours later, he put down his pencil and stretched. Several of the others had already finished; a few were still marking answers on their pages. Colonel Golubko stood up. "We will be finishing, now," he said, looking at the clock over the rear door. It is time to eat—but you should eat lightly—this afternoon we will be going to another location for 'physical tests'." Terenty thought he detected a grin on the man's face. "After eating, go to your quarters and bring your toothbrush and a change of clothes back here."

189

An hour later, the colonel had a surprising announcement. "We are going to *'Star City'*, where you will have the same endurance tests they give the cosmonauts."

Star City! The young men looked around at each other; everyone in the Soviet Union had heard of the big space center outside of Moscow where the cosmonauts lived and trained.

At the rear of the main building, two cars, drivers at the wheel, awaited them. When Terenty eased into the rear seat of a blue Moskvitch sedan, he saw it was the same vehicle that had been invisible onstage during the demonstration of the new technology.

As the crowded vehicles drove around the main building toward the driveway, Terenty observed that the driver was wearing the yellow eyeglasses; inside the car, the tinted windows made it seem as if it was already dusk.

As they passed out onto the street, Gennady gazed up and down at the brooding, black-painted fence that now seemed to symbolize his new, confined life. At the next intersection, when the car accelerated out "Soyuz Novaya Zemlya Prospekt" northeastward, he noted glumly that they were driving in the opposite direction from where Galina lived. Gennady hoped it was not an omen—he was afraid to guess what the two cousins now thought of Terenty and him for not going to see them last night.

He settled back into the seat and stared out the darkened windows at the dim shapes that passed by. While they rode past unending blocks of apartments, a deepening gloom settled over him with the realization that every rhythmic thump of the tires on the pavement was carrying him farther from Galina; he longed to be with her again. Once, as the Moskvich jolted over a big bump, the rumble of noises that came from underneath the sedan seemed to be saying that she did not want to see him, anymore. Somehow, he would have to try to make it up to her—*if* she would let him. Gennady tried to bolster his spirits by reminding himself that this excursion into the countryside would only last a day or so; in the meantime, he was sure there would be enough to do at "Star City" to keep him busy.

Sometime later when they passed a sign, he sat up in his seat; they had arrived at the training center. Gennady watched as they drove up to a lift-gate. Two guards holding assault rifles stepped up; after a conversation with the driver, the gate opened and the sentries waved the vehicles through.

The cars drove down a road through the woods. Before long, a modern concrete-and-glass building came into sight, then a row of new-looking office and apartment structures intermixed with a number of older, Soviet-styled yellow brick ones; all separated by open, grassy spaces.

Colonel Golubko motioned toward some of the buildings. "All the cosmonauts and their families live here," he said, "everything they need is on this base: stores; a recreation center; a culture hall; schools—" He rolled down the darkened window and waved at some children on a playground. "Over there is a kindergarten," he went on, as some of the youngsters waved back.

Terenty smiled to himself at the gruff, older military man's surprising manner toward children; he guessed there was still a lot to understand about him.

Several young women pushed baby carriages along the sidewalks. Terenty thought these were probably the wives and children of researchers or cosmonauts, since Soviet space travelers tended to be younger than their American counterparts. Then something else occurred to him: since several women had already been to the *Salyut* and the currently orbiting *Mir* space station, some of these young mothers might actually *be* cosmonauts who had already flown in space, or were training for an upcoming mission; this place was, after all, the home of the cosmonauts.

Gennady was struck by the space center's rural-like atmosphere—unless one knew what went on here, a person would never guess its role in the nation's space program.

The vehicles pulled up in front of a building shaped like a outsized barrel. When everyone was out of the cars, the colonel spoke. "We shall now see how well you digested your lunch!"

Wondering what he meant, Terenty joined the others as they passed through a door into a lobby, where a man in a white

191

smock coat awaited them. "These are the candidates?" With the colonel's nod, he motioned toward a door. "The dressing room for the centrifuge is in there."

Terenty gave a start. *The centrifuge!* So *that* was why they were here! Colonel Golubko came up just then, with a smirk. "*Now* we will find out the truth about your physical condition!"

"Colonel, have *you* been on the centrifuge?"

"Many times . . . and you are in for the ride of your life!"

In a few minutes the first of the group came out of a fitting room in a head-to-ankle jumpsuit. An attendant motioned him toward a door. "This way, please . . . the rest of you can watch from up there." He pointed at a stairwell that led to a glassed-in observation deck on the third level.

The others watched as a pair of technicians strapped their fellow student into a contoured seat facing inward at the end of a blue-green tube about two meters wide and twenty meters long that loomed over what looked to be a motor equipment room in the middle of the circular space. The fellow in the cockpit looked up, and, spotting his friends staring at him from the glassed observation deck, gave them a grinning thumbs-up.

An attendant gave an ironic smirk."We will see how he smiles *after* the gravity run . . ."

"How big is the centrifuge?" someone asked.

"It is the world's biggest—and can deliver up to thirty-one times the force of normal gravity. Today, we will operate at about four times the weight of gravity to simulate the liftoff of a manned rocket and at six-and-a-half times earth gravity to equal a 'Soyuz' re-entry from orbit."

The two white-coated men worked inside the capsule for a few minutes, then made their way back across a walkway that began to retract into the outer wall at the second level.

A buzzer sounded; red lights began flashing around the big circular room. With a loud "click" and a whining noise, the bulky, blue-green tubular arm began moving; barely noticeable at first, then after a minute it was whirling around in a blur. Terenty shuddered to think what the rider was enduring inside the end of that streaking boom.

The machine's humming motors swirled the capsule for ten minutes, then began to slow down. After it had decelerated to about a revolution per second, with loud clicks and a grabbing sound, the big arm shuddered to a stop.

As soon as the walkway extended to the capsule's hatch, the two white-coated men trotted back across and leaned inside. In a couple of minutes they were lurching back across the ramp with the rider's arms slung across their shoulders. The young man's jaunty bravado of before was gone; the fellow's face was pale; his bloodshot eyes were sunken back into their sockets. The trio disappeared through the second-level door in the side of the circular space.

A loud voice crackled from a nearby loudspeaker. "Terenty Suslov report to the preparation room!" Terenty gulped as the others looked at him with mixed expressions of awe and pity. He gave a lame grin and turned toward the stairwell.

"Terenty Suslov?" A man in a white smock coat with a tape measure around his neck sized-up the young officer and reached for a space-suit-looking outfit. Two other men in white coats came into the room. "These doctors will apply sensors so we can monitor your vital functions." He motioned at a door. "Use the restroom, now, so you will not be sorry, later."

In a few minutes, Terenty, wearing a head-to-foot outfit that squeezed his body so snugly he could hardly breathe, stood up. A bundle of thin wires and a rubber tube dangled down from the front of the suit. "During the test, the suit will inflate and form a pressure cuff around your body to keep the blood from pooling in your back as the gravity-forces build up."

With a feeling of dread Terenty remembered how wasted the first fellow had looked after his rounds on the centrifuge. The only consolation was that it would all be over in a few minutes; then he could watch the others undergo *their* turns on the machine.

"Good luck!" One of the doctors offered, with a sardonic smile.

An elevator lifted the three to the second level, where a few meters across the skywalk stood the open end of the bulbous capsule on the end of the blue-green tubular arm. To Terenty, the whole contraption looked like an enormous cannon. He glanced up and caught the faces of the others staring down at him through the observation windows.

The two technicians eased Terenty into the upright seat mounted in a frame. With a practiced air one of the workers strapped him into the harness; the other attendant snapped the sensor wires to a plug on a control panel and hooked-up the rubber tube to a valve.

Terenty looked around; in front of him was a small television camera and a microphone. "We will have two-way communication with you during the test," one of the men said. "Push down on this lever all the time the machine is operating . . . if you let it go, the experiment will stop at once." He looked at Terenty and grinned. "But no one, not even a *female* cosmonaut, has ever ended the test before its time!"

After one more tug on the harness and a final look-around, the technicians backed out of the capsule. Terenty's heart was racing as he heard the telescoping platform behind him retracting into the wall of the big circular room, then come to a stop with a thump that had a sound of finality about it.

A voice sounded in his helmet earphones. "This is the control room . . . can you hear us?" Terenty looked around the tight space, trying to locate the speaker. "Look at the camera," the voice went on

Terenty stared at the video eye and nodded. "Yes, I hear you."

Now alone in the mysterious machine, all this seemed unreal; an hour ago he would never have imagined himself sitting here in the world's largest centrifuge, about to be assaulted by a force many times his own weight.

Terenty heard the sound of rushing air. At once, the pressure suit began to tighten around him; in a few seconds the outfit, snapping and popping, drew snug, as if a blood-pressure cuff had inflated all around his body.

"Push down the lever!" came a command in his earphones. Hardly able to move his hand against the pressurized suit, he groped on the seat arm for the stick and pressed it down.

"Remember to hold it down the whole time of the test!" the voice added.

A vibration ran through the seat. For a moment he felt nothing out of the ordinary, then a pressure started building against his backside. In another minute, he was unable to lift as much as his little finger. "Keep the lever down!" the communicator shouted in his earphones. In his excitement he had almost forgotten the all-important device—fortunately, the gravity force pushed his fingers down onto it. He doubted he could have pried them off in any case; his forearms and hands were being shoved backward as by an enormous, unseen weight.

The laconic voice came back. "We will simulate third-stage ignition of the booster rocket." Over the next few seconds the forces increased to where Terenty could hardly breathe. "This is the maximum acceleration . . . four times the force of gravity as the 'Soyuz drives toward orbit." Since Terenty could not see outside the capsule, he had no sensation of actual movement, even though he knew the machine was whirling him around at tremendous speed. If this was what the cosmonauts went through, Terenty thought, he believed he could handle it.

"Now we will simulate re-entry . . ."

Gravity forces began to build-up on him far beyond what they had been before. Terenty found himself gasping for breath against a stupendous weight pushing down on his chest; his lips parted in a grin he could not control. As the forces increased, his eyes felt wet, but when he blinked, a cloudy red mist appeared in front of him—it seemed as if his eyeballs were being pushed to the back of his head. Without thinking, he tried to lift his left hand, but the attempt was useless against the uncompromising force that held his arm to the seat.

"The re-entry forces are now six-and-a-half-times normal gravity! The simulation will continue for six minutes!"

Six minutes! Fighting to stay conscious, realizing that only his pressure suit was keeping him from blacking-out, he held the lever down with all his might.

"One minute!"

By now, Terenty's body felt like a block of wood; he only wanted the ordeal to end.

"Thirty-seconds to completion of re-entry!"

Terenty tried to lift the fingers on his free hand, but could not; the weight was too much.

The young man again tried blinking against the red curtain before his eyes; all he could see were vague, pinkish shapes.

"The end of the test! Simulated parachute deployment!"

The whine of the motors gave way to the swishing of air; the forces on his backside began to let up. After three more minutes the machine shuddered to a stop.

"Are you all right?" boomed a voice over his right shoulder. Terenty ached all over; he felt giddy and exhausted.

A technician reached for the console and turned a lever; the rubberized garment began to shrivel. The other attendant unstrapped the restraints and pulled the sensor's wire connectors from the console. "Now, you can stand up."

Terenty put his hands on the seat arms and tried to push himself out of the seat, but was unable to do so. Grasping underneath his shoulders, the two men lifted Terenty from the contoured couch. So *this* is what the cosmonauts go through, he thought, as the three lurched across the skyway to the elevator.

In the preparation room, Gennady was sitting in the suit-up seat, getting dressed for his encounter with the centrifuge. Terenty gaped at him with bloodshot eyes. "Are you next?" he croaked.

Gennady was shocked at his friend's appearance. "How *was* it?"

"I—am glad it is over," Terenty gasped, as the men eased him into a seat and started removing the flight suit, "it was an— *experience*."

As quickly as he could, Terenty dressed back into his civilian clothes and stepped out onto the third level just as the centrifuge was starting to move. As the tubular machine accelerated, Terenty remembered what it had been like for him in that same claustrophobic cubicle a few minutes earlier; he hoped his friend would make it all right through the crushing ordeal. The streaking arm swept through its circular course for the alloted time, then at last the droning motors let up. With a grabbing groan the big blue-green tube once more shuddered to a stop.

But Gennady was not moving.

A strident voice barked from the loudspeaker. "Doctors to the centrifuge immediately!"

Two more men rushed out and bent over the seated subject. *What was happening?* Another doctor ran across the opening with what looked like a respirator. As Terenty and the others watched, alarmed, the attendants lifted Gennady from the seat and laid him out on the walkway.

It was then that the observers saw the blood all over his face and on the flight suit. After a few seconds his legs moved, he put his hands to his face and seemed to be coughing. The doctor said something to Gennady, who nodded.

Terenty and the others clattered down the stairway to the fitting room where the doctors were easing Gennady onto the examining table. "What happened?"

"He suffered a nosebleed at the end of the centrifuge run," a doctor said.

"He choked on blood," another doctor put in, "it was fortunate we were right there when it happened."

Gennady hauled himself to a sitting position, blinking. "I am a fine one," he groaned.

A doctor nodded. "You will be all right—it happens, sometimes."

As two attendants began helping Gennady out of his suit, another doctor ran his finger down a list. "'Viktor Grishinov' is next."

One of the young men gulped and raised his hand.

The others made their way out of the room. Gennady stayed behind. "I will be up there in a few minutes!" he said, in his still-quavering voice.

As they stood looking down at the massive machine on the circular floor below, those who had not yet ridden the centrifuge had nervous questions for Terenty.

"Does it hurt?"

"How does the gravity force feel?"

In a few minutes the next rider and the two attendants emerged through the second level door and strode across the rubberized walkway to the open back of the centrifuge. The fellow had a determined look on his face as he glanced up at the others.

Once more, the machine streaked through its routine. After the run had finished, the young man gave a thumbs-up when he walked back across the skyway without help.

"Comrade Viktor is in very good physical condition," someone said.

Just then, Gennady came through the doorway. Terenty gave him a pat on the back. "How are you feeling? We were worried about you."

"I am much better—how are the others doing?"

"Viktor came through the test very well."

"All remaining subjects to the fitting room!" the loudspeaker blared.

One-by-one, each student took his turn on the sweeping arm; in another two hours all six of the young officers had completed their tests. "I am embarrassed that I was the only one who had problems," Gennady said, as they returned to the fitting room.

A doctor, who had overheard him, tapped his clipboard. "Actually, it is not unusual for subjects to become ill," he said to Gennady. "The machine causes great stress on the body . . . that is why we consider it to be a good measure of the true physical condition of those who perform on it."

"Well, comrades, I see you finished the centrifuge!" came a familiar voice from just outside. Colonel Golubko strode into the room dressed in a flight suit.

"Colonel, are *you* going to ride on the centrifuge?"

The older man nodded as he stepped toward the corridor with the two attendants.

"Colonel Golubko is one of our most important subjects," a doctor put in. "He is in such very good physical condition that we have used him for special medical tests before the cosmonauts go on missions." The others' eyebrows went up as the man went on, "we have learned much from the colonel. In fact, he could have been a cosmonaut, himself."

"He even *walks* better in the flight suit than we did!"

Another doctor spoke up. "Perhaps you should go to the observation deck, now, to watch the colonel's centrifuge test—I believe you will find it impressive."

When the young men again trooped upstairs to the viewing room,.the red light was already flashing over the main door. Then the buzzer sounded and the big arm began its majestic sweeps around the circular room, gathering speed by the second. In a minute, it was racing considerably faster than it had spun with the students on board.

One of the technicians came onto the deck. "The forces on the colonel are now ten times the normal weight of gravity," he said, his eyes following the streaking centrifuge, "this is one of the fastest runs ever performed with a human."

The young men gaped in awe at the whirling metal arm. Based on their own earlier experiences on the machine, what Colonel Golubko must be enduring right now was unimaginable. Any lingering doubts about their leader's nerve, conditioning and courage were being swept aside by the spectacle down there.

"Why does he do these experiments on the centrifuge—at his age?"

"He has a reason—a personal reason—but *you* must ask him."

Terenty started to speak, then changed his mind and focused instead on the streaking cylinder with the colonel inside.

Then came the "click" as the brake clutches kicked-in. As the centrifuge arm slid to a stop, the young officers could see the back of the man's head and his shoulders.When the technicians bent over him, he gave a nodding thumbs-up. The others watched as he made his way unassisted across the walkway into the main building.

"How does he do it?"

"He must be fifty years old!"

When they filed into the preparation room, technicians were already pulling off the silver-haired man's flight suit. He gave a wry grin to his students. "How was *that*, for an 'old' man?" .

"We are impressed," one of the young men said; the others nodded.

A doctor motioned toward the door. "Step outside, please. We will perform some medical tests, on the colonel, now."

A half-hour later, again dressed in civilian clothes, Colonel Golubko stepped out to the lobby, where the young men were standing, still talking about the older man's feat.

Gennady was the first to speak up. "Now I *really* feel foolish for getting sick in there!"

The colonel shrugged. "It has happend to me, too."

"Colonel, we were wondering—*why* do you still do all this at your . . . your—"

". . . age?" The older man's eyes crinkled at the fellow, whose face turned crimson. He motioned toward some nearby chairs. "Take seats, comrades, I shall tell you a story." As the others settled into armchairs, the man went on, "Back in the mid-'sixties, I was training for space flights. One of my mentors was a cosmonaut named, 'Vladimir Komarov,' a good man—a good man, indeed—who had flown on *'Voskhod-One'* with two other fine fellows I knew. But later, Komarov was killed when something went wrong on the first 'Soyuz' flight. It was a terrible blow; not only to the space effort, but also to me, and I resolved to train extra harder. The space program in those days was much more political than it is, now."

Colonel Golubko looked around at the younger faces staring at him.

"One day the 'Political Officer' called me. 'We have information,' he said. I had no idea what he was talking about, then he pulled out a folder. An uncle I had forgotten had been captured by the Germans during the 'Great Patriotic War' and had gone over to the other side." The silver-haired man shrugged. "That made it impossible for me to keep training for space flight—but they said I could still be a human test subject . . . since I hoped to someday return to flight status, I went along."

"You kept training on the centrifuge?"

"The doctors said I had what they called a 'perfect physique' for the gravity machine . . . something about my body shape." Rodion Golubko grinned. "Just remember, I am perfect!" and the others laughed. "When I finally understood I would never fly in space, I left the cosmonaut program. Then, I joined 'Special

Forces', and have been there ever since. I still do experiments on the centrifuge."

A major with a clipboard came up. "Your quarters are ready." When the men filed out, to everyone's surprise, night had already fallen. The major led them across to a glassed, modern-looking building.

The man read off quarters assignments: as usual Terenty and Gennady would bunk in the same room. True to form, when the two stepped into their quarters, their kits were already there. "These people think of everything," Terenty said, as he dropped onto a narrow bed.

Gennady sat on a cot, put his head in his hands and groaned. "I have never been so tired in my life!"

"And the Colonel said tomorrow will be even busier."

"What is this?" Gennady picked up a small package labeled, "Rations". He opened the box and found several objects inside that looked like toothpaste tubes. "I suppose this is our dinner." He twisted off the top of one of the tubes and squeezed some of the contents into his mouth. "Sausage, I guess it is. Not bad, actually."

Terenty opened a tube and tasted what came out. "I suppose this is cosmonaut food."

"The centrifuge was an ordeal."

"Can you believe Colonel Golubko?"

"He rode it like it was practically nothing—and *I* got sick!"

"*I* feel sick when I think about running out on the two girls. They probably hate us, by now."

* * *

Moscow, 7:34 PM, Friday, August 16, 1991:

Tamara Kuznetsova pulled the stale muffins and the homemade blintzes from the refrigerator. As she stared down at the aborted dinners that lay flat and soggy on the cold plates, waves of sadness rolled over her. Had she done or said something wrong? She had had such high hopes for herself and the little girl. Perhaps she had been too optimistic. And poor Galina—her cousin had had to force herself to go to work, this morning. The young woman tossed the wasted food into the trash can; there must be nothing to remind her of those two fellows. Somehow, life would have to go on.

* * *

Star City, 8:12 AM, Saturday, August 17, 1991:

"Comrades, I trust you rested well . . ." Rodion Golubko, looking refreshed, gazed around at the half-dozen young men who were gathered in the dormitory lobby. "We will have no breakfasts, since your physical tests will continue."

A man in a white smock coat came out. "Colonel Golubko?"

The middle-aged officer nodded.

The others followed the man across the grassy expanse to another building. In a preparation room much like the one back at the centrifuge, the smock-coat man turned to them. "In here, you will prepare for the treadmill."

A man with a stethoscope stepped up. "Viktor Grishinov?"

The young man raised his hand.

When the two had disappeared into a smaller room, another medical man appeared. "Candidate Suslov, come with me."

As Terenty followed the man into an examining room, he could hear other names being called out behind him. These people seemed to waste no time.

"Onto the treadmill." The doctor motioned to the tracked machine. "We will control the various speeds and monitor your physical reactions."

At first, the machine ran at a relatively slow pace, but then the speed increased. After a while, the moving belts became sheer torture. "At least on the centrifuge, we were s*itting down*," one of the sweating students gasped through his oxygen mask, as his shoes pounded the rumbling treadmill belt.

In the early afternoon they finished with the stationary exercise routines. "I believe my legs are made of wood!" one of the men moaned, as he wobbled toward the shower room.

"I can hardly stand," another called across the steamy stall, as water cascaded over him.

"My legs are numb."

"This 'Star City' is a tough place!"

When they had finished dressing back into street clothes, Colonel Golubko was waiting for them outside. "Comrades! I trust you enjoyed your exercise!" The man motioned at a parked bus. "Let us now go to have our lunch."

When Terenty took a window seat, his legs muscles were tightened in painful knots. "I do not believe I will ever walk again," he groaned aloud to Gennady, who had dropped into the aisle seat next to him.

Gennady moaned, rubbing his legs. "I am tired and hungry!" He shook his head. "Tell me—how did we ever get ourselves into *this?*"

"They selected us."

"Right now, I believe wish I had been more anonymous!"

* * *

Moscow, 2:25 PM, Saturday, August 17, 1991:

There was a rapping noise at the front door of the apartment. Then another knock; louder and more insistent. Tamara Kuznetsova squinted through the peephole. In the hallway stood two middle-aged men, their features distorted by the tiny glass. Both seemed to be wearing gold-braided, military-style hats.

"Yes?"

A muffled male voice came back through the door."We wish to speak to "Tamara Drubkina'."

"Who are you?"

". . . Army—"

Frowning, the young woman opened the door. A pair of uniformed military men stood in the corridor; one held a sheaf of papers in his hand. "Tamara Drubkina?"

"I am Tamara 'Kuznetsova. 'Drubkina' was my former married name."

"You were married to Pavel Drubkin?"

203

"Yes—but what is this all about?"

"Come with us, please. We wish for you to make an identification."

* * *

Star City, at the Same Time; 2:25 PM, Saturday, August 17, 1991:

As the men were finishing their lunch in the *Cosmonaut's Cafeteria,* the colonel rose to speak. We had intended to perform other tests this afternoon," he said, "however the facilities are not ready. Instead, we will tour 'Star City'."

A trim, athletic man Terenty recognized as a cosmonaut stepped to the head table. "You will follow me." Over the next two hours the experienced space traveler led the young men around the training center, through several laboratories where the cosmonauts trained on full-scale mock-ups of real space hardware.

Colonel Golubko sought out the students. "Comrades! We will have our dinner very soon!" he announced. "Tomorrow you must have strong, empty stomachs!

Terenty groaned. *Tomorrow?* That meant they would be here at Star City for least one more day! For Gennady, any lingering hopes he might have had about seeing Galina that evening were now gone. The young soldier had a sinking feeling that, after one more night away from Moscow, the slender, dark-haired girl might never again want to see him.

* * *

Star City, 7:04 AM, Sunday, August 18, 1991:

"Comrades! We will now prepare for weightless flight!" A man in a white smock coat with a stethoscope around his neck addressed the officers.

Another man picked up a scale model of an airplane from a table and held it up. "We use this type aircraft to train

204

cosmonauts in weightless conditions." The man gave an ironic smile. "The Americans have a name for the airplane they use for this purpose: they call it the *'Vomit Comet'*, The practitioner grinned, "So far, we have cleaned up several hundred liters from inside our cabin!"

A doctor handed out little packages to the men. "I would suggest you take one of these, since it could decide what kind of experience you will have!"

A man wearing flight gear came into the room. "Follow me this way to the dressing area," he said.

In a few minutes the Academy men, including the colonel, were outfitted in blue jumpsuits. As the young men stood around, fidgeting, the doctor returned, dressed in a jumpsuit that was a lighter shade of blue than the others'. "I will be aboard the aircraft should you need medical attention."

After the officer had told the young men what to expect during the weightless ride, he led them out to a bus.

In a few minutes, the vehicle pulled up at the far edge of the airfield alongside a white, four-engined jet transport airplane. The men climbed aboard and took their places in jumpseats arranged around the outside bulkhead. Then the engines rumbled and the aircraft lifted from the runway. While the big Ilyushin climbed out, the doctor shouted some final instructions over the roar of the four turbofan jet engines.

Then as the aircraft's nose pitched up into a forty-five degree angle, every passenger's weight doubled. Since he had already experienced a far greater gravity pull on the centrifuge, Terenty found it tolerable.

"Here we go!" the doctor called out, "remove your seat belts!"

The engines throttled back; as the big transport glided upward; the only sound other than the idling engines was the air outside whispering against the airframe.

All at once, Terenty's stomach felt as if it was about to come up into his throat. The airplane's padded floor was now a half-meter below him . . . then a full meter . . . then two meters. He was floating in midair! Loud whoops sounded throughout the cabin as the young men twisted and flipped from side to-side and from floor-to-ceiling.

Gennady turned three complete somersaults to the middle of the cabin; then back-flipped to the forward end of the padded space. One or two hung motionless at first, stupefied by what was happening, before they, too, pushed off. By now, all the others were doing the same.

"Stand by for gravity!" The deck rose to meet the men, who settled gently onto the pad just as the engines roared back to life. Once more, they were pressed down onto the deck at twice their weight while the airplane accelerated nose-up.

"In orbit, most cosmonauts adjust quickly to weightlessness," the doctor called out to them.

All too soon, it seemed, the flight was over and the bus carrying the laughing, rollicking young men drew up at the hangar, Colonel Golubko, puffing on a Cuban cigar, was waiting for them. "Get dressed into your civilian clothes—we will now have a feast to make-up for the short rations of the past two days."

* * *

"Cosmonaut's Cafeteria"; 1:10 PM, Sunday, August 18, 1991:

"Comrades, your physical tests are finished." Colonel Golubko stood and addressed the young men as they downed their post-flight lunch in the cosmonaut's private cafeteria. "The doctors tell me that you could all be cosmonauts." He gave a little smirk. "But I told told them the nation needs you for other things—"

* * *

Moscow, 5:35 PM, Sunday, August 18, 1991:

The iron gates swung open for the two cars; the Zhiguli and the Moskvitch eased into their regular parking spaces at the rear of the Academy's main building. Colonel Golubko handed each of them a piece of paper. "Well, comrades, you earned this," he said, switching his cigar from one corner of his mouth to the other, "these are your passes . . . you are free until Tuesday morning."

Gennady clasped the precious pass in his hand motioned to Terenty. "Come on!" Both broke into a run, leaving the others gaping at them.

The remaining young men looked around at each other, amused. "Why are they in such a hurry?" one observed with a shrug, "you would think they had lost their best friends, or something!"

In their room, the two scrambled into clean clothes. Then they bolted down the straircase, out the front door and through the exit gate to the street. "This way!" Terenty said, as they turned and jogged up Soyuz Novaya Zemlya Prospekt, then down a shaded boulevard, past the place where the little girl had chased the tin can into the street.

At a kiosk, Gennady held up his hand. "Let us get them flowers." They dropped some coins at a young lady florist, who handed both ot them bouquets wrapped in tissue paper.

They made for the row of apartments where the two girls lived. Taking the steps two-at-a-time, in a few moments they were standing, out of breath, in front of a familiar-looking door.

With a straightening of clothes and a quick glance at each other, the two took nervous breaths and knocked on the door.

-16-

Vera Kuznetsova, in bathrobe and slippers, stood frowning at the young men and the floral bundles they were holding. "These are two very decent girls," the woman glared, "if you think you can buy them with flowers, you are mistaken." She moved to close the door.

"*Nyet!* Please!" Terenty stepped forward. "Let us explain what happened—"

"Explain it to *me*, then," came another female voice. Tamara came up beside her mother, who turned and flounced off. "Where have you *been*? Galina and I gave up on you."

Terenty caught his breath at the sight of the beautiful girl; he felt his face flushing. "We were—called away by the—*'school'* on a special—assignment," he stammered, swallowing. "They sent us out of the city and we could not talk to you."

"I am sure you *really* missed us while you were off, somewhere, doing *whatever* it is you do!" There was sarcasm in Tamara's voice. "And did you know that Pavel is dead? He was killed by an Army truck!"

"An Army truck?"

"He was riding in a taxicab! An Army truck ran into it!"

"But I thought he—" Terenty caught himself just in time. Since he already knew first-hand that Pavel had been shot dead inside the Academy, they must have told Tamara he had died in a cab collision with a military vehicle. Then he remembered something else: *Galina's former boyfriend had also supposedly been killed by an Army truck while riding in a taxi!* Had he, too, trespassed onto the Academy grounds and was shot? If so, the authorities were using the same cover for both deaths! Someone was playing a deadly serious game.

His senses swirled back to reality. Tamara was staring at the flowers he was holding. "I . . . brought you these—" He offered the long-stemmed arrangement to her.

The auburn-haired young woman hesitated, then took the bouquet from him. "Come in," she said in a flat voice. She stood aside as Terenty stepped into the small parlor, followed by Gennady, still grasping the flowers he had brought for Galina. But the slender, dark-haired cousin was not there.

Just then, Larisa stepped through the archway with her thumb in her mouth. When the mother lifted her daughter, the little girl reached out to Terenty. As he took the grinning child into his arms, Tamara gave a slight smile.

Gennady looked around the room. "Where is Galina?"

"She is at her new flat—but she may not want to see you." A stricken look came over Gennady. With the little one in Terenty's arms, the girl and the two young men trooped up the stairs to the next level. "Wait here," Tamara said. She gave the door a couple of knocks, and, finding it unlocked, stepped inside. Through the door came muffled sounds of female voices in conversation as the young men stood fidgeting in the corridor.

After an interval the door opened and Tamara motioned for Gennady to go inside. "She wants to talk to you . . . alone."

Gennady took a deep breath, then eased into the small, plain parlor. The cousin was sitting on the edge of a sofa with her hands clasped between her knees. The girl's eyes were red; she had been crying.

"Galina . . ." the nervous young man sat down, "I—I want to explain what happened." He offered the flowers to her. I brought you these—"

She stared at the arrangement for a moment with liquid eyes, then without a word put her arms around his neck. He could feel the flowers in her hand dangling down his back; her tears were wet on his shoulder.

In a small voice the dark-haired girl spoke. "What *happened*? I was so worried about you."

Gennady brushed her cheek. "The school called us away on a special . . . *'assignment'* . . . and we had no way to let you know where we were." He caressed the nape of her neck; she squeezed his shoulder.

"Did you think about me?"

"All the time."

"Are you telling me the truth?"

"I promise."

There was a knock. The two dis-engaged from each other; with quick motions Galina wiped her eyes and patted her hair. Tamara peeped around the door. "May we come in?" Terenty, with Larisa in his arms, followed her into the room. "Terenty told me how they had to go away on a special job." She seemed to be in better spirits.

Galina dabbed at her face. "Gennady told me the same thing."

Terenty spoke up. "Let us make it up to you. We can go down to the 'Arbat', tonight."

Tamara's eyes darted back and forth at the others. "My mother could take care of Larisa—"

Gennady turned to Galina. "How about it?"

Galina glanced at Tamara, who was nodding at her. "All right . . . but let me change into something besides these old clothes. I have been moving from the burned flat into this place."

Terenty, Tamara and the child went back upstairs; Gennady stayed behind. In the living room Vera Kuznetsova was arranging trinkets; Terenty suspected she was there because she was curious about what the young people were doing. "Mother, could you take care of Larisa? We are going to the 'Arbat'."

"With Galina?"

"She and Gennady are going with us."

As the lady lifted the youngster from him, Terenty detected disdain on the older woman's face; he guessed their absence had turned her against them. As the "babushka" passed through the archway, the little girl, her face beaming, waved back over the woman's shoulder at him.

"I believe she likes you," Tamara said. She looked down at herself. "Oh! I must get dressed! I will be right back."

Terenty paced back and forth, too nervous to sit down—he was going out with Tamara!

Knocks sounded on the door. Galina, in tight jeans and a red halter top, strode into the room on shiny red stilletto heels. Gennady followed, grinning.

Tamara came under the archway just then. Terenty's eyes went wide at the sight of her in a mini-skirt, white blouse with a red scarf tied around her neck, and shiny black boots; her auburn hair was pulled back. The girl looked young enough to be a teenager, Terenty thought; he had to remind himself that Tamara was, in fact, in her 'twenties and the mother of a child.

The foursome boarded a tram out in front of the apartment block. In a half-hour, they were standing in a crowd of people in *'Arbat Square'*. Gennady pointed toward several lighted, gold-domed and red-brick towers a few blocks distant over the tops of some buildings. "The 'Kremlin'," he said.

Galina entwined her arm with his. "Perhaps we could go there."

Tamara leaned her shoulder against Terenty's as they joined a lively throng of mostly younger people surging down the lighted pedestrian *'Ulitsa Arbat'*, past outdoor cafes, jugglers, sidewalk poets, bistros, restaurants, pastel-colored, multi-storied buildings and shops that lined the popular outdoor pedestrian mall. As they made their way along the bustling concourse, Terenty could hardly take his eyes off Tamara; he noticed that others were also admiring the pretty, mini-skirted young woman with her smooth, easygoing stride; made even more alluring by her shiny black boots. At one point, she nudged him with a grin and a wink toward Gennady and Galina who were walking along ahead of them, arm-in-arm, gazing at each other, looking as if the problems of the recent separation were now in the past.

At the far end of the promenade, they stopped at a hulking, many-storied, tan-colored building that took up an entire city block; a structure surmounted by pointed towers soaring into the sky.

Galina stared up at the enormous lighted structure that cast its presence over the entire Arbat District. "*The 'Foreign Ministry Building'*," she said, "Sergei's brother works in there."

With the mention of her dead boyfriend, there was an awkward pause. The girl eased closer to Gennady, who looked uncomfortable; putting her arm in his. As they turned about, Terenty noticed Galina glance back at the so-called *"Stalin-Gothic"* building; with that tiny gesture he knew that Sergei's death was still an issue with her.

In the warm night air, the little troupe made their way up the popular "Ulitsa Arbat".

Before long, they were back at Arbat Square. Gennady motioned toward a yellow, triangular-shaped restaurant on a nearby corner. "How about some food?"

* * *

In the restroom, Galina powdered her nose. "What do *you* think? Do you believe their stories about having to go out of town on 'school-business'?" She gave a side glance at her cousin, who was touching-up her own face.

The other girl looked at herself in the mirror for a long moment. "I *want* to believe them . . . but I keep feeling they are holding something back from us—"

"I agree."

"What should we do?"

"We must be careful."

* * *

The two young men had watched as the cousins disappeared into the restroom. Terenty looked across the table at Gennady and gave a sigh. "I do not feel right, carrying on like this—" He looked around to make sure no one was overhearing them.

"But what can we do?. We are bound by the oath!" He stared perplexed through the big window at pedestrians parading past outside. "We will have to be careful."

"Galina seems to like you."

"I was worried she would never again want to see me after what happened."

"We must make it up to them.

"I congratulate you . . . Tamara looks beautiful, tonight."

"She certainly—here they come!"

The two young women threaded their way up to the table by the window. "Your turn!"

Galina took her seat, facing the fellows. "We will wait for you—but hurry, I am hungry!"

212

"Relax, will you?" Galina chided her cousin as the young men moved away from them. "This is better than sitting at home doing nothing. Besides, I think I am falling in love."

"Galina! What about Sergei?"

"I realized back there at the Foreign Ministry building that I had to move on with my life. I guess looking at that thing was a sort of healing for me. And it is time for *you* to see that things are really over with Pavel, now that he is also gone."

"But what about Larisa? As long as Pavel was still alive, at least there was *that* connection for our little girl. What will I tell her?"

"Tell her *nothing*. Pavel was a brute—both you and Larisa are now much better off."

Tamara started to speak, then held back as Galina shook her head with a slight wagging of her finger. Turning, she saw Terenty and Gennady making their way toward the table.

An hour later, the foursome left the emptying eatery and set out across Arbat Square. The Sunday evening crowd had thinned; it was getting on toward midnight.

Tamara pointed beyond some nearby buildings toward the looming, lighted, onion-shaped, golden-topped spires of the Kremlin in the distance they had seen earlier. "Let us go there," she said, tugging Terenty's arm, "I have never been to the Kremlin at night."

"It is getting late," Galina put in, "The *Metro* line will be closing."

"We can take a taxi," Gennady said.

"Taxis make me nervous—Pavel and Sergei were both killed in taxis."

Galina gave a shudder and shook her head. "Do not remind me of that!"

Gennady looked at Galina. "I am sure that was only a coincidence," he said, trying to casually deflect the topic that he knew was incendiary—the young officer was concerned the girls could put facts together and start asking questions. "I would also like to see the Kremlin." As the little troupe headed down another street, the seat of the Soviet government soon came into clear view. At a tiny square they stopped and gazed up at the lighted towers and the immense brick walls of the famous fortification that followed the curve along the Moscow River until it bent out of sight to the left at *'Red Square',* hundreds of meters in the distance.

"Let us go onto the bridge," Terenty suggested, and the quartet turned right onto the broad span that crossed the Moscow River to connect the Kremlin with the district to the south. This night, there was no traffic and few others on the walkway as they turned about and admired the mighty, illuminated buildings within the massive red brick wall and its towers, several topped with a glowing red star.

Terenty's thoughts went back to earlier times when he had been in there. "One day, when I was a teenager," he told the others, "my father and mother took me to a Kremlin reception. I remember meeting 'Brezhnev' and 'Gromyko'."

Tamara's eyes were wide. "You met *'Brezhnev'?"*

"My father was a diplomat and it was his *job* to know those people—having connections like that probably had a lot to do with our next posting, which was to Washington."

"Did you meet a lot of American girls?" Tamara was eying him with a sideways stare.

"The girls over there were all right." *He had had a wonderful teenage social life in the United States; American females of all ages were fascinated by the fact he was a "real" Russian. He had been invited to a lot of parties.*

Tamara let go his hand stepped to the railing. The girl stared down into the dark river water, at the reflections of the lights along the riverbanks. When Terenty came over, she turned and looked at him. "Why did you come back to me?"

Her question caught him by surprise. "I wanted to see you again . . . to be with you."

Terenty looked down the way; the other couple had stopped at an overlook

The girl pressed on. "Do you have any *idea* how disappointed I was when you did not show up when you said you would? Galina and I made food, hoping you would come, but we had to throw it all away. I did not want to see you anymore—"

Terenty caught his breath.

"... and then you came back like nothing had happened with some story about the 'metal school' sending you out of Moscow! Did you expect me to *believe* that?"

Terenty felt a terrible guilt about what the girl had gone through on his behalf; especially about the food. There was a rushing in his ears. "What I told you was the—"

"Understand—I cannot endure another bad relationship . . ." Her eyes were filling with hot tears.

Terenty silently cursed Semen Putridchenko and the damnable oath; he was caught between his duty to the country and this girl, who deserved better. He could tell her *everything,* hoping she could keep a confidence—but the vision of a firing squad came back. Terenty put his elbows on the masonry bridge rail and buried his face in his hands. He stared down at the black river gurgling beneath them, then turned to Tamara. "We really *are* working with metals . . ." *But soon the "metals" we will be working with will be deadly paramilitary weapons.*

The only other people on the bridge other than Gennady and Galina were about fifty meters away. He took a deep breath and leaned toward her. *What he was about to say would put him before a firing squad if General Putridchenko ever found out. There was another concern: were there listening devices nearby that could record his words?* Terenty looked about, then decided to take the chance. He spoke in a hoarse whisper. "Tamara, I cannot tell you much, and what I will say must always be a secret between us." He looked straight at her "Well?"

"All right," she said, swallowing.

"We are involved in a national security matter."

The girl's eyes went wide. "Then you *are* military men!" Her voice was dusky.

"Well . . . not exactly. We are not in the *active* military, but we work through the—" He almost said the 'Academy'— "through the *school . . .* in something different and very important to the Soviet Union. I wish to God I could tell you more—but I cannot."

"Tell me—do you believe in God?"

The question took him aback. "Years ago, my mother used to talk to me about God—but always when my father was away. He is an atheist."

"Are *you* an atheist?"

Terenty looked uncomfortable. "When I joined the 'Komosomol', the State became the most important thing in my life. Later, I joined the Communist Party."

"You are a *Communist?*"

Officially . . . yes." The girl reeled back. "But I only joined to further my military career and did not think much about it."

"I will tell *you* a secret." The girl reached for his hand. "Every day you were gone, I lit a candle and prayed for you. Galina did the same for Gennady."

"I guess no one has done that since my mother prayed for me when I was young."

"Your mother sounds like a good person."

"My mother is dead—cancer. My father lives in Moscow."

"Oh, I am sorry!" She touched his forearm.

"And *I* am sorry I caused you to worry." He gazed into the auburn-haired girl's beautiful hazel eyes that sparkled in the Kremlin's reflected light. "Please—you must trust me."

"All right, I will trust you." Tamara stood on her tiptoes and gave him an impulsive kiss.

* * *

Gennady and Galina watched the other couple down by the railing. "Let them have their privacy," Galina said. She reached for the young man's elbow and tugged him toward an outcropping where the walkway stood out on a battlement over the river. "We also need to talk." The two stepped onto the projecting parapet and looked down at the black, slow-moving water underneath them. Down-river, past the Kremlin, a barge-towboat chugged along, its probing spotlight beam searing the bank with a dancing circle of light.

On her spike heels, the young woman looked straight into Gennady's eyes. A puff of wind ruffled her short, dark hair. "When Sergei was killed, I was sure I would never become involved with another man." Gennady started to say something, but she went on. "Sergei was young and he was sometimes impulsive . . . but he was a good, decent person." She looked down into the water for some moments. "I always believed there was more to what happened to him than what they were telling me." She shook her head. "Now, *Pavel* is killed just like Sergei was—in a taxicab by an Army truck! Do you not see how suspicious that looks?" Galina stared expressionless down at the water and shrugged. "I feel like some big, invisible plot is going on all around me."

"Galina, I—"

The girl put her fingers to his lips, stopping his words. "Before I knew you, I was just a little schoolteacher with a small job and a dead fiancé. And then you came along and danced with me and made me forget about all that for a while—and then you went away!" She shrugged. "After I had given up hope of ever seeing you again, you came back with a story about having to go off with some 'metallic school,' or whatever it was." Her dark blue eyes flashed. "I want to believe what you say, but I think you are holding something back." Galina looked straight into his eyes. "Tell me—*who are you and what do you really do?*"

Gennady reddened. He knew if he ever wanted to again see this girl, he would have to level with her, right here and now. But there was the oath. The young man looked down the concrete walkway where the other couple were arm-in-arm and smiling at each other; Terenty and Tamara seemed to have straightened things out between themselves. His story would have to be at least as convincing to Galina as Terenty's must have been to Tamara.

The girl was still staring straight at him. "Well?"

"All right, I will tell you what I can," he began in a rasping whisper, "but there are some things I cannot reveal to you, or to anyone else. I am bound by an oath."

"An oath?"

Gennady held up his hand. "We must not raise our voices." He glanced around; no one else was in earshot on the bridge. "It is very complicated—"

217

All at once, his voice had to compete with a heavy rumble that seemed to come from somewhere on the far side of the Kremlin. He stopped, frowning, and stared off in the direction of the sounds that faded away after some moments.

He went on. "I must have your promise that you will not reveal any of this to anyone—the penalties will be a firing squad for me and the *'Gulag'* for you."

The girl's hand flew to her mouth. "I am not sure I even *want* to hear of it!" Galina stared into his eyes. "All right, I promise . . . but what are you *doing* that could cause such horrible things?"

Gennady gripped Galina's shoulders—as much to calm and steady himself as to reassure her; he was now heading into territory that could have enormous consequences for both of them. "There are things I cannot talk about, but you must trust me."

The girl's face looked pale in the shadowy lights of the bridge; her chest rose and fell in shallow gasps; he became aware she was holding his forearms. He took a long breath. "The part about working with metals is true." *We will be working and training with deadly, secret weapons made of metal.* "We are in a . . . 'developmental' program that is—vital to the security of the Soviet Union." *We will be "developing" our skills to counter enemies of the State.*

"Then you *are* military men!"

"Right now, we are . . . ah, classified as 'Reserves'."

"How about *later?*"

"I promise you that what we are—will be—doing is of great value to this country. You must believe that."

The girl was shaking her head. "No . . . no—I do not like the military after what happened to Sergei—and Pavel."

"Please believe me when I say our work is very important to the 'Motherland' . . . in ways you cannot imagine.*"*

"Will you be going away?" Her voice was low.

There came another heavy roaring-like noise, along with some thunder-like "booms" from the direction of the far-side of the Kremlin; he could barely hear her speak. Then the sounds subsided.

He again looked into her face. "We will be working and training in and around Moscow for a while . . . then we will probably be sent—somewhere . . . hopefully, not for very long." *Spetsnaz units may be deployed anywhere in the world on instant-notice.*

The young woman put her hands on the thick railing and gazed across the water toward the illuminated Kremlin buildings. By the lights of the bridge and the reflections from the river, Gennady could see she was thinking.

"You say you want me to trust you—but how can I trust *anyone* from the military after what I have been through?" She turned and looked into his face. "What makes you think you are different from other military men?"

"Look at the heart!" Gennady tapped his chest. "Even *military* men have thoughts and ways of feeling—" He stopped, embarrassed.

"Feeling?" Galina was shaking her head. "After you disappeared, I thought you had no feelings; now you come back and tell me *this!* I do not know what to think."

Thinking about *you* kept me going all the time we were—we were—out of Moscow."

"Where did you go, 'out of Moscow'?"

"I must not tell you; it is part of the oath. But it was not far from the city."

"This 'oath'—how long is it before you can say anything?"

"I can never talk about certain 'things'—*ever.*"

"It is *that* important?"

Gennady wanted to change the subject. He looked down the way at Terenty and Tamara, who were holding hands and talking to each other. The young officer reached his arm around the slender brunette's waist. "Let us join them," he said.

Even though she was not completely satisfied with Gennady's answers, Galina went along with him down to where the other couple stood looking at the sights. "Let us walk around the Kremlin," Galina said to them, "I have never seen it up close at night."

When they stepped up, Terenty had his arm around Tamara's shoulder. "We can walk around the walls, then take a taxi to your home."

The young people came off the bridge and made a right turn onto the narrow roadway that skirted past the rust-colored brick ramparts of the Kremlin wall. Below, on the other side of the street, a stone embankment made a slight curve as it followed the Moscow River.

The little troupe came up to the corner of the Kremlin and made a sharp left turn up the eastern wall toward Red Square. *"Saint Basil's!"* Galina pointed to the famous building with its multi-colored, onion-shaped spires. "Building that church was probably the only worthwhile thing *'Ivan the Terrible'* ever did."

Tamara looked up at the big clock faces on one of the Kremlin towers. "It is past midnight."

As they trooped past *'Lenin's Tomb',* which, after hours, had no lines of people in front of it, Terenty was puzzled that the whole expanse of Red Square and the buildings inside the Kremlin were ablaze with lights. "I read somewhere that they only turn on all the lights for ceremonial and special occasions— is *this* a 'special occasion'?" he wondered, aloud.

Tamara pulled herself closer to Terenty. "This is *our* 'special occasion'!"

Galina spoke up. "I am glad we all went out together." She rubbed her fingers across the back of Gennady's neck. "It is a beautiful night."

The foursome had just about reached the narrow space between the *'Saint Nicholas Tower'* of the Kremlin wall and the quaint brick facade of the *'Historical Museum',* where the pavement nosed downhill along the northeastern corner of the ancient fortress, when there came sudden roaring noises from behind the *'GUM'* department store on the opposite side of Red Square. At the same time, heavy rumbling sounds erupted from the streets farther beyond. At once, bright, flickering lights seared the sky, outlining billowing clouds of engine-exhaust smoke that started drifting across the tops of the buildings.

Gennady and Terenty looked at each other, surprised; those were the sounds of armored personnel carriers! *"What the hell is going on?"* Gennady muttered.

Just then, a massive Army vehicle, followed by a half-dozen others, burst around the end of the GUM building and roared across Red Square straight at the little group, who were standing transfixed in the glaring headlights! At the same time, another line of dark-green personnel carriers full of soldiers in battle gear whined up the short incline from behind the Historical Museum. More armored personnel carriers were now converging onto the square from several directions. All the big, smoking vehicles howled directly toward the four young people!

Terenty pulled Tamara behind him; Gennndy grabbed Galina. Both girls were shaking.

The leading machine slewed to a stop; an Army man with a major's insignia on his helmet leaned out of the cab and looked down at Terenty. "You must evacuate the square at once!"

"What is the matter?"

"Orders—"

"Are these 'maneuvers'?

The officer was not answering any questions. "Leave the area *NOW*—or I will place all of you under military arrest!"

The two young men needed no further prodding. But as Gennady tugged Galina, the spike heel of her shoe got caught in a crack in the brickstone pavement and the shoe came off!

When Gennady turned about to retrieve it, an infantryman in the nearest carrier aimed his rifle at him. There was a loud click as the safety came off—for a long second, the young man in civilian clothes stared up into the gun barrel. *"Spetsnaz . . ."* he mouthed, pointing at himself. The soldier lowered the weapon. Gennady deliberately reached for the shoe and handed it to the girl behind him, who slipped it onto her foot.

The four ran down the incline to a space behind the Kremlin wall where they held up. Galina grabbed Gennady around his neck and burst into tears. "You could have been shot because of me!" The girl held onto him as her tears coursed onto his shoulder. "Oh, Gennady . . . do not leave me—ever!"

Nearby, Terenty and Tamara held each other. She looked up at the looming wall, with smoke roiling over the top of it, then at Terenty. "What is happening?"

"I do not know." The engine noises seemed to be subsiding—were the soldiers leaving the square, or had they just turned off their engines? "I want to see about this," Terenty said. He made his way back to the corner tower; crouching in the shadows he could see that the personnel carriers were still parked on Red Square, but men milling around the vehicles did not seem to be doing anything in particular. He returned to the others. "Whatever they are doing up there does not seem to concern us— I hope."

Galina wiped her eyes. "I want to go home."

Gennady nodded. "I believe we should get away from here, at once!"

Terenty reached for Tamara. "Let us go back to Arbat Square and find a taxi."

* * *

Moscow; 7:32 AM, Monday, August 19, 1991:

Terenty's eyes flew open. Someone was pounding on the apartment door! Gennady stirred from his place on the living room floor and came to his elbow, blinking.

"Open up, quick!" someone shouted from the corridor.

Vasily Kuznetsov, in his nightshirt, bustled through the arched opening and pulled open the door. An agitated-looking man stood in the hallway. Tamara's father gaped at the newcomer. "Comrade Renko . . . what—?"

"They have overthrown the government!" The words tumbled out of their neighbor's mouth. "Turn on your television!"

"What!"

"Gorbachev is out! Finished!" The man dashed to the next door and rapped on it. "It is on the television, right now!"

Vera Kuznetsova stepped into the living room, along with Tamara and Galina, who had stayed over at her cousin's apartment. "What is going on?" the older woman asked her husband, "I heard voices."

"Something is happening with the government."

The father came back with a small television set. In a hurry he set it on a table and turned it on. While he adjusted the pointed aerials, the black-and-white receiver came to life. On the screen a newscaster was in mid-sentence. ". . . is reporting that Mikhail Gorbachev is unable to perform his duties because of health reasons. 'Vice President Gennady Yanayev' has taken over his powers . . . the *State Committee for the State of Emergency* decrees all media organs to be under official control. All strikes and demonstrations are banned."

"'*State Committee for the State of Emergency*?'" Tamara's father frowned. "What is *that?*"

A scene of eight men came on the screen. "Oh, my God!" Terenty blurted out, "There is Yazov!" Sure enough, the Defense Minister, the man who had addressed the students at the Academy the other day, was one of the new rulers!

Tamara turned to him, puzzled. "Who is 'Yazov'? Why is he so important?"

Terenty reddened. He had almost said too much! "Ah, 'Yazov' is the—top military man—in the whole country . . ."

"This is revolution!" Gennady said. Galina came over and sat next to him. She reached for his hand.

Vera Kuznetsova spoke up. "I knew things were bad under the current régime, but this is not the way to go about change!"

She motioned to the two young women. "Girls, we must go to work, this morning."

Just then, there was another knock at the door. When Tamara's father tugged it open, a man he recognized from a nearby apartment was standing in the hallway. Another neighbor came up; then a third and a fourth. "There is opposition to the coup!" the first man said, red-faced. "We are going to the *White House*—to protect Yeltsin!"

"Yeltsin is *opposing* the new régime?"

"*Da!* He says that the overthrow is illegal and is calling for citizens to guard the loyal government! Come with us!" Several more men came up; all seemed anxious to leave at once.

"I will get dressed." Vasily Kuznetsov turned to Gennady and Terenty, "Let us go with these fellows!"

Tamara burst through the archway, wide-eyed. "You are leaving?" She looked at Terenty. "My father says you are going to the White House! What is happening?"

He pressed her hand "No time for explanations! You and Galina go to work and we will be back here as soon as we can!"

Just then, the slender cousin came out and made for Gennady's side. "Oh, be careful!" She gave, him a quick kiss on his cheek. "I will pray for you—"

At the street, a tram was just coming down the block. "Come on!" someone called out, "this streetcar will take us as to the Arbat!" The men crammed into the jammed coach; all on board seemed to be headed for the White House.

As the railcar rumbled toward the center of the city, everyone was talking at once:

"Why is the 'Committee' taking over?"

"What happened to Gorbachev?"

When the tram pulled in at the "Arbatskaya Station", Terenty and Gennady looked around in disbelief. Arbat Square, where they had been with the girls only a few hours before in a festive-like atmosphere, was now crowded with thousands of grim-faced men and women.

"Comrade Boris is resisting!" a man shouted, raising his fist, "we must hurry!" The men joined the surging throng making their way out "Ulitsa Novyy Arbat".

When they had gone about a kilometer, they came upon a crowd of people massed in front of the Parliament building. The atmosphere was electric; everyone seemed to be in a state of frenzied excitement.

Yeltsin is in there!" came a shrill voice above the others. The crowd cheered.

Terenty, Gennady and Tamara's father elbowed their way through the throng up to a spot in front of the big white structure. From time-to-time, someone would come to a window and look out.

Lines of ordinary-looking citizens continued to file from all directions into the big open spaces around the Parliament headquarters, milling about, shouting, applauding, whistling; raising their fists.

"Most of these people are young," Vasily Kuznetsov observed. Terenty saw it was true: most of those gathered about in the streets looked to be in their 'twenties and 'thirties.

Gennady climbed up onto a tall curb and scanned the crowd. "There must be twenty thousand or more out here!" he said from his vantage point. He looked about some more, then pointed. "Something is happening back there!"

Shouts started coming from about two blocks away. From the same direction came a growing, surging rumble of big engines. A column of gray-green Army tanks and armored personnel carriers came clattering up Ulitsa Novyy Arbat and began squirming into position around the Parliament building, forcing people aside. In a few minutes, dozens of the military vehicles, loaded with armed soldiers, had moved to the front of the White House, followed by other machines that stopped along the roadway.

A sullen crowd converged around them. "Shame!" shouted the onlookers.

A stringy-looking young man in scruffy denims jumped onto a tank and began beating on the armored turret with his fist. "Why are you here?" the fellow shouted at the surprised tank commander.

The officer lifted his earphones from his leather helmet. "We have orders . . ."

Others yelled questions and insults, to little response from the military men. One tank driver stood up in his hatch with a camera and took pictures. Several others alighted from their armored vehicles and stood around, smoking cigarettes, acting casual. As he watched the tentative, uncertain behavior of the soldiers, Terenty was puzzled: *Do these Army people not know why they are here?*

Shouts came from the direction of the White House. "Yeltsin is coming!" Others began calling the President's name. From his perch, Gennady saw a phalanx of men in business suits stepping out toward the crowd. Standing on tiptoes, Terenty spotted the combed, white hair of the President of Russia headed straight toward him. Yells and shrieks rose up as the well-dressed man strode with purposeful steps toward a nearby tank. The man climbed onto the bristling machine and shook hands with the surprised military man on the turret.

Then Boris Yeltsin turned toward the crowd and raised his fist, provoking a crescendo of noise from the massed onlookers, who surged forward, shouting.

The President raised his hand. "People!" he shouted. The throng quieted down. Everyone stood transfixed as the leader of Russia began to speak. "Citizens!" he shouted, "this is an illegal coup!" The crowd roared. "I call on the people of the Soviet Union to fight back!" His words met with thunderous applause, shouts and loud whistling. "The reactionaries will not triumph!" He looked around at the military forces facing him. "Soldiers! I appeal to you not to turn against the people!" The men at the tanks and personnel carriers were impassive. "This coup is a new reign of terror!" Boris Yeltsin raised his fist. "I am the 'Guardian of Democracy! I call for massive civil resistance!" Whistles and applause rent the air. "I call for a general strike, tomorrow!"

The electrified crowd cheered and clapped as the portly, white-haired man dropped from the armored machine and made his way back through the admiring throng toward the Parliament building.

A man climbed onto a stone abutment and began waving to get the attention of the crowd. "People!" he shouted, raising his fist, "we must protect Comrade Boris!" The man gave a look over his shoulder at the White House. "The President is—"

His words were cut off by yells from a nearby street, followed by more loud voices.

A moment later, a dozen or more rag-tag-looking men ran into the crowded square, shouting and waving their arms over their heads. One of the scraggly-looking men climbed onto a curb and cupped his hands to his mouth. "Listen to me!" the fellow shouted, as his compatriots formed a line in front of him. "We are the veterans of Afghanistan—!" There was scattered applause. "We must build barricades!" He pointed toward the tanks and armored carriers. "We must use '*Molotov Cocktails*' if the Army becomes the enemy of the people!"

Gennady nudged Terenty. Some of the soldiers in the military vehicles had reached for their weapons; they seemed to be looking toward their commanders. *For instructions to shoot?*

A thin, emaciated-looking old woman, her head covered by a threadbare shawl, detached herself fom the main mass of people, and with slow, measured steps made her way toward one of the tanks. In her hand was a basket of flowers. The ancient lady pulled one of the flowers from the basket and left the colorful petals sticking out of the end of the tank's main gun barrel! The crowd quieted as she shuffled to the next tank and slipped another flower into the muzzle of *its* gun. A young woman reached into the wizened woman's basket, and began going down the line in the other direction, leaving a flower in each tank's gun. A bearded young man came up, took some petals for himself and went to the nearest armored carrier, where he stuck them underneath a windshield wiper.

Vasily Kuznetsov glanced over the woman's shoulder and gasped, wide-eyed. Behind her, the gun barrel of a tank was swinging toward her head! In a flash, he pushed the surprised woman out of the way! But he lost his balance, tripped, and fell onto the pavement..

"My wrist!" the older man moaned, as he tried to get up.

As the others stood back, the two young men helped the man to his feet. "It does not feel broken; I believe it is just a sprain," Terenty said.

"Make way for us!" the young men called out as the three made their way out of the crammed arena and headed back along Ulitsa Novyy Arbat toward the Metro station.

* * *

After some insistent knocks, Tamara pulled open the door. Her father staggered into the little parlor, grasping his forearm.

"Papa!"

Vera Kuznetsova came out of the kitchen, wiping her hands on an apron. "Vasily! What happened?" The man's wife helped him to the sofa. Tamara and her mother sat with their hands cupped over their mouths while Terenty and Gennady told how he had kept the woman from being smashed by the big rotating gun.

"You are heroic!" the man's wife gazed at him, caressing his sprained wrist.

Gennady glanced at the television set that was turned on. "Look!" he said to the others, reaching to turn up the volume. On the screen several men, dressed in civilian suits, sat behind a long table facing the cameras. To the left was Marshal Yazov, who had exchanged his bemedaled military uniform for a dark business suit. The young men gave each other quick looks, shaking their heads; they did not recognize the others at the table.

The man in the middle, evidently the new leader, was speaking. ". . . I have taken over the duties of 'President of the USSR', in keeping with *'Article One-Hundred-Twenty-Seven, Clause Number Seven of the Soviet Constitution'—"* The man, whose hands appeared to be shaking, went on. "Mikhail Gorbachev is unable to perform his duties due to health reasons."

Gennady stared at the lineup on the little screen. "They do not look right . . . those men all look scared and the man in the middle looks sick."

The camera moved-in for a close-up of the gray-suited individual, who had identified himself as the "Acting President". His face had a gray, waxen cast; his greasy-looking hair was unkempt and drooped down over his forehead; the man's spectacles, that exaggerated the size of his eyes, kept sliding down his nose. The man was gulping. "The 'Committee' is taking-over to avoid a national catastrophe—" The nervous-looking "Leader" turned to the man next to him and whispered something, then again looked straight ahead; his glasses momentarily reflecting a studio light back into the camera. "We issue a 'stern warning' against Boris Yeltsin's 'provocations'."

A voice off-camera asked: "When will Gorbachev be back?"

The man clasped his trembling hands together. "Maybe later—who knows?"

"Enough of these politics!" Tamara's mother turned off the television set. "Let us now eat."

There was knock at the door. The others heard Tamara's father and Renko's voice coming from the living room. In a moment the two stepped into the kitchen.

The man rolled his cap in his hands and looked at the window. "Is there a fire escape out there?" he asked in a whisper. Vasily Kuznetsov shook his head; Renko looked relieved. "I do not wish to be overheard." Terenty looked hard at the man as the neighbor went on in a low voice, "I have a secret receiver and I have been listening to short-wave broadcasts—there are many things happening that we are not being told."

What do you mean?"

"There are demonstrations—big demonstrations—all across the Soviet Union against the coup. The people are calling it 'illegal'!" The man had gripped his cap so tightly his knuckles were white. "America is supporting Yeltsin and Gorbachev against the plotters!"

"America!" Everyone in the tiny kitchen looked at each other; this was surprising news.

"There are demonstrations in Red Square, right now—rumors the Army may fire on the people. Yeltsin is appealing to the military not to shoot citizens."

Terenty was frowning. "Where are you getting all this?"

"On the short-wave radio! I heard it from the 'BBC' and the 'Voice of America'."

Gennady turned on the television set. A grim-faced news announcer was denouncing Mikhail Gorbachev and Boris Yeltsin.

"I am telling you the *real* situation is completely different from what is on the television!" The neighbor was insistent. "The people are all for Yeltsin."

Vasily Kuznetsov turned to the others. "We must go back to the White House!"

His wife put a hand on his shoulder. "You cannot go because of your arm!"

The older man looked at the two young men. "Then *you* must go there."

Tamara looked at Terenty. "I am going."

Galina reached for Gennady's hand. "I am going, also."

"It may become dangerous," the neighbor told the young women, "are you *sure* about this?"

"Yes!" Tamara and her cousin spoke together.

Vera Kuznetsova wiped her eyes.

The neighbor spoke up. "We will wait until evening."

On the television, the "Emergency Committee" was proclaiming a ban on demonstrations.

* * *

Arbatskaya Station, Moscow; 8:37 PM, Monday, August 19, 1991:

"Oh!" Galina gasped. Someone had elbowed her as she and her friends squeezed through the Metro station that was crammed with people. Gennady gripped her hand; Terenty held on to Tamara as the four young people and Renko, the neighbor, joined the crowd streaming onto Arbat Square.

"Omigod!" The cousin's eyes went wide at the scene before them. The broad plaza was crammed with thousands of shouting, jostling citizens who were using the square as a staging area to begin their march out to the White House. Terenty tugged Tamara into the throng, followed by Gennady and Galina. Renko elbowed ahead of them through the crush of people as the crowd surged out along the broad, straight thoroughfare.

At the *'Garden Ring Road',* the streaming line of people became a solid mass of humanity. Terenty gazed about them in the fading light of dusk. "This way!" he called to the others, gesturing at an opening.

"Look at that!" Gennady pointed down a side street. A cloud of smoke, highlighted by an orange fire underneath it, rose from an overturned tram car. Even as they watched, sweating, shouting men threw timbers and lumber onto a growing pile of debris around it. Beyond it, another rail car was also on fire.

A bewhiskered, middle-aged individual with stainless-steel teeth grinned at them. "We are barricading the streets!"

Molotov cocktails—!" another man shouted as he brushed by. In the fellow's arms were Vodka bottles half-filled with gasoline; each glass container was topped by a twisted cloth stuffed into it. The foursome backed away from the man and his fire-starting explosives.

From where they stood, to Terenty, the scene seemed much more intense than what they had seen there earlier that day. Gennady looked around the jammed arena. "There must be a hundred-thousand people here, now!"

A bearded individual in a faded, tattered military uniform mounted some steps at the front of the Parliament building. Standing in the lights, his face outlined by the flickering orange glow of burning railcars, the fellow raised a megaphone and began shouting to the crowd. "Citizens!" he yelled, "all those who have courage and are willing to defend this building, come forward!" There was a movement toward the beleaguered building. Dozens, then hundreds of Muscovites shuffled past where Terenty, Gennady, the girls, and Renko were standing.

A metal-toothed old "babushka" pushed Terenty aside and elbowed her way toward the building. "Give me a *'Kalashnikov'* and I will kill them, myself!"

Another older woman shuffled forward. "Let the people live in peace!" she croaked.

As the citizen barricade grew bigger, applause and cheers swelled louder. In a few minutes, thousands of people surrounded the big white structure with locked arms, facing the crowd.

Just then, the coughing, stuttering sound of diesel engines starting up carried across the square. Heavy noises of the tanks and armored personnel carriers parked all around the crowded mall rumbled to life. Hundreds of shrieking onlookers, drawing back, became enveloped in black, choking engine exhaust as the big vehicles started moving.

People looked at each other: *Was the Army going to open fire on the demonstrators?* Tamara grabbed Terenty's arm; Gennady reached for Galina's hand in case they had to make a run for it.

Renko frowned at the lumbering tanks, then shook his head. "I do not believe they are going to attack—they seem to be pulling back."

As the tense crowd watched these maneuvers, more engine noises sounded from the direction of the Moscow River. A minute later, shining headlight beams flickered onto the nearby bridge as heavy machines came into view. *More tanks!* Two dozen of the tracked vehicles roared across the span toward the Parliament building!

But the tanks began turning about until their guns were facing *away* from the big building and those standing shoulder-to-shoulder around it! Their engines sputtered to a stop.

A trim, athletic-looking Army officer dropped from the lead tank and stepped toward the hushed, uncertain crowd that was shrinking back. "Comrades and citizens!" the man shouted, "I have been given orders to secure the building!"

An unarmed officer from the original Army group was making his way forward. He saluted the new man, who Terenty recognized as a major general. The officer turned about and strode toward the citizens standing around the White House. Another officer came up, until there were dozens of military men standing alongside the citizens around the Parliament building.

A circle of citizens gathered around the new military commander. Terenty tugged Tamara after him. "Come—we must hear this man!" Gennady, Galina and Renko followed, threading their way to the front where the man was speaking and gesturing to some citizens.

Terenty elbowed himself and Tamara up closer so they could hear what the man was saying. ". . . my friend, Yeltsin—" they overheard the man say.

A man turned to Terenty, grinning. "He is 'General Lebed'!"

Gennady listened as another new officer was speaking to someone. "We were ordered to take this building by force, if necessary—but General Lebed wants no bloodshed . . . he is well-acquainted with President Yeltsin."

Gennady turned Galina about and eased her through knots of people back to the others and relayed what he had just overheard.

Terenty stood on a curb and looked out over the gathering. From the streetlights and by the flickering orange light of the fires burning nearby, he could see that men from the original Army units who had been in position since that morning were mingling and talking with citizens and the newly-arrived soldiers. General Lebed was speaking with officers Terenty had not previously noticed. When he eased himself and Tamara close enough to read the shoulder patches, he was startled to see that they wore the insignia of *'Alpha Spetsnaz'* troops.

Terenty looked at his watch. "We must be going!" he said to Tamara. He spotted their friends nearby and guided the girl through the throng toward them.

* * *

Tverskaya District, Moscow, 6:52 AM, the Next Day; Tuesday, August 20, 1991:

Terenty and Gennady stepped up to the main entrance of "Vulkon Metallurgical School No. 6". But when Gennady tried to open the door, it was locked. Terenty pointed to a piece of paper tacked to the door frame:

-ALL CLASSES CANCELLED UNTIL FURTHER NOTICE-

The two young men stared at the message in consternation. Gennady groaned. *"Now what are we going to do?"*

Just as they were about to turn away, the door cracked open, revealing the pale face of Rodion Golubko staring back at them! "Ah, Suslov and Lychin . . . I thought I recognized your voices." The senior officer motioned for them to come into the darkened entryway.

The pair stepped past the door that the man closed in a hurry. "I am glad you are here—we need to talk." He led the way down a short, shadowy corridor to a small office. Terenty noticed that all the window blinds were drawn shut. The colonel pointed toward a couple of battered chairs. "So far, you are the only ones who have come here this morning." After the two had sat down, the trim, silver- haired officer leaned back against the edge of the desk. "With the way things are, I am relieved to see you here."

Terenty glanced at Gennady, then back to the colonel. "Sir, it is our *duty* to be here."

Just then, there came knocks from the direction of the main door up front. In a minute, Colonel Golubko returned with Grishinov, Kerebets, Blagron and Malinovsky, the four others from the group, who tugged chairs into the little room. "Well, you fellows have bolstered my faith!" Then the officer became serious. "As you know, there is much confusion, right now."

"Gennady and I were at the White House yesterday and last night," Terenty said.

"I was at Red Square," one of the others put in.

The colonel looked over his eyeglasses at the young men. "If I were you, I would leave politics to the politicians." He narrowed his eyes "I wish some senior officers had done so."

The man dug around in his coat pocket, pulled out a cigar and lit it up. "Comrades, there may be great changes in our country soon, and since we will be working together, *there are some things you must understand.*"

Well-built, blond-haired Misha Kerebets raised his hand. "Colonel . . . why is the school closed?"

"Many of our faculty are away on duties concerned with . . . 'matters'."

Terenty got the impression the colonel was measuring his words—*were some of the 'Academy's' senior officers involved with the coup?*

Dark-haired Viktor Grishinov, a talkative soldier of strong physique, spoke up. "What about the dormitory and the dining-room? We have no place to stay."

"You are allowed in the dormitory . . . and the dining-room will be open, for the time being. If you have arrangements outside, you may use those. Just do not talk about the Academy."

Andrey Malinovsky, a balding, restless, muscular young man, frowned. "Sir, how long is this 'unrest' going to last?"

"I assure you that the Academy will open again very soon."

Husky, red-haired Petr Blagron had a question. "You said there were 'some things we must understand'—what did you mean by that?"

Rodion Golubko took a long draw on his cigar and blew a contemplative puff across the room. "As professionals, our mission is to carry on without regard to politics . . . even our adversaries are the same." The colonel looked away for a moment. "In a strange sort of way, *all* military men—whatever country they represent—are like that. Or *should* be." He went to a window and lifted a blind for a moment, then turned back to the young men, shaking his head. "You may not know this, but the Soviet military is in serious trouble, right now. Our military leaders believe that Gorbachev's policies have caused a decline in the power and the influence of our armed forces, both here in this country and abroad. We still have the advantage in strategic rockets and warheads, but our ground forces are shrinking. I am told the Navy and the Air Forces are also having a hard time."

Kerebets was frowning. "Colonel, is there anything they can do about that?"

"Some of our highest-ranking officers tried to gain political influence to stop it from happening, but were unable to do so—now the country is faced with a crisis." The young men in the crowded little room were staring at the colonel as he went on. "Today was the day Gorbachev was to sign a treaty with the 'Republics' that would have been the end of the Soviet Union as we know it."

There was a general stir in the room.

"Now a group of men, including the heads of the Party, the military, the KGB and the police are trying to take over the government. There are a lot of legal questions about this, and I, for one, do not believe they will succeed." He puffed on his cigar. "I am speaking in confidence, of course."

"How will this affect us?" The question came from Malinovsky.

"Soon, I am sure, we will return to our normal duties."

Blagron raised his hand. "Sir, are we permitted to go to the barricades?"

"If you go, I would advise you to watch, only—*do not participate*—there will be serious consequences for those on the losing side." Terenty and Gennady glanced at each other: from now on, they would have to be careful.

Terenty had an idea. "Comrade Colonel, do we still have our accounts at the G-R-U store?"

"The shopping privileges continue—at least for now." He shrugged. "After that—who knows?"

"Then, could we go there while it is still . . . *open?*" Terenty looked around; some of the others had picked up on what he had meant.

The colonel gave the student-soldiers a wry grin. "Ah, now that you mention it—I believe a shopping trip *would* be a good idea—we must 'take advantage of the advantages' while we can!"

Gennady nudged Terenty as they filed into the store. "Let us get things for the girls . . . this is an opportunity we may not have much longer."

"I will buy something for Tamara's parents and the little girl!"

Later, at the guardhouse, the colonel held up his hand. "Remember to check at the main door every day for the latest information about the school . . . I am sure we will return to our regular schedule in a few days. Whatever happens—the country will survive and will need us."

* * *

Galina Gavrona stared in wonder at the French cosmetics case, the lipstick, the nail polish and the American nylons. A bulging bag on the floor held bathroom necessities. When the "student" had handed her the bundles, he had told her to sit down. "I was able to find these . . . I hope you like them." The young woman gaped at Gennady, who was sitting on the sofa beside her, grinning.

"How—?"

"Connections, my dear . . . connections."

The dark-haired schoolteacher pulled him to herself and put her lips to his.

* * *

Tamara Kuznetsova caressed the case with the tips of her fingers, not believing what she was seeing. The packages of nylon stockings the floor at her feet; little Larisa swung her new doll in her arms with a wide smile. "Terenty, this is . . . this is—" She ran out of words and flung her arms around his neck. Her eyes were brimming. "But, why . . . *how did you do this?"*

Before he could answer, Vera Kutsnetsova bustled through the archway, prompting the two young people to disengage in a hurry. When the lady saw what her daughter and granddaughter were holding, and the scattered cellophane packages of nylon hose, her eyes went wide. "Where did *these* come from?"

"There is a store near the . . . school—" Terenty handed a shopping bag to Tamara's mother. "I was able to find these for you."

The woman looked into the bag and gasped. "Soap . . . towels . . . dishwashing soap . . . even toilet paper!"

Terenty did not want her to start asking a lot of questions. "Our 'school' is not open."

The grandmother sighed. "Our school is also closed— according to the television, the whole country has stopped because of what is happening."

Tamara squeezed Terenty's hand. "The store where I work was closed when I got there—by the way, where is Gennady?"

"He is with Galina; he bought her the same things as these—except for the doll, of course!" Terenty rumpled the child's blonde hair; the little girl grinned up at him.

Vera Kuznetsova bustled toward the kitchen. "Would you like some kvas and cheese?"

Of course." He was in favor of almost anything that would keep the older woman's goodwill going.

The door opened. Galina and Gennady came, laughing, into the front parlor. "Wait until you hear what Gennady—" Galina spotted the packages and stopped in mid-sentence.

"Terenty brought me these things." Tamara motioned at the bags that were lying about.

The little one stepped up with her new doll cradled in her arms. "My mommy's friend gave me this."

Terenty gave Gennady a grin. The idea to bring gifts had been superb.

Just then, Vasily Kuznetsov came into the room, hitching his suspenders. "There is something happening at Red Square," he said. "It is on the television." The man disappeared back through the archway, returning with the television set that he lifted onto the table and plugged it up.

On the screen, a sullen-looking man was decrying Boris Yeltsin and the others in the White House. From the way he spoke, it was obvious "The Committee" still controlled the news media.

The picture then switched to the big open plaza in front of the Kremlin, where armor and troops faced crowds of citizens; the scene looked tense.

Gennady turned to the others. "We should go there." Vera Kuznetsova, just returning to the room with a tray of refreshments, spoke up. "Please do not go . . . it is dangerous."

"This is important, mother," The auburn-haired young woman looked around at Terenty and the others, who nodded.

"Then you must have something to eat and drink," the older woman insisted. If she stalled for time, she thought, perhaps she could talk them into staying put. To her, right now, Red Square did not look like a safe place to be.

As the little group sat around eating, the television cameras switched to the White House. According to the newsman, even though Boris Yeltsin was still inside the building, he had no authority. The crowd, described in heavy tones as an illegal assembly, was still massed around the Parliament building.

Terenty suggested they go first to Red Square; then to the White House.

Mrs. Kuznetsova looked agitated. "Is it really *necessary* for you to be out in all of that?"

"Those people are standing up for Russia—we must join them," Tamara said. Terenty reached for her hand.

* * *

The foursome made their way from the tram station into a teeming mass of people, all of whom seemed to be headed toward Red Square, about a half-kilometer distant. All during the bumpy, crowded ride, Terenty had been thinking about the emotional send-off Tamara's mother had given them—the woman been adamant that the young people should "stay away from trouble". And he was haunted by the crying episode little Larisa had put on. Had the child somehow understood that her mother might be going into danger? If something should happen to Tamara, he knew he could never forgive himself. More than once he had been at the point of urging that they all turn back, but he had kept his thoughts to himself as they pressed on; now it was early evening as they joined up with the crowd surging in the direction of the Kremlin.

When the young people came up to the big open space behind the Historical Museum, they were confronted by about a dozen parked tanks surrounded by citizens. Squads of soldiers stood around.

Terenty thought they looked unsure as to why they were there.

A female news reporter with a camera crew was grilling an Army officer who seemed to be in charge of the armored force. The military man's face was flushed as if he was upset about something. He spoke with fervor into a microphone the woman held out to him. Gennady glanced at Terenty; both knew that military officers were not supposed to show emotional opinions. Terenty tugged Tamara's elbow; Gennady held Galina's arm as they squirmed and threaded through the throng.

". . . fed up! You hear?" the uniformed man was saying, "I have had enough of this incompetence!"

Terenty noticed the reporter indiscreetly nodding as the officer kept talking, "Our men have no rations . . . there is no sanitation . . . we have been on the move for a day-and-a-half without rest!" The officer, whose insignia identified him as a "Tank Corps Major" wrung his hands. "Enough of this!" The man looked straight into the camera. "And you can tell the people who sent us here I said that!"

Onlookers gasped—he could face a firing squad for saying such things. Terenty and Gennady glanced at each other—should the camera swing around and catch their faces, the wrong people might recognize them! It was time to move on.

They topped the slight rise between the museum and the Kremlin wall into a sea of people massed shoulder-to-shoulder in Red Square. Many of were holding little white, red and blue "Russian Federation" flags. On their faces looks of grim determination held sway. Here, more tanks had taken up positions; their big turret guns were trained toward the crowd. To Terenty, these soldiers looked better prepared, more confident than those behind the museum had been.

The two young officers had a quick conversation out of earshot of the girls. Terenty shook his head. "I do not like the looks of this . . . there could be trouble here, soon."

"Perhaps we should go to the White House."

"Good idea." The two pushed through the throng back to Tamara and Galina, who were watching a soldier, his hat a jaunty angle, who had climbed up onto the bed of a truck and was waving a Soviet flag on a pole to cheers and whistles from the gathering. Terenty was startled to observe that the hammer and sickle had been cut from the banner. Was the "Emergency Committee" losing its grip on events?

The two couples elbowed their way back through the jostling crowd to the Metro station. In a half-hour they were once more standing in Arbat Square in a huge gathering of citizens. The surging mass of humanity moving out Ulitsa Novyy Arbat toward the seat of Parliament reminded Terenty of a glacier composed of thousands of people.

They came into the wide open space in front of the big building, where tens of thousands of Muscovites were packed together in the broad expanse. An expectant, festive air prevailed throughout the orderly throng. In the evening darkness, flickering reflections of fires at barricades all around gave the Parliament and other nearby structures a pulsating, orange cast.

Holding hands to keep from becoming separated, the foursome pushed and shoved in single file in the direction of the hulking White House. When they got closer, Terenty saw that most of the lights in the building were turned off; there seemed to be few people in the place; the soldiers and the military vehicles of the previous day were absent. Terenty turned to a man next to him. "Where are the tanks? Where are the people?"

The fellow shrugged. "Lebed's tanks left this afternoon . . . all the women in the building left a little while ago. We heard there could be an attack to seize Yeltsin!"

As they shouldered up close to the building, a man with a bullhorn appeared on an elevated stairstep. "Comrade citizens! Comrade citizens!" The crowd quieted; the man looked out across his massed audience. "Comrades! I have good news! Good news for all of us!"

"What is it?" a piercing voice called back from the crowd, to scattered laughter.

The smiling man went on, "I have been told that 'our friends', the 'Emergency Committee' have issued a curfew!" His remarks were greeted by catcalls and whistles, then the fellow again raised the bullhorn. "The 'Committee' says we must be off the streets and back in our homes by eleven o'clock tonight!" Laughter spread across the plaza, as the fellow, still grinning, once more spoke. "Will we obey these 'orders' comrades—?" There was sarcasm in his voice.

The crowd broke into laughter, with handclaps and whistling.

"We have an-hour-and-a-half to obey this order!" The fellow looked out across the swelling throng. "Are we going to listen to our 'New Leaders'?"

There came a rolling roar of derision, then applause.

"We will defend the barricades!" The man punched his fist into the air to a thunderous response.

A frizzy-haired young woman came by handing out what looked like ribbons. When she came to Terenty, the girl dropped a circular piece of cloth into his hand another into Gennady's and then to Tamara and Galina. "Armbands!" she said, going along, passing out more of the white, red and blue insignia to others. Terenty looked at the cloth piece in his hand and glanced at Gennady, who was shaking his head. Both knew that, as Soviet officers, they had no business wearing the Imperial colors. The armbands dropped to the ground. The girls had already put on theirs, as had most of the others nearby.

There was a shout, then a rising hubbub of voices. "Look!" A man standing next to Galina pointed at the Parliament building. Terenty turned about to see a balloon, at least ten meters long and five meters in diameter, ascending above the rooftop on a tether. The shouts became louder as a spotlight focused on a outsized white, blue and red Imperial Russian flag that was draped over the dirigible-shaped craft. It cleared the roof-line like some ghostly apparition and hung in the air, yawing back and forth. The bottom edges of the draped-over flag caught the light breeze and started flapping. There were more handclaps, whistles and cheers.

Terenty leaned toward Gennady and spoke into his ear over the crowd noise. "What happened to the flag of the Soviet Union?"

The same man who had earlier jeered about the curfew re-appeared on the steps out front with his bullhorn. "Comrades!" Thousands of pairs of eyes turned to look at him. "We need more men to work the barricades! Tanks are coming!" As hundreds of men began moving in the direction of the flaming barricades, the fellow again bellowed into the microphone. "Come and stand around the building!" All across the plaza, people—men and women—stepped toward the big white edifice. "Comrade Yeltsin and our country need us now!"

A bearded Orthodox priest in clerical regalia came forward and reached for the bullhorn. As the crowd became quiet, the man pulled a little black-leather prayer book from his robe, and turning toward the ranks of citizens standing guard in front of the building, in a resonant voice read aloud the "Lord's Prayer".

Tamara clutched Terenty's arm. "I am frightened, she said.

Galina pulled herself closer to Gennady. "So am I." He put his arm around Galina's shoulder; Terenty reached for Tamara's hand. The four edged their way back through packed masses of people. Bumping and jostling, they came out onto the thoroughfare, which was jammed with pedestrians, most of whom were going against them toward the White House.

Terenty cast about. "This street is too crowded—there must be a better way."

Galina pointed to the left. "There is a Metro station in that direction . . . I used to get off there when I was going to teacher's college." The quartet turned up the side street.

They were just past the United States Embassy when they came to a barricade where an overturned tram bus was piled high with lumber, ripped-up Metro crossties and telephone poles. Wooden doors and other combustibles were also shoved up against the front of the barrier. Flame crackled and sizzled around the bottom of the pile in a light drizzle of rain that was starting to fall. Terenty pulled out a folded umbrella that popped open over the two couples' heads.

Just then, a man came running toward them, waving his arms. "Take cover!" he called out.

Shouts arose from down the street where people were scurrying pell-mell toward the barrier. A runner leaped behind the barricade. "Tanks are coming!"

The long protruding snout of a big gun nosed around a building down on the far corner, followed by the green armored hull of a tank that skidded into a turn, followed by another, then several more. Exhausts billowing, the clanking column picked up speed toward the roadblock.

"Get back!" Terenty shouted, grabbing Tamara's elbow. Gennady tugged Galina toward the pile of jammed jetsam that stood across the road in the tanks' path.

As the big machines barreled straight at the barricade, a young defender jumped aboard the leading tank and tried to throw a towel over the driver's armored viewing slit. While he was doing this, the turret swung its big gun, catching the boy from behind and knocking him to the ground! As horrified bystanders screamed and shouted, the tank ran over the youth, its churning treads crunching him underneath; blood and gore gushed from the tank's sprockets and treads! As the heavy vehicle backed away, a severed hand lay on the pavement, sticking out of a sleeve. The hand's fingers were opening and closing.

One of the defenders took one look at the ghastly sight and ran to a curb, where he dropped down on all fours, retching. Others were doing the same. The two girls put their hands to their faces and screamed.

At the sight, Terenty grabbed Tamara and turned her away. Hysterical, she fell to her knees, gasping and choking. Terenty knelt down and held her.

Galina leaned over, shaking and crying. Gennady pulled her to him, cradling her head, just as another chorus of shouts arose from the barricade. The second tank had slewed past the first and was aiming for the barrier. Another defender, running in front of it, was unable to leap aside. The armored vehicle rammed him against the barricade in a clatter of falling and splintering timbers. Then it backed off, leaving the fellow crumpled motionless on the ground. As it churned in reverse, a soldier took a glancing blow from the machine and fell with a groan to the street. A squad of soldiers ran up and lifted his inert form onto the hull of the tank.

All at once, Galina went limp in Gennady's arms and sagged to her knees, moaning; the girl had fainted. He cradled her in his arms as she went to the ground; there seemed to be no end to the horrors of all this. The young man held her close and caressed her head and her shoulders; in a few seconds she shuddered all over and blinked through tears coursing down her face. "Oh, Gennady, I want to go home—"

Searing blue-white flashes and the staccato sound of rifle shots came from a nearby darkened side street. As bystanders looked on, appalled, some defenders dragged the bloody, convulsing bodies of two comrades out into the garish light of the burning barricade.

While the men stood there, some cursing in frustration, an open-top Army command car whined up to where they were. A lieutenant colonel hopped out, frowning, and was confronted at once by several grim-faced defenders, one of whom stepped forward and planted his feet in a wide stance. Hands on his hips, the scruffy-looking citizen glared at the uniformed officer. "Who are you for— Yeltsin or the 'Committee'?"

The military man looked around and shrugged. "Who the hell knows *who* I am for?" He motioned to the tank commander standing in the top hatch and at the soldiers nearby. "Get this armor and these troops away from here! Go to the White House!" The tank commander saluted. The officer got back into the car.

The big machines began treading in reverse from the barricade, followed by the loping infantrymen. The motionless soldier was still lying atop the second tank.

Attracted by the flashes and the noise, more citizens were running toward the fiery, shoved-in barrier. At the gruesome sight of the bodies on the pavement, the newcomers stopped. Some of the men took off their hats; others turned away. Several dropped flowers and petals in puddles where blood and rain mixed together and ran in rivulets down into the gutters.

Gennady, still holding Galina close to his chest, looked over at Terenty, who was trying to comfort the shaking, auburn-haired girl in his arms. "We must get out of here!"

As they stumbled away from the somber scene, Terenty glanced back. In the misty darkness, the fires cast macabre shadows onto the surrounding buildings; backlit people, outlined by the dancing orange flames, stepped about in jerky, surreal movements. He remembered his mother used to tell him about "Hell". This must be what Hell looks like, he thought.

* * *

Tverskaya District, Moscow; 8:20 AM, Wednesday, August 21, 1991:

The four young people and Vera Kuznetsova sat around the kitchen table, talking over the events of the previous night. The older woman buried her face in her hands as Terenty and Gennady told her what had happened at the barricade. "You all could have been killed!" She wiped her eyes on a napkin. The child, who had no understanding about what they were talking, sat in a chair on a stack of books, happily eating and flinging about her cream of barley with a spoon. For once, the little one's mother and grandmother did not mind the mess she was making.

Terenty caught Gennady's eye and made a slight motion with his finger toward the door. The other officer understood; they must go to the door of the Academy to see if there were any new instructions from Colonel Golubko. A glance at his watch told him it was past the time they should have checked for a message. "We will go now and take our running exercises," Terenty said.

Tamara's face lit up. "We will go with you! Galina and I need exercise, too."

Terenty shot a look at Gennady; at all costs the girls must not know the real reason they wanted to go out! He gave Tamara an indulgent nod. "Ah, but our exercise is strenuous . . . it is too soon after breakfast for you to exercise."

Galina's eyebrows went up. "Oh? Well, you just had *your* breakfast, too!"

Gennady held his hand up in a casual gesture. "Yes, but we are *used* to exercise right after breakfast—is that not right, Terenty?" He arose from the table. "We will only be gone for a short while." The young men made for the door before the others could react.

That was close!" Terenty shook his head, as they bounded down the stairs and turned toward Soyuz Novaya Zemlya Prospekt. "I hope we have not missed a message from the colonel!"

When they trotted past the entrance of the "metallurgical school," it turned out that all their efforts had been unnecessary: out of the corner of their eyes they could tell there were no messages on the door. A little farther along, they pulled up at a bus stop and dropped onto a concrete bench.

After catching their breaths, the two jogged toward the flat from a roundabout direction, to take up some time so as not to make the girls suspicious. A few blocks from the apartment, Gennady pointed at a playground. "Look at that park . . . maybe we can bring the others here."

* * *

When the door had closed behind the two young men, Galina had risen from her seat and edged around out of the line of sight of the older woman. "Come with me up to my flat," the dark-haired girl said, narrowing her blue eyes at Tamara, motioning her head toward the door. "I want to show you my new apartment." The grandmother lifted the child from the food-spattered seat.

Galina gestured toward the door. "Let us go upstairs and talk," she whispered.

On the next level, Galina closed her apartment door. "Kvas?"

The girl poured the amber liquid into two glasses. Tamara took a sip. Galina downed a swallow, fingering her glass. She looked straight into her cousin's eyes, "Tell me—what do you know about Terenty?"

Tamara's eyes widened for a moment, then narrowed. "He told me the other night on the bridge by the Kremlin that he is doing work for national defense . . . or something like that."

"Was that all he said?"

"He told me about being in the Communist Party 'to help his career,' as he put it." The girl shook her head. "Now that you mention it, he really did not tell me much."

"Exactly! Gennady said something about 'working with metals' and that he was in the 'Reserves', and that he was bound by an oath not to say much."

247

"So that brings us around to the question: 'Are they *really* going out for their 'exercises'?"

'We must find out what they are doing . . . for our own sake."

"And for the sake of my daughter."

"I have an idea—if they 'go out for their exercises', tomorrow, let us follow them!"

"We owe it to ourselves to get some answers."

* * *

The two fellows puffed into the parlor. "That was a good run!" Gennady gasped, as the perspiring pair sank into seats to catch their breaths.

The two cousins came into the room, smiling. They swung their arms around their young man's neck with a flourish and put a glass of kvas to his lips. "A drink for the exercisers!" they said together.

Larisa climbed onto the sofa next to Terenty and handed him her doll. "My doll is sleeping," she said, with childlike gravity. Tamara sat on the seat arm and leaned across the back of the sofa while Terenty stroked the doll's face and hair as the child beamed up at him. Tamara took in all this with interest; all along she had been watching his behavior toward her daughter—so far, he had passed all the tests; she would try to put aside for the moment the nagging questions she still had about him.

Gennady, wiping his face with a handkerchief, grinned at the little girl. "We saw a playground while we were running . . . how about a picnic?"

"Of course!" Tamara tossed back her head and laughed."The *'Patriarch's Pond'!* It has a children's playground!" The young mother swung off the sofa and scooped her daughter into her arms. "A picnic will take our minds off politics."

* * *

The Playground at Patriarch's Pond; 1:40 PM, Wednesday, August 21, 1991:

Tamara took a swallow of mineral water and smiled to herself. Out on the playground Terenty was pushing Larisa on a swing; the little girl squealed every time he gave her a shove. Sitting cross-legged on a sun-drenched picnic cloth, she watched as the young man and the little one enjoyed themselves. It had been a wonderful idea of Gennady's to come here, she thought; the young woman was enjoying the secluded tree-lined park, just a few blocks from the apartment. Other families and groups were gathered about on the grass and under the shade trees. In the middle of the space was the *'Patriarch's Pond'*, named after the head of the Russian Orthodox Church, who used to own this little sanctuary in the northwest part of Moscow. Squinting in the sunlight, she spotted, out among the clusters of citizens enjoying the day, Galina and Gennady, who had been off by themselves, walking toward her, swinging their clasped hands between them like a pair of newlyweds.

All at once a shadow fell across the grass in front of her. She looked up to see a fierce-looking, shaved-head, tattooed youth, wearing a black T-shirt with obscene symbols on it, pointing at her. "Fascist!" he shouted. Three others, clubs in their hands, were running in the direction of Terenty and Larisa.

"Terenty!"

The Army officer turned about just as the first *'hooligan'* ran up to him and swung his heavy wooden weapon. Terenty, reacting by trained instinct, ducked as the thick weapon came close over his head. Before the assailant could pull back for another try, Terenty did a half-turn and delivered a mighty kick with the heel of his foot on the man's jaw. The fellow's head snapped to the side and blood spurted from his nose as he spun to the ground, insensible. The club wobbled through the air and landed a few meters away.

At the same time, the first youth had grabbed Tamara's long hair in his fist and pulled her to her feet. When she tried to push him away, screaming, his club struck her a glancing blow in her side. The young mother doubled over and sagged to her knees.

Terenty charged toward the fellow, who released his grip on the girl and turned to face the enraged young fellow coming at him. In the split-second that the bald-headed attacker pulled his weapon back to strike a new blow, Terenty launched himself feet-first, catching the assailant in the chest. The fellow fell, motionless. Terenty knelt beside Tamara, who was gasping and holding her side. "Are you all right?"

She nodded through tears that were coursing down her face.

A child's cry rent the air.

"Larisa!" Tamara shouted, pointing.

Two intruders were dragging the little girl toward the trees!

Gennady dashed up and grabbed one of the abductors by the shoulders. The fellow let the child go and turned to face him. As the other youth kept tugging the kicking, screaming child by one arm toward the nearby woods, the assailant swung his club at Gennady, catching him on the shoulder. Stunned, he spun around as the fellow hauled back for another blow.

There was a blur of motion. With a moan the man fell to the ground on all fours. A thick club struck him again on the side of his head, sending him sprawling senseless onto the grass!

Galina dropped the wooden weapon and leaped to Gennady, who was leaning over, dazed.

There came a shout from some distance away. Terenty, runnng after the fourth man, caught up to him just as he reached the edge of the woods with the little girl. The would-be kidnapper took one look at the charging defender and let go the crying child. Before he could turn about to flee the fray, Terenty landed a right on the fellow's jaw. With a groan, the bald male fell backward onto the grass, not moving.

Terenty knelt down to the hysterical child. Tamara ran up and pulled the little girl to herself; the two hugged each other and cried.

Just then, a pair of policemen huffed up. "We have been looking for these fellows!" one of them said, hauling the moaning man to his feet. By now, more officers were handcuffing the other three. "Skinheads!" he said in disgust, "they have been terrorizing this neighborhood . . . we believe they are Chechen sympathizers."

"Chechens!" Gennady blurted out, surprised. "I remember how—" He stopped, realizing he should say no more.

"These hoodlums have been assaulting citizens and kidnapping children." The man looked at Larisa, who had calmed down in her mother's arms. "Especially *younger* children, and holding them for ransom. Some were killed when their parents could not afford to pay."

Tamara gasped and pulled the little girl closer to herself.

The officer glared at the sullen prisoners. "Well, we have everything under control, now.It was fortunate we were already in the area." The man tipped his hat.

Tamara shuddered. "I want to get away from here!" The others nodded in agreement. In quick order, they gathered their picnic things and headed out of the park

"Who are they?" Galina asked, "and why did they attack us?"

"Probably Chechens trying to break away from the Soviet Union," Gennady spoke up. "They are violent people." *Deadly violent. That day in Grozny he had been the only Soviet soldier to survive the rocket attack on the troop carrier. Were the separatists bringing the violence to Moscow?*

They came upon a small Orthodox church. "We must light candles of thanksgiving!" Galina tugged Gennady up some stone steps toward the front door "I used to come here with my mother when I was a girl."

"This church was *open,* back then?"

"Some were allowed to be open. This church was one of them."

In his entire life, Gennady had never been inside a house of worship. "I do not know what to do in a church."

Galina pulled on the door handle. "We will give thanks that we got away from those awful men."

When their eyes had adjusted to their surroundings, they saw that they were at the rear of a little wooden, peaked-roof structure; icons of saints reposed in alcoves; an elaborate altar with an Orthodox crucifix took up the far end; the aroma of incense permeated the place. Larisa pulled her arms around her mother's neck.

251

Galina put her hand on Gennady's shoulder and guided him toward an altar of candles just inside the front doors. Terenty followed Tamara in silence. She took a lighted candle and lit another one in a holder with it. Galina did the same. Both girls stepped back, made the sign of the cross, and clasped their hands together.

Gennady, looking confused, glanced at Terenty, who was gazing up at the images.

"I greet you in the name of our Lord and Savior," a man's deep voice came from nearby. "I heard you enter." A garbed, gray-bearded priest stepped up. "Can I be of service to you?"

"We are giving thanks for—saving us from danger." Galina measured her words.

"I—see." The priest looked in turn at those in front of him. "In these difficult times, the Heavenly Father will protect us if we believe it so."

Terenty, who long ago had heard those same intonations in church with his mother; knew what the priest meant. But the man's words made no sense to Gennady, who stole a look at Galina, then at Tamara. The two cousins were standing with their heads bowed; their eyes closed; their hands clasped together. In the dim, yellow candlelight he could see their lips moving. The little girl's arms were around her mother's neck. Even though all this was a complete mystery to him, Gennady could not deny that their recent escape from the skinheads had been miraculous. He was always in favor of whatever worked; maybe there was something to this "religion" thing, after all.

The cleric faced the little group. "I bless you in the name of the Father, the Son, and the Holy Ghost." He made the sign of the cross in the air. "May the Saints be with you."

Terenty fumbled around in his pocket and dropped a coin into an ornate box by the door. Galina glanced at Gennady; in a few seconds his own coin clinked into the container.

* * *

When they trooped into the flat a short time later, Tamara's father met them at the door in a state of excitement. "Can you believe it? It looks like the coup is about over!"

"What!"

It is on the television, right now!"

The black-and-white receiver was set up on the kitchen counter. Terenty pointed at the screen. "Look! There is the *old* newscaster!" The familiar middle-aged man who had done the news for many years was back on camera. "What happened to the news-people who were supporting the coup?"

Vasily Kuznetsov turned up the volume. ". . . are reported fleeing Moscow," the television man was saying. The scene switched to Red Square, where an enormous Imperial Russian flag, covered with flowers, held aloft by the people, was snaking around the plaza.

"We must go there!" Tamara burst out.

Her mother turned to her, frowning. "But you said you were not going there, any more."

"Look at those people—those are happy people."

The newscaster was speaking. "The members of 'The Committee' are under arrest!"

Someone handed the man a piece of paper. "Boris Pugo shot himself today, and is dead . . . his wife is in a hospital."

Pugo! The unpopular Interior Minister, who had crushed an uprising earlier in the year in the Baltic States, was, according to the report, now dead by his own hand.

The newsman leaned away for a moment, then turned back holding a note. "Kryuchkov of the KGB and Defense Minister Yazov are under arrest!" Someone handed the man another paper that he scanned over. "Now to the Parliament Building, where President Yeltsin is to about to speak . . ."

The scene dissolved to a podium where a dark-haired man was standing. The camera panned across an audience seated in a big room; the man grasped a microphone. "Comrades! I present the President of the Russian Federation, Comrade Boris Yeltsin!" The lawmakers rose to their feet, cheering and applauding as the familiar, white-haired leader came up. He clasped his hands over his head, grinning, as the applause went on, then he motioned for quiet.

"Comrades and citizens!" he spoke in a clear voice, "I bring you great news!" A murmur ran through the assembled multitude, then he went on, "The coup is crushed!" Cheers rang out, then the smiling speaker went on. "I spoke with Comrade Mikhail Gorbachev and he is safe. He will be returning to Moscow later today! The traitors are all under arrest!" Everyone was applauding. The leader motioned for quiet. "That is not all, comrades . . . Boris Pugo shot himself and is dead! The chamber became quiet as the President again spoke. "The conspirators tried to flee Moscow, but were caught before they could escape. They are being brought back to face charges!" There was more applause. "I proclaim the end of the illegal censorship that was imposed by the criminals . . . I have ordered all troops to return to their barracks."

Tamara's father switched off the TV. His daughter, her eyes shining, arose from her seat. "We must go to Red Square!" She turned to her mother, who was not speaking. "Is this not exciting?"

"But things are uncertain."

Galina touched Gennady's arm. "I believe we should join the celebration."

Tamara's father spoke up. "Let the young people have their fun," he said, nodding at his wife.

* * *

When the two couples alighted from the tram near the Kremlin, crowds of people were surging toward something that was happening behind the Metro station. Gennady motioned to the others. "Let us see about this!"

When the four rounded the corner of a building, they saw a snaking line of tanks and other military vehicles that were roaring away, stirring up dust and gray-black exhaust smoke.

Terenty stopped an applauding, whistling bystander."What is happening?"

"The troops are going back to their barracks!" The fellow grinned as he waved at green armored personnel carriers rumbling past. Many of the crewmen waved back. Up on a battle tank, its commander stood in the turret hatch, smiling at the bystanders, many of whom were throwing flowers at the big machines. Other military men clasped their hands over their heads. Terenty noticed one tank man in particular whose cigarette kept falling out of his mouth every time he grinned. "The siege at the White House is over!" the soldier shouted.

This is exciting!" Tamara called up at a tank driver as his machine clattered by.

For some time they stood there, along with the thousands of others who were celebrating the evident end of the coup.

"Come on!" Galina tugged Gennady's shirt-sleeve, "We must go to Red Square!" They turned in the crowd and pushed their way toward the Kremlin, whose walls and towers loomed over the nearby buildings.

"Look at all these people!" Tamara shouted as they came up onto Red Square. Thousands of laughing, dancing, singing citizens were jammed into the vast expanse; to Terenty, it seemed that there was hardly any room to breathe. Out in the middle of the throng, a white, red and blue Russian Federation flag, that looked to Terenty to be thirty meters long, undulated above hundreds of people who were holding it up over their heads. As the foursome elbowed their way closer, they could see that bunches of flowers had been tossed onto the enormous banner.

Galina tapped her cousin's shoulder. "We can help them hold up the flag!" The two squirmed through the humanity to the edge of the huge banner and grabbed the edge of it, joining the dancing flag-bearers as the symbol of change wove its way around the jammed plaza. Shouts and singing filled the air alongside the Kremlin's brooding brick ramparts.

When the girls had moved off, Terenty and Gennady held back, remembering Colonel Golubko's admonition to not get involved in the demonstrations.

After some time, Tamara caught sight of the young men and nudged Galina. "There they are!" she shouted. The two let go the banner and made their way back to their companions.

"We must go to the White House!" Terenty said above the noise of the crowd. It took some time for them to make their way back through the throng—more people were coming up all the time. When they again came in sight of the Metro station, it was getting on toward dusk.

They found themselves in the rear of another crowd that was moving in a direction that seemed to be headed away from the station. Gennady turned to a shabby-looking older man who was hobbling along on a lame foot, holding a crippled arm. "Where are all these people going?"

"To *'Dzerzhinsky Square'* . . ." the bewhiskered fellow croaked; his eyes watering as if he had a fever, "for revenge!" Gennady glanced at the others, who were staring askance at the man's cadaverous face and his mouth of green and silver teeth. "The K-G-B killed the others—" His ulcerated lips twisted into a sneer, ". . . but I never told them what they wanted to know—not what they *really* wanted to know!" He gave a lopsided grin, revealing several stained gaps in his metallic mouth; with a drawn-out moan the man pulled his threadbare jacket close around his shoulders and shuffled off into the shadows.

"Something is happening at 'Dzerzhinsky Square!" someone called out.

Galina pulled Gennady's hand. "Let us follow them!"

The foursome fell into a moving mass of citizenry that came into the open space. One side loomed the notorious yellow facade of *'Lubyanka Prison'*, long the headquarters of the KGB; its orange bands at the roof-line enveloping the big building like a structural strait-jacket. Everyone knew about the prison beneath the square, where hundreds of thousands of people had been held, tortured and killed over many decades. Now the edifice looked down on a scene of shouting, gesturing citizens who had gathered in the center of the lighted space around the hulking gray statue of 'Felix Dzerzhinsky', the founder of the "Secret Police".

From somewhere, came the sound of glass breaking and shouts along nearby streets. Terenty nudged Gennady. "We had better go now to the White House."

A half-hour later, they were once more pushing their way out through shoulder-to-shoulder pedestrian traffic toward the seat of

Parliament. When they got there, they found themselves in yet another dancing, laughing throng gathered around the lighted White House. Above it, fluttered the Russian Imperial flag.

"This is wonderful!" Tamara exclaimed, squeezing Terenty's hand, as the dancers passed by, waving and singing.

After they had watched the crowds for a while, Galina stifled a yawn.

"Perhaps we should go back to the flat."

"We must get up early in the morning and exercise," Gennady put in.

Tamara and Galina glanced at each other.

* * *

Tverskaya District, 7:15 AM, Thursday, August 22, 1991:

Terenty nudged Gennady, who was wrapped in a blanket on the parlor floor of the Kuznetsov apartment. "We must get up," he let out in a groaning whisper to the other young man. They had planned to leave the flat, make their run to the door of the Academy, and return before the others stirred. The two pulled on their shoes, tiptoed to the door and went out.

As soon as the fellows had closed the front door, two female faces peeped around the edge of the archway. "They are gone!" Tamara said in a dusky voice.

"It was a good idea to set our alarm clock," Galina whispered. *"Now we will see where they are really going!"* She pulled open the door and peered out. "No one is in sight!"

The two made their way down the stairs to the front entrance of the apartment building. When they came out onto the sidewalk, Tamara grabbed Galina's sleeve. "There they are!" She pointed at a pair of receding figures on a sidewalk two blocks away, rounding a corner. The young women crossed the street and dashed down the sidewalk after them. But when they ran around the corner, they skidded to a halt, their eyes wide. The fellows were only a few dozen meters ahead of them! The two ducked into some tall, thick bushes next to the sidewalk and held their breaths. Peering through the branches, they watched as Terenty and Gennady jogged down to the middle of the next block, then trot up a couple of steps and through a doorway. Above the traffic noise came the faint thud of a door closing. Galina looked at Tamara and made a "come-on" motion. "Let us see where they went!" In a minute they were standing in front of a concrete building whose outer wall was part of the fence-line. Behind the structure were some dense woods.

"'Vulkon Metallurgical School Number Six'—" Galina read aloud from a sign next to the door.

"They said they went to a 'metal school' and this looks like it."

"I want to know more about this place—are you with me?"

Tamara nodded.

Galina pushed on the door. To her surprise, it yielded to her touch. After a quick look-around to make sure no one was watching them, the two young women stepped up into the murky interior of "Vulkon Metallurgical School Number Six"!

-18-

Colonel Golubko snapped his fingers. "I am not certain I locked the front door!" The two younger men followed as the officer re-traced his steps back through the leafy tunnel into the shop building.

Rounding a corner, he was astounded to discover two females standing in the dim hallway.

"Oh!" A young woman with reddish-brown hair gasped, putting her hand to her mouth. A slender, short- haired brunette stood next to her, wide-eyed.

The middle-aged man glared at the intruders."Who are you? Why are you here?"

"I . . . we—"

Just then, Terenty and Gennady stepped up behind the Colonel. "Terenty!" the first girl blurted out.

The older man turned to the younger officers with a thunderous expression his face. "Do you *know* these two—two?"

"They are . . . friends," Terenty stammered, his face turning red, "but I do not know how they got here."

"Please, sir," Tamara's eyes were welling with tears, "it is all our fault . . . we just wanted to know where they were going." Gennady was appalled; Terenty's face was ashen—if the two girls had gone any farther into the place their very lives would have been in grave jeopardy. Because of what Tamara and Galina had done, the young mens' futures and even the colonel's career might now be seriously at risk.

The man in plain clothes frowned at the two young women, then at the civilian-dressed men under his command. "Suslov . . . Lychin—you will escort these *'females'* from here at once. This is a dangerous place!" The jagged blue vein stood outlined on his temple.

"Yes, sir; right away, sir." Gennady took Galina's arm; Terenty nudged Tamara toward the exit.

"You will meet me here in the morning at *'oh-eight-hundred'*." The older man gave Terenty and Gennady a significant look. "We will talk." He shoved the door shut with a loud click.

Just then, there came the pounding of jackboots. Two guards in battle gear with automatic rifles quick-timed up the corridor. When they spotted the older man in the gloomy half-light, they drew up short and saluted. "Colonel, sir, the alarm light for the outer door was on, and we were coming to investigate."

"Yes . . . the door *was* open—I was just letting out two of my officers after a brief meeting with them concerning the—resumption of school. Since they did not go any farther than this office, they did not activate the chip sensor."

"Everything is all right, then?"

"The situation is normal." He nodded in a gesture of dismissal to the young men, one of whom had been the sentry who had shot Pavel a few days ago. "Thank you, corporals, for your prompt attention." The guards saluted and turned about.

The colonel decided to not tell General Putridchenko about any of this; he would handle the matter of the foolish young women and their consorts, himself. And he was becoming aggravated by the way Suslov and Lychin kept running afoul of procedure and drawing attention to themselves. First, the intruder the guard shot a few days ago had had their names on his person; now this. The two were otherwise fine officer material and had promising futures, but somehow they were going to have to get these misdeeds under control or they would not last long in this program.

As he strode back through the verdant passageway toward the guardhouse, it occurred to him that he had not seen General Putridchenko since the start of the coup. Unusual—the "Chief of Security" always kept a high profile. The officer walked across the campus to the Security Office at the rear of the main building and went inside. "Is the general in?"

"No, colonel, he is not." The major on duty looked perplexed. "In fact, I have not seen General Putridchenko for some days, now."

Rodion Golubko went outside with a feeling of unease—the general's unexplained absence was out of character for the normally punctual officer. As he made his way back across the

Academy grounds, a startling thought came to him: *Had Semen Putridchenko been involved with the coup?* He recalled their conversation of several evenings ago over drinks when the Security Chief had hinted about a possible *'putsch'* in the near future. Had the general known more than he was letting on? Had he already thrown in his lot with the plotters? Had his remarks been a subtle suggestion to join him? If that had been the case, it was his good fortune he had not done so, given how things had turned out.

* * *

Outside, the four young people shuffled up the sidewalk without speaking. Terenty and Gennady were seething; Tamara was breathing in gasps; Galina brushed back tears—Gennady was squeezing her elbow. At the corner, she stopped and pulled her arm away from him. "All we wanted was to find out where you were going!"

"Can you not trust us?" he shouted back at her above the traffic noise.

Terenty fumed at the girls. He was torn between maintaining the secrecy of the Academy and telling them more than he perhaps should. "The 'metal school' is a dangerous place," he said, "it has all kinds of cutting saws, and lasers and electric wires all over the place—you could have been cut by the blades or electrocuted!"

When they reached the apartment, the tension between the Army men and the young women was still high. "I am not ready to accept this 'explanation of yours!" Galina glanced at her cousin, who was glaring, then back to Gennady, "I believe we deserve to know more!"

Gennady closed his eyes; this was not going to be easy. "We are involved in important national security work that we cannot talk about . . . we work with 'special' materials . . . in the future, our military forces will take these materials on actual missions. That is all I can say."

Tamara frowned at Terenty. "But why was the man at the school so angry at us?"

Terenty looked straight at her. "Because you were only a few seconds away from being shot dead!" Both girls sucked in their breaths; their eyes went wide. "Just beyond you were armed guards with orders to shoot to kill! In fact—" Terenty held up; nothing would be served now by divulging what really happened to Galina's late boyfriend, Sergei, and to Tamara's now-dead former husband, Pavel, ". . . in fact, we may be in trouble at the school, now, because you went there."

Larisa, in her night clothes, came into the parlor holding a little blanket. Still half-asleep, she climbed up onto the sofa and lay back, blinking. Tamara sat down beside her and stroked her hair. "Are you ready for breakfast, sweetheart?" The little one nodded, sucking her thumb.

Terenty, still appalled at what had happened, caught Gennady's eye. The other young officer let out a long breath. This had indeed been a close call.

They were just taking their seats around the table when Tamara's father bustled into the small kitchen. "Gorbachev is back in Moscow!" He turned on the television set.

When the picture popped onto the screen, the General Secretary of the Communist Party of the Soviet Union was shown making his way down a set of wheeled steps from an airliner. A crawler on the bottom of the picture told that the event had happened several hours earlier, in the middle of the night, at an airport outside the city. To Terenty, the haggard-looking man wearing casual clothes, his form outlined by the inky blackness of the night against the white airliner, looked more like a tired tourist than the supposed leader of the whole country. Then Gorbachev's wife—who looked to Terenty to be unsteady, perhaps unwell—appeared at the door of the jetliner. Holding onto the shoulder of a young girl, she took some time to descend the spindly stairsteps. As flashbulbs seared the scene, the balding man in the light-colored jacket, managing a wan smile, stepped down onto the glistening tarmac where a battery of floodlights had been set up. Both the airliner and the contrasting black pavement glistened in the glare of the lights—it had been raining. One-by-one, Gorbachev's family and some men who Terenty guessed were probably his aides, came to the bottom of the steps.

Mikhail Gorbachev steadied his wife by her elbow, then, following after her, ducked into a waiting limousine. In a few minutes the procession of vehicles moved off into the darkness.

The announcer came back on the screen. "The General Secretary says he is again in control of the nation and will meet with President Yeltsin later today."

Vasily Kuznetsov patted his wife's shoulder. "I am sure the country will survive all this."

Terenty had an idea. "Since the schools are still closed, how about all of us going to the circus?"

Tamara brightened. "I have never taken Larisa to the *'State Circus'*."

"I am ready to get away from all this!" Galina spoke out, to the agreement of the others.

* * *

When Rodion Golubko returned to the officer's quarters, the soldier at the front desk handed him an envelope. The colonel tore open the cover, pulled out a piece of paper and read the handwritten message:

Colonel Golubko,
Come to my office at once.
Important.
Antonin Krolov
Colonel General
Commandant

Frowning, the officer stuffed the missive inside his shirt pocket and once more crossed the Academy grounds to the main building. What is *this* all about? Had the general already found out about the incursion into the building by those two idiot females? Would he have to once again try to defend Suslov's and Lychin's follies? These and other thoughts crowded into his mind as he knocked on the outer door of the Commandant's office.

A major opened the door and saluted. "Ah, Colonel Golubko . . . the general is expecting you." The younger man stood aside to admit the colonel to the ornate office.

At the far end of the gilt-trimmed, high-ceilinged room, the Commandant, in civilian clothes, returned the colonel's salute, then motioned for him to take a seat. "I suppose you wonder why I summoned you here," the stocky man said, lighting his pipe. General Krolov took a few puffs, sending an aromatic blue cloud over his head, then lifted a piece of paper from his desk. "I have here a report from the Soviet General Staff's *'G-R-U Counter-Intelligence Directorate'* that implicates General Putridchenko in the coup!"

Colonel Golubko sat up straight. "I am not completely surprised—"

The general's eyebrows went up. "Explain what you mean, colonel."

Rodion Golubko recounted the conversation with Semen Putridchenko in the apartment.

General Krolov leaned forward, frowning. "Did you not find his remarks to be—shall we say—strange?"

Yes, but this was *before* the coup attempt."

"That is true." While Colonel Golubko fidgeted, the Commandant scanned the General Staff's report, puffing his pipe between clenched teeth; its crackling seconded by the ticking of a wall clock. The officer handed the paper across the desk. "Colonel, I have an assignment for you,. I want you to find out all about General Putridchenko's activities. You have my permission to go through his office, his quarters—everything. It is urgent that we determine his involvement in the conspiracy."

"Yes, Comrade general."

"One more thing . . . do not tell anyone about this." The general stood. "Handle this matter without delay."

Colonel Golubko saluted, did an about-face and left the room.

The officer walked to the security director's nearby suite and approached the major at the front desk. "I want all the keys to General Putridchenko's office and his living quarters."

"Sir, the general told me not to allow—"

"I am acting on orders from Colonel General Krolov!"

The young man was perplexed. "I must confirm this," he said, lifting the telephone receiver. After a short conversation, he rang off and reached into a desk drawer. "I am very sorry, sir, but I was under orders not to let unauthorized persons into the general's office and quarters."

"That is fine, major, you are just doing your job."

Inside the Security Chief's office, using the keys, the colonel rifled through Semen Putridchenko's private files, cabinets, papers, and documents; even tapping the walls for hidden panels.

But after two hours, he had to admit that if the Ukrainian had committed any crimes, the man had concealed the evidence. Rodion Golubko picked up the telephone receiver on the big wooden desk, dialed a number and spoke some short sentences into it. Then, pocketing the keys, he walked back to the outer office. "Do not let anyone else into General Putridchenko's office," he told the major at the front desk. "I will return the keys, later."

When Colonel Golubko stepped inside Semen Putridchenko's private quarters, he gave a start of surprise—the place had been ransacked; piles of papers and other items were strewn about; drawers and contents of emptied shelves were on the floor. He shook his head as he recalled the well-kept place where he and the Director of Security had talked just a few nights earlier.

The officer pulled back furniture; tapped on walls; looked for a tell-tale seam; listened for subtle changes in the pitch of his knocks. But after some time, the colonel's search through General Semen Putridchenko's jumbled belongings had turned up nothing incriminating.

Then, as he rapped along the wall behind where a bookcase had stood, there came a hollow sound and an empty feel to his knock—it seemed there was an open space behind it. A close look revealed an almost-invisible, square-shaped seam enclosing a wallboard space about a half-meter in area. Using a kitchen knife, he worked the blade down along the narrow, tell-tale line.

All at once the section came loose. Pulling aside the piece, he saw a small safe on a ledge behind it. "Aha!" the colonel muttered to himself. The gun-metal strongbox was surrounded by cables that would prevent its discovery by metal detectors. A wire-shrouded storage battery, probably a back-up power source, was next to it.

Now he would find out if he had remembered his Spetsnaz safe-cracking techniques. Easing the wires back and away, he cocked his ear and turned the knob-dial until he detected a faint *"click"*. Then, back the other way to another tiny click. Then another. He recalled that this type of safe used *four* turns, instead of the usual three. Sure enough, halfway into the next rotation there came a *"snap"* inside the mechanism, as if something had loosened, along with a slight movement of the stainless-steel handle. With a groaning creak of hinges, the dusty door swung aside.

The colonel reached inside and pulled out a handful of papers. Even as he scanned the first sheet, he saw it was just what he had been looking for. He sat down in a stuffed chair and began reading about Semen Putridchenko's role in the coup. As he followed down the pages it became evident that the Academy's Chief of Security had been tapped by the plotters to assassinate Boris Yeltsin in his White House office, using his familiarity with their security people to gain entrance At the bottom of the message was the signature of a KGB mid-level functionary whose name he recognized. When he held up the paper to the light, sure enough, there it was—a faint "KGB" watermark.

With a start, the colonel realized that the assassination attempt was set for this very evening at the Parliament Building when Mikhail Gorbachev would also be there!

On the pages, a sordid picture of the Academy's security director began to unfold. From the papers, it was obvious that General Putridchenko for some time had been feeding information to Chechen rebel warlords about Soviet military plans. As he read along, Colonel Golubko swore under his breath; based on this evidence, the general's damnable treachery had caused the deaths of hundreds of Soviet Soldiers down there. Colonel Golubko was surprised that the general had been so indiscreet as to have kept the records of payoffs to him from the breakaway region's leaders in his own safe; without a doubt, the man had either never expected anyone to ever find them, or he had forgotten them in his hasty departure.

There was more. In a separate bundle were messages from the same individual at the KGB to General Putridchenko showing that the Intelligence agency had found out about his Chechen connection and had blackmailed him into joining the KGB-backed coup against Gorbachev.

The colonel had a grim grin at this information. Given the KGB's usual policy of killing off such operatives after their usefulness was over, General Putridchenko had probably extended his life by going on the run. How long it would take the spy agency to track him down, however, was another matter; in any case, the man would have to look over his shoulder for the rest of his life—however long or short that might be.

Then he remembered the papers General Krolov had given him. He pulled the folded sheets out of his pocket and set them alongside the Putridchenko papers. The contents were similar; somehow the GRU had discovered the Security Director's perfidy and had passed along the information to the Commandant. How interesting, the colonel thought, that the General Staff's Intelligence Directorate had caught their rivals, the KGB, red-handed in the plot against the General Secretary! Someone over there would pay plenty for those indiscretions. Kruychkov, the KGB's head, reputed to be one of the main conspirators, was already under arrest; who else at the agency would be brought down?

When the colonel arose from the chair, he noted it was the same one he had sat in several evenings ago when he and the now-fugitive General Putridchenko had drunk copious quantities of Vodka and talked about anti-government plots and coup attempts. How ironic, he thought.

He remembered that Semen Putridchenko in his earlier days had been a champion pistol marksman. The colonel went to a closet rack where the general had once showed him his collection of handguns. There, an empty, dust-free slot in the cabinet was mute evidence that a pistol had recently been taken from the space. The missing weapon's label described it as a *"Walther PPK"*.

Colonel Golubko realized that should the general carry out the assassinations of Yeltsin and Gorbachev, the results would affect not only the Soviet government but its relationships with other countries. At all costs Semen Putridchenko had to be stopped tonight before he could get into the parliament building.

Based on this information, Rodion Golubko timed his encounter with the traitorous general for five minutes past ten o'clock that evening.

* * *

South Moscow, 9:28 PM, Thursday, August 22, 1991

I liked the animal acts best!" Tamara reached for Terenty's hand as the two couples and the little girl came out onto the street from the big tent-like concrete building of the *'Moscow State New Circus'*.

Terenty was carrying Larisa. How about you, little one?"

The child put her arms around his neck."I liked the clowns!" He ruffled his hand through her hair as the troupe stepped along toward the nearby Metro station. Ahead were several transfers before they reached the apartment near Soyuz Novaya Zemlya Prospekt in the near-northwestern part of the city.

At the Arbatskaya Station, they alighted and went outside; it would be some time before the connecting ride came along. Galina pointed across Arbat Square at some people who were making their way out Ulitsa Novvy Arbat. "Let us go to the White House!" She looked at a timetable on a nearby poster. "The last train is at ten-forty; we have time to go there."

* * *

At that moment, a half-dozen blocks behind the White House, Rodion Golubko alighted from a Moscow taxi and stepped away into the shadowy darkness that was only relieved by a street light here and there. Looming above the treetops up ahead was the enormous lighted bulk of the Parliament Building.

He looked at his watch; if Semen Putridchenko was as punctual as he usually was, he would be there right on time. Since the White House's security people already knew and trusted the Academy's Director of Security, the colonel knew the general could talk his way into the building with ease—if that were to happen, there would be no time to sound an alert—he would have to brazen his way past the guards to stop the man, himself.

* * *

The young people came onto the plaza that fronted the gargantuan white building. A good-natured, late-evening crowd milled about; it looked as if everyone wanted to be a part of the now-historic place over which the Russian Federation flag was flying; the tri-color banner waving in the breeze seemed to symbolize the great changes now taking place all across the vast country. According to reports they had seen on the television, inside the building at that very minute, Boris Yeltsin and Mikhail Gorbachev were discussing many of those changes.

As they stood there, Gennady noticed a figure lurking near the side entrance, some distance away. The individual was pacing back and forth in the shadows with his hands in his pockets; he kept looking up and down the sidewalk and at the building. Once, when he turned in the direction of the young men for a moment, Gennady's eyes went wide. He nudged Terenty. "Look!" It is General Putridchenko! What is *he* doing here?"

Terenty recognized the Academy's Security Director, who was in his dress uniform. The two stepped around to the girls' other side and discreetly gazed over their shoulders at the strangely-acting man.

"There is Colonel Golubko!" The two watched as the trim man, dressed in plain clothes, strode toward the pudgy general.

Rodion Golubko stepped up to the man and touched his shoulder."General Putridchenko!"

The other officer whirled around in surprise. "Golubko! What are you doing here?"

The colonel narrowed his eyes at the other man. "*I found the strongbox in the wall*. . . I know everything about you—about the

'Chechens' . . . about the 'K-G-B '. . . about your part in the coup. It is all over, general—you must give yourself up!"

The senior officer blanched, then pulled a pistol from underneath his medals' sash; Colonel Golubko felt the insistent muzzle of the Walther's silencer pressing into his stomach. The general looked right into the other man's eyes. "Do not make me shoot you, colonel," he spoke in a guttural voice through clenched, nicotine-stained teeth.

Rodion Golubko nodded toward a nearby thicket. "You will get nowhere with this."

The uniformed senior officer glanced sideways; for the first time he saw the armed guards who were in position around the building; all had blended into the background with subtle presence.

Colonel Golubko smirked. "For your information, Gorbachev is *not* in the building—we warned him to stay away."

Semen Putridchenko's eyes bulged. "You lie!" His chin quivered. "Yeltsin and Gorbachev are meeting here, tonight."

"I assure you that *'Comrade Mikhail Sergeevich'* is not in this building—or, shall we ask one of these guards?" Rodion Golubko could feel the silencer trembling against his stomach; the general's hand was shaking. The colonel moved his hand. "Just give me the gun and everything will be all right."

Across the way, the younger men stared transfixed as the two older officers seemed to be having an intense discussion that Terenty and Gennady could not follow because of the intervening distance, the darkness and the crowd noise.

All at once, Semen Putridchenko, scowling and shaking his head, turned and ran off. The colonel started to follow him, then stopped as the other man disappeared into the night. Putting his hands in his pockets, Rodion Golubko walked away.

Gennady gaped at his friend. "What do you make of that?"

Just then, Galina spotted the two young men a short distance behind herself and Tamara. "We should be getting back to the Metro, unless we want to walk home!"

With Terenty once more carrying Larisa, who was now sleeping, they made their way back to the station just in time to catch the last ride home for the night.

At the door, Terenty handed the child back to her mother. "We shall stay tonight at the—the 'metal school'." He swallowed, having again almost given away the name of the Academy, "we have a meeting early in the morning with the man you saw."

A disappointed look crossed Tamara's face.

"We will return as soon as—"

The auburn-haired girl put her free hand behind his neck and put her lips to his.

* * *

"Taxi!" Two-hundred meters behind the White House, Semen Putridchenko stepped from the curb, his hand upraised, waving. When the cab slid to a stop, the general jerked open the door and dropped inside. "To the *'Kievskiy Station,'*" he told the driver, puffing. As the yellow-colored taxi pulled away, the military man turned about; no one seemed to be following him. He leaned forward. "How long will it take us to get there?"

The driver glanced back. "A few minutes . . . not much traffic this time of night."

Semen Putridchenko felt in his breast pocket; the ticket was still there.

As they rode along, he pulled off his uniform tunic and wrapped the officer's hat and the sash in it. From a pants pocket he pulled out a brown beret and adjusted it on his head, taking care to cover his graying, combed-over hair.

The vehicle made its way across the bridge over the Moscow River. In minutes, the taxicab pulled up in front of the blocks-long train station that was lighted from end-to-end. After paying the driver, the man stuffed the rolled coat under his arm and walked in a hurry to the public locker where he had earlier stashed the luggage bag.

Pulling out the case, he stuffed his tunic with the sash and the hat wrapped in it into the locker; by the time any pursuers found it, he would be out of Russia. Looking around, he located a nearby public restroom. In a stall, the man pulled out a razor and dry-shaved his head, then his mustache; flushing the hair down the toilet. After a quick change of clothes, the now-bald-headed man with the clean-shaven face picked up his valise and went back outside to another locker. There, he pulled out another pre-positioned travel bag and put the one he had been carrying inside it. The man clicked shut the metal door and set the lock and with a deep breath of relief and satisfaction—along with a new appearance and a complete change of wardrobe he even had a new name: forged papers now identified him as *'Leonid Efimovich Retchko'*.

According to the "Departure" board, the train would pull out at midnight. The man with the new look and the new identity went down to the platform level and located the train to Kiev that was already loading by the tracks. He showed his ticket to a conductor, who pointed to a compartment car in the middle of the train.

As he stood there talking to the train official, another man was lurking in the shadows, watching and waiting for him. But the agent did not recognize the general in his new guise as he walked right past him to the railcar.

In a few minutes, when the train began moving, the man, frowning, squashed his cigarette with his shoe, stepped into a nearby red telephone booth and made a call.

* * *

8:02 AM, Friday, August 23, 1991:

Colonel Golubko leaned back against the.edge of the wooden desk in the small classroom; his arms crossed. "Now, I want to know about those females who were here, yesterday."

"Comrade Colonel, sir, they are two girls we met a few days ago," Terenty said.

Gennady swallowed. "They are decent people; they—"

"They came very near to being shot!" The blue vein stood out on the colonel's temple.

"Yes, sir . . . we have told them it is a dangerous place." Terenty was downcast.

"They do not know what actually goes on here?"

"We told them that we go to a 'metal school.'"

"You should know that the G-R-U was preparing to pick them up for questioning!"

The young officers looked at each other, dismayed. "Sir, we—" Gennady gasped.

Rodion Golubko lifted his hand cut him off. "Since I had left the door unlocked—this time, *only*—I will accept some responsibility for a mistake . . . *their* mistake, you must understand."

"Yes, Comrade Colonel."

"You are about to embark on a very rigorous training régimen that will take you away from *women*—do your 'female' friends know that?"

"We have discussed it with them—in general terms."

"Your 'Special Forces' training will begin Monday at oh-eight-hundred . . . the country will go on, as will the Soviet military. The Imperialists must not be allowed to take advantage of us."

The two young officers let out deep breaths; it was time to get back to work.

There is something else I think you should know . . . Marshal Akhromeyev was found dead this morning in his office—a suicide!"

"What!" Terenty's jaw dropped. "When he spoke to us last week, I was very impressed by him."

Gennady's eyes were wide. "Why? How? He seemed to be an honest man."

"Perhaps, but there was some evidence he was at least sympathetic to the coup—he left a note that he thought the country was being ruined; he could not bear to see everything he had worked for all his life be destroyed."

A long pause filled the room.

Colonel Golubko broke the silence. "I will see you here on Monday morning. And say your farewells to your friends—you might not see them again for a long time."

* * *

273

Tverskaya District, 9:10 AM, Friday August 23, 1991:

As Tamara deposited the breakfast dishes into the kitchen sink, there was a knock at the hallway door. Vasily Kuznetsov returned a minute later with their neighbor. "Comrade Renko is here!"

He offered a chair at the table to the man. Vera Kuznetsova set a cup of tea in front of him.

The visitor stirred the hot drink. "Have you seen the television this morning?"

"No, we have not—is something going on?"

"Just the overthrow of the K-G-B!"

Vasily Kuznetsov turned the switch; in a matter of seconds the television picture blossomed up. A male newscaster stared into the camera. ". . . the statue in Dzerzhinsky Square came down a short time ago. Toppled by young men who climbed onto it with ropes and pulled it over."

The screen cut to a report. The big statue of the founder of the "secret police" stood with ropes draped around it. Around *'Iron Felix's'* neck a crudely-lettered sign proclaimed in Russian: "The Junta is Finished". The lines tightened as a truck-tractor pulled on the big burnished brass figure. It leaned forward for a few seconds, wobbled, then pitched onto its face on the ground. The cameras cut away to cheering men whose arms were upraised. As the little group in the kitchen watched the televised scene, a crane picked up the statue and lifted it onto a flat-bed truck.

Renko sneered at the screen. "Maybe they can put it in a graveyard for statues!"

Tamara left the room; in a minute she came back with Larisa. The little girl was wearing a blouse Terenty had bought for her at the G-R-U store that went with her pleated skirt and canvas shoes.

"My, you look pretty, this morning!" her grandfather said. The child looked up at him with a grin and wagged her turquoise-rimmed sunglasses back and forth on her scrunched nose.

"We will be back in about two hours," Tamara said, reaching for her red canvas purse, "we are going to *'Gastronom Number*

One'." With a wave from the little girl, the young mother and the daughter stepped away, holding hands.

For a while the two men sat the table, drinking cups of tea and talking about the political developments taking place in the country. Russian Federation President Yeltsin had finally had his meeting with Mikhail Gorbachev at the Parliament Building; the white-haired one had forced the reluctant General Secretary—the President of the Soviet Union—to read aloud the names of the eight main conspirators to the skeptical parliamentarians. Gorbachev had personally selected all of them; now, they had turned against him.

"It looks as if the power is now going over to Yeltsin," Tamara's father said. The television image they had just seen of Boris Yeltsin pointing his finger at a cowed-looking Mikhail Gorbachev on the stage in front of hundreds of jeering lawmakers was fresh on his mind.

"Comrade Mikhail Sergeevich is finished," Renko put in.

Just then, there was a knock at the front door. Terenty and Gennady came in.

Vasily Kuznetsov motioned toward chairs. "Sit down, boys! You remember Comrade Renko, of course." The men shook hands.

Terenty looked around. "Where is Tamara?"

"She has gone to the market—'Gastronom Number One', they call it—the big one down on *'Tverskaya Ulitsa'*. She took Larisa with her."

"How long will they be gone?"

"She said she would be back in two hours." He looked at the clock. "They left a half-hour ago."

Gennady spoke up. "Is Galina in her apartment?"

"I am sure she is . . . she had breakfast with us, earlier."

Gennady excused himself and left.

Renko was staring at the television screen. "Turn up the sound," he said, frowning.

". . . are looking for four escapees from a police wagon." The announcer was in mid-sentence. "Authorities say the missing men—described as 'shaved-head hooligans'—may be part of a Chechen terrorist group . . . this morning, as the four were being

275

taken to a detention center in the Tverskaya District, they overpowered three guards, took their weapons and ran off."

Vasily Kuznetsov, his forehead creased, turned down the sound. "Did not Tamara and her friends encounter hooligans the other day? I hope those men who escaped are not the same ones!"

Terenty did not like what he was hearing. "I am going to look for Tamara!" he said, pushing back from the table.

In the corridor, he realized he could use reinforcements; he would ask Gennady to go with him. The young man took the stairs two-at-a-time. At the fifth level he rapped on Galina's door.

The girl peeped out, then opened the door, patting her hair. "Terenty . . . !"

He gave her a wry grin and looked into the room. "I hate to disturb this lovely moment, but I need Gennady to go somewhere with me."

His friend came up behind her. "What is happening?"

"Perhaps nothing . . . perhaps everything." He told them about the escapees.

The dark-haired cousin put her hand to her mouth. "Oh, my God! Those awful men—*escaped?*"

"I am not sure if they are the same ones, but I want to go look for Tamara. Larisa is with her."

Galina went for her handbag. "I am going with you!"

-19-

In a few minutes, the three were making their way past a crush of people into the bustling, Moorish-looking marketplace. Terenty looked around at the garish emporium, jammed with rows of items of all description. He called out to Galina over the hubbub of people in the surging marketplace. "Is *this* where Tamara goes shopping?"

"She comes here often . . . even with the shortages, this place has nearly everything."

Terenty looked about for the auburn-haired young mother and her daughter. "Then, where *is* she? I do not see them."

After jostling up and down the crowded aisles, they still did not discover any sign of the two. "Perhaps they went outside," Gennady suggested.

The three elbowed their way back to the main entrance. Looking up and down the sidewalk, Galina spotted a red canvas handbag on the edge of the dusty sidewalk down the way. She tugged Gennady after her. "Tamara has a purse just like that!"

When she picked it up and drew it open, the girl gasped. "It *is* Tamara's purse!" She pulled out an envelope addressed to her cousin. "This proves it!"

Gennady picked up a pair of stepped-on sunglasses from the sidewalk and matched the two turquoise halves together, frowning. "Did not Larisa have sunglasses like this when we went on the picnic, the other day?"

Galina took the broken, child's-sized frame from Gennady; her eyes wide. "Oh, my God! I gave these sunglasses to Larisa for her birthday!"

Terenty felt as if a hammer had struck him in the chest; his mouth all at once went dry. As he stared at the scuffed, red-canvas purse and the child's shattered sunglasses, the implications were obvious. "Something has happened to them!"

Casting about, Terenty spotted a security guard standing in the crowd of shoppers milling about on the sidewalk. His face flushed with anxiety, he elbowed his way over to him."Please, sir . . . a friend of ours and her little girl are missing."

"'Missing', you say?"

Terenty told the man of his fears for Tamara and Larisa.

Galina came up with the handbag and the broken sunglasses. "We found these on the sidewalk," she said, "they belong to them."

The detective motioned toward a door. "Come with me!" Inside a small, cluttered office they described Tamara and Larisa while the man took the information down on a form. "What were they wearing?"

Galina thought for a moment. "When I had breakfast with Tamara his morning she was wearing jeans and a pink T-shirt with a red 'kiss-lips' design on it. She always liked it. She thought it was funny."

The man's eyebrows went up. "Do you not think it might be considered by some to be—shall we say—*'provocative'?*"

"She would never think of it that way."

The detective shook his head. "There are those who would, unfortunately."

A sinking feeling came over Terenty. He knew the man was right—a pretty girl wearing something like that would be irresistible to some unsavory types of men.

"How about the little girl ... what was she wearing?"

Galina shrugged. "I did not see her, this morning. Sorry." The others also shook their heads.

The man lifted a telephone receiver and spoke some words into it. "I have asked assistance from Moscow police." He stood up. "Let us go back outside and look around ... perhaps we will find a clue, or something." The officer led the way to the front sidewalk. "Look for anything else that belonged to them. I will ask around ... perhaps someone saw something suspicious."

But when the three young people and the man re-grouped at the front door some minutes later, none of them had anything to show for their efforts.

A blue and white Moscow police car swept up to the curb and a plainclothes officer got out, brandishing a badge. The policeman and the house detective huddled in conversation for a minute, then came over to the others. "This is 'Inspector Samosky'," the security man said, as the police detective nodded,

"I gave him the information and the evidence; he will take over the investigation."

The new man scanned the sheet. "When was the last time you saw these subjects?"

Galina bristled. "These 'subjects' are my cousin and her daughter . . . I saw Tamara, this morning."

Terenty and Gennady glanced at each other. "We have not seen them since last night."

"I see." He looked up and down the sidewalk and at the mass of shoppers milling around the front of the big market, then turned back to them. "People do not just drop their purses and sunglasses on the sidewalk, then vanish—I am sorry to have to say this, but it looks like they were kidnapped."

Terenty paled as the man went on. "We will secure the area where you found the items and question some people." He returned to his car, spoke into a two-way microphone, then came back. "Does the subj—does the 'woman'—have any enemies? Do you know of anyone who would want to harm her?"

All three shook their heads and shrugged. Galina wiped away tears with her hand.

Terenty remembered the television report about the escapees. "The other day we had a run-in with some bald-headed men—" He told the officer about the encounter at Patriarch's Pond.

The detective's eyebrows went up. "Yes, I remember that report . . . they are the same ones who escaped this morning!"

"You think they might be the ones who took—" Terenty did not want to finish the sentence.

"That would be a possibility. They escaped not far from here."

Gennady snapped his fingers. "Perhaps they recognized her and decided to take revenge!"

Terenty clenched his fists; Gennady's idea made sense.

Samosky looked at the hopeful faces before him with a feeling of pity. "Let us try to find them soon," he said. *If the Chechen criminals follow their usual pattern, they will demand a ransom, then kill them.*

"How soon will we know?"

"The laboratory will analyze these things; perhaps we will find useful fingerprints or other clues. Return to your homes and we will work on this." He put the handbag and the glasses in evidence bags.

* * *

12:40 PM Friday, May 23, 1991:

On the sofa Vasily Kuznetsov held his wife close to him. "Vera . . . I am sure they are doing all they can—" His voice quavered.

Gennady held Galina; the dark-haired girl had not stopped cying ever since they had told the older people about what had happened.

Terenty paced the floor, slapping his hands together. "I cannot endure this!" The young man picked up a picture of the mother and child and stared at it.

There was a knock on the door. Renko and his wife came into the room. "We heard what happened!" the man said. The woman embraced Tamara's mother.

As the afternoon went on, other neighbors from the apartment building came by; some brought food. An older woman from down the corridor set a tray on the kitchen table. "You must eat!" Terenty tried to sample a homemade blintz, then set it down; he was not the mood for a meal right now.

Galina excused herself, then left. Upstairs in her flat, the girl lighted an incense candle and prostrated herself before an icon of Saint Peter. After a while, Gennady wondered about her and went up to her apartment. When he pushed on the door, he found it was not completely closed. Easing inside, he saw her on her knees in a darkened corner before her simple altar, tears streaming down her cheeks, her silent lips moving as she fingered a string of prayer beads. He stood there a moment without making a sound, then backed out and went downstairs.

When he got there, Inspector Samosky had just arrived. Gennady went back up to Galina's flat where he tiptoed in and touched her shoulder. "The police are here."

280

"... new information," the detective was telling the anxious little gathering in the parlor as they came in, "when we interrogated the people at the market, several told us they had seen people matching the subjects—excuse me, the woman and the child—with some bald-headed men at the sidewalk. One of the men had the child in his arms. The witnesses said they did not seem to be going willingly."

"Did anyone try to help them?"

"No one wanted to get involved . . . one woman said she thought at the time it might be a family matter of some sort."

Terenty wrung his hands. "Did anyone see where they went?"

"They were last seen going up the sidewalk toward *'Pushkin Square'*."

Terenty gave a start. "'Pushkin Square'! That would be in *our* direction—we went by there on our way to and from the market!"

The investigator read down a paper in his hand. "The laboratory found fingerprints on the sunglasses lens that matched one of the fellows who escaped this morning."

"Then they *did* recognize Tamara and Larisa and decided to kidnap them! If they are somewhere around Pushkin Square, then we must look for them!"

"Our officers are searching the area, now, but it will take time. There are a lot of buildings in that neighborhood."

"We must help them!" Gennady looked around at the others who were nodding.

"There is one more thing. We know for sure that the escapees are involved with a cell of Chechens that carried out the recent apartment bombings in the city."

Terenty motioned to the officer to step outside into the hallway with him. In the corridor, he closed the door and looked at the man for a long moment, then spoke in a low voice. "My friend and I are in training for 'Special Forces'. I want the truth."

"The *truth?*" Samosky glanced up and down the corridor; no one was overhearing them. He went on in a whisper. "Those kinds of people—those *'terrorists'*—will stop at nothing." He shook his head. "We will do what we can, but—" The plainclothes officer shrugged. "Sorry."

"But is there not *something* we can do to help?"

"You may come with us and join the search."

They went back to the others. "The police want to know if we can help them in the search."

"You can go along with officers as they look through the neighborhoods," Samosky put in.

Gennady looked at those gathered around. "I am ready to get going," he said.

Terenty and Vasily Kuznetsov nodded in assent; Renko did the same.

"Let us now go," the Inspector said. Leaving the women, the men bounded down to the street where Samosky motioned to a waiting police car.

At Pushkin Square, a plain-clothes officer tugged open the car door. "We have found nothing," the man, whose name-badge identified him as "Restov", told the Inspector.

"Thank you, Lieutenant." He introduced the four newcomers to the officer. "These people are friends of the missing woman and child. They will walk with your men."

Restov called to several nearby investigators who came over to Terenty and Gennady. With the two other men, they broke into search parties and made off down side streets lined with rows of three and four-story apartment buildings.

When they came back at sunset, no one had anything new to report. "We talked to many citizens," the man who had gone with Terenty said, "but no one has seen anything unusual." The other men reported the same.

"We will keep patrolmen on the beat, here, tonight," the Inspector said, "let us meet here again at eight-o'clock in the morning."

Terenty was agonized by the thought that Tamara was being held against her will—perhaps close to where they were at that very moment! "I will keep looking here, tonight..."

Gennady nodded. "I will do the same."

Samosky held up his hand. "Conserve your strength—it may take some time to find them." *The prospects of finding them alive now in the hands of the Chechens are very small.*

After the investigators had left, Terenty and Gennady headed back toward the square. "This is a nightmare," Terenty's voice broke, as he and his friend shuffled along. He kept looking up at lighted apartment windows, hoping to see a silhouette or some other evidence of Tamara. After a while, the two young men were almost the only people still on the street. "I guess we better go back to the apartment," he said, "the policeman was right about getting some rest."

With one last despairing look around at the now-empty sidewalks and at the shadowy apartment rows, the two friends made their way up Tverskaya Ulitsa.

* * *

6:58 AM, Saturday, August 24, 1991:

The two young men, Tamara's parents and Galina sat around the kitchen table, trying to eat some of the food that the neighbors had brought them the day before. The samovar on the counter gurgled; everyone wanted hot tea to try to clear their bleary eyes after a sleepless night. "I never thought a cheese blintz would make a breakfast," Terenty mumbled, idly stirring the cup before him, as he took an indifferent bite.

The grandfather turned on the television. In a half-minute, when the picture came up, a newscast was just starting The man on the screen was saying that Gorbachev and Yeltsin would share power, and that they had purged some top officials of the Communist Party and government ministries. As the announcer read off a list of those who were now gone and their replacements, their pictures flashed on the screen.

Terenty squinted at the photographs. Gennady shook his head. "I do not recognize any of them except Yazov." He remembered how impressed he had been when the Defense Minister had spoken at the Academy the week before. Now, the same "Marshal of the Soviet Union" who had once directed the country's entire defense apparatus was sitting in a jail cell—an accused conspirator.

The man was reporting that three Baltic States had just declared independence. Vera Kuznetsova switched off the television. "The country is coming apart!" she declared, her voice breaking, "while my daughter and granddaughter are lost . . ." The veins in her thin neck stood out. Then she slumped down into the chair and put her hands to her face; her shoulders heaving.

Terenty pushed his chair from the table and stood up. As Galina reached for her handbag, her eyes fell on the little framed photograph of the missing young woman and her daughter. On impulse, she dropped it into the purse.

Thirty minutes later, at Pushkin Square, Inspector Samosky and Lieutenant Restov hailed them. "We have found someone who may have information," the Inspector said, walking up to them. "A woman says she recognizes the suspects from the police pictures we showed her . . . she says she has seen them around the neighborhood, but is not sure where they live."

Terenty let out a breath. "That narrows it down. If we just knew *which* flat was theirs'."

Restov looked down his nose at the young man. "But it may not be *their* apartment . . . they may be transients staying there for a short while on their way to somewhere else." To the others' questioning looks, he went on, "If they are who we think they are—'terrorists'—then they move around a lot. These 'cells' have a constant parade of people in and out to try to confuse the authorities." The man shrugged. "That makes it difficult for us."

Galina looked at the detective. "What can *we* do?"

"Walk the streets; ask people questions—everyone is trying to do the best they can."

She pulled out the little photograph from her handbag. "I brought this picture of my cousin and the little girl."

Samosky squinted at the two in the framed picture, then handed it over to Restov. "Make copies of this and hand them out. Put them on poles, on fences; everywhere." After the lieutenant had left, the inspector turned back to the others. "We must now get started."

Terenty went off with Samosky toward a row of flats on a side streeet; Galina and Gennady headed out from the square on a different slant. Other officers scoured the neighborhoods in other directions, showing everyone they came across pictures of the criminals; asking questions. Lieutenant Restov returned with a boxload of the picture of Tamara and Larisa. He handed them out to the others.

"Tape these on poles, put them in shop windows; ask lots of questions."

The investigators and the missing mother and daughter's relatives and friends trudged about in a widening circle from where the two had last been seen. By now, the story had made the evening television newscasts; the picture was being beamed all across the city. In mid-afternoon, Tamara's parents tottered to the scene and dropped onto a Metro bench, where they sat, holding on to each other in a daze as the search efforts went on.

At nightfall, there was still no sign of the young mother and child. Terenty, frantic from worry, lack of rest, and from having eaten hardly anything for two days, was about at the end of his endurance.

"You must go and rest," Inspector Samosky told the distraught young man.

Terenty shook his head. "I must keep trying . . . *we must keep trying—*"

Galina touched his shoulder. "Come . . . we must let the police handle this; we can all be back in the morning, if they have not found them by then." She hoped he had not noticed the tears on her face.

"Take these people to their homes," Restov told a policeman, motioning at a squad car.

* * *

6:40 AM, Sunday, August 25, 1991:

Lieutenant Restov looked around at the glum little knot of friends and relatives of the missing pair gathered on the corner across from Pushkin Square. "We will make one more pass through the neighborhood; after that, we will have to conclude they are—somewhere else."

"You would *give up?*" It had never occurred to Terenty that the police would put a time limit on the search.

Galina turned away, hot tears stinging her cheeks. For the first time, she had to confront the possibility she might never again see her cousin and niece. Gennady put his arm around her shoulder.

"We will try to resolve this today." Samosky looked uncomfortable. "I know how this sounds but I assure you we will pursue the search in other ways, should it become necessary."

"*What* other ways?" Terenty could hardly speak

"Forensics, undercover methods."

"That is a death sentence!" The young man clenched his teeth. "We all know *that* would take so long they would never—"

"Let us make one more search . . . perhaps someone in the neighborhood saw the picture and remembered something. We will certainly try."

"Then, let us get going."

The little groups branched off as before and began combing the neighborhood; showing the picture to residents; asking questions.

It was late morning as Gennady and Galina were trudging down a back street when the girl happened to look up—and did a double-take. "Stop!" she said hoarsely. Galina grabbed Gennady's arm and pointed up at a third-story window on the backside of the apartment row. "Look at that T-shirt hanging outside the window! It looks just like the one Tamara was wearing when she disappeared!" `

Waving in the light breeze was a pink pullover with a "kiss-lips" design on it!

"Are you sure?"

Galina gave a vigorous nod. "Yes!"

Gennady grasped her hand and ran with her toward the main street. Looking about, he spotted one of the police officers of the search detail. They huffed up to him and gasped out what they had seen.

The policeman frowned. "You are positive it is the same shirt?"

"It is just like the one my cousin was wearing—it must be some kind of signal! They must be up there!" She was speaking so fast the officer could hardly understand her.

The man spoke some words into his portable radio. "Samosky is coming right away!"

The Inspector and Restov ran up. Stumbling over their words in haste, the young people told the detectives what they had seen.

"All right, we will first evacuate the lower floors . . . *quietly,* so as not to tip-off the people in the top-floor apartment what is happening." He said some words into his pocket-sized transmitter, then officers began knocking with a light touch on residents' doors on the first two floors. One-by-one, the dwellers came out, some wondering what was happening, and were led away. A block off, the officers explained what was happening to the questioning citizens.

"I *knew* there was something strange about those people!" one lady neighbor declared, as officers huddled with them, "every time I tried to be friendly, they glared back at me!"

"It seems like the people who live there keep changing."

Two squad cars of policemen drove up. Inspector Samosky directed the reinforcements into positions inside doorways, on rooftops and behind stairwells. "Now it will be a waiting game!"

Before long, four bald-headed young men, all wearing black pull-over shirts, came down and got into a car out front. They drove about two blocks in the direction of Pushkin Square, when all at once four police cars shot out of a side street and cut them off! With a screech of tires, the out-of-control vehicle bounded up onto a curb and buried its front bumper in some shrubbery.

The four passengers jumped out and started to run, but changed their minds when an officer fired a shot over their heads. The suspects stopped; their hands went up. "You will not get away this time!" Restov hissed. More policemen ran up. "Shackle these subjects!"

Inspector Samosky pulled a flier out of his pocket and compared the pictures on the information sheet with the men before him. "These are the escapees, all right!"

The officer gestured to Terenty and Gennady. "Come with us—we may want you to make an indentification."

The two detectives, with other officers and the young men, crept up the staircase to the third-floor landing. When they came to the suspect's door at the top of the stairs, the plainclothesman held up his hand. "Wait here!" he mouthed. Three men stood shoulder-to-shoulder in front of the door; their handguns at the ready. On a hand signal, the three men rammed the door with their shoulders. With a splintering crash, the door burst into a living room.

A female wearing a scarf on her head backed away, her hand groping for a handgun on a table behind her. A young auburn-haired woman was tied-up in a nearby chair, gagged and blindfolded. A little girl was lying on a sofa. The child's eyes were closed; she was not moving.

Lieutenant Restov grabbed the woman and spun her arms behind her. With a couple of "clicks" the detective snapped handcuffs on her wrists and twisted around the sullen suspect to face a pair of uniformed officers who tugged her toward the stairwell.

Tamara!" Terenty bounded into the room and spotted the trussed-up auburn-haired young woman in the chair. He rushed up and pulled the blindfold from her eyes.

When she recognized him, she closed her eyes that filled with tears. In another second, the gag came off. "Terenty! Terenty!"

One of the officers whipped out a pocketknife and sliced the ropes binding her. As soon as she was free, she stood up, grabbed the young man and held him in a tight embrace. Then she spotted the little girl lying on the sofa. *"What did they do to Larisa?"*

The child blinked as Tamara picked her up; she seemed to be groggy. "Probably they gave her some sort of sleeping medicine," one of the policemen said.

Galina ran into the room and flung her arms around her cousin. As the officers stood by, the two and the child, now awakening, had a cry; Terenty and Gennady held them.

"How did you put the T-shirt outside?" Terenty asked, when Tamara could speak.

"I told the girl I was hot. She untied me and I took off the T-shirt and put on this sort of wrap-around sheet." The young woman looked down at herself with a grin. "The sheet is actually hotter than the T-shirt, but she never knew it! When she untied me for a while, she said that if I tried to escape, she would kill Larisa, but it would not have made any difference since the door was locked from the outside." Later, when she went to sleep by accident, I hung the shirt outside the back window. She never noticed it was gone and I was hoping you would recognize it."

"Thank goodness, I did!" Galina said.

"I was tied-up most of the time." Tamara left the room to put back on the pink T-shirt.

When she came back, the Inspector was again talking on his pocket transmitter. "We shall inform your parents that we have found you and have arrested the suspects," he said.

As forensic investigators began arriving with their equipment, the detectives and the others went back downstairs to the outside; Galina carried the still-sleepy Larisa.

"May we go, now?" Tamara looked at Samosky, "we have not eaten since yesterday."

"If we need you for further questioning, we have your address."

Looking across Pushkin Square, Terenty spotted a golden-arched sign on the opposite corner. "When I was in America, I used to eat at a place called *'McDonalds'* . . . a very popular place. Right over there is their Moscow restaurant." He offered her his arm. "Tell me . . . have you ever had a cheeseburger and fries?"

* * *

7:22 PM, Sunday, August 25, 1991:

Tamara's mother and Galina were clearing the kitchen table; a number of the residents of the building, including the Renkos, were there to celebrate the safe return of Tamara and Larisa from the clutches of the kidnappers.

"I saw on the television what happened, and we came here right away." An older man with a mustache, who lived on the first floor, grinned as he swirled a glass of kvas.

"We recognized your picture," his wife put in.

"How fortunate you were able to hang your shirt outside the window," Renko's wife said.

The little one bounced on Terenty's knee while Tamara, sitting next to him, told how she and her daughter had been grabbed on the sidewalk just as they were about to go into the food market; how the men had forced them to the apartment; about being tied up, blindfolded and gagged for hours at a time during the whole experience; the hypodermic injections that made her drowsy and put Larisa to sleep for two days; how they had threatened to kill them both; tricking the abductors' young woman accomplice into letting her take off the T-shirt on the pretext she was overheated; about the rescue. At one point, through the open window, she had actually heard Galina and Gennady talking to each other on the street below, but was unable to cry out because she was tied up at the time, unable to pull the gag from her mouth.

There was a knock at the door. Inspector Samosky came in holding a sheaf of papers in his hand.

After introductions, he spread out the sheets on the table. "When we captured those fellows and that woman, we broke up a Chechen cell that was already responsible for several criminal acts in Moscow, including the recent apartment bombing." The detective glanced up; the others were staring at the pages. "In the flat, we found the names and addresses of other Chechen cells here in Moscow. We have already rounded-up several more suspects; police in other cities are now on the lookout for others." Noting everyone's rapt attention, Inspector Samosky went on. "From information we found, it looks as if they were preparing to invade a crowded theater and blow up themselves—and maybe hundreds of innocent people."

The investigator glanced at Tamara. "If the young lady here had not been kidnapped, forcing us to find her . . . then many people might have been killed!"

Terenty put his arm around the shoulder of the auburn-haired girl and pulled her close to him.

She reached up and put her hand in his. "But why did they kidnap Larisa and me? Why *us*—and no one else?"

Samosky gave Gennady a look. "Your friend's theory that they recognized them and decided to grab them for revenge was probably correct."

"Would they have really harmed them?"

"They were terrorists—anything would have been possible." The Inspector gave a satisfied smirk. "One more thing: they have all been taken to Lubyanka, where they will *never* get out."

* * *

10:27 PM, Sunday August 25, 1991:

Galina Gavrona gasped; her eyes were wide. "Tomorrow? You are going away—*tomorrow?*"

"With all the worry about Tamara and the little girl being missing, I did not want to say anything. But we are being called back to the school for 'advanced training.'"

The girl shook her head. "No! You cannot do that!"

Gennady leaned back and pulled Galina to him. The young man stroked her hair, her face; her neck; her back; caressed her shoulders. "We will be going away for a while."

"Away? For how long?" Her voice sounded thin.

"I am not sure." He felt the girl's tears starting to drop onto his shoulder; the mounds of her chest pressed onto him as she breathed; her wet eyelashes batted against his cheek.

"How much I am going to miss you." He fingered the fine hairs at the nape of her neck.

"You will miss me?"

"More than you could ever imagine."

"What will you be doing?"

"We have been assigned to Special Forces."

Galina raised up. "But you said you were not 'military'."

"When we went to talk to that man you saw . . . he told us we have to report in the morning to start the training I told you about."

Gennady pulled her once more against him; as the two held a lingering, wet kiss; he ran his fingers down the inside of her T-shirt; the little hooks came loose; he began to ease the garments upward toward her shoulders.

The girl shook her head. "Not here . . . not now—please . . ."

He drew back and looked into her face.

Her head moved from side-to-side; she tapped the end of his nose with her fingertips."Not until I am married."

* * *

"She is so beautiful," Terenty whispered. In the shadowy darkness of the bedroom he and Tamara looked down at Larisa, reposed in relaxed slumber in her bed; her arm around her new doll. Terenty ran his fingertips through the little one's fine blonde hair "So different from last night." He put his arm across the young mother's shoulder. "I was afraid I would never again see the two of you."

Tamara looked into his face, reached up and entwined her fingers in his. With a motion she tugged him into the hallway, under the archway and out into the front parlor. "Hold me . . ." she whispered, pulling him down beside her, "hold me close." She dropped off her shoes and tucked her feet underneath herself, then leaned against him; her arms around his neck; her warm breath on his ear; her luxurious auburn locks draping over their faces. A tear, followed by another; then a steady flow dropped onto his shoulder. "While I was in that awful place," she whispered with a shudder, "I thought I would never see you again, either . . ."

Terenty turned Tamara's face to his and kissed her, tasting the salty tears that were running down her face; caressed her hair, her neck, her shoulders.

He drew back and took a deep breath. "There is something I must tell you."

The girl tossed her long, reddish-brown hair over her shoulders. She saw in the dim light that he looked serious. "Is something wrong?"

"I suppose you could call it that." He looked straight into her eyes. "We have to report tomorrow morning—for 'advanced training.'"

The girl shook her head. "I do not understand."

"We have been assigned to train with 'Special Forces'."

Tamara's eyes were wide. "You are *leaving?*"

"We will train in the Moscow area at first, but after that, we may be gone for a while."

There was a gasp from her, then more tears welled-up. "I cannot endure for you to be gone!" She put her hands to her face.

"I will write you often, and I am sure there will be times we can see each other." He leaned back and drew her down to him. "It will not be forever."

In the darkened room, as her tears fell onto his shoulder, his eyes wandered across to the dim outline of the arch—the entryway that seemed to symbolize all the things that had happened since they had met less than a fortnight ago. His mind went back to that first night when the beautiful young woman had spun under the archway into the room wearing her party dress; the barefoot dancing; Tamara coming softly into the parlor and kneeling down to him, her long, auburn hair falling over his face; the little girl turning and waving over her grandmother's shoulder at him as they passed through the archway; all the times when Tamara had stepped with her easy, fluid stride underneath the curved opening with a smile for him.

A dreadful sadness came over Terenty. To where would he travel—and how long would it be—before he would ever again see that archway, the child, and this young woman?

~~~~

PART THREE

THE CARTEL

-20-

Kiev Station, 9:20 AM, Monday, August 26, 1991:

"Kiev!" The train conductor's strident voice came from the corridor of the railcar. "Leonid Efimovich Retchko" raised the curtain and looked out at a passenger platform slowly parading past his private sleeper-compartment window; a glance at his watch told him it was already mid-morning in the capital city of his native Ukraine. With a lurch and a rumbling squeal of brakes, the *'Moscow Express'* shuddered to a stop. The *incognito* "General Semen Putridchenko" patted his inside coat pocket to make sure the new identification papers were there and reached for his hand luggage.

The stocky, bald-headed man dropped to the platform and moved along in a bustling crowd of other passengers toward the main terminal.

After clearing local Customs, using the new identity documents, he stopped at a red telephone booth and made a call. After a short conversation, he stepped back out and made his way toward a line of taxis outside the building.

* * *

KGB Headquarters; Lubyanka Square, Moscow, Wednesday, August 28, 1991:

Livshits read the summary report, frowning. That traitor, Semen Putridchenko, the man who he learned had tried to assassinate Yeltsin, had vanished; a development that could adversely affect his own career. Since all the exits from Moscow were being monitored by trusted agents, the missing general wanted for complicity in the plot must still be in the city—but where? Probably in hiding; afraid of what the old Kremlin crowd, now back in conrol of the situation, could do to him. He must be found.

With Kruychkov, the former KGB boss, under arrest as the alleged mastermind of the aborted coup, he knew that if he could bring the Putridchenko affair to a quick and successful conclusion, he could be in line for advancement.

'The Deputy Intelligence Officer of the Moscow Directorate' reached across his desk for the scrambled-line telephone. "Livshits, speaking . . . I am assigning myself to the 'Putridchenko' case. A pause, then, "Yes, I will have full control. Tell 'The Committee' to meet me here in half an hour."

* * *

Nigerian Embassy; Madrid, Spain, Tuesday, September 10, 1991:

The very dark-skinned man leaned back in the leather chair and regarded Retchko with the coldest, most impersonal eyes the white man had ever seen. "You say you are a 'Soviet Major General'?"

"Yes, that is true—but I also knew some 'coup leaders', so it was necessary for me to leave the Soviet Union." Retchko handed over his new, inflated credentials to the African.

While the Nigerian read down the pages, the Academy's former "Security Chief" looked about the room. A nameplate reading, *'M. Adwadube, Assistant Legal Attaché,* faced outward on the desk; diplomas and other documents with the man's name hung around the walls. Above the two men a lazy overhead fan was having little success in moving around the humid Madrid air. Retchko pulled a handkerchief out and wiped his bald top. The lawyer seemed to be taking a long time reading the documents. *Did he suspect that they were actually forgeries?*

At length, the man put down the papers. "Tell me, general— why did you come here?"

"I was told you wish to establish a 'security division' in your organization. That is my specialty."

"How did you know about us?"

"I have . . . ah, 'Chechnya' connections. I advised their 'security apparatus' on methods of apprehension and interrogation. They gave me your name."

"You did all that from *Moscow?*"

"I operated outside of the 'usual' channels.

"You were involved with Chechen rebel warlords?"

"I would prefer to call it *'realistic activity'.*"

Adwadube shook his head. "I must say, general, you have no scruples."

"Scruples?"

"It means you do not give a damn about what you do to other people." The Nigerian reached for the telephone. "It also means you are probably the very man we are looking for."

* * *

INTERNOL Headquarters, Geneva, Switzerland; Thursday, September 12, 1991:

Tarliani squinted through his bifocals at the first report from the new agent in Lagos, Nigeria. The individual, who had been recruited at great risk, had just passed to the Agency new information about the crime organization that INTERNOL had learned had been set up in Nigeria. The decoded missive stated that the venture involved hijacked oil, smuggled weapons, nuclear materials, computers, secret bank accounts, extortion, and some other things about which the agent had heard rumors but had not yet been able to confirm. The airport at Lagos kept coming up, the message said, but its role was unclear. "Chechnya", "Madrid", and "Tanuta" were also somehow connected—but so far, the agent had not been able to determine how they fit into the scheme. In addition, a Soviet individual would soon be involved, whose identity was, for now, a mystery. To the Chief Inspector, it looked as if the international police force was facing a criminal Cartel whose tentacles already extended worldwide.

* * *

299

Murtala Mohammed Airport Lagos; 8:21 PM, Sunday, September 22, 1991:

As he came down the stairsteps from the airliner, Lagos's soggy humidity hit Retchko like a steam bath—before he had even made it to the tarmac his clothes were already sticking to his pudgy bulk from the rivulets of sweat rolling down him..

A very black middle-aged man, dressed in a white shirt and khaki pants, stepped up to him. "Retchko?" His eyes bored straight at the newcomer.

The Ukrainian nodded.

"Identification?"

The former Soviet officer pulled out the serrated-edged card the Nigerian Embassy in Madrid had given him and held it up. The other man shoved an identical-looking card with a notched edge at his; the two were a perfect match. "Come with me!"

The men walked around a corner to a darkened, dingy-looking, dead-end corridor. The Nigerian motioned at a row of stiff-backed benches. "Put two hundred dollars in your passport."

Retchko pulled from his wallet the strange-looking American currency. Fingering the cash, he picked out two green-shaded bills, both with an oval picture of a bald-headed man and "100" at its corners, that he took to mean one-hundred dollars, and stuck it into his forged passport.

The Nigerian took it from him. "Wait here for me . . . I shall return—"

When the other man disappeared around the corner from where they had just come, the incognito Soviet general sat down next to his travel bag. Facing him on the opposite paint-peeling wall was a mural-sized poster proclaiming about something called, *'Pepsi'*, that he had never heard of.

The African came back with the passport. "Follow me!" he said, motioning. As the two crossed the main terminal that was jammed mostly with people in native dress—some balancing enormous loads on their heads, he saw—the Academy's former Security Chief observed that all the men and women working the ticket counters and the gates wore their airline uniforms; he would replace them with his soldiers. As for the Nigerian troops who were about, the Ukrainian military man detected a general lack of discipline—but that would soon change.

The men strode down a curving sidewalk, past beggars and other people of the night, to a curb alongside a thoroughfare. "Get in!" the black man told the Caucasian, motioning to a blue, four-door Toyota parked underneath a street light, its engine running. The stocky Soviet swung his bag onto the rear floorboard and got in. The other man eased himself into the opposite back seat.

Whlle the driver waited for a break in the traffic, Retchko stared at the front occupants: a young man who gripped the steering wheel and a fellow in the right front seat who looked several years older; both had very dark complexions. The two looked straight ahead without speaking.

A frowning policeman in an outdated-looking "Colonial-style" uniform motioned for the car to move on. The driver put the Toyota in gear and nosed the vehicle out into the flow of traffic to the impatient stare of the officer who was tapping a billy-club.

Near the edge of the airport they made an abrupt swing down a dimly-lit road and made their way into a district of large metal-sided hangars and warehouses. Gazing about as they wove down the rutted, shadowy street, Retchko observed the ghostly shape of a large cargo airplane parked out on the concrete apron. He guessed it belonged to the organization of which he was now a part.

The Toyota drove up to one of the metal hangar buildings and stopped. The man in the left-rear seat opened the door. The front-seat rider hopped out and pulled open the passenger's rear door. The man led the way toward a door at the side of the building. In a conference-room, the fellow nodded toward some leather-backed chairs around a long mahogany table. "Ah, take seats . . . the others will soon be here."

A short time later, to the shuffle of footsteps, into the room came several very dark-skinned men. All stared at the pallid, bald-headed stranger. One of the newcomers, a shiny-faced, rotund African wearing a baggy, flowery outfit, his black wing-tip shoes sticking out, stepped forward and put out a huge hand.

"I am 'Masobe Busa' and I will be showing you around and getting you acquainted with ''The Organization', which is the code name for our group."

The Ukrainian, not sure of what to make of all this, shook the other man's enveloping grip. The fellow in the voluminous outfit gestured at the bald white man. "This is 'General Retchko'" he told the others, "he was with the Soviet military." There was a scraping of shoes as the African went on, "he is joining us to improve our security measures."

Busa gestured for all to take seats. The other Nigerians sat expressionless. "These are the men you will be working with."

He nodded at one of the men. "This is 'Doctor Mobustu', with the 'Nation Bank of Nigeria', where the funds of 'The Organization' are—'processed'." The man gave a slight nod.

Busa motioned to a trim, middle-aged individual who was wearing a pin-striped suit. "This is 'Doctor Krasheev', who also has a regular position at the 'Nation Bank'. He arranges for shipments of our funds out of the country to overseas banks *'and to other entities'* under various cover." The well-dressed man nodded at the newcomer.

"This man—" Busa gestured to a powerfully-built, very dark man—"is 'Norbert Ezego', who travels *'incognito'* as our overseas operative. You two will work together to develop means to protect our interests around the world." Retchko's instincts, told him the fellow looked like a hard individual. He would keep a close watch on him.

The Nigerian motioned toward another man standing in the doorway. "'Doctor Nkrume' is the general manager of the 'Tanuta Refinery', where we process our crude. He also controls our 'diversion' operations, which we will show you later in detail." Nkrume gave a nod.

Busa gestured to the next Nigerian, a wispy-looking, baldheaded man in a brown three-piece suit. "This man is the 'Chief of 'The Organization', and we all report to him."

The white man stared at the slight, middle-aged fellow, who nodded back at him, his fingertips tapping together. Retchko found it hard to believe that this little man was at the top of the whole operation.

"We use 'Chief 'as his identification—never his real name." Busa rapped his own chest. "As for me, although I am officially with the 'Nigeria Oil and Gas Corporation', I arrange to move products from the 'Tanuta Refinery', our central plant, into regular channels."

All eyes focused on the bald Ukrainian. "I am glad to be here," he said, sounding awkward.

Busa went on. "Tonight, the general will be at the hotel. After we return from Tanuta City, he will transfer to the apartment." He pointed at the two men who had ridden with him earlier; both had been standing back during the introductions. "You will take him to the hotel and make sure he is comfortable." Busa looked around at the other Africans, then at Retchko. "Tomorrow, we will start our business at the refinery."

A few minutes later, the blue sedan pulled up onto a curved driveway in front of a stucco-sided, six-story building with a lighted sign on the front that identified the place as the "Roomland Hotel". All four men got out and made their way into a carpeted lobby. "We will go directly to your room," the older man said, "everything is arranged." They trooped up six flights of stairs to a brilliantly-lit hallway. At the far end, the leader of the group rapped on a door using a syncopated sequence of knocks that Retchko detected as a code. In a moment the door cracked open. "We are here," he said to a young man.

The three stepped into a fair-sized room, comfortably-furnished. The space reminded Retchko of his quarters back at the Academy in Moscow.

"Ivan, here, will be your bodyguard for the night."

The Soviet looked the adolescent up and down. He seemed very young.

"I will be here at eight o'clock in the morning," the older Nigerian said. He and the other fellow stepped into the corridor and pulled the door shut. From pronounced "clicks" of a certain quality, Retchko recognized special door-locks. This must be an important room, he decided.

* * *

303

8:42 AM, Monday, September 23, 1991:

The *'Aero Commander'* arose from the runway and climbed out over the swampy wasteland that surrounded the International Airport at Lagos. "It will take us about two hours to get to Tanuta City!" Busa called out to the new "Security Chief" above the airplane noise.

As they flew down the boggy coast toward the southeast, Retchko read the materials the African had given him about the operations of "The Organization's" refinery. According to the papers, the plant was secretly taking crude oil from the next-door refinery, using hidden valves along the main pipeline that happened to run underneath a corner of the "Tanuta Refinery", diverting it in a manner that the other company could not detect. The re-routed oil, the existence of which was concealed by computers, was then mixed with their own regular crude and processed by the plant as part of its normal operations. The refined products were sold through several layers of dummy companies that the banker Krasheev had set up. Working with legitimate contracts as a cover, they had offices in Lagos, London, Amsterdam, and Madrid; and at Dallas and Houston in the United States.

Reading on, he learned that the funds generated by the transactions were wired from the "Nation Bank of Nigeria" into Swiss accounts, and from there into banks in the Cayman Islands. Most of the profits were funneled to a profitable weapons-smuggling operation that supplied arms to well-financed rebels in Chechnya and other places around the world.

The "Academy's" former security director grunted to himself in satisfaction at this last revelation; his activities with the breakaway Soviet republic's warlords had been his connection to this new job.

Other papers concerned 'The Organization's" involvement with certain "Third-World" countries *and private concerns* that were seeking to obtain materials for so-called terror weapons, such as "dirty" nuclear bombs and chemical-biological devices. It was evident that some people were willing to pay huge sums for those goods. The Communist-grounded Ukrainian's eyes narrowed as he thought about how he could enrich himself personally as well as his new employers. Maybe there was something to this "Capitalism", after all.

The Aero Commander swept the Niger River Delta and thumped down onto a runway lined with tall African grass. In a few minutes the aircraft rolled up to a rusty hangar building, A peeling sign on it declared: "Tanuta City". A limousine drove up to the airplane's side.

As the newcomers ducked into the back seat, a man in the middle-row-jump-seat turned about. "I am sure you remember Doctor Nkrume," Busa said. Retchko and Nkrume shook hands.

Before long, they were speeding past a huge operation that Retchko recognized as a petroleum refinery. "That is the other company's plant," Nkrume pointed, as the silvery complex swept past.

A half-kilometer farther on, the luxury sedan drove into another refinery and pulled up to a white- painted, clapboard-clad office building. A sign announced the name:

TANUTA REFINING COMPANY

TANUTA CITY

RIVERS STATE, NIGERIA

Everyone got out of the car except the driver, who stayed inside the limousine. The others stepped onto a wooden covered porch where Busa pulled aside a squawking screen door to let the others pass into the place. Inside, Retchko was greeted by a slender, attractive young woman whose creamy skin was noticeably lighter in shade than that of any of the other Africans he had yet seen in Nigeria. "I am 'Lisa Anaya'," she said in a British accent, extending a hand to the pale, baldheaded European, looking straight into his eyes. He observed that her's were green.

"'Retchko—'General' Leonid Retchko'."

"'Miss Anaya' is the manager of our 'design operations'."
Busa turned to the young woman. "General Retchko is joining us
to set up a security division."

Nkrume spoke up. "We will leave, now, and tour the
facilities."

The men stepped out a back door, where the Plant Manager
motioned to an open-top, military "half-track" truck. Lisa Anaya
stayed behind. As they climbed in turn up a ladder to bench seats,
the driver handed each of them a hard hat. Retchko grimaced; the
helmet felt blisteringly hot against his bald head.

The topless truck rumbled off, its bulldozer-like rear tracks
buzzing against the hard ground, past the refinery towers, of
which several slender ones had plumes of orange flame crawling
around their flared tops. Seeing Retchko's concerned look, Busa
pointed at one of the fiery tongues. "The flames burn excess
gases from the towers!" he called out over the truck's noises. The
general shook his head; setting fires in a petroleum plant looked
dangerous to him.

The half-track slithered to a stop at a low, un-marked metal
building at the far edge of the complex. Two guards were
standing by the chain-link gate. Retchko frowned. "What is this?"

"This is the most important building in the refinery."

Inside the air-conditioned structure, a large-diameter pipe
emerged from the cement floor at one end and ran for several
meters before disappearing back into the concrete slab at the
other end of the room. Metal tubes connected the big pipe to a
bank of electronics.

As they stood there, a loud *"CLICK!"* that made Retchko
jump came from inside a metal box, followed by the whine of an
electric motor. From inside the pipe came rushing noises. After
some seconds, with more clicks and a moan from the motor, all
again.became quiet. "This is what this refinery is all about!" Busa
beamed at Retchko, who stood blinking at what he had just seen.
"Come, let us go back to the main building and I will tell you all
about it!"

In a few minutes, the tracked truck whizzed up to the rear of
the refinery headquarters. The light-skinned young woman
directed them to a meeting room, where everyone took a seat

around a long conference table. The female took her leave. "I will be in my office," she said.

Busa took a pointer and pulled down a color-coded diagram on the wall. "This refinery is the key to the whole international operation . . . and much of the current income for our activities is generated here." Retchko stared at the board as the man went on. "Back in the 'British Colonial' days, there was a 'Royal Navy' pipeline that ran underground from a tank farm next door to a dock two kilometers south of here on the water. Warships used it as a refueling stop. When the British pulled out in nineteen-sixty, they abandoned the dock and the pipeline. When this refinery started, the pipeline that ran underneath part of this property was being used by the refinery next door to bring crude from the offshore field."

"Did the other refinery know that some of the pipe was under this land?"

"We guess they had no knowledge that the pipeline ran for a short distance under a corner of this property before it turned to the coast and on to the offshore tanker docks."

Busa went on. "One day I discovered that part of the pipeline ran underneath a corner of this property. What if we—that is to say, *this refinery and I*—could draw off some of the incoming crude and refine it for ourselves in secret?"

Retchko narrowed his eyes; it was obvious to him that Busa had no—what had that man in Madrid called it, "scruples"?—about working for one company, while at the same time stealing its goods and re-selling it to a competitor for his own gain! Busa would bear special attention.

The Ukrainian leaned forward as the Nigerian went on, "I told him the end-products would bring a premium price on the open market—but we would first have to make sure the other refinery did not know what was going on."

Nkrume held up his hand. "That was where my sister-in-law came in." He stepped to the doorway and called for Lisa Anaya.

Even though he knew very little about Africans, when the slender, cream-skinned young woman with the short, curly brown hair stepped into the room, Retchko was once more struck by how nice- looking she was. As soon as she started speaking in her

British accent—not in the thick brogue of most Nigerians—the new Security Chief realized she had not only looks, but brains, as well. She was not yet thirty, he guessed. Age differences had never been a problem for him. He would arrange to get to know her better.

"When 'Lester', *my sister's husband,* asked me to come here to design a system, I thought the idea sounded interesting, although I stay away from the *'down-stream'* details." Lisa Anaya popped the pointer into her palm as she spoke. "The stated objective was to buy part of the oil from the other refinery."

Busa narrowed his eyes, nodding—Retchko was frowning. *What she had just said was not correct! Did she not have full information? Retchko knew they were actually stealing the oil.*

The young woman was going on, "Mister Busa got copies of their computer software that I analyzed and modified . . . from then on, we drew out twelve-percent of the crude that flowed from the offshore well-heads and the docks that came across our property. At the same time, our computer would draw off our wholesale-quota into our tanks for refining."

"Tell me about the building from which we just came."

"The 'computers' you saw in the 'pump-house' were actually 'motor controls'. Flow sensors report when and how much crude is moving past. The main computer, which is located in another building, tells a valve on the main line to open and a pump draws the oil out of the pipeline into our tanks in the correct, twelve-percent proportion. When the oil stops flowing to the other refinery, the sensor detects this and tells our computer, which then orders the pumps to stop and to close the valve. This takes place many times a day. The actual quantities of crude we obtain this way are very large—thousands of barrels a day, as a matter of fact."

"You say the building is close to the property line . . . what security measures do you have in place, there, at this time?"

Lisa Anaya looked perplexed. "I am not sure—"

Busa spoke to Retchko. *"You* are here . . . to make sure our *'interests'* are well-protected."

"Then I must have total and absolute authority over all security matters, anywhere and everywhere that 'The Organization', as you call it, does business."

"Our scope is worldwide."

"Then, *my* scope will be worldwide."

I am sure that will be acceptable to ''The Chief '. You were brought here for that purpose."

"Very well. I must see all the other parts of this operation, then I will plan out the details and get started."

Just then, a steward appeared at the door, bowing. "Luncheon is served," he said. Everyone around the conference table made their way into a corridor, where the man directed them to a small paneled dining-room. "This way," he said, gesturing at several tables that were set with formal silver place settings over white tablecloths. In the middle of each stood lighted candles in silver candelabra; the place reminded Retchko of the officers' dining-room back at the Academy. As they made their way toward the tables, the new Security Chief made sure he would be at the same table as Lisa Anaya.

As they took their seats, the youthful female computer expert glanced at the very white, blue-eyed Ukrainian. He was not particularly attractive, she thought; the paunchy man was bald-headed and much older than she was. But he was reputed to have been a powerful officer in the Soviet military. "They say you are a Soviet general—"

Retchko fidgeted. "I *was* a Major General in the Soviet Army. I left Russia after the . . . 'coup'." He did not want to discuss anything that might lead back to his involvements in Moscow."How about you? I was impressed about how much you know about computers."

"I have a Master's Degree in Electronics," Lisa said.

"You talk like you are British."

"My father was a Nigerian diplomat stationed in London . . . my mother was English. My sister, my younger brother and I were all born in London."

"Did I hear you say that Nkrume is your brother-in-law?"

"He is married to my sister, Betty. They live here in Tanuta City."

Retchko thought about that for a moment. "Where did you go to school to learn about computers?"

"I went to an engineering school in the United States, at the center of their computer industry."

Since it is obvious there is almost no security at this refinery, and if she is familiar with the American computer companies— we can work together to obtain hardware; it will be a legitimate reason to be with her.

The food arrived just then and the talk soon turned to other matters. Toward the end of the luncheon, Lester Nkrume leaned over and nudged the general. "I want you and Lisa to do a survey of the refinery. Let me know what measures we must take to make it more secure."

"It would be"—Retchko glanced at Lisa Anaya—"a very good idea."

"You should start as soon as we are finished, here," the refinery manager added.

After the meal, the general and Lisa Anaya put on hard hats and walked toward the kilometer-square silver forest of rumbling, steaming, cracking towers and pipes and other machinery of the oil operation. As they stepped along, Retchko observed that some of the workers were wearing dark-colored clothes—he knew that dark apparel absorbed heat and could cause severe burns in case of a fire or explosion. He would direct that everyone in the refinery must wear white or silver outfits. As they went about the sprawling industrial space, other issues came to his mind. What about their hiring policies—did they screen the applicants? Did they have a system to monitor the workmen? How about sensors for hazardous gases? Could they shut down or isolate a part of the refinery in an emergency? Did they have an evacuation plan? It looked like there was much work to do here.

"This is the operations building," Lisa Anaya said, as the two came up to a one-story, corrugated, metal-sided structure with a rusty tin roof. Through several un-shuttered windows they could see people moving about inside the fluorescent-lighted space.

Retchko noticed that the day had darkened. Turning about, he saw towering black clouds rolling in from the ocean to the south. "It will rain, soon," he said.

"It has not rained in a while," the girl remarked. Even as they gazed at the distant clouds, there came a yellow flicker low on the horizon, followed by a faint rumble.

When the two went inside, a young man came up to them. "Miss Anaya, I am glad you are here," he said, "we are having some dropouts in the data link from the pump-house."

The woman frowned. "Let me see about this." She motioned for the African, whose badge Retchko read as "Frank Ogawan, Office Manager". He and the new security director followed her into a room of computers. "This is where we monitor all the refinery's operations . . . it's where we control the 'pumps' on the pipelines."

The young woman squinted at one screen with a frown. "There is something not right at the pump-house . . . let us go there."

Outside, they saw that the darkening clouds were rolling closer toward them; flashes of peculiar, green-hued lightning spiked around the edges of the billowing black thunderheads. "We must hurry!" Frank Ogawan called to the others, bounding down the steps.

The scurrying trio were still about fifty meters from the pump-house, near the refinery's fences, when a sudden, stiff breeze came up. Then a stronger gust, a weird mixture of warm and cool air, slapped their faces and clawed at their clothes. Retchko's hat flew off, bounding away with flying gravel and dust. Across open spaces, tall grass whipped in the wind. Just then, the dancing orange plumes of fire at the tower tops started giving off stacatto popping noises as the rising wind fanned the flaming flares.

Kettle-drum-like booms of thunder shook the ground. The portly Retchko glanced over his shoulder at the sky behind them—the non-stop lightning behind the clouds looked as if someone had turned on a giant light-bulb. The flickering flashes betrayed the man's flushed face and bulging eyes. "We must run faster!"

Lisa Anaya's eyes went wide. "Look!" she pointed. A kilometer away, a churning mass of very dark, low-lying clouds was scudding directly at them across the flattened field-grass, chased by the continuous, kaleidoscopic green lightning. Overhead, the swirling sky had turned sinister and threatening. The three, now caught out in the open running for their lives, stumbled their way through the graying gloom. Up ahead, two guards at the pump-house were shouting and waving for them to run faster.

There was a flash, an ear-splitting noise and a blast of heat that threw everyone to the ground!

Retchko came-to a few seconds later to a loud roaring noise in his ears. Pushing himself up, he saw that the others were sprawled in the thrashing field-grass. Near the fence, one of the guards raised himself onto his elbows, shaking his head. The other tried to sit up, then fell back and became still. Casting about, Retchko saw that the young office manager was moving his arms and legs and seemed to be unhurt, although obviously shaken.

But Lisa Anaya was on her back; her unblinking eyes were staring at nothing. When Retchko crawled over to her, he saw she was not breathing. Remembering his training, the former Soviet general grabbed a fistful of hair and pulled back her head. Pinching her nose, he put his mouth to hers, then blew a breath into her lungs and pulled back as she exhaled. After several tries, the young woman coughed and shook her head. In a few moments, she managed to sit up. By now, all except the stilled guard seemed to be coming around. And all this time, the wind was blowing ever stronger.

Frank Ogawan's eyes went wide. "Over there!" he pointed. Hanging from the bottom of a seething purplish cloud was a white waterspout, outlined by the lightning, writhing along the shoreline down the way. As they stared, stupefied, the rotating column veered off from the open water in their direction!

Just then, a howling wind blast bellowed across the grassy landscape, slamming a maelstrom of flying objects into the side of the metal building. "Get inside! Quick!" Retchko ducked as a barrage of airborne missiles flew all around and huge drops of rain began pelting them. The Ukrainian pulled the young woman to her feet and pushed her toward the pump-house entrance. The others, except for the insensible guard, stumbled after them. After the others had lunged inside, Retchko paused a moment to steal a glance at the motionless man still lying out there and at the raging weather—then shoved the door shut.

At that instant a wind blast of unimaginable power slammed against the front of the pump-house! The corrugated metal building reeled under the sudden onslaught; the roar of the twister became mixed with great wrenching and crashing noises. The lights went out. A booming racket rang their ears and the whole place heaved as a massive object slammed against the front door! The four inside cowered underneath the thick, raised oil pipe in the middle of the pump-room

Then after some seconds there was only the rain pounding the place. In another minute it came to a stop

Retchko and the guard tugged open the door. Blocking their way was an enormous, silver cylindrical object that he recognized as a refining tower lying on its side. Where the front fence had once been now lay a twisted steel electrical tower; bare cables draped over the pump building.

Frank Ogawan came up behind them and gazed at the sight. "Those are power lines!"

Retchko surveyed the drooping wires. "Are they still on?" The three men looked at each other, wide-eyed; knowing that if the cables were still charged with electricity, the rain-soaked ground could electrocute them on the spot. Then Retchko remembered that live, high-tension lines made a buzzing, snapping sound—these were silent. "I am sure these lines are dead."

"What happened?" A female's voice was behind them. Lisa Anaya came up and stared at the wreckage outside the front door.

"The storm blew a refining tower over here," the office manager said, "and that is an electrical tower—what is left of it."

The girl spotted the power lines that ran over their heads onto the roof. "Are they—?"

"The power is not on."

With the men helping the girl, the four crawled over the big cylinder and picked their way around the building, over objects that had been blown by the storm that were scattered about on the ground. On the backside, they came to a chain-type fence. Across the way, on the other refinery's land, was a line of electrical towers with a gap where one was missing. It looked as if the wind had picked up the tall, spindly steel structure and had carried it from across the way, over the top of the pump building, just missing the roof, and had dropped it in a heap at the front door, its dangling cables trailing back over the building's topside and the outer fence.

The security officer looked around. "Where is the other guard?"

The others followed as the youth ran toward the front of the building. When the others came up to the wreckage of the tower, the young man was on his knees; his head in his hands.

Lisa stopped short, dropped to her knees and put her hands to her face. "Oh, my God!"

Sticking out from underneath one of the twisted beams was a hand. It was obvious that, at the end of its headlong flight from the other field, the tower had landed squarely on top of the unfortunate fellow.

Retchko scowled. "He was already dead."

The girl gave the Security Chief a withering look. "Have you no feelings?"

"We must not let emotions get in our way," he came back, "the important thing is to get the refinery operating again."

Frank Ogawan was inspecting the crushed cracking tower. "It's not our's; it must have blown here from the other refinery."

Retchko nodded. "That is very fortunate for us."

The whine of an engine caught their attention. The half-track truck whirred around the corner of the refinery and splashed up to where they were standing. Nkrume and some other men jumped out. The Plant Manager looked aghast at the jumbled wreckage around the pump-house. "Is everyone all right?"

Retchko gestured at the twisted tower. "One of the guards was killed under there."

Nkrume winced. "Most unfortunate."

Frank Ogawan looked across an open space at the towers. "How is the refinery?"

"Only a little damage . . . everything will soon be operating normally." The refinery manager motioned at the truck. "Let us return to the main office, now."

Retchko glanced down at the body of the guard and gave an impatient motion. "They need to bury him right away." Lisa blanched; flies were already buzzing around the lifeless form.

One-at-a-time the troupe climbed into the rear of the truck. As Lisa Anaya pulled herself up the metal ladder ahead of the new Security Chief, the man could not help but notice how her tight skirt hiked-up, revealing substantial bare thigh. The young woman, oblivious to this, sat down on a side bench seat; the perspiring Ukrainian dropped onto the one opposite her. Now that the clouds were gone, the equatorial sun once more beat straight down onto them; here and there little puffs of vapor came out of the ground.

When Retchko pulled out a handkerchief and wiped his glistening bald pate, Lisa's eyes narrowed. *Was that the shadow of hair roots on his head?*

The half-track rumbled up to the rear of the main building. Inside, Busa was walking around, flustered and exasperated; slapping his hands together in impatience. "I must be going to the other refinery!" he wheezed, his eyes bulging. "If I stay away, they will suspect me!"

Nkrume gestured toward the door. "Go back . . . work with them to get their plant once more in operation—and, of course, keep us informed about what they are doing."

The portly man strode out the door. From outside, came the thud of a car door closing.

Retchko frowned. "Is he going to ride over to the other refinery in *our* vehicle?"

Ezego spoke up. "Busa will transfer to another car with which the other people are familiar. We are certain they do not suspect he is with us."

The white man thought about that, then nodded. "Each of you will now discuss the nature of your jobs with me." He turned to Lisa Anaya. "I will start with you." The bald European motioned toward the conference room. "I wish for you to explain to me about your computers and your other duties . . ."

315

Twenty minutes later, the two came back out, just as the ceiling lights came back on.

Retchko gave a quick toothy grin, then looked serious. "What facilities are there for maintaining electric power here when the regular current is off?"

Frank Ogawan spoke up. "We have a generator, but it is out of operation right now."

Retchko shook his head and looked hard at the Plant Manager. "I must speak to you about these matters." The door closed behind them.

Sometime later, when the two emerged, there were serious expressions on both men's faces. The Ukrainian motioned to Ezego. "Come inside, now . . . we have many things to discuss."

Seated at a desk, Retchko stared across at the African. "How does the other refinery not know that what comes out of the wells is *not* the same as what they receive? Do they not have flow-meters?"

"Our software causes their wellhead meters to display the wrong figure . . . since their computer senses how much crude is coming into the pipeline and automatically deducts the twelve-percent from the total and records it on their meter logs, no accurate records show what is actually going on . . . the software I devised for their computer can never reveal the diverted crude—therefore, there is no way for them to know that the amount coming from the wellhead is more than they actually receive."

"What if they should change their computer program, themselves? Would that not make your system useless?"

"Busa planted a 'cookie', as they call it, in their computer that automatically notifies our computer of any changes in their program or operating system. It transmits the information back to us . . . our computer automatically re-programs theirs back to our configuration."

"How about Lisa Anaya? Does she know about all this?"

"She is ignorant of the details." He gave a smirk. "She believes we are 'buying' the crude from the other refinery. Actually, we are obtaining it through subterfuge."

316

A satisfied look crossed Retchko's face. So they really *were* stealing the oil! He could relate to that.

* * *

7:35 PM; The Same Day:

Retchko winced—the setting sun flashed straight into his eyes as the Aero Commander's nose came around over the Niger River Delta onto a northwest heading out of the little airport at Tanuta City. The Ukrainian rubbed his eyes and settled back into his seat; he must be mentally alert during the ride back to Lagos while he reviewed the day's events. Retchko was glad Busa was still back at the other refinery; something about the man irritated him. In his place in the middle seat slumped Nkrume, who was returning to the capital city on what he had said was a personal matter. The Plant Manager's head was already nodding, which meant the Security Chief could reflect about this day without having to carry on a conversation with the man. He needed some time to think.

What he had learned about the refinery both impressed and unsettled him. Those people were living on the edge of a gold mine—*black* gold, it was—but at the same time, their security procedures were so slack he wondered how they had gotten away with stealing the crude from the pipeline all this time without being caught. On the other hand (an expression he had heard the locals use), the computer-controlled secret siphoning of oil from the other refinery's supply was pure genius.

Lester Nkrume, the Plant Manager and the brother-in-law of Lisa Anaya, and who looked to be not particularly strong, would not get in the way of coming changes. *If he did, he would be eliminated.*

As for that fellow Ezego, Retchko had gotten the impression he would kill his best friend—if he had one—with little or no prodding. "Special attention to Ezego'," the new Security Chief noted; from his own experiences with double-crossers and other dishonest types—sometimes including himself, he would admit—an indefinable "something" about the very dark-

317

complexioned man set him on guard. On the other hand (there was that phrase, again), he could be the perfect ally in the struggles that would soon come.

The young Frank Ogawan, the earnest office manager, had caught his attention for a different reason: his seeming innocence and honesty were characteristics he had found to be in short supply in Nigeria. For those reasons the fellow would have to be watched; people with little fortitude in this business could be dangerous to the overall enterprise. What might lie ahead would demand a cold, calculating nature such as he, himself, possessed, along with Ezego and Busa, but not with Ogawan. And there was Lisa Anaya.

Lisa Anaya. He would never forget the look on her face when he had told her in their private meeting how he had saved her life by breathing into her mouth. She thought he was exaggerating until Ogawan, the fawning office manager, had told her that he had seen the European put his mouth to hers and force air into her lungs. "Your eyes were glazed," Retchko said, "without me, you would be dead, right now!" She put her hands to her cheeks, wide-eyed. *"You owe me . . ."* the portly Ukrainian had smirked, not altogether in jest. From the expression the girl's face he was sure she understood exactly what he had meant. *I am not sure she can be trusted. But I will use her for my own purposes.*

This new job was turning out to be far more interesting than he would have ever thought it would be.

* * *

7:50 AM, Tuesday, September 24, 1991:

Someone was rapping on the front door. In a minute, the servant, "Mickey", who had been loaned to the Security Chief while his usual master, Busa, was gone, came to the entrance of his dressing quarters.

"The driver is here for you," the slight, stooped, middle-aged, bald-headed fellow said, leaning forward in a deep bow, pressing the palms of his sinewy hands together.

318

"Very well." Stowing the shaving kit, and with a rake of his stubby fingers across his hairless head to make sure he had shaved his bald top to shiny sufficiency, the stocky man turned toward the door.

* * *

The blue Toyota drew up to a sentry post. A white-gloved guard motioned the sedan forward into the fenced compound. For Retchko, this tropical Army base was familiar-looking territory—he was glad to once more be back in a military environment.

The vehicle drove past parked Army vehicles to a corrugated-metal building. A soldier stepped forward and pulled open the rear door. The young man saluted. "Colonel Ajiboy is expecting you." The civilian-dressed European hoisted himself out. "Right this way, sir," the soldier said. The men made their way down a central corridor to a glass-paned door. The fellow knocked twice, then pushed it open.

Inside, an intense-looking female soldier stood up from a receptionist's desk and looked the pale newcomer up and down. "General Retchko?" The Caucasian nodded. "Come with me."

At another door, she rapped with a subtle sequence Retchko detected. The young woman ushered the white man into a spartan office where a trim, very black man in a summer military uniform, wearing green-shaded eyeglasses, stood behind a well-worn desk. "You are General Retchko?"

The Ukrainian nodded.

"I am 'Colonel Ajiboy'—'*Solomon*' Ajiboy'." A gold bracelet on his wrist reflected the sunlight. "Cigarette?" The Ukrainian took one and accepted the light proffered by the African. The two men sat down.

Ajiboy gestured toward the window. "This Army post is at the service of the 'Organization'. *As I understand it*, the military government of Nigeria provides cover in return for a portion of the profits from the activities of the group." He spoke slowly; measured-like, Retchko noticed.

The Ukrainian studied the African face. *Did the man have reservations?* "Go on."

319

"The 'Organization' is in control of the Lagos airport—this allows it to move goods in and out of the country without interference."

"What manner of goods?"

"They bring weapons here from Cuba and Angola. Then, they ship them in mis-labeled crates with matching paperwork on their own transport plane to Libya. From there, the goods move by 'fishing boats' to a Black Sea port in northern Turkey that is friendly to the 'Organization' ... from there, Chechen operatives take the arms across Iran and around the Caspian seacoast to Grozny."

"That explains the steady supply of *matériel* the warlords have always had."

Ajiboy took a deep breath. "Now, general, tell me about *your* involvement with the Chechens."

Retchko realized *he* was being interrogated. The white man lifted another cigarette from the desk holder. After lighting it, he settled back, his eyes narrowed. He would measure his words. "When I was with the 'Liaison Group' of the Warsaw Treaty Forces, I happened to meet one of the Chechen warlords while I was there. Later, he contacted me with a proposal: if I would provide him with information about the Soviet military, he would set up an account for me in a Swiss bank. From then until I left Russia I sent them advance notices of Soviet military operations. They told me the information was very valuable to them."

"I can see how that would be."

Retchko wanted to change the subject. "I wish to see your operations at the airport."

The colonel reached for his hat. "We shall now go there."

Outside, an olive-drab officer's field-car awaited; its sweating, uniformed driver, standing beside it, pulled open the rear door.

* * *

Thirty minutes later, the big vehicle pulled into a parking lot behind the main building of the "Murtala Mohammed Airport

Lagos." Retchko cast about, frowning. "I do not see your security men."

Ajiboy glanced at his wristwatch. "It is tea time."

The 'Organization's' new "Security Chief'" shook his head. There was much to do.

Inside, the African led the Ukrainian down a hallway to a door marked, "Security Office". As the two stepped into the masculine-looking space, a man in a sentry's uniform set down his teacup in a hurry, stood and saluted.

The colonel motioned at the bald white man. "This is General Retchko, who will be working with us here at the airport." The second officer and the newcomer nodded at each other.

Just then, a uniformed man came out of an inner office. "Solomon! I thought I recognized your voice! I was—" The fellow stopped in mid-sentence when he saw the white man standing there frowning at him.

"Call the officers to a meeting at 'oh-eleven-hundred' in the conference room," Ajiboy broke in, "this man"—he nodded at the general—"will be speaking to us."

"Yes, sir." The fellow stood up straight, saluted and disappeared back in the direction from where he had come.

"Come with me—" The black man closed the door, then moved behind a bare desk, motioning to Retchko to take an opposite seat. "General, I am sure there is much to do to make this airport more secure."

Retchko narrowed his eyes at the colonel; an instinct told him the other man was unsettled. He decided to press his advantage. "Yes, I see a need for substantial improvements." Ajiboy fidgeted as the Ukrainian went on, "When we arrived, the security people were taking a break—a 'tea break', or whatever it was—all at the same time."

"It is a tradition from when Nigeria was a British Colony."

"Yes, but *we must not let the past rule the present.*" Retchko's eyes narrowed. "We must have these 'breaks' at different times of the day so people will always be on duty."

"Yes, of course."

Retchko decided to give the African some slack; he might need him later for his own purposes. "Colonel, we are all working toward the same objectives . . . "

Ajiboy seemed to pause for a moment. "Of course."

There was a knock at the door. A security officer shuffled into the little office. "The meeting is ready." With a hesitant glance at the pale newcomer, the man backed out of the room.

A half-dozen Africans in military uniforms stared at the bald European as the new Security Chief settled heavily into a seat around the conference table. Ajiboy squinted at the small gathering through his tinted glasses. "This is General Retchko." The officer nodded at the white man. "He will be working with us here at the airport." The other men sat like statues. "He is a former Soviet security officer." The men, frowning, glanced about at each other.

The Ukrainian, taking notice of this, stood up to speak.

-21-

Retchko settled back in the stuffed chair in his quarters and sipped his whisky. He must remember to thank Mickey for coming up with the bottle of *"Johnnie Walker"*; it had been a while since he had had a really good Scotch. And he needed it; even as he had arrived at the airport this morning, he understood there was a major task before him. Tea breaks—by the gods! Did those people live in the real world, or what? His immediate objective must be to tighten-up the whole operation.

But he had sensed a resistance to his new régime. *I do not care what they think about my ideas—they will either go along with my strict way of doing things or I will eliminate them. I will start by replacing the civilians at the airport with military personnel under my command.*

There would be a chip-identification system like the one at the Academy.

Retchko leaned back in his easy chair and took another long, satisfying swallow of Scotch. How ironic, he thought, that everyone back at the school was on the chip-monitoring system he had conceived—*except himself.* He had taken a convenient absence the day the faculty and students had had the chips implanted and had thus avoided having the tiny identification and locating device placed in his arm. What a turn it had been for him to have escaped being tracked by his own contrivance!

To re-create the chip program would require the services of an electronics expert to design and put the system in place. He smiled to himself. That person, of course, would be Lisa Anaya.

A satellite would be a more involved proposition. He would have to use an American or a European satellite channel, which might take some time to arrange. For this, he would again use the Organization's electronics expert.

At some point, I will exact my "just and due payment" from her for saving her life.

There were glaring deficiencies at the airport that would require immediate attention. To him, it was inconceivable that the police were not armed. He would replace the jocularity he had observed among the security officers with strict protocols of rank. And when they had driven him around the edges of the airport, he had even seen gaps in the fences; there should be multiple rings of electrically-charged barriers plus anti-personnel mines at the outer perimeters.

Other changes would soon be on the way. A departure tax, already in use at many European airports, would generate vast amounts of revenue for the Organization. He would set up an important-sounding "company" as a cover to operate the airport under his control. He would put up large-sized picture posters all around the airport of the Nigerian government's Leader in military dress. This would bring the government to his side. He would tell Ajiboy to march troops inside the terminals as a show of force.

Another method of control would be to have soldiers take passengers into custody *as their aircraft were loading.* The security men would extract personal information and ransom from the detainees. Anyone who resisted would be taken to a sound-proof room where much more intense force would be applied. A high proportion of those subjects would not survive. An on-site crematorium would dispose of the physical evidence.

There would be thorough searches of all departing passengers' luggage. He would make it illegal for passengers to have electronic devices, either in their luggage or on their person. To enforce this, he would impose a heavy penalty to violators—a visit to the sound-proof room.

Only currency with specific dates on them would be acceptable to pay the departure tax. Anyone without the correct bills would be detained in the "usual" manner.

These types of measures had proved effective at a certain airport in a Warsaw Treaty country where there had been security problems. Soon, stories of such happenings at that airport had led to fear of the authorities and became a deterrent that ensured compliance from the masses. It would be reasonable to assume he could achieve similar results here at the "Murtala Mohammed Airport Lagos". Under his control, he expected the airport to soon have universal respect and a fierce reputation for its strict methods and procedures.

When they had driven him down the flight line of un-marked aircraft the Organization used to transport the contraband goods, he was surprised to learn that the biggest airplane he saw parked in front of the group's hangar had once been a part of the modern *'Iraqi Airlines'* fleet that had fled from the Americans during the recent so-called "Gulf War." When the bombings had started, all the airliners flew to Iran and were interned. Through special connections with the Iranians, the Organization had obtained a Boeing 747 that they had stripped-out and strengthened to carry cargo. The huge airplane now picked up weapons from Cuba, Angola and North Korea and delivered the armaments to Libya, Sudan and Afghanistan. He would seek to soon include others on the Organization's customer list.

Inside the hangar, Retchko had noticed several tarpaulin-wrapped pallets with the international "nuclear" symbol on them. "What is that?" he had asked.

"These gas centrifuges, along with plutonium pellets and carbon control rods, came from North Korea," came Ajiboy's answer. "They had intended to carry the centrifuges and the nuclear materials to Iraq, but the so-called 'Gulf War' happened, and now the Organization has all of these here. "Several countries *and some private organizations* are interested in it."

Retchko poured himself another Scotch. Gas centrifuges and nuclear materials, indeed! The scope of the Organization was far more than he had even imagined it to be.

His thoughts were interrupted by a knock. Turning about, he saw Mickey, framed in the doorway, bowing; his hands pressed together. "You have a guest," the fellow said.

Busa bounded into the room, his flowery outfit billowing behind him. "Retchko!" The agog African pumped the white man's hand. "You must come with me to meet some important people!"

Busa led the Ukrainian to his next-door townhouse where a well-dressed gathering of Nigerians was on hand. Mickey appeared with a glass of Scotch that he handed to the guest.

The host nodded at a bald, slightly-built man. "This is Doctor Nomoah . . . you remember him, of course." The banker, whom Retchko recognized, was wearing the same brown three-piece suit as the other night at the first meeting in the airport hangar.

Nomoah shook the Security Chief's hand. "We will meet in the morning," he said.

From across the open space, Nkrume waved a drink to the newcomer. "Hallo, Retchko!" he called out above the hubbub of voices and the soft African music coming from a stereo console.

A young woman holding a *'Martini'* glass came up to him and extended a manicured hand. "I am 'Betty Nkrume'," she said, presenting a smile of perfect white teeth. Even as he shook her hand, the Ukrainian could see that she was related to Lisa Anaya. A look up-and-down, without any pretense at being discreet, also told him that she was at least as attractive as her sister.

Across the room, the husband, feigning indifference, turned toward the bar.

The youthful-looking female smiled at him again and looked straight into his eyes. "Lester tells me you have joined the 'Organization'," she said in a British accent.

Retchko nodded. "That is so . . . I will be involved with security matters."

"My sister says you are an Army man in Russia."

"Lisa said that? Yes, I *used* to be in the military in the Soviet Union."

"Then you are no longer—?"

There was a nudge on his elbow for which Retchko was relieved; the girl's questions were heading in a direction he wanted to avoid.

"I am sorry to interrupt," Busa said, looking at both of them, "but I want General Retchko to meet someone." The white man nodded at the refinery manager's young cream-skinned wife, who gave him a smile in return.

Busa directed Retchko into a palatial, paneled, indirectly-lighted office.

A soft African man's voice came at his shoulder. "The *'Bhagwan'* will see you, now." Retchko turned about as an older man, dressed in a long, white robe with a crown on his head and holding a bejeweled scepter in his hand, shuffled up to him.

"He is our 'spiritual advisor'," Busa said. The robed cleric bowed at the white man and at the host. Retchko, not sure what to do, nodded back, all the time trying to keep a straight face as the "holy man" raised his shining scepter and waved the top end of the thick jeweled rod to and fro.

"I am pleased to see you." The older man spoke in English, in an accent that Retchko detected to be Middle-Eastern.

"The *'Docteur'* is the *'Adept of the Terrarianists'*." The younger fellow spoke, with a smile at the bald Caucasian, and went on, "he draws from the powers of the Earth to dispense good health and prosperity to the believers." The youth kissed an enormous bejeweled ring on the man's index finger. Retchko became aware of a scent of incense in the room.

"Tomorrow, you will come to visit our *'Terrarim'*," the "Adept" said, nodding. Without another word, he nodded, turned and went out, followed by his white-robed assistant.

Busa, who seemed to have been in a sort of trance, blinked at his guest. "We will return, now, to the others."

In the living room, people were gathered by the front door; shaking hands and saying their farewells. "Ah, here you are . . ." came a feminine voice. Betty Nkrume stepped past several other guests and came up to Retchko. "I was afraid you had already gone." She reached for his hand. "The party is about over . . . I wish we had more time to talk." With the hand-touch, she leaned forward, allowing her low-cut party dress to expose a considerable expanse of chest. He gave a thorough, obvious look at the sight. The girl held her gaze into his eyes for a long moment. "I trust we will *see* each other again, *soon*—"

Just then, her husband came up. "There you are, my dear . . . we must go, now." He put the palm of his hand on his young wife's bare upper back and guided her toward the door in what Retchko took to be an exaggerated gesture for his benefit. He saw the refinery manager give a quick look back at him as the two stepped out into the steamy Nigerian night.

* * *

8:25 AM, Wednesday, September 25, 1991:

"There is the 'Terrarim'!" Busa pointed out the open window as the blue Toyota raced along the highway toward the center of Lagos City.

Retchko stared at the green-domed, multiple-sided yellow stucco building, partially hidden back in a grove of palm trees.

"We will go there today after we see Doctor Krasheev!"

The car came onto a bridge that went on so long Retchko began to wonder if they should ever reach the other end. As they thumped along in the humid equatorial morning, the European gazed out at the scene of fishing boats plying their trade. As far as he could see, waves of heat shimmered above the surface of the mirror-still water. Busa pulled out a white handkerchief and wiped his shiny face.

Finally, tall buildings materialized ahead of them in the haze; before long the sedan bumped off the causeway past a sign that read, "Ikoye Lagos." To Retchko, it seemed as if some of the structures they were going by were in a drastic state of disrepair; one or two in particular appeared to have been completely burned-out. "What happened to those buildings?"

"The Nigerian grunted. "Political factions".

The Toyota made its way down a narrow street and pulled up in front of a two-story, cream- colored stucco building. Retchko and Busa stepped into a paneled lobby with fixtures the Ukrainian recognized as identical to what he had seen in Busa's home the previous evening. Just a coincidence? Or was there a connection between the two places that went beyond the surface details? Other things about the room interested him. Over the front door hung an unimportant "native art" painting—a stern-faced portrait of the nation's "Leader" in a military uniform would be a far better use of the space. Since in the Capitalist system the bank was the centerpiece of everyone's personal finances, what better way to confront the people with an unmistakable symbol of State power than at such a place? He would bring up the subject to Nomoah. Looking about the waiting area, Retchko made other observations. Not only was the bank's guard unarmed—the man was dozing! And where were the security cameras? The laser intruder alarms? The "Chief of Security" shook his head; wherever he went, the task before him became ever more involved.

A woman employee holding a clipboard pulled open a glass door, admitting into the room the raucous clatter of business machines. "Doctor Nomoah will see you, now."

The visitors followed her through an open work space, past clerks staring at computer screens; others fingered keyboards and operated clacking calculators. At the rear of the room, she rapped on a mahogany door in a subtle sequence that Retchko detected— much the same as the knock at the hotel room door and at Colonel Ajiboy's office. *A common code?*

A compact-sized man stood up behind an executive desk and shook the crease out of his brown, three-piece suit. Retchko wondered if the man had any other outfits; every time he had seen the banker he was wearing the same clothes. The financier extended his hand. "I.M. Nomoah."

"You have met General Retchko, of course," Busa interjected.

In the few seconds during which everyone shook hands and settled into leather chairs, Retchko took in his surroundings. The scene was dominated by a formal outside garden, visible through a full-size picture window behind the banker. The Head of Security recognized the wall paneling, the light fixtures and other decorations as being just like Busa's, which meant there probably *was* a connection between the two places.

The new Security Chief launched into his observations that set Nomoah nodding with approval.

" . . . hang a portrait of Nigeria's leader wearing a military uniform above the front door of the bank", Retchko went on, "and put large pictures of him in *many* public places. Such has been most effective in *'Eastern Bloc'* countries."

Nomoah regarded Retchko with a pleased expression. "Very good suggestions." The banker spread his hands. "We have a good relationship with the government . . . I am sure they will act on these ideas."

Observing the man's positive reaction out of the corner of his eye, Busa spoke up in what Retchko detected to be

329

exaggerated *(favor-currying?)* haste. "Doctor Nomoah is an expert in financing."

The little bald-headed man gave a modest shrug. "My function in the Organization is to obtain funding from outside sources—most often from investors in American and Europe . . . we always structure these 'investments' so that those who put money into our ventures are not aware of the true nature of where it is going . . . when we have made our profits from the oil refinery at Tanuta City and from our weapons sales, we use our connections in the Cayman Islands to 'launder', as they say, the money into construction in America. We have a company, there, that builds high-rise apartments and condominiums that are very profitable. By the time the money gets passed through America, it is completely legitimate."

"How do the 'investors' get their money back?"

The banker looked at his watch, and stood up. "We will discuss *that* matter another time," he said, ending the conversation.

When the Toyota drove away from the bank, Busa was beaming. "I believe Doctor Nomoah was pleased with your suggestions!"

"His duties seem important."

"Now, we shall visit another bank." He leaned forward and tapped the driver's shoulder. "Take us to 'Dinubu Square'."

Retchko looked at his watch. "How about food? I have not eaten since this morning."

"Have patience . . . a little longer, and we will have a most memorable meal."

Before long, the car pulled up to a block-square open space in the middle of the city. As the men climbed out, Retchko observed that workmen were tearing down a large residence across the way.

Seeing his interest, Busa spoke up. "Many of the British officials' homes are being removed . . . the 'Leader' wants no more reminders of the colonial period in our country." Retchko grunted; in the Soviet Union, such a "reminder" would have long ago been divided into multiple apartments. But then he had to remind himself that he was no longer in the Soviet Union, and would probably never return there.

The two men left the driver sitting in the parked car and walked down the street to a hulking, multi-storied building whose graystone exterior reminded Retchko of some buildings he had seen back in Moscow. They tramped up stone steps to a pair of impressive-looking bronze doors, on each side of which was a shiny brass plaque proclaiming the institution to be the "Nation Bank of Nigeria." Inside, the very dark African and the pale, bald-headed man crossed the shiny stone floor of the main lobby, made their way up marble steps to the second floor and made a turn to the left. At the end of a hallway, Busa led the other man into an office.

Behind a desk sat angular, well-dressed African whom Retchko remembered from the first gathering in the airport hangar's meeting room. "Doctor Krasheev, General Retchko—" Busa said. As the two shook hands and took their seats, the Ukrainian scanned a name plate on Krasheev's desk that identified the man as the bank's "Director of Intercontinental Remittance".

"I am impressed with the scope of the Organization," Retchko said. "It covers the world."

Krasheev leaned back in his big leather armchair and tapped his fingertips together. "It is indeed a big operation," he said, with the barest suggestion of a smile. "My function is to place our financial assets into banks abroad." Retchko nodded; the man went on, "Since this bank is one of Nigeria's most important financial institutions, it gives me the cover to conduct the affairs of our 'group' with no difficulties. It is easy to transfer our funds into overseas accounts when I handle the transactions in the name of the 'Nation Bank of Nigeria'."

"How do you do the transfers? In person?"

Most of the time, we make the transactions by wire. But sometimes, we do it by *'courier'*."

"Courier?"

"We have someone to carry the money on their person to a foreign bank. Sometimes, we bring it here. When we do that, we use a chemical process that turns the currency to a black color. At

331

the destination, we have a procedure to return the bills to their original state. The system is foolproof—it is not traceable by any conventional means."

BANG! came a loud noise from the outside. Retchko, startled, gaped out the open window at an older brick-and-glass building across the street that took up the whole view. "That is a factory the government is converting to manufacture clothing for the military," the banker said.

Krasheev nudged his executive chair back and came to his feet, which Retchko took to mean that the conversation was ended.

"I am sure we will speak again, soon," the "Director of Intercontinental Remittance" said, shaking the two visitors' hands.

Before long, they were again on the highway, headed away from the city center.

Just after crossing over the long bridge, the Toyota turned off into a grove of palm trees and drove up onto a circular drive in front of an octagonal-shaped stucco building. When Retchko hauled his pudgy bulk out of the rear seat and gazed up at the dark-green dome on top of the structure, he recognized the place as the "spiritual" man's "Terrarim" they had driven by that morning. The black man motioned the European toward a pair of tall bronze doors with a flaming wall torch at each side.

As they stepped up to the massive double entryway, as if on cue the two gilt barriers swung inward, revealing in the yellowish half-light of the interior a white-robed man, his head wrapped in a turban, bowing at the visitors. Busa and Retchko followed the fellow into a corridor flanked by flickering torches strung along multi-colored ceramic walls. An older-looking individual in a white robe came out of the dusky darkness and bowed with the palms of his hands pressed together."This way," he said. The mysterious man led them into a circular, torch-lighted room with a mosaic floor; smoky candles gave off a strong aroma of sweet incense. The man waved the visitors toward reclining couches next to a low table laden with fruits and other dishes. "Be comfortable," he said, bowing.

The two were just settling onto the futon-like sofas when a loud gong sounded. Startled, the white man squinted across the murky space and saw a turbaned fellow holding a leather-tipped wooden striker in his hand; the suspended brass sounder still moving metronome-like back and forth on a rope.

Two youths in white robes sidled into the room and raised tubular wooden instruments to their lips. To hollow, wavering notes, an oiled youth in a loincloth stepped through the opening and made his way in long, measured strides around the circular room to a pre-planned spot. As the wailing music went on, other young fellows followed around the curved wall to evenly-spaced positions.

As Retchko stared, fascinated, a barefoot girl in a diaphanous wrap-around outfit that outlined her taut figure in startling detail leaped through the opening and twirled toward the white man at his couch. To the beat of the music, she bowed and swung around his recliner, then took a place on her tiptoes in front of one of the young men; the palms of her hands pressed together over her head.

While the music went on, another girl, then another, all in identical attire, came into the room and went through the same twirling, twisting routine until about a dozen couples were arrayed around the torch-lit, circular space.

As the two musicians again played their instruments, the dancing couples spun around the floor; the girls' outfits whirling to their frenetic rotations. Then the young men backed away to the edge of the room. With one motion the girls pulled their outer garments away and held the shifts at arms-length. Now clad in only the flimsiest of tops and bottoms, as the tempo increased, they twirled their former wraps over and around themselves, undulating to and fro.

All at once, the music stopped. The girls froze in position, unblinking. With a start, Retchko realized they were all staring at him. Then with long leaps the dancers swept across the glazed floor and out through the exit.

The cymbal crashed out a brassy note. Silver smoke drifted in wafting tufts about the room.

Out of the murky haze stepped an apparition in a white, flowing robe. Peering into the cloudy vapor, Retchko recognized the white-bearded "Bhagwan" of the night before. The gong sounded again; the "Adept" swayed through the swirling mist across to the European on his low couch. Putting the palms of his hands together, the man took a deep bow.

The wooing notes of the woodwind instrument stopped. The turbaned mystic nodded at the European, who was staring at him.

"I am pleased to have you as my guest . . . I shall join you." The older fellow eased onto a reclining couch between the other two men. As soon as the important man was comfortable, he reached across the table for a bunch of grapes, pulled off a couple and took a squishy bite. The leader motioned to an attendant. The youth put the palms of his hands together and bowed.

The turbaned young man came back bearing a tureen of fruit, followed by another youth holding a dish of what looked to Retchko to be some sort of skewered worms or snails that he set in front of the guests. Seeing the Ukrainian's hesitation, the robed man motioned at the serving plates. "It is the bounty of the Earth," he beamed, grasping a strange-looking morsel in his fingers and popping the brown mass into his mouth. "You must eat!" he said to the foreigner, as an attendant handed him a flopping leather wine-skin. The "holy man" upended the wobbling bladder for a long drink, then wiped his chin with the back of his hand.

Hunger overcame hesitation; the European picked up one of the strange-looking pieces, shoved it into his mouth and chewed it in a hurry. Swallowing, the white man frowned at the worm-like objects on the plate. "What are they?"

The Terrarianists' leader rubbed his stomach. "Baby leeches . . . from the Niger River."

"We believe they give us increased powers of preservation," Busa put in, patting his own paunch, "we begin every meal with them."

The Bhagwan upended the wine bladder again and took a long, deep drink, then wiped his mouth with a lopsided smile. "We 'Terrarianists' honor the Earth . . . from where all riches flow. The ground and its natural foods give our people the will and the strength to live." He plucked another of the slimy creatures from the plate and lifted it to his lips.

Just as Retchko was wondering if these distgusting objects were to be the only course of the entire meal, several servants appeared with dishes of vegetables and other foods. Busa filled his plate with his hands; the robed man did the same. "Eat!" he smacked, licking his fingers with a dripping grin.

The bald Ukrainian picked off a brown, fleshy, cooked vegetable from a serving dish and put it into his mouth. To his surprise, it had a sweet taste. "What is this?"

"Plantains," Busa said through a gigantic mouthful, "fried bananas—they came to Africa from the Americas during the slave-trading times. Very popular here, now."

After a while, the bearded man clapped his hands; a servant rushed to the table. "Bring the 'dessert'!" In a moment the fellow re-appeared with a large bowl and a stack of smaller ones balanced in the crook of his elbow. The "Adept of the Terrarianists" glanced at the Ukrainian. "You like our food, no?"

Retchko, still not used to eating with his hands, nodded. A servant came around passing out towels.

Busa rubbed his stomach some more. "We 'Terrarianists' eat well."

The spiritualist took another turn at the wine-skin. "Drink!" he directed with a grin. A pair of servants helped the others lift the burbling brown bladders. "We do all the work for you!" the bearded man giggled, wiping his mouth. He clapped his hands with exaggerated motions then gave a wobbling wave. "Water pipes!"

"We finish our meals with a good smoke," Busa put in.

The three servants came back, each holding a pot-bellied brass tub with charcoal embers glowing in a grate at their bottoms. From the top of each dangled a rubber hose with a brass mouthpiece at the end. Taking care not to spill anything, they placed one of the objects next to each of the men. The leader put a nozzle to his mouth and took a long draw as the sound of bubbling liquid came from inside the bulbous smoker. Retchko took the hose of the one beside him and inhaled. The smoke tasted cool and smooth: he guessed the water filtration had something to do with it.

Across the way the flute and a woodwind struck up their woofing notes as another all-female troupe whirled onto the dance floor. While the sarong-clad girls, who looked to be hardly beyond adolescence, pranced about in the wavering orange light of the torches, the men puffed on their gurgling water-smokes.

The "Adept" spoke up. "These *'maidens'* are 'priestesses' who invoke the 'bounty of the Earth' through dancing," he said, following the fluid momements of the svelte young women with admiring eyes. "Later, through rituals, they will carry the seed of our renewal." While Retchko pondered the only possible meaning of this, the "Dokteur" spoke again over the reedy music. "You will meet my nephew," the Leader said.

Retchko looked at the older man who was nodding to the beat of the music.

"He is a 'freedom fighter'."

The general frowned. "*'Freedom fighter'?*"

"He is now in *'Sudan'*, where he is preparing to do battle."

"We are supplying weapons to him," Busa said.

The "Adept" clapped his hands; the dancers dashed out through an archway.

A veiled, light-skinned young African woman in a translucent, wrap-around garment whirled out of the swirling smoke and began a dance on her tiptoes with fluid motions to a throbbing, pulsating beat. As Retchko stared transfixed, the glistening girl spun about the space, each time passing a little closer to him; then all at once the music stopped and she leaped out through an exit. A sudden silence came over the space.

The turbaned man smiled at his pale male guest. "You like her, no?"

"Ah . . . yes, of course."

"Then it is arranged." The "Adept" clapped his hands twice. A robed young man stepped out of the smoky shadows over to Retchko's reclining sofa and motioned for him to arise.

The youth led the Ukrainian down a curved ceramic-tiled corridor to a brass door. Pushing it open, the young fellow motioned. The white man stepped across the threshold into a bedroom. The servant put the palms of his hands together, bowed low, and turned away. The door closed.

By the flickering lights of torches, the general looked around the space. In the middle stood a high brass bed with golden side-curtains closed on three sides; across the top ballooned a golden satin canopy. The purple satin sheets were pulled down. An aroma of sweet incense permeated the place.

The door creaked aside and a veiled, tawny young female, clad in a loose, gauze-like shift, eased through the opening. As she pushed the door shut with a bare foot, Retchko recognized her as the solo dancer with the creamy coloration he had seen on the dance floor a few minutes earlier. With a single motion, the wide-eyed girl pulled the mask from her face.

Retchko gasped. *"Betty Nkrume!"*

-22-

Livshits and the two other plainclothes KGB agents strode with purposeful steps across the sidewalk. At the curb, the ranking Russian raised an impatient hand; a taxi drew up alongside them. The three men piled into the back seat. The driver turned about. "Destination?"

"To the airport—and hurry!"

The Intelligence officer reached into his coat pocket and pulled out the folded piece of paper with the statement they had forced Semen Putridchenko's brother to sign—the evidence they needed to prove that the fugitive had been in Kiev since fleeing Moscow. Of course, they had had to use "persuasion" to extract the needed information from the man, but that was standard procedure in the interest of "State Security". Under such "influences", Arvid Putridchenko had revealed that his younger brother Semen had passed through Kiev on his way to Gdansk, Poland to see their sister, then he was going to Madrid, Spain, which was the last place the man's brother had known concerning his whereabouts. The three KGB men warned the frightened fellow they would return in force if he held back anything. The general's brother swore it was all he knew. His signature sealed his story. It would go into his file.

The ticket stub inside the general's uniform pocket at the Moscow train station had led them to Kiev, where they knew Semen Putridchenko had relatives. The alert maintenance man who became suspicious of the untouched storage compartment and notified the security office had certainly deserved the bottles of Vodka and the hundred-ruble reward the KGB officer had arranged for him. Close examination of the evidence had revealed strands of hair on the clothes, suggesting that the suspect had shaved his head while still at the station. Now, they would search in Madrid for a stocky, baldheaded man who spoke with a Slavic accent. Not much, but it was something to go on.

* * *

INTERNOL Headquarters, Geneva, Switzerland; The Same Day:

Tarliani sat back and puffed on his curved smoking pipe as he read the latest decoded dispatches from the three agents in Nigeria. The trio had lately been feeding INTERNOL some intriguing new details about how the strict new security measures at the Lagos airport now made it the most dangerous airline destination in the world. The newest recruit had even learned the name of the man behind it all: a certain "Leonid Efimovitch Retchko", supposedly a Ukrainian who was claiming to be a former Soviet Army general who had left Moscow after the failed "August Coup". Not only was the information important, but it was remarkable how the operatives often crossed paths down there—yet only two knew of each other. The third was gathering Intelligence for the same international police agency, but was not aware of the existence of the other two agents, who in turn did not know of him. The setup was perfect for double-checking and triple-checking their reports.

Tarliani called his assistant on the interphone to come to his office.

"*Ja?*"

The Swiss spymaster handed a piece of paper with Retchko's name on it to the other man. "Bring me the *'dossier'* on this person."

He fumbled in a pocket of his tweed coat, pulled out a tobacco pouch and re-filled his pipe. As a blue cloud rose over him, he gazed out the fourth-story window at the people bustling along down below. Damn! he thought, squirming in his seat. He just could not place this "Retchko" individual. Perhaps the mysterious man was one of those nameless—yet important—Soviets who occasionally surfaced from obscurity, like Gorbachev had done. Another possibility: the fellow could be

339

someone about whom they already knew who was now operating under a cover name. At any rate, INTERNOL's records would have all the information.

But when the other man stepped back into the office, he was shaking his head. "I am sorry, sir, but there are no files on any 'General Leonid Efimovitch Retchko'."

* * *

Tanuta Refinery, Tanuta City, Nigeria; At the Same Time:

General Leonid Efimovich Retchko stood sweltering in the hot sun; his bald head baking inside the oven-like safety helmet. The sweating Security Chief, encased in one of the new silver-colored protective jumpsuits, watched as workmen dragged lengths of pipe into a part of the refinery that had been damaged by the storm.

Frank Ogawan came up with a sheaf of papers in his hand. "The new computer links have passed all the tests," he said, handing a printout to the sun-burnished white man. "Miss Anaya did a wonderful job supervising the repairs to the electronics."

Retchko turned away with a scowl. The earnest African irritated him, particularly when the boy talked about Lisa Anaya, which was often, he had noticed. *I suspect that the fellow's interest toward Lisa is more than just business. At some point, I may have to "neutralize" him.*

Retchko motioned to the refinery's manager. *Someone else I will have to deal with, for much the same reason.* "Nkrume! Now that the plant is ready to start-up, we must concentrate on making it more secure." He motioned at the half-track. "Let us return to your office."

Back at the main building, the Plant Manager sat in his executive's chair as Retchko sketched on a wallboard. The Security Chief aimed a pointer. "We will start with a review of all the staff and the workers, here. I want to know all about everyone at this refinery—their backgrounds; their lifestyles . . .

anything that might turn out to be important *or interesting.* I have a necessity to find out such things."

"I trust the people, here."

"*'Trust'* is not a good word for me. The important thing is *'control'*—I must know what everyone is doing *wherever they are.*" Retchko bored his eyes straight into those of the other man. "I will use my methods from Moscow—methods that were very effective, there."

"What . . . 'methods'?"

The Security Chief held his direct gaze. "I expect you will follow my directives."

The bald man paused for effect.

"I will implant a computer chip into the wrist of all employees. The chip will have identity codes and other personal information on it." He described the satellite system he had used in Moscow, without going into specifics about the Academy. "I will do this with all personnel, both here at the refinery and at the Lagos airport." *And, later, at other locations.*

Retchko held his stare all the time he was speaking in a measured, monotone pace; an intimidation technique he had perfected. *Nkrume is weakening. I will pay special attention to him—and not only because at the "Temple" I had the closest possible encounter with his wife.*

Nkrume gripped the armrests of his chair. "Of course—"

"Lester?" Lisa Anaya came in with some papers.

Retchko frowned. *The girl is ignoring me. I will get her attention.*

"Miss Anaya?" Lisa turned to him. "I wish to speak with you . . . alone."

He frowned at the Plant Manager. Lester Nkrume stepped from the room.

The Security Chief closed the door and stared for a long moment at the short-haired, cream-skinned young woman in the short skirt. *How would she look in a bedroom out of that dress and everything else? Like her wanton sister? She still owes me my "reward" for saving her life.*

The Ukrainian motioned for her to sit down. He took the executive chair behind the desk lately occupied by the other man.

Lisa Anaya hesitated, then eased herself into the opposite stuffed seat. The pale foreigner leaned forward and gazed straight at the girl's unblinking eyes; her throat bobbed. *Staring at these people with intent seems to put them in a compliant state of mind; almost like hypnosis. Cultural, perhaps? My natural force of personality? I prefer the latter explanation.*

The Ukrainian moistened his pudgy lips. "I need your—" he fumbled for the right words in English—"expert . . . *'talents'*."

The girl's expression graduated from indifference to interest as Retchko went on. "I want you to build a satellite transmitting and receiving station."

While the man described the wrist implants and how they would be tracked from orbit, along with the other electronic devices and programs he wanted her to design and put in place, she decided she had perhaps mis-read this crude-looking, bald-headed foreigner. The man was offering her an opportunity to put her specialized knowledge to work in a way she could never have imagined. Up to now, except for the storm repairs, her duties had been mostly routine; she had even considered returning to London to look for another job. But as the older man talked on, she knew that leaving the refinery was no longer necessary. "I will need specifications—"

"Unfortunately, when I left Moscow, I had to leave all the blueprints behind. I am not an electronics expert—*you* are. You will design and build the system from the beginning, and it must be done as rapidly as possible. There is not much time."

The girl spread her hands. "This will require a laboratory . . . equipment . . . hardware. Our facilities here are limited."

"You will have whatever you need. But time *is* important."

"What do *I* get out of this?"

"I will put in for a substantial increase in your salary. I can arrange other things, as well."

Lisa Anaya frowned. "What 'other things'?" Several times during the conversation she had noticed him watching her with an interest that looked almost clinical.

A grin flicked across the man's mouth that lacked any pretense at being subtle. "We will address those at the proper time."

"When my sister returns, she will be glad to hear that I will be staying here."

"When she *returns?*" Retchko tried to sound casual.

"Betty has gone with the 'Adept' and the *'temple girls'* to Amsterdam." Lisa Anaya noticed the man's puzzled look. "Twice a year, she goes there with them. While the old man does his business, they earn money in the Amsterdam brothels."

"Your sister works in a *brothel?*"

"She says she just goes along to make sure the other girls do not get into trouble. She tells me she stays busy . . . she likes to go shopping . . . sometimes she goes with the 'Dokteur' when he meets with the European 'Terrarranists'. Last time, she visited with our brother in London. He is now on holiday in America."

"What does her *husband* think about all this?"

"I have noticed he gets moody when she leaves." She twirled her short, curly brown hair in her slim fingers. "There are times when I think he does not trust her."

I can see how that *would be. At the proper time, this knowledge could be very useful to me.*

The stout man stood up and extended his pudgy hand. Lisa Anaya shook it. For the first time in his presence, she was smiling.

-23-

When Lawrence J. "Lucky Larry" Landay huffed into his office, the telephone on his desk was ringing. Still puffing from his morning run, the sweating sales company owner dropped into the high-backed leather executive chair and lifted the receiver. "'Landay Marketing'."

"'Lucky Larry'! Is it *you?*" A British-sounding female voice crackled in the earpiece.

"Who is this?"

"Lisa Anaya! I'm calling from Nigeria!"

"Lisa! Of course! How *are* you? And how did you find me? It's been a while!" *Too long a while*, he thought, warming up to the enthusiastic, youthful-sounding, speaker on the other end.

"There was an article about you in the alumni magazine about how you had started an electronics sales company there," she said, "I got the number from the operator."

"Well . . . what did I do to deserve this pleasure?"

There was a pause. "Larry, I need your help."

"My help? What's the deal?"

"I'm involved in a project with—satellite communications. It is very secret."

"That's okay . . . I'm used to working with secrets."

"Tell me—do you still have your machine we put together in lab to decipher codes?"

Larry looked across the room. On top of a filing cabinet sat the shoebox-sized wooden case. Back in school, as laboratory partners in a class, he and Lisa had built from scratch a pair of the simple code machines using computer keyboards and store-bought electronic parts and two wooden boxes. Even though he had intended to throw it away several times, he had never gotten around to it; after a while, the peculiar-looking device became a conversation piece. "As a matter of fact, I'm looking at it, right now."

"Really? I still have mine, too. Do you have your little code book? The one we wrote?"

"It's probably around here, somewhere." He wondered where this was leading.

"Wonderful! Connect the machine to the telephone line . . . I am going to send you a message in the 'S-*Twenty*' code like we used to do. What is your number, there?"

He told her his fax number. "I will hook it up, right now."

"Good." There was a little pause, then, "this is just like old times, right?"

The American felt a flush come to his face. "Yes—this is just like 'old times'."

"I will ring off, now, " she said in her proper British brogue. The receiver went silent.

Larry Landay hung up the telephone, leaned back and took several deep breaths. The room was spinning around a little. Oh, yes—he remembered Lisa Anaya, all right. How could he ever forget the brainy girl of the English accent and the creamy skin and green eyes back in grad' school? The very thought of her still sent up his blood pressure. He was surprised and pleased to hear her voice after all this time; wouldn't it be great to see her, again! But why did she want to communicate with him in a *code?*

Larry went on thinking; remembering. It had all started when he and Lisa had gone as part of a school group to the "Big Island" of Hawaii to study the design and construction of a deep-space tracking station and an observatory. At the time, they were only casual classmates, but that had all changed one evening when he and the girl had borrowed a car and drove down to a deserted black sand beach on the South Shore. Ignoring a billboard-size sign warning of dangerous surf, the girl had dashed barefoot out into the breakers. "Come on in!" she shouted to him, splashing and giggling, in the foaming, incoming tide, "are you afraid of a little water?"

"The sign over there says there are undertows—"

"Are you a 'weenie'?" She cupped her hands and flung a jet of saltwater at him on the shore. Not to be outdone by a *girl*, he pulled off his shoes and splashed out to her just as a roller cascaded over, drenching them both.

Larry looked out with misgivings at the heaving, rolling black ocean, backlit by the rays of the rising quarter-moon. It occurred to him that those undulating wavetops marching straight at them, could, at any moment, become less than friendly. As much fun as he was having rollicking in the surf with this carefree girl, maybe it was time to get out of the water.

As if to punctuate his thoughts, the moon brightened, spotlighting the sign warning swimmers that the waters along that beach were dangerous.

Just then, a giant comber slammed into them, causing the two to totter in the surging current. With a shriek, Lisa grabbed Larry's arm as a mighty out-tow pulled at their legs, almost causing them to lose their balance. "Let's get back to the shore!" Larry shouted. Holding on to each other, the two fought their way, slipping and sliding, back through the crashing, roiling, clawing waves, up the sloping sand to the safety of the foaming beachhead.

When they finally splashed ashore, she had pulled away from him and took off, laughing, across the bubbling wet sand. "We must be getting back to the hotel!" he called to her, "people will be suspicious!"

Lisa laughed over her shoulder. "Let them *be* suspicious!" As he reached for her arm, she skidded to a stop, causing him to stumble, sprawling, into the water's edge with her following after him. The girl's gasping, breathy voice was lost in the rolling, roaring, surging sandy sea swells washing over and around them on that isolated moonlit black sand beach down on the South Shore of the Island of Hawaii.

Larry Landay closed his eyes and flooded his mind in the memories of that supercharged night on the volcanic beach, which he had learned later was at the very southernmost point of the country—in the surf that night, the trysting two had been the most "southern" people in the whole United States.

But after they had graduated with their Masters Degrees in Electronic Engineering, he and Lisa had gone off to their separate careers. Along the way, he had started his own marketing company in Mountain View, California. One time, he had read in the alumni magazine that she was somewhere in Africa, but he hadn't remembered where it was. Her call just now had been the first time they had spoken to each other in a long while.

Larry stepped over to the filing cabinet and pulled down the little homemade code machine that had been the reason for her telephone call. It had seen no use since that lab class back in school; when he rubbed its top and then blew on it, tiny dust-balls fled off into the air.

He unplugged the fax machine; in its place went the decoder. He found an old dot-matrix printer, a keyboard and a stack of fan-folded paper on a closet shelf and hauled them out.

Lisa had said she would use the "S-Twenty" code—the same one they had used most of the time back in school. Since they had developed three different codes the machine could use, Larry opened a panel and looked down at the little cogwheels and cams inside the case. A tiny arrow pointed to the numerals "20"; the machine was already set. He closed the cover, stabbed the plug into a wall socket and flipped the power switch. A green light on the front lit up—for the first time in a long time, the little machine was "live." He turned on the printer and stepped back.

Something was missing. The code book! Larry's eyes drifted over to the filing cabinet. He pulled open a middle drawer and there it was: in a manila folder were the typed, stapled-together pages that had held the keys to the cryptology course.

Larry set the little book on the desk by the machine. Everything was ready. Now, he would see if she was really serious about sending him a message.

While he waited for something to happen, still sticky from the run, he stepped into his private bath for a quick shower.

When he turned off the water, he heard the buzzing of the printer in the next room. Toweling-off in a hurry, he pulled on a change of clothes. When he stepped into the office, the device was printing out numbers in four-numeric-digit sets. "Well, I'll be—it's the 'S-Twenty' code!"

When the printer stopped, he tore off the paper, sat down at his desk and opened the code book.

An hour-and-a-half later, Larry leaned back and looked at the results. Spread out before him on several sheets of paper was a list of electrical and electronic items—some of which would be

347

very large and heavy—that Lisa was requesting for delivery to Nigeria. Included were a pair of ten-foot-diameter parabolic dish antennas with all the hardware and equipment that went with them; fiber-optic and copper transmission lines; remote-control transmitters and receivers; other devices relating to sending and receiving signals to stationary satellites. Larry noted that most of the gear she wanted would be pre-tuned to what he knew were United States military frequencies.

"Wow!" he said under his breath, "what sort of business is Lisa *into*, down there?" She had not mentioned anything about being involved with the American military.

Larry picked up the code book and composed a message back to her; he would need a few days to locate sources and give her the prices on the things she wanted. Then he had another idea: If he got the order, he could go along with the shipment to Nigeria and help her set it up.

* * *

Lisa Anaya felt a flush come to her face. Larry could come here! I say, she thought, *that* would be grand! Ever since yesterday, when Retchko gave her the new assignment and she had started trying to locate the American, the young woman had been remembering and thinking about their old times together back in school. It would be great to see him, again. Maybe they could even rekindle their relationship.

* * *

Soviet Embassy, Madrid, Spain; the Same Day:

Livshits stared at the flickering images on the screen; in the darkened room, he and the KGB's Bureau Chief for Spain, along with other agents and technical experts, leaned forward in their seats.

"There he is!" one of the technicians called out. "Hold that picture, right there!" The man strode forward with a pointer. "This man—" The agent tapped the image of a baldheaded individual in the background of a long-shot.who was walking alongside a railroad sleeper car— "we believe is Putridchenko." The projectionist zoomed-in for a close-up of the subject.

"Show the next picture." A full-face image came up of a heavyset, hairless man carrying a valise. "These pictures were taken by a security camerat the Moscow train station at the time we believe Putridchenko boarded the train to Kiev."

"Alternate the comparison picture with this one in rapid sequence."

A stock photograph of the missing General Semen Putridchenko flashed on the screen, depicting a dark-haired man with bushy eyebrows and a dark mustache. After a couple of seconds, the picture of the hairless man by the train took its place. Several times the two sets of photographs shot up onto the screen, one after the other. It was clear to everyone in the room that, aside from the changes in the subject's hair, the features were very similar.

"Now, for the technical analysis of the facial shapes . . ." Thin, concentric yellow lines appeared on the screen, superimposed on the full-face photograph of the man in the train station. Everyone in the room stared at the wavy, saffron shapes that followed the contours of the subject's face. Then the picture of General Putridchenko flashed up. The lines on the screen also seemed to match the bald individual's face.

One of the agents shifted in his seat. "Everything about the man's face is the same in both pictures."

Livshits motioned for the projectionist to turn on the lights. "Ah, comrades—all this is very interesting, but the matter has already been settled." The others in the room turned in his direction. "I have showed you these comparison pictures in order for you to become very familiar with this subject. This morning our agents in Kiev showed General Putridchenko's brother the picture of the man at the train station . . . after a certain amount of—shall we say, 'encouragement'—he confirmed that the man *is* Semen Putridchenko. Based on his testimony and some other information, I believe he is here in Madrid." The agent picked up a stack of photographs and began handing them out. "Take these enlargements to all our agents and operatives. If Putridchenko is here, I want him found—I want him dead."

Tanuta Refinery, Two Days Later:

Leonid Efimovich Retchko leafed through the pages of "Landay Marketing's" quotation. "This source in America can supply all these things?" The man's eyes bored into Lisa Anaya's. "How soon can this source deliver these goods?"

Lisa Anaya crossed her legs in the chair on the opposite side of the desk. "That will depend on how they ship it. By air would be the fastest way. But this equipment will be heavy."

"After it arrives, how long will it take to get the system operational?"

"The agent in America can come here and help us install it."

"He will come *here*?"

Lisa thought it better not to divulge that she and "the agent" already knew each other. "It is rather common practice in America for suppliers to work with their customers on jobs like this."

"How much extra will it cost?"

"He says it is already in the price."

Retchko shrugged. "Very well, place the order . . . payment through the usual channels. I will give you the shipping arrangements."

Yes, sir." Then she noticed that her brother-in-law's personal things that had been in the office yesterday were gone. "Where is Lester?"

The man glanced at her over his reading glasses. "His desk is in the open office. From now on, I will be using this room."

* * *

Mountain View, California; The Next Morning:

Larry Landay was stepping toward the coffee maker when he happened to glance in the direction of the code machine and did a double-take—a folded-over printout was bunched-up all across the top of the printer! Forgetting about the coffee, he lifted the chaotic pile of paper up and away from the machine. Thank God, it hadn't jammed, he thought, as he took it to his desk.

Two hours later, when he had deciphered the message, what he saw was a purchase order from a "Tanuta Refining Company," located in Tanuta City, Nigeria. At the bottom was Lisa Anaya's name. On another sheet was a "freight forwarding" order directing that the merchandise go by ship from the Port of Los Angeles at San Pedro to Acapulco, Mexico. A truck would then carry the shipment to Mexico City. From there, according to Lisa's instructions, a special cargo plane would fly the goods to Lagos, Nigeria, where it would be put onto an inter-coastal ship to Tanuta City, down at the mouth of the Niger River. He would go with the shipment all the way to its final destination, then stay and help with the assembly and installation of the equipment. All the arrangements and special paperwork would be handled from Nigeria.

There was a note. *"Larry, secrecy is very important. Be careful about this. Lisa."*

The American shook his head. "Secrecy" he could understand, but what kind of "freight-forwarding" was *this?* As he re-read the purchase order, he realized that much of what they wanted had once been classified as "Top Secret" or "Embargoed" by the U.S. Government—in fact, some items had only very recently been released for limited sale outside the country. Several items on the list, due to their potential military applications, were still forbidden to certain countries. In any case, the shipment would require clearance from the Commerce and State Departments; perhaps even the Defense Department. These things would take time, and the purchase order made it clear that the goods had to be shipped right away, which he knew would be impossible if they followed the rules. And what did Lisa mean by "special paperwork?" Was there a secret plan to go-around the regular channels? Being arrested for illegal technology transfer was not on his agenda. What first had seemed like a perfect excuse to see Lisa again was now looking much more complicated. Perhaps even dangerous.

* * *

351

Lisa Anaya read Larry's return message with a frown. Why was he concerned about the shipment being legal? It seemed to be a straightforward business deal; that it could be anything else had not occurred to her. She would discuss the matter with the Security Chief.

* * *

After he had sent his coded note to Lisa, Larry Landay called up his friend, Joe Anglin, and asked for his help to put the package—his biggest deal, so far—together.

When Joe looked over the purchase order, he whistled. "Larry, what are those people gonna *do* with all this stuff?"

"I didn't ask . . . all they told me was that it had something to do with 'satellite communications'."

Joe Anglin flipped through more pages, shaking his head. "Well, maybe you *should* ask—you know 'Uncle Sam' doesn't like having his secret stuff getting into the wrong hands." He scanned down the sheets of paper with raised eyebrows. "And how about all this laboratory and test equipment they want . . . some of those things look pretty sensitive."

"I'm sure it's all right." Larry was trying hard to believe his own words.

"Okay, buddy—but I wouldn't want to put *my* butt in the crack over this."

"I wouldn't be going with the shipment to Nigeria if I didn't think everything was okay."

Joe Anglin's gray eyes went wide. *"You're going to Nigeria?"*

"I agreed to take it there and to help their people get it up and running."

"Man, you have more nerve than I do."

Larry swallowed. "There's a lot of work to do . . . let's get started."

* * *

352

Tanuta Refinery; The Next Day:

". . . and those who follow my instructions will have no difficulties—" Retchko held his un-wavering stare into Lisa Anaya's green eyes as he handed her a manila envelope across his desk.

The girl shook her head; blinking—it seemed as if the pale Ukrainian had put her under a spell; had physically measured her. For how long? All the while he had been speaking to her these past several minutes? Before that, even? Had she missed anything he had said?

". . . are the payment instructions—" The bullet-headed man was speaking in a metronomic-like voice. "I expect both you and this 'agent' in America to proceed with haste."

Lisa stepped into the corridor and felt chilled—her clothes were clammy—like she had been in a meat locker. Patting her blouse, as if to somehow remove any leftover taint from the conversation, Lisa turned in the direction of her work-station to send the coded instructions to Larry.

As she walked toward the open common office, Lester Nkrume stood in its doorway; beckoning. "I wish to speak with you," he said in a hoarse voice. Lisa thought he looked distracted—not the usually-confident, self-accustomed Plant Manager. He gestured toward another door at the far end of the hallway. "Let us go to the meeting room," he said.

The man hesitated, looked up and down the corridor, then followed her. He closed the door behind him. "I—wish to discuss with you these new 'designs' you are doing for General Retchko."

"Yes?"

"Lisa, these things are—*drastic.*" Lester Nkrume wrung his hands. "He seems suspicious of everyone! He is going after all of us in a way that makes me uneasy." He gestured at the open work-stations. "Look at me—he has taken over my own office! I am now sitting in a room with *clerks!*"

"I am sure you will get back your office as soon as the security system is put in."

Lester Nkrume shook his head. "I believe you are mistaken. These changes are permanent. And he is taking over *everything.*"

"Well, he has given *me* much freedom. But, if it will please you, I will try to be more careful, from now on." She reached for the door handle. "I must be going now." She waved the papers in her hand. "I must get this message ready to send to America."

She had taken only a few steps down the corridor when Frank Ogawan came up. "Miss Anaya," the office manager said, "I understand we will have a satellite installation here very soon."

Lisa gave the young man an indulgent nod. "Yes, and I am sure it will help you keep up with the latest developments."

With a half-smile, she side-stepped the fellow, who watched as she turned into her cubicle.

In his new office, Retchko snapped off the under-desk loudspeaker; he had heard every word of the conversations between Lisa Anaya and Lester Nkrume and with Lisa and the office manager. *My earlier impression that the Plant Manager was not strong was just proved correct. Now, I will begin to isolate and reduce the man to insignificance; moving him from his office was only the first step. I will allow Nkrume to stay around—as long as he behaves himself—so as to not arouse any suspicious talk among the employees. But his days of having any real authority at the refinery are over. And Frank Ogawan, that fawning, simpering fool of an office manager, will never amount to anything enough to be a threat. As for Lisa Anaya—I will continue to "cultivate" her for my own purposes. Very carefully, of course; the girl must never realize that I am using her for my own objectives . . .*

Retchko narrowed his eyes and grunted; the new hidden microphones in every room of the office buildings were already providing him with much useful information.

* * *

Port of Los Angeles, San Pedro, California; Three Weeks Later:

"Sign here, sir." The ship's Fourth Officer thrust a clipboard at Larry Landay's outstretched hand. "All your goods are loaded and in good order." Since Larry had already been on board the

'*Beacon Trader*' for two days, watching the stevedores loading his merchandise and other cargo, he knew the signatures were only a formality. The officers had even allowed him to put on a hard hat and go down into the cargo hold to check his items himself as they came on board.

The other man tipped a finger to his officer's cap and turned about into the charthouse.

Larry stepped to the ship's starboard handrail and gazed across at the shipping company's metal-sided warehouse on the wharf that was topped by the sign of the '*East Pacific Shipping Co.*'

While he stood there, his shirt fluttering in the morning harbor breeze as the ship prepared to cast off, some concerns about the shipment intruded into his thoughts—and not for the first time. For one thing, his Nigeria-bound cargo came on board without being inspected by United States Customs, which was unusual. Not only that; it seemed as if every scrap of paperwork had originated in Nigeria, since he had not seen any documents about the shipment from the American side, save for the waybills affixed to the individual crates and pallets by the shipping company and the ship's own manifest that he had just signed.

His gaze wandered to the bow of the freighter where crewmen were dogging-down the forehatch with a metal cover. Down on the dock a quartet of longshoremen were casting off the *Beacon Trader's* lines as a pair of tugs came up. Soon the space between the side of the freighter and the dock widened; the ship swung around into the channel. Larry felt a rumbling vibration coming up through his shoes; a big puff of black smoke shot from the stack; then a column of diesel exhaust billowed into the air above the midship superstructure. The passenger-freighter, as long as two football fields, began to make its ponderous way down the channel, past other ships tied-up at wharves; its masts clearing close under the big suspension bridge; then began to pick up speed.

A half-hour later, when the ship rounded the westernmost opening in the low, two-mile-long breakwater, the engine vibrations increased and the freighter lunged into the long Pacific swell. Larry, holding onto the railing while trying to get used to the up-and-down and unceasing side-to-side and back-and-forth motions of the ship, made his way around to the aft end of the superstructure and stood in the salty sea breeze for some time as the Southern California coastline dissolved into the morning haze over the ship's boiling silver wake. Turning about, squinting, he could just recognize, low on the horizon off the starboard side, the blue-green humps of Santa Catalina Island. As the freighter plowed along in the sunshine, a squadron of screaming seagulls dipped close by the ship's stern.

Just then, a nearby loudspeaker crackled out an announcement: "Now hear this! Luncheon is now served in the dining salon!"

Good idea, Larry thought; he could forget for a while the mission to Africa and concentrate on his appetite. He dropped down a set of steep companionway stairs to the second deck. In the paneled, carpeted dining-room, that Larry thought was rather plush for a freighter, several passengers were already seated at well-set tables. The steward motioned toward a big oval-shaped table in the middle of the space. "You will be at the Captain's Table."

A white-haired, middle-aged man looked over the top of his wine list at Larry. "You like to sail on freighters?" Larry picked up a European accent. The others were staring at the American.

"It's the first time for me."

"We take a freighter holiday every year," the foreign-sounding man said, nodding at a somewhat plumpish, dark-haired woman whom Larry guessed was his wife. "We took freighter trips in the Baltic back when we lived in Poland—'Gdansk', Poland—we just came back from visiting my wife's brother, there."

"Most people don't know about these kinds of ships," a gray-haired lady put in, "it's a lot more casual on freighters, compared to regular cruise ships. The food is good, the people are friendly and I like the way they let us have the run of the ship. "

"As long as we behave ourselves!" another fellow spoke up.

While the others were talking, Larry had been trying to follow a conversation taking place at the door. ". . . at *that* table," a slightly-built, cream-skinned individual who looked to Larry to be in his late-twenties was saying, nodding toward their gathering in the center of the room.

The steward led the man over to where they were sitting. "Right here, sir," he said. The light-complexioned young black man, with a self-conscious look on his face, took a seat.

A thin, red-headed man spoke up. "Welcome to our crowd," he said, spreading his hands, "it looks like we'll all be eating together for the next few days . . . let us get acquainted."

The newcomer gave a half-hearted smile. "I have always wanted to sit at a 'Captain's table'," he said, in British-sounding accent.

"I am a retired dentist," the white-haired European man said.

"I teach high-school science," the orange-topped fellow put in, with a grin. "I take long vacations to get away from all those kids!"

"I am a real estate agent," the gray-haired woman said.

"I am into marketing," Larry put in.

The white-haired man nodded at the newest arrival. "How about you?"

The fellow with the light-chocolate skin looked at his hands for a moment, then around at the others with a slight grin. "I am a—photographer. I am taking pictures for a magazine."

Another passenger looked interested. "Oh? Which magazine?"

"The . . . biggest . . . ah—travel . . . magazine."

Larry's eyebrows went up. "You're taking travel pictures on a *freighter*?"

Before the man could say anything, a ship's officer appeared at the entrance and spoke to the dining steward. After a moment, the two made their way toward the center table, to the admiring stares of everyone in the room. "Captain Parkins is joining you," the steward said, pulling out the chair at the head of the table for the man. The others started to rise.

"As you were," the white-uniformed officer boomed in an authoritative voice, placing his gold- braided hat on the table, "I always take the first meal of the journey with our passengers."

"How many days will it take for us to get to Acapulco?" someone asked.

"Four days, usually. The ship will be there for one day, unloading some goods and taking on stores. Then we will go to Panama City; then to Buenaventura, Colombia; and on to Valparaiso. After that, we'll go back to Los Angeles. We follow this schedule every six weeks."

A steward came up with a big tray and started placing heaping, steaming plates in front of the passengers. Another attendant served the captain. The subject became freighter food, which Larry was discovering compared favorably with that of some cruise ships on which he had traveled. The only complaint he could muster was that there seemed to be a smell of diesel exhaust all around the ship, which he guessed was usual for freighters.

As the convivial conversation carried on, several times Larry caught the photographer looking hard at him.

* * *

Tanuta Refinery, The Next Day:

When Lisa Anaya dropped a report onto Retchko's desk, her eyes fell on a paper on top of some others. Since she could hear the general's rasping voice coming from down at the far end of the corridor where he was having a conversation, she picked up the sheet and started to scan it in a hurry. As she read down the page, her eyes went wide; her hand went to her mouth to stifle a gasp. All at once the Security Chief's voice sounded louder, along with a shuffle of footsteps. He was coming back! Hastily, she stuck the paper back in its original place and turned away from the desk just as the bald man's stocky bulk came through the doorway. "I left the report about the storm on your desk," she said, trying to appear at ease.

The Ukrainian dropped into the seat and nodded at her in his standard gesture to leave.

Back in her cubicle, the young woman sat motionless for some seconds; there seemed to be a roaring in her ears. She must try to get a message to Larry.

* * *

At Sea, the Next Morning:

On the third ring a sleepy Larry lifted the telephone receiver. "A *'Radiogram'?* I will be there in a little while . . . thank you."

It was then he became aware of lurching motions of his cabin. Through the open porthole came the sounds of roaring seas and the pounding of the hull against the ocean that were not there when he went to bed last night. It would seem they were now in rough waters.

* * *

In the radio shack, the operator stuffed the message into an envelope and put Larry's name on it, then dropped it into the countertop basket. Then, he printed a duplicate, put it in another envelope, and placed it in his own desk drawer. It would later be picked up just as the other person had arranged that he do with any correspondence either to or from the American. Not a usual procedure—it was a violation, in fact—but the passenger had slipped him some money to do so.

* * *

Larry paid the radio operator and tore open the envelope. The import of the message hit him after he read it the second time:

==*RADIOGRAM*==

—LAWRENCE J. LANDAY ABOARD BEACON TRADER—

YOU ARE BEING FOLLOWED. BE CAREFUL.

L. A.

"L.A.?" The message was from Lisa Anaya! He looked at the radio operator. "When did this come in?"

"A little while ago . . ." The fellow acted casual, as if the reception was routine.

But as soon as the American had closed the door, the radio man reached for the telephone and placed a call to one of the passenger cabins.

* * *

Stuffing the paper into his pocket, Larry dropped down two decks to the dining salon; the mysterious message from Lisa still fresh on his mind. Stepping into the room, Larry observed that the Polish man's wife was not there. At the head of the table, the captain's chair also sat empty. As Larry and the others took their seats at the center table, everyone was commenting on the heavy seas through which they were now sailing and the exaggerated motions of the ship. Larry noticed that the dining-room attendants were having to move about with careful steps and deliberate balancing motions as they went about their duties.

About the time they were situated around the big table, the cream-skinned young man who had said he was a photographer came through the doorway and made his way toward them. The American pointed at an expensive-looking camera slung around the fellow's neck. "Taking pictures, today?"

"Ah, yes—I want to use my camera . . ."

"Oh, I *like* your camera!" the real estate woman gushed, "we use a lot of pictures when we sell a property—do you do real estate pictures?" The fellow hesitated; the lady seemed to be having somewhat of a hard time getting the fellow passenger to talk. "Pictures of houses?"

He shook his head. "No . . . travel pictures, only."

"Travel pictures of *'freighters'?*" Larry put in, with sarcasm. "What kind of camera *is* that?"

The fellow turned the device around and looked at the front of it as if reading the name for the first time. "It is a—'*Hassel* . . . *blad*'—a 'Hasselblad'." The fellow pulled it from around his neck and set it on the table by his coffee cup.

The Polish man looked interested. "My wife and I take nature photographs as a—hobby. We do close-up pictures of plants and insects and small animals . . . and other things."

The science teacher was also staring at the camera. "A very good camera," he said. "The American astronauts took their pictures on the moon using a 'Hasselblad'." This information did not seem to impress the photographer, who said nothing.

Larry wanted to keep the stranger talking; most photographers, it seemed to him, would have reacted to the others' comments about his camera. "What kind of film does your camera use?"

"Ah, I believe it is 'one-twenty'."

"Color? Black-and-white? Slides . . . Prints?"

"Ah—pictures." The man paused, as the steward poured a round of coffee in everyones' cups, then he went on, "I take black-and-white pictures."

"Oh!" the schoolteacher said, "like *'Ansel Adams'*! He used to shoot really terrific outdoor pictures in black-and-white, a long time ago."

The cream-colored young man looked uncertain. "'Ansel Adams'?"

Just then, the stewards arrived with the food and the topic of photography dropped away.

* * *

After the breakfast, Larry stood gripping the handrail, his feet spaced wide on the heaving main deck forward of the superstructure, as he watched the foaming seawater gush by the side of the plunging, pitching ship. Overnight, the wind and the seas of the eastern Pacific through which they were passing had risen; the cargo-passenger freighter now slammed along in a roaring seaway, its rising and falling bows booming as it rode over swells and plowed through deep troughs, shoving aside green-white walls of water that flung upward and outward, cascading back onto the foredeck in a swooshing silvery spray that drenched everything. Overhead, the wind hummed and moaned in the masts and the rigging. Larry braced himself against the shuddering ship's sudden motions that every few seconds caused him to nearly lose his balance as he gazed outward at scudding, dreary-looking gray clouds that were dropping almost to sea-level in the blustery winds.

While he took in all this, The American's thoughts were dominated by the conversation at the breakfast table, just now. He was certain that the light-hued black man was no real photographer—everyone in that business knew about Ansel Adams, arguably the best and certainly the most famous landscape photographer of all time. *'Black-and-white'* pictures, did the fellow say? These days, travel magazines tried to outdo each other with splashy *color* layouts, he knew. And the British-speaking fellow sounded like a newcomer to the 'States, based on his accent and his seeming lack of knowledge about current American topics.

His musings were interrupted by a touch on his shoulder. Larry whirled about to discover the same "photographer" from the breakfast table standing next to him! The young man gave what Larry suspected could have been a pre-planned grin. "You are traveling on holiday?" he spoke loudly over the noise of the roaring, swishing sea and the kettledrum-like "booms" of the big ship's hull attacking the roiling waters.

Larry was caught off-guard by the fellow's sudden appearance and the question. "Yes . . . no—it's somewhat of a— 'business trip', I would say!" He fairly shouted over the sea-noises.

"You are going to Acapulco?"

"I plan leave the ship at Acapulco—yes."

The other man sidled up beside him and held onto the rail. "You will stay there?"

Larry felt a prickling sensation the back of his neck; he did not like the direction these questions were going. The American glanced at the fellow. "You say you are a photographer?"

"I am new at this picture-taking business." The traveler fingered his camera case. "I took a photography course in London, where I live. I hope to sell the ship-story to a travel magazine."

Larry stared out at the hypnotic up-and-down motions of the undulating seascape as the freighter pushed along. He reminded himself that the reason he was on this ship was to ensure the safe delivery of the cargo to Nigeria. The stranger's story sounded plausible, yet his questions struck Larry as pushy. The American now regretted divulging he was getting off at Acapulco. He turned and for the first time noted that the fellow had green eyes. "Well, I wish you all success in your photography career."

The passenger looked ill at ease. "I will go to my cabin, now," he said. Clutching the camera case, he turned toward the companionway leading to the second deck. As the young man trudged up the steep steps, Larry watched him go with misgivings; his story had sounded contrived.

Perhaps it would be a good idea, he thought, to check on the electronics shipment down on the cargo deck. Holding onto the handrail, he made his way forward a couple of hundred feet on the rising-and-falling spray-splashed main deck; past a shimmering, wet-steel forest of white-painted masts, cargo booms, cranes and other machinery to a dripping, canvas-topped companionway entrance up near the ship's bow. He clattered down several sets of narrow steps to the third cargo deck into a big space that was groaning from the wracking forces of the ship's movements. In the shadowy light of bare bulbs, Larry swayed down a lurching, working alleyway; his ears assaulted by the thunderclaps of the ship's hull wrestling with the forces on the outside; past goods stacked high to the overhead, to where his shipment was situated near a vertical hatchway shaft. As he groped around the wooden crates and pallets that were secured by ropes to the juddering deck he detected a strong odor of—what was it? *Diesel fuel.*

Then Larry noticed something else unusual: the shipping company waybill inside a clear plastic envelope that was affixed to one of his crates was *wrinkled.* When he looked closely at the envelope and ran his fingers over it; sure enough—it had been slit-open and cleverly re-sealed with cellophane tape! Since it was intact the last time he saw it, it must have been opened in the meantime! He tugged at an envelope on another crate—it also came open! Larry's eyes went wide. *What's going on, here?*

Bracing himself, he clambered about the rest of the pallets and crates and found that *all* of his waybill envelopes had been opened and re-taped! He knew for sure that the manifest he had signed the day they left port had listed the same information as these company · documents—so why would anyone want to tamper with the envelopes—unless the person about whom Lisa had warned him had found the cargo and now knew its contents! A quick inspection of some other shipments nearby revealed that *their* envelopes were intact, which told him *his* goods had been singled-out by someone for special attention. Perhaps that someone was watching him at that very moment! Larry spun around, hoping to catch any such individual spying on him. But he seemed to be the only one on the rolling, pitching third level of the forward cargo hold.

He idly kicked at a folded paper on the dingy deck next to a nearby pallet. A page from one of his envelopes? But when Larry opened the new-looking sheet, he had an even greater shock: *It was a duplicate of the radiogram he had received that morning from Lisa Anaya!*

-24-

Acapulco Harbor, 7:35 AM; Three Days Later:

Larry stood at the rail next to the Polish doctor and his wife as they looked down on a plunging, black-hulled cutter swinging up alongside the ship's accomodation ladder. When two men in civilian clothes hopped onto the platform, the red-haired school teacher pointed at one of them. "That guy's the 'harbor pilot' . . . the other is the 'Customs' man."

In the sea-breeze, the stocky Polish woman pushed her dark hair out of her face. "This is just like when we used to take our Baltic cruises."

An hour later, the *Beacon Trader* was warping alongside the commercial wharf. Looking down, Larry spotted several semi-trailer trucks parked on the pier, their drivers standing beside them with papers in their hands. Already the freighter's cargo cranes were swinging around over the ship's open hatchways.

By the time the gangway dropped into place, most of the passengers were ready to disembark. Even though he was ready to get going, Larry had come to know and like most of the people on the ship—the exception had been the aloof "photographer" who had stayed off to himself most of the time. On the occasions Larry had observed him wandering about the freighter with the camera slung around his neck, he had never seen the fellow actually take a picture. One day at lunch when the young man was absent, the others around the dining table had talked about it. "I always thought photographers took pictures," someone had said, "and I don't see him shooting any."

More than once, Larry had wondered if the light-skinned black man was the person on the ship Lisa had radioed about who was supposed to be following him. Even though the guy had behaved strangely, he had no proof that the mysterious passenger was anyone other than a bumbling neophyte who, like he said, was trying to sell pictures of his journey by freighter to a travel magazine. But then he had drawn attention to himself by *not* taking pictures. Perhaps the person who was supposed to be on his trail was someone he did not suspect! He would have to keep looking over his shoulder until the shipment reached its destination. And it was still a long way to Tanuta City, Nigeria.

Larry felt in his pocket for the peculiar little card Lisa had faxed him just before he left Mountain View. "You must have it," she had written, "for identification." It was a rectangle about the size of a business card with a serrated top edge that he had pasted onto a cutout piece of index card.

A ship's officer swung a gate aside and touched the brim of his hat. Larry, who was carrying his luggage bag, nodded back, then he and the other departing passengers, including the "photographer," lurched down the gangway to the pier. At dockside, when he inhaled the sweet Acapulco air, he realized how much he had become used to the diesel smell of the ship.

As the American cast about, trying to get his bearings, a brown-skinned man wearing a cap with a *"Mack Truck"* logo on it was stepping toward him. Black, very stiff-looking hair stuck out underneath the cap's edges. In the man's hand was what looked to Larry like a small paper.

"Señor Landay?" he spoke in a heavy accent.

The American nodded.

"Identificación?" The man thrust out the object, that Larry realized was a card just like the one in his pocket. In a hurry, he scrambled around for the pasted-on paper from Lisa and lifted it to the other man's card. The jagged edges were a perfect match. The man motioned in the direction of a nearby tractor-trailer. "Come with me, señor . . . everything is arranged."

His heart pounding, Larry followed the fellow around to the left side of a dirty "Mack" truck tractor. Larry noticed the rig had no markings and its license plates were covered with dried mud. When the Mexican banged on the bottom of the driver's door, a dark-haired young man stuck his head out the window. The man with the cap gestured toward the moored ship. The truck's diesel roared to life shooting skyward a cloud of greasy black smoke. With an agonized-sounding grinding of gears that made Larry wince, the truck shuddered toward the edge of the pier, where the cranes had already unloaded several pallets of cargo from the ship.

As Larry watched, another man came up with some papers in his hand and drew the trucker aside. For some moments, the two talked to each other out of earshot of the American, their heads close together. The dock man turned and bustled up the gangway to the ship's deck. The fellow with the cap came toward Larry. "Señor, we will have your—shipments off the boat—very—soon," he said in his heavy, halting English.

Larry looked up as the freighter's cargo derrick swept out with a ten-foot long wooden crate slung underneath it that Larry recognized as part of his load. With jerks and shudders the crane lowered the box onto the dock. As the lines dropped and the cargo boom began moving once more above the ship's rail in the direction of the open forward hatch, a very large forklift whined up. The Mexican truck driver motioned at the rig, shouting something in Spanish. The machine scooped up the crate and hauled it to the front of the flat trailer where it lowered its load onto the bed. Before long, the entire load of crates and pallets was lashed down onto the trailer.

The dock man shuffled up to where Larry and the other man were standing. In his hand was a clipboard. "Sign here, señor." The American put his signature at the bottom of the top page. The fellow turned to leave.

"Don't I get a copy of that?"

The Mexican shook his head. He nodded at the driver, then stepped away before Larry could say anything else.

The man with the cap made an impatient gesture toward the truck. "We must go, now," he said, "they are waiting for us." Larry, wondering who "they" were and with an uncertain feeling, followed the fellow around to the right side of the tractor. The man climbed up and opened the door. "Get in," he said, motioning to Larry, who stashed his travel bag into a space behind the seat and took the middle position. With a rumbling growl from the diesel, the lurching truck, with the driver furiously working his hands and feet through the shifter, turned about and made its way across an expanse of stacked containers to the edge of the dockyard. As they came up to a gate, the barrier swung open. Without slowing down, the roaring rig rushed right through.

In a few minutes, the truck turned onto a highway and started out along the undulating landscape of southwestern Mexico.

The American glanced through the rear window at the load behind them, then at the men on either side who were staring straight ahead without speaking; there was an air of unreality about all this. His hands were sweating. "How long will it take us to get to Mexico City?" he shouted over the roaring engine to the man with the cap.

"Señor, do not worry about that—the *'Organization'* has—arranged everything!"

Larry decided he would just have to trust these two un-talkative men to know what they were doing. *But what was this "Organization" about which the man had just mentioned?*

The young man downshifted and the truck began to labor up a long grade into mountains.

* * *

United States Customs, Los Angeles, California; at About the Same Time:

Carside looked up as his assistant came into the office. "These are the cargo manifests of ships that left San Pedro in the past seven days." The young man handed a stack of papers to the man and glanced at the brass nameplate on his boss's desk: *"Auditor of Commercial Cargoes"*.

The older man flipped through the sheets, remembering some of the ships' names, even what their holds had looked like when he was an inspector. Though he was no longer at the docks, he still liked to keep his finger on the pulse down there.

The younger fellow was hanging back. Carside frowned. "What is it?"

"We found a discrepency." He handed his superior a photocopy of a manifest. The pages were about a cargo-passenger ship called, *"Beacon Trader"*. Carside's eyebrows went up in recognition; one time he and his his wife had taken a cruise on

368

that particular ship to Acapulco and flew home as it went on to destinations farther south. In fact, according to the itinerary that was attached, she should be in Acapulco about right now. There was a notation that on its last trip the ship had encountered a fuel system breakdown and its propulsion plant was due for a major dockyard overhaul. Carside scanned down the list that ran several pages: machine tools, exercise equipment, textiles; refrigerated produce from the Imperial Valley. He knew that one reason the *Beacon Trader* was popular with shippers was its big refrigerated cargo holds that took up the entire back-half of the ship. On its return trips, it would bring to California huge loads of tropical fruits from Chile and Costa Rica. And its passenger accomodations were practically on a par with many cruise ships.

"What's so unusual about this particular shipment?"

"Look at this—" The younger man ran his finger down to a section of "exercise equipment". "See this shipment?" The manifest showed a consignment of two crates, each of two-hundred cubic feet, plus three pallets of goods each weighing about three-thousand pounds. Carside knew that—even in this exercise-crazy world—*that* particular load looked like a lot of workout stuff. At the bottom of the page he read that the goods had been assigned by a company in Amsterdam, Holland, by the name of "Hannecker-Johannanvelt, Ltd." to the "East Pacific Shipping Co.". A declaration stated the cargo would be off-loaded at Acapulco to a trucking company called, "Guerrero-Federal Transporte, S.A."

"I checked on this forwarder and did not find any such company in Amsterdam—and there was nothing about the Mexican trucking company, either."

"Maybe they are new outfits."

"I made sure our list is up-to-date."

Carside gestured for the other man to stay in the room, then lifted the telephone handset and called the Customs agent at the San Pedro dock where the *Beacon Trader* had loaded the cargo. By the tone of the Chief Auditor's voice and from his facial expressions, the assistant got the impression that something was indeed unusual about that particular shipment.

The man hung up the receiver. "You were right—some things don't add up about that load." He looked thoughtful for a moment. "The shipment was supposedly inspected at the point of manufacture, at Él Segundo, near the Los Angeles International Airport. When it arrived at the San Pedro dock with seals on the crates and pallets and the paperwork that stated it was already inspected, the Customs inspector passed it straight through to the ship." The young assistant started to speak, but Carside raised his hand. "Wait—here's where it gets interesting: *There are no manufacturers or wholesalers of that type of exercise equipment in or around Él Segundo!*"

The assistant snapped his fingers. "Él Segundo is where—"

"*. . . the big defense electronics plants are!*" Carside reached for the telephone. "I'm calling the agent in Acapulco."

At length, Carside put down the receiver. "Mexican Customs says there is no written record of the shipment . . . but they say some people at the dock do remember seeing a truck loading what looked like the goods. They will notify the police to be on the lookout for the truck."

* * *

After some hours of steady pulling up a mountain grade, the terrain began to level-out. The dark-haired man with the "Mack" hat pointed at a small building alongside the road. The heavy rig pulled up in front of the yellow stucco place with a sign out front that announced the establishment was a *"Cantina"*.

When the American dropped to the ground, he saw they were in a hamlet that looked about like what he would have imagined a typical Mexican town to look, complete with a bored-looking burro tied up to a hitching post in front of a tiny store across the road.

He followed the other two through a squeaking screen door into a room furnished with several tables covered with red-and-white checkerboard cloths, each surrounded on four sides by high-backed ladder-chairs that looked to Larry as if they had seen a lot of use.

As the Californian took his seat in one of the battered seats, off to the side, a mustachioed man lifted a telephone receiver and spoke in a low voice into the mouthpiece. Putting it down, he came over to the three customers. His teeth gleamed beneath the bushy black brush below his nose. *"Buenos dias, señors!"*

* * *

An hour later, after they had finished their lunch, the trio climbed back up into the cab and the big rig roared off. They had gone but about a kilometer when the truck came up behind a long, slow-moving line of dump trucks and construction machinery. Kilometer after kilometer the snaking procession crawled along on the winding, narrow, two-lane road while the young driver and the dark-haired man with the "Mack" hat cursed at the slow-up. Finally, when they came a straight stretch of road with no opposing traffic ahead, the youth jammed the shift lever into a lower gear and floorboarded the accelerator pedal. The big combination waddled out into the opposite lane, gathering speed as fast as the fellow could work the engine and the gearbox. Finally, after what seemed to Larry like an eternity out in the exposed lane, he twisted the wheel and the truck swung back into the right lane. The speedometer was pointing at 140 kilometers an hour. Larry glanced back wide-eyed at the load that was rocking back and forth against the flat-bed tie-downs. The fellow let off the accelerator and eased back on the rig's speed.

Even as they were still slowing, all at once, there came a siren behind them! Larry turned about and stared in consternation at the flashing red and blue lights of a police car pulling up alongside the truck. A uniformed officer was waving a pistol out the window at them!

The truck pulled off onto the shoulder in a cloud of dust. The flashing police car drew up behind it. Shaking his head, the man in the right seat climbed down from the cab.

Two grim-faced officers came up to the side of the trailer. One whipped off his metal-rimmed, green sunglasses and looked the man from the truck up and down with a sneer of contempt, while the other officer stooped under and around the truck trailer, poking here-and-there with his billy club.

As Larry stared out the rear window, his heart pounding, the man jerked back the corner of a canvas cover, exposing part of a pallet bearing the antenna system meant for Tanuta City. The man with the hat said something and a loud argument broke out in Spanish.

At length, the Mack-hat man pulled himself back up into the front seat, shaking his head, groaning. "Oh, señor . . . we have much trouble!"

The powerful patrol car swept around the truck, its tires spinning up a dust cloud. "We must follow them,." the man moaned.

Swaying from side-to-side, the rig rolled back onto the roadway behind the police cruiser.

Two minutes later, the car ahead of them turned off the pavement and pulled up at a ramshackle white stucco building set about fifty meters off the highway, at the edge of some woods. It appeared the structure had until recently been a store and gas station. A crudely-lettered sign that read, *"CORTE"*, was nailed above the doorway. Remembering his school-days' Spanish, Larry took the word to mean, "Court House," which, given the nature of their cargo, suggested all sorts of possibilities; none encouraging. A gnawing feeling, abetted by the spicy Mexican meal he had just eaten, came into his stomach. The driver set the truck's brakes and turned off the engine.

The man to Larry's right pulled on his mustache. "We must go with these *'hombres'* . . ." The three occupants of the Mack dropped down and followed the troopers inside. The American's heart was pounding—*what is this all about?* One of the officers called out something in a loud voice to no one in particular, as there was no one else in sight. A second later, however, a grossly overweight individual with thinning black hair and a bushy handlebar mustache brushed aside a dingy muslin curtain at the rear and shuffled through a door opening, hitching up his pants. He spotted the officers and grinned, revealing several missing front teeth. The remaining ones had a decidedly green cast.

Larry's puzzlement as to who he might be was answered when the trooper again spoke. *"Él juez!"* The fat, green-mouth man was a "judge"! The American was sure he saw the officer wink gravely at the official, who narrowed his eyes in return. Then followed a jabbering conversation in Spanish between the two officers and the frowning "judge", who was shaking his head. Larry glanced at his companions; the man with the hat had a stricken look on his face.

The officer grinned, pointing to Larry. "'Americano'!"

One of the policemen jabbed Larry's ribs with his billy club. The hat-man gestured. "He wants us to follow him, señor!" All went back outside to the truck. One of the officers pulled back the canvas from the corner of the same pallet as before and spoke to the gap-toothed fat man, who was nodding.

"He wants us to go back inside," the Mack-hat man told Larry, whose side still smarted from the officer's club. They stepped down a short musty corridor and made a turn into a disorderly room with a half-dozen rickety ladderback chairs situated about.

Larry looked around. Is this a courtroom? he wondered.

An officer motioned for the truckers to stand in front of a cluttery pile of planks where an old door, minus its handle and hinges, was laid across a pair of scuffed carpenter's saw-horses. With a start, Larry recognized the conglomeration as the "judge's" bench!

Puffing, the obese man settled heavily into a groaning ladderback chair and pulled on his enormous mustache. One of the troopers handed him a piece of paper, that he glanced over. The official then spoke something in Spanish to the man with the hat, who seemed to be draining of color. "He says we were speeding when we passed the other trucks . . ."

All at once Larry had a prickly feeling. *This was a setup! The slow-moving dump trucks and road-building machines had been creeping along on purpose in order to cause their truck to have to speed-up to get around them, so the officers could swoop down, catch them, and haul them off to this so-called "court"! Were they now in the clutches of a gang of roadside racketeers who could very well be desperate, dangerous men? Was there a secret jail nearby? A torture chamber? Shallow graves? He had read stories about places such as this.*

Larry turned to the man in the hat. "Ask the 'judge' this: 'Why couldn't the road graders and the trucks try to stay out of the way of other vehicles driving through? Maybe if they'd pull off to the side of the road every now and then, people wouldn't have to drive so fast to get around them'—"

At this the man reddened, then looked up at the fellow behind the "bench" who was staring at them. He said something in his native tongue to the man, who sucked in his breath. For an eternity the pudgy man riveted his eyes on the American. He shot a glance at the troopers, who had thunderous expressions on their faces.

The magistrate whacked down his gavel on the makeshift bench so hard Larry thought he had cracked it; the saw-horses scooted a couple of inches sideways on the dusty floor. The policemen grabbed Larry and the young truck driver by their shoulders and shoved them, stumbling, back out the front door. One drew his pistol at the gasping, wide-eyed American and the quaking driver. The two prisoners raised their hands. The officer's revolver swung back and forth at the two young men's midsections. As they stood there, through the screen door Larry could hear what sounded like a heated discussion in Spanish between the "judge" and the man from the truck.

Then, things became quiet. The officer glanced at the empty door opening, then back at his captives. His gun wavered for a second, then he caught himself and with both hands aimed the pistol straight at the American's stomach.

The other officer came out just then and signaled for the policeman to lower his weapon.

The man in the hat burst out the doorway and motioned for the two other riders to follow him.

"Let us go at once," he gasped, hastening toward the truck. Larry turned and stepped in a hurry after the others toward the truck. "Get inside! *'Rápido'!*" the man went on, with furious gestures, as they clambered up into the cab. The diesel engine rattled to life. Without waiting for the usual warm-up, with a loud "swoosh" of releasing air brakes the driver maneuvered the rocking rig back onto the pavement. As they drove away from the creepy "court-house", Larry took a quick look back through the rear window and saw the two officers and the "judge" standing outside the weatherbeaten building with hands on their hips, staring at them.

Larry was still shaking. "What happened?"

"I gave them *'pesos'*, señor . . . many pesos. They will not bother us, now."

When they had driven about a kilometer up the road, the men saw—headed toward them—the same slow procession of trucks and construction machines that had been their nemesis an hour ago. Behind them was a line of frustrated-looking drivers. Larry turned about and watched the leading car pull out into the other lane to pass. A minute later, when he again glanced around he saw—far back in the distance—the flashing red and blue lights of a police car.

The officers were making another arrest.

* * *

As the rig swayed back onto the road, inside one of the crates the load shifted, causing a switch to close, activating a rado transmitter whose coiled output cable happened to be touching a metal plate. Powered by its fresh battery, the unit began broadcasting a signal.

In a synchronous orbit, 22,300 miles above Manaus, Brazil, a Signal Intelligence satellite of the United States's "National Security Agency" detected the transmission. The onboard computer calculated the source of the signal to be at ninety-two-point-seventy-one-kilometers south-southwest of Mexico City. The satellite started relaying the continuous broadcast to a ground-receiving station at Sunnyvale, California.

-25-

Eleven-hundred miles east of Sunnyvale, hundreds of feet under Cheyenne Mountain at Colorado Springs, Colorado, a flashing, highlighted message appeared on the screen at Lieutenant Dixon's console. The young officer pressed a button that brought up current U.S. Military activities in the region where the signals were originating. The screen showed nothing. Frowning, he punched a button that connected him to the Watch Officer of the section that monitored interceptions of surface signals in the Western Hemisphere. "Colonel, we are intercepting a signal on 'D-Console' from a ground-based source in southern Mexico that is transmitting on a restricted U.S. Military frequency."

The colonel touched a button on his console and the same screen as Lieutenant Dixon's came up in front of him. "Yes—I see it." The senior officer struck another key and the type of the intercepted signal displayed onto his screen. "The transmission is on a channel used by United States commanders in the field to send coded burst signals to a military satellite that relays the information to the theater commander."

The colonel scrolled down some more on the screen. "The channel is also used by the theater commanders to communicate with the Joint Chiefs at the Pentagon."

"Colonel, we do not have any operations in southern Mexico, right now."

"Thank you, lieutenant . . . I will take-over from here."

The colonel jabbed a button marked, "Mexico". On his screen came information about the U.S. Embassy in Mexico City. He scrolled down to *'SIGINT'*, the long-standing acronym for "Signal Intelligence" and tapped a button. He would speak to his opposite number, there.

In his earpiece came a series of clicks, then a man's voice. "Major Blackburn—"

On the secure scrambler, the colonel described to Blackburn the unaccountable transmissions originating from south-

southwest of Mexico City. "We have no operations going on down there."

"Relay the screen to me."

The colonel pressed a button that copied the screen onto a secure circuit for uplink to another satellite. In less than half a second, the image appeared on Blackburn's console in Mexico City.

* * *

Carside hung up the telephone and called for his assistant to come into his office. "We might have a break on the whereabouts of the 'exercise equipment'! A little while ago a truck with a load of electronics equipment was ticketed for speeding near a town about sixty miles south of Mexico City. Just after the truck had left, they got the teletype bulletin. The small-town cops gave a good description of the truck to the Federal Police. They say the rig was headed north. By now, it's probably somewhere in Mexico City. They are on the lookout for it."

* * *

Larry had no idea that Mexico City was so big—it had been almost two hours since the truck had passed the sign that marked the boundary of the *'Distrito Federal'*. A glance at his watch told him that they had been on the road for eight hours, including the episode back at the strange "court-house". The sweating driver was steering the rig up to the Cargo Terminal at the *'Aeropuerto Internacional Benito Juárez'*.

"Wait here, señor." The hat-man dropped down from the cab and stepped across to the glass entrance of an office. In a minute, he came back out with another man, who pointed at a "Boeing 747", parked by itself out on the edge of the apron. As the truck lurched up alongside the huge airplane, Larry gaped up at the enormous aircraft. Strange, he thought, that there were no markings on it.

Reaching for his travel bag, he dropped down and made his way over to the two other men who were gazing up at a pair of big open double-doors in the left side of the 747's fuselage behind the rear edge of the wing. Up on the cargo deck two very dark-skinned men in work-clothes looked down as a scissors-type freight elevator lowered a forklift to the ground.

As Larry stood aside watching, over the next hour the forklift and the elevator hauled the crates and pallets up into the 747, where the men tied-down everything to the cargo deck.

* * *

Blackburn was speaking to the colonel in Colorado Springs. "We have a new fix on the transmissions. They are now originating from the Cargo area at the Mexico City International Airport. I am going there now with a detachment of Marines. Keep me posted by radio as to the cargo's whereabouts."

* * *

Three pale-looking, round-faced men, casually dressed in short-sleeve shirts, stepped across the pavement and rode up the elevator to the 747's cargo deck, where they turned toward the front. "Those are the pilots," the airport man—who seemed to be working with the loaders from the plane—said in a heavy Spanish accent. He pointed at Larry's luggage."You need to get aboard, now, señor . . . you will be leaving in a few minutes."

The Mack-hat man stepped up and shook Larry's hand; the young driver, who had hardly said anything the entire trip, also put out his. "I wish you well, señor," the older man said.

A voice came from the airplane's cargo door; one of the dark men was motioning for Larry to get aboard. He stepped onto the forklift platform that hoisted him upward. At the doorway of the 747, he turned about. Down below, the two truckers were climbing up into the Mack's cab.

* * *

Quintana lowered his binoculars and motioned to the traffic controller standing by him. "Have 'Security' contact me at once."

He pointed toward an aircraft far out on the apron. "And get me the flight plan and the manifest of that 'Seven-Forty-Seven'." From his perch high in the control tower, the senior duty-officer at "Ground Control" squinted again through his spyglasses at the big Boeing parked in the early-evening twilight across the way at the Cargo Terminal. The truck that had been unloading its cargo onto it for some time seemed to match the description of one he had just learned was being sought by United States authorities. Once more he read the teletype printout, then gazed out again. The people who had been walking around it had now boarded either the truck or the airplane; its cargo doors were closing; the yellow portable elevator and now the semi-truck itself were starting to pull away. Even as he stared through his binoculars, the red lights on the top and bottom of the plane's fuselage began flashing; the big aircraft was about to depart. A man handed Quintana sheet of paper; on it was the filed flight plan of the 747 with its listed owner—*"Patagonia Heavy Air Transport"*—and the destination, Caracas, Venezuela.

"Caracas?" Quintana clapped his hands. "Where is that manifest—hurry!" He turned back and stared once more at the cargo apron. The other man handed Quintana an inspection declaration from Él Segundo, California, showing the shipment—"exercise equipment"—had been inspected at the manufacturer's location

The bell on the teletype was ringing. A moment later the assistant handed Quintana a new page. The man's eyes went wide. He snatched up the console telephone handset and punched in some numbers. "Quintana, here . . . send a military detail *'on the double'* to that 'Seven-Forty-Seven' at the Cargo Terminal! Yes, the one that is parked by itself! Its taxi light is on. I am putting a hold on its departure . . . and stop that truck that is there beside it! Arrest the *'hombres'* with it!" He handed the paper back to the other man, who read it himself. It was a dispatch from INTERNOL to Mexican authorities to arrest the occupants of the truck and sieze its cargo on an International Warrant that had just been issued by United States Customs. Since the cargo was already aboard the 747, Mexican Security would detain the plane and arrest those aboard it.

* * *

Come this way!" a heavy voice sounded from up forward in the fuselage that was loaded with crated and palletized goods. One of the dark men Larry had seen earlier stepped out and motioned for the American to follow him. The two made their way forward through the cavernous main deck that was outfitted with rollers, past the just-loaded cargo and a forklift that was strapped to the floor, to a spiral staircase. Climbing up to the second level, Larry came into a passenger cabin of about forty plush leather seats. Looking about, he was surprised to see a wet-bar at the rear of the cabin. Beyond an open door up front, on the darkened flight deck the three pilots were sitting at their consoles surrounded by banks of lighted instruments and blinking lights. The half-dozen very black men he had seen working the cargo inside the airplane were strapping themselves into seats, laughing and joking among themselves in a resonant dialect Larry did not understand. Just as Larry dropped into a window seat toward the rear of the cabin and reached for his seat belt, the cabin lights dimmed for a split-second; at the same time a rumble ran through the floor, then the muffled whine of jet engines starting.

* * *

"This is 'Patagonia Heavy Air Transport Seven-Forty-Seven' requesting permission to taxi." The metallic voice grated into Quintana's earphones in English, the international air transport language, in an accent the fluent Mexican recognized as Eastern European. But before the control tower could reply, the airplane commenced a slow left turn off the apron onto the taxiway that led to the west end of the main runway

"Hold up!" Quintana shouted into his mouthpiece. "Permission not granted!"

But as all eyes in the tower stared in surprise, the plane, still moving, leaned into a turn onto the taxiway. The massive aircraft, its landing lights spraying white light ahead of it, the red lights flashing on the fuselage and its red-and-green navigation lights blinking, continued to roll along the cross taxiway.

* * *

"Patagonia—this is 'Benito Juárez' Ground Control! You are instructed to pull to the next exit and hold!" As if deaf, in the evening gloom the un-marked 747 continued its hurried pace toward the takeoff point.

There was a shout from a man at a radar console. Quintana glanced at a radar screen and his eyes went wide. *Another airplane was on final approach—if it maintained its present course and speed it would collide with the 747 on the runway!*

"Approach Control! What aircraft is on final?"

"Mexico Avion 'D-C-Nine'!"

"Send him around! Clear all traffic! Clear all traffic, *now!*"

Nothing but hisses and an occasional crackle sounded in the Mexico Avion co-pilot's headset. It would only take him two or three seconds to snatch it off—worth the chance, he figured. In a hurry he pulled the earphones away and wiped his forehead.

"Mexico Avion D-C-Nine—go around! Repeat . . . go around! Abort your landing! Another aircraft is on the runway!"

* * *

The headset was back on. The hum and crackles were still there.

* * *

The "Humvee" skidded to a stop at the Cargo Gate. A man in a United States Marine uniform gestured at the gatekeeper. "Let us through!" he shouted in Spanish, "we are here on a special security mission!"

The man in the glassed enclosure gaped at the military vehicle and its half-dozen armed soldiers in combat uniforms in the rear; their *M-16's* were cocked and pointing up. The guard hesitated. "Señor, I must see some *'Identificatión'.*"

Blackburn jabbed his finger at the white star on the side of the olive-drab vehicle. "There is your 'Identification'!"

"Señor . . . I must—"

381

The driver floorboarded the Humvee's accelerator sending the splintered red-and-white wooden gate flying into the air! The gatekeeper ran out, pulling on his service revolver as the big vehicle's taillights faded away. Running back inside, he snatched-up the emergency telephone and punched-in some numbers.

* * *

As soon as the cabin lights went out, Larry Landay leaned back in his leather seat; for once there were no flight attendants to tell him to return his seat and tray-table the upright position for takeoff. He looked out the window as the lights of airport buildings blurred by. They must be running late, or something, he thought; it looked as if they were rolling along the taxiway pretty fast. Then came a lurch and his elbow pressed against the left seat arm. The 747 made another thumping lean into a turn. Larry frowned. That pilot up there must really be in a hurry, he thought. A couple of rows in front of him, two dark men glanced at each other, frowning, and said something in an incomprehensible brogue.

* * *

There it is!" Blackburn pointed, "get in front of it!" The Humvee hurtled through a taxiway intersection and howled forward at the massive rear of the airplane.

"He's going at least sixty!"

Blackburn knew the aircraft's taxi speed was much too fast to be safe. From straight behind it, the circular orange exhausts were outlined at the rear of each of the four engines; the dozen-and-a-half wheels of the landing gear stood backlit in the landing lights as the airplane kept up its overspeed pace out the taxiway.

Another pair of headlights was coming up behind the Americans. The Marines lowered their 'M-16's' at the overhauling stranger—after a couple of seconds, Blackburn recognized the newcomer as one of the airport's armed security vehicles; at its rear stood a soldier holding on to a twenty-millimeter cannon a pedestal. A man motioned at the Americans that he would try to shoot out the airplane's tires. Blackburn gestured he would attempt to get ahead of the aircraft. The driver pressed the pedal to the floor; the huge bulk of the Boeing grew larger as they drew closer.

"Hurry!" In a moment the plane would be on the runway and accelerating to a speed the military vehicles could never match. Even as he looked, the huge aircraft swung onto the runway. The driver twisted the wheel and the spinning tires leaped from the pavement.

Then over the screeching vehicle noises came the deep, rolling thunder of the turbofans—blue-orange flame appeared at the rear of the engines.

"Ready weapons!" The officer pointed at the bottom of the airplane. "Aim for the tires!"

* * *

Quintana, after shouting for the DC-9 to abort the landing, had turned again to the 747, which had made its turn onto the runway and was beginning its takeoff roll.

All at once the white shaft of another airplane's landing lights outlined the end of the runway! Quintana's eyes went wide—*against his orders, the Mexico Avion DC-9 was still on its final approach!* To his horror the ponderous 747 was squarely in the path of the DC-9, and was just starting to accelerate!

Quintana grabbed the Approach microphone. "DC-9 abort your landing! Go around!"

* * *

In the smaller airliner, the co-pilot's ears rang from the sudden loud voice in his earphones.

Then, he saw it: below and just ahead of him was the silver top of a huge airplane, its running lights flashing and its landing lights on, at the exact spot where the DC-9 was about touchdown!

The captain shoved the engine throttles foward; the twin jets went to full thrust. The aircraft leveled-out.

Racing alongside the enormous aircraft, all at once Blackburn saw a bright light flood the 747! Looking up, he was staggered to see the landing lights of another airplane aimed at the airliner that was taking off! Just as it seemed as if the newcomer would pancake onto the top of the Boeing, it lifted a little and shot up and over the 747's vertical fin with a strident roar heard above the bigger airplane's own jet engines!

Meanwhile, the Mexican Humvee, which had closed to within a few meters of the plane's wing, all at once exploded in a ball of fire! As the flaming wreckage cartwheeled through the air, Blackburn saw that the vehicle had veered into a jet exhaust and the five-thousand degree plume had blown it up.

The American vehicle lunged back onto the runway, just ahead of the massive aircraft. Blackburn stood up and motioned at the dark cockpit, but the uncompromising airplane continued its accelerating roll. The Humvee, outlined in the landing lights, going flat-out, began to lose ground. Then the lights moved ahead, plunging the vehicle into darkness as the outline of the end of the right wing, its strobe light flashing, passed so close overhead that Blackburn thought it would scrape the Humvee's top.

"The tires! The tires!" The rattle of M-16s firing full bursts added to the din as the rounds slammed into the wheels. Two of the big rear tires on the right outer main landing gear truck blew apart with loud *BOOMS!* Chunks of rubber and shards of steel belting flew through the air, some striking the bottom of the airplane as the alloy rims commenced bounding along in a shower of sparks. But the big Boeing was drawing away, and after a few more seconds its bulbous nose lifted and the 747 became airborne; the shot-up wheels still trailing thin streams of smoke even as the gear began to retract. "Hold your fire!" Blackburn shouted as the black shape of the airplane thundered over the rooftops of the *'barrio'* that crowded the far end of the runway and climbed away into the night.

-26-

Out of habit, when Larry heard and felt the rumble of the engines and the airplane began to creep forward, he gripped the leather armrests and looked out the windows. As the white runway edge-lights shot past faster and faster, all at once there came a bright light outside—like night had turned into mid-day—and a roar that seemed to come from over the top of the airplane—then it was night, again! Even while everyone looked at each other, frowning, there came an orange flash and what sounded like the "Boom!" of an *explosion* outside louder than the jet engines; at the same time, Larry felt a thumping vibration on his backside. For a fleeting moment he thought he also saw a dark-colored vehicle racing alongside in the glare of the landing lights, then just as quickly vanish behind the right wing. "What was *that*?" he said aloud. Then came some quick flashes; at once there was a pounding to the seat of his pants; the airplane swayed violently from side-to-side! *Had an engine exploded or they collided with something on the runway*? As the 747 continued to accelerate, the pounding vibrations became so intense he thought the airplane was going to break apart. Then the shaking stopped and the ground dropped away with the familiar take-off thumps and thuds.

* * *

Up in the glassed tower, Quintana looked at the clock: from the time the "Patagonia" airplane had started from the apron until its wheels lifted from the runway had only been about five minutes. Then he realized his clothes were soaked from sweat.

"Sir, Departure Control is on the line!"

"Quintana, here . . . what—?" A questioning look came onto his face; the others in the control room stared at him. He hung up the receiver. "Departure Radar has lost the 'Patagonia' airplane!"

"Has it crashed?"

"No reports of any crash."

* * *

Twenty-two thousand, three-hundred miles above the Amazon, the satellite now placed the spurious signal at a location twenty-one kilometers east-north-east of the center of Mexico City, moving on a heading of eighty-two degrees at a ground-speed of three-hundred sixteen kilometers an hour. The information passed to the receiving station at Sunnyvale, California, and on to Cheyenne Mountain. At the monitoring console, the colonel in charge looked at the signal displayed on his screen and made a decision. He pressed a button and sent the intercept to the "Signal Intelligence Office" of the "National Security Agency" in Washington, D.C.

* * *

Shaking, Larry unbuttoned his seat belt; others in the upper cabin were doing the same. All had the same wide-eyed expression their faces from the takeoff, which was by far the roughest he had ever experienced. As the engines continued to roar at takeoff power, the airplane made a shallow turn to the right. Looking out and down he saw that they were flying at a very low altitude; individual street-lamps and even house-lights raced past just below them; it seemed as if a tall tree branch could reach up and grab the bottom of the aircraft. "Why are we flying so low?" he said aloud.

Holding on to the seat backs, he groped his way up the aisle to the open door of the cockpit.

Inside the darkened space the three crewmen, surrounded by glowing dials and switches, were working levers and talking in a language he thought sounded like Russian. The nearest man, directly behind the co-pilot, glanced up as he adjusted a lever and noticed Larry standing there. "You are the passenger?" he said in English in a heavy accent.

The American nodded.

The fellow turned and said something to the captain, who was staring straight ahead, gripping the control wheel with both hands. "The jump-seat—" The man gave a quick motion to an empty canvas seat with a tubular frame at the rear of the center console. Larry climbed around the spindly chair and dropped into it. As he tightened the seat belt, the co-pilot glanced around at him. "You are the *American* passenger?"

Larry answered above the rush of air against the airframe and the engine noises. A splash of bright lights like a small town swept past just below them. "Why are we flying so low?"

The second pilot glanced at Larry and went on. "We are flying below radar," the man said in stilted English, "we can fly close to the ground without hitting anything. We have turned off our running-lights and the transponder. We cannot be detected." The man saw Larry's frown. "We have the same 'terrain-following radar' as the Soviet *'Tupelov One-Sixty Bomber'*."

"I didn't know airliners had this kind of radar."

"This aircraft used to be an Iraqi airliner. When you 'Americanskis' attacked Iraq a few months ago, this airplane flew to Iran. They took it over and sold it to the 'Organization'. When we stripped it for cargo service, it still had the special radar we Soviets had installed for the Iraqis." He pointed at a display on the instrument panel. "That is the 'terrain-following radar'."

Larry stared at the unit on the front panel with letters in Russian. "I am an electronics engineer . . . how does it work?"

"Before we left Mexico City, we programmed our flight plan into the computer. The radar locked-onto a Soviet military navigation satellite—the two are in constant communications, right now—the radar on this plane is connected to the automatic pilot." Even as the co-pilot spoke, the four levers on the center console nudged forward, which brought about more speed from the engines. Larry watched, fascinated, as the control yokes in front of the two pilots and the pedals on the floorboard made constant movements, which he guessed were operated by the automatic pilot and the onboard computer—all controlled by a Russian military satellite.

The second officer scanned the instruments. "We are now flying at a ground speed of seven hundred ninety kilometers an hour." Another small town shot by in a blur close underneath. "Our altitude is one-hundred meters."

"One hundred meters—that's practically on the deck!" The lights of another little town tilted under the end of the right wing as the 747 banked to the right; the end of it seemed about touch the streaking treetops just below. "You are *sure* the radar knows where we are going?"

"Soviet fighters and bombers and cruise missiles use this same system. It is very accurate."

* * *

Armando Cruz's coffee cup stopped in in midair in front of his face. Why were his chickens squawking like they were suddenly struck *'loco'?* Now the dog was barking. Frowning, he glanced at his wife who was rocking the cradle; in the crib, the baby was grimacing and squirming.

Then he felt it as much as he heard it: a low-pitched, growling rumble. The floor and walls began vibrating to a noise that seemed to be coming from—*an earthquake?* His eyes wide, the young farmer set down his cup and made for the door in a hurry.

Just as stepped outside, a dark, massive object bolted out of the starry sky and swept over the top of his house with an earsplitting roar, shaking pictures off walls and dishes from shelves! In a second whatever it was disappeared, leaving the tops of trees in his yard swaying back and forth.

His ears ringing, Armando saw the shape of a huge airplane, the biggest he had ever seen, dip its wing and vanish from sight beyond the east side of town. *Was it about to crash?* But he did not hear any explosion.

In the yard, the frowning hens were arranging their feathers back down as they stalked around, muttering among themselves about the big noise; the harried rooster was trying to restore order; the dog threw itself back down in the doorway; its tail swishing from side to side.

Shaking, the young "Señor Cruz" turned and stepped back inside, where his wife was trying to calm their shrieking infant.

* * *

388

The engines went once more to full power and the aircraft straightened-out into a steady climb. The flight engineer called out something to the co-pilot in the right seat, who had a chart in his lap. "He says we are climbing and turning to avoid a mountain peak that rises thirty-four-hundred-eighteen meters above sea level to our left . . . we will turn, again, to go past another tall peak to the right . . . we are climbing to go through a pass between the two mountains."

'There it is," the pilot said. He turned and scanned the instrument panel, then glanced back at Larry as yet another town swept past below them. "The 'Soviet Air Force' developed this system for our bombers."

"Are you Russian?"

"Ukrainian . . . we used to be in the *'Strategic Bombing Forces'* before we left to do other— 'things'."

Larry shook his head; it was hard to believe he was flying in an American-made airliner that was under the remote control of a system from the Soviet Union! Just then, the airplane made a sudden bank to the left, then to the right. From the pressure in his ears, he could tell they were still climbing.

The co-pilot leaned over and pointed at the map. While he and the pilot spoke for a minute, the airplane gave another twist to the right, then to the left.

The sound of the plane's engines dropped and the 747 pushed over. The co-pilot said something to the captain, who nodded.

"He says we are over the mountain pass and are now dropping toward sea level." After a few minutes of descending by remote control, the engines went once more to cruise power.

The captain turned to Larry. "We are five kilometers from the edge of the land-mass." The American had been watching, fascinated, as the Soviet-made computer piloted the airplane almost at ground level through mountain passes. Now over the coastal plain, the 747 straightened out, still sweeping over the terrain at an altitude of one-hundred-meters. The airspeed indicator was holding at eight-hundred-sixty kilometers an hour.

A smudge of light came into view on the far horizon to the right. The co-pilot looked out at the glowing lights, then at the chart. "Vera Cruz at seventy kilometers."

Then the surf-line swept past just underneath. The captain reached over and twisted a knob, at the same time gripping the control wheel. "I have control," he said, pushing the four throttle levers forward. The engines gave a surge of power; Larry felt the nose of the 747 begin to rise. "Over water, we will fly better at higher altitude."

Four minutes later, a sudden, strong vibration ran through the airframe. The pilot, frowning, turned and said something to the flight engineer, who had some quick words in reply. As the shaking went on, Larry looked at the third pilot behind him, who was scanning his instruments. The man called out to the captain in a loud voice. At once, the pilot pulled back on the engines and Larry felt himself shifting forward against his seat belt as the airplane nosed over. The vibration lessened, then stopped. The pilot eased forward on the throttles and once more the aircraft flew level.

"What's the matter?"

"We are losing cabin air pressure." The captain looked around at the co-pilot, and at the American. "Take some of the cargo handlers back there and find out what is wrong."

Larry unbuckled his seat belt and followed the other man into the upper passenger cabin, where a half-dozen anxious faces greeted them. "We are going to the back of the airplane and investigate . . . the captain wants some of you to help." The husky men looked around at each other, then two arose from their seats.

The procession filed down the spiral staircase to the main cargo deck. A man flipped a switch and a row of lights came on down the middle of what had once been a huge passenger cabin, now loaded with cargo that seemed to Larry to stretch away forever. As they made their way down the aisle flanked with stacked and palleted goods, the layout reminded him of the hold on the third cargo deck of the *'Beacon Trader'* until he remembered that this particular deck and its contents were hurtling through the air at hundreds of miles an hour.

The men stepped up to a bulkhead door that led to the tail cone at the extreme rear of the airplane. When the officer opened it, Larry and the others could hear a rush of air. The officer knelt and pulled on a hatch. One of the black men produced a flashlight. The co-pilot leaned through the opening and shined the light around the space at the very rear of the main cargo deck. "Everything looks normal," he said.

When he lifted another hatch, at once there was a very loud rush of wind and the thunder of the jet engines that sounded to Larry to be very close. A cold draft of air along with a strong odor of kerosene-jet exhaust came up at them.

The co-pilot aimed the flashlight down into the lower hold and pulled back up at once. "The right-rear lower cargo door is open!" he shouted over the noise. "It is almost off its hinges! We must secure it or the deck could collapse! If that were to happen, the airplane might go out of control!" He reached for a telephone on the bulkhead and spoke some words into it. "The captain says to try to make emergency repairs! We may have to divert to Havana and repair it before we can go on to Lagos!" The co-pilot motioned to the others. "Find some wire!"

"There is a shipment of wire in the second compartment!"

As the two cargo-men headed toward the front of the airplane, the co-pilot located a light switch. When a bulkhead fixture came on, the man grabbed a support frame and dropped into the lower cargo hold. Larry and the others followed him into the empty cavern-like space. Holding on against the shrieking slipstream, the officer leaned toward the damaged door that was knocking against the bottom of its frame. "It is broken—the frame is bent! When we took off, something hit the bottom of the door and loosened the lock . . . when we climbed to a certain altitude, just now, the air pressure in the cargo hold pushed out the door. That was the vibration we felt—the loose door hitting the side of the plane. When we came down to a lower altitude and reduced speed, the vibrating stopped."

The two who had gone after the wire appeared at the top of the hatchway. A roll of insulated cable thumped to the lower deck. In a few minutes, the wire held the door fast in its frame. The men went back up to the flight deck

* * *

In its geo-synchronous orbit 22,300 miles above the Amazon jungle, the satellite had re-acquired the signal that was lost when the 747 had flown through the mountain passes. The orbiter was once more following the crated cargo's every move.

* * *

At the National Reconnaissance Office, Major Coltrane stared at his monitor screen, puzzled—the intercepted signal was on a frequency that until lately had been reserved for secure United States military traffic. Even though some of the transmitters were recently approved for release to certain reliable U.S. allies; so far, none had been delivered outside the United States. Yet, here was a broadcast on one of the restricted channels originating over the Gulf of Mexico.

He punched a button that brought a supercomputer on line. The calculations on Coltrane's monitor screen showed that the signal source was on a probable course to take it over Havana in two-and-a-half-hours.

* * *

The flight engineer had been watching a particular instrument that registered hydraulic pressure to the landing gear. "Captain, we have low hydraulics on the right outer main gear—the primary and two secondaries . . . we may have to do a 'gravity-drop.'"

"Brakes?"

"No hydraulic pressure . . . no pressure on the backup air brakes."

The pilot glanced back. "Take some men and go down there and see what is the problem."

The co-pilot looked at Larry. "We must make another inspection."

As before, the four men trundled down the spiral staircase to the main deck and turned aft. Half-way back, they stopped at a

392

square metal hatch-plate on the deck. One of the black men knelt and loosened some thumbscrews. When the man pulled up the plate, at once there came the roaring noise of air against the outside airframe. The co-pilot eased himself down through the opening that was just wide enough for his shoulders into an open space, using handholds on a bulkhead. The probing beam of his flashlight stopped at a light switch. He moved it and several powerful lamps came on. Looking up, the man motioned to Larry to drop down into the space. "I may need your help!" he called out over the wind noise.

The American wedged feet-first through the narrow opening in the deck and lowered himself down onto a narrow aluminum platform. Over toward the middle of the fuselage bottom was the right-center main landing gear tucked up against the bottom of the main deck. The Ukrainian shined his flashlight over its tires and the wheel rims, then along the big struts and hydraulic lines and hoses and shrugged. "The gear over there looks all right."

Then he turned about to face a low bulkhead beside them. "The outer right-hand main gear is behind this plate," the officer said, handing Larry the flashlight and tugging on some clips. When the inspection plate came away they were confronted by a strong smell of brake fluid. The man took the flash and shined it into the well. "Oh, my God!" he muttered.

Larry peered over the man's shoulder and gasped. The two rear tires on the four-wheel outer truck were almost gone—only a few chunks of rubber still held onto the metal rims. "They shot away the tires!" The second officer shined the beam around the well and gave another groan. Pungent liquid was sloshing around in the bottom of the wheel doors. He directed the light around the tightly-packed space and shook his head. "The hydraulic lines are gone."

Larry gaped at the scarred wheel rims. "I guess that was the vibration we felt when we took off."

The other man snapped off his flashlight. "I must speak to the captain about this."

Back on the flight deck, Larry stood by as the co-pilot, speaking in his language, talked with the captain and the flight engineer. From Larry's rudimentary knowledge of Russian, the conversation was about the ruined tires and the broken hydraulic lines. All three pilots were shaking their heads.

The captain turned over the controls to the co-pilot and reached for the radio microphone. Speaking in his accented English, the man called Havana Control. Larry recalled that "Aviation English" was the international air transport language. The captain hung up the microphone and turned to the others. "We will go to Havana for repairs . . . they suggest we try to take from the rims what is left of the shot-up tires . . . they say it will better for both the airplane and the runway if we have smooth rims to land on." He nodded to the co-pilot. Take some men and go back there and scrape the wheels . . . do the best you can."

For the third time the Ukrainian pulled himself out of his tight seat and crawled over the center pedestal. "Come with me," he said to Larry. He stopped to get a tool box from a locker. The two went out into the upper cabin where the officer shook awake the pair who had gone with them the two other times. The four trooped back to the open manhole, where the co-pilot and Larry dropped down into the small space. As the two black men knelt by the opening on the main deck with the tool box, Larry and the pilot went to work chisling and scraping the remaining chunks of rubber and steel belts from the shot-up rims.

* * *

As soon as the 747 captain opened his microphone and began transmitting, the satellite picked up the signal, converted it to digital, and at once relayed it to Coltrane's console at the National Reconnaissance Office—now there were two signal sources coming from the airplane. As the pilot and Havana Tower talked to each other, their conversation was displayed on Coltrane's monitor in phonetic English by voice-recognition software.

* * *

Coltrane punched a button and spoke into his headset microphone to the Duty Officer at the '*Defense Intelligence*

Agency'. "We are intercepting what looks like a distress signal from the source of the first transmission over the Gulf of Mexico."

"Forward the screen to my console." The English lettering displayed on the second screen.

Frowning, the colonel scanned the read-out, then pushed a button that connected him to the *'North American Air Defense Command'*, underneath Cheyenne Mountain at Colorado Springs.

* * *

"Ordway—" The major at the console spoke into his headset microphone.

The colonel in Washington came on the line. "Unknown aircraft transmitting a signal on a United States classified frequency . . . latest co-ordinates twenty-three-point-two-two north . . . niner-zero- point-zero-fiver west . . . the aircraft was speaking to Havana Tower about some sort of in-flight emergency."

The spoken words and the other information appeared on Ordway's screen. Ordway pressed a button that connected him to the Duty Officer at Homestead Air Force Base in Southern Florida.

* * *

"Burke—" The captain jabbed a button that engaged the buzzing voice circuit on his console from Cheyenne Mountain. "Homestead . . ."

"Unknown aircraft calling Havana Tower about an in-flight emergency. Coordinates twenty-three-point-two-four north, eighty-niner-point-niner-one west." The translation and the other information flashed onto Burke's screen. The captain pressed another button.

Sixteen minutes later, two *F-16's* left the runway and set a course to intercept the Boeing.

* * *

The pilot shook his head. "With no brakes on the outer gear this landing is going be very—" The man's sentence hung in the air. Larry heard the co-pilot mutter something about "ground-loop". Even though he didn't know all that much about airplanes, he could certainly figure that two missing tires would make for a hard landing. He would just have to trust that the captain and his flight crew knew what they were doing. Larry was sweating. Just then the pilot wiped each hand in turn on his pants legs. To the American, the pilot's own sweaty palms meant things must be even more serious than they were letting on.

The Ukrainian captain again spoke. "We will use the thrust reversers all the way." The man took a deep breath. "At least the engines are performing well," he said, turning to the flight engineer. "Do a check-out of all systems. Prepare to lower the damaged gear by gravity when I call for it."

The co-pilot pulled out the flight manual and began familiarizing himself with the procedures for a gravity-drop-down of the right outer main landing gear.

* * *

McHard set the rate of climb at three-thousand feet a minute. "*Weapons Control*' . . . request information about the target."

"Altitude and type of subject aircraft not known," came the voice at the other end. There was a pause. "Come about on a vector of two-four-zero."

"Wilco." He and Werner, his wingman, swung their F-16's onto the south-southwest course and maintained their climb. In six minutes, when they leveled-off at twenty-one thousand feet, the flight officer gazed out the bubble canopy of his streaking interceptor at a beautiful and clear nighttime sky. Just off and behind his right wingtip, he could see, in the reflection of the instrument panel in the cockpit of the other aircraft, the vague outline of Werner's helmet. Down below, the black ocean was invisible except for the glimmer of a wavetop that every now and then caught a fleeting beam of the half-moon.

McHard watched his "heads-up" radar display—nothing, yet. True airspeed was holding at eleven- hundred-forty knots. Five, ten, fifteen minutes went by. Then a blip appeared on the head-screen at five-thousand feet altitude. "Contact!" he called to Weapons Control. "*Bogey'* at one-o'clock! Range ten nautical. Altitude fiver."

Homestead came back on the circuit. "Reduce speed to six-hundred knots . . . lower to altitude fiver . . . 'shadow'—" The two pilots pulled back on their throttles; their aircraft began rapid descents. Four minutes later the two interceptors leveled-out at five-thousand feet. The "heads-up"screen showed they were two miles from the target. "Closing!" McHard scanned the sky ahead—then he spotted the black bulk of an unlit aircraft moving to his left against the starry horizon.

"Tally ho! *'Bogey* in sight! We commit!"

"Shadow and eyeball!"

The pilots swung their F-16s around and took up stations behind the rear quarters of the airplane. McHard gave his engine more thrust; as if tied together the two fighters pulled up in close formation behind the subject aircraft's tail. In the pale moonlight he could make out the silhouette of a very large airplane flying too low and much too slowly for an airliner on a regular international flight. He opened his microphone. "Bogey is a 'Boeing Seven-Forty-Seven . . . altitude fiver . . . no running lights . . . we are performing an *'Armament Safety Check'*—"

Both pilots re-viewed their armament switches to make sure they were "safe" against an inadvertant launch of the *'Sidewinder'* missiles or any accidental firing of their cannon while they examined the stranger.

McHard eased his plane underneath and to the left of the target's tail. Pulling out a flashlight he shined its beam through his plexiglas canopy at the big airplane's undersurface; his wingman, to the right and just outside the larger aircraft's slipstream, did the same. "Discoloration at the right wing root," Werner said, "looks like fresh lubricant or hydraulic fluid." The inspection at close quarters that went on for some minutes brought no response from the 747. "Don't those guys know they have company?"

McHard opened his microphone. "Seven-Forty-Seven has no markings, Repeat—no markings or identification numbers on it."

Weapons Control came back. "Description matches an aircraft that made an unauthorized takeoff from Mexico City—continue shadowing."

"Wilco."

McHard, growing restless, decided it was time for the shadowers to introduce themselves. He opened the radio to his wingman. "Let's make a *'Seven-Forty-Seven Sandwich'* . . ." With the wing leader on the left and Werner on the right, the two interceptors moved up alongside the Boeing; slightly above and just forward of the end of each wing. A few touches on the controls brought the cockpits of all three airplanes onto an even line with each other. McHard was close enough to see the glowing dials of the flight engineer's console behind the co-pilot. Then he and Werner flipped on their F-16 navigation and landing lights. "Merry Christmas!" he grinned into his microphone.

Larry was just returning from the wheel-well with the co-pilot and was buckling his seat belt in the jumpseat when all at once there came flashing red, green, and white lights outside on both sides of the airplane! The outlines of the shadowers off both sides were plain to see in the flickering reflections of their navigation lights against the bigger aircraft.

The 747 pilot gazed out the windows to his left and right and swore in Russian. "We have—as you Americans say—'company'." He shook his head. "'*NATO*' aircraft used to do this all the time over the North Atlantic and the Barents Sea. They will follow us for a while, then break-off when we get close to Cuba."

Larry remembered something. "While we were in the wheel well, I *thought* I saw a light coming up through the crack between the wheel doors. At the time, I figured you had turned on the landing lights, or something. Guess it was those guys looking us over."

The pilot, who seemed to be used to this sort of cat-and-mouse-game, turned around to the flight engineer. "Determine the gross weight of the airplane when we reach Havana . . . we will be overweight." He glanced at the co-pilot. "Get the checklist to dump fuel—'wheels-down' will use more fuel and we will let the gear down early to make sure they operate."

Larry stared at the pilot. "What do you mean, 'make sure they operate'?"

The captain flexed his fingers on the control wheel. "This could be a very—'different' kind of landing . . ."

The flight engineer spoke up. *"With the extra-range fuel tanks,* our current gross weight is three-hundred-sixty-two-thousand kilograms . . . we will use an estimated eight-thousand kilograms of fuel between now and arrival at Havana airspace." There was a pause. "The maximum allowable landing weight will be two-hundred eighty-six-thousand kilograms. We will need to dump sixty-eight thousand kilograms of fuel."

What is our estimated time of arrival at *'José Marti'?*"

The engineer punched some figures into his computer. "One-hour, six minutes."

The pilot looked out the side windows; the shadowers were still there. He reached for the radio microphone and called Havana Tower.

* * *

From its geo-synchronous orbit, the reconnaissance satellite continued evesdropping on the conversation between the pilot and the Havana airport and relaying the information to the California ground station. The dialogue appeared in "real-time" letters on Burke's screen in South Florida.

-27-

The countdown clock now estimated twenty-seven minutes to touch-down on the Havana runway. The captain turned about. "Co-pilot! Take your men to the wheel well! Use the telephone to tell me what happens when I try to lower the gear."

In a few minutes, the second officer and Larry were once more balancing themselves on the narrow beam between the right-center and the right-outside main gear wheel wells. One of the black men dropped the intercom handset on a long cord down through the manhole above. The co-pilot said something in his own language, then handed it back up and grabbed a nearby hand-hold. Larry, taking the man's cue, braced himself on his precarious perch for whatever was about to happen.

There was a whine, then the outer gear doors began to open. As the doors swung down and out, a blast of wind tore into the wheel-well, nearly dragging out the two men out who were holding on for dear life. The hydraulic pistons continued to push open the doors, finally locking into place with a solid "THUD!" Behind him, Larry felt bumping and heard loud groans as the heavy bulk of the center gear started down; the whole airplane began shuddering as other pylons and their wheel trucks descended into the slip-stream. Both men held their breaths and watched as the crippled outer gear trembled and started to swing away. But a torrent of liquid was spraying all over the inside of the wheel well from broken hydraulic lines—Larry and the other man had to duck-aside as fluid shot through the inspection manhole past them. The hydraulic pump to the outer gear screamed as the reservoir ran dry, then became quiet. After dropping only a few inches, the outer landing gear stopped moving.

The co-pilot looked up at the wide-eyed African at the manhole staring down at the fluid- smeared space below him. "Call the captain and tell him we will have to lower the right outer main by gravity!"

The fellow shouted into the handset, then after a moment turned back to the men hanging-on in the wheel well. "The flight engineer says to hurry—they are going to have to dump fuel, soon!"

"Tell the Captain to try the electrical gravity release!" On the deck above them, the dark-skinned man relayed the co-pilot''s message.

Another pause; then the black man once more looked down into the space below him. "He says they are going to do it now! " Just then there was a loud *BANG!* from the wheel well. Sparks showered from a junction box just inside the inspection opening; the overhead sealed-beam light-bulb flickered.

"There is a short-circuit!" Larry looked over the shoulder of the second officer as the man reached inside and twisted a thumb-screw. The plate on the electrical box swung aside. The second officer stuck his head through the opening. After a moment, he pulled back and looked at the black man above him. "Give me some pliers with insulated handles!" The fellow handed the tool down to Larry. The American relayed the piece to the officer, who twisted his shoulders back inside the opening. A moment later, he called back, "Tell the pilot to try the release switch!" The man above spoke into the telephone. There came a snapping noise—then all at once the big wheel truck dropped away into the void below with a shudder and a slam that shook the whole airplane.

It worked!" Larry grabbed the handholds, almost losing his balance off the narrow wing spar on which he was standing.

With one last look down at the ghost-like landing gear now hanging in midair below the airplane, Larry and the Ukrainian pulled themselves back to the main deck.

On the flight deck, the flight engineer pointed at a display of green lights on his instrument panel. "All the gear are now down and locked!"

The pilot turned to the flight engineer. "Prepare to jettison fuel!" The third officer reached for a switch, then moved a lever

Fuel jettisoning!" the flight engineer called out, "three-thousand liters a minute!"

The pilot reached for his radio microphone and told Havana Tower he was dumping fuel.

* * *

Something in the murky shadows underneath the forward fuselage of the 747 caught McHard's attention. Did his eyes deceive him, or was the nosewheel dropping? The flight leader pointed his sealed-beam flash at the lower front of the big airplane. Sure enough, the landing gear was deployed! He radioed his wingman. "Take station underneath the aircraft and eyeball the undercarriage."

* * *

At his console, Burke stared horrified at the screen's electronic translation of the 747 pilot's intercepted radio transmission to Havana Tower—he had just overheard McHard's radioed order to his wingman to pull out and drop below the 747. But the controller knew the big Boeing was now dumping jet fuel into the air from the ends of its wings. *If the fighter flew into the volatile mist, its jet engines would explode!* "Wingman! Cancel that order!" Burke shouted into his microphone. "Repeat—cancel that order! Do not move from station!"

* * *

When Werner heard McHard's order to change station, he cut power and pulled away from opposite the 747's cockpit. As the fighter dropped behind the end of the behemoth Boeing's right wing, all at once a spray of liquid burst onto its bubble canopy! Before the pilot could react, the F-16 erupted in a ball of orange fire, then a deafening explosion rent the darkness, blowing the interceptor and its pilot to bits!

* * *

The flight engineer moved a pair of levers, all the while keeping his eyes on the wing-discharge fuel flow meters. "Rate of jettisoning now six-thousand liters a minute."

His words were hardly out of his mouth when all at once there came a bright orange fireball outside and below the right cockpit window that disappeared behind them along with a thunderous, shaking blast! The big Boeing rocked as chunks of *shrapnel* peppered the fuselage.

"What was that?"

"One of the American airplanes flew into our jettisoning fuel! It blew up!"

Status check!" The pilot scanned his instrument panel.

"Readings are normal . . . cabin pressure normal."

* * *

"Delta Sierra'!" McHard burst out in the jargon pilots use for a disastrous development. "My wingman has exploded!" Inside the orange fireball, the destroyed fighter's "Sidewinder" missiles were going off. Bits and pieces of metal clattered against McHard's fuselage.

Stung by the sight of his wingman vaporizing in a ball of fire, the flight leader, seeing that the 747 was venting fuel, pulled his F-16 away so as to stay outside the spray. The interceptor straightened-out on a course above and behind the lumbering Boeing. McHard set his jaw. "They did that on purpose!" he said out loud. On impulse, he flipped all the armament switches to the "On" position. "Two can play this game!" he cried into his oxygen-mask microphone, forgetting his words were being overheard by the weapons controller, "Sidewinders armed!"

A voice burst out of McHard's helmet earphones: *"'Cleared Dry'! Repeat—'Cleared Dry'!"* The order not to engage rang in McHard's ears, jolting the angry pilot back to reality.

* * *

403

The 747 pilot pointed to a line of lights on the horizon forward and slightly to the right of the airplane's direction of flight. "Cuba," he said.

The co-pilot looked at the map. *"Pinar del Rio."* The display from the Soviet positioning satellite showed they were now in controlled Cuban airspace. The aircraft was on autopilot.

* * *

At his Weapons Control console at Homestead Air Force Base, Burke had been watching his display of the radio transmission from the 747. The blip on the screen showed the source was now beyond interception. "Disengage and egress!"

"I have the aircraft in sight!"

"Knock it off! R-T-B!"

The Weapons Control officer's order to "Return to Base" could not be defied. "Damn!" McHard stared for one last, long frustrated moment at the big Boeing, backlit against the lights of Cuba, still trailing a comet's tail of fuel from the ends of both wings. "Roger," he said into his helmet microphone. He swung the stick to the left and the F-16 rolled away, leaving behind the lumbering 747 and his wingman—now just a crimson smudge bobbing in floating wreckage on the black water, far behind and below the streaking fighter and its thwarted pilot.

* * *

Two loud *WHOOPS!* sounded, startling the American.

"I have control!" The 747 captain reached forward and disengaged the autopilot. "Set the *'V-O-R'* to Havana frequency! First Officer . . . give me a heading to *'José Marti'!"*

The co-pilot consulted the "Havana Approach Manual", then rotated a knob to the Havana *'Very-High-Frequency-Omni-Range'* channel. While the big airplane leaned into a shallow turn, he kept his eye on the needle as it swung around to point onto a heading toward *'José Marti International Airport, Havana'.* "Course zero-niner-zero!"

The flight engineer moved a hand across his control panel. "Fuel jettisoning completed . . . estimated landing weight two-hundred-sixty-four thousand kilograms."

"Manual landing! Airport coordinates!"

"Runway elevation seventy-six meters . . . length of runway four-thousand meters."

The flight engineer spoke up. "Estimated time to arrive—eight minutes.

"Tell Havana to have their emergency vehicles ready!" He pulled back slightly on the four engine throttles, then glanced back at Larry. "The escape hatches are at the side windows."

"Escape hatches?"

The pilot ignored him; Larry guessed he had too much on his mind right now to reply.

Ten degrees flaps!" Larry noticed the three Ukrainians were now speaking altogether in English.

The co-pilot moved a lever. From somewhere came a whine.

Flaps twenty degrees!" The sound pitch of the four big engines dropped a little more; Larry could feel the airplane start to sink rapidly. The lowered landing gear was causing a buffeting motion to the airplane

Below them, lights of a great city were starting to show up. "Airport beacon!" the co-pilot called out. Larry spotted the distant flashing alternate green and white lights.

A disembodied voice burst out of the overhead speaker in Hispanic-accened English: "Patagonia Boeing Heavy come about to compass heading one-fifty . . . two-twenty knots ."

The right wing dipped as the big 747 swung into a shallow turn.

"Speedbrakes up! Flaps twenty-five degrees!"

Havana Tower came back. "Descend to five-hundred meters." From the pressure in his ears, Larry knew they were losing altitude at a steady rate.

"Patagonia Heavy come about to heading zero-six-zero, one-seventy knots . . . descend to two-hundred meters." The airplane leaned to the left for some seconds, then straightened out, dropping even more rapidly.

Ahead and below them Larry could see the lighted parallel lines of the distant runway lining up end-on—a sight he had never before seen from an airplane. As the runway came closer, Larry's eyes went wide—it looked awfully short. They were going to land on *that?*

A loud crackle; the tower voice once more came out of the speaker. "Patagonia Heavy . . . cleared to land." The pilot gripped the control yoke wheel with his left hand; his right hand palmed the four throttle levers; his feet maintained a light touch on the rudder pedals.

The pilot opened his microphone. "Patagonia Heavy on Final. Two-hundred meters."

"Speedbrakes down! Landing lights on!"

The co-pilot reached up and moved a switch. A white glow appeared outside the cockpit side windows. The aircraft continued its descent down the glide slope.

"One-hundred! Approaching minimums!" came an automated, hollow-sounding male voice from an overhead loudspeaker. "Minimums!" the voice said.

Larry stared transfixed as they moved toward—then over—a display of red lights, flashing in rapid, repeating sequences toward the line of yellow that marked the squared-off end of the runway. The landing lights splayed a brilliant carpet of white far down the pavement.

"Thirty" . . . "Twenty!" . . ."Ten!" . . ."Five!" . . . "Two!" the synthesized voice counted-down in a quick sequence of altitudes in meters as the runway rushed up at them.

With his left hand the pilot eased back on the control yoke. At the same time, he pulled the throttles all the way back.

There was a suspended silence, then a shock slammed the seat of Larry's pants that reminded him of the time his elementary-school principal had paddled him in his office. A violent shaking came up through the entire airplane—the instruments on the panel dissolved into a blur. Then the streaking runway came back into sight as the pilot pushed the yoke forward and nose wheels skidded down.

"Speedbrakes up! Manual brakes!" The pilot's right-hand fingertips pulled on the reverser-levers, then at once he palmed the throttles full-forward. With the engines at full reverse-thrust power, Larry felt his chest shoving into the pulsating center-seat's shoulder harness. As the runway lights shot by outside, the vibration in the airplane became ever greater as more weight settled onto the landing gear. The airliner began to swerve to the right as the two bare wheel-rims settled shrieking onto the surface.

Larry gripped the thumping armrests—the right-side runway lights were shooting by directly below them!

The pilot let out a yell. *"I cannot control it!"*

-28-

The desperate captain held on to the juddering control yoke as if in a death-grip. Larry grabbed the center jumpseat's vibrating tubular frame and watched, wide-eyed, as the lights at the right side of the runway streaked past underneath the wing. Then the solid line started to edge away from them.

The bounding aircraft slewed toward back toward the middle of the runway.

"One-hundred!"

"Eighty . . . sixty . . . holding straight!"

"Thirty!"

"Reversers off . . . speedbrakes down!"

The aircraft slowed, then came to a shuddering standstill in the landing lights; the pounding against the seat of Larry's pants had stopped. The only sound came from the idling turbofans. The American looked out at a low-lying line of lamps squatting in front of the airplane and gasped. The lights were at the end of the runway. *Another fifty yards and they would have run off it!*

A voice came from the loudspeaker "Patagonia Seven-Forty-Seven . . . turn left onto the taxiway and hold—" The pilot advanced the throttles and rotated the nosewheel control wheel.

The aircraft waddled forward, and with a groaning shudder lurched into the turn. Outlined in the landing lights, the taxiway came about before them. The captain touched the brakes.

Just then, a small truck swung in front; on its rear was a sign in block letters: "SIGUEME".

The pilots frowned. "What does it mean?"

Larry spoke up. "I believe it means, *'Follow Me'*, in Spanish."

The 747 started moving, again. As it crept down the side taxiway, Larry could feel the rumble of the two bare rims on the pavement.

* * *

At his console beneath Cheyenne Mountain, Major Ordway's screen blinked once then displayed: "LOSS OF SIGNAL".

Frowning, the officer queried the surveillance satellite. The same result. Something had caused the mysterious radio transmission to cease.

* * *

A man with a lighted orange wand in each hand hopped off the vehicle and ran to the end of the left wing. Turning about, he made motions toward a space in front of a hangar. With a burst from the engines, the pilot maneuvered the airplane to the spot. The flight engineer moved some switches and at long last, the whine of the engines subsided. The three crewmen set about setting levers and turning off the electronics.

Larry wobbled out into the upper passenger cabin, where the other men, whooping and laughing with relief, were pulling their things out of the overhead. Behind him, as the three crewmen came from the cockpit, one of the black men, then another, clapped his hands. Someone gave a whistle. Even though Larry knew nothing about the Ukrainian pilots, the way they had safely brought down the damaged airplane had been a masterpiece. They were either very skilled or very lucky. Probably both.

Snatching his luggage bag from a bin at the front of the cabin, Larry joined the others bumping down the spiral staircase. As he followed them back through the warehouse-like cargo space, he noticed that some of the pallets had snapped their tie-downs—from the hard landing, he guessed.

When he spotted his load of electronics toward the rear of the plane, he could see that several of the cartons were dislodged; one mid-sized wooden box had even fallen off onto its side. As Larry slowed to stare, the man behind him bumped into him. "Keep moving!" someone further back called out. He would have to see about it later.

At the left rear main-deck cargo door, the Cubans had rolled up a metal staircase to the side of the fuselage. As Larry and the others clumped down the steps, the American looked around at the well-lighted airport that was far larger and more up-to-date-looking than he had expected it to be—*was this really Havana?*

He knew that Americans were officially barred from coming to Cuba—what would happen if the United States Government found out he was here? Would anybody in Washington believe that this was an unscheduled stop? What about the shoot-out at the Mexico City airport? How would they take it if they knew he was on the 747 that had caused the American fighter plane to blow up in midair? *What was he doing on this airplane in the first place?* With a groan Larry now understood he would probably have a lot of questions to answer before he would ever again see Mountain View.

A truck with spotlights mounted on it roared up. By the time the three pilots had stepped underneath the fuselage to the right side of the airplane, the lights were already shining on the outer wheel truck and up into the well. Curious, Larry followed them. ". . . all power and hydraulics—" the captain was saying to a uniformed man.

The Cuban spotted Larry and stared at him with a frown.

The pilot noticed the man's interest in the blond newcomer. "He came with us . . . he is a technician with the goods for the 'Organization'."

"Organization!" Larry gave a start—had he not already heard *that* word, somewhere? But before he could ponder further about it, the Cuban was again speaking.

"I am informed of the—nature of your—cargo," the man spoke in measured English. The official looked at the three pilots and the American. "It is exceedingly—fortunate you are—here. We will send some—shipments—with you when you leave." The three crewmen nodded.

Maybe it was his imagination, Larry thought, but *did these men already know each other?*

A vision of Lisa Anaya flashed across his mind. Even though it was hard to believe she could be involved in anything out-of-the-ordinary, the unusual happenings and unanswered questions were starting to pile up. Ever since that warning message from her about someone following him, there had been one unexplained incident after another: the opened waybills and the copy of the Radiogram in the ship's cargo hold; the highway "court;" the shoot-out at the airport; the exploding airplane. Now, here they were—in Havana, Cuba—where these men were talking matter-of-factly about hauling goods from this island to his own destination in Africa.

Looking up, for the first time he saw the magnitude of the destruction wrought by the bullets. The fluid-soaked wheel well glistened in the garish light; big drops of liquid landed on the pavement with audible *"plops"*; already a pungent puddle was forming. Mangled cables, hydraulic tubes and shards of sheet-metal hung askew; a whole section of the front panel was torn away from the aluminum bulkhead; broken wires drooped down in disarray. The men gaped at the incredible sight of a couple of runway lights that had been ripped-up by the damaged landing gear when they ran off the pavement and were now wrapped around the right-side wheel truck by their power cables. The American stared at the damaged metal wheel rims. Getting down safely after all the airplane had been through had been a miracle. But how would they ever again take off?

Someone called out to them from the direction of the tail of the aircraft. A maintenance man was pointing up at the overhanging rear fuselage. The fellow shined a flashlight at the right-rear cargo door they had tied-down with wires during the flight. "This will take many repairs," the mechanic said, speaking in Spanish. Larry translated the words for the others.

The headlights of a vehicle, moving fast, shined on them. A small bus whined to a stop with a loud screeching of brakes. The side door folded open and a no-nonsense-looking man in green Army fatigues dropped from the running board. Larry saw the 747 captain give a significant glance to the two other pilots, then step forward and turn the military man aside. He watched as the two carried on a conversation for a couple of minutes in a language incomprehensible to the American. Then the Ukrainian pilot came back, motioning to Larry and the others. "We will all go with this man—to take care of official matters," he said in broken English.

Larry and the crewmen, along with the Africans, who had been standing nearby, shuffled up into the paint-peeled conveyence. With a gritty grinding of gears the machine lurched around. As they chugged off, Larry glanced back. In the glaring banks of lights, maintenance men were already at work on the 747.

The bus rattled up to an enormous, lighted-up hangar. Through open doors at one end, Larry could see several very large aircraft inside in various stages of repair. The machine squealed to a stop in front of a one-story structure attached at one side of the building. As he stared out, the American observed that lights inside were shining. Were these people expecting them? Larry remembered the radioed conversations between the pilots and the Havana Tower while they were still flying. He guessed they had made some sort of preparations for them.

The bus's jerking front door flapped back. The Army man stood up and faced his uncertain-looking passengers. "Comrades! We will now go inside!"

Larry realized the man was speaking in Spanish, to the puzzlement of the others. "He says to follow him!"

The Cuban aimed his beady eyes at the source of the voice, as if analyzing the upstart newcomer, then eased back when he realized Larry was translating to the other men. Without another word, he turned about and dropped down the steps.

The passengers stepped from the bus where a serious-looking man in fatigues pointed toward a door at the side of the building. "In there!" Larry repeated the man's order out loud in English, prompting the fellow to single him out with a glowering glare. The Californian could feel tension all about; his stomach was gathering in knots. His sweaty hand gripped the handle of his travel bag as he joined the line of men walking in a hurry toward the entrance. As Larry paced past the critical Cuban, he could sense the man's steady gaze on him; his skin prickled as if a "Bulls's-Eye" target was painted on his back.

Inside, they blinked in the bright lights of a hallway, where another Army man directed the troupe—minus the pilots, who were not with them—down the corridor to an open space inside the hangar. The stark concrete floor bore painted lines that seemed to define an assembly area. Another soldier came up and pointed for the men to line up on some evenly-spaced marks.

While the others formed up, Larry looked around. The inside of the gigantic structure was painted white, with open-riveted steel beams along the outside walls supporting a tall, curved roof. Every minute or so an announcement of some sort in what Larry recognized as Russian blared out from horn-shaped loudspeakers that were situated all around the place, punctuated by several seconds of rousing martial music that, to the American's ears, sounded decidedly non-Caribbean. Looking about, Larry focused on some men who were working on a nearby airplane. With their pale, cherubic faces they were obviously not native Cubans—these men resembled the pilots. He decided they must be Soviets.

A tanned, fit-looking military man about his age, with insignia that seemed to denote he was an officer, strode up to the front of where they were assembled. In his hands he held a sheaf of papers that he shuffled against his chest, and with a searching, skeptical face surveyed the rather ragged ranks. "Comrades! Listen to these announcements!" the man said in passable English.

Larry was relieved he was speaking in a language all the new arrivals could understand—but the term, "comrades," which was the second time he had heard it spoken, was a forceful reminder he was in a Communist country where its use was common. The American felt himself stiffening; nervous drops of sweat were dripping from his underarms, dampening his shirt. Where was all this going? Larry closed his eyes and took a deep breath; he must try to remain calm. He took a glance around at the Africans whose grim, sweaty faces seemed to suggest that they felt as he did.

". . . a list of you men—" the man was saying in a strident voice, bringing back Larry's attention, "answer when I say your name." All in the group spoke up when he read their names aloud, except for the three pilots, who were still somewhere else. Larry wondered how they already knew their names—perhaps the captain had radioed them ahead, he decided. The officer led the men down a narrow corridor to a classroom-like space with desks. On a side wall was a life-size color portrait of Fidel Castro in his fatigues. Larry stared at the scruffy-looking "Leader's" picture and wondered how he ever got to be so important, looking like that, and if he ever took a bath. "Take seats," the man said.

A lighter-skinned fellow in a blue-and-gray uniform with a holstered pistol hanging at his belt came through the doorway. Larry guessed he was a policeman of some sort. The man stepped up to a paint-faded podium. A silence hung in the room as the official, his lips pursed, gripped the lectern and ran his eyes across each newcomer's face.

"Comrades! I am 'Inspector Camarena' of the—*'Nacional Revoluciónary Police'* . . . the *'P-N-R'.*" Once more Larry gave a start at the word, "comrades," which he now realized was used all the time in Cuba. "It is—fortunate you are—here with us."

"Fortunate?" The American fidgeted in his seat. Did he mean it was "fortunate" they had landed safely here in Havana, instead of crashing at sea? Then Larry recalled something else: a little while ago, a man in a uniform had said something about "sending shipments with you when you leave." Perhaps it was "fortunate" for the *Cubans* that the 747 had arrived just now so it could carry goods somewhere to Castro's confederates!

The P-N-R Inspector went on in a bookish, stilted-sounding style that sounded unnatural to Larry's ears. "The highest authorities will—furnish you with all appropriate—things for your stay, here. We will—dispense with formalities. The *'Revoluciónary Government'* understands the importance of— your visit and wishes for your—stay to be pleasant."

Larry remembered a language professor back in college who had once told him that government-run spy schools often used the halting technique to force-teach a language to people who would be imbedded in a foreign country and needed to speak without an accent. Perhaps Inspector Camarena had learned his English at such a school.

Just then, a trim, tanned young woman with short hair the color of copper, wearing a blue-and-gray skirted uniform, came into the room and stood by, holding a leather satchel.

"This is 'Officer Montoya'. She has—documents for your— stay in Cuba."

The policewoman stepped forward, elbowing the man aside. "Give me your passports!"

There was a scramble as the men dug around for their documents. Larry pulled his from his rear pocket, where he always kept it. As he passed it along with the others', he noticed that all the black mens' passports had *"Angola"* on the covers. So *that* was where they were from. He remembered that Cuba had sent thousands of troops and weapons to a civil war in Angola.

Officer Montoya culled through the passports—until she came to the dark-blue one Larry recognized as his own. She looked about the room until she found the American and held him in a long stare.

"A tourist card is twenty-five dollars United States Currency!" She spoke in a piercing voice that sounded to Larry as if it could penetrate concrete. "But the 'Revoluciónary Government' recognizes your importance and will not charge you for this."

The other men looked relieved. Larry was frowning. What did she mean by "recognizes your importance?" The P-N-R guy had just now said practically the same thing.

Officer Montoya went down the row of seats and gave each of the men a card. When she handed Larry his, she held her gaze straight into his eyes for a long moment. The policewoman returned to the front and held up a card. "This is your 'tourist card' . . . without it, you can be arrested." Larry glanced at the rubber-stamped one in his hand did a double-take: *his name was already typed on it*! On the reverse side someone had hand-written his occupation as "Consultant".

The American looked up; the Cuban woman was staring at him. "*'Norte 'Americanos'* . . . we stamp your tourist card—not your passport," she said in her accented English, "your being here is of value to us. We will not cause you problems with your government."

The policewoman's comments added to his questions. "What did she mean by, *"your being here is of value to us"*?

Just then, the Army officer came back into the room. "Come with me, comrades." He motioned for the men to follow him. As Larry stepped past Officer Montoya, out of the corner of his eye he caught the forceful young woman's unwavering gaze still on him

Outside the hangar, the Army man led them to a long black limousine. Little red flags with yellow stars in their centers fluttered on both front fenders. He motioned at the open trunk. "Put your bags in the rear compartment."

As the visitors piled into the capacious vehicle that had a window dividing the driver from the passengers, the Army man gestured with his cigar. "You should feel honored—this is a Soviet general's field car." He took the right-front seat.

By the big vehicle's interior lights, Larry read an engraved plate that said, *"ZIL"*, in the Cyrillic alphabet he recognized from his two semesters of Russian at the university, and that the car had been manufactured in Moscow. *"Pavel Drubkin"* was also on the label; someone by that name had installed the sumptious interior at the ZIL factory.

After a short ride across the airport's military section, they pulled up to a unimportant-looking one-story building. The destination turned out to be a small, cafeteria-like eatery; definitely a welcome sight as none of the newcomers had eaten since before the airplane had left Mexico City. The aroma of Cuban food was in the air. Looking around, the American spotted the three pilots already at a table.

Right away, Larry discovered that this cafeteria line was like no other he had ever seen. For one thing, there were no plates. A server directed the men to a stack of divided trays that obviously functioned as such. As they moved down the serving line, some of the foods they ladled onto the trays appeared thin and anemic-looking, as if re-constituted from various powders. There was a green, slippery, gelatin-like substance, certainly containing more water than anything else, that kept sliding around in its compartment on the tray. A stringy brown object that Larry never identified, had, to his surprise, a tangy good taste. Something else looked like a sponge inside a moistened roll.

The coffee was served black, in miniature white-porcelain mugs with no handles. From his first tentative swallow, Larry found that the molasses-like Cuban brew was much heavier and stronger than the coffee he was used to back in the 'States. The Army man, dropping into a chair at the same table, saw him frowning at the little cup. "That is *'Cuban coffee'*, señor—drink it . . . carefully!" Judging from the amount of the thick stuff the Cubans around him were gulping in quantities he would not dare

416

try to match, the American deduced that the military people down here were wired on caffeine.

The Army officer was looking at Larry. "You are Norte 'Americano', no? What do you think about Cuba?"

"I find it 'interesting'." Larry, surprised, groped for words. "I am into—sales," he went on, not wishing to reveal any details.

"Señor, I know about you and your equipment. You are an 'electronics engineer' taking a satellite tracking system to Nigeria for the 'Organization'!"

Larry felt his face reddening. *How did this Cuban know these things?* The military man seemed to be amused at the American's obvious surprise that he was already aware of the real mission of the guest who had literally dropped from the sky. His ears burning, Larry tried to look calm—but now that his cover was blown, he would go ahead and try to do some probing of his own."This 'Organization'—I keep hearing about it, but I don't know what it is."

The Cuban looked astonished. *"You do not know who you are working for?"* He cocked his eyebrow and leaned forward over the table. "It is *'muy gigante'*, señor." The fellow's rasping voice was barely audible above the background conversations in the dining-room. "All I can say is that it is secret and they will pay you *'mucho dinero'!*"

A queasy feeling was developing in the pit of Larry's stomach not caused by the Cuban food or the high-octane local coffee. Somehow, he had become involved in something that was beyond anything he could have ever imagined. Here in Havana, they even knew about his Nigerian deal! It was beginning to look as if the Cubans, the pilots, Angola, the airplane, his cargo and the "Organization"—whatever it was—were all tied together! Then there were the Soviets he had seen in the hangar. No wonder these people were so willing and ready to repair the damaged 747! And there was no telling who or what else were involved. Larry thought about the happenings back on the ship and in Mexico. Were they all, too, part of this?

The fellow across the table unbuttoned a breast pocket of his fatigues and pulled out two cigars. "Smoke?" Larry could smell their leaves. "They are the finest Cuban—the best cigars in the world."

"I'm not a smoker."

The man lit-up and projected a long, aromatic puff toward the ceiling. "It is unfortunate you 'Americanos' have not had any of our excellent cigars for many years."

Larry shrugged. "I try to stay out of politics."

"You understand, we send most of our cigars to the Soviets."

Larry did not want to be pulled into a political discussion by someone he did not know; it could well be a trap. "Like I say, I'm not political—not here in Cuba, anyway."

The Cuban gave a smirk. "Since you will be on our 'friendly' island while your airplane is being repaired, I am sure you will want to see Havana while you are here."

Larry detected an ironic tone at the word, "friendly". "I don't know much about Havana."

The man gave an enigmatic shrug. "We can take care of that." He looked about. "We will leave, now."

A few minutes later, the big ZIL pulled up in front of a two-story stucco building on a narrow street not far from the airport. A sign hanging out over the screened entrance proclaimed the place to be the "Noches Hotel". The travelers retrieved their luggage bags from the rear trunk and joined up at a dimly-lighted registration counter. A night clerk wearing gaudy suspenders handed out room keys.

"Señor Landay, I will return in the morning for breakfast. You will have big day, tomorrow." The military officer stuck out his hand.

The American shook the Cuban's. "All right, Mister—ah, 'Señor—'"

"Barrientos'—*Major Teófilo* Barrientos." The Army man turned and marched out.

On the third level, down a shadowy hallway, Larry found his room number at the rear of the building. Since the night was warm and the space smelled musty, he raised a window. A mesh-screen covered the outside frame. After pulling down the covers, Larry turned off the lights, stripped down to his shorts and dropped onto the mattress sheet.

A couple of minutes later, when he was almost asleep, he felt something like a feather go across his face. "There was something on my face!" he said half-aloud. Larry reached over and pulled on a lamp switch. When the weak yellow light came on, he looked around and gasped.

An enormous black cockroach, almost the size of his hand, was crawling on the pillow! He swatted at it with the palm of his hand. To his horror, the hideous creature spread its wings and fluttered through the air to the lampshade, where it wobbled a moment, then took off again, this time heading into the bathroom where it slapped itself onto the edge of the toilet bowl. In a flash, Larry knocked it into the water with his foot and grabbed the flush handle. The huge insect dropped out of sight, kicking, down the swirling whirlpool.

His heart pounding, he searched about the room; under the bed, in and behind the *amoire* that served as a closet; but didn't find any more vermin. The tired traveler turned off the light and dropped again onto the pillow.

But as he lay back, there came a scratching from the direction of the window. Propping himself on his elbow, he blinked at the source of the sound. Backlit by a streetlight, scuttling across the outside of the screen was the outline of a roach every bit as big as the one he had dispatched down the drain. Larry prayed the screen had no holes in it. Even as he gaped, from off to one side a foot-long lizard shot across, grabbed the flailing creature in its mouth and vanished.

His skin prickling in the humid Havana night, the exhausted American rolled over and pulled the pillow over his head. Bugs or no bugs, he was going to have to get some sleep.

* * *

Someone was rapping on the door. "Señor!" A man's voice called out in an Hispanic accent. Larry opened his eyes. Sunlight streamed in the window. Where was he? Then it all came back: This was a seedy Havana hotel room. More knocks on the door. "Señor Landay!" He got up and cracked open the door. The burnished face of Teófilo Barrientos stared back at him through

419

the narrow space. "Ah, señor, we will be leaving in twenty minutes—bring your luggage with you."

Larry hopped into the shower and washed the residue of yesterday off him; the water ran clear and the soap was at least halfway decent. As he toweled off, he remembered the major had said something about showing him around Havana—maybe he could salvage *something* out of this un-planned stop-over on this complicated island.

When he bumped his baggage down to the first floor lobby, the major and two of the Angolans were waiting for him. "Ah, Señor Landay—it is good to see you, again . . . you had good sleep, no?" Larry gave the Cuban a half-hearted nod.

Just then, the four other Africans clumped down the staircase with their luggage. "Let us go, now!"

Outside at the curb was the same bus that had carried them from the airplane, enveloped in its usual cloud of diesel exhaust. "The *'bolo'* general is in his big car, today so we go by bus."

Once more, Larry caught the ironic tone to the man's voice—it was obvious the major had little regard for the Soviet general, whoever he was. What had he called him—"bolo?" It did not sound like a compliment.

The bus rattled up the short street and turned onto a big thoroughfare. A little farther on, they lurched through an intersection, and a couple of minutes later the bus sputtered past a sign announcing they were at the *'El Aeropuerto Internacional José Marti Habana'*. The driver maneuvered the machine, trailed by its tail of smoke, through a gate. In traffic that was heavier than Larry would have expected, the bus drew up behind a line of stopped taxicabs; all shiny American vehicles, Larry noted, that were from the nineteen-fifties.

"Let us go inside, comrades. We shall now have breakfast!" As they headed toward a concrete-and-glass structure, Larry's ears rang with the scream of nearby jet engines and the slam of pile-drivers; it looked as if a good deal of construction was going on around the airport. The American was struck by how much alike—except for all the old cars about—this gateway to Communism looked, compared to other airports he had seen.

The major cleared the way through a milling throng of people and lines of ticket-holders queued at airline check-in counters. Except that all the airport signs were in Spanish, as were the public address announcements, the place could have been almost anywhere in the 'States, Larry thought. The passengers he saw in the waiting lines looked prosperous; none of the impoverished-looking types he had expected to see in this Communist country. But all these people were *leaving*, Larry noted—which suggested they were probably *not* from Cuba.

Barrientos led the men down a concourse to a restaurant. From the first bite it was evident to Larry—and judging by their facial expressions, to the others, also—that this "food" would have to be endured, not savored. But hunger overcame hesitation; the American and the Angolans bit into hard-boiled eggs with marble-hard yolks a startling purplish-green in color; sliced, room-temperature ham, warm cheese, and a hard, lumpy biscuit that Larry thought could do well as construction material.

Three-quarters-of-an hour later, after the strange—though, filling—meal, the men were back aboard the smoky bus. "We will return to the airplane," Barrientos announced, as the swaying vehicle lumbered past a guard gate into the airport's military section. He turned to the black men. "You will assist with the cargo."

When they drove up, they saw that the 747 had been moved into the hangar; its tall vertical tail now stuck out the end of the building into Havana's tropical sunshine. Inside, the airliner rested on jacks; the damaged landing gear and the dented lower-deck right-rear cargo door had been taken off. Once again, it seemed to Larry that this airplane must be very important to rate such intense attention.

One of the Soviets came up and motioned for the passengers to follow him. When Larry turned to join them, the European held up his hand.

The major motioned to Larry. "You will go with me."

When they stepped through the doorway into the office reception area they were met by a wispy-looking, middle-aged man with salt-and-pepper hair. "Teófilo!" The fellow pulled the officer to him in a bear hug.

"Trini!" Barrientos returned the grasping greeting. He turned to Larry. "This "Norte Americano" says he is bored and wants to see Havana!"

The American shook the suntanned Cuban's leathery, calloused hand. "Larry Landay . . . but I'm *not* really bored."

"'Trini Torres'." Humor lines creased the older man's face. "You are 'Norte 'Americano', no?"

The officer spoke up. "He is working with the 'Organization'"

Larry gave a start—there was that word, again.

"You are not finding Cuba exciting place?" Trini Torres looked incredulous, then brightened. "Señor, I offer my services." He looked the Californian up and down. "You speak Spanish?"

"Enough to get around."

"My English is not so good." He nodded at the Army officer. "I will show our Havana to the 'Capitalist'. Come with me, señor!" Larry followed the fellow outside.

"Trini Torres" loped around the corner of the hangar office in the direction of an old car—quite old, the American saw, with enormous fins at the rear—that was snugged into a space on the pot-holed parking lot where the painted lines were barely visible. Several other American vehicles were parked nearby; none newer than what Larry guessed would be late-nineteen-fifties vintage.

The older man saw Larry's look-around. "Ah, señor, we clever Cubans get by with whatever was here when Fidel took over." He grabbed the handle of the gargantuan two-door "hardtop" and tugged open the squawking driver's door. "Get inside, señor . . . we will go see city, now."

Trini maneuvered his colossal car out onto the avenue. As they drove away, Larry gazed across the way at the hangar. From the distance, he could see that the 747's wide cargo doors were now open; it looked as if the Africans were loading more crates into the aircraft.

* * *

"Yes, I'm sure this is the airplane . . ." The middle-aged *female photo-analyst at the "National Security Agency" stared*

into the computerized magnifying viewer at the three-dimensional slide. The woman motioned to the supervisor, who was standing next to her.

The man leaned over and squinted through the 'stereo-optic' viewfinder. "But only the tail is visible outside the hangar—do a side-scan."

The technician clicked a mouse; the software rotated the vantage point around to display the right side of the tail fin. "Yes . . . it's the Seven-Forty-Seven, all right—there's the vertical stabilizer." The man stared again into the viewer at the blowup of the picture the satellite had captured on its pass two-hundred-eight-miles above Havana earlier that morning. He turned to the assistant. "Call 'NORAD' . . . tell them we found their baby—it's in the military hangar at José Marti!"

* * *

Larry gaped around at the outsized vehicle's faded broadcloth-and-vinyl seats and its gaudy, painted-chromed dashboard trimmed in gold lettering. Trini kept pushing some buttons on the left side next to the wrap-around windshield that the American decided must be the gear selector. To Larry, the two-toned, slightly-oblong-shaped, translucent steering wheel looked oddly oversized, compared to vehicles he was used to back home. Although he had heard his parents talk about these kinds of cars, he had never before ridden in anything like it. "What kind of car *is* this?"

Ah, Señor Larry—this is one of your 'Capitalist' cars . . . a Nineteen-Fifty-Seven 'Chrysler Three- Hundred'!" The Cuban pressed the accelerator pedal; a growling like an aroused lion came from underneath the hood. The acceleration jerked back Larry's head as the tail-finned machine bored through an intersection. "My car she has three-hundred-ninety-horsepower!" He pumped the brake pedal; the hood dove as the speed dropped. "Power brakes!"

From out of a side street, an old orange Chevrolet pickup, full of children in the back, lurched across in front of them with a brassy blast from a fender-mounted horn; its driver gesturing at them.

"Where are we going?" Havana was already looking a lot bigger than Larry had expected it to be.

"You will see everything, Señor Larry. Have patience!" At an intersection, the Cuban spun the oversize steering wheel. "We are getting close to where *'Él Máximo*` lives!"

"You mean—*'Castro'*?"

"It is his favorite *'casa'*. He has many *'haciendas'* depending on what 'mood' he is in."

The car made a right turn onto a one-way street. "There it is, señor . . ." The driver pointed at a row of pine trees. "Fidel's *'primero casa'.*"

As the big Chrysler moved at a slow, measured pace past an iron gate in the fence that ran alongside the roadway, two soldiers with automatic rifles glared at them. Larry stared at the heavy foilage beyond the fences. "I can't see anything."

They say he has a big house and a place to play tennis. Did you know Fidel plays tennis?"

Larry said nothing. He did not know Castro liked tennis.

"He also plays basketball."

The American rolled his eyes; this guy talked as if he really *liked* the Bearded One. "Is Castro popular with the people?"

"Ah, señor, *''The Revolución''* brought us better life. Better than before."

The car made a right turn onto a one-way street. "There sure are a lot of 'one-way' streets around here," Larry said.

"Señor, you are most observant. Around the 'hacienda' of *Él Commandante, all* the streets are one-way—*away* from his place!"

Trini pointed straight ahead. "That is the marina, señor— *'Marina Hemingway'* they call it. They named it after your writer. He stayed in Havana lot."

Over the rooftops of some low buildings were the tips of masts. From their shiny looks, Larry found it hard to believe that Cubans could own such vessels. "Whose boats are they?"

"Señor, they come from all over the world." He glanced at Larry. "Not everybody shares you Norte Americano's hatred of 'The Revolución'."

"We don't even *think* about Cuba all that much." Larry was starting to suspect that these people were obsessed with resenting the United States.

A truck, trailing the standard swirl of blue smoke, passed them in a hurry. In the back, on piles of straw, sat about a dozen youths of both sexes, all wearing red 'kerchiefs tied around their necks. Larry stared at the peasant-looking young people, some of whom held up long-bladed machetes for the men to see. The truck made a turn down a side street. Larry frowned. "Who are they?"

"Students . . . going to the sugarcane fields. Everyone donates to collect the harvest."

"Why don't they use machines?"

"Fuel shortages! Your damn embargo—even the *Russians* are talking about cutting us off! So now everybody works in the cane fields."

Trini gave the big car more speed. "You 'Americanos' made good cars!" the Cuban shouted over the whoosh of the air. He jerked the wheel to avoid a man on a bicycle. "Too bad you Capitalists have such bad ideas about Cuba." Larry started to say something, then decided not to be drawn into a political discussion. These people were quite adept at baiting him, he was discovering.

As the hardtop swept past a sign that said *"Miramar District"*, the driver pumped the brakes; the long, important hood dipped as the speed fell off with a wobble. "Needs shock absorbers. These Russian truck ones did not last long—"

"You have *Russian* shock absorbers on your car?"

"Señor, the carburetor came from an East German personnel carrier! The 'bolos' left it in a field. We did it ourselves. Works good, no?"

A red, early-'fifties Plymouth convertible, its top down, passed them headed in the opposite direction. Trini swiveled about in his seat. "Ah, see that car? It belongs to my cousin, 'Mojo'. He put *'Sovietica'* carburetor and tires on it, too!"

A light-green station wagon with rust streaks down its sides was meeting up with them. Larry stared at the car as it came closer. "Is that a 'Volvo'?"

Trini snorted. "You are probably the first person who ever mistook a *'Lada'* for a Volvo!" He gave the smoking vehicle a sneer as it went by. "Ha! There are very few Volvos in Cuba, and most are forty years old." He glanced at the decrepit automobile in the mirror and shook his head."That Lada is a Russian car—a very *'simple'* car." A grin flickered across his face. "All I will say about Ladas is that they always *start*—but with their brakes, you cannot always *stop* them! And they ride like farm wagons! They are made of heavy Soviet steel. Did you know that Stalin's name meant, 'Steel'?"

The American thought he had heard that before, but his attention was now focused on a huge house off to his right. The thoroughfare was leading them into a district of large, older-looking houses; some that were set back into groves of trees and erratic landscaping were the size of mansions. As Larry looked more closely, he could see that many of the once-splendid homes were in varying states of neglect and disrepair. "Is this where the rich people live?"

A smirk creased the swarthy Cuban's face. "Señor, here in Havana we are *all* rich with 'The Revolución'. This is *'Miramar'*—rich people *used* to live here until most of them left to Miami after Fidel arrived. Now, are workers' clubs and schools. Some are *'clinicas'*."

"You mean *doctors' offices*?"

"Señor—the peoples of Cuba are the healthiest in the world! You can see it for yourself!" Trini gripped the two-toned steering wheel and glanced at his passenger. His expression was adamant. "Under 'The Revolución', Cuban health is the best anywhere!"

The American had never before connected Cuba with health care. Maybe sometime he could check on the man's claims. But first, he would have to get *off* this island.

The boulevard dove through a short tunnel then came back into sunlight onto a beachfront thoroughfare. "We are now on the *'Malecón'*, señor—this road goes around to *'Old Havana'*." The man glanced at his passenger. "You will like Old Havana."

Larry took in the enormous houses and storefronts they were driving past. To his right stood block after block of hotels and big apartment buildings."This is where the *'Mafioso'* lived before 'The Revolución' overthrew Batista . . . you 'Norte Americanos' *helped* Batista! He and the mobsters ran Cuba. You see, most of the people suffered until Fidel got rid of both them and the CIA." The man's tanned, leathery face was animated. "Now, things are better with 'The Revolución'!"

The big Chrysler drove along, past small parks, each with a monument of some sort that Larry guessed somehow figured into Castro's scheme of things. After a while, he began to notice that there were not that many regular autos out and about—apart from smoke-belching Soviet-looking trucks and buses, most Cubans they were now encountering were riding bicycles. "Looks like a lot of bicycles."

The older man winced. "We are conserving fuel for 'The Revolución'. The 'bolos' may not be here much longer." He noticed Larry's questioning look. "We get our oil from the 'Sovieticas' and we give them our sugar." The man paused as if thinking about something, then went on, "there is talk that 'counter-Revoluciónary' activities in the *'U-R-S-S'* may mean less for Cuba—this 'Comrade Yeltsin' does not look like Gorbachev." He sighed. "Our best times were under Brezhnev." The man shook his head. "Now, we have *'mucho'* shortages, señor. Soap; toilet paper; *cerveza'*—beer. Even *beer*, señor! But we are strong. Yankee Imperialism cannot match 'The Revolución'."

Larry was listening with interest as they drove past more faded apartments and other buildings along the beachfront boulevard. If anything, he was getting an education about what Cubans thought about the Soviets and the Americans. "You talk about 'bolos'—who are they?"

"We call the Russians that because they do not wash their hands—ever!" Seeing Larry's frown, he went on. "Señor, we Cubans are very clean people! We take baths before we go out at night, and we change into our best *'camisas'* and *'pantaloons'*. And the señoritas . . . oh, my—see how *they* dress!" He made a gesture of a woman's figure. "But those 'bolos'—bah! Dirty people." He took a glance at the American. "We will buy you a *'guayabera'.*"

"A what?" Lary frowned. "Camisas" and "pantaloons" for shirts" and "pants" he understood, but this word was new to him.

"A 'guayabera'." Trini pointed at his own white cotton shirt that hung outside his pants. "Every *'Habañero'* wears one. Good in Cuba weather."

The man squinted ahead. "Ah! The *'Artesans's Market'* . . . we will go there!" He pulled off the main road into a pot-holed parking area. "Señor—here is where you start to look Cuban!"

The bustling place reminded Larry of the big "flea market" back in San Jose, not far from his office in Mountain View. Trini led Larry down several aisles, past jostling shoppers, to a booth near one end of the sawdust concourse. He held up a white pleated cotton pullover shirt with a row of clear buttons down the front. "This is what you want." After a half-minute of gestures and loud talk, Trini flipped the merchant some coins and handed the shirt to the American, who had not said anything.

The trader motioned to a fitting room. In a minute, Larry came back out wearing the guayabera.

Trini beamed. "Señor, you are now perfect Cuban!"

"Thanks . . . I guess." Larry spoke in English.

The shopkeeper's eyebrows went up. "Norte 'Americano'?" The man glared, jabbing his finger. *"You filthy, damn-bastard Imperialist pig!"* The fellow stepped up to Larry's face with fists upraised and let go with a volley of obscenities in Spanish.

Trini tugged Larry's elbow and with a forced smile at the red-faced shopkeeper, turned the American back out into the corridor.

"What was *that* all about?"

"He was about to attack you! He lost his father at what you call the 'Bay of Pigs'. He blames *all* 'Americanos'—"

* * *

Soon after they left the market place, the Malecón bore to the right, still hugging the shoreline. Trini slowed the Chrysler and motioned toward the water. "Right here, señor, is the closest

Havana comes to Florida—to Key West. It is only a hundred-and-forty kilometers from this spot."

Larry stared at the rolling breakers foaming against the rocks at the foot of the seawall and thought how different it was just a few dozen miles across those wave-tops, compared to the way things were here on this island.

As they rode along, he saw people fishing from the rocky shoreline; when the road took a bend where they could see the waterline, here and there a young man would be rolling a huge inner tube along the boulders. Other tubes lay at the edge of the surf along with what looked like fishing gear. Then he noticed that around each of the inflated rubber doughnuts was tied what seemed to be a fishnet that covered-over the hole in the center. "What are they doing out there with those inner tubes?"

"The *'él Neumáticos'*—they paddle out at night and fish for Red Snapper."

"Why don't they just go out in boats?"

"Señor, *there are no boats.* But there are many tire tubes. You remember the 'bolos'—?"

So they purloined the inner tubes from the Soviets. "What do they do with the fish they catch?"

"We will be having *'Siesta'* in 'Old Havana', today, señor. Do you like Red Snapper?"

As the Chrysler drove along on the broad oceanfront thoroughfare, Larry watched people lolling about on top of the concrete seawall, soaking up the mid-day sun. Along the broad sidewalk, lovers held hands and gazed into each others' eyes. He wondered how much they actually knew about the outside world in this Castro-controlled environment. Not much, he guessed, based on his conversations so far with Trini and Major Barrientos.

The Cuban turned the Chrysler toward the City Center. As they drove through a crowded neighborhood, Larry did a double-take—looming over a grove of tropical trees, was what looked to the American like a "flying saucer". A line of customers stood out of the place and all the way back down the street; knots of people milled about in its park-like setting. "What is *that?*"

Trini's eyes followed to where Larry was looking and laughed. "Ice-cream!"

Larry gazed out at the two-level, white circular building that soared above the treetops on outsized crab-like legs. "What does that thing have to do with ice-cream?"

The Cuban pulled into a parking space and gestured with his cigar at the white, odd-looking structure.

"That is *'Coppelia'*, señor, the most famous ice-cream store in the world."

"If it's so famous, how come I've never heard of it?"

Trini sighed. "You 'Americanos' do not have anything to do with Cuba, no? So how *would* you know about 'Coppelia'?"

Larry thought about the ice-cream places back home and their many flavors. All at once, he had a craving for the stuff. He reached for the door handle. "Can we go in there?"

The man looked over at the place, then back at Larry with a shrug. "Maybe we can have ice-cream." He popped open his door. "Do not say anything . . . I will do all the talking, señor."

The two made their way across grassy grounds shaded by palm trees and other tropical plants into the pavilion. Trini took one look at the shuffling procession of people that went all the way to the outside and beyond and raised a finger. "Wait here, señor, I will return," he said in Spanish. The Cuban spoke to a white-clad man behind the counter, who nodded.

"It is all arranged—come with me." Larry followed the islander outside to an unoccupied marble table under a shade tree. All around them, convivial Cubans dipped their spoons into bowls of their creamy concoctions.

A waiter came up with two metal containers. "Enjoy!" he said in Spanish.

"Vanilla—my favorite, and the best," Trini slurped, motioning for Larry to do the same . . . "real cream and Cuban sugar."

With the first spoonful, the American had to agree it was the most luxurious frozen creamery he had ever tasted. "How did Cuba come up with such good ice-cream?" *He had forgotten not to speak aloud.*

"It is all from Fidel."

While he and his companion tackled the contents of their bowls, Larry took in the alfresco scene of smiling, laughing citizens who seemed to be enjoying themselves. "I have never seen so many people eating ice-cream at once!" *A man nearby took notice of Larry talking in English.*

"Thirty-thousand people a day come here, señor. It is the biggest ice-cream parlor in the world!"

As Larry dug into his dish, he found it hard to believe that this time yesterday he was sitting in a sweltering cantina many miles south of Mexico City with the two truck drivers, trying to down a spicy Mexican meal. The strange "traffic court"; the shoot-outs; the plane ride; the mid-air emergencies; the landing—all had happened in the past twenty-four hours. And now, here he was, at an enormous ice-cream parlor in Havana, Cuba.

"Señor, we were lucky . . . I told the manager you were from Canada . . . he let us go to the front of the line." The man leaned back and lit another cigar. "If he knew where you were from, or if you had been a 'bolo', he would have thrown us out!"

"Why do you Cubans despise those 'bolos' all that much? I thought you and the Soviets were all in the same—"

". . . Señor, we are now in the 'Special Period'. Do you know what that is?" The swarthy fellow looked down his cigar at the American. "I will tell you. In the Soviet Union, Gorbachev is soon going to be gone and this new 'Comrade Yeltsin' is going to have to cut back. And where do you think he will start? Cuba! In fact, it has already started."

Trini frowned. "Not long ago Fidel went on the television. He told us that we will have to do without a lot of things. Things like soap, toilet paper, perfume; *'dinero'*—'money', to you. Especially money. All these things come from our 'friends', the Soviets. He called it the start of the 'Special Period'—a time of sacrifice for all Cubans. Next, they will probably cut off the oil. If that happens, things here are going to be terrible. That is why we do not anymore like the Russians. But Cubans are strong, señor! 'The Revolución' will go on, no matter what. Of course, if you *'gringos'* would let up on your embargo, things would not be like this. *Por favor,* señor! Cubans do not hate 'Americanos'—just your government that is trying to starve us!"

Larry took in all this without any outward response. Regardless of how the man felt, the American doubted the embargo was at the root of all of Cuba's problems. Already, in the short time he had been out and about in Havana, he had seen all kinds of things that could be improved upon without anything added from America: a coat of paint all around, for one thing, would work wonders. And he detected a subtle lethargy, perhaps the by-product of a bland system that failed to reward hard work or punish slackers. Even though he had been impresed by the clever energy of many Cubans, he suspected that many of these people were barely surviving. Trini had been right about that.

A shadow came over the table. Looking up, Larry confronted a scowling, dark-haired man with a pencil mustache who was pointing at him. "'Americano'! I heard you talk!" The man clenched his fists and stepped toward Larry.

-29-

Customers at nearby tables stopped what they were doing and gawked at them. Trini stood up, put his hand on the fellow's shoulder, and turned him aside. The Cuban led the agitated man a short distance away, where the two had an animated conversation, during which the stranger glanced around at Larry several times. The American could feel the penetrating stares of people sitting at the other tables. Larry saw Trini slip a sheaf of U.S. greenbacks into the man's hand. The fellow thrust his fists into his pockets and stepped away into the crowd.

"We must leave at once, señor!" Trini said, motioning to Larry. In a hurry, the older man led the visitor through the line of people to the curb, where the Chrysler was parked.

The two men dropped into the car. "What was *that* all about?".

"That man was an agent of the *'Ministry of the Interior'*. He heard you talking—he was going to arrest you for 'Counter-Revolucionary Activity' until I told him you were transporting 'friendly' goods through Cuba. Of course, I had to pay him."

Trini nudged the car back out into the traffic. "We will soon have 'Siesta' in good place." He gave a nodding smile at a tanned, leggy *se*ñorita in a microskirt crossing in front of them. The young man with her caught the driver's leer and put his hand around her waist.

"Señor, Cuba has the most beautiful girls in the world . . . you agree? Lots of skin."

Larry had already decided he had never seen such skimpy everyday outfits in his life. Some of the girls looked as if their clothes had been applied onto their bare bodies with a spray gun.

At the next intersection a dark-haired *'Cubana'* with startling good looks crossed the street on the arm of a florid-faced, overweight, Anglo-looking man who was decidedly older than she was. Trini narrowed his eyes at the snuggling, unevenly-matched pair. *"'Jinetera'* . . ."

"'Jinetera'?"

Trini puffed on his cigar; its smoke whisked out the open windows into the humid Havana air. He gave the Chrysler more gas; the big-finned hardtop pulled away into a neighborhood of piled tenements whose fronts were painted in garish colors. "Señor," he said, flicking the cigar in the direction of an overflowing ash tray on the dashboard, "a 'jinetera' is a female jockey who 'rides'—" He paused while Larry caught on what he meant. "That girl you saw back there . . . she is not a 'chica'—a prostitute. She sees the foreigner as her ticket out of Cuba—that is, if she *wants* to get out of Cuba." Larry was frowning. "It is like this: the girl has parents and some brothers and sisters. Maybe a child or two. If she gives herself to a male tourist, she can make some real pesos for herself and her family; get some clothes, jewelry; spending money. Plus, she can visit places like clubs and good restaurants and bars where she would not usually be able go, except with a foreigner."

"What do you mean by, 'give herself to a male tourist'?"

"Just like what it sounds, señor." Trini twisted the steering wheel to avoid clipping the rear of a smoking Soviet car pulling away from the curb. "Of course, she does not *think* of herself as a prostitute, or immoral, or anything like that. Maybe she can get the foreign hombre to marry her—it happens, sometimes. If not, there is always *tomorrow's* foreigner. Look, señor—this is the most sex-charged country on earth. Sex is everywhere! Look how the girls dress and behave. A student showing a lot of skin or a nice-looking female dentist in a short dress might come up and grab your crotch and proposition you in the middle of the day! 'Sex for Siesta'—how about that!" Trini laughed at his own wit. "Men on business trips come here from just about everywhere but the United States. As soon as a girl finds out a 'hombre is a foreigner—it is 'Hola!' And Cuba has the healthiest, best-looking real prostitutes in the whole world—the government says so!"

"The government?"

The older man blew another long puff of cigar smoke that swirled away. "The government says it helps the economy! But it is officially against the law for a Cuban to be in a hotel room with a foreigner. They are very strict about that. So, tourists and the women have to be careful." He gave a little smirk and went on.

"The girl's family probably has a special bedroom set up for her. It goes on all over Cuba. But . . . if you are a *Cuban* and you find someone you want to spend some time with, there are the *'casas de amor'.*"

It was Larry's turn to grin. " *'Love houses'?* "

"You catch on *'rápido',* señor! Mostly in the outer parts of Havana, there are official little 'hotels' that sell rooms for—say, three hours for a few pesos. If you do not have privacy at home, you and your lover—maybe you and your wife, even—can go there and catch up on things. The hotel even gives you a bottle of wine! A lot of little Cubans got their start in one of those places."

They came up to a vast open space. Trini stopped the car and made a sweeping gesture. "Señor, this is the *'Plaza de la Revolución'.* This is where Fidel gives his speeches before a million people."

Larry's eyes cast about at the unadorned, stark celebration of cement.

"When Comrade Fidel speaks here, it is the center of the world!" Trini pointed at a concrete building. "That is the Communist Party headquarters."

The American stared across the way, shaking his head. Facing the wide paved plaza before him on the facade of a slab-sided concrete structure was a huge painted picture of a bearded man's face. The Cuban followed Larry's gaze. " *'Che Guevara',* señor . . . the hero of 'The Revolución'."

The Cuban pointed the Chrysler down a two-lane street into a bustling neighborhood where every driver seemed to be testing his car's horn. To Larry, many of the side streets looked to be too narrow for more than one vehicle.

"This is *'Havana Viejo',* señor—'Old Havana'." From apartments and storefronts came loud Latin music; Larry felt a lot of energy in the air. He had never before pictured Havana like this. The American also thought the place had a seedy look and feel to it. There was a vague, sweet aroma that seemed to be everywhere. He decided it was mildew.

The big automobile passed through a plaza; the open area in the center was packed with ancient American-made cars. Trini swung the steering wheel to avoid an oddly-shaped bus with a dip

435

in the middle, pulled by a truck-tractor, overflowing with passengers. "They are called, 'Camels', señor—many of them in Havana."

Trini aimed the car down a broader boulevard, past rows of apartment buildings painted in faded pastel hues; many with shops and bars on the first floor. Down a narrow cobblestone side street, Larry saw shirtless, brown-skinned youngsters kicking a soccer ball. "Is soccer a big sport in Cuba?"

"Si, señor. Many Cubans play *'fútbol`'.*"

"We call it 'soccer '. . . 'football' is a different game where I come from."

Trini's leathery face produced a grin. "Cuban games are better than your Norte Americanos'."

Larry ignored the gibe; instead, his attention was riveted on a huge, stone-faced, domed structure. "It looks like our Capitol in Washington." As they drove past, Larry found it hard to believe that a U.S. Capitol look-alike sat here in this bastion of Caribbean Communism.

"Fidel moved the government into the other buildings we saw back at Revolución Square. This is now a science building."

The Chrysler took several turns and came to a small park with a big statue in the middle, around which men were sitting on benches. "That is *'Parque Central'*, señor . . . the most *importante* place in Old Havana."

"Why is it so important?"

"Because they are talking *'el béisbol'*."

Larry frowned. "Why are they talking about 'baseball' around a statue?"

"There is not much else to—" Trini stopped; a flush came to his face.

Larry caught on that the man was flustered. Was he embarrassed by Cuba? Up to now, Trini had seemed solidly on board with the "Revolución"—almost boring, at times—ignoring or glossing-over shortcomings that Larry could readily see. A newly-landed tourist would think he had arrived in **a** time-warp, with old cars everywhere and the shabby buildings of bygone eras all around. It was becoming obvious to Larry that the island's inhabitants lived in a closed environment, oblivious to the realities of the outside world. In Havana had discovered a society who actually thought they were better off than everyone else on the planet. He had to admit that Fidel had done a good job of convincing the citizens about that. But was there nothing else to do in this city but spear fish, eat ice-cream, talk about baseball and cheer the Revolution? Larry thought it remarkable that in less than a day he had made the transition from accidental visitor to sage observer of the island's social structure.

The Chrysler slid into a space in the middle of a paved-over plaza. "Ready for 'Siesta', señor?" The older man led Larry in the direction of a four-story building

"*Bueños tárdes,* señors." The *maitre d'* led the two men to a table at the edge of the dining patio where several other guests were having lunch. As they took their seats, at a nearby table another waiter was pulling out a chair for a well-dressed, middle-aged woman.

Larry gazed about the open-air, awning-covered outdoor restaurant, with its panoramic view of the parking plaza.

"This is the oldest hotel in Cuba, señor. It has been here since eighteen-seventy-five."

The Cuban narrowed his eyes at the woman who had just come in, then looked straight at Larry across the table. He gravely shook his head and wagged his forefinger in a slight back and forth motion over the tabletop that Larry took to mean: "no talking".

Larry stole a glance at the female newcomer, who was looking down at her menu. *Was her head cocked, as if she was listening to them?* Trini was still discreetly shaking his head.

All at once, the woman shoved back her chair, stood up and strode away.

Trini watched without speaking until she had disappeared through the column-flanked entranceway and out of sight into the lobby. After a furtive look-around, he pulled closer to the table. "Señor," he said in a hoarse whisper, "that woman followed us here—she is *'C-D-R'.*"

"The what?"

"*'Committee for the Defense of 'The Revolución''.* Every neighborhood in Cuba has one. I knew who she was by the way she sat . . . she was watching us—and listening." With another glance around the dining room, Trini crossed his arms on the table and leaned forward. "The C-D-R is supposed make sure everyone supports 'The Revolución'. They tell us they clean up parks and keep streets clean, but—"

The Cuban held up speaking and frowned at the back of a heavyset individual at a nearby table who had stopped a conversation with another man, who also sat silent. Trini again wagged his index finger across the tabletop that Larry caught as another signal to remain quiet. After some seconds, the men resumed talking.

Trini leaned closer across the table. "But every C-D-R 'leader' is really an informant—a government spy. No Cuban would dare speak against 'Él Presidente'' and 'The Revolución'." He pulled a card from his pocket. "Major Barrientos gave me this." He gave it a quick read, then spoke again in a lowered voice, "You will be going to a very good hotel, tonight, señor . . . to the *'Nacional Hotel'*. You will like it. *Muy diferente* from last night." The man glanced at a waiter stepping toward their table. "Ready for your Red Snapper? It came from the 'Neumáticos'!"

The American looked up at the waiter. "Two Red Snappers . . . and no inner tubes!"

The attendant frowned at the two men. *"Que?"*

"Dos 'Snappers y dos cervezas, por favor," Trini ordered in Spanish two Snapper-servings and a couple of beers.

Trini squinted again at the two men at the nearby table for a long moment, then seemed to relax. "They are not 'State Security', I am sure of it," he breathed in a hoarse whisper, "but informers are everywhere." The Cuban glanced around the dining pavilion once more. "We have signals when we believe one is nearby." He tapped his left shoulder with the fingertips of his right hand. "When you see somebody do this, be careful—an informer could be listening."

Larry leaned over and lowered his voice. "How do you know somebody is one of these . . . .'informers'?" .

"By their looks. They wear white guayabaras, new pants and shiny shoes—they *always* have shiny shoes. And the mustache . . . for some reason many informers have what you Americans call a 'handlebar' mustache—I got that name from watching Miami television—and they like to wear dark sunglasses so they can watch *you* but you cannot see who *they* are watching. But the eyeglasses always have heavy, black plastic frames that give them away, every time." Trini gave a smirk. "Sometimes I wonder just how smart they really are, when the agents look the same!" He glanced up; the waiter was coming toward them with a tray held high.

Larry frowned at a mass of slimy-looking yellow objects on his plate. "Red Snappers, I know— but what is *that*?"

"Ah, Señor Larry! You will now eat like real Cuban! That is fried *'plantain'*. It is like banana. But better."

After the meal, the two made their way out into the high-ceilinged lobby. While Trini stepped away to make a telephone call, Larry took in the yellow room with the stuccoed arches and its dark-varnished, wooden overhead beams. As he looked about, he remembered the time years ago when his parents took him to New York and they had stayed at a hotel just off Times Square. That long-ago lobby, with its rich woods and heavy furniture had looked almost like this one.

Trini came back, stuffing a paper into his guyabera breast pocket; a cigar jutting from his mouth at a jaunty angle. He pointed a nicotine-stained finger toward an archway. "One more drink, señor?"

A waiter seated them in the middle of a Moorish-Victorian room with wicker tables and chairs. Casting around, Larry thought he would not be surprised if a slicked-down Humphrey Bogart in a white coat and black bow tie, a cigarette between his fingers, should saunter into the place just now, just like in a movie he had once seen. The American's eyes stopped on a life-size bronze statue of a woman in a provocative pose. "What's that?"

"Ah, 'The Spanish dancer!' The statue is famous in Cuba, señor."

Once more, Larry was taken by the blatant sexuality on this island. Some of the Greek and Roman statues he had seen in museums had been pretty life-like, but never before had he observed the female form expressed in such sensuous, suggestive detail as this one.

"Two daiquiris," Trini told the waiter. When the man turned about and left, the tanned *'Cubano'* reached into his back pocket and pulled out a billfold. "I have relatives in Miami," he said, fingering a clear plastic pack of photographs. A grin, with what Larry thought had a rueful cast, flicked across Trini Torres's face. "They all think I am the 'bad hombre' of the family for staying here."

"They . . . escaped—?" The American was not sure what was the correct word to use.

"Señor, they *abandoned* 'The Revolución'! My brother and his wife and some others left one night in a boat. Much later, I got a letter—they were in Miami. They had a baby girl. She was the first Cuban baby born in Miami. He sent me a piece they cut out of the paper about it. They named her 'Sabina'. But that was many years ago. She used to be on television in Miami—did you know that?"

Larry shook his head; Trini went on. "My cousin Mojo and I rigged up a television aerial in his attic on the Malecón—it is against 'The Revolución' to do that—and we saw her on a station out of Key West." The man flipped through the little pictures and pulled out one. "Here she is . . . we took this of her off the television screen 'bout three years ago."

Larry focused on a tiny photograph of a long-haired brunette giving a newscast; even in the grainy, wallet-sized reproduction he could tell she was extremely attractive. "Very nice-looking."

"Ah, señor, Sabina Torres is beautiful, no? But I have never seen her in person! Just the pictures they sent me and when I saw her on the television. She is not on the television, now. She got married."

Just then, the waiter came back with the drinks. Trini fingered his icy glass, then raised it. " *'Salud'*, señor, to success!" After downing a huge swallow, the islander narrowed his eyes at his glass and gave a knowing smirk. "Did you know that 'daiquiris' were named after a town in eastern Cuba?"

Larry shook his head.

Trini brightened. "We will order more drinks!" He caught the waiter's attention. "My friend, here, needs a *'Mojito Perfecto'*. One for me, also."

When the waiter stepped away, Trini leaned back with an expansive gesture. "Cuba has good drinks!" With a look over Larry's shoulder toward the bar, he upended his daiquiri and took it down beyond the last drop. "Better hurry, señor . . . here comes the next round."

The new concoction had a snappy, sweet flavor with a tangy aftertaste. "What *is* this?"

Trini downed half his glass with a rapturous expression. "It is the Cuban favorite . . . rum and mint and lime and sugar and ice and other things. You like it, no?"

Larry, feeling mellow from the drinks, was now almost glad they had made the forced landing here in Havana, for all he was learning. He took another swallow and suspected that the concoction was probably more potent than Trini was letting on. Gazing about the room that was looking ever more cheery by the minute, he realized that riding around Havana with this intense, inexplicable Cuban in his outdated Chrysler had opened a door for him into a society he had before known about only in negative terms. In a way, he felt concern for these people.

Larry waved off Trini on another drink; after the beer, the daiquiri and the Mojito Perfecto, he figured he had had enough lubrication to last for a while.

At that moment the lights went out, plunging the whole place into darkness. Only pale, indirect light from outside the hotel made its way through the main lobby into the bar.

"Oh, señor!" the Cuban groaned, "*'Granma'* said this could happen."

"Your *'grandmother'* said this could happen?"

"'Granma'—the Communist Party newspaper in Cuba—it said if the 'Sovieticas' cut our oil, there could be blackouts. I fear it is happening, now." He called for the waiter, who came over in the gloom with a flashlight and handed the bar tab to Trini.

Back outside, as Trini was about to open the car door, he gazed about the open square for some moments before dropping into the driver's seat. "I want to be sure no one is following us."

He paused once more with the key over the ignition and turned to Larry. "We must be careful, señor. Some of the things we talked about in there were 'counter-Revoluciónary'." He jabbed the key into the switch and started the engine.

* * *

Across the way, a man with greasy black hair, wearing a white guyabera, squinted through his dark glasses. The two male occupants of the Chrysler leaving the plaza matched the descriptions the female agent had telephoned to him from the hotel. He started the red "Lada's" engine. He would follow the target American car until the next agent took over.

-30-

"Where are we going?"

"Many more things to see and do in Havana, señor." The Cuban maneuvered the massive hardtop around pedestrians scuttling out of their way, then down a narrow side street. As Trini motored the car through another crowded square, the American stared at a big yellow stucco facade with two bell towers, both topped by a cross. He noticed people making their way through some big wooden doors.

"Is that a *church?* I thought there weren't any churches in Cuba."

"Ah, that is the 'Cathedra', señor. It is not used much—that is true." The man glanced at the building, then had to swing hard to avoid an old lady in a crosswalk. "The government says we are atheist, but not long ago they told us we could have some religion, again. I heard the Pope may even come to Cuba, soon. The Pope!" Trini shrugged. "Now why would he want to come here? 'The Revolución' and *'Santaria'* take care of us. You will see 'Santaria', soon."

The car drove into an open area surrounded by multi-storied buildings. At the center, in a park, stood a statue of some man Larry figured was another "Hero of The Revolution". Trini motioned with his cigar. "This is the *'Plaza de Armas'*, señor. This is where Havana was founded hundreds of years ago."

Larry gazed around at the elegant buildings that looked as if they had all been refurbished and painted only yesterday. "This area looks almost brand-new."

"'The Revolciónary Government is putting the plaza back like it was in the old days." He nodded at a señorita who was eyeing him from a crosswalk. "People like to come here for the— what do you 'Americanos' call it? The *'flea markets'?"*

* * *

443

One block behind them, the man in the white guyabera was speaking into his two-way radio microphone. A blue Lada pulled away from the curb and fell in a hundred meters behind the Chrysler. The red car dropped back several blocks behind the other two vehicles as the old American machine continued down a side street. The second driver spoke into his microphone. "They are heading for the waterfront."

* * *

The big hardtop came out from behind a row of well-kept apartments onto a thoroughfare fronting a body of water, its surface glistening in the golden, late-afternoon sunshine. Trini made a gesture with his cigar. "That is 'Havana Bay', señor . . . it is the biggest harbor in the Caribbean." A little farther along, they drove past vast, warehouse-like shells of buildings jutting out over the water, like spread fingers pointing at the other side of the bay. As they went by, Larry could just make out the faded logos of shipping companies. "Those are the old ship docks," the Cuban said, "many cruise ships used to come here . . . and the flying boats to Miami and Key West and San Juan." The older man shook his head. "Those were the days, señor. Those were the days—"

"What happened to the ships?"

An uncomfortable look crossed Trini's face. "After 'The Revolución', all except some East German ships and some others—mostly Russian—went away. Now, even they are all gone."

* * *

The blue Lada pulled out of line; the orginal red Lada, the same one that had started the surveillance back at the hotel, swung-in behind the Chrysler. The driver stared ahead through his thick, black-framed dark glasses as the big- finned old American hardtop made a turn away from the port district. It looked to be going in the direction of 'Plaza Vieja'.

444

* * *

Trini was looking at the rear-view mirror. "Señor," he
frowned, taking a quick look again at the view to the rear, "I am
almost sure I have seen before the car that is behind us "

* * *

*At that moment, the red car turned into a side street. At the
same time, a faded green Ukrainian "Zaporozhets" sedan pulled
away from the curb and swung behind the Chrysler. The driver
tugged on his waxed handlebar mustache and stared ahead
through black-framed sunglasses as the old 'Yanqui' car made its
way into a district of concrete apartment buildings.*

* * *

Trini looked at the mirror and narrowed his eyes. "I wonder
if we are being followed." Larry turned about, but the only
vehicle in sight behind them was an odd-looking little green car
some distance back that he took to be one of the Eastern
European jobs he was becoming used to seeing. And even as he
watched, it turned away onto a side street. Except for one of the
"Camels" that roared up alongside them just then, the only
vehicle in sight was a smoking blue car about a block behind
them. He looked at Trini and shrugged.

* * *

*In the blue car the driver ran his hand through his shiny
black hair and peered ahead. It was the Chrysler, all right, and,
for sure, it was headed for 'Plaza Vieja'. Following the
instructions on the two-way radio, he would trail it there. He
spoke into the microphone.*

* * *

445

Trini turned the big car down a ramp into a dank underground parking garage. Larry gaped askance; some of the concrete pilings holding up the cracked cement roof forming the plaza above were buckling; several looked as if they were about to give way. Some sort of fuzzy green growth climbed up the bricked and cemented walls. A movement caught his eye—a pair of gray rats the size of house cats loped across the uneven pavement and after a quick glance at the newcomers with their shining eyes, the creatures nosed down into a nearby drain, their long tails disappearing.

Larry blanched. "We are parking *here?*"

Trini opened his door. "Everything is arranged, señor . . . we are going to a nearby place."

Even before they trudged up to ground level, an eclectic mixture of Latin music and other sounds funneled down the cluttered concrete stairwell. At the top of the steps, the orange light of dusk greeted them as they emerged into an unkempt open space surrounded on all sides by the faded old buildings and sagging mansions of another time. On a nearby sidewalk a scruffy-looking sextet blared away in a frenzied Cuban rhythm. The sounds of television shows burst out the open windows of tenements, adding their buzz and chatter to the din.

A couple of giggling, pony-tailed girls sitting on the bottom step of an apartment entrance playing a game of "jacks" paid no attention to the men as they strode past. An ancient Plymouth four-door sputtered by; its gesturing male occupants shouting obscene cat-calls at a youthful hombre and his *'señorita amor'* who were locked in a passionate embrace in a doorway.

As the American followed his companion across the square, he was struck by the electric vitality of the closely-knit neighborhood, whose teeming inhabitants appeared to embrace their disintegrating surroundings with surprising verve.

"This is 'Plaza Vieja', señor!"

"Where are we going?" Larry gasped, as they headed in a hurry down a narrow cobblestone byway lined with two and three-story apartment buildings.

"You will see, señor . . . just a little farther." As the men jogged along, a light breeze came up, flapping a row of underwear on a clothes-line that drooped overhead between two buildings. All along the way the sounds of the television programs they had heard back at the plaza came from open windows. Out of breath, Trini slowed to a brisk walk. "Hear those televisions?" he huffed, "they are the *'novelas'* . . . very popular in Cuba . . . most of them come from Mexico and Colombia."

Larry could hear what sounded like intense dialogue in stacatto Spanish coming from inside almost every apartment. "What are they—'soap operas'?"

The Cuban, stepping along in a hurry in the gathering gloom, gave the American a questioning look. "I do not believe they are about 'soap', señor! 'The Revoluciónary Government says that by watching them we will see how decadent the Capitalists are." He glanced about as they strode along. "We also see that the Capitalists are using our advanced ideas."

"What 'advanced ideas'?" The two rounded a corner and made their way down a street even more narrow than the one they had just left. Larry noticed an aroma of incense coming from the some of the tenements.

"Well, señor," Trini puffed, "like in Miami Beach—in Florida—they now have buildings just like those we have had on the Malecón all along! I saw *that* on Sabina's television station." He glanced at Larry and went on. "'Americanos' are *so* far behind Cuba, señor . . . we can see it right there on the television!"

Larry doubted that any Miami or Key West television station would broadcast such propaganda. He knew about the "South Beach" restorations that were returning that neighborhood to its original "Art Deco" look; probably the Cubans had seen those things in the background of the soaps they watched and believed the "Capitalists" had copied the Malecón facades—which, as an engineering student, he had learned were built in the first place by *Americans* back in the nineteen-twenties and 'thirties. Once more, he was struck how indoctrinated were these people.

As the chatter of the "novelas" faded behind them, from somewhere up ahead came the hollow, syncopated beat of conga drums, along with deeper thumping sounds and chanting voices.

447

Trini motioned to Larry to move faster. "We must hurry, señor . . . it is starting!"

They stepped under a peeling stuccoed archway flanked by flickering torches into a stone-and-brick courtyard where cross-hatched trellises held up a canopy of honeysuckle-like vines against the purple sky. Wavering orange flames danced on iron pylons; palm fronds swished in the light evening breeze.

At a double-doorway, they held up and squinted into a darkened, smoky room where Larry could make out bobbing heads and the undulating forms of scores of people swaying to drumbeats. In a corner, two men were slapping drumheads. A young woman, clad head-to-toe in a white robe, stepped up; a small jar in her hand. "*Bueños noches, señors!*" she shouted over the noise, "you are here for the initiations, no?" The girl stuck her index finger into the glass and marked first Larry's, then Trini's forehead with oil. The girl gave a wide-eyed, lopsided grin; her head bobbing along with the drumbeats even as she spoke. Larry thought she looked giddy, almost in a trance. She motioned the two into the crowded, pulsating room.

The stuffy place reeked with a smoky incense that seemed to be trying to crawl down Larry's throat. His nose was tingling; right away, a metallic taste came to his mouth. He rubbed his eyes---already they were smarting. As he gaped around in the wavering light he could see that many of the people were wearing white robes like the girl at the door; what looked like sparkly beads hung around their necks.

Trini and Larry sidled into the shadowy, low-ceilinged place jammed with chanting islanders. Larry glanced at Trini; the swarthy Cuban's face had a euphoric expression."*What is this*?" the American called out.

"*'Santeria'*—the religion of Cuba!"

Larry stared at two black men in the corner whose hands were slapping drums in a blur. One was beating a pair of tall drums he remembered to be 'congas'; the other was palming a wooden box that gave off deep thumps that seemed to set the rhythm for the chants. Every few seconds the conga man leaned back his head and shouted something; the roomful of people loudly returned it back to him.

Trini gestured for Larry to follow him. The two elbowed their way around the outer wall to the left side of the room. From there, they had a clear view of an open area at the front. The American's eyes focused on a wooden cage on a card table where a nervous-looking rooster stared out.

A muscular, shaved-head, dark-skinned young man in a tight-fitting black T-shirt stepped up and took the hand of a young woman on the front row. The box-drummer took up a thumping cadence; the congas came in with a beat that settled into a singular syncopated sound. The dancing pair began gyrating around the floor to the beats.

At length, there came the shout of a man's voice, ending the dance. The lamps went out, except for a few around the open floor. The dancers were gone. The crowd fell into silence.

At that moment, Trini seemed to snap out of whatever otherworldly mind-state he had been in. "We will leave, now, señor." Larry, relieved at not having to watch any more of this, followed him through the throng toward the rear exit. As the two pushed past the pressed-together people, for a split-second, Larry thought he recognized a white-robed man as he passed him by. When he glanced again, the man's eyes were locked onto his! At once, the frowning bystander looked away and took a couple of steps backward into the shadows.

* * *

After the two had gone out into the courtyard, the waiter from the hotel's bar, the man in the white robe, stepped out through another door into an alleyway and pulled a tiny two-way radio from a pocket in his robe. Cupping his hands, he spoke into the microphone.

* * *

Outside, evening was coming on as Trini and Larry retraced their steps back up the street. For some distance as they went along, the American could hear the rumble of the assembled multitude behind them.

449

"We must hurry, Señor Larry," the older man huffed, walking faster, "it will soon be starting."

Where are we going?"

"You will see, señor . . . you will see."

In a few minutes, Trini was maneuvering the Chrysler out of Plaza Vieja. As they drove up a narrow side street Larry was full of questions about what they had just seen. "What was *that* all about, back there?"

"Ah, señor, the people in the white robes were being taken into 'Santeria'." Trini caught the American's puzzled look and went on. "Santeria goes back to the early slaves. When they got here, they wanted to keep their African religions, but the Spanish would not let them—they told the slaves to convert to 'Christianity'. So, the blacks came up with a clever way to fool their masters. They started worshiping statues of Christian saints during the day. The Spanish thought the slaves had become Christians, and laughed at them. They called them 'Santerias'. But at night, when they were out of sight of the Spanish, the slaves prayed to the same statues, giving them *African* names. The Spanish never knew what they were doing." Trini glanced at the American. "Many Cubans are still doing it."

As they steered through one tenement neighborhood after another, over the grumble of the automobile's big engine the American could hear the loud, emotional dialogue of another "novela", as the man had called it, rolling out of open windows. Every television seemed to be tuned to the same station. Larry remembered Trini had said the programs were from Colombia and Mexico.

* * *

When the Chrysler emerged from the underground parking garage, the driver of the blue Lada sat up straight and stubbed out his cigarette. The subjects were leaving. The man eased the little sedan out of the side street and fell in about a block behind the hardtop. For now, he would keep his headlights off, since he could see where he was going by the reflected lights of the apartments and the intermittent street-lamps. The high-finned tail-lights of the target vehicle were easy to follow, in any case. He reached for the microphone.

* * *

The Chrysler turned onto a dimly-lit, six-lane thoroughfare that Larry recognized as the Malecón. As they rode along, the humid Havana night air blew through the open windows as he watched the black ocean swells, their silver wavetops catching the low-hanging, almost-full moon, undulating in stately ranks toward the shore to fling themselves, roaring, onto the rocks; the shearing, sibilant surf sounding above the drone of the car's engine. Every now and then a tall breaker would climb up and over the top of the seawall; at those times he could taste the salty spray mist. Down on the glistening boulders, hardy "Neumáticos" were shoving their mesh-covered inner tubes out into the heaving surf for another night of pursuing Red Snappers.

It had been less than a day, he thought, since their crippled airplane had made its emergency landing here in Havana. Since then, he had found this Communist-led city at the United States's doorstep to be far different from what he had supposed it to be— so far, the only discordant notes had been the episode at the shirt-store and that guy at the ice-cream place. He would leave "Santeria" alone. With some changes, he figured Cuba could someday even be a robust tourist destination for Americans. Larry settled back in the pliant, nineteen-fifties' plastic-and-polyester front seat and stared out the window at the starry sky. It had become an altogether warm, pleasant Havana night. "Where did you say we are going?"

"To the world's greatest nightclub."

"In *Havana?*"

"The *'Tropicana'*. There is nothing else like it. You will see."

Trini turned down another broad avenue. In a few minutes, they pulled into a crowded parking lot in front of a brightly-lit place that rose above the palm trees. Even as he alighted from the Chrysler, the tempo of fast Latin music came to Larry's ears. Trini gestured at the place. "The 'Tropicana', señor".

While Trini stepped over to the ticket office, the American took in the scene. The vast place was exploding in lights and sound; the very air vibrated to the pulsating, high-energy of frenetic music and the hubbub of hundreds of people, all punctuated by the non-stop clinking of slot machines and other organized noise. Off to one side, in a chandeliered room, well-heeled-looking people sat around gaming tables, drinks at hand. Larry saw that the gatherings consisted mostly of well-dressed, middle-aged, cigar-smoking Caucasian men and much younger, very attractive, darker-skinned women who seemed to be hanging on their every word, gesture and movement. Wealthy foreigners and their "jineteras", he decided.

While Larry stood in the bluish neon lights, out in the club, a live band kept up a hot tempo of Latin music; from where he stood he could see the rear tables of what looked to be the darkened main show-floor. Judging by the shouts and clapping, it sounded like a big crowd was out there.

Just then, Trini came back, grinning, holding up two tickets. "Would you believe the hotel had already made reservations for us—they were even paid-for!"

An older man in a tuxedo stepped up. "*Bienvenidos á 'Tropicana* señors," he purred in Spanish that Larry understood, "the show is starting." The man nodded at a younger fellow, also dressed in formal wear, and handed him a card. "A reserved *'large'* table for these guests."

* * *

Out on the parking lot, a blue Lada, its lights off, pulled into an empty space between a red Lada and a green Zaporozhets. A man wearing a white guayabera, his black hair slicked grease-like, emerged from the red car and sidled over to the driver's door of the new arrival. Another individual with a bushy mustache stepped from the shadows, then a middle-aged woman in a business outfit appeared. The shiny-haired man in the guayabera nodded toward the direction of the well-lit front of the structure from where the loud Latin music was coming. "They

452

*are in there." The four made their way between the rows of
parked vehicles toward the source of the lights and the sounds.*

* * *

Larry's first impression, while his eyes adjusted to the dim
light, was the hollow rumble of voices as if in a huge open space,
along with a peculiar sensation of vibrating heat.

* * *

*The man in the white guayabera pointed at Larry as the
American and the other man vanished into the darkened
nightclub. The fellow gestured, expressionless, with his eyebrows
and his forehead for the head-waiter to lead the four Cubans
after their quarry. The maitre d', without a word, motioned for
the others to follow him. He always had a spare table at the
ready for important guests.*

* * *

No sooner were Larry and Trini seated at a side table close
the front, than a spotlight seared the darkness, outlining a
smiling, middle-aged man in a tuxedo standing on a thrust stage,
holding a microphone in his hand. After a burst of applause, the
man, showing lots of white teeth, spread his arms. *"Showtime!"*
his voice boomed out over the sound system in resonant Spanish
to expectant handclaps and cheers. "Señores and señoritas . . .
'Tropicana'—the geatest and most famous nightclub in the
world—welcomes you to *'Paradise Under the Stars'!"*
At once, an explosion of light and sound tore through the
place: the Cuban dance band crashed into a salsa beat; at the
same time dozens of spotlights opened up, bringing an astonished
gasp from the many hundreds of people in the place, then loud
applause. Larry looked around—and his eyes went wide. Down
every aisle between the tables, scores of smiling showgirls—
everyone with knockout good looks and a shapely figure that
filled-out their lavish costumes—were strutting toward the front.

453

But what riveted his and everyone else's attention was the lighted, full-sized, crystal chandelier perched atop every girl's head! As they jiggled toward the stage, prancing and kicking to the music, an equal number of young men in pastel, skin-tight bodysuits danced from the wings onto the stage platform. To a faster tempo, the troupe broke into a frenzied dancing and singing routine across the whole stage; all the while the sequined, sashaying showgirls managed to keep the glowing, top-heavy-looking light-fixture headpieces in perfect balance on their heads.

Trini poked Larry. "Look at those 'chiquitas'!"

The audience roared as more colored lights came on above them. When the American, already reeling at the overwhelming spectacle, looked up, his jaw dropped. In the palm trees overhead, outlined by the colored lights, more copper-colored girls were swinging over the awe-struck crowd on trapeezes and ropes to conga rhythms and pulsating salsa music at a volume that drove into Larry's chest. As he watched the girls swaying above, he saw for the first time that the nightclub's glitzy showroom was outdoors.

Then the performers dashed off the stage as the lights swung about and focused on a new troupe running out from the wings. As much as the first girls had worn elaborate petticoats and bustles, some with huge chokers and necklaces, elbow-length gloves and spike heels, feathers, and the stupendous chandelier headdresses; the leggy new bunch wore sequined thongs and barely-there micro-tops that hardly covered the essentials of their shiny tan bodies as they whirled and kicked across the stage to throbbing Latin beats in an orgy of hormone-charged frenzy.

On and on the high-energy routines went, as girls came out wearing ever more heart-hitching costumes that devolved down to string bikinis that showed nearly everything while they strutted across the stage and swung in the trees to the constantly-changing colored lights and the non-stop salsa and conga beats that kept getting faster and louder and faster and louder while the audience's roars of approval and the sibilant sound of handclaps rose out of the vast arena, past the leafy, towering palms, into the clear, starry-black night of tropical Havana.

After more than two hours of dazzling non-stop routines featuring the incredibly beautiful girls who literally oozed sex from their tight, glistening brown bodies, and the pulsating, non-stop music, Larry was in a realm far beyond sensory overload. Trini was right: he had never seen anything else like it.

The middle-aged Cuban slapped Larry on his back. "How about those chiquitas!"

As the crowd began to file out, Larry scooted back his seat and started to stand. Trini touched his shoulder. Not now," he said, looking about, "the others will be here."

"The others?" The American settled back into his seat.

A waiter came up with a bottle of rum in an ice bucket and several glasses that he started setting around the tabletop in front of several empty seats. With the lights up, for the first time Larry saw he and Trini had been sitting at one of the larger tables. The tuxedoed man looked around. "Señor, your guests are here."

"Trini! *'Hermano'!"* came a tittering female voice. Larry turned about in his seat and looked straight into the buffed midsection of a girl who had stepped up close behind him. Blinking, he looked up and recognized a brunette dancer he had noticed in particular as one of the most eye-catching performers in the entire show. "Trini, 'eet ees *so* goode to see you, ahgeen!" the glamour-girl squealed. The curvaceous creature stepped around and presented a cheek for the air-kiss that Larry had seen done several times since he had been in Havana. As she bent over, Trini patted her rounded bottom, prompting the girl to wiggle the tuft of feathers attached to her outfit. The giggling girl took a seat next to him. "We deed goode, tonight, no?" the dancer chirped in staccato Spanish, shaking her glistening, jiggling, chest and shoulders—much skin, Larry observed—and her outfit that plunged down to where he knew it would not be legal outdoors in the 'States.

The older man's eyes took in her luscious shape. *"'Mi amor '...* you have never looked or danced better."

"Oh, Trini, you always say such goode theeings to me!" The young woman shook her shoulders and took quick, deep breaths that the two men could not help but notice.

Larry realized the showgirl was looking at him. "The 'hombre' is your *'compadre'*, no?"

"Erica', this is—'Señor Larry' . . . he is—visiting Havana."

The female looked the younger man up and down and at his light-colored hair. "You are German?"

"Ah, you must join us for a drink!" Trini changed the subject.

There was a shufflling of shoes. Larry turned about to see two other men who were now standing behind him.

* * *

When the two newcomers stepped to the table down front, a man with the plastic-framed sunglasses, the oily-headed man in the guayabera, the mustached individual, and the woman in the business suit, all of whom had been sitting at a rear table observing the two men during the performance, faded out of sight into the lobby. "It is not necessary to remain here," the woman told the others in a brittle, edgy voice, "Comrade Erica will take care of things and report soon. I found out from the box office that their tickets came from the 'Hotel Nacional' . . . they will go there, later . . . we will leave now and dispose of the suspect at the proper time."

* * *

Trini embraced one of the men, then turned to the American. "This is Mojo, my cousin!" The other man grabbed Larry in a smothering hug. "'Señor Larry' is the hombre I told you about." Trini flicked his cigar. Larry dis-engaged himself and took a couple of gasping breaths; the second man stepped up and pumped his hand.

"José Alcantra—Mojo's neighbor . . . he wanted me to meet you."

"How about me?" the girl spoke up.

"The *'chica'*, here is Erica."

"*'Chica!'* I eem *not* a—"

456

Trini chuckled. "Of course, not, *'mi amor'* . . . all Cuba knows you never charge for your favors!"

The showgirl tugged Larry's wrist and went on in her sing-song accent. "Señor Larry, do not beleeve theem . . . Trini—tell heem I am good girl!"

"*Senorita, 'mucho Havana hermanos'* know just how *'good'* you really are!"

Trini—I hate you!" The brunette fumed for a second, then caught the older man's smirk. "Ah, Trini, you always putting me on!"

". . . and taking you off!"

The girl gasped, pretending to be annoyed. Larry grinned at the seduction game that never seemed to stop in Cuba. The older man lifted the rum bottle from the bucket with a flourish. "A drink to the 'goodness' of our favorite 'chica'!"

The young woman took a glass of rum, set it down and rubbed around the rim with her finger. She shifted her gaze to Larry. "You are weeth beesineess, no?"

"I, ah, flew to Havana the other night." His Spanish was rusty, but the girl seemed not to notice.

"You are here een Havana, long?"

Larry took a long swallow of the sweet rum. "I plan to leave, soon."

"Soon?" Like tomorrow?"

"Maybe—maybe not . . . I cannot really say when I might be leaving." The American glanced at José. Mojo's friend was staring at the girl.

"You have known Trini seence you came here?"

"Since this morning."

José's eyes were darting back and forth from Trini, to the girl, to Larry, and back, again. The friend noticed she had not yet taken a swallow of her drink.

"You like Havana, no?"

"It's a lot different than what I had thought it would be."

"They did not tell you about Cuba where you came from?" She drew a deep breath, attracting attention to her spectacular bosom, then took to rolling the glass between her hands; her flashing brown eyes never leaving Larry's. "*Mi* handsome hombre, where deed you say you are from?"

"He is from another country!" Trini's face wore a stony expression, but his eyes were also now shifting back and forth between the girl and Larry.

Erica finally took a sip of her drink. She batted her eyes at the American. "Did you see the government *'beeldeengs'*, today? Did you like theem?" What part of Havana did you like best?"

Larry was watching José, who had leaned forward, his arms crossed on the table. Frowning, the man caught the American's eye. He was slowly shaking his head.

"I . . . ah, saw some buildings, yes; they were—interesting. And you have good ice-cream."

"*Oy*, you weent to 'Coppelia'! The girl shook her cantilevered chest. "You see lots of *'parteecular'* peeple there, no?"

Larry took a quick look at José, still leaning on the table with his arms crossed—and did what he hoped was an un-noticed double-take. The man was slowly patting his left shoulder with his opposite fingertips, at the same time gravely moving his head from side-to-side. Larry's eyes narrowed; Trini had told him earlier it was a signal that an informer was nearby! He glanced at Mojo, who seemed to have picked up José's furtive signal and was discreetly motioning his head toward the exit.

"You hombrees are not leestening to me!" Larry turned back to the girl, who was wiping her eyes in pretended dismay. "Trini! Thees foreign *'mon'* have no time for Erica!" she broke into accented English for the first time. "Do I make heem tired of me?"

Larry tried to construct a believable smile on his face. "Actually, I *am* tired, you see . . . we have had a busy day." Without thinking, Larry had spoken out in English

"'Americano'!" The girl pointed; her eyes big.

Trini spoke up in a hurry. "Ah, he has important business in Cuba."

Just then, the house lights went out, leaving only a few fitful lamps in the cavernous showplace.

458

Erica gave a start. "I have not beene heere for thees lights out, before!"

José blinked at the others. "We should all be going, now." He shoved back his chair.

The girl grabbed Larry's forearm. "I weel see you ahgeen, soon?"

Trini put his hand on her taut shoulders. "My pretty one, the 'Americano' is . . . 'taken'."

Larry thought for an instant she looked a little crestfallen. "I weel go, now. I am *mucho* tired." With a kiss on the cheek from Trini and proffering her's to the others, the dark-haired dancer turned away.

The four men watched as the costumed "Cubana" vanished through a stage entrance down front.

"Interesting . . . 'señorita'." Larry said, as they made their way back up through the now-darkened lobby toward the parking lot..

"I have known that little 'chica' ever since she started here, years ago."

"She's really not that little!"

"Ah, you noticed, no?" Trini's grin cut through the darkness.

"You know how they get those dancers?" This was from Mojo."They go all over Cuba, searching for *'mulattas'* with talent and looks. Every Cuban girl wants to dance at 'Tropicana'. These are the most beautiful girls in Cuba, no? Their beauty is a national treasure. They exercise and practice for hours every day to do this show."

José spoke up. "And this place has been here since nineteen-thirty-nine! Did you know that?"

"I really didn't—"

"It is true, señor! In the old days, even the 'Mafia' left it alone. And when Comrade Fidel took over from Batista, he kept this place going, it was so famous! 'Tropicana' is the biggest and most beautiful nightclub in the whole world, you agree?" He made a sweep with his arm around the place. "I heard that it is thirty-six-thousand square meters. There is nothing else like it!"

As they paced across the nearly-empty parking lot, Trini pointed to the tops of trees, outlined in the moonlight, that surrounded the club. "All around this place are tropical gardens." He made the outline of a girl's figure with his hands. "You and your favorite señorita could go into those woods there at night—even when the club is full of people—and nobody else would ever know about it!"

Larry chuckled to himself at the ways of this island. And all this was happening just a few dozen miles from Florida.

* * *

Alone in the girls' dressing room, Erica lifted the telephone receiver and dialed a number. She spoke some words into it, then hung up. The others would now do their part.

-31-

"How well do you know this girl . . . this Erica'?" José was speaking to Trini. "I think she was asking a lot of questions—not like a showgirl would usually talk. I do not trust her."

Larry had noticed the same thing, but said nothing.

Trini frowned, then chuckled. "Oh, I am sure she did not mean anything—she just likes to know what I am doing. I think she is jealous."

José was not going to be put off. "She sounded like an informer, to me. I thought we should leave right away."

The men were stepping up to a convertible with its top down that was parked out near the edge of the almost-empty lot. When they came closer, Larry recognized the red Plymouth he and Trini had seen earlier that day as they drove through one of Havana's neighborhoods. "*Mi 'carro',*" Mojo said, "is nineteen-fifty Plymouth." He glanced at Larry. "It is *'muy bueno',* no?"

The American ran his hand across the hood. Its shiny medallion caught the glimmering light. "It is well preserved, all right."

"Cubans must keep cars running good a long time. It is the 'embargo', señor . . . your damn 'Americano' embargo—" A pause hung in the air.

Trini glanced at Larry. "We must be going, now."

In a few minutes, the big Chrysler was rumbling along at a fast clip. "We will go to the hotel, now, señor!" The older man pointed at the dashboard clock. Larry was surprised to see that it was well-past midnight.

After a looping drive around the Malecón, the car turned into a tree-lined, divided driveway. The American's eyes went wide as they pulled up in front of an enormous lighted structure surrounded by illuminated palm trees. The American looked around at the place that to him looked like some sort of fantastic, outsized sandcastle. "Señor, the *'Hotel Nacional de Cuba'* is the most famous hotel in the Carribbean!"

461

Larry looked about at the splendid surroundings. "I am staying *here*?"

"Si, señor . . . everything is arranged."

A uniformed man slid behind the wheel. Then the car disappeared down the bending driveway and out of sight.

As the two headed toward the arched, Moorish-like entrance, Larry could hear the muted crashing of surf; they were near the ocean, he guessed.

Inside, the lobby was mostly empty, except for voices coming from a bar off to the side. Trini gestured toward an archway. "One more drink to finish the day, señor?"

As the two came up to the entranceway of the lounge, Larry's attention was caught by some old-looking pictures hanging on the wall. The Cuban looked at the gallery of photographs and grinned. "Ah, Señor Larry, these are some of the famous people who have been in this bar and at this hotel."

"*Winston Churchill* was here?" Larry recognized the cherubic face and the trademark cigar of the wartime British Prime Minister."All these people stayed here?"

"They were here—and more. Singers, politicians; almost everybody who was anybody in the 'forties and 'fifties came here at one time or another." A dreamy look came over the man's face. "This was the biggest and best hotel in the Caribbean in those days. It still is."

The American frowned at several other pictures of mostly dark-haired, business-looking men he did not recognize. "Who are they?"

"Let us get a drink and I will tell you about *those* people." The two took seats at a table. "Two 'daiquiris'." The white-coated waiter took the order and went off. The Cuban gave a sweeping gesture. "This is one of the most famous hotels in the world."

"It is very nice. But I have never heard of it."

An aggrieved look crossed Trini's face. "Of *course*, you have not heard of it! You 'Americanos' sit up there looking down on Cuba, but you cannot stop 'The Revolución'. The *'Hotel Nacional de Cuba'* is one of the best anywhere. People come here from all over the world, señor!"

462

The waiter came back with the daquiris. Trini lifted his glass. "To peace." Larry thought he detected a tone of irony in the man's voice. The Cuban took another swallow and looked at his glass with a smirk "Did you know that daiquiris were invented in this very room?"

"I had no idea."

A fleeting frown crossed Trini's face. "You 'Americanos' have *many* ideas, all right—many *wrong* ideas about Cuba, señor!" Several customers at other tables glanced over at the man, whose features had taken on a crimson cast. A man got up and with a side-glance, left the room.

"What about those men you were going to tell me about?"

The Cuban brightened. "We all love Fidel, of course . . . but the times *before* 'The Revolución' were very good for my family and me." Larry's eyebrows were raised as the older man went on. "The men in the pictures were *'Mafioso'*. You see, when Batista came into power after the war, the casinos were very big—big and *empty*."

"Why was that?"

"Everybody knew they were crooked."

Larry snorted. "What's so unusual about crooked casinos? Aren't they all?"

Trini grinned as he hailed the waiter for more daiquiris. "During the war, some of the 'Mafiosos' came down here from the 'States to set up businesses that did very well. Much of the sugar and rum that Cuba made went to markets up there. In those days, 'Americanos' had all these ration stamps for everything, but there were always shortages. The *'Mob'*, as they use to call it, printed counterfeit stamps for sugar and other things and they made a lot of money for themselves and for Cuba smuggling black-market goods to America."

"That sounds pretty bad."

"Not so fast, señor! Most of the mobsters were Italian, you see, and America was at war with Italy. But the Mafia wanted to show they were loyal Americans, if you can believe that."

"What did they do?"

"You see, one of the big chiefs—an Italian hombre named *'Lucky Luciano'*, was in prison. The Mob ran the New York docks through payoffs and in a lot of other ways." A wry grin came to Trini's face. "Now comes the part that is hard to believe, but it is true! The United States Navy wanted to be sure there was no sabotage at the port. And what better way to make sure the port was safe than to use the dock workers whose unions were controlled by the Italian Mafia! So the mobsters gave the orders *and during the war, the American Navy paid the Mafia to patrol the New York docks!* And there was no sabotage! The Italian gangsters looked patriotic and the NewYork docks were safe—I swear it is true! Luciano even got a better prison cell for arranging it, and after the war he was let out many years early and sent back to Italy. Later, he came here to Havana."

Larry shook his head in amazement. "How does that figure with the casinos?"

"I am coming to that. Like I said, after the war the casinos had a bad reputation. Now, Batista remembered a Mob man named *'Meyer Lansky',* who had worked with Cuban businesses during the war. He called him back down and gave him a lot of power to clean up the casinos, which he did. Before long, Havana had the biggest, most-honest gambling operation in this whole part of the world! The casino that was right here in this hotel— the 'Hotel Nacional de Cuba'—was the biggest casino in the Caribbean."

"How ironic that the Mafia had a reputation for being honest!"

"It was Mister Lansky who did it. He knew it was better to have honest casinos doing a lot of business, than a few crooked ones losing money. *Mi papá* said he was a great businessman. Now comes our family's part in all this: Papá was a bartender at this hotel, and he knew all the Mafia people and the entertainers who came in-and-out. One time the 'Mafiosos' had a big meeting, right here at this hotel. Big men came from all over 'Norte America'. I was just a little boy, then, but I still remember them. They were important, but they treated me and my father and my mother and my little sister good. Papá drove those men around Havana while they were here, and I got to ride with some of them. I remember they gave me candy and gifts. Lucky Luciano was here from Italy, and he came into the hotel and I saw him. Mister Lansky became very rich and powerful running the casinos here in Havana, and all that time, he was very good to us."

"What happened to him?"

"With 'The Revolución', Fidel closed the casinos and Mister Lansky went away. We never again saw him. And some of our family went to Florida to get away from Castro. Things became very 'different', after that."

Just then, the lights blinked. The waiter stepped up."We are closing, now, señors."

Trini dug some pesos out of his pocket and pushed back his seat. "Let us go get your key. It is at the front desk."

When Larry gave his name at the counter, without hesitation the clerk handed over a key to him. The American stared at it in his hand, surprised, then at the Cuban.

"Everything is arranged," the desk man said, "your luggage is already in the room."

Trini motioned toward a nearby bank of elevators.

In the suite, as advertised, the travel bag was already on the bed. Larry watched as Trini walked around the elegant space, poking here and there, looking behind the curtains, in bureau drawers and in the closet; under the bed.

"What are you doing?"

"Checking the room. You never know when it might have eyes and ears." He put out his hand. "It has been an interesting day, señor, and I will see you in the morning."

After Trini took his leave, Larry looked around at his sumptious surroundings—a vast improvement over the first hotel with its bugs and lizards. Someone—he did not know who—had "arranged" all this.

* * *

As soon as the elevator door closed behind Trini, the door to the room next to Larry's cracked open. After a second or two the door opened fully and a heavyset, dark-haired figure with a huge mustache emerged. After looking up and down the corridor, he sidled over to the American's door. Putting his ear to it, the fellow could hear water running in the bathroom. Satisfied that the foreigner was preparing for bed, without making a sound, he tiptoed back into his room and closed the door. The man lifted the telephone receiver and dialed a number.

* * *

The telephone on the nightstand was ringing. After a second, Larry recognized Major Barrientos's voice. "*Bueños dias,* Señor Larry. You had good sleep, no?"

The American was learning how to play along with these talkative Cubans and the way they stretched their greetings before they got down to business. "Yes, I did."

"Meet us at the cafeteria in twenty minutes."

* * *

"Over here, Señor Larry!" A voice called to him in the buffet restaurant. Looking about, the American spotted Major Barrientos waving at him from a table at the back. After a trip down the self-serve line, he took a seat. To his surprise, the three pilots were also sitting there.

"It is good to see you—again," the 747 captain said in his broken English, as the two other Ukrainians also put out hands, nodding in turn as they shook Larry's.

Larry dug into the tropical breakfast in front of him. "Where's Trini?" he asked between bites, "he said he would be here this morning."

"Trini should be here in a little while." The major took a hefty swallow of his Cuban coffee and smirked at the grimacing Europeans, who were making feeble attempts to sip the thick brew from tiny cups. "They are still trying to get used to this coffee of ours!"

"Repairs to the airplane are about—finished," the pilot said in his hesitant accent, "we will be—leaving Cuba, soon."

The American picked at his food and looked around. "This is a really nice hotel," he said, almost blurting out that he would never have thought such a splendid place would exist in Cuba, but catching himself in time.

"The government is just restoring the hotel, señor. You are about the first to stay here, now." Barrientos gave a smile." This is the 'Palace of the Caribbean', as they say. It has quite a history. We can walk around and see it, if you like."

Before going outside, the men stopped at the business counter in the lobby to pay their room charges. The pilots had expense accounts, Larry noted, pulling out his own credit card. When his turn came, he made his request in Spanish. The clerk scrolled down the computer screen for his room record, then shook his head. "It is already taken care of, 'Señor Americano'."

Larry was surprised. "Someone has already paid for my stay, here?" *Since he had only spoken to the clerk in the local Spanish language, how did the hotel employee know he was an American?*

The man shrugged. "Do not concern yourself, señor . . . everything is arranged."

It occurred to Larry that he had heard that phrase repeated any number of times since he had left California.

Larry and the others stepped out to an enclosed courtyard of palms and flowering tropical plants; a perfume-like aroma suffused the morning air. From beyond, came the rumble of vehicles along the Malecón and the distant booming of the surf.

A man in a tuxedo stepped up. "Major Barrientos?" The uniformed Army officer nodded. "There is *'teléfono'* call for you—this way, por favor."

While the officer was gone, the Ukrainians said they had been following the repairs to the cargo jetliner. "We may be—leaving tonight," the captain said.

There were loud footfalls. Teófilo Barrientos came running up, out of breath.

"Señors!" he gasped, "We must leave, *pronto!*"

"What's going on?"

"Trini has been arrested!" He pointed at Larry. "The P-N-R is looking for you, too! All of you get your luggage! Meet me at the front entrance! I will have the limousine!" He turned and dashed off.

When Larry opened his room's door, he stopped short. *The suite of rooms had been completely ransacked; all his things were strewn about; every bureau drawer was pulled out and emptied; even the mattresses and box springs were sprawled over in disarray!*

Scrambling around, his heart pounding, Larry located the luggage bag under the pile, stuffed his things back into it, and dashed for the elevator.

At the front entrance, the black ZIL, with the pilots already inside, was waiting for him. The major tossed Larry's bag into the trunk in a hurry, then shoved a Soviet military officer's hat the American. "Put on this!" Larry dropped into a jump seat and slammed the door.

The outsized Russian car, with the two red general's flags flapping on the front fenders, accelerated down the short driveway. At the intersection, in the opposite lane, a red sedan, followed by a blue four-door vehicle, a little green car, and four police cruisers were pulling into the hotel drive. Barrientos glanced back at Larry. "Get down! You pilots, sit up! Look like military men!"

As Larry ducked behind the division panel, the driver moved a switch on the dashboard; dark glass panels slid up behind the regular bullet-proof panes, turning the sunshiny outside into a murky twilight inside the car. As all the vehicles passed each other, the hunkered-down American's eyes focused for the second time on the little brass plate from the factory on the back of the division glass frame. The name on the plaque, "Pavel Drubkin", Larry remembered from the other night as someone or other in Moscow who had installed the car's interior. If the clever shielding-glass that was keeping him from his pursuers was also the fellow's handiwork, he would like to someday shake his hand.

On the Malecón, Barrientos stepped on the gas. "You can sit up, now!" he called back to Larry. The outsized car raced out the broad thoroughfare, looking for all its official flags at the front and the vague outline of the driver and four passengers inside wearing military hats, like a general's staff car transporting high-ranking Soviet officers to somewhere important.

A half-hour later, the black limousine shot through the military entrance at the International Airport and swept up to the familiar hangar. Jumping out, Barrientos jerked the luggage out of the trunk. "I am going to the Interior Ministry! I am sure there has been mistake about Trini's arrest!" He hopped back into the big car and drove off.

Inside the hangar, the 747 sat on padded hydraulic jacks; its tail fin, too tall to fit inside the hangar, soared outside the big sliding doors into the sunshine. Larry's eyes followed the sound of a gasoline engine to a tractor-like "auxiliary power unit" that was parked underneath the airplane's nose; a thick, black cable connected it to the bottom of the fuselage. Focusing on the wheels that had been shot up, he noticed the repaired rims were now a shiny green-yellow in color—probably some kind of metal primer, he thought—and the tires looked new.

As they stood around, all at once there came loud whining noises. The American gave a start as the landing gear gave a jerk and started moving, then all the wheels and pylons retracted in stately fashion into their wells and the doors closed with thumping noises; then they re-opened and the gear came back down into landing position.

Larry gazed up at where the damaged cargo door had been. To his surprise, it was back in place, looking normal. The American shook his head in admiration; these Soviet airframe repairmen had performed a miracle in just two days.

A pale, round-faced specialist came up, wiping his hands on a towel. He spoke in rapid Russian to the pilots, who were nodding.

The pilot turned to Larry. "He says the airplane is—functioning perfectly and we can—take off as soon as we—wish. We will wait until—tonight to—"

A slamming car door interrupted the man. Turning about, they saw the female P-N-R "Officer Montoya" from the other night coming toward them with quick steps. In her hands she held the mens' passports.

Larry's eyes opened wide. "Am I glad to see these! I was beginning to—"

"Come with me!" The uniformed policewoman pointed toward a door. Larry and the three pilots glanced at each other and followed her out of the hangar down a hallway into a space that Larry remembered as the same classroom where they had been two nights before. The Angolans were already there, slumped casually in their seats. With a nodding glance at Fidel on the wall, the American dropped into a desk chair.

"I hope you enjoyed your—stay in Cuba," the P-N-R officer said in measured English, as she shuffled the little books, "even if we had some—*difficulties*." Before Larry had time to ponder what she meant, the young woman went on. "You will transport some shipments for us to your destination."

Then she went around giving back the passports to their owners, keeping Larry's until the last. The female officer handed to the American his precious dark-blue book while holding a long look straight into his eyes. For the first time, he noted her hazel eyes complimented the shade of her short, slightly wavy hair and tight, copper-hued skin. He judged she was in her late-'twenties and actually right nice-looking. But her abrasive personality ruined everything, he thought.

"*Señores,* you will remain here at the military section of the airport until you leave. You will—take food and water with you on the airplane. It will be—a long trip."

Larry wondered just how much she already knew about all this. "We can eat, now?"

"Yes—but do not leave this part of the airport." She hitched her police-purse onto her shoulder and with a perceptible look back at him, strode from the room.

The men made their way back outside. One of the Africans pointed across the way. "There is the food place," the fellow rumbled in a deep, resonant voice. Shielding his eyes, Larry spotted the same eatery where they had gone the other night for the midnight meal.

As they stepped across the taxiway, Larry happened to look in the direction of the guard gate they had driven through a while ago—and looked again. Through the torrid heat waves rising from the pavement were several squads of armed guards spaced around the outer fences who had not been there, earlier. Had the soldiers taken up positions for their benefit? Were they getting special protection from something or someone? First, Trini's arrest; then his room charges paid by an unknown person or persons; the torn-up hotel suite; the sinister-looking caravan as they were leaving the hotel; now this. And hadn't the policewoman told them to stay in the *military* part of the airport?

* * *

An hour later, after another round of Army food and one more try at Cuban coffee, Larry joined the others as they trudged back across the blistering expanse of concrete toward the hangar. Each of the men carried a sack of food and bottles of water for the long flight. The pilot glanced up at the afternoon sun. "We will be—taking off in a few—hours."

When they walked around the edge of the hangar, the men saw a trailer truck loaded with pallets and several crates parked underneath the aircraft near the cargo door. As they came closer, Larry observed that the jacks that had been supporting the 747 were gone; the big airplane now rested on its own wheels and tires. At the front of the aircraft a pushing tractor was hitched to the forward landing gear strut. It looked as if their departure was not far off.

One of the technicians with a clipboard in his hand pulled aside the captain and the two began a low conversation in Russian; their heads close together. As they talked, Larry overheard the word "Organization" pass between them.

A man in a Cuban Army uniform pointed at the Angolans, who were standing around. "Load those pallets onto the airplane!" he said in an accent, gesturing at the tractor-trailer. The American figured the trucks' loads were the "shipments" he had heard mentioned several times.

Larry walked around the hulking 747. Although he was not an expert on airplanes, the big cargo jetliner now looked to be in perfect shape. No wonder the Soviets had been such capable "Cold War" adversaries, he thought, if this superb-looking repair job was any example of their technical expertise. He had to remind himself that they were only ninety miles from Florida.

As he came around the airplane, a forklift with a pallet on it was about to rise to the cargo doors. On impulse, Larry hopped onto it just as it started upward. At the top, he leaped over the

471

open space and made his way up the working aisle to his goods. He found that the cargo handlers had re-tied everything back down to the deck. A quick inspection told him the sliced-open and re-taped labels that had been such a mystery on the ship were just as they were. The crowded cargo deck was now crammed with big pallets and shipping crates almost all the way to the rear bulkhead

Just as he stepped off onto the concrete, a small truck with a police insignia on its doors roared into the hangar and pulled up behind the first truck. On it was a wooden crate about two-meters square. The driver, outfitted in a police uniform, dropped from the cab and motioned to one of the black men. "This is part of the shipment! Load it onto the airplane!" The brusque newcomer looked around. "Get me the captain of this aircraft!"

Larry pointed to a door over at the side of the hangar. "He's in there."

Curious, the American followed the man into the office, where he was speaking to the pilot. After the fellow turned about and left, the captain stared at a copy of a document. Written in Spanish, it listed an "additional" item of cargo for the flight, and gave its weight. The pilot picked up another printout and scanned down the page. "The aircraft is now—ready. We will leave— after dark." Larry dropped into a tubular chair to pass the time. A frantic "novela" blared from the television.

Later, when he went back outside, the pusher-tractor was shoving the enormous airplane out of the hangar. Except for the left-rear cargo-deck doors that were still open, to Larry, the aircraft looked to be buttoned-up for the flight. As he stood there in the late-afternoon sunlight watching it roll to a stop, from around the building came the whine of several vehicles. After a few seconds, the sounds resolved into a pair of big fuel trucks, followed by motorized steps. Both of the tankers stopped behind a wing; the rolling staircase drove around and pulled up at the open cargo door. From the amount of fuel the airplane was taking on, it looked to Larry that the next leg of their journey was going to be a long one.

The Angolans drifted out of the offices and stood about, laughing and telling ribald jokes back-and-forth among themselves. Larry guessed they were glad to be getting away from this island. He could relate to that.

By the time the fueling was completed, early evening had come to Havana; the big Boeing shone in a glare of floodlights. The pilots stepped out carrying their bags, which reminded Larry that his was still inside the office.

When he started back out with his luggage, the Russian chief mechanic in charge of the 747's restoration looked up from behind the counter. The American stepped over and put out his hand to the fellow, who looked surprised. "Very fine repairs," Larry said in his rudimentary Russian, with a nod. The round-faced Soviet gripped the American's hand, nodding back.

Outside, a line of Africans was mounting the stairsteps. As Larry came forward, looking up at the flight deck he could make out the pilots' ghostly faces outlined in the dim reflected lights of the instruments. The co-pilot slid open a side window and looked down at him. "Hurry aboard, comrade—we are leaving, now!"

Just as the American reached the stairsteps below the left-rear cargo-deck doors, there came the sudden sound of a car horn, followed by the screech of tires. Larry gaped as a big black *ZIL* popped into view around the corner of the hangar, zoomed across the lighted pavement straight at him and skidded to a stop at almost where he was standing. The right-front door burst open and out stepped a grinning, familiar figure.

"Trini!" Larry dropped the handbag and embraced the slender Cuban. "What happened? I was afraid you were in jail, or something!" He pumped the man's hand and slapped his back.

"They said we were doing 'counter-Revolucórnary activity'!"

"What—!"

"Remember the hombre at the ice-cream place?"

Larry nodded.

"He heard us and called the 'P-N-R'. A woman followed us to the hotel restaurant."

"You *said* she looked suspicious!"

"And those two men at the next table—we thought they were not listening . . . well—they *were* overhearing what we said! It was they who heard us talking about at which hotel you were staying," "I saw them at the Interior Ministry."

The major came around the car. "P-N-R agents were following you everywhere you went! It was they who bought the tickets for the 'Tropicana' show . . . those agents arranged to have your luggage taken there and even paid for your room!"

"After I left you at the hotel last night, they arrested me at my car."

"That explains why you were not at breakfast, this morning."

Trini touched a bruise on his cheek. "I was there all night and all day."

Major Barrientos pointed a finger at the American. *"They were next coming after you!"*

"Me? Why?" Larry was glad he had ducked-down in the limousine to escape being seen.

"They thought you were a spy, or something! That was also why they tore up your hotel room— they were looking for evidence . . . they left you alone at the time because they thought you would lead them to more suspects!" The Army man pushed his officer's hat to the back of his head. "When I went to the Interior Ministry and explained the air shipments, the Security Chief ordered them to let Trini go and stop everything against you. They had not known who you were."

A rueful look came over the older Cuban's leathery face. "And I have some things to say to that little 'chica' showgirl, Erica. I found out she was an informer!" Trini was indignant

All at once, the red light on the bottom of the airplane began flashing beams of scarlet all around. "We are leaving!" a voice came from above. At the open upper cargo doors, one of the Africans was gesturing down to the American. At the same time, a ground-crewman dropped into the driver's seat of the motorized steps and started its chattering engine.

Larry shook the two Cubans' hands one more time, grabbed his travel bag and pulled himself up the aluminum stairsteps, two-at-a-time. As soon as he stepped inside the cabin, two black men closed the wide rear doors and dogged them down. Even as the American and the Angolans made their way up the cargo corridor toward the spiral staircase at the front, from the outside, they could hear the big jet engines coming to life.

On the upper passenger deck a festive atmosphere was breaking out; the Africans were shouting and laughing. One of the men poked Larry's arm, grinning. "We are going home!"

Larry heard someone calling his name; through the open door to the darkened cockpit, the flight engineer was gesturing at him. The nodding man motioned to the jump-seat behind the center console. The American dropped into the tubular canvas chair and strapped himself in. The captain, reading from a clipboard, was calling out short sentences in rapid Russian that the other two acknowledged; the pre-flight checklist, Larry figured. It all reminded him of a countdown to launch a space rocket. The pilot punched some figures into a console keypad. The co-pilot and the flight engineer nodded back at him.

"Everything is normal," the two said in Russian that Larry understood. Then the captain spotted Larry behind him. "Ah, 'Comrade Americanski'—" He switched to his halting English, "You will be with us for the—takeoff, I see."

The co-pilot pulled down the microphone. "Havana Ground Control—this is 'Patagonia Seven-Forty-Seven-heavy' request permission to taxi," he said in his Ukrainian-flavored English.

A crisp-sounding voice came back at once. "Patagonia Seven-Forty-Seven-heavy cleared to taxi."

The same vehicle with the "Follow Me" sign on it they had seen the other night swung into the shiny path of the landing lights. The captain nodded to the co-pilot, then advanced the four throttles on the center console with the palm of his right hand; from underneath the wings, the jet turbines responded with a muffled roar the crew could hear up on the flight deck.

The diminutive truck led the mammoth aircraft out into a twinkling world of little purple and orange lights strung along the edges of the taxiway. With its landing lights splaying on the pavement ahead of it, the gigantic airplane went on at a smooth, steady pace into the darkness; the impatient whine of the turbofans pushing it along. What a difference, Larry thought, compared to the crippled hobbling on the bare rims of the other night!

"Patagonia Seven-Forty-Seven-heavy request permission to take-off."

"Patagonia heavy cleared for take-off."

The captain glanced at the first officer. "Take control, twenty-degrees flaps." An answering moan of hydraulics and servo motors came from below the deck. "Speedbrakes down."

Larry watched, fascinated, as the hulking aircraft made a deliberate turn and a broad, lighted path opened up before them, marked at the edges by orange lights that converged far in the distance. The co-pilot stood on the brakes and with a distant-sounding squeal the airplane came to a stop, lined-up on the center stripe.

The co-pilot gripped the control yoke. "I have control!"

With a glance at the instrument panel, the captain fingered the four engine throttles. "Thrust!"

The flight engineer swiveled about in his seat, leaned forward and grasped with his right hand a set of rearward-facing handles on the four center-console throttles. At the same time, the captain's right palm, along with the engineer's hand, slowly, steadily, shoved the throttle levers forward. Outside, the four hulking turbofan-bypass engines responded with a rising whine and rumble as the levers continued their advance. As the sound beyond the windows became ever louder, Larry began to feel a shaking in the tubular seat.

The first officer released the brakes and the center stripe started moving underneath them; slowly at first, then faster as the engines came up. "Takeoff power is set!" the captain called out. As the turbofans thundered at maximum thrust, the interrupted center marker became a rushing blur in the headlights.

"One-hundred!"

"Check!"

The little marker lights along both sides of the runway were racing past faster and faster. Larry felt himself being eased back against the seat canvas.

"Vee-One!" the captain called out. He dropped his hand from the throttle controls. and scanned the instruments. At the same time, the flight engineer released his own fingers from the ivory-plastic grips on the backside of the throttle levers. Larry

knew that meant the airliner was at the point where, should something happen, due to the diminishing runway length they would have to take off, regardless.

"Vee-Two! Rotate!"

The co-pilot pulled back on the control column; the nose came up; the streaking runway lights dropped out of sight. The thumping of tires on the pavement abruptly ceased, followed by the thuds of the gear struts extending.

"Positive climb!" the first officer called out. "Gear up!"

The captain leaned forward and moved upward a lever on the center of the instrument panel, prompting moans Larry recognized as the hydraulics sucking the landing gear up into the wheel wells, followed by muffled thumps as the outer doors slammed shut.

The 747, pulling out at full engine power, dropped its right wing, revealing the panoramic lights of the city and the airport they had just left behind, then straightened.

"Climb Power!" the captain called out. The flight engineer reached forward and pulled back slightly on the throttles; the sound of the engines dropped a little; the airplane settled into a steady ascent into the night. In a few minutes the lights below began to scatter as the eastern outskirts of Havana slid by below.

The captain called out to the second pilot. "Flaps zero degrees! I have control!"

The co-pilot centered the landing gear control lever to the "off" position, at the same time scanning the instruments, then twisting little knobs on several automatic controls. "Course heading one-two-zero-degrees true!"

Glancing back, the Ukrainian captain gave the American sitting behind him a quick smile. "Well, señor," he said in English, with a touch of irony," did you enjoy your—stay in Cuba?"

"It was not what I expected."

"They all say that."

To Larry, The captain's cryptic comment more or less confirmed that the airplane and its crew had been in Havana before—perhaps many times. Whatever was the cargo they were carrying to Nigeria, he figured it must have been important enough that the Cubans had arranged for the 747's hurried repairs.

"How long will it take us to fly to Nigeria?"

The pilots looked at each other, then at him. "You did not know? We are going first to Angola!"

"But I am supposed to take—" Then the American remembered what the African had said earlier about going home. "Home" meant "Angola", of course.

"In Luanda, we will get more shipments for the 'Organization', then we will go on to Nigeria."

There was that word, again. Larry felt drops of uncertain sweat roll down the inside of his shirt. "How long will we be in Angola?"

The captain shrugged. "A few hours, perhaps."

Even as Larry took one more look out the darkened flight deck's windows before turning-in for the night, the great airplane broke through a band of clouds into a brilliant canopy of stars on its climb toward cruising altitude.

Returning to the dimmed passenger cabin, Larry observed that all the Angolans were sleeping, doubtless lulled by the hypnotic droning of engines and the rush of air against the 747. At the rear, the American located a row of triple seats and some blankets and settled in.

Sometime later—he was not sure how much later—something nudged his shoulder. Opening his eyes, Larry, blinking, thought he must be dreaming: before him stood an apparition of a female. Then he sat up straight and gasped; his eyes wide. For the young woman who was looking down at him was real; very real, indeed.

"Officer Montoya!"

-32-

Larry had never been so surprised; shocked; stunned—whatever it was—in his life. His jaw dropped; his eyes were wide. *"What—!"*

In the semi-darkness the "Cubana" groped her way down into the aisle seat next to the American and stared at him, doe-eyed. To Larry, the usually-overbearing policewoman looked different from before—then he realized she was wearing faded jeans and a white blouse; until now, he had never seen her in anything but the blue and gray P-N-R uniform. And she seemed nervous—almost frightened; not at all like the brittle professional she had been back at the Havana hangar. "Señor Landay . . ." the young woman spoke in dusky, accented English, "you must not be angry with me—"

"Angry? My God! What're you *doing* here?" Larry was still thunderstruck, gasping for air. "How did you get on this airplane?"

"I was in the *'cajon'*—the big 'box' they brought on a truck before you . . . we . . . took off."

Larry remembered the wooden crate that came up on a truck. It was a police truck! *"You were inside that box?"*

"Si, Señor Landay. I had help from a . . . 'friend'. When your plane came the other night, I knew it was my only chance—"

". . . to *escape* from Cuba? (*There was that word, again.*) Do you know where we're going?"

"Si, señor. The airplane is going to Nigeria. I must get there. Por favor—help me."

This was almost too much for Larry to take in all at once. "Does the *captain* know you're here?"

She shook her head. In the dim yellow light the girl's tan-shaded skin had almost a green tint.

"We'll have to tell the captain you're on board."

"Oh, señor, what if he will do something bad to me?"

"I believe he'll be more surprised than anything else."

479

A quick grin crossed Montoya's brown lips. "Like *you* were surprised?" She eased herself out of the seat. "I must tell the pilot I am here." Larry hauled himself from his own seat and followed the young woman up the shadowy aisle past the sleeping Africans toward the flight deck.

At the forward door of the cabin, he caught up with her just as the captain turned about in the dimmed cockpit to say something to the flight engineer. A look of astonishment came across the man's face as he caught sight of the slender female's form, outlined by the low cabin lights, standing in the doorway.

"Who are you? What are you doing here?" Then he spotted Larry coming up behind her.

"Captain, this is 'Officer Montoya' of the 'P-N-R'— remember her?"

The three Ukrainians gaped at the unexpected newcomer. "Yes ... *but why is she here?"*

"Por favor! I had to leave Cuba for my—safety. I must go with you to Nigeria."

Larry spoke up. "She says she was inside the crate they delivered on the last truck."

The captain's eyes darted between Larry and the stowaway, then he gave an aside wave. "Very well ... take care of the—the female—for now. We will talk about this—later."

The two made their way back out into the passenger cabin. Larry grinned. "So, I now have orders from the captain to 'take care of you'!"

At the top of the spiral staircase the Cuban girl turned down the steps toward the darkened main cargo deck. "I must get my things ... come and help me."

The American followed the former P-N-R officer back through the open alleyway, with its rollers on the deck for moving cargo, past a score of lashed-down pallets and crates, to the rear of the enormous airplane's cargo deck. Flipping on a reading light, a holdover from the 747's days as a passenger airliner, he saw her aim a flashlight through a low opening in the side of the wooden crate that came on board just before they had taken off from Havana. He shook his head. She had been inside it all along! "Officer Montoya" squeezed through a hinged door and shoved out a suitcase, a briefcase, the P-N-R purse he had seen her carrying, and bulging plastic bags of food containers and bottled water. It looked to Larry as if she had prepared for a long stay in there. "Why did you do this?"

The female stowaway stood up and patted her hair. "Por favor, help me take these things upstairs. Then, I will tell you."

The two lugged her things up the spiral staircase and stowed everything except the food containers in the overhead. As they again took seats on the back row, a faint aroma from the plastic parcel reminded Larry it had been some hours since he and the crew-members had eaten back at the airport's military cafeteria. He turned to the girl, who was staring at the bag; swallowing. "Hungry?"

"Si`, señor ... much so."

"So am I."

At the very back of the upper passenger deck was a small galley, a holdover from the 747's former *'Iraqi Airlines'* career; after Larry figured out how the microwave food-heaters worked, their boxed dinners were soon steaming on plates from the tiny pantry.

All the while as they ate their midnight meal, the American kept watching the young Cuban woman out of the corner of his eye; it was hard to believe she was the same aggressive policewoman he had been so determined to avoid. Had it all been just an act? He remembered how she kept looking at him in those meetings and that she had held his passport to the last. Something indeed drastic must have happened to cause her to cut all ties to the homeland and stowaway on this Africa-bound cargo airplane. And from the way she was going after her meal, it looked as if she had not eaten in a while.

When she was finishing, Larry decided to do some probing, starting with the obvious question: "So tell me—why did you come on this airplane?"

The female stowaway stared down at the food tray. "Ah, Señor Landay ... it is complicated—so complicated."

We have a long trip ahead of us; we may as well use our first names. I'm *'Larry'* Landay. Call me 'Larry'."

The Cuban policewoman put out her hand. "*'Marisol'*— 'Marisol Montoya'." Larry saw that her fingernails were perfectly manicured. Whatever had brought about the change, the non-threatening young woman sitting next to him was a definite improvement over the abrasive "Officer Montoya" from back in Havana.

"Marisol" let out a sigh. "You 'Americanos' do not understand what it is like in Cuba."

"For two days, I went all over Havana. I saw and heard a lot—you might be surprised how much I 'understand' about Cuba."

A reading light across the aisle caught her tight, tanned skin and her short, orange-golden hair; her ever-so-slightly broad nose. The American decided she was a mixture—along with Spanish-Cuban, he figured she could also be part-West-Indian; some African; maybe even a little Oriental thrown in for good measure. Her lean hands, toned, buffed arms and shoulders; her sinewy, sandal-shod feet, all outlined in the backlight, left him no doubt that, as an officer of the law, she had kept herself in top form. And beyond whatever advantages the dim yellowish cabin light gave her—in everyday clothes, he thought the young woman's features added up to a right nice-looking package.

But right now, she looked defiant. "Señor`Larry, I say you know *nothing* about Cuba!" Her hazel eyes flashed below rather thick eyebrows; a crimson flush fanned across her bronze complexion. "It is very bad! Except for my uncle Trini—I was the *only* one in my family who had not at least *tried* to escape!" She caught his questioning look.

"Did you say, 'Trini'? 'Trini Torres'? Drives an old Chrysler?"

"Si, Señor Larry . . . you know him?"

"He took me all around Havana!"

"Oh!" It was Marisol's turn to be surprised. "He is my only relative still in Cuba. *Mi papá* and *mi mamá* and my little brother and some uncles and aunts and cousins all of them left one night in a boat. I stayed behind because I had the police job. But after that, things became difficult for me. My superiors were suspicious of me because of my family's 'desertion' to Florida.

There was no reason for me to stay in Cuba. I had seen this airplane coming to the airport many times. So I started making plans to get on it, somehow."

"You saw this airplane *many times?*"

"Si. This airplane picks up weapons and takes them—somewhere."

"How did you get into the box . . . the crate?"

"Another officer—he was the truck driver—had helped me get a shipping crate and put things in it. Then you showed up the other night on the airplane, and—you saw him when he drove the crate with me inside it up to the airplane—we were afraid they would not take it aboard."

Larry remembered the driver had been pretty aggressive in getting the crate onto the airplane.

The girl stifled a yawn. She fumbled for the seat-back button and dropped into a reclining position. "I am very tired, now." Even as Larry punched-off the reading light, Marisol Montoya was asleep.

The American watched her for a minute, still hardly believing the dozing female beside him was the dislikable policewoman of the airport. Then he pushed back his own seat and in a couple of minutes was himself gone for the night.

* * *

Bright sunlight was shining into Larry's face. Blinking, he looked up to see a semi-circle of very dark men staring at him. After a second he realized their interest was focused on the passenger in the seat next to his. Larry looked over at the sleeping female and it all came back.

One of the men spoke up in his thick African accent, pointing. "Who is she?"

"The policewoman from the airport, remember? She's going to Nigeria." Larry decided not to say much about her. The fellows looked around at each other with smirks.

The stowaway Cuban policewoman stirred, then came awake with a start. "Oh!" She looked around, wide-eyed, then seemed to regain her bearings. "Where are we?"

"Somewhere over the South Atlantic, I would guess." Larry glanced at his watch; they had been flying about thirteen hours. "We're probably not far from Angola." He looked out the right-side window at a clear azure sky; far below, a white carpet of clouds crawled by underneath them in brilliant sunshine; as the men in the aisle moved about, the sun shone into his face through a window on the left side, forward.

An African came back to the others standing in the aisle. "The captain wants to speak to the American," he said, motioning at Larry, "bring the woman, too."

Just as the two passed through the open door to the flight deck, the chief pilot came out of the crew's restroom. "Ah, the new passenger." He looked the stowaway up and down. "No uniform? Are you no longer a police—woman?"

"I do not know what I will do when I get to Nigeria."

The Ukrainian looked at Marisol. "Perhaps you will already have a job when you get there." Larry and the girl glanced at each other as he sat down at a narrow table in the crew's quarters. "I radioed the 'Organization's' Security Chief' at Tanuta City about you. He wants to use your police experience in his 'system' . . . you will go there."

Marisol brightened. "I have heard of 'The Organization'. P-N-R people in Cuba speak of it."

To Larry, it seemed the girl knew more about his mysterious customer than he did.

Just then, the sounds of the engines dropped; the deck took a dip beneath everyone's feet. The round-faced Ukrainian stood up. "I must take over and prepare for the landing . . . we will be on the ground at Luanda in about thirty minutes."

Larry spoke up. Ah, captain, how long will we be there—in Angola?"

"One hour—or less." His eyes darted from one to the other of the two in front of him. "You should stay on the airplane . . . it is not safe in that country. They are having a civil war, there."

As soon as the Africans had felt the airliner push over, a festive air that rivaled their Havana departure broke out; by the time Larry and Marisol stepped back into the passenger compartment, bawdy laughter and high-fives—along with some other gestures—were going strong. Animated conversation about their homecoming then went on for some minutes.

"Take seats!" the flight engineer called out. "We are landing!" The airplane was in a tight turn. Larry watched as a coastal plain of scrub grass and marshland swept by close below. When the wheels brushed the concrete, the Angolans gave out more loud shouts, whistles and handclapping.

In a few minutes the cargo liner pulled up in front of a weatherbeaten hangar. Fuel trucks and a semi-trailer loaded with crates moved in.

The whooping black men, pulling their things from the overhead, called to Larry for a round of handshakes and back-slapping. As soon as the portable steps were alongside, the happy-looking men made their way down the spiral steps and on to the outside.

* * *

The Chief Photo Analyst stared at the satellite pictures in consternation: the military hangar at Jose' Marti was empty. "It's gone!" The man made several calls. In a few minutes all American agencies interested in the 747 knew that it had gotten away sometime during the past twenty-four hours. The man did some fast figuring. By now, the airplane could be anywhere within a five-to-eight-thousand mile radius of Havana. They would now have to start all over.

* * *

Larry watched as a squad of forklifts unloaded some of the crates and pallets the 747 had brought from Havana and others were being lifted on board. Off to one side sat the wooden box in which Marisol had hidden; the little trapdoor was still hanging open As she stared down at it, sitting forlorn-looking on the foreign tarmac, lines of tears rolled down her face

The American reached into a compartment and handed the girl a paper towel. "I'm embarrassed," she said with a wan grin, wiping her eyes, "this is a big thing for me."

"I guess it's because you've never been out of Cuba?"

Marisol looked surprised. "Señor Larry, I trained at the Police Academies in Mexico City and Caracas and also in Moscow! I served with Soviet Special Forces in East Asia!"

"In Russia?" It had never occurred to the American she had done such things. So Montoya was well-traveled.

"I am a trained professional, señor!"

"The captain says you have a job waiting for you in Nigeria. A security job of some sort."

"It gives me something to look forward to—I guess." She pointed out the window. "Look, the trucks are going away." Larry followed her gaze to the outside where the forklifts were moving back.

Just then, the flight engineer burst out of the cockpit. "Get into the restroom! Hurry!"

"What?"

"The Customs and the Immigration men are coming aboard! If they find you, they will take you off the airplane!"

The two passengers scurried to the very back of the cabin, to the tiny cubicle across from the galley. Crowding inside, Larry locked the door. But the light and the loud exhaust fan came on! Larry's wide eyes met Marisol's—the noise would give them away! In a hurry he moved back the lever; they would have to take their chances with an unlocked door. Their hearts pounding, the two stood breathless in the stuffy, unlighted space. Larry could feel Marisol's heaving chest against his.

From the direction of the flight deck, heavy, male, African-sounding voices of two men were speaking to the crew. Larry heard the words "kilograms" and "cubic meters," which seemed to suggest the men were examining the cargo manifest.

"No passengers?" The answer was indistinct. Then came quiet. Wide-eyed, the two hidden in the little space held each other, hoping the men out there were finished.

Then a voice said, "You go on . . . I will use the restroom and follow you!" Tramping footfalls started coming down the aisle!

"You can do that later—we must hurry!" came the other man's voice from farther off. The footsteps stopped, receded a bit, then paused.

"Oh, my God!" Marisol breathed, "I left my purse out there!"

After some long seconds, the footsteps sounded as if they were going away. After that, they heard the unmistakable clumping of shoes on the aluminum spiral stairs; in another minute there came the muffled thump and the vague vibration of a door closing in the side of the aircraft. Marisol was gasping. "Are they gone?"

Larry cracked open the door; no one was in the passenger cabin. Through the open cockpit door up front he could see the flight engineer in his seat, facing the right-side instrument panel. The American shrugged; everything looked normal out there. As if to re-assure them, the lights blinked, then came the whine of a jet engine starting.

By the time the two buckled into their seats all four of the big turbofans were up and running.

The 747 lurched and bumped across the cracked concrete onto the pavement of the narrow taxiway. To Larry, it seemed as if they were rolling as fast as they had back at Mexico City.

The airplane made several leaning turns, then Larry saw that they were on the runway. At once, the big jets went to full power and the huge aircraft began to accelerate. Then the nose came up and the Boeing lifted from the ground with the familiar thumps of the gear retracting.

As the aircraft banked into a sharp climbing turn, from outside the airplane all at once, there came the *BOOM!* of a loud explosion, then another that shook the fuselage! Sounds like metal fragments peppered the windows and the slab-side of the airplane! Marisol grabbed his arm. Larry looked out in alarm at puffs of black smoke racing past. "They are shooting at us!" As he gaped, appalled, a missile, riding an orange contrail, shot up past the end of the right wing and disappeared into the sky.

The engines throttled back; to Larry, the airplane dropped off like a skipped stone in a millpond. Then the jets came back up as the 747 careened into alternating tight turns. From the airplane's violent gyrations, the American figured the pilots must be using evasion maneuvers such as they had probably done in Soviet bombers. After another minute, the noises outside stopped and the airplane started into a steady climb.

* * *

The CIA analyst read the decoded report, then reached for the scrambler telephone. "Grayson, here ... our operative at the Havana airport says the cargo Seven-Forty-Seven is bound for somewhere in Africa— he believes Angola." The man listened, then said, "Our man also knows there was a lot of electronic equipment on the airplane. There was another pause while the person the other end spoke, then he came back with, "One more thing: there was an American on board ... we believe he was the California guy with the electronic equipment. Yes, from Mountain View. Suggest the 'Agency' look there."

The man hung up the telephone with a satisfied nod; that secret agent down there was worth everything they were paying him. He again lifted the receiver. "Place a scrambler call to INTERNOL in Geneva—to Tarliani. I have information for him."

* * *

"My purse! Where is it?" Wide-eyed, Marisol slapped her palm to her forehead and pointed at the aisle. "It was right there!" The girl frantically scrambled around. "It is gone! It has my papers and everything in it!" She burst into tears.

"Maybe they just moved it."

The distraught young woman shook her head. "Now they know who I am ..."

Larry unbuckled his seat belt. "Let's look for it."

The two pulled their way along the upward-slanting aisle; the airplane was still climbing. At the top, as Larry and Marisol stepped onto the tight flight deck, the third pilot looked up and saw them. "I am glad that is the last time we will be going to Angola—" Larry noticed the captain shoot a fast frown in his direction. The remark confirmed to Larry that this airplane's career was quite varied. He remembered it had no numbers or markings on it and that the pilot had said it had extra-range fuel tanks. Who owned it? The mysterious "Organization" about which he kept hearing? And whatever they had loaded at that last stop must be pretty important, given the way they had rushed it on board.

"They took her purse," Larry told the pilots.

The captain thought for a moment and shook his head. "I watched them on the ground after they left the airplane. I do not remember seeing either of the men carrying it."

"Then maybe it's still on board!" The girl bounded toward the steps and clambered down the spiral rungs toward the cargo floor. The two made their way back through the long cargo deck. "They left by the rear passenger door . . . let's look there."

But when they came to the back exit, the handbag was nowhere in sight. The young woman put her hands to her face. "My purse—my papers . . . all gone!"

He put his arm around her shaking shoulders, at the same time noting how firm and fit she felt. "I'm sure everything'll be all right."

"Now those people know who I am and I do not have any 'identificación' . . . I do not even have any 'dinero'! "

Larry cast about the space where they were standing. The crates tied-down back here in the far-rear of the cargo deck, he realized, were the ones they had loaded at Luanda. Some of the others further forward had been pushed closer together to make room for the Luanda crates. A look up the long working alleyway toward the front of the airplane, the windows dimmed by cargo, revealed no crewmember to be in sight. In the shadowy light, he spotted a familiar object a short way up the aisle alongside a pallet: the flashlight Marisol had used to remove her things from the stowaway crate. "Let's look around."

He shined the yellow beam back and forth across one of the boxes; on the side, some letters in both Cyrillic and Spanish were stenciled in black on the plywood. "Look at this!" He pointed at the label. *"Two Hundred Kalashnikov A-K-Seventy-Four"*. He gasped at the import of the markings; the contents of all the big boxes were of Soviet manufacture. "These are automatic

489

weapons!" Larry aimed the light up and down the aisle and whistled. "There are thousands of automatic rifles, here! And look at all these pallets of ammunition—this airplane is an arsenal!"

Marisol ran her hand across a crate. "I trained on these weapons in the Soviet Union."

Her remark reminded Larry that she was without a doubt very handy with those things. Pretty face and trim figure aside, if necessary, this petite young woman could probably put up a furious fight using all manner of weapons and self-defense tactics. In California, he had known a San José policewoman who once told him she could arrest him if he came on too strongly to her. He figured he might do well to remember those facts in future dealings with Marisol Montoya.

All at once, there was a glow of light in the far forward part of the cargo deck—someone was coming down the spiral staircase! Larry flipped off the flash and set it aside. The two turned toward the front, where they encountered the co-pilot stepping toward them in the shadows. "Ah, there you are. Did you find the missing—object?"

The young woman hung her head. "No . . . it is gone."

"The captain wants me to look around back here to see if there was any damage from the anti-aircraft shells." He moved past them and on toward the rear of the aircraft.

* * *

Far out in the South Atlantic, in the trackless seas northeast of Ascension Island, a low pressure trough was rolling over warmer tropical water and beginning to generate surface winds; in a few hours, this unstable airmass would be moving forward at thirty knots. An ocean swell about three meters above mean sea level would soon develop ahead of it and start advancing to the northeast in the direction of the coast of southern Nigeria.

* * *

There came the familiar drop in the sound of the jet engines and the airplane pushed over. "Well, here we go . . ." Larry took his seat with a jab of nerves; he had read some recent stories about how dangerous the Lagos airport was supposed to be.

Marisol stared out the window at the cottonball clouds scudding by as the 747 continued its descent; her thoughts kept going back to the lost handbag. How foolish she had been to leave it out where those horrible men could find and take it!

As the Boeing began a series of sharp, dropping turns, Larry observed what looked to be marsh-lands sweeping beneath the alternate dipping ends of the wings. Then the airplane straightened out and with a rumbling swish the enormous airliner's probing committee of tires grabbed the uprushing pavement.

The bulky cargo liner eased into a space in front of a large hangar among several smaller airplanes that were also without numbers and markings. The American gazed out at them. More "Organization" planes? Larry turned to Marisol, who was staring out the window, swallowing; her fingers absently rubbing the seat-arm. "Looks like we're here," he said.

Outside, at the portable steps, a very black man in a military uniform and a black beret came up, squinting at them through metal-rimmed green sunglasses."Larry Landay?"

The American nodded.

"I am 'Colonel Ajiboy'—Airport Security'," he said, in an African accent. The athletic-looking man turned to Marisol. "And this is Miss Montoya?"

The young Cuban woman stole a quick glance at Larry, then looked up at the tall military officer. "Ah, *si*`—yes," she said in her uncertain English.

The Army man nodded at the female. "General Retchko sends his regards and he will see you in a few days at Tanuta City." He looked her up and down, then back at Larry. "You both will come with me to the office." He turned about and with the two following, paced across the pavement in the direction of the main terminal building.

The officer led Larry and Marisol down a corridor, finally going into what looked to be a conference room. Around a long table sat several men; two in military uniforms; a half-dozen others were in civilian outfits. Ajiboy motioned at a couple of empty chairs. "Take seats." The American and the young Cuban woman sat down.

At the head of the table, a small man in a brown three-piece suit leaned back in his armchair and tapped together his fingertips. "I am 'Doctor Nomoah'," he said, nodding at the new arrivals, then turning to an overweight, extremely dark man in a billowing, flowery, full-length outfit.

"'Masobe Busa'," the man rumbled in a deep voice.

The others gave their names, all of which, to Larry, sounded complicated and were lost to him, for now. Knots of tension began working their way up from the bottom of his stomach.

The colonel nodded at Marisol, then looked at the others in the room. "Miss Montoya is from Cuba, where she was on the 'National Police Force', and is highly qualified." Larry noted that the emotionless men around the table seemed to be sizing-up the youthful-looking woman. "She trained in the Soviet Union and will be working with General Retchko."

With that, Larry noticed the expressionless men loosened up. Having the approval of this "General Retchko"—whoever he was—seemed to carry a lot of weight with these intense-looking individuals.

". . . instructions are for you to remain with the shipment," the Army man was going on, "we will issue you proper weapons for your journey to Tanuta City." His eyes swept over the faces of the other Africans. "The equipment they have brought to Nigeria is very important to your 'Organization'. I will assign a squad of my soldiers to go with them."

Ajiboy motioned for Larry and the female to follow him. The three made their way out to the corridor, where the three pilots were stepping toward them. The flight engineer held an object in his hands that he thrust at Marisol with a grin.

"My purse!" The girl caressed the handbag, wide-eyed. "Where did you find it?"

"It was on the airplane, just inside the rear passenger door— next to a pallet."

The captain gave a slight mile. "I guess they found the female's things not so interesting!" He put out his hand shook her's. "We must be—leaving now."

The five who had flown together shook hands all around. Larry watched as the three men, whose flying skills had saved his life several times, walked away. He wondered if he would ever again see them.

The girl scrambled around in her handbag. "They got my 'identificación'! Now, for sure, they know who I am and where I have gone."

"What difference does it make? You're a long way from Angola."

She was downcast. "They will give all the 'información' to Cuba!"

The Army officer motioned to them. "We are leaving for the docks, now." The three, with Marisol still unhappy over the missing items, made their way outside where an olive-drab Army car awaited; its engine idling.

A young soldier held open the rear door of the command vehicle. "Your luggage is in the trunk," he said. Larry dropped into the rear seat next to the girl.

The car swung around, followed by a trailer-truck carrying their shipment from the airplane. An armored personnel carrier fell-in at the rear; another of the heavy-looking military machines pulled in front of the car. In the bright midday sunshine the bunched procession moved away from the 747, past the other airplanes and several hangars, then out through a gate at the far backside of the airfield onto a pot-holed street.

As they bumped along, Larry saw that the airport's outer fences swarmed with armed troops. Then he remembered that soldiers had also surrounded the military section of the Havana airport. Could it be that the electronics shipment was so important that it warranted all this protection in such widely-separated places as Cuba and Nigeria? An unsettling thought came to the American: *How many people know about these goods—and about him?*

* * *

493

Carside hung up the telephone. According to his just-completed conversation with Washington, the sensitive electronics that had been spirited out of the United States from San Pedro were now likely somewhere in Africa. Into whose hands had those goods been delivered? Someone very clever was behind all this.

* * *

The caravan lumbered past a peeling sign that spelled-out, *'Apapa Quay'*, into a roaring, bustling area of shipping docks. In the front seat, Ajiboy turned about. "Lagos is the biggest port in West Africa!" The procession made its way down a crowded concrete pier past a row of dingy-looking warehouses; beneath a hulking hammerhead crane; past trucks alongside freighters loading and unloading goods; to the far end of the dock. There, they lurched to a halt at a modest-sized vessel tied up to the wharf. Larry read the name, *'Coast Adventurer,* on the little ship's rust-streaked stern.

Ajiboy got out, motioning to the others. "We must hurry . . . General Retchko wants the ship to leave while it is still daylight."

As Larry and Marisol with their travel bags made their way toward a nearby gangway, the American gazed up at the ship's superstructure with some misgivings. The three upper decks looked as if they had been piled on top of the freighter's tubby hull without much thought; the vessel's fading paint competed with a layer of orange rust that poked through here-and-there all around the ship.

When they stepped on board the main deck, a muscular navy-blue-clad African seaman motioned to them. "Follow me to your cabins," he said, in a heavy accent, leading them toward the superstructure. The fellow swung around a handrail and pulled himself up a steep companionway. Larry and Marisol trooped upward behind him. At the second level, they went forward a short distance, then stepped across a high door frame into a narrow, white-painted corridor. Looking at a paper, the sailor gave a mahogany door a push. It retreated inward with a dismal groaning of hinges. By the light coming through an open porthole they saw a very small, old-style, nautical-looking room with varnished wooden built-in cabinets and mesh nets for personal items. Under the single porthole was a narrow bunk; at the inboard bulkhead stood a dark dresser. The man clicked a switch; a weak, yellow-tinged light-bulb flickered on in the middle of the overhead. "This is your cabin," he said to Marisol.

Leaving the girl, the deckhand stepped a short distance down the corridor and opened a door into a similarly gloomy-looking room. "This is *your* cabin," he repeated to Larry.

The American nodded to the seaman, then stepped inside and closed the door. From the looks of his tiny space on this little ship, he was glad the journey down to Tanuta City would probably take at most only a couple of days; any longer, he thought, and he could develop claustrophobia in here.

Larry stepped back out into the short corridor, where Marisol was closing her cabin door, shaking her head. "Look at the bright side," he grinned at her, "at least you're not traveling in a wooden box! And a poster on the wall says you can have all the salt-water showers you want."

The two strolled to the forward part of the superstructure. Standing at the solid rail under the ship's overhanging bridge, they watched in the fading daylight as the crates and pallets of electronic gear rose swaying into the air, then with jerks and the squeal of pulleys dropped down into the forward cargo hold.

Marisol glanced at him. "You brought these electronics all the way from California?"

He pointed at a re-inforced plywood box suspended in midair on a cable. "This is the second time I've seen these crates loaded onto a ship." While they watched the seamen stow the goods below decks of the little freighter and pull canvas covers across the broad tops of the hatches, he told her about his journey from Mountain View up to the time they had landed in the shot-up 747 at Havana.

A sudden seabreeze came up; the girl's short hair fluttered for a second, then dropped back; Larry ran his hand through his own unruly, blown-about hair.

"There is something else I might as well tell you." The American gave a side look at the young Cuban woman. "The first few times I saw you, I did not like you at all."

"*Que?*"

"That night when we first met at the airport, and then later, I decided to avoid you as much as possible." Marisol gaped at him. "I thought you were too 'aggressive', or 'bossy', or something like that."

"Señor Larry! You must try to understand that, in Cuba, I am—that is, I *was*—in a struggle to survive!" It was the only way I could be."

"Then it was all just an 'act'?"

"With my family gone, you see, I had to be like that to stay alive. That is why I wanted to get away from—"

Their conversation was interrupted by the noise of a half-dozen troops in battle gear, holding automatic weapons, tromping up onto the main deck; the colonel was with them. Larry guessed they were the soldiers the Army officer had said would be going with them on the trip. By now, it was obvious to the American that his cargo of electronics was important enough for these people to give it all this special protection. But from whom? And why?

Colonel Ajiboy pulled up the steep steps to them. "All the shipments and the papers are in order," the military man said, "I will notify General Retchko that you will be at Tanuta City in two days." He pointed at the soldiers down on the main deck. "My men will go with you for protection." The Nigerian put out his hand. "Good luck on your journey."

With that, he turned about in a rigid military step, strode across the deck and clambered back down the companionway. As the two watched from the second superstructure deck, the tall, slender man bounded down the gangway onto the pier. He seemed to be all right, Larry thought.

All at once, there came a sudden, brassy blast of the ship's horn, causing both of them to jump, then a gray cloud of smoke roiled down from the topside smokestack. Sniffing the air, Larry nudged Marisol. "That's coal smoke! This must be a really *old* boat."

Even as thicker and blacker fumes tumbled out from the ship's funnel and rolled over the pier, a tug chugged alongside. Except that this vessel was much smaller and older than the *Beacon Trader* had been and that the Lagos docks here were rather seedy-looking, as they stood watching the swearing, sweaty seamen casting off the mooring lines, to Larry, everything else was much the same as it had been back in San Pedro when that other ship had sailed.

Before long, the cargo vessel had eased away from the dock and soon rounded the breakwater. Then came a throbbing beat from under their feet as the engine went faster. Foam churned off at an angle; the breakwater receded; the freighter commenced a slow side-to-side motion; they were underway. As the steamer waddled along in the seaway, the engine's relentless surging set off rattles, creaks and groans that, to Larry, seemed to come from every corner of the ship.

Larry and Marisol stepped around the deck to the after end of the superstructure. Astern, the top rim of the orange setting sun was dropping into the ship's silver wake. In a little while, the white glow of Lagos's lights took over in the western sky, catching the silver-crested tops of the rolling black waves as the little ship pushed on.

There came the brassy beat of an electric gong that Larry recognized from his days on the *Beacon Trader*. "Ah, dinner!" He nudged the girl. "Let's find the 'chow hall' or whatever they call the eating place on this barge." Holding on to the mahogany rail, the two clumped down the steep companionway stairs to the main deck, to the source of the aroma of cooked food.

Inside, a native man in a white chef's outfit motioned at an empty table. "The captain will be with you, shortly."

* * *

In the nighttime South Atlantic, the black wall of water rolled on, pushed by the forty-knot wind behind it. The low-pressure trough was now a little less than fourteen-hundred miles from its landfall in forty-two hours on the reefs and sandbars of the Niger River Delta.

497

They were just taking their seats when a slim, baldheaded white man with gold bands on both shoulders of his starched white shirt appeared at the room's entrance. As Larry watched, the greeter said something to him, then gestured toward the table where he and Marisol were sitting.

"Hallo," the man said in a booming voice, pulling out a chair for himself, "you are our passengers for this trip?" Larry and Marisol nodded as the angular man offered his hand. "I am 'Captain Imwalley' and I welcome you aboard." He nodded to the white-dressed man at the door, who seemed to be the steward, and went on, "I trust you find our little ship to your liking?" The American detected an European accent; perhaps German or Dutch.

The girl spoke up. "We are all right . . . so far," she said, "when do we arrive at—what was the name of that place.?"

"Ah, your shipment goes to 'Tanuta City'. We will get there two afternoons from now. The ship will stop tomorrow afternoon at Port Ibom to take on more cargo."

The steward set a bottle of *'Bordeaux'* and some glasses on the table. Larry noticed there was an extra glass. "Someone else coming?"

Before the captain could answer, a very black man in a military uniform stepped to the entrance. The waiter pointed toward their table. The newcomer came over and took a seat, nodding.

"This is 'Major Banjo'," the ship's captain said, prompting a round of handshakes. "He is in charge of the military detail that is making this trip."

The Army man looked the young Cuban woman over. "General Retchko's orders are for me to instruct you in the 'A-K Seventy-Four' weapon."

"I trained in Russia on all the 'Kalashnikovs'."

A momentary look of surprise came across the Nigerian's face. "Well, fine." He looked at Larry. "You are trained in these, also?"

"I am an American . . . why *should* I know anything about these . . . those—things?"

Banjo glanced at the captain, whose face was serious, then back at Larry. "Well, *'Mister American'*, these are dangerous waters." He shook his head as if finding it hard to believe this pale foreigner was so uncomprehending. "Pirates—"

It was Larry's turn to be surprised. *"Pirates?"*

"General Retchko is taking all precautions,' he told the American. "The safety of your cargo is of great concern to the 'Organization'."

There was that word, again. And the way these people kept talking about this "General Retchko," he was sounding more important all the time. Lisa had never mentioned him.

Larry glanced at Marisol. How would his former girlfirend react when she saw him with this attractive young Cuban woman?

* * *

Mountain View, California, at That Moment:

Joe Anglin looked up from the desk; the Venetian blinds on the front door were clattering. Two close-cropped men wearing razor-pressed trousers and sport coats stepped into the little front office, looking about, as if taking in everything. Both reached into coat pockets and produced badges that they held up. "*'Federal Investigation Agency'* . . . you are Lawrence J. Landay?"

Joe swallowed. "He—he's not here."

"Where is this individual?"

"I'm not sure . . . he was going to . . . that is, he said he left for—"

"He left for where?"

"He didn't say."

"Who are you? Give me some identification."

Joe pulled his driver's license from his wallet. "I am keeping the place open until—Larry gets back." The man compared Joe's face with the picture.

"That's his name—'Larry'?"

The second man withdrew a document from his coat pocket. "We have a search warrant signed by a federal judge." He spotted the coffee-maker. "Make us some coffee. We'll be here a while."

As the agents turned away, Joe Anglin looked across at the filing cabinet and went pale. On it was the little cypher machine with the code book beside it! *And the Tanuta purchase orders were in the files!*

* * *

The native steward placed dishes of food before the diners at the captain's table. Larry pointed at some shiny-looking yellow objects one of the hot servers. "I saw those back in Havana," he said, "I believe they are called—"

". . .'plantains'—" the captain put in. "They came from the Caribbean back when this coast was involved in the slave trade," he went on, between bites, "ships that carried slaves to the 'New World', as they called it back then, came back with all kinds of new foods. Yams and white potatoes and corn and tomatoes all came to Africa and Europe that way."

"So did sugar," Marisol put in. "I am from Cuba."

Larry had been listening to the captain as he talked. "You have an interesting way of speaking; did you come from France?"

"'Belgium'. Before we Belgians gave up the Congo, I was involved in cargo trade on the Congo River. I left and came here. That was some years ago." What Larry took to be a rueful expression came onto the man's tanned face. "Now, of course, things are much different down there—they do not even call it 'The Congo' anymore."

* * *

500

The trough's forward motion was slowing; after sunset, the rate of condensation, the engine that drives such weather systems, had decreased. The wave surging ahead of it dropped to an average height of three meters; its forward progress toward the Nigerian coastline, now twelve-hundred miles ahead of it, lessened to twenty knots. As the weather system moved northward during the night, warmer water closer to the equator would keep it organized.

* * *

The Army man caught Marisol's attention. "We must go now and get you checked-out on your weapon." He motioned to Larry. "*You* should also learn how to handle the 'Kalashnikov'."

"I should? What for?"

"We must take all precautions." He stood and nodded at the captain.

The military man, followed by the Cuban woman and the sandy-haired American, made their way up two steep companionway sets of steps to a small chart-room directly behind the wheelhouse. When all three were inside the stuffy space, the major closed and locked the door. Selecting a key from his pocket, he opened a mahogany case and pulled down the most deadly-looking rifle Larry had ever seen. Banjo balanced the dull-black weapon in the palm of his hand, then handed it to Marisol.

The policewoman turned it over and scrutinized its features, all of which were a complete mystery to Larry. She nodded. "It is in order."

The Army major reached into a cabinet and pulled out a bandolier of bullets and a pair of curved magazines, weighted with rounds. He helped her mount the bullet belt across her shoulder; one of the magazines went into a slot on the belt. The girl snapped the other magazine onto the bottom of the weapon and took off the safety. "I trained on these weapons with 'Soviet Special Forces' ... this model is used by 'Spetsnaz'."

A surprised look of recognition came across Banjo's face. Larry frowned. "Who—what is this 'Spetsnaz'?"

"Soviet Special Forces . . . the finest in the world. No other country can compete against it."

"I heard *our* 'Navy Seals' and the 'Delta Force' are the best."

"Sorry, comrade." Marisol's eyes bored at his. "They do not stand a chance against Spetsnaz!"

My God, Larry thought, with a mixture of male envy and respect; the further along with her he went, the more he realized she came from a world of experiences such as he could not have imagined.

Banjo pulled out a second dull-black automatic weapon and handed it to Larry. Grasping it like it might at any second start shooting off without warning, the Californian discovered it was somewhat lighter than its hefty appearance would have suggested. The soldier watched with an expression of restrained amusement as the electronics engineer ran his hands across the assault rifle.

"It doesn't weigh all that much." Larry tried to sound as if he knew at least something about the weapon in his hands—which he didn't.

The major took the automatic rifle from the American and put it back into the cabinet, alongside the one Marisol had been holding, along with the bullet belts. "In the morning, we will do some live target shooting." Larry felt both excited and anxious. If they wanted *him* to use one of these things, then the ship must indeed be sailing into dangerous waters. "For tonight, I have posted my squad of men on the corners of the ship." The Army man looked the other two over. "You should get lots of sleep . . . starting tomorrow, we will be very busy."

* * *

Mountain View, California, at the Same Time:

"Send a lab detail to comb through this place," the agent was saying, "yes, we have the warrant." The crisp-looking man was speaking on the telephone, evidently to his superior. At length, he hung up the handset and looked hard at Joe Anglin. "You must come with us, for questioning."

Joe's legs felt as if they were going to give way beneath him.."Am I under—arrest?"

"Not for now. But I would suggest you get a lawyer."

* * *

At Sea; the Next Morning:

Major Banjo's eyes scanned the cable towline that dropped off the ship's stern into the churning wake. He nodded at the Cuban policewoman. "You will take the first shots." She lifted the weapon's stock to her shoulder, released the safety and peered down the gunsight at the towed wooden target bobbing along one-hundred meters astern. As Larry watched, Montoya squeezed the trigger with a professional touch. At once, the Kalashnikov exploded to life with a stacatto roar; bursts of flame shot from the muzzle; spent cartridges clinked onto the deck. Out on the water, slugs tore into the target; chunks of wood spun off with loud *CRACKS!* Larry's ears were ringing; he had not reckoned with the earsplitting noise of automatic rifle fire. Acrid puffs of blue-gray gunsmoke rolled away in the breeze. In a few seconds, when he could hear again, there were only the sounds of the freighter's propeller thrashing the water below them and the sibilant slap of seawater and spray sluffing along the sides of the ship in the seaway. With a satisfied smirk, the young woman lowered the weapon.

"Good shooting!" From the Army man's expression and the tone of his voice, her performance with the Soviet automatic weapon was far better than he had expected. He turned to Larry. "All right, 'Mister American', let us see *you* shoot."

Marisol stepped up to Larry and tugged on his weapon's curved magazine. "Make sure the magazine is locked-in," she said. He tried to move it around, but it was fixed in place. "Pull this handle back." She pointed at a lever-like projection near the rear of the barrel. There was a click. "Curl your left fingers around the fore-stock and your right index finger at the trigger, thumb across the rear stock." She showed him how to do this. "Lift the weapon so the stock is just inside your right shoulder." The American hoisted the gun, which he figured weighed less than ten pounds, to his shoulder. She looked him over and nodded. "Move the selector lever to the lower position." Marisol guided his fingers as he went through the motions. "In the lower positon, you will shoot a round every time you pull the trigger."

Once more Larry was awed at this compact young woman's knowledge of these kinds of things; her life had certainly been different from his. And he thought it remarkable that he was holding this "Cold War" weapon from the "other" side in his hands. He had heard of the "A-K-Seventy-Four", but never expected to ever *see*, not to mention, to *use* one.

"Aim through the front and rear sights," Marisol was saying in her Cuban accent, "aim a little higher than the target to allow for the fall of shot." He squinted down the barrel, which brought a quick response from her. "*Both* eyes open! Now squeeze the trigger—"

Larry swallowed and sighted the target that was sawing back-and-forth in the ship's roiling wake. He gave the trigger a slow pull with his finger. The weapon responded with an earsplitting bark and a mighty shove against the small of his shoulder. Out in the water, a splash rose several feet above and to the left of the target.

"Do it again!" he heard Montoya say, sounding far-off over the ringing of his ears.

He squeezed off anorhwe round; this time the splash was in front of the wooden platform.

"Keep at it until you hit it!"

He fired the weapon several more times, then a chunk of wood flew off the target. I hit it!" He lowered the weapon and grinned.

"Keep shooting! Keep hitting it!"

It took several more rounds before he registered another hit.

"Next time, do not look up—your job is to keep hitting your target." She pointed to another lever on the rifle. "Lift that handle." Larry moved the projection, which he remembered set the rate of fire. "Now, it is in the 'automatic' mode. Fire it again—hold down on the trigger."

He positioned the weapon his shoulder and squeezed the trigger. What felt like a jackhammer beating on him slammed against his shoulder; splashes shot up in front of the target. As the weapon kept firing, he raised the barrel a little and pieces of the wooden target flew off.

Then the rifle stopped shooting. "You are out of ammunition," she said. "The magazine holds thirty rounds . . . you must learn to be accurate." She gave another smirk. "That comes from practice."

Banjo looked at Marisol, then at the American. "We will go to breakfast, now."

Larry turned about and glanced up. For the first time he saw the soldiers on the top deck above them, scanning the seas; weapons at the ready. He felt his shoulder. It was already starting to ache.

* * *

The Photo Analyst at the 'National Oceanic and Atmospheric Administration' peered at the satellite images—a tropical wave had developed in the past twenty-four hours four hundred miles northeast of Ascension Island. A little late in the storm season, perhaps, but from past experience he knew this type of activity had the potential to strengthen and produce intense surface wave action as it moved northeastward toward the equator. He would notify the "Forecast Center" to compare these images with those of the next satellite pass that would take place in about twenty-one hours.

* * *

Larry and Marisol stood by the rail as the *Coast Adventurer* edged against the dock while deckhands tossed heavy hemp lines down onto the wharf, where they were grabbed by shouting African longshoremen and snubbed to cleats. Larry looked about the tiny landing; at the top of a corrugated metal warehouse was a sign that read PORT IBOM in faded block letters, along with a logo for a cola drink. Behind the storage building, small structures and houses, some on pole-like stilts, lined a muddy, pot-holed street that faded back to the edge of the jungle. At one side, a concrete ramp led from the water's edge up to a drydock, where a good-sized wooden-hulled fishing trawler hung suspended in slings. Larry squinted as the late-morning sun glinted off the boat's twin stainless-steel propellers; at the same time he saw the name, *'Ocean Gatherer'* on the craft's stern transom and the numerals *"12"* on the side of its wheelhouse.

Above the sounds of dockside machinery, a chugging, whoofing sound came from behind the warehouse, then a little steam locomotive puffed around the edge of the building, tugging several miniature flatcars behind it, each loaded with a wooden crate. The tiny switch-engine rattled to a stop on the pier alongside the freighter in a wheezing cloud of blue wood-smoke and steam.

* * *

An hour later, as the vessel pulled away from the dock, a man in the weatherbeaten shipping office watched through an open window. The fellow lifted a telephone receiver and, cupping the transmitter with his hand, told someone on the other end of the line in a low voice that the "Coast Adventurer" was leaving port.

* * *

". . . and are some of our best and most-trusted men—" An infantry lieutenant was talking about the shipboard guards to the American and the Cuban woman, who were sitting with him and Major Banjo in the dining salon. "General Retchko is most anxious to get these goods to Tanuta City in safe order."

Larry spoke up. "I heard something about 'pirates'."

The younger Army man shrugged and gave a glance at his superior officer. "I trust they will not bother us."

Banjo gave an indulgent smile."But we are taking precautions."

* * *

At midday, the wind's motion was carrying the wave east-northeasterly across the equator over warm water at twenty-five knots. Now a second ridge of water was forming on the surface about a kilometer to the rear of the first; both waves were being pushed ahead of the main weather pattern at a height of four meters above average seas. The entire system was moving along toward a landfall on the Niger River Delta in twenty-nine hours. It had begun to rain.

* * *

As they were leaving the dining-room, Marisol announced she was going to her cabin to take a nap. Larry decided to explore the ship. He climbed the steep steps to the top deck, where Captain Imwalley spotted him standing at the rail. "You want to steer the ship?"

The African helmsman stepped aside and pointed at the spoked wooden wheel on its brass pedestal. "Keep the arrow in the binnacle on the compass heading," the fellow said in a heavy brogue.

Larry grasped the varnished projections and stared at the dial in front of the steering post.

"Come about to the right," Imwalley said.

Larry rotated the wheel.

"Come about to one-two-zero." The ship heeled to the left, the compass dial continued its rotation under the arrow until "120" appeared under the arrow. "Center the wheel!"

The ship straightened out and resumed its easy roll and pitch across the dark gray water. Larry stared ahead at the featureless seascape. "The helmsman must always follow the indicated course," the captain said, "since there is nothing else out here to go on."

"It's a bigger job than I figured it would be."

After a while, the American's legs and arms started to get stiff from staying in the same position. The captain noticed him rotating his shoulders and moving about from one foot to the other. "It takes a lot of stamina to man the wheel for hours at a time," he said. "You want to see the rest of the ship?"

Larry nodded, trying not to look too relieved.

The officer called out to the regular helmsman who was standing outside at the rail, The fellow flicked overboard his cigarette, stepped back onto the bridge and again took the helm.

The captain led the passenger down several steep sets of steps to a grated deck next to a pair of ten-foot-high barrel-shaped boilers in the hottest place to which Larry had ever been. Through clouds of steam, several crewmen, stripped to their shorts, were shoveling coal into the ends of flaming fireboxes. "This is the boiler room!" the officer shouted above the rumble of the furnaces.

The two passed through a heavy steel door into another room where a three-story high machine was bolted to the deck. "This is a 'steam reciprocating engine'!" Imwalley called-out above the thrashing noises of the machinery. Larry watched, fascinated, as the four swinging connecting rods within the heavy frame rose and fell about once each second, turning a crankshaft in the bottom well. A man stood at a control platform, scanning dials and handling levers. The captain pointed at a rotating, two foot-thick shaft at the rear of the engine that disappeared through the next bulkhead. "It is connected to the propeller at the stern of the ship."

"How fast are we going?"

"About eleven knots an hour." The officer caught Larry's calculating expresson. "That is not very fast, of course, but it is sufficient for what this ship is used." The man looked up at the bulk of the engine, with its thrusting piston rods and eccentric valve links. "This ship is one of the last to use a reciprocating engine. The 'Titanic' had a pair of engines like this, although they were much bigger and more powerful than this one."

Captain Imwalley pointed at the foot of steep, grated stairsteps leading upward. "Come, we will go back up on deck." Outside, the tropical heat and humidity that had seemed so heavy to Larry, before, now felt almost frigid by comparison with the hellish heat down in the bowels of the ship.

"How's my cargo?"

The ship's master called to a nearby deckhand. "Show this passenger the electronic shipment . . . it is in the forward hold."

"Aye, aye, sir." The fellow motioned for Larry to follow him. The two made their way forward along the main deck of the superstructure, past masts and derricks, to the front of the ship where steep steps took them down one level to the cargo deck, lighted by bare bulbs on the overhead. "It is over here," the dungareed fellow said, leading the American past rows of general cargo. The setup reminded Larry of the cargo hold in the *Beacon Trader*, except that this space was much smaller than on the other freighter. Up ahead, he spotted the familiar wooden crates and pallets tied-down to the deck at the edge of the forward hatchway. Larry sniffed the dank air; he had, without realizing it, compared this musty hold with the strong diesel smell of the first ship. Here, there was no odor of fumes.

* * *

United States Federal Building, San Francisco, California; at the Same Time:

The Federal agent gave a wave of dismissal. "All right, Mister Anglin, you are free to go—but not too far—we may want to question you further."

Larry's friend breathed a long sigh of relief, slid back his seat, and left the glass-walled interrogation room.

When he had gone, the first agent leaned back from the table and tapped his fingertips together; shaking his head. "This guy is small fry—the big fish is somewhere else." He reached for the telephone. "I'll notify the Federal Prosecutor . . . based on what we have found so far, I believe we have enough evidence for the Grand Jury to indict this 'Lawrence Landay' for 'Illegal Transfer of Technology, Conspiracy, and Racketeering'."

-34-

At Sea, the Next Morning:

Captain Imwalley leaned back as the dining steward poured after-breakfast coffee. "This is the most dangerous part of the trip and I am glad we will be arriving at Tanuta City this afternoon."

Larry cocked his eye at the man. "Why is it more dangerous?"

The Army major, stirring his coffee, spoke up. "These are the worst pirate waters." The officer looked up to see that everyone around the table was staring at him. "Ah, most of the time, they attack offshore drilling platforms. But they have also gone after ships, so we have posted all our armed guards."

"We have additional lookouts," the captain put in.

Marisol glanced at Larry, then looked around the table at the others. "The American and I can help since we are both checked-out on the 'A-K-Seventy-Fours'."

The captain pushed back his seat and motioned to the others. "Then, let us go topside."

* * *

At the Severe Storm Forecast Center, the meteorologist pored over the wavy millibar lines on his computer-generated chart and at the satellite pictures of the equatorial Atlantic south of the bulge of West Africa. His attention fell on the tropical wave that had come up the day before; it was now a much more organized system than it had been twenty-four hours ago. He sat down at his keyboard and typed out a bulletin for transmission to coastal interests and to ships at sea. Very soon, there could be dangerously high tides along the Niger River Delta.

* * *

Larry and Marisol stood on the ship's bridge, gazing out over the featureless water. As the American's eyes adjusted to the glare of the sunlight, he noticed a "dot" straight ahead on the seascape horizon. He pointed at the object low on the water. "What's that, out there?"

The captain reached for the telephone, spoke into the handset, then hung it up. "The crow's nest says it looks like a fishing boat. We see them all the time." He glanced at Larry and Marisol, who were wearing bullet-belts slung over their shoulders. In their hands were the automatic rifles. Larry saw she was wearing a red bandana around her neck. "Stay here on the bridge," the master said. The officer stepped to the engine-room telegraph and rang for "Full Ahead". Larry felt the deck beneath his feet surge as the steam engine turned faster revolutions. Thick, black, oily-looking smoke commenced tumbling out the top rim of the single funnel, drifting away to port in the seabreeze, hanging low on the water for some distance before dissipating.

Soon the dot became a trawler towing nets. As the freighter passed it by at a distance of several hundred meters, Larry could make out men in shorts and dungarees moving about on the deck. Most wore all-black, he noticed. After a while, the fishing vessel dropped astern as the *Coast Adventurer* plodded along on its east-southeasterly course.

The ship's navigator stepped onto the bridge, holding a chart. "We are 'here'," he told the captain, pointing at a penciled-in "X" on the sheet. Larry edged over and glanced at it; from the marking it looked like they were only a short distance offshore from Tanuta City, traveling parallel to the coastline.

Several sharp, sudden gusts of wind from starboard whooshed up just then, churning the gray sea into tossing whitecaps. Larry looked out from the bridge to his right. Across the water, a long bank of black clouds was rising above the southwestern horizon. Even as he watched, a yellow flash tore through the cloud's jagged silver edge, outining the churning clouds, still some distance away. "Looks like we may have some rain before long."

Captain Imwalley frowned at the approaching cloudmass, then stepped to the compass. "Come left to heading zero-forty-five-degrees!"

"Aye, aye, sir!" The helmsman spun the wheel; the numbers in the circular binnacle in front of the steering pedestal began to creep around. "Heading is now zero-forty-five degrees."

"Very well." Imwalley turned to Larry. "We will put our stern to the storm." The master glanced at the clock, then went back to scanning the seas over the bow.

The Army man took his leave and went out onto the starboard bridge wing. In a minute he came running to the door. "Look behind us!" he shouted, pointing astern. "The fishing boat is coming back at us—fast!" The crow's nest telephone was ringing.

-35-

"Come on!" Marisol bolted for the starboard bridge wing, motioning with the snub muzzle of her Kalashnikov for Larry to follow her. The young woman ran out, turned and pounded up the steep steps to the roof of the wheelhouse with the American huffing after her. There, two uncertain-looking soldiers were lowering their weapons at the boat that was plowing through the choppy seas toward them. A rumble of powerful engines was becoming louder by the second. The plodding fishing boat of a few minutes before had transformed into a menacing-looking commerce raider bearing down on them..

The lookout shouted down, pointing astern."Pirates!" The oncoming boat was now only a hundred meters behind them. Up forward on the ship's bow, the gesturing Major Banjo was yelling orders to his men to get ready to repel boarders.

A female voice pierced above the shouting soldiers and crewmen. "Ready weapons!" With a loud *'SNAP!'* Marisol set the selector of her AK-74 to "fully-automatic" "Get down into firing positon!" she shouted to Larry and the two soldiers. The men each knelt onto one knee. Seeing what they did, Larry did the same. He lifted the lever and pulled back the handle that cocked the weapon like he remembered having done earlier on the ship's fantail.

Larry felt the deck tilt toward the right; looking astern, the ship's wake had curved into a frothy cresent as the vessel bent into a sharp left turn; it looked as if the captain was running for the shore. As the fleeing freighter straightened-out on course for land, Larry had a fleeting impression of a long line of indistinct treetops coming into sight above the horizon.

When he turned back, he saw that the "fishing trawler" had pulled even with their ship; even as he looked, a man on the boat's foredeck pulled a tarpaulin from a pedestal revealing a machine gun pointing straight at him! At the stern, another renegade lifted a slender, stalk-like object to his shoulder. A trail of reddish smoke arched through the air! A glowing object the size of a tin can slammed into the side of the middle deck where it exploded with a loud *WHOOM!* A ragged billow of smoke and flame shot upward just aft of where they were standing on the top deck.

"Rocket-propelled grenade!" Marisol Montoya yelled. "Get down! Get down!' The four dropped to the deck, sprawling, as the machine gun unloaded a volley that raked the superstructure, splintering the ship's starboard wooden lifeboat. Loud crashes of shattering glass rent the air. Another rocket grenade plowed into the starboard companionway stairs. The spindly structure buckled, then sagged downward onto the second deck. A column of brown smoke climbed up the side of the superstructure and blew off in the wind toward the shore.

Marisol motionioned toward the port stairs, now their only means of escape from the top deck. "Get off! Get off!" Cradling the AK-74, Larry scooted backward, along with the others, to the top of the steps as more shots whanged into the right side of the ship. One-after-another, they scrambled down to the portside deck, opposite from the exposed side, where the attackers were raking the ship with grenades and automatic fire. The *'Cubana'* pointed toward the fore and aft corners of the superstructure. "Over there! Take cover and open fire on them!" The two crouching soldiers loped around the front of the deckhouse. One of the Army men fell; his rifle clattered to the deck. The girl hunkered down and peered around the after bulkhead, then motioned for Larry to follow her.

A fiery explosion rocked the vessel amidships. Chunks of decking erupted into the air.

Gunfire sounded from the direction of the forehatch. The major and his men up front had opened up on the fake fishing trawler with AK-74s. The black-clad pirate at the machine gun on the boat's foredeck flailed backwards onto the deck; not moving

Smoke was now billowing out of the stern house. *Fire!* Appalled, Larry thought about the delicate electronics in the fore-hold. Had he come all this far to lose the shipment to *pirates?*

The wind was now blowing harder; to the rattling din of gunfire was added the booming of thunder.

Marisol shook his shoulder. "Cover me!" The young woman worked her way around to a square metal structure. Looking around, she gestured a "come on" signal to Larry. He crawled around the rear of the jutting superstructure and came up next to her. Peering around it, he saw that the wooden trawler had swung around and its stern was turned toward the freighter. Larry squinted at the name on the boat's transom: "Ocean Gatherer"—where had he seen that name before? The number *"12"* came into sight on the side of its wheelhouse. Larry gasped. *It was the same fishing boat he had seen in the drydock back at Port Ibom!*

Larry pulled the trigger; a burst from his Kalashnikov tore into the attacking boat's waterline

Another projectile zoomed through the air and plowed onto the freighter's main deck. A burst of flame shot up from the area of the dining salon; gray smoke billowed forward from the superstructure in the wind that was now blowing harder from the open water. As Larry popped another magazine into the weapon, the pirate vessel rocked from side to side in the wind and waves of the storm that was now upon them. Lightning flashes and booms of thunder, louder than the noises of the gunbattle, crashed across the water. Big drops of rain began to fall.

Crouched on the deck, Larry glanced over his shoulder; through the rain, not far away over the bow of the still-moving freighter, he could make out an indistinct line of white surf washing onto a low beach; behind it, some woods rose beyond the shoreline. *Was the captain going to run the ship aground?*

Just then, a pair of hooks popped onto the top of a nearby railing. Attached to them, shaking chains dangled down and away, over the side. "They are coming aboard!" Montoya shouted. A dark face appeared the edge of the deck, then the attacker scrambled up the wobbling ladder and hopped onto the rain-slicked teakwood deck. Holding a curved scimitar, the man lunged at Larry.

A slender form streaked out from behind the other end of the big winch. The edge of a swinging shovel blade connected with the intruder's neck—red froth shot into the air, mixing with the rain. As the fellow doubled over, Montoya grabbed the handle with both hands and with a yell, shoved the intruder overboard!

But at the top of the wobbling ladder, another boarder was lifting his foot over the rail. The girl swung the shovel again and caught the thief in his windpipe with the sharp edge of the blade. The gagging fellow gripped his his throat that was gushing red and dropped away.

Larry staggered back; his eyes wide. In the space of a few seconds, the Cuban girl had saved his life twice!

But the attacking boat had moved in closer for another assault. At the same time, as the rain continued to drench the ship's upperworks and pepper the water all around, the wind was pushing the freighter ever closer to the nearby parallel shoreline.

Another rocket-propelled grenade swished through the air, straight through the open starboard side of the bridge and exploded with a thunderous *'BOOM'!* inside the wheelhouse! A blast of orange flame and gray smoke billowed up; the forward windows shattered out over the foredeck, along with chunks of the compass binnacle, the ship's wheel and its dismembered pedestal.

Marisol pointed out to sea. "Look!" Off in the distance, a dark ridge of water with a white crest as far as they could see to the horizon was rolling fast in the direction of the shoreline.

"Tsunami!"

-36-

All at once a blast of wind blew into their faces, shoving them back against the superstructure. As they stood there, Larry stared stupefied at the green-black wall of water that was upon them. He grabbed the girl and shoved her to the deck. A split-second before it struck the freighter, the pirate trawler reared up on its beam ends and rode the crest of the enormous wall of water—then it turned completely over and splintered apart in the roaring, foaming breaker that was carrying it ashore! As the water slammed against the side of their ship, Larry felt the deck heave upward. The two slid backwards as the ship's rail lifted toward the sky. With a shriek and a *'BOOM'!* the wave slammed against the slab-sided steel hull, rolling up and over the side of the ship, drenching those on the deck. Larry flung his arm around the girl and the two held on to each other. As Larry stared grimacing into the wall of water, he saw that not only was the mighty wave pushing the ship toward the shore—the heaving wall of water was carrying the thrashing, shrieking pirates past the freighter's still-smoldering stern into the unyielding trunks and branches of the woods beyond the shoreline!

The ship fell back into the trough, raising an enormous splash. At once there came a shudder and the screech of tearing metal. The ship was aground!

Marisol looked up and pointed, wide-eyed. "Another wave!"

"Get inside! Get inside!" Larry pulled the girl to her feet, bundled her into a machinery space, and pulled on the door. At that moment, the second wave plowed into the ship, lifting the whole vessel once more and throwing the two into a heap. The lights went out. From outside, there came terrible wrenching and grinding noises of mangled metal as the ship settled onto a ledge of submerged rocks.

Larry pushed open the door. The water below churned with lumber and other flotsam from the disintegrated pirate trawler. Several bodies floated in the eddy current. But the wind and rain were now letting up.

The vessel commenced making awful metallic shrieks as the pounding waves now seemed to be wrenching apart the steel plates of the ship's bottom. Judging by the rocking motion of the deck, Larry guessed it was balanced on an underwater reef just off the beach. He took the girl's hand led her around to the forward superstructure platform. On the bows, the Army major and three of his soldiers were pulling themselves up the companionway handrails from the forward hold. Spotting the two, the officer waved. "Are you all right?" he called out to him over the wind and the surging sea.

The American cupped his hands. "Yes . . . but we had better get off this ship." Larry pointed at a big crack in the main deck just forward of the superstructure that was opening and closing with the motion of the impaled vessel in the pounding surf. Larry realized the bow was yawing back and forth; it looked as if the ship could break in half at any moment. "She's going to break up!"

Even as he called out, the freighter seemed to settle more onto the rocks; its bow jutted out of the water at angle. Groans and screeching sounds came from the hull as big waves slammed against the side of the stranded ship. Leaving Marisol, Larry dashed around the superstructure and looked aft down the open port promenade deck. Through the opening at the rear, he saw that the stern deckhouse that had been afire earlier was now awash; every few seconds a wind-driven sheet of silver spray rolled completely over it. There was no sign of the two soldiers who had been stationed back there. Nor did he see anyone from the engine or boiler rooms—likely, they had drowned when the submerged reef tore open the ship's bottom.

He ran back to the fore end of the main-deck superstructure, where the lookout was calling down to Marisol from the crow's nest. "Where is the captain?"

"I do not know."

Larry remembered the grenade that blew onto the bridge; so far, no one there had called to them. "I'll go up and find out." As he turned toward the companionway, he had an uneasy feeling about what he might find up there.

At the top of the steps, Larry turned into the pilot house and stopped—the place was completely wrecked. Captain Imwalley lay in a mess of gore; blood was splattered on the rear bulkhead. The mutilated bodies of the helmsman and the navigator were sprawled next to him. He turned away just as Marisol stepped up. She took one look at the horrific scene, rushed to the rail and was sick. "The captain seemed like a nice man" she moaned, her hands over her face.

"I guess they all were." He turned the shaking girl toward the stairs. "Come on . . . we must save ourselves." *And the cargo.*

While Marisol stopped at the second deck to see about her things, Larry dropped down to the main deck and hopped across the yawning crevasse that ran all the way across the ship. As he made his way forward, he could feel the deck moving beneath his feet as the freighter's forepart swayed back and forth when a breaker pounded against the hull. At the forward hatch he came across the major and his two remaining soldiers, who had pulled back a corner of the canvas cover. One deck down, the electronics and the other equipment, to Larry's relief, were still dry. But for how long? As they stood gazing down at the stranded shipment, there came more cracking, groaning noises.

The Army man cast about their unstable surroundings, then at the goods lashed to the wobbling deck one level below. "We must get everything off the ship—fast!"

Larry was trying to fight down a growing feeling of desperation. *At the last minute, were the elements going to destroy the electronics?*

"I see someone on land over there waving at us!" The lookout on the foremast was pointing over the port side. Sure enough, on a platform across the water about five hundred meters away, a black man in a white shirt was waving his arms over his head, jumping up and down. "He's running toward shore!" Those on the shipwrecked freighter watched as he hopped onto a bicycle and sped off up a lane. For the first time, Larry noticed a factory of some sort situated a little farther up an inlet, not far from where the ship was stranded. *Their refinery destination?*

A sudden, terrible yell came from the woods off the ship's submerged stern. A shoeless pirate ran from the edge of the forest toward the water, clawing the air as if it could make him go faster. The gasping fellow tripped on a piece of driftwood and fell face-first onto the sand. As those on the freighter gaped in horror, a twenty-foot-long crocodile running on all fours bolted from the woods behind him. Before the hapless bandit could get back up, the enormous creature grabbed the screaming fellow in its gaping jaws and rolled him over and over, leaving a broad crimson stain on the wet shoreline. Then the hissing reptile dragged the limp, broken body into the sandy surf in a slurry of splashes and disappeared with its quarry beneath the waves.

Marisol buried her face in her hands and turned to Larry, whose face was ashen. He pulled the shaking girl to his chest and held her; her tears running through her fingers.

"Some people are coming!" The lookout was pointing in the direction from which the man on shore had gone a few minutes earlier. Everyone except Marisol, who was still distraught, turned and watched as several trucks splashed along the narrow road toward the shoreline. Larry observed that one flat-bed vehicle had what looked like bulldozer treads at its rear. The procession slithered to a stop at the water's edge, two hundred meters across the sandy bar from the freighter's bobbing bow. Several people hopped off and stood around, pointing in the direction of the grounded ship. Squinting, Larry thought he saw a short-haired, young-looking female in the group. *Lisa Anaya?*

Marisol looked up from his embrace, wiping her eyes with her hand. The problem Larry had foretold to himself was now at hand: *How would he explain the two young women to each other?*

Several people on land were waving at those on the ship. Larry and the others waved back. Then they saw a couple of men haul an inflated life raft off the back of the truck and drag it into the surf. Jumping in, they paddled through the breakers out to the ship. In a few minutes, when the Nigerian men drew close alongside the broken hull, one of them cupped his hands and shouted up at the people standing by the rail, "We have a barge coming to take off the cargo!"

Just then, the deck gave a big heave; at the same time a scream of tortured metal sceeched from the twisting break; a sheet of water shot into the air across the front of the superstructure. Marisol grabbed Larry's arm, even as a couple of the others lost their footing and stumbled to the deck. The Army major shouted at the would-be rescuers. "Hurry! The ship is breaking up!"

"We will take you off! Find a rope or a ladder!"

Marisol pointed at the rail on the first deck. "The pirates' ladder! It may still be back there!"

Larry turned, and, crouching for balance, loped back down the slanting deck to the break that was now yawing five feet wide. Leaping across it, he ran around the superstructure. In a hurry he pulled the chain-linked steps up the sloshing side of the ship onto the deck, then dragged it back to the opening.

"Throw it across!" Major Banjo shouted. With a mighty shove, Larry heaved the limp, rattling ladder over the break onto the foredeck The Army man gathered it and made his way up the deck to opposite where the life raft tossed below in the surging breakers.

"I'll get our things!" Larry shouted at Marisol. He pulled himself up the unsteady companionway to the second deck. On the port side, he found the door leading to the cabins swinging back and forth with the swaying of the ship. At the end of the athwartships corridor, in the little cabin he madly stuffed his clothes into the carry-all, and with a last look around, made his way to Marisol's cabin. Her kit was on the narrow bed, already packed. He snatched it up and dashed into the passageway, just as the ship gave a big lurch. The door to the outside slammed shut. It would not open! Larry dropped the luggage and shoved against it. The door was jammed! In desperation, he looked about and spotted a red object mounted on a nearby bulkhead. A fire-axe! Tugging it from its mount, with several furious swings at the wooden frame, with a splintering crash, the door broke open. Gasping in relief, he dropped the tool, grabbed the travel cases and scrambled back down the steep steps to the first deck. At the break, he flung the bags at a soldier braced on the other side of the ever-widening gap.

"Get the weapons!" Marisol shouted across at him.

Larry pulled himself back around to where the two AK-74s lay soaked on the sloshing deck. With the two dripping automatic rifles looped across his shoulders, he jumped across the yawning gap once more and groped up the slanting foredeck to where the ladder was now hooked across the top-rail.

Banjo tapped Marisol. "You go first!" He motioned to Larry, "Then, you!"

The Cubana swung her leg over the rail and felt for the deck edge, then dropped down a couple of rungs. The major steadied Larry onto the ladder. With Marisol going down first, the two descended the wobbling chains. "Take it easy!" she called up to him. As the raft lifted at the top of a wave, big hands reached up for her waist, hauled her in, then grabbed Larry. The two dropped onto a narrow bench seat. The Army men lowered first one bag, then the other, into the heaving boat with a rope.

"We will be back!" the fellow shouted at those looking down at them from the ship's rail, reaching for the oars.

After a wave-tossed trip across the shallow, rolling surf, the rubber raft ground onto the sandbar.

As the American climbed out, there came a feminine squeal. "Larry! Larry! It is you!" A slender young woman was running across the sand, her arms outstretched. "Oh, Larry!" The cream-colored girl grabbed him and held onto his neck.

"Lisa—!" His arms went around her and he spun her around. On impulse he kissed her neck. He glanced over Lisa's shoulder where Marisol was just climbing out of the boat, her eyes wide; a surprised look on her face. Larry felt his own face reddening as he dis-engaged and turned to the Cuban policewoman. Both females were staring at each other with wary expressions.

"Ah, yes—" He was groping for words. "Marisol Montoya, this is Lisa Anaya." He looked at Lisa. "Montoya came with us from Cuba . . . she will be working with security, here." He motioned to Marisol, then to the other girl. "Lisa is an electronics engineer." He caught the perplexed look on Marisol's face. "We went to college together back in the 'States."

Their eyes narrowed at each other, the two young women shook hands.

The awkward introductions were interrupted just then by loud sounds of another truck splashing down the rutted, sandy road in their direction. Everyone turned to look as it slid to a stop. A stocky, baldheaded man dropped off the truck's rear onto the soggy ground.

Lisa spoke up. "Oh, General Retchko . . . this is Larry Landay."

The hairless man strode up and put out a pale, puffy-looking hand. "'Leonid Retchko'—'*General*' Leonid Retchko'." He spoke in an accent that the American guessed was Eastern European. Larry noticed that the bald white man had no eyebrows.

The Cuban woman put out her hand. "I am Marisol."

The Ukrainian shook it, looking her up and down. "You will be working with us."

"She has already saved my life, twice," Larry spoke. Lisa Anaya frowned.

The white man looked at the American. "Miss Anaya has spoken about you."

"Favorably, I hope! "

"The electronics are safe?" The general did not seem to be interested in banter.

"Yes . . . but the ship is settling." As they stared out over the sandbar at the canted freighter grinding on the reef, Larry told him about the pirates and the storm. "We were shipwrecked."

Just then, the late-afternoon sun broke through. Marisol looked up. "This looks a lot better than the tidal wave!" she said, with a glance at Lisa. Larry noticed this; perhaps, he thought, she was trying to get on more friendly terms with the other young woman. The last thing he needed right now were two competitive females going after each other with himself caught in the middle.

There came a chugging sound from upriver. Around a nearby bend, a barge-like, flat-bottomed boat mounting a derrick nosed into view, pushed by a tiny diesel tugboat. "I have ordered this boat to take the electronics from the ship," Retchko said. Everyone watched as the rig floated past them and turned at the sandbar.

The stubby, low-hulled craft nosed alongside the listing freighter, just as the rubber raft with the three Army men and the lookout, the only surviving crewman, scraped ashore on the sand. While Major Banjo introduced himself to General Retchko and discussed security matters, across the inlet, stevedores were working fast. While everyone looked on, the first canvas-covered pallet rose from the forehatch, swung in the air, then was lowered to the barge. In turn, the second pallet, and all the wooden crates were hoisted out onto the lighter.

With the setting sun casting a backlit orange fan-in-the-sky over the sagging ship, the laden barge pulled away and plodded around the mouth of the river into calm water.

There was a commotion in some nearby underbrush, then two disheveled-looking men ran out. Spotting the group standing on the beach, they turned to escape back into the forest. Marisol pointed at the pair. "Pirates!"

Retchko scowled. "Kill them."

Two of the Nigerian soldiers took aim with their automatic rifles and sprayed the fleeing men with a long volley of bullets. The thrashing thieves staggered forward, fell onto their faces and were still. A crimson stain spread beneath them; soaked up at once by the wet sand. Blue smoke curled from the muzzles of the weapons. Spent cartridges lay on the ground.

The Cuban girl stared at the bodies with a look of contempt. Lisa gasped and turned away.

Retchko shrugged. "The crocodiles will eat them." The general nodded at the soldiers with a professional air, then at the others. "We will go now to the refinery."

The general's young driver, who had been loading luggage and the surf-soaked automatic rifles onto one of the trucks, came up to Larry. "I saw the wrecked ship and went to tell the others." He put out his hand. "I am Frank Ogawan . . . the office manager."

The American shook the fellow's hand. "I guess you saved us."

"I was inspecting the platform when I saw the ship on the rocks. I rode my bicycle back to the refinery to get help."

General Retchko was frowning. *"I said—'we will go now to the refinery'!"* He gave a sharp glance and an impatient gesture at Frank Ogawan. The African subsided.

As Larry pulled himself up onto the rear of the truck, he glanced back at the two men lying dead on the sand; "General Retchko" had not hesitated to mow down the two thieves. Did they say he was the "Security Chief"?

The two girls climbed aboard the tank-treaded truck and took seats on opposite-side benches. Although Larry caught both of them stealing glances at him, he thought they seemed more to be sizing-up each other.

Just then, there came a loud *"BOOM!"* from the direction of the abandoned ship. As everyone turned to watch, the grounded vessel gave off a squealing noise and a *"WHOOSH!"* A frothy column of water gushed into the air from the forward hatch. As agonized screams of tortured metal rent the air, the freighter that was tearing apart started moving backward; more water washed over the twisted decks that were submerging. While the sinking ship continued its slow, steady, wrenching slide off the reef, in another minute the bow stood straight up. Then the vessel's name, *"Coast Adventurer"*, was enveloped in a geyser of spray and foam as the last of the little freighter dropped out of sight in a rumbling welter of huge bubbles and pieces of wreckage popping to the surface from somewhere now far below.

-37-

The truck caravan splashed past a sign that read,'TANUTA REFINERY', through an open gate into a fenced compound. Looking about, in the early-evening twilight Larry spotted ghostly vertical tanks and lighted towers across the way that he recognized as an oil refinery.

The line of vehicles pulled up to a white clapboard building. The young office manager hopped out and motioned for the others to follow him. "We have dinner for you," he said. All at once, Larry realized how long it had been since they had last eaten.

When he helped the girls off the truck, Lisa caressed his arm and gazed into his face, smiling. "I cannot believe you are actually here!" Larry grinned back at her, his eyes catching her's.

Marisol Montoya caught the expressions of the two and turned away.

Frank Ogawan pointed toward a door. "Come this way . . . we will now eat."

The group filed into a fluorescent-lit room where a long table was set up. Lisa sat next to Larry; Marisol took a seat across from them; the bald white man dropped into a chair at the head of the table. Lisa pointed to an empty chair next to her's. "My brother will be joining us," she said, "he is on his way from town."

* * *

Interior Ministry, Havana, Cuba, at the Same Time:

The Inspector looked the report over, then frowned at his assistant, who had brought the paper to him. "You are sure it is 'Marisol Montoya'? *In Angola?*"

"She has not been at work for two days. They found her purse and her identification on the airplane at Luanda when it arrived there. I learned the airplane's next destination was Lagos, Nigeria."

The officer looked at the clock: it was a little after two in the afternoon in Havana. He shoved the paper back to the other man. "Bring that uncle of her's—that 'Trini Torres'—back here. This time he will not get off so easy. Work him over . . . I want some answers."

* * *

Federal Building, San Francisco; at That Moment:

"At this time, You are not charged with a crime." The Magistrate looked down from his bench at Joe Anglin and went on, "But you must not leave California without permission of this court, while we locate Lawrence J. Landay. In the meantime, you should get a lawyer."

* * *

Tanuta Refinery, Tanuta City, Nigeria:

Frank Ogawan looked at the clock on the wall then around the dinner table at the newcomers; it was getting on toward evening. He gave a nodding smile. "We have rooms in the dormitory for all of you."

". . . and you will begin the construction in the morning." Retchko interrupted the young office manager, who became subdued. The white man cast his eyes on Marisol. "I will tell your duties at that time, as well. We must begin our work at once."

The stocky general turned to the major. "I have arranged with Colonel Ajiboy for you to work at the airport in Lagos . . . we are increasing the security, there." He narrowed his eyes at the two nervous-looking younger soldiers. "I observed the efficient way you disposed of the two 'pirates', as you called them, on the beach. You will remain here." The uniformed young men sat still in their seats, swallowing. "Consider that a promotion." The soldiers seemed to ease a little.

Larry, taking it all in, sensed that at this place, the hefty, bullet-headed man was in total control.

Lisa spoke up. "My sister Betty is married to the refinery manager . . . they will be returning here, tomorrow. She was in Amsterdam on holiday."

Larry thought he detected a flash of disdain cross the general's face at the mention of the husband.

"Officer Montoya saved my life from the pirates," Larry said, with a glance around the table, "she used her training to kill two of them who were attacking me."

The Cuban girl's eyes narrowed at him, then at Lisa. "*'Mister Landay'* protected *me* from the storm. On 'life-saving'—we are even." From the edge to her voice, Larry had no doubt, now, that Marisol was jealous of Lisa and had used sarcasm to get back at him.

Lisa's eyebrows were up. "What type of training did you have?"

"I trained in Caracas and in Moscow. I served at Vladivostok, in the Far East."

"In *Russia*?" Lisa's reaction was the same as had been Larry's.

Retchko had been listening. "At what school in Moscow did you train?"

"At the Moscow 'Central Police Academy' and at the 'Spetsnaz' training facility."

The general gave a visible start at this information. "We will discuss that further, tomorrow."

Someone tapped Larry's shoulder. "May I take your picture?" The American looked around and his jaw dropped.

Lisa nodded at the newcomer. "Larry, I believe you have met my brother!"

Her brother was the "photographer" from the 'Beacon Trader'!

Larry was incredulous. "You're Lisa's *'brother'*?"

"I was on holiday, so Lisa asked me to go on the same ship with you," he said, taking the empty seat next to his sister, "I needed a cover story, so I tried to be a photographer." The cream-skinned, green-eyed young man shrugged. "I did not think you believed me."

Larry remembered the fellow's lack of knowledge about his camera and of photography in general and his bumbling picture-taking attempts about the ship. "I thought you were a spy!"

Lisa Looked at Larry. "The electronics cargo was important and I needed some way to keep track of it." She held her gaze on him. "And I wanted to make sure *you* were safe . . ."

"I was sending radiograms to my sister about how things were going," the brother said.

"But when he got back here, we realized the messages he sent were not the ones I received!"

"What do you mean?"

"We believe the radioman on the ship was manipulating the messages."

Larry sucked in his breath. "Of course!" He told them about finding the copy of the radiogram on the cargo deck next to his shipment.

Larry did not notice that Retchko, who was overhearing their conversation, was frowning. *The American must not know that my sister and her husband, upon my instructions, were observing him on the ship and were prepared to 'eliminate' him if he deviated from the procedures.*

"The radio guy was up to something, all right," Larry said. He thought for a moment. "In fact, there was something creepy about that whole ship."

"Like the *'smell'?*" The "photographer" wrinkled his nose.

Larry snapped his fingers. "That's right! The ship smelled all over like 'fumes'."

"I almost forgot!" Lisa got up and left the room. In a minute she came back with a newspaper in her hand. "Look at this!" She thrust a section in front of the two men. Both read a circled article and gasped at the same time.

NO SURVIVORS IN SHIP EXPLOSION

(Valparaiso, Chile)—Port officials say there were no survivors when a cargo-passenger liner blew up outside the harbor of Valparaiso, Chile, today. The Assistant Harbormaster told a press conference

that the ship, the "Beacon Trader," had just arrived on a scheduled run that originated at Los Angeles, when a fire broke out in the engine room. Before passengers and crew could be taken off, a series of explosions tore through the vessel, that sank off the outer harbor.

The ship's owner and operator, "East Pacific Shipping Co.", said there were three passengers and thirty-two crew on board. All were presumed lost. Most of the ship's passengers who had sailed from Los Angeles had gotten off earlier at Acapulco, Panama City, and at Buenaventura.

Marine Investigators say the ship had experienced fuel leaks recently that were likely aggravated by some heavy seas through which the ship had run several days earlier.

The ship had been due for drydocking for engine and fuel-system repairs after its return to Los Angeles in three weeks.

The two gaped at the article and at each other, astonished. "We could have been killed!"

Marisol's eyebrows went up. "That was the ship you were on?"

Larry nodded, then told the others about the voyage down the coast to Acapulco with the electronic equipment. "All the time, we smelled fumes." He shook his head. "It was a wonder it didn't blow up while we were on board!"

General Retchko's eyebrow-less eyes bored at the newcomer. "Well, the crates are now safely here." He glanced at Lisa. "Tomorrow, we will start on the project."

Just then, several waiters in formal attire stepped into the room bearing trays. The topics around the table turned to other subjects.

Larry observed that the two young women were talking. "You are from Cuba?" Lisa Anaya was asking Marisol Montoya.

"I was a policewoman in Havana before I—'caught the airplane' to Lagos." Larry picked up that she did not want to tell them how she had stowed-away on the 747.

Retchko, staring across the table at the trim Latina, broke in. "She will be working with our 'security'." Larry noted his extended gaze. To the American, the man looked to be, at the very least, clever. Perhaps ruthless, even. He decided that the pudgy "general" would bear watching.

Marisol turned to the cream-skinned other young woman and spoke in measured English. "Larry says you and he will be working together on the electronics."

Lisa gave Larry a quick glance, then went on speaking to the Cubana. "We will be setting up a new communications link with other offices of our—'organization'."

To Larry, Lisa seemed to be holding back something from the female detective. It occurred to him that he did not, in fact, know much about what he was supposed to do, beyond installing the equipment—something Lisa, herself, could handle, given her training in electronics. If that were so, then why was he here? Was it because his former girlfriend wanted to renew the relationship from their college days and this was a convenient way to do it? Or—did she want him around to protect her from a malign influence—*something or someone?* Already, he had detected a subtle tension among those already here. He glanced down the table at the pallid, bald-headed man with the accent. Did it originate with the hairless foreigner? Was Lisa in fear of him? Were the *others* in fear of him? He recalled how the dark-skinned young "office manager" had seemed intimidated by the aggressive-acting man. Larry remembered how the Army major on the ship had talked about "General Retchko" in terms that had left little doubt the "Security Chief" would stop at nothing to enforce his edicts. Already, he had ordered the soldiers to shoot the two fleeing pirates in cold blood.

Larry ate with few words of his own as he listened to the others talking while they became better acquainted with their new colleagues. He wanted some time to think.

When he finished his dinner, Larry excused himself and stepped out onto the front porch of the main building. Leaning against a column of the overhanging porch, he gazed out. Across the way were dozens of silvery cracking towers, surrounded by beam-scaffolding, all illuminated by countless lights. Here and there, workmen outfitted in silvery-looking jumpsuits moved along on the high catwalks. The sky glowed orange from flames belching at the top of slender towers all about the enormous industrial operation.

Even though the refinery was at the edge of a tropical jungle, he shuddered. The expatriate Californian couldn't shake off a feeling that there was more to this assignment than simply installing a satellite communications link. The vision of the forceful baldheaded man at the table wouldn't go away.

As Larry took in the impressive sight and listened to the night air resounding with the whine of machinery and the varied animal sounds from the nearby jungle, there came a rub at his shoulder. Lisa Anaya stepped up, her shoulder touching his. The girl wrapped her arms around herself and looked out. "It is a big place."

Larry shrugged. "Yes, but there's something about all this that—"

"You feel it, too?"

"It's my imagination, of course—I've only been here a short while."

"I've felt it ever since I came here, last year." Lisa glanced at his face, reflected in the light. "It became worse when General Retchko came here not long—"

All at once, there was a blast of noise, causing both of them to jump. After some seconds, the racket stopped. "That was a 'blow-off'," Lisa said, catching her breath. "They say gas blows through the system and makes the noise. It happens a lot—but I never get used to it." She reached for his hand. "I am happy you are here. Did you think about me?"

Her question was like a bolt of electricity to him. "Of course, I thought about you. I thought about you a lot."

"You did?" There was a pause, then the cream-skinned girl squeezed his hand. "Larry, when we finish this project, I want you to take me away from here."

He started to say something, but the young woman touched her fingertips to his lips. "Before you say anything, I want to tell that you that leaving here will be very difficult—perhaps impossible." Lisa was shaking her head. "Larry . . . I know Retchko. He will keep giving us things to do and putting us off until we give up—I have already seen it happen to people." Her voice was edgy. "The ocean and the jungle are all around us! The nearest 'civilization'—if that is what you want to call 'Lagos'— is hundreds of kilometers up the coast from here . . . and, no one—*no one*—gets in or out of Tanuta City without Retchko's say-so."

Larry frowned. "We'll talk about it, later. Right now, I guess we have a lot of work to do."

* * *

While they spoke, Marisol Montoya had stepped up behind them in the gloom. Overhearing their words, she backed away. Larry and Lisa didn't see her.

* * *

As the two turned in the other direction, Larry glanced back over his shoulder at the dozens of vertical silver cracking towers, shimmering in the ghostly light, their surging sounds rumbling across the night.

When they finished this assignment, they would leave this place, of course.

Wouldn't they?

~~~~

EPILOGUE

Somewhere West of the Urals;, Sunday, December 29, 1991:

Terenty Suslov fingered the precious piece of paper and grinned. "We have worked hard for this!" he said to Gennady Lychin, his friend and fellow Special Forces officer.

Gennady watched as Colonel Golubko handed out the passes and the rail tickets to the others of their paramilitary group. "I wrote Galina we would be there on Tuesday," he said. The frigid air rang out with the happy voices of the young men. Even the usually-serious colonel seemed to be in good humor. "Galina and Tamara are looking forward to us being there for New Year's," she said in her latest letter."

"I cannot wait to be with Tamara and Larisa—and her parents, too."

"It has been a long time since we have seen them." Gennady's gaze carried across the cold, snowy wasteland surrounding the isolated training camp to the white peaks of the Urals, far to the east.

Trim, rugged-looking Andrey Malinovsky came over to the two, holding his pass. "The train to Moscow leaves in an hour," he said, "we had better get going."

The three officers of *'Vityaz Spetsnaz Russian Special Forces'* turned and stepped in the direction of the plain barracks building that had been their headquarters and home for the past four months while they trained for the secret mission to penetrate the United States of America.

~~~~

(TO BE CONTINUED AS *'PLAZA MAYOR'*)

~~~~

DISPOSITIONS

The "Academy"—The super-secret school in Moscow continued in operation as an adjunct of the 'G-R-U', the Intelligence branch of the "Russian General Staff".

* * *

"Mike" Adwadube—Mike (not his real first name) Adwadube, the lawyer with the "strange" eyes, stayed in Madrid as a recruiter for the "Organization".

* * *

Lisa Anaya—The young electronics engineer continued working at the Tanuta Refinery.

* * *

Joe Anglin: His lawyer eventually cleared his name from involvement in the transfer of technology to Nigeria.

* * *

The "Boeing 747"—The ubiquitous cargo aircraft continued to fly contraband military goods around the world in the service of "The Organization".

* * *

Masobe Busa—The overweight African kept luring unsuspecting people to Nigeria.

* * *

Dominique 'Nicky' Ferry—As a teenager, he began calling himself "Nick". Following his last year of high school and before he started at the university, his parents invited Larisa Kuznetsova, who was beginning her first term at Moscow State University, to visit them in West Dallas. The two became fast friends and Nick planned to visit her in Moscow the next summer.

* * *

Ned Ferry—The detective turned his investigation business over to his daughter, Sloane, and retired in 1999. In honor of his late wife, Browning O'Bryant Ferry, he established a scholarship for Australian international students at the university.

* * *

Sloane Ferry—Sloane was de-briefed by Jim Randolph at secret locations in New Mexico and Washington State. After the subsequent event at "Plaza Mayor", the two continued to see each other.

* * *

Nixie Garten—The "Woman of Mystery" who sat next to Kip on the Lagos flight remained with the airline. Later, she did translation work for Kip in Madrid, where the two renewed their acquaintance.

* * *

Galina Gavrona—The "slender, dark-haired cousin" and Gennady Lychin continued their relationship.

* * *

Rodion Golubko—Colonel Golubko became a general in 1993 and retired the next year. He later did consulting work for various organizations, including the Russian Space Agency, the Russian "Federal Security Bureau"; INTERNOL, the international police organization; and the Russian Special Forces, "Spetanaz".

* * *

Brad Holdon—In 1998, Brad and Kip Leeds merged their firm, 'H & L Petroleum Marketing' with a company in Houston. Brad was still un-attached; still making pointed observations about women.

* * *

The 'Invisible Technology'—The United States's program was cancelled in 1993, a victim of budget cuts—a powerful Congresswoman on the "Armed Services Committee" known to be not entirely sympathetic to the military had claimed that the concept was "unworkable" and had stopped it. In Russia, meantime, research went on, finally achieving a measure of success in a couple of years. But, as in the U.S., the project fell to budget constraints—in Russia's precarious first years without Communism, there were no rubles available for such expensive pursuits, and the project was shelved. In 2013, with Russia now enjoying unprecedented prosperity from petroleum exports, the Kremlin resurrected the program and was nearing production of the devices in great secrecy.

* * *

Larisa Kuznetsova Suslova—The little blonde girl grew up to become an exceptionally attractive young woman and a distinguished student at Moscow State University.

* * *

Larry Landay—When the California electronics engineer learned he was wanted by the authorities, he stayed in Nigeria, later learning the true nature of his work with the Cartel.

* * *

N.B. Krasheev—The "Nation Bank of Nigeria's" "Director of Intercontinental Remittance" continued as the financial head of the "Organization."

* * *

Marisol Montoya—The former Havana policewoman stayed in Nigeria as an assistant to General Retchko, nurturing growing suspicions about the actual aims of the "Organization".

* * *

Gennady Lychin—Gennady stayed with the "Spetsnaz", taking part in several dangerous missions. He and Galina Gavrona continued their relationship.

* * *

Kip Leeds—Kip traveled to New Mexico on the government airliner with Sloane Ferry and Ned Ferry. There, they were de-briefed by James Richard Randolph, of the "Investigation Agency", about Sloane's abduction and rescue.

* * *

Dr. Mobustu—The director of the "Technical Section" of the "Nation Bank of Nigeria" had demonstrated to Kip how to clean the black money in Busa's living room on that incredible afternoon. After the subsequent event at "Plaza Mayor", the banker dropped from sight and was being sought by the authorities. To this day, he has escaped the international police dragnet and is still at large.

* * *

Murtala Mohammed Airport Lagos—Under the control of General Retchko, the international airport at Lagos became even more fearsome, which was his intention. Goose-stepping soldiers continued their high profile. A "torture-chamber" and a "crematorium" were kept busy disposing of travelers dragged from the concourses and off airliners to be shaken-down, such as Kip Leeds had witnessed.

* * *

"Betty Nkrume"—The sister of Lisa Anaya continued to live at Tanuta City with her "husband", Lester, who was the manager of the refinery.

* * *

"Lester Nkrume"—The Plant Manager of the Tanuta Refinery continued to work under the watchful eye of General Retchko, who disliked him.

* * *

I.M. Nomoah, "The Chief"—The diminutive banker remained in charge of the international crime Cartel.

* * *

"The Organization"—The crime Cartel known as "The Organization" continued to grow in influence and power, supplying international criminals and terrorists with weapons and training

* * *

General Leonid Efimovich Retchko, aka 'Semen Putridchenko'—The Ukrainian strengthened his grip as the "Chief of Security" of the growing, ever-more powerful "Organization". Later, he joined the Cartel's forces with a robed insurgent in Afghanistan to train and equip the terrorists who would, in time, bomb the "Twin Towers" of the *'World Trade Center'* in New York City.

* * *

"Star City", Russia—The first-rate Russian spaceflight center at "Zvezdnyy Gorodok", better-known as "Star City", continued to train cosmonauts (and later, American astronauts) for flights into orbit aboard *'Soyuz'* spacecraft to the "Mir", and later, to the "International Space Station".

* * *

Terenty Suslov—Terenty stayed with Russian Special Forces for a number of years, rising to the rank of Colonel. He and Tamara Kuznetsova continued their relationship.

* * *

Tamara Kuznetsova—Tamara and Terenty continued their relationship.

* * *

Tanuta Refinery—The plant continued operating as the cash-generating and "money laundering" arm of the crime Cartel, under the firm direction of Leonid Efimovitch Retchko.

* * *

Trini Torres—The wispy, somewhat-eccentric Cuban remained on the island. Over time, he began to question the "Revolución" and to consider if he should try to leave.

<p style="text-align:center">~~~</p>

AFTERWORD

This story had its origins with a business-related journey to Nigeria I took some years ago, where I encountered people and events much like those portrayed here. As I told others about my adventure, some said it would make a good tale and that I should write about it. After a while, I started a short-story that soon became much broader in scope.

My own involvement in the narrative paralleled when Kip Leeds hauled his luggage into the airport to catch the flight to Frankfurt and ended when the airliner landed back in Amsterdam. Most of what took place in-between happened to me just like what happened to Kip, which forms the heart of the story. Much of the rest is based around actual historical events.

For me, the Lagos airport was, without a doubt, the most intense place to which I had ever been. For some years, horror stories abounded about other peoples' stop-overs there. A doctor who had also been through that airport once told me a security man had divulged to him about a secret room where they found it more "convenient" to beat people to death as opposed to shooting them—so as to not waste bullets. Hearsay, but it would fit the reputation the airport had for a long time. Now, I'm hearing that things are better there. But travelers invariably bring up the sweltering heat and humidity in and around the vast terminal, almost always mentioning the ever-present "baby-diaper" smells—I guess those things have never changed.

While in Lagos, I encountered the whole crowd of people and the places depicted here, most under other names. Some were memorable. The character I named "Masobe Busa" was really there, flowery outfit and all, as was the banker, 'Dr. I.M. Nomoah' (a play on words; say the name aloud). The banker I called "Krasheev" was real, as was the 'Technical Director', "Dr. Mobustu" (pronounced, "Mob-used-to"). The Army officer in that room, whom I well remember, became the pattern for "Colonel Ajiboy", although the real officer was much more coarse than the efficient but mannerly colonel in the story.

Others in this unsavory mix included the attorney I named "Mike Adwadube", who really did have the most un-nerving eyes I have ever seen, and the attractive, light-skinned girl in the bank's waiting room, who became "Betty Nkrume". The real people I encountered in Nigeria made excellent prototypes for the characters in this story.

The scene in "Busa's" living room with the Army people, the bankers, the armored personnel carriers, the money and the chemicals, took place just as depicted here. I still find it hard to believe it all happened like that, but it did.

Lagos really did look like a war zone and I sweltered in the traffic jam and witnessed the scene at the fuel yard just like it was in the story.

The blonde young German woman, the "Woman of Mystery", turned heads at the Frankfurt airport and we really had an "antique car" conversation on the airplane. Her sudden appearance next to me rendered me near-speechless and just like Kip, she didn't believe me, either. The girl was as attractive and intriguing in person as was the "Nixie Garten'" character, and she actually was a flight attendant. But I didn't get her name and telephone number like Kip Leeds did.

As for the "Invisible Technology"; several electronics manufacturers make sound-cancelling equipment, and to reverse light waves to render things invisible would almost seem to be the next logical step. I naively thought the "wrist-implant" computer chip idea was original—until I read that they were doing it with farm animals, using much the same type of satellite technology as in the story. Now I see where a few *people* are trying it. Truth can, indeed, be as strange as fiction, and the "Invisible Technology" concept figures greatly in *'PLAZA MAYOR'*, the next volume.

Much of the research for these stories came from documented Internet sources. Although once panned, the Internet has become a prime source of information of all types, regardless of those who seem to only spotlight its more salacious aspects. Additionally, the colorful *"Moscow"* travelogue by *DK Publishing*, and the *"Lonely Planet"* book about Moscow, both of which I hereby acknowledge, helped me set the locations of events in that sprawling, enigmatic capital city of Russia.

The fictional people in Moscow who found themselves in the tumultuous tides of August, 1991 were in the midst of actual events. *"Newsweek", "Time" and "U.S. News and World Report",* from my personal collection, were vital in helping to establish a time-line framework upon which to fit the various scenes. Using these and some other sources, I was able to draw everything together into what happened during that unforgettable week as anxious crowds jammed "Arbat Square" and the world held its collective breath.

My heartfelt thanks go to the cordial staff of the *'Consulate General of the Russian Federation in Houston'* for their wonderful help and advice; in particular to Vice-Consul Tatiana Shustrova, who graciously gave me much helpful information concerning social customs in her country.

On a topic far-removed from the palatial surroundings of the Consulate General's suites, the "Academy" that figured so prominently in the story was loosely patterned after an actual one in Moscow—a super-secret, advanced "War College" for rigidly-selected officers of all branches of the military that was organized to function very much like the one in this narrative. Graduating from it was mandatory for Soviet officers who aspired to the very highest ranks; i.e., "Marshal of the Soviet Union" and "Fleet Admiral of the Soviet Union".

The "Spetsnaz G-R-U" actually exists, and continues to be the most efficient, the most lethal—and the most respected—Special Forces, anywhere. The background as presented in the story about that topnotch paramilitary organization is authentic, insofar as I could determine, and there is a considerable body of information available. One with an interest in such things would do well to check out their website. Another source of information about "Spetsnaz" and other countries' Special Forces is *"The Encyclopedia of the World's Special Forces",* by Mike Ryan, Chris Mann, and Alexander Stilwell, published by Barnes and Noble Books.

"Star City", where they train the cosmonauts, the Russian equivalent of the "Johnson Space Center" in Houston, is an actual place and is just as described. The Internet has interesting websites about it, including pictures of the big centrifuge. A few years after the time of the events depicted in this story, the Russians began offering rides to the public on the body-flattening contraption. For adventurous types who would want to go in the opposite direction from heavy weight, they now also sell rides on the zero-gravity airplane—the "vomit comet"—for a hefty price that includes the "little bags" in the fare.

Concerning the sections about Cuba, once again, the Internet filled many gaps, including how "Santeria" influences the culture of a festive people who cope with chronic shortages with verve and ingenuity, along with the social (and sexual) mores that make Cuba such a fascinating study. Three travel books about the island country were helpful: Frommer's *"Cuba";* Odyssey's *"Cuba",* by Andrew Coe; and Moon Handbooks' *"Cuba"*, a hefty tome by Christopher Baker. All were useful for putting things in their proper perspectives in and around Havana.

If one should go to Cuba, one of the first places to visit would be the "Tropicana" night club; going strong since 1939 and still reputedly the biggest, flashiest cabaret in the world.

Another destination of note is the "Nacional Hotel", in its restored state once again the gem of the Caribbean as hotels go, and the site of what was once the most magnificent casino, anywhere. In the old days, the spectacular showplace was run in ship-shape fashion by *'mobster extraordinaire'* Meyer Lansky, who, along with the Batista government, was swept away in 1959 by Fidel Castro's own rag-tag mob. Good reading on the subject of Havana in its casino heyday can be found in *'Playboy's Illustrated History of Organized Crime',* long out of print, but worth a look if you can find it. One more stop would be at the "Coppelia Ice-cream Bar", about which several sources insist actually does serve its world-beating frozen concoctions to thirty-thousand customers every day. (Some say the number is closer to fifteen to twenty-thousand; still a whopping crowd of ice-cream enthusiasts.) As a side note: one time I was in Santiago, Chile, and came across a colorful "Coppelia" store in a mall.

Another thing I learned about Cuba and was corroborated by multiple sources was the strong support most native Cubans give—and have always given—to the Castros. One will pick up this theme in the story. This "Castro-mania" would seem to fly in the face of the conventional wisdom unceasingly presented by many Cuban expatriates in Florida, who believe they would be welcomed with open arms at the shoreline should they return someday to "rescue" the native population from their "misery". What I learned about the actual state of affairs on that island would strongly suggest otherwise—Cubans overwhelmingly would react to such an attempt as an invasion of their beloved homeland to be forcefully repelled.

Another consideration: since their free-wheeling culture-core is considered by many to drive the most sensuous, sexually-charged society on the planet, it might be yet another inducement for many Cubans to fight for the *status quo* as opposed to the prospect of having to take orders from their presumably more prissy relatives from Florida. Some "boat people" do leave the island. But they are the exception.

During the preparation of this story a number of people, including Joe Barfield, Paul Caver, Tamara Gajewski, Tony and Diane Noriega, Brian Ross, and Salem Thannoon, among others, were there at crucial times with helpful suggestions and encouragement, which I hereby and gratefully acknowledge. Rodrigo Aguilera's cover artwork was masterful. My wife, Cecilia, never stopped urging me on to finish the project. On the production side, Bobby Bernshausen and his intrepid staff at Virtualbookworm.com Publishing worked wonders to whip the draft into the proper formats. And there was Cate Kahn, who kept insisting that I write about the time I journeyed to Nigeria that became this story.

John S. Halbert
Katy, Texas